Praise for Anjana Appachana

'Appachana's writing is eloquent in detail… But the detail illuminates a larger subject and the writing is in service to something greater than the novel – a view of humanity, a sense of what is moral and lasting. *Listening Now* is a large book in every sense, a panorama filled with insight and surprise, inviting, absorbing and satisfying' – **BOSTON GLOBE** on *Listening Now*

'In an eloquent interweaving of perspectives… Appachana succeeds in drawing us deep into a complex vision of shattered happiness and withered dreams' – **NEW YORK TIMES** on *Listening Now*

'Anjana Appachana's almost quaint tale fleshes out old stereotypes and stresses the transformative power of storytelling' – **INDIAN EXPRESS** on *Listening Now*

'Appachana can imbue the texture of women's quotidian existence with solidity and substance… Much of this has been said before, but not with such vividness and urgency, the cumulative impact of which is quite extraordinary… It takes courage to write a book like this today' – **MEENAKSHI MUKHERJEE** on *Listening Now*

'Appachana's accomplished first novel reveals her capacity for insight into experience, which she communicates with unflinching courage' – **MARIA COUTO** on *Listening Now*

'*Listening Now* has been worth the waiting… It has a rich tapestry of women's lives, very fully and sympathetically drawn; a fine ear for the rhythms of spoken Indian English, a plot that is fully engaging and intriguing, and a finely suspended final moment, the beginning anticipating the end, the end recalling (and illuminating) the beginning' – **LAKSHMI HOLMSTRÖM** on *Listening Now*

'Appachana succeeds in rousing our sense of outrage and righteousness without resorting to glib gimmicks… She allows the characters room to breathe… And in the end she succeeds splendidly in moving you as well as enlightening you' – **ASHOK BANKER** on *Listening Now*

'By restoring the lushness of narratives routinely reduced to pathetic caricatures and afternoon soap operas, Appachana has paid a long overdue tribute to the millions of ordinary women who use stories to weave security blankets, to spin safety nets' – **MINI KAPOOR** on *Listening Now*

'Anjana Appachana is an extremely gifted writer' – **SUNDAY OBSERVER** on *Incantations*

'Subtly and skilfully combing comedy with the intimation of tragedy, Appachana's stories proclaim a versatile and exciting talent' – **NEW STATESMAN AND SOCIETY** on *Incantations*

Also by Anjana Appachana

Incantations and Other Stories
Listening Now

FEAR AND LOVELY

Anjana Appachana

VERVE BOOKS

First published in 2023 by VERVE Books,
an imprint of The Crime & Mystery Club Ltd,
Harpenden, UK

vervebooks.co.uk
@VERVE_books

ISBN
978-0-85730-834-4 (Hardcover)
978-0-85730-833-7 (eBook)

2 4 6 8 10 9 7 5 3 1

Typeset in 11.1 on 13.5pt Garamond MT Pro
by Avocet Typeset, Bideford, Devon, EX39 2BP
Printed and bound in Great Britain by Clays Ltd, Elcograf S.p.A.

MIX
Paper from
responsible sources
FSC
www.fsc.org
FSC® C018072

For my daughter, Malvika, who, more than anyone, understands how,

and

for my parents, Parvathy Appachana and ST Appachana, who are always with me.

Prologue: More than one

In 1976, four years before I left New Delhi for America, I had a concussion and lost a few days of my memory, and not long after I lost most of my mind.

Everyone commiserated about my lost memory. They said, 'Poor thing, but never mind, only a few days of memory she has lost, so much worse it could have been.' Of course, there was no poor-thing-but-never-mind-so-much-worse-it-could-have-been about losing your mind. Nothing was worse than that. *Mallika's become mental*, everyone would have said, had they known the truth. Mental meant mad, mental merited no excuse, better dead than *that*.

Now, had my mothers been different, they would have married me off, because – of course – marriage cured all ills. Marriage was more effective than any psychiatrist. A psychiatrist merely treated mental, whereas marriage cured mental. After marriage, crazy people became normal. Homosexuality became heterosexuality. Heavy periods became normal periods. Irregular periods became regular periods. Recalcitrant girls became adjustable girls. Even pimples disappeared after marriage!

But clearly the magical powers of matrimony failed to convince my mothers. Instead of marrying me off, they constructed a story about my illness, and they did a fantastic job of it. You see, the secret to a credible story is for the teller to believe it too. As my mothers told friends and neighbours what had happened to me, so persuaded were they by their own fabrication that everyone else was too. Ma and Shantamama were sisters, and they had practice creating stories from the time I was in Ma's womb. If they could have reconstructed history for my sake, they would have somehow also accomplished that. As far as they were concerned, any lie you told to protect your loved ones was the truth. And when it came to telling stories, no one could beat my mothers, whether it was their versions of the Mahabharata or their versions of our lives.

In this case, their version of my life was that I had tuberculosis.

'Haii! Poor thing!' everyone said and kept their distance.

Thus, in one stroke my mothers achieved the impossible: they ensured complete sympathy and absolute isolation. No one visited me. No one called me mad, mental, lunatic, nuts, crazy, paagal, cracked, cuckoo. No one put a finger to their temple and moved it left and right to indicate a screw was loose in Mallika's head, poor thing. After all, TB wasn't your fault. How could you help it? Mental certainly was. Mental was entirely your fault, and so what if you were suffering through it, you had better suffer for it.

Not a soul knew that my mothers were taking me to that rare and ominous breed of doctors, a psychiatrist. Such a discovery would have demolished my future, including, of course, my marriage prospects. Which were abysmally low anyway since Ma was a widow without much money, I was 'little-darker-than-wheat' complexioned, and, worst of all, I was shy. Only one thing could have trumped the absence of a father, lack of money, and my little-darker-than-wheat complexion, and that was love. But I didn't talk, so what chance was there of anyone noticing me, let alone being blinded by love for me? As Shantamama had once said, 'You'd have been better off with a wart on your nose than with that shyness – at least with a wart you'd be noticed.' When I had replied that I was fine not being noticed, Shantamama had snorted, 'Modesty is one thing, but foolishness is another! My god, your answer *reeks* of foolishness.'

You see, shyness was almost as bad as mental. People had every word for shy except shy. In our colony, these were the words all the aunties, uncles and grandmothers had: such-a-good-girl, not-at-all-opinionated, not-at-all-Westernized-totally-Indian, modest, adjustable, sweet.

As for boys?

'Boys think you're snobbish or stupid,' my friend Mahima informed me. That stung like hell. I said that Arnav had once talked to me for two hours; he wouldn't do that if he thought I were a snob or stupid. 'Huh! That was only because he was high,' Mahima said.

Before I go on, I must make it clear that Mahima wasn't being mean to me. She had a sharp tongue, and there was a hard edge to her beneath her soft and lovely countenance, but we had lived next door to each other since we were babies, and she knew me deeply and tenderly. Mahima was just trying to get me to be less socially inept, and this was her way of doing it, just like Shantamama's way was the wart.

Although I didn't talk, I loved to listen. Besides my mothers and friends, I could also listen endlessly to our neighbours, to their mothers and mothers-in-law, to their guests, to my college mates, to the sabjiwalla, the phalwalla, the mochi, the kabadiwalla and the voluble stranger in the train. This too exasperated my mothers and friends. Why was I wasting my time listening to every Tom, Dick and Harry? Why was I so gullible? Why did I believe everything I heard?

But what does listening have to do with believing? Listening is like being lost in a book. For me, every story was music, every storyteller the Pied Piper of Hamelin. And I was every child that followed him. All the children that disappeared forever into the mountain with the Pied Piper were me. And the one lame child that didn't disappear, who bore witness to the disappearance of all the enchanted children, and who lived to tell the tale – that was also me.

The best thing about listening to people's stories was that I didn't have to talk. Those who spoke to me were the storytellers, and my ear (my sympathetic, fascinated, cornucopia-like ear) was their page. If the talkers had been asked what Mallika was like, they'd have said, *so nice*, that ubiquitous word always used to describe me, a word that my mothers took great exception to.

So, there we are. Such-a-nice-girl. Not-at-all-opinionated. Not-at-all-Westernized-totally-Indian. Modest. Adjustable. Sweet. Snob. Boring.

So many words for shy, except shy.

It was a fatal combination, mental and shy. At least you could lie about mental, but how did you lie about shy?

Anyway. I didn't have to lie about anything, because my mothers did it for me with their TB story. For the first time in our lives no one dropped in to visit us. No one asked to see me. Like many others those days, we didn't have a phone, so there were no endless phone calls enquiring about me. To isolate me from the prying, gossipy world was what my mothers had desperately hoped for, but they hadn't expected such spectacular success.

So, to all appearances, everything was normal. After all, what is normal? Normal is pretence. Normal is silence. The better you can pretend or the deeper your silence, the more normal you are, aren't you?

Having succeeded in isolating me and ensuring that no one could see, suspect, or gossip, Ma and Shantamama continued feeding normal a steady diet of lies and fabrications till normal grew nice and plump and wholesome. But the more wholesome normal was, the more I deteriorated, and the more devastated my mothers became. It was the opposite of what had happened in *The Picture of Dorian Gray*. If you remember, Dorian Gray's picture, locked up in that room, grew older, uglier, more dissipated and ravaged, while to the outside world the flesh-and-blood Dorian Gray remained young and beautiful. That was the secret to his eternal youth: the picture grew old instead of him. Well, in our case, the opposite happened: while the outside

world continued to see and believe our picture of normal, the picture
ravaged my mothers. They kept me so safe, and hid the truth from everyone
so fiercely, that over the months their flesh burnt away, their eyes sank into
their sockets, and lines appeared on their faces. Ma's long black hair became
streaked with grey, and Shantamama's equally beautiful hair fell out in
clumps.

The possibility of my never recovering and of my never living what's
called 'a normal life' held my mothers in a state of terror.

'Padma, do you think she is like this because of her concussion?'

'But the psychiatrist said it has nothing to do with the concussion,
Shantacca.'

'But, Padma, she lost her memory when she had the concussion.'

'Only lost three days, Shantacca. Three days is nothing.'

Periodically, my mothers comforted each other. At least it wasn't the kind
of mental where I had to be locked up somewhere. I wasn't hysterical or
violent. Nor was I staring into space, talking to myself, and roaming around
unbathed, with uncombed hair. All wasn't lost, they reassured each other,
all wasn't lost, was it?

All was lost. I was lost to them. I was lost to myself. I – who, all my life,
had cared so deeply about everyone and everything – no longer cared about
anyone or anything.

It was hell for my poor mothers. But not for me. Before I fell ill, I had
been holding a cactus in my heart. It grew, as do all things hidden. I was
in excruciating pain. Then one day, suddenly, my body relinquished it. The
pain vanished, and I was left blessedly dead. If being dead to everything and
everyone meant I was mental, then mental was a benediction.

But my story is by no means only about mental. It is also a love story, and
love is never one. All of us loved each other, and our love stories belonged
to each other, even the ones we did not know. Just as a single banyan tree in
a grove of banyan trees cannot have one story, for each tree is born of the
roots of another, so it was with us.

Yet, for all the love we bore each other, we had no idea of each other's
silences. We didn't even understand our own.

Know this too: this story isn't only about what we hid from each other, or
what we hid from ourselves. Because it is possible to be utterly silent about
a central thing in your life and simultaneously live the happiness of other
centres, even as one quietly seeps into the other. Central is so much more
than one. At least, it was for me.

Part I

Mallika: What to do?

August 1980

Three days before Arnav and I left for graduate school in Pennsylvania, I quietly left my house, walked swiftly to the row of houses behind, and surreptitiously climbed up to his barsati. It was five a.m. and still dark.

I was staggering under the weight of all that I was carrying up to his room. My buried story, for one. The earth under which it lay was moving. Not that I had any intention of speaking about it to Arnav. How could I when I couldn't even speak of it to myself? Yet, as I went upstairs to his room, it was what I bore.

On top of it were the two lies which I had practiced all night. One lie was in anticipation of Arnav's question, why. In the spectrum of lies, this was a small and harmless one, yet as I climbed up to his room, its weight was threatening to break my back. I had practiced the lie all night, not just to get my words right, but also my tone. I had to utter it without looking guilty, without stuttering, and without going red in the face. The last was the most unsurmountable. But, as one of our neighbours had charitably said, 'Such-a-good-girl this Mallika is, only problem is, she is little-darker-than-wheat complexioned, that is the thing.' That was, indeed, the thing, and I was grateful for it because most people couldn't see me blushing. Perhaps Arnav would not notice either?

The second lie was in case Arnav's landlady, Mrs D'Souza, the biggest gossip in our colony, caught me going up to his room. I was breaking her rule of No Girls Allowed. That too, at five a.m. Of course, she would assume the worst if she caught me. Even my Sati-Savitri, pure-as-driven-snow reputation wouldn't withstand the scandal that would follow. She would immediately inform my mothers and then proceed to discuss my transgression with everyone in the colony. For my part, I'd never sneaked into a boy's room at five a.m. At any a.m. At any p.m. What Arnav's reaction would be, I couldn't imagine.

My nerves were shot.

But what to do? Randhir, whom I'd known my entire life, wasn't here. He was studying in America. Otherwise he was the one I'd have asked. And there would have been no sneaking around at five a.m., because he lived right next door with his family. His mother and Ma were best friends. At the age of fourteen, weeping and blowing my nose copiously into his pristine white handkerchiefs, I had confessed to him the true story of my life. It was a story straight out of a Hindi film, but alas, without the happy ending. Rapt, sixteen-year-old Randhir had given me sage advice, and after that we were irrevocably bound to each other. You can't imagine what it was like to be bound in this manner to someone who looked like a cross between a Greek god and Heathcliff, or at least what I imagined Heathcliff looked like, dark and brooding. Except that Randhir was fair and brooding. Although, I suppose, Indian-fair is Heathcliff-dark. It was heavenly, his brooding look. On the rare occasions that I felt less than charitable towards him, I told myself he cultivated it. But Randhir knew how to wheedle me out of such moods. He had mastered the art. All he had to do was look at me as though we were kindred souls. That was it. Nothing made me levitate more rapidly than Kindred Souls Day.

So, I couldn't ask Randhir for help. My mothers were out of the question. And my two childhood friends who were still in Delhi didn't have that kind of money. Which left Arnav. Who was neither Heathcliff nor a Greek god. He was sunshine. He had lovely, startlingly light brown eyes against that deep brown skin, eyes fringed with thick lashes and always full of laughter. That is, when he wasn't smoking marijuana – in those instances, he looked sleepy and heavy-lidded but still lovely. He was tall, lean, and often unshaven; he wore the same old jeans and carried that dishevelled look with a carelessness that was horribly appealing. My heart could barely withstand his presence in those days, and it would retreat into a place deeper than shyness. As for him, he just about knew I existed. During the course of our unexpected friendship, I had trained my heart to withstand him a lot better. But... Well, I'll come to those *buts* later.

Randhir and Arnav had been bosom buddies since they were in the first class in primary school, and then later in boarding school, and you couldn't think of one without the shadow of the other falling into your consciousness. Although I never felt I was on steady ground when I was with Arnav, there was no questioning his fidelity. He was fiercely loyal to Randhir. To me too. As a friend, that is.

I breathed in deeply, exhaled, and knocked.

There was no response.

After half a minute, I knocked again. Not loudly, because Mrs D'Souza had a reputation for hearing everything.

After a minute, I knocked a third time. Still no response.

I heard a sound below me and panicked. I turned the handle down, the door opened, I rushed through and softly shut it behind me.

An hour later, I rushed out equally precipitously. Shutting the door again, I stood on the landing, breathing so hard that it was as though I'd been running. I needed a minute to compose myself. Closing my eyes, I took a couple of slow, deep breaths.

When I opened my eyes, Mrs D'Souza was standing below the stairs at her door, looking up at me, arms akimbo, eyes glittering avariciously.

'I must say you're breathing very heavily, my girl. That too, with eyes closed. What all have you and Arnav been up to?'

I looked at her in horror.

'Don't keep standing there – come down.'

I went downstairs.

'Good morning, Aunty. I just… I went up to ask Arnav if he wanted to go for a walk.' This was the lie I had prepared and practiced the previous night in case she caught me. The blood rushed to my face as I uttered it.

'You went inside Arnav's room at *five a.m.* It is now *six a.m.* It takes *one hour* to ask him to go for a walk?'

She'd seen me going in. She must have been peering out. I hadn't prepared a lie for this.

'Answer me, my girl, I'm waiting.'

I searched hard for an answer.

'And now you're going for your walk *without* him?'

I shook my head. Then I nodded. Then I became paralyzed.

'Listen to me, my girl. I know you and Arnav are going to university in America in two-three days, that too, together, and who is to say what all you'll do there? In America, anything and everything goes, but right now you are still in India, and don't think that just because Indira Gandhi has come back as Prime Minister that changes anything – a young woman does not go into a young man's room. I had expressly forbidden it when I rented my barsati to that boy.'

'Aunty, we were *talking*,' I burst out.

The boulder of emotions that I had been rolling up the hill Sisyphus-like all these years must have surged to my face, because her expression changed. Her eyes filled with tears. She was overcome. In trembling tones, she said, 'I shouldn't believe you, but I do.'

My body sagged with relief.

'To anyone else, I would say, "this is a cock-and-bull story, a girl asking a boy for a walk from five a.m. to six a.m.," but not to you. My *dear, dear* girl, even if it is not the entire truth, I believe you are innocent. My own son, Mark, I do not believe, but *you*, I believe. I said to your mother the other day, "Padma, Mallika is so good, not only does she not go out with boys; she does not even talk to them. Where will you find such a girl in Delhi in the year nineteen-hundred-and-eighty?" That was what I was telling your mother.'

My Sati-Savitri reputation had come to the rescue.

'"Only Randhir and Arnav she talks to," I told your mother, "but so nicely she talks to them, no fluttering eyelashes, no come-hither looks, nothing. So naturally they treat her like their sister. Naturally they respect her." That is what I told your mother. I am the first person to defend you, you know that?'

I nodded. I knew nothing of the sort, but I was so grateful for the tears that filled her eyes. I was also galled by the naturally-they-treat-her-like-a-sister approval.

'Everyone in our colony says, "Such a nice girl Mallika is, so modest, such a loving, giving, dutiful daughter!" I told Mrs Nanda, "See how she wears such beautiful cotton sarees, and at the end of the day her saree is not even crushed! No tight-shite pants and shirts with her bums and her bosom sticking out – no – *that* is not Mallika."'

True, that was not me. With no money to spare, and unable to keep up with Delhi fashions, I stuck to handloom sarees and blouses, which gave even more impetus to my Sati-Savitri reputation.

'My dear, be very careful in America, alright?'

I nodded.

'America has Influence my dear. Even if you don't go there. Look at my son, Mark – *such* a good boy he is, never been to America – but once I found *five* naked American women under *his* bed! Can you imagine?'

She registered my shock with pleasure and launched into her story.

'Yes, my dear, five dirty *Playboy* magazines with shameless naked women, under his mattress. I said to Mark: "So, what is this?" He goes red in the face and says, "Mum, Pondy forgot them here. His cousin from America gave them to him – I haven't even *looked* at them." I shouted, "You big, fat liar!" And he says, "Mum, I read this magazine *only* because it has *excellent* interviews – there's one with President Carter." I gave him one tight slap. "You think I am a stupid fool or what!" I said. Then he opens one and says, "*See.*" And there it was – an interview with the President of America! My dear girl, you could have knocked me down with a feather. The next day I confronted this Paramvir, who knows why they call him Pondy, whom I've known since he was ten, and he has the cheek to say, "These aren't mine, Aunty, Randhir's cousin got them from America." I said, "Indeed? Does America breed dirty Indian cousins or what?" Mallika, my girl, I read Jimmy Carter's interview in that dirty magazine. He says, "I've looked at a lot of women with lust." He says, "I've committed adultery in my heart many times." What is the *need* for this kind of talk? This is a very American thing, I'm telling you, talking about sex and religion. But the fact is this – the President of America has spoken the truth about *all* men. So be *very* careful.'

'I will, Aunty. Bye, Aunty.'

'They can't help it, my girl. Even the best of men are like that. It is called' – she spelled it out in a whisper – '*L-U-S-T*.'

I nodded. 'Aunty, I have to go, bye.'

'Men are ruled by it, my girl. *We* – now *we* are different.'

I began edging my way towards the door.

'How is your mother?'

'Which one, Aunty?' It always aggravated me, the way she said mother in the singular when she knew I had two.

'Your real one, my dear.'

'They're both real ones, Aunty. They're fine. Bye, Aunty.'

Before I could rush out, Arnav came bounding down the stairs, radiating energy and good cheer. 'Morning, Mrs D'Souza! Let's go for our walk, Mallika.'

I looked at him in fascination. How had he managed to switch it on so rapidly?

Mrs D'Souza looked at him and then at me.

'I asked her to wait outside so I could change,' Arnav explained.

'My dear boy, you think I'm a fool or what? This poor girl was trembling like a leaf outside your door.'

'Aunty, I wasn't,' I said, mortified.

'Trembling like a leaf,' Mrs D'Souza said rapturously. 'Her eyes closed. Frozen like a statue. Breathing as though she'd run a mile.'

Arnav said comfortingly, 'Mallika, you don't have to feel bad. I've accepted it.'

I looked at him startled. What on earth?

Then I realized what he was doing. He was improvising.

In addition to being a fantastic actor, Arnav was a member of the Theatre Improvisation Group in Delhi, the TIG. You could throw any sentence at him, and he would make a story out of it – always the most hysterically funny story. He must have heard everything Mrs D'Souza said to me. Now he was determined to save my skin.

'Mallika came to tell me something in confidence,' he said.

'What did you tell him, my girl?'

Arnav said, 'Mrs D'Souza, it was about me. Mallika won't betray my confidence.'

'Of course,' sighed Mrs D'Souza, clasping her hands. '*Such* a nice girl!'
'Yeah,' said Arnav, warmly.
'Do not say "ya," my boy, that is a very rude way of talking to your elders.'
'Yes, Mrs D'Souza.'
'Arnav, I'm going by myself for my walk,' I said.
I charged out of the door, leaving him to play centre stage.

I walked briskly, trying to shake off my unwieldy emotions. Walking had saved me during the time I was recovering from my illness, and now I did it every day.

A loud, untuneful singing bumped, rolled, and stumbled across our colony.

Usually in the summer I started my walk at six a.m., so by the time our neighbourhood singer made his morning debut, I was almost a mile away from his orbit. But now it was six-fifteen a.m. The old singer had emerged for his morning walk and was singing a Hanuman bhajan at the top of his voice. The dissonance of his bhajan grated noisily against my early morning experience. During the monsoon, he set all his bhajans to the Malhar ragas. 'Which is all very well,' my Shantamama always said, 'but the old man's voice is like chalk scraping on the blackboard.' Randhir used to say that the old man's ability to carry a tune was inversely proportional to his love for the Almighty. Early in the morning, his bhajans stumbled noisily onto balconies and terraces, through windows and doors. 'Man, it's worse than a bloody alarm clock,' Randhir would groan. Those days, before he left for America, Randhir would shut his window every night in an attempt to shut out the sound, but his mother, Madhu Aunty, quietly opened it early in the morning, because, as she said, 'If there is no ventilation then there is no health.' Soon the sounds of the singer were joined by the sound of the Mulla praying from the nearby mosque. And sometimes Mrs D'Souza, not to be outdone, played her record of Handel's *Messiah* full blast. 'The Music of the Spheres,' Randhir called it. Once at six-thirty a.m., as the three sounds filled the neighbourhood, Randhir had sprung out of bed and put on a Grateful Dead record, also full blast. His father leapt out of his chair in the veranda, dropped his cup of morning tea and burnt his hand. If it hadn't been for Madhu Aunty's rapid intervention, his father would have broken the record. 'Padma, what is the meaning of all this Grateful-Shateful-Dead,' Madhu Aunty complained to Ma later. 'How can dead people be grateful?'

Madhu Aunty was Ma's beloved friend and lived like a sentinel to the immediate right of our house. I had known her all my life. She and her husband were in their veranda drinking their morning tea as I walked back from Mrs D'Souza's. 'Good morning, Aunty, good morning, Uncle,'

I waved to them, and they smiled and waved back, 'Good morning, good morning, Mallika.'

It was Madhu Aunty who had told Ma's tragic story to everyone when I was a baby. 'Better everyone knows,' she had declared to Ma. Meaning the men in our colony shouldn't think Ma was fair game, being a young and beautiful widow, and the women should know without a doubt that she wouldn't ensnare their husbands. 'That is everyone's mentality, hai na,' Madhu Aunty had said. With this in mind, she had told everyone how Ma and my father had got married against their parents' wishes, and how both parents had disowned them. Then, when Ma was pregnant with me, my father had died in a terrible car accident. This part Madhu Aunty had dramatized beautifully, with tears streaming down her face, telling the rapt neighbours how Ma's sister, Shanta, and her husband took care of Ma. Then Ma got a job as a lecturer in Delhi University, and Ma's mother gave her the money to buy our house. 'Now, Padma's life is her daughter; men and all she is not one bit interested in,' Madhu Aunty announced. And everyone had seen that this was indeed true. Madhu Aunty could quell gossip and speculation in an instant if it threatened her family and friends, and to no one had this skill extended more fiercely than to Ma and me.

Walking past Madhu Aunty's house and then my own, I waved to Anu Aunty, who, like another sentinel, lived to the left of our home and was also Ma's beloved friend. As usual, she was plucking jasmines in her garden for her morning puja and for her hair. 'Namaste, Aunty,' I said, and she smiled and replied, 'Namaste Beti, live long.' When Anu Aunty prayed for her family, she also prayed for Ma and me. She had done so every day for twenty-three years, and I, who never prayed, had unwavering faith in her prayers. The sight of Anu Aunty in her garden, plucking jasmines early in the mornings, was itself like a prayer.

We knew most people in our colony, and almost everyone knew Ma and me – not just because we'd lived here all my life, but also because Ma and I tutored the neighbourhood children. Ma had been tutoring since I was a baby as it was difficult to make ends meet on her lecturer's salary, and I, much against Ma's will, had insisted on doing the same at sixteen after I finished school. I taught English and Biology, and Ma taught English and History. I loved the children I tutored. I loved listening to them and to their mothers, who told me everything about their lives and loves.

Randhir said I had no discrimination. I suspected it galled him that I listened to his talk with as much interest as I did to our neighbour's mother-in-law's sister's gossip. But I did have discrimination. For example, I knew the difference between Dickens and a Mills & Boon romance, but I read both. In those days, when none of us could afford to buy more than three or four books a year, and the only decent library, the British Council, allowed us to borrow only two books at a time, and the lending library in the market only had time-pass books, I read every single book I could borrow. Listening was just like that.

In any case, our neighbour's mother-in-law's sister's gossip was *not* Mills-&-Boon-ish; it was Dickensian. I had said so to Randhir, and he had rolled his eyes.

But listening to gossip was one thing, whereas being the subject of it, another. Mrs D'Souza, a widow, had been our neighbour for fifteen years. She was always dropping by for a cup of tea or coffee. She believed that Ma and I upheld the unflinching moral standards that she upheld. Today, I had sorely shaken that belief. Of course, she had no idea about the secret stories in our lives, which were sealed and invisible in their vaults. Our visible lives were lived in an exemplary manner, complete with starched handloom sarees, nicely covered bosoms and bums, nothing tight-vight or sticking out. At some point today, Mrs D'Souza would land up at home and inform my mothers about my transgression. Lies of omission were all very well; I was a master of those. But to look my mothers in their eyes and blatantly lie? I couldn't do that. And the truth was impossible. So, what was I supposed to say?

Randhir, who had been studying in Pennsylvania for a year, said that was the bloody problem about living in India; your business was everybody's business, all the bloody time. When he had got a teaching assistantship the previous year to go to his university for a brand-new degree – a Masters/PhD in English with a specialty in creative writing – the entire colony had been in turmoil. 'He is going to America to write stories-shories?' they asked his mother. 'What kind of useless degree is that – that too, for a boy!'

Madhu Aunty had told everyone that Randhir had a scholarship for a PhD in English without mentioning the specialty in creative writing. After all, a PhD – even in that useless subject, English – was better than writing stories-shories, although obviously a PhD in English couldn't touch the feet of a degree in Engineering or Medicine or an MBA. But Madhu Aunty's lie got out. So, when the neighbours expressed their astonishment that Randhir was going all the way to America to write stories-shories, Madhu Aunty said, 'What does it matter, Randhir has scholarship, how many boys get scholarship in America?' True; until this year when both Arnav and I had managed it, no boy or girl in our colony had got a scholarship or assistantship to go to an American university. Going to America without one was out of the question. Hardly anyone we knew had been abroad. Most of us hadn't even sat in a plane. Everything Foreign was wondrous, especially music, jeans, perfume, underclothes, and underarm deodorants.

Even plastic bags from abroad smelled exotic. Indian plastic bags just smelled.

Randhir said the best part of being in America was living without that constant interference and unasked-for advice. Even your best friends didn't interfere in America, he said. He wrote to me twice a month from his university, his frustration about India spilling out onto the pages even though he had got away. Randhir was always simmering. He was upset about people poking their noses in your business, and he was frustrated about his parents' inability to understand his dreams. He had been furious about the Emergency. He had been briefly joyous when Indira Gandhi was voted out, then once again full of ire against the Janata Party government and even more ire about our Prime Minister, Morarji Desai, drinking his own pee for health benefits. Now that Indira had been voted back in, Randhir was furious all over again. But even though he simmered endlessly, Randhir was gentle and kind. This, combined with his magnificent looks, meant that every girl in sight was smitten by him.

Before he had come home this summer, Randhir had written to me, *I'm only coming back because of you.* Which should have been a declaration of intent, but it wasn't.

Now, I too was going away. My mothers and friends nodded without conviction when I assured them that I would come back every year. I was holding on fiercely to Randhir's incredible information that, in America, anyone could take loans, any time, and pay them back too. He and his friend Vineet had explained to me the wonders of credit history, a concept that I couldn't grasp. The things he told me about America, I'd never have known from Hollywood movies, *Time, Newsweek, Life*, and the *Reader's Digest*. What it boiled down to was that I could – if I had the courage to take a loan, and the means to pay it back – come home every year.

'It's not easy,' Randhir had said frankly. 'But it can be done.'

Given the fact that, in India, people went into debt only when they had to marry off their daughters or buy a house, it was no small thing that I was contemplating. But if I couldn't come home every year, then I wouldn't go. And Randhir knew this. He had assured me that loans in America didn't carry the kind of weight they did in India. 'But how will I pay it back?' I had asked him. He said teaching assistants got paid extra in the summer, and that extra money would help me pay it back. Then he tried to explain the wonders of credit cards to me, but when I couldn't believe that Americans took loans for everything, all the time, their entire lives, he groaned and gave up.

Now, the morning sun had lit up our neighbourhood. It was early August, and in another hour it would be too hot to walk. I had taken three rounds of the colony, and the surge of emotion that had been banging on my walls like a little demon was finally taking a nap with a snuffle here and a snuffle there. Finally, it was quiet within and without. I was one of the few who walked so early. It was the only time my breath was my own, my thoughts my own; the only time when lovely silence itself was the story, wrapping itself around me like a shawl, the sounds around me like embroidery around its edges – a solitary dog barking; the sound of the milkman's cycle and the ting-ting of his milk containers; the thud of newspapers being thrown into verandas; the familiar argument between the milkman and Mrs D'Souza, the milkman protesting that she was doing him great injustice by accusing him of watering the milk. In the winters, I walked later because it was so dark. But there would be no walking in the Delhi winter this year, no walking through that heavenly morning mist, breathing in the smell of distant woodfire, the cold sharp against my face, I bundled up in my sweater and coat and shawl, and all the gardens full of flowers, some like babies, their petals closed, stems bowed down, waiting to be touched by the sun.

Time to go home, have a bath, breakfast, and then pack before the children I tutored, their mothers, and our neighbours started coming home to say goodbye to me. Although I had already said my goodbyes, everyone was determined to come by and say several more. My tearful children and their mothers came daily to commiserate. They were not merely mourning my departure; they were also mourning my mother losing her only child to that vast and distant country. They kept assuring my mother I would come back: Mallika wasn't the kind to lose her Indian values and gain an American accent and an American husband.

Going to Anu Aunty's garden, I plucked jasmines and put them in my hanky. I needed to make the phone call to the gynaecologist today to make sure her clinic was open tomorrow, Saturday.

The hurdle rose like a spectre before me.

We didn't have a phone. There was one public phone in the market, which was out of order half the time, and the rest of the time the line was always unclear. You had to shout and there was always a line of people behind you, listening to everything you said. Which meant I would have to use Madhu Aunty's phone. But if I went to her house, she would hear me. Which meant that I would have to use her kitchen phone.

But this strategy also had its problems.

Those days, when most of us didn't have even one of anything, Madhu Aunty had two or more of everything – two phone instruments, two houses, two cars, two gas cylinders, two Godrej almaras, two record players, and *five* bedrooms. The main phone, a sleek blue, was installed in the sitting room. She had paid her cousin from England an arm and a leg for the instrument and the customs duty on top of that. The eternally unprepossessing Indian phone, black and square, served as the extension and was installed in the kitchen. Madhu Aunty had acquired the second phone to eavesdrop on Randhir's conversations and make sure he wasn't falling into the clutches of a Muslim girl, a Christian girl, a forward-shameless girl, or a crazy girl. She had already lost her older son, who had married a Muslim girl in Bombay and been disowned by his father. So, whenever Randhir received phone calls, Madhu Aunty listened in the kitchen. As she told Ma: 'So fair and handsome he is, and hundred and one girls are after him, I have to listen, no? Otherwise one more tragedy will happen.' Because her foolish son said that religion didn't matter. And he had already had one dangerous involvement with a crazy girl. His mother wasn't going to let it happen again. How exactly she could prevent Crazy, Forward, Shameless, Christian, or Muslim from happening to Randhir were he so inclined, none of us were sure – but Madhu Aunty had her ways, and the second phone was one way. Of course, Randhir, true to the stereotype of oblivious Indian men, had no idea about his mother's machinations.

Ma and I used Madhu Aunty's phone whenever we needed to, and we didn't even have to go next door to do so. Our kitchen windows were just three feet apart, and Madhu Aunty was constantly passing us kadhi, samosas, mooli parathas, and fresh garden grown vegetables through the windows. On the rare occasions that someone phoned us or we needed to make a call, Madhu Aunty's kitchen phone suffered the same fate as the food and the vegetables. Squat and recalcitrant, the phone took a lot of manoeuvring through the window bars even with the receiver off. Its cord stopped short of our windowsill, and we would be pressed against the bars for the course of the conversation, unable to turn, and if the pressure cookers weren't on, everyone could hear everything. That normally didn't matter, since secrets weren't meant for the phone, and privacy, like credit cards, was an alien concept.

So, the dilemma was this: the only phone I could use to make my call to the gynaecologist was Madhu Aunty's, but I had to do it when no one could overhear. Which meant using it when Madhu Aunty was *not* in her kitchen, and when my mothers and grandmother were out of *our* kitchen, and when Madhu Aunty's servant Ramu (who didn't know English) *was* in her kitchen so he could give me the phone.

My after-walk serenity had disappeared.

As though to affirm my rising agitation, a tremendous bellow pervaded our neighbourhood. It came from three-year-old Subramanium, who was in the throes of a tantrum. Other children with tantrums shrieked, but Subramanium bellowed. It was a deep, long, continuous OOOOOO sound which emerged not from his throat, but from somewhere deep inside his small but sturdy chest and sounded like a dog baying. Once he began, he couldn't stop. He could go on for an hour or more, baying with utter abandon, a terrible sound that our entire street, as well as those who lived in the street behind his house, dreaded. He was now rolling on the floor of his veranda and bellowing while his young mother sat, exhausted, on the lawn chair next to him. Every time Subramanium had a tantrum, his mother would pick him up and dump him on the veranda, where he could bellow and roll around to his heart's content. So what if the entire neighbourhood could hear, she said. That was better than people thinking she was beating him. She saw me and cried out in relief: 'Mallika!' I walked to their veranda and picked up the bellowing Subramanium, rocked him in my arms and stroked his heaving back. I was the only one who could stop his tantrums – god knows why, because I was by no means a lover of children. But this child loved me, and subsequently, I loved him too. 'You'll be fine, everything's alright, such a good boy,' I murmured, stroking him.

But this time, Subramanium didn't stop. After ten minutes of rocking and crooning, I was exhausted. 'Subramanium,' I scolded. 'Enough of this. Stop crying now.'

Subramanium bellowed, 'I *want* to stop, I *want* to stop, but I don't know *how* to stop, *you* tell me, *how* to stop? *How* to stop?'

This was exactly how I was feeling.

In that moment, I had a profound glimpse into the nature of little Subramanium's big tantrums. I realized that even though the tantrum was born inside him, it had a life of its own beyond him. It was larger than him. Subramanium's tantrum came out because he was three; mine stayed in because I was twenty-three. But this didn't mean I couldn't feel it. It was yelling and drumming its feet through my entire body. I know you can stop yourself from saying or doing something because you shouldn't, but how do you stop yourself from *feeling* something because you shouldn't? To those of you who say, 'of course you can,' let me say this: you haven't stopped feeling it. You've just shoved it away into a place where there's sufficient darkness for it to hide and quietly grow into a monster. And that monster's going to come out one day and swallow you up in one gigantic gulp. And when the monster is no longer in you, you are in the monster.

'Now, Subramanium, make Mr Tantrum your friend,' I said.

Subramanium paused mid-bellow. 'How?' he asked, his chest heaving.

'Say, "Mr Tantrum, I am your friend."'

'Mr Tantrum, I am your friend.' Subramanium sighed, looking deep into my eyes.

'See. Mr Tantrum's happy.' I kissed him and put him on his mother's lap.

'Mallika, what will I do when you go to America?' his mother sighed, as Subramanium sat on her lap, hiccupping.

I said bye and went home, thinking about the various hurdles involved in making that phone call and praying that my two mothers and my grandmother wouldn't make me talk. I could feel the beginnings of a headache on the left side of my temple and neck.

Shantamama, Ma's sister, lived in Bangalore with her husband and two sons. Her husband was in the railways, and they got first class railway passes, so Shantamama came and stayed with us two or three times a year. My grandmother, Ajji, lived with her son in Bombay, but also spent a few months of the year with Shantamama and Ma.

All three were in the sitting room, having their morning coffee. They greeted me, full of love.

'Darling, you're wearing an *orange* blouse with this *magenta* saree! It clashes so badly!'

Shantamama.

'And how come you've plaited your hair? You always put it up in a bun for your walks.'

Ma.

'Child, surely you haven't put *rouge* on your cheeks!'

Ajji, my grandmother.

I looked at my blouse. They were right. It didn't match with my saree. As for the rouge – oh, no, was it that obvious? Suppose Arnav had thought I went to his room in the hope of a tryst, in addition to the help I needed? Many girls did. Seek a tryst, I mean, not the help. A dash of kajal was the only thing I usually wore first thing in the morning. This morning, I had applied what I thought was a mere touch of lipstick to my cheeks and spread it, in an effort to add some colour to my pale, overwrought face. I had four lipsticks – orange, magenta, red, and maroon – so I chose maroon for the rouge. If it wasn't subtle, that was because it was still dark, I couldn't find my hand-held mirror, and there was no mirror in my room. As for the small mirror above my bathroom washbasin – it had fallen and broken a month ago. It hadn't been replaced. Ma and I couldn't spend money on useless things like mirrors with the going-to-America expenses mounting up. As for my blouse, it had looked like my magenta one in the darkness.

They were looking at me expectantly.

'I didn't notice in the dark,' I said and quickly went to the kitchen where my Ayah-ji was weeping over my tea. Quickly, I rubbed off the rouge with my palm.

Ayah-ji wiped her eyes as she strained my tea. 'Who will look after you in Amreeka?'

I put my arm around her. 'Ayah-ji, I'm coming back in one year to see you.'

'Without you I have to live for one year?' Sobbing, she gave me my mug of tea.

'Don't cry, Ayah-ji.' I gulped my tears down a throat already raw with swallowing emotions. Ayah-ji had looked after me since I was a baby. That I was going across the oceans to study was beyond her comprehension. What need for so much studying, she kept asking me, hadn't I studied enough?

I went to the sitting room to join my mothers and grandmother.

'But why the rouge?' Ma asked, puzzled.

'I was looking washed out,' I said.

'But you always look washed out when you're tired, and you've never worn rouge,' said Shantamama. 'That too, for an early morning walk!'

'I thought I'd try it. I'm going for a bath now,' I said, edging my way upstairs with my mug in one hand and my handkerchief of jasmines in the other.

'But, child, why aren't you having your tea with us?' I could hear my grandmother saying as I went up the stairs to my room.

Separately, my mothers and grandmother were contained. Together, they were like the Brahmaputra in flood.

My grandmother saying, 'My granddaughter has got a scholarship to go to America, it is a very great thing.' Shantamama saying, 'But all alone in that country, Deva, Deva.' Ma saying uncertainly, 'She won't be alone, Randhir and Arnav will be there too.' Shantamama snorting dismissively. My grandmother saying, 'Be happy for her, Shanta.' Shantamama saying, 'Suppose she marries an American – then? I'll never understand his accent, and he will divorce her within a year!' Ajji saying, 'Control yourself, Shanta.' Shantamama saying, 'And if she has a child by the time he divorces her, then what will she *do* all alone in a strange country with no one to turn to?' Ma saying, 'All I'm praying for is for the TB not to come back.' TB being their code for mental.

This was how it always was when the three of them were together.

Ma saying, 'Find a man who can stand up to his parents. Marry someone who knows your heart, not someone for whom looks are all.' Shantamama bursting out, 'Mallika, don't get taken in by all that high-flown talk; looks are *very* important. Why don't you ever make the best of yours? Look how tightly you plait your hair; wear your plait a little looser, your face looks so much softer. And why don't you wear more sleeveless blouses in the summer? Your arms are so nice and slender. You don't even bother powdering your nose, it's always oily. And what's the point of all that kajal in your eyes if you don't even *look* at a man, let alone smile at him?'

But now that I was going to America, my grandmother could say, 'Uff, leave it, Shanta. Mallika has got a scholarship to study in America! Stop harping on marriage.' At which Shantamama snorted.

I knew exactly what that snort meant. What was the point of excellence in all areas of life if it didn't lead to The Ultimate Happiness – marriage? For here I was, twenty-three years old, unmarried, and flying to America for a PhD, accompanied by Arnav, this eligible boy from IIT – the Indian Institute of Technology – who knew me so well and liked me so much but didn't want to marry me. And the minute I landed in America, I would be welcomed with open arms by that other eligible boy, Randhir, who knew me even better than Arnav, and was even better looking, but also didn't want to marry me. What kind of tragedy was this?

'Don't worry, Shantacca,' Ma would say. 'Mallika won't be alone. Randhir and Arnav will be there with her. They'll see to it that no harm comes to her.'

'But suppose the harm that comes to her comes from *them*?' Shantamama demanded.

As usual, Shantamama had the last word. Because *this* was the crux of the matter.

Four hours later, as I packed, my headache becoming worse, their siren calls flew into my room.

'Trunk call, trunk call from America, hurry!' Ma.

'Mallika, child, come down!' Ajji.

'It's Randhir, the seconds are ticking, quickly, quickly!' Shantamama.

I ran downstairs to where all three stood, calling me.

'Kitchen, kitchen,' Ma gestured, and I rushed into the kitchen and to the window where Madhu Aunty's servant was handing the phone to Ayah-ji through the bars.

I grabbed the phone from Ayah-ji. Oh, god, why was Randhir phoning from America?

'Hullo, hullo? Randhir?'

'Mallika, no need to shout, I can hear you.'

'Randhir, what's wrong?'

'Nothing's wrong.' He sounded as if he were right next to me. 'Listen, have you been to the dentist?'

'No.'

'You better go, then. It can be up to a thousand dollars to get a root canal done here, so get your teeth checked before leaving.'

'A thousand dollars?' I shrieked, feeling my headache stab at me even harder.

'Yeah. Don't go to Dr Chopra in the market. If you have a cavity, he'll just pull out your tooth. Go to Dr Mukherjee in Def Col. He saves teeth. He's the best.'

'But, Randhir, Dr Mukherjee charges a hundred rupees for a filling!'

'God, Mallika, do your Maths. Hundred rupees is about eight dollars. You'd rather pay a thousand dollars than eight dollars?'

'I know, I know, but I haven't even packed and –'

'If you have tooth problems in America, you're done for. You'll never be able to go home to India. You'll be in debt for the rest of your life.'

I felt faint.

'Hullo?' he said.

'I'll go, I'll go.'

'Good. See you at JFK. Safe journey, OK? Bye.'

'Bye, Randhir.'

I gave the phone back to Ramu through the window and turned to find my mothers and grandmother gathered in the kitchen, listening worriedly.

'Nothing's wrong. Randhir wants me to go to the dentist because American dentists charge a thousand dollars for a tooth.'

They were speechless. For once.

Then Ma said, 'I'll give you the money, you must go to the dentist.'

'I'll go tomorrow, Ma.'

They were still standing dazed in the kitchen. The thousand dollars had knocked them out cold.

'Why are you still in the kitchen?' I scolded.

They slowly left.

Ayah-ji began washing the dishes.

'Ramu,' I said, going back to the kitchen window, rubbing my temple. 'Just give me the telephone directory.'

He handed me the directory through the windows. I looked up the phone numbers and wrote them down on the little pad Ma had kept next to the window. Then I went outside to check. Ajji was lying down in the downstairs room, listening to classical music on All India Radio. Shantamama was sitting at the desk next to her, writing a letter. Ma was changing the sheets in her room.

I swiftly went back to the kitchen and peered through our kitchen window into theirs. No Madhu Aunty.

'Ramu,' I said. 'Phone.'

Ramu gave a long-suffering sigh and handed me the phone through the windows.

Pressed against the window bars once more, I dialled the dentist and got an appointment for ten a.m. Then I dialled the gynaecologist's number and made an appointment for one-thirty p.m.

I gave the phone back to Ramu and let out my breath. Done!

By the time we finished lunch, the migraine had taken over.

My mothers and grandmother didn't engage me in conversation during lunch. They could see the migraine on my face. 'Go to the Phuknewalla,' Ma said after I finished eating.

'What will she do in America when it happens,' Shantamama said unhappily.

'America, it is full of pills for pain,' my grandmother said ominously.

'India also has pills for pain, Amma,' Ma said.

'But there, it is only that,' my grandmother sighed.

I went into the kitchen, where Ayah-ji had just finished washing the dishes. She looked at my face and asked, 'It has started again?'

'Yes, Ayah-ji.'

'Chalo.' She wiped her hands with her saree palla.

The Phuknewalla, who lived in the servants' quarter behind our houses, had healed me of my worst migraines when I was fourteen. The migraines came less often now, and when they did, I was no longer prostrate with pain, but when they returned, I always went to him.

The Phuknewalla was sitting on the charpai outside his quarter, smoking a beedi.

'Why do we have to keep coming back?' Ayah-ji demanded. 'Why can you not cure Baby for good?'

'Bilkul, I have cured Baby,' he said. 'Now, her headache is two, three times a year only. At first it used to be ten, fifteen times a month. If that is not a cure, then what is?'

The Phuknewalla and Ayah-ji had the same preliminary exchange every time we went, Ayah-ji belligerent, the Phuknewalla serene. Ayah-ji believed that it was her right to take away my migraine and that he had usurped that right, even though she was the one who had brought him home to me all those years ago. I don't think she had anticipated that he would be helping me for such a long time, and it only served to exacerbate her jealousy.

We went inside his quarter, where he made me sit on a plastic stool. Ayah-ji squatted opposite me, glaring at the Phuknewalla for his presumption. I was familiar with the routine now. He never touched me. He gathered the air around my head and neck in a sweeping motion with both hands, ending at the side of my neck where the pain was always the worst. Then, with one fist, he drew out the pain as though he were drawing out a rope from my neck. I felt the pain even more sharply as he did this, and then, as he kept pulling, the pain began to diminish. His hands were still closed. Then he went to the door, opened his hands, and blew the pain out of his palms.

'Alright, Baby?' Ayah-ji asked me, getting up.

I nodded. The worst of the pain was gone. Now, I would go home and lie down, and then, over the next couple of hours, the rest of the pain would slowly disappear.

'You need Shanti inside you, peace,' he said. He said this every time.

'Shukriya, Phuknewalla, a lot of thanks,' I said. I got up and gave him money.

'So much?' he said, looking at the notes.

'How much you have done for me,' I said. 'And now I am going to America. You stay well.'

I was washing the last few dishes that Ayah-ji had forgotten about when Madhu Aunty called me from her kitchen window.

'Mallika, you finished lunch, no? Accha, then for one minute, come home.'

Placing the last of the dishes on the counter, I rinsed my hands and went to her house. She was standing in their sitting room, deep in thought. She took me to her bedroom and said, 'Sit.' I sat on her bed. She sat next to me. 'Beta, why you phoned the gynaecologist for appointment this morning?'

I almost choked.

'Beta, vaise, you are truthful girl, but I know that about some things we women cannot be truthful. No need to lie to me; I am your Madhu Aunty, I am like mother to you. By mistake, I picked up the phone in sitting room same time when you were phoning from kitchen. Everything I heard. Now, tell me?'

I could feel my knees trembling.

'Beta, you are like my daughter. That you know. Tell me.'

I couldn't say a word.

Then, to my horror, she began to cry.

'Beta, scholarship or no scholarship, if you are pregnant you cannot go to America. It is *very* backward country; do you know in some places in America there is no abortion clinic? And more money than gold American doctors take!'

I tried to say something, but nothing came out.

'Beta, do not hide from me. The way you made that phone call, so secretly-secretly, you think I am a fool? Who is it – Randhir or Arnav? I will kill whichever one it is, I promise you. I will get Randhir from America, and I will strangle him with my own hands.'

'No, no, no!' I gasped.

'No – what? No, it is not Randhir, or no, it is not Arnav, or no, I am not pregnant?'

'Aunty, all three, no.'

'Promise on your mothers' names that you are not.'

'I promise.'

She fished out her handkerchief from her blouse and wiped her eyes. 'Then why you are going to gynaecologist tomorrow?'

I couldn't come up with a single lie.

Her eyes narrowed.

'Accha, accha,' she said, ominously. 'I know why. *Now* I know why.'

What did she know? I could hear my heart thumping like crazy.

'What, Aunty?' I asked against my better judgment.

'*Now* I know why,' she said grimly once more.

She couldn't possibly know. I was beginning to feel a little sick.

'Aunty, what do you – know?'

'What I know is the truth which you are not telling me.' She was examining my face minutely.

'Aunty, *how* could you think it was Randhir or Arnav?' I burst out.

'No other boy you know,' she said simply.

'I've *never* –'

'I know, Beta, I know. You are *very* good girl. Sorry, Beta, but with all this love-shuv and all, you know what all things can happen.'

'There's *no* love-shuv or *anything*, Aunty.'

'Yes, Beta, you are very good girl, but your phone call – it gave me heart attack.'

It was too much. 'Alright, Aunty. Bye.'

She exhaled noisily. 'I am telling your mothers this evening about phone call. It is my duty. It is out of love. Beta, it is for your sake that I am telling.'

'Yes, Aunty,' I said, and fled.

'Mallika darling,' Shantamama called me from Ma's room as soon as I entered.

I went to their room. Ma was asleep. Shantamama was lying with her book next to her.

'Darling, how is your headache?'

'Much better, Shantamama. Almost gone.'

'Good. I had a horrible dream this morning.'

'Oho. What happened, Shantamama?'

'I dreamt I was dead, and all of you were so lovingly washing my body and *so* lovingly dressing me up in a beautiful magenta saree and *so* painstakingly painting my fingernails and toenails with pink Cutex and applying this lovely magenta lipstick on me. Everything so perfectly matching. So, I should have looked beautiful, no? But I didn't, because I had all this hair sprouting out of my upper lip and chin. Imagine, being cremated with hair on my face. When I woke up, I looked at myself in the mirror and I found the dream was telling me the truth. I thought, Deva, thank you I'm not dead yet, before Mallika leaves, I have to ask her to do my deforestation.'

'Of course, Shantamama.' I went to the bathroom, took the small scissors and tweezers out of the cabinet, and went and sat by her.

'That's not to say I'm going to die any time soon, but you know, one always has to be prepared, no? Darling, wait till you reach menopause. It's terrible the way hair sprouts out where it shouldn't.' She shuddered. 'When you're –'

'Shantamama, I can't cut while you're talking.'

She subsided. I carefully cut the hair above her lip. 'It isn't much. You should let me wax it.'

'No, no, too painful.'

I finished her chin with the tweezer. Then I picked up the Charmis cream from next to her and rubbed it over her upper lip, chin, and under her chin. I spread what was left over her cheeks and forehead. How soft her skin was. I wouldn't be able to touch it for the next... How long? One year? More? My throat closed.

'Thank you, darling. My neighbour in Bangalore went to America and came back with these beautiful small curved scissors and nice, sharp tweezers. When you come home, you can get them for me. If it's not too expensive.'

'Alright, Shantamama,' I said, putting the cream back and kissing her.

'Go and rest my darling, go. Try and sleep.'

Lying in bed, my thoughts went round and round. At some point this evening, Mrs D'Souza would drop by and inform my mothers about my early morning visit to Arnav's room. And Madhu Aunty would inform them about my appointment with the gynaecologist. What on earth to tell them? I *had* to meet the gynae before we left for America. I *had* to. The lies were making me sick. What to *do*?

Randhir: What is there to hide?

1970 and after

When he was sixteen, one of their neighbours, Mrs Sood, had dropped in to see his mother, full of news about her trip to America. She was the only one in their neighbourhood who had been there. He was in his room and could hear her talking loudly to his mother.

'*Very* nice people these Americans are, Madhu, I can't even *tell* you how friendly. They are always saying hi, always smiling, even to strangers.' The Americans had loved her sarees and said how much they wanted to visit India. There were so many things that amazed her about these Americans. 'Imagine, Madhu – Americans just throw their things away! And nice people, educated people, they pick up these things from garbage dump.'

'From rubbish dump!' his mother exclaimed in horror.

'Madhu, garbage dump in America is very different from rubbish dump in India,' explained Mrs Sood. 'Beautiful things you find there. Perfect-condition dressing tables, beautiful lamps, chairs, and sofas, oh, Madhu, I can't even *tell* you!'

'Imagine!' his mother marvelled.

There was a silence as his mother and Mrs Sood contemplated rubbish dumps full of beautiful things, there for the picking.

Then Mrs Sood said, 'But so much divorce and all. Such funny reasons the Americans have to divorce, you wouldn't believe!'

His mother said, 'In *Reader's Digest*, I read one wife left husband because of snoring.'

Mrs Sood said, 'That is nothing! My sister's neighbour in America, she divorced her husband because she said she did not love him.'

The two women screamed with laughter.

'Tell me more, tell me more,' his mother said.

'No maternity leave in America,' Mrs Sood said triumphantly.

'Haii!' his mother exclaimed in disbelief. 'Why?'

'Don't know.' She added in a sibilant whisper: 'Abortion also, it is illegal.'

'*Hanh?*' his mother said in disbelief.

'And, Madhu,' said Mrs Sood. 'This also you will not believe – their children *all* leave home when they are eighteen! Parents, they *expect* that!'

He pricked up his ears.

'That cannot be,' his mother said.

'By God, it is like that only. One American woman – Madhu she was *overjoyed* when her son left for college. She sold all her son's furniture and made it into her painting room.'

'Kamaal hain! But when her son comes home?' his mother had asked in astonishment.

'That is not how Americans think. When their children leave, they *leave*. Relationship itself is different.'

'Children, they do not come home?'

'Once a year, maybe. For few days. And when parents go to see children, they stay in hotels.'

'Why?'

'Who knows. Americans are *very* nice, but some things I do not understand about them.'

After he overheard the conversation, it became one of his favourite fantasies. Of leaving home and not coming back. It wasn't even a guilt-ridden fantasy, because in it his parents weren't longing to see him, so there was nothing pulling him back. In his fantasy, his father didn't take it for granted that he, Randhir, would join the family business as soon as he finished college. In his fantasy, his father said, 'Your older brother, Akhil, will help me, you do whatever you like.' It was a fantasy in which no one was appalled that, instead of joining the family business, he wanted to do his BA Honours in English, of all subjects, and his writing wasn't a fierce secret diluting every word he penned. In his fantasy, it was the writing which was fierce, for his winged heart was free.

That day, when Mrs Sood was talking about America, Randhir had just finished school. A few months later, the results came out, and he'd done as well as everyone expected: five points in the Indian School Certificate exams, above ninety percent in every subject, and he'd topped his class. Then the news from school that he would be getting the President's Gold Medal for topping, as well as the President's Silver Medal for the Best All Rounder. His parents had been ecstatic. They had said he should apply to all the Indian Institutes of Technology, and so he had. After he completed his five-year Engineering degree, he would join his father and Akhil in the family business.

He applied to the IITs for Engineering and took all the exams.

And then, just for the heck of it, he quietly applied to St Stephen's for an English degree.

'Just sent off my application to Stephen's for English,' he told Arnav, laughing. He knew how ridiculous it was. They were on their motorcycles near Palam airport at three a.m., watching the planes land, something they did periodically for the thrill of it.

Arnav's face lit up. 'Fantastic! You'll get in like a shot.'

His laughter disappeared. 'I can't do it.'

'Then why the hell did you apply?'

'Just... for the heck of it.'

'It's going to *kill* you not to go when you get in.'

He was conscious of a sinking feeling in the pit of his stomach.

'What's the use of an English degree when I join my father's business?'

'If you're joining the family business, then what's the use of an Engineering degree?'

He didn't tell Mallika. If his mother ever asked Mallika if she had known Randhir was applying for a BA in English, Mallika wouldn't know what to say. She wouldn't betray his confidence, and she wouldn't lie to his mother either. But she'd try to do both anyway and tie herself in her inevitable knots. Whereas if Mummy asked Arnav, he'd find an answer that wasn't a lie. His calm demeanour and sunny disposition had disarmed all their teachers at school. It had saved him from many a consequence. In boarding school, Arnav and Vineet broke all the rules − smoking on the hostel terrace, climbing over the school walls and spending nights out, and, once, stealing the skeleton from the Biology lab and dangling it front of the Hindi teacher's window in the middle of the night. The teacher almost died of fright. The only reason Arnav and Vineet weren't suspended was because they were amongst the school's toppers. And also because Randhir was the headmaster's favourite student and begged him not to suspend them, saying *he'd* see to it that they didn't misbehave. Soon after that, Arnav had hidden a cigarette filled with dope in his desk and was discovered by the warden. Arnav had had a lucky escape − the warden and headmaster thought it was just a cigarette.

Arnav got into IIT Delhi, and Vineet got into St Stephen's for Economics. He, Randhir, also got into all the IITs and, as Arnav predicted, Stephen's for English. He didn't tell anyone about the latter. His mother boasted about his admission into the IITs to the entire colony. People came in droves to congratulate him and were greeted with pedas and laddoos by his parents. Every congratulation that he accepted, smiling, felt like another nail in his coffin. Burn your bloody boats, he heard that voice inside him saying.

Without telling a soul, not even Arnav, he wrote to every Engineering college, withdrawing his admission, and accepted his place at St Stephen's for a BA Honours in English.

Then he told his parents.

'You have refused admission at *all* the IITs?' his father had said, his face pinched.

'It's St Stephen's,' he said.

'But it is *English*,' his mother said. 'And you are a *boy*!'

'Beta,' his father added, 'writing poems and stories is alright, but it will not get you anywhere in life.'

Randhir felt his head jerk up. How did his father know he wrote?

His mother was smiling lovingly. She'd been snooping around in his room. Anger began pooling into his stomach.

'Daddy, if I'm joining your business, it doesn't matter if I do an English degree or an Engineering degree.'

'Engineering degree, it is prestigious degree. English degree is alright for girls. Not for you.'

His father was talking very earnestly, very lovingly. He couldn't bear it.

His father got up. 'We will send telegram to IITs and tell them to ignore your letter and say you are accepting admission.'

He followed his father. 'Daddy.'

His father turned. His face was heavy with unhappiness.

'Daddy, please don't talk about my writing to – anyone. Please.'

'What is there to talk about?' his father replied.

Randhir went into his room. He didn't shut the door. Whenever he'd tried before, Mummy had driven him nuts with her nagging about how rude it was. Only at night, after everyone went to bed, did he shut his door. Of course, first thing in the morning, his mother would open it, and the morning sounds of the dishes, the doorbell, and the constant arguments with the servant would wake him up.

His mother followed him into his room. 'Beta, please think properly.'

'You told Daddy I write?'

'Beta, why are you sounding like that? So *beautifully* you write!'

He waited.

'Only two things he has seen, Beta. I promise. One poem and one story. Bas.'

He could feel his anger corroding his insides.

'I showed your Daddy, I said, "So beautifully our Randhir writes."'

'Mummy, you shouldn't be looking at my things.'

'I was just *cleaning* up your room, Beta, so *untidy* you keep it. Bas, one poem and one story was on your desk.'

'They weren't *on* my desk. They were *inside* my desk.'

'But what is there to hide? It isn't gold. Or letters from any girl. It is only stories. I was *praising* your writing to him, Beta.'

She'd never understand.

'Mummy, please don't discuss my writing with anyone. Promise me.'

'Beta, there is no shame in it. It is not good for *college* degree, that is all.'

'Promise me, Mummy.'

'Accha, accha, I promise.'

His mother would sooner break her best crockery than a promise made to her children.

'Beta, Engineering is *good* degree,' she said again.

'Like the BA that Mahima will get one day, so you can get her a good husband? So that you can boast about my being in IIT to everyone?'

'Sometimes' – his mother's eyes filled – 'you give my heart so much of pain that I cannot believe it is my own son who is talking to me.'

'I'm sorry.'

She didn't answer and went out of his room.

He didn't want to give her pain. He didn't want to give anyone pain. But not giving pain to your family usually meant giving it to yourself. It was like ingesting small doses of poison daily to give yourself immunity against it: the small doses made you ill, and you retched and heaved, and eventually, after months and years, you became immune to it. But this kind of immunity wasn't strength; this kind of immunity, over time, was also death.

He had always known he'd one day work in his father's factory, but during those idyllic boarding school days, it had seemed very far away. He was the Head Boy and House Captain, loved by his teachers, worshipped by the juniors; the one who excelled in everything and walked away with the first prizes in academics, in sports, in debates, and in elocution; the one whose behaviour was so exemplary that the headmaster would call him to his office and ask him to counsel recalcitrant students. He was the Golden Boy. The Shining Example.

Yet, even in those happy days, something inside him had smouldered and constricted his heart. In fact, after he won the All-India Gold Medal for the On The Spot Essay Writing Competition, that feeling became worse. The subject of the essay was 'Courage.' He found himself writing about the courage to be yourself. About how it meant swimming against the stream. Courage, he wrote, is a solitary journey because those who love you most can be the very ones who condemn you.

A couple of months later, it was announced in the school assembly that he had won the All-India Prize for the best essay. When his essay was published in the school magazine, he reread it with wonder. Later that night, he wrote in his diary: *Where did my essay about courage come from?* He answered his own question: *From the pen of someone who wishes he had it.*

On the heels of that, Arnav casually asked him, 'Hey, why d'you think you'll be condemned for being yourself?'

He didn't answer. Arnav had got to the heart of it. As usual.

Though Arnav didn't read much fiction, he *wanted* to read Randhir's work. When Randhir wrote his first story in the ninth class, Arnav had read it and burst out, '*Fantastic*, yar, but why is this guy so bloody miserable?' Taken aback, Randhir had asked, 'Where have I said he's miserable?' And Arnav had declared, 'You haven't *said* it, but, I mean, look at the way he reacts to every damn thing!'

After that, he'd shown Arnav every story and poem he wrote. Then he'd go back and rework it. Even in those early days, he'd known that his first draft was not his last.

School was now behind him. After college, his life in his father's factory would begin. Now was the heaving and retching stage for him, of ingesting the poison of inevitability, of getting used to the idea of living a life that wasn't his own. Three years, maybe five, to build up his immunity, the immunity that was a living death.

After his blow-up with his parents, he'd gone for a long ride on his motorcycle. When he came back, he saw Mallika walking towards the market with a cloth bag hanging from her shoulder. He parked his bike and sprinted down the road to join her. Within a minute she asked, 'What's happened, Randhir?'

She was fifteen then, and he seventeen. He told her about his blow-up with his parents. Her large eyes, like black holes, consumed every word he said. It would have been easier if his father yelled at him, he told her. He didn't want to be the child who would fulfil his father's dreams. He wished his father hadn't been such a fantastic example of hard work and success, indulgent with his children's needs, and so kind to them, never interfering in what they did, always ready to give Randhir money to buy books, always filled with the absolute belief that he, Randhir, would never let him down. His father had no expectations of him except that he would join his business, and even *this*, he didn't want to do.

'What do you mean, "even *this*?"' Mallika said. '*This* is *everything*.'

He looked at her, startled.

'His expectation of you,' Mallika continued indignantly, 'is your *whole life*, Randhir.'

They walked the rest of the way to the market without talking. She returned her books at Bittu's Books, the lending library, and picked up two more, and then they walked home. It was a shitty lending library, full of third-rate bestsellers and stupid romances; he didn't understand why Mallika and her friends read that rubbish, but anyway.

He was still grappling with Mallika's absolute comprehension.

This was the moment to tell her about his writing.

But the words – 'I write stories, I want to be a writer' – were stuck in his throat.

For the entire walk, he was trying to get these words unstuck. But they wouldn't come out.

When he went back home, he pulled out the trunk that he kept under his bed, unlocked it, took out his diary and spent an hour vomiting out his frustration and misery at the prison-like life ahead of him. Then he found himself writing about how people viewed him as this perfect boy. He wrote about how, one day, a Delhi University boy, a couple of years older than him at another college, had committed suicide with an overdose of sleeping pills. Everyone was shocked, uncomprehending. He was a topper in school and college, popular, a fantastic debater, loved by his friends, a beloved son and brother. Everyone said he lacked nothing; how could this have happened? Randhir understood how. He understood that boy's despair, so deep, so profound; he often felt *he* was that boy, he wrote in his diary. He didn't write why. You could only dig so deep. There was no point in digging till you reached the centre, no joy in finding a rotten core.

The next night he talked to Arnav. They were upstairs on his terrace at midnight, on the other side, away from Mallika's house, sharing a cigarette. Maybe he was a little paranoid, but sometimes he felt that if they talked on the side facing Mallika's room, she'd hear them, and sometimes they talked about stuff he didn't want her to hear.

Arnav smoked in silence, then said, 'OK, fine, but do your MA in English too. IIT would have been five years. So at least give yourself five years of freedom doing what you like.'

Five years doing what he wanted. He felt heady at the thought.

'Remember that DU guy, Amit, who committed suicide?' he asked Arnav.

Arnav looked slightly taken aback at the change in subject.

'Everyone thought he was perfect. But I guess he wasn't,' Randhir said.

'Meaning what?'

'Meaning... we all think we know the people we're close to but... we don't.'

There was a brief silence.

Then Arnav said, 'You mean, *we* don't know *you*?'

Randhir laughed. 'Of course not! Just thinking aloud.'

The next morning, he told his parents that he had thought it over and that he was going to do his English degree at Stephen's. His father left the room without saying a word. His mother wept again.

He could never tell his parents the plain, unvarnished truth – that to join the family business and live that life, would kill his spirit. 'Kill your spirit,' they would say, bewildered. 'What do you mean? You will make plenty of money, you will live in luxury, you will get offers from so many beautiful girls, your children will not lack for anything, you will not lack for anything – what do you mean, kill your spirit?'

Family was overrated. Family meant no freedom. Family meant claustrophobia. He hated himself for feeling this way, but he had nothing in common with his family. His father had started his factory from scratch, and now it was thriving. It was his life, his passion, his everything. He would fail his father. He had nothing in common with his brother, Akhil, who was now studying in Bombay. He didn't understand his sister, Mahima, who wanted nothing more than to get married and have children and whose greatest love was watching Hindi films. And he was constantly embarrassed by his mother, who behaved as though she were the presiding deity of their neighbourhood.

He rarely wrote in his diary about the despair that periodically almost felled him. Here he was, a beloved son who had done exceptionally well in everything, living in a secure home with parents who gave him more love than he wanted and had more money than he needed, and he felt this kind of despair? He had no right to feel it.

He began collecting Mummy's sleeping pills. Two or three every month from her packet of pills; she never noticed. He couldn't buy too many of them from the chemist, who still asked for prescriptions, so sometimes he'd buy a packet from other chemists on the way to college. He would take the pills out of the shiny foil and put them in an empty bottle he kept behind the large bottle of Old Spice aftershave in his bathroom cabinet. The bottle began filling up. Like having savings in the bank. It was just in case. Just in case, if one kind of freedom was denied to him, then, if need be, if it came to it, maybe he could have another.

A little before he began college on his seventeenth birthday, his mother gave him fifty rupees, and while he was at his favourite bookshop greedily buying books, she had a mirror hammered onto his wall. A full-length one. 'Happy birthday to you!' she sang happily when he returned from the bookshop.

He looked at the mirror, aghast. 'I don't want a mirror in my room,' he said.

She laughed, 'Beta, mirror is more important in rooms than books. How you can go to college in crushed shirts and pants? You never notice – but *now*, you will notice.'

It was her way of placating him. It was her way of saying, 'I have accepted you are doing English.'

She always gave him the most spectacularly unsuitable presents. The previous year it had been a gold ring with a large coral – it would bring him luck, she said. He had refused to wear it, and she was still nursing her hurt about that. But this time, since it was the I-have-accepted-you-are-doing-English gift, he couldn't reject it outright. He knew his friends would laugh their heads off; he could already hear them saying, 'Hey, man, Randhir's got himself a full-length *mirror* in his room!' He'd give it a few days.

But a few days later, he found he couldn't prise the damn thing off without destroying the wall. He called the colony carpenter and told him he wanted it out, and the carpenter said, 'Bhaiyya, just few days ago I put it in and now you are saying to take it out?' His mother came back home just as he was trying to persuade the carpenter. 'But, Beta, it is my birthday present to you,' she said. He saw that she was about to cry. He couldn't handle it. So, he hammered two nails on the wall on either end of the mirror, and every day he hung a bedcover from there so that it covered most of the bloody thing. And every day, without fail, his mother removed it as soon as he stepped out of the house. His friends howled with laughter at the sight of the full-length mirror, exactly as he'd anticipated. So, that was that. He was stuck with the mirror just as surely as he was stuck with his family, he told Mallika.

'How can you even *think* about your family like that?' Mallika said, shocked.

'At least I *think* my thoughts,' he said teasingly.

She looked at him the way she'd looked at him a year ago, the day she'd poured out her life story to him. '*As* if!'

He'd known Mallika all his life; she'd lived next door to him since she was a baby, though, of course he hadn't really *known* her. She and his sister, Mahima, and their friends Prabha and Gauri – the quadruplets – lived in the world of giggling girls, endless gossip, stupid romance novels, and silly games like langdi tang, hopscotch, and gitta. Meanwhile Randhir, Akhil, and their friends lived in a world of cricket, football, hockey, and endless music. These two worlds never collided.

Then, that day, he was home from boarding school for the summer holidays. He was sixteen. His father was at his factory, his brother at a friend's place, his mother and Mahima at the cinema. He had just slogged for four hours, studying for the ISC exams he'd be taking in December, and now he was in the living room, pondering whether to go to his parents' room, flick a cigarette from his father's packet, and smoke it before everyone came home, or whether he should go out in the heat to the paanwalla at the other end of the colony. It was a peaceful moment, the anticipation of the forbidden cigarette, and the knowledge that, after the cigarette, he'd be blissfully alone, discovering the poem that was brewing inside him. When Mummy was at home, she was a magnet for noise – servants, neighbours, phone, her own loud and constant talk – it was endless. But now, in her absence, even the sound of the pressure cooker and the clatter of dishes being washed in the kitchen were a kind of silence.

The silence was shattered. Mallika, sobbing, burst into his house, barrelling into him and knocking him over. It spoke volumes for her wretched state that she wasn't embarrassed. She heaved herself off him, 'Sorry, sorry – where's Madhu Aunty, where's Mahima?'

'They've gone to see a film,' he said, getting up from the floor.

'Oh, noooo,' she wailed.

'Stop crying,' he said, helplessly. This was the end of his cigarette and writing. He was stuck with her. Her nose was streaming, her eyes were streaming, everything was streaming. What the hell was he supposed to do?

'Come with me,' he said finally, and she followed him to his mother's room.

'Sit.'

She sat on the bed, heaving.

What a blundering idiot he'd been that day. He had taken the glass from Mummy's bed to the bathroom, washed it, and filled it with water. Then he'd dropped the water all over the bedroom floor and mopped it up with the towel. After that, as Mallika kept sobbing, he grabbed the packet of Mummy's pills from the side table and gave her two. 'Have.'

She had them.

The pills always calmed Mummy down. She swore by them.

'Is it a boy?' he asked her.

Once a boy at the other end of the neighbourhood had followed Mahima home, talking filth behind her. She'd run home and told him. He'd found the boy and given him a thrashing. That he'd do the same for his sister's friends was a given.

'No,' she said.

'Then what?'

She began sobbing again. He took out a handkerchief from his pocket and gave it to her, and she blew her nose like a trumpet. God. The way girls cried wasn't funny.

'I went to the lending library at the market, and Gullu and Sweetie were there. You know them, no?'

He nodded. They were friends, eight or nine, who lived down the street.

'When I went in, they looked at me, and then Gullu said to Sweetie, "See, *Mallika* is a bastard."' She began shuddering with sobs again.

'They're stupid. They don't even know what "bastard" means. Stop crying.'

'No,' she wailed. 'It's true, I *am*.'

'Huh?'

'And now everyone will get to know, and what will Ma do, we'll have to leave the colony, but where will we go, we don't even have any money, what will we *do*?'

This was too much. 'Hold on.'

He got up and took out a cigarette from the packet by his father's bed, switched the fan to the fastest speed, and pulled back the curtains, letting out the smoke and letting in the blinding summer light. 'Don't tell Mummy I smoke, OK? OK, now tell.'

'This man who's been coming home for a year – you've seen him, no?'

'That tall man? Ya.'

'He got my mother pregnant and never married her. So, I *am* a bastard.'

His mouth dropped open. 'I thought your father was dead.'

'I also thought. But that was made up. A year ago, Karan found out about me. That's why he came back. That's when I got to know.'

Oh. He mouthed the word, but it didn't come out.

She was jerkily opening and closing his handkerchief. She'd tear it to shreds at this rate.

'He and Ma knew each other in college, in DU. He wanted to marry her. After his MA exams, he took the IAS exams and went home to Lucknow from college. That same day, his mother got him married off to another woman.'

Unbelievable!

She blew her nose again and wiped her eyes with her palm.

'His mother had arranged the wedding on the day he was to come home from college; all the guests were arriving; his mother said she'd have a heart attack if he backed out of it – I'm telling you, that mother of his is worse than that Lalita Pawar.'

'Lalita Pawar?'

'You don't know who *Lalita Pawar* is?'

'No. Who?'

'She's the actress who plays the mother-in-law in Hindi films.'

'I never see Hindi films.'

'Such a snob you are. That Lalita Pawar is horrible; her eyes are always twitching, and one eye is smaller than the other, and she does horrible things to her daughter-in-law behind her son's back. When you see her, you think, god, people aren't like that in real life. But they *are*. Karan's mother called Ma a *randi*. You know what that means?'

'I know, I know.' He tried not to cringe.

She had stopped crying. 'Yes, it means *whore*. *Her* son makes Ma pregnant and marries another woman, and *Ma* becomes a randi? If *Ma's* a randi, then what does that make *Karan*? What's the word for a male randi?'

'Stop saying that word.' He was squirming.

'I'm just repeating what *she* said. Why are you being so fastidious?'

Fastidious? He managed not to laugh.

'At least I'm using it for a reason. You and your friends use bad words because you think it's cool.'

Hurriedly he asked, 'So, then?'

'Ma wrote to him that she was pregnant, but his mother hid the letters. When he finally got around to coming to Delhi to tell her, he saw Ma with a baby – me – so he thought she had got married and… that was that.'

'God, it sounds like one of your Hindi films.' Then he wanted to hit himself for saying it.

But she wasn't upset. 'I know. In Hindi films also the Hero always believes his mother.'

'If that's the way you feel then why d'you watch that shit?'

'You boys laugh at us and think we have no brains because we read romances and watch Hindi films? *You* read James Bond. *I* think James Bond is brainless.'

That was the problem with females; they went off on a tangent. His mother was a prime example. Ignoring Mallika's last outburst, he said, 'How did your father find out about you?'

She went back on track immediately. 'His younger sister found Ma's letters and told him. Then Karan – don't call him my father – went to my grandmother in Bangalore and found out where we live. But after he came to us, Ma wouldn't marry him like everyone wanted.'

'Everyone?'

'Shantamama, Madhu Aunty, Anu Aunty, Prabha, Gauri, Mahima.'

'They all *know*?'

'Of *course* they know.'

He whistled. 'Wow! I didn't know Mummy was capable of being discreet.'

'How can you be so *mean* about your own mother?'

He blinked.

'I mean – how *much* she's done for Ma and me. All our *lives*. She has *such* a big heart.'

He couldn't bring himself to say, 'that's not all she is,' because a deep sense of shame was running through him at Mallika's words. He didn't want to look at it. Shame was like a subterranean creature that metamorphosed into a monster the moment you glanced at it, rising from the ground and swallowing everything in its wake. What the hell – he was Head Boy at school, he got prizes for everything, he topped every class, he damn well wouldn't feel that way.

'Sorry,' he said.

What the shit was he doing? Apologizing because *he* had said something about *his* mother that had upset *her*?

She looked somewhat mollified.

'Your Ayah-ji knows?' he wondered.

'She pretends to be like Mrs Gummidge, but she knows everything.'

'Who on earth is Mrs Gummidge?'

She quoted, "'I'm a lone, lorn creature, and everything goes contrary with me.'"

He looked at her blankly.

'I thought you loved Dickens?' she said as though he'd betrayed her.

'Of *course,* I love Dickens. I have all his books.'

'You *have* them, but have you *read* them?'

'Obviously!' he said, affronted.

'Mrs Gummidge is in *David Copperfield*.'

A vague memory came to him. 'Oh, she lives in that boat house!'

Mallika nodded.

'But she's hardly memorable!' he protested.

'She's *very* memorable.' Mallika spoke as though she were defending a close friend.

In the silence that followed, she observed him.

'You don't have all Dickens' books,' she continued. 'You don't have *Our Mutual Friend*.'

His amusement disappeared. '*You've been going through my books*!'

'As if!'

She said it scornfully. Stupid girl – how dare she.

'Then how d'you know what I have and what I don't?'

'I looked at your bookshelf through Mahima's binoculars. From *outside* your room.'

'Why?' He was astounded.

'Because I can't go *inside*, obviously!'

She was mad.

'People keep borrowing my books and not returning them,' he said.

Mummy didn't even know which of her gaggle of friends 'borrowed' them. And she didn't understand why it maddened him. Now, he locked up all his books before he went back to boarding school.

'*I* always return books,' she said.

'I'm not lending you my books.'

'Who's asking you for them?'

'God, *binoculars*! Looking at my books through *binoculars*!'

'Why not? Looking isn't *borrowing*. Looking isn't *touching*.'

Weird wasn't the word for Mallika.

'OK, OK, go on with your story.'

'After he came back, Karan wanted to marry Ma. But Ma said no.'

'So, he comes home to see you now?'

'Sometimes he comes. But mostly I spend two weekends a month with him. At his sister's house in Old Delhi.'

All this drama going on next door, and he hadn't had the foggiest idea.

'What's he like?'

She looked away from him.

She hates her father, he thought.

She looked up and burst into tears. 'I don't hate him.'

Had she read his mind or what? His second handkerchief was sodden. She wiped her eyes with her hands. He got up and got her another clean one.

She sobbed, 'I just feel so bad for him. He keeps trying but... I can't.'

'Can't...?'

She kept crying.

It hit him. 'You can't love him.'

'I should. But I can't.'

He wanted to say, you can borrow my books, take as many as you want.

'That's OK, Mallika. No big deal.'

'What d'you mean "no big deal?" It's *very* big.'

He said helplessly, 'I mean, you can't force love.'

She stared at him.

'But... he's so alone, Randhir.'

'Mallika,' he said earnestly. 'You can force yourself to *do* things, but you can't force yourself to *feel* things.'

The tears were diminishing. 'Oh.' Then she said, 'He takes me to bookshops and all... but sometimes... I just want to come home.' She spoke as though she were confessing to a crime.

He was feeling upset now. 'Have you told your mother?'

'I can't. If I tell her, she'll never let me spend time with him. Then they'll start fighting about me again. I'm sick of their fights.' She took in a deep breath and yawned.

He said, 'What's happened to his wife?'

She yawned again. 'She left him to go to an ashram.'

'No children?'

She shook her head. She was looking extremely sleepy.

'What about your mother's brother?'

'Huh! *Him*! He also abandoned Ma when she got pregnant. Never even writes to her.'

She was looking sleepier and sleepier.

'You better go home and sleep.'

Her words were slurring. 'What to do about Gullu and Sweetie calling me a bastard?'

'I'll deal with that. Chalo, get up, I'll take you home.'

'Ma has no money. We'll have to sell the house, and it won't get us enough to buy one in another colony. What'll we do?'

'Oho, stop worrying about money, money doesn't matter.'

She snorted. 'Only people with money say money doesn't matter.'

He began to laugh. 'Come on, you're falling asleep.'

She got up, with difficulty, and he walked her the ten steps next door.

Then he went to Gullu's house and told her mother what Gullu had said. The mother said, 'Impossible, Gullu doesn't even know the meaning of that bad word.' Gullu, who was listening, said she *did* know the meaning of the word and she *had* used it. Her mother slapped her.

Gullu wailed, 'But bastard is someone who doesn't have a father, and Mallika's father is dead, so what is wrong with what I said?'

So that was that.

He went back home and had lunch and wrote the first draft of his poem.

But later that evening, around six p.m., he heard sounds next door and strolled out to see a crowd of neighbours gathered around Mallika's house. 'What's happened?' he asked one of them, and she replied, in dire tones, 'Mallika, she is very serious.'

He pushed past the crowd and went into Mallika's house. Everyone was there – her mother, his mother, Anu Aunty, a hysterical Ayah-ji, and the colony doctor, Dr Wadhwa. The doctor was assuring them that Mallika was sleeping, not unconscious – had she taken any medicines earlier?

He said to the doctor, 'She was crying so I gave her a couple of my mother's pills.'

Everyone turned to look at him. Padma Aunty's eyes were red with crying.

His mother gasped, 'Which pills?'

'The ones next to your bed.'

His mother shrieked, 'Buddhu, bevakoof, ullu ka pattha, are you mad?'

'But you take them every night, Ma!'

'Stupid fool, I take *one*. Gold Medal in essay writing, but no sense in your head! Go get the pills, hurry up.'

When he came back with the Calmpose pills, Dr Wadhwa examined the packet and said Mallika would be fine; she would probably sleep till late the following morning. When she woke up, she should drink plenty of water. Then he turned to Randhir and gave him a lecture about dispensing other people's medicines with such impunity. When they went home, his mother yelled at him some more.

He went to check in on Mallika the next evening and told her that Gullu thought a bastard was someone whose father was dead.

Mallika gave a huge sigh of relief.

Towards the end of the summer holidays, when he was walking back home from the paanwalla, a packet of cigarettes hidden in his pocket, he saw Mallika's father driving her back home. Her father helped her out of the car. She was looking ill.

He went home, hid the cigarettes in his cupboard and went to Mallika's house. The house was smelling of Amrutanjan. Karan and Padma Aunty were at the dining table, talking, looking grave. Padma Aunty told him that Mallika was lying down; she had vomited. Her migraine was very severe. She'd been having them for months now, and they had no idea why.

Mallika had been suffering for *months*?

He summoned up his courage. Even though he was upset, it took a lot to do so.

He said to Karan, 'Mallika's getting migraines because it's very difficult for her to spend time with you.' He heard his words coming out like gasps.

He saw their shock.

'She... *wants* to spend time with you,' he stammered. 'But it's very... difficult for her. Because –' he stopped.

He didn't have the words to say, because she's trying so hard to love you. How can you help what you feel? You just shove it away and don't feel it, but not feeling it kills you even more.

Karan said gently, 'Come, sit down, Randhir.'

He sat at the dining table. For some peculiar reason, there were tears in his throat. He stared at the table, at the white-and-blue checked tablecloth. In the silence, he heard Karan swallow and Padma Aunty's uneven breathing.

The room was dense with emotions. It was like being stuck in something thick and viscous, and he couldn't pull himself out.

'I'll make tea,' Padma Aunty said. 'Randhir, will you have tea or lime juice?'

'Lime juice, Aunty, thank you,' he muttered.

After she went into the kitchen, Karan said, as gently as before, 'Did Mallika tell you that she didn't want to spend the weekends with me?'

He looked up at Karan. 'She *wants* to. But…'

He saw the dawning of understanding on Karan's grave face.

Padma Aunty came out with a plate full of thick slices of homemade chocolate cake. She put two slices on a plate and gave it to him. 'Ayah-ji's just getting the lime juice,' she said.

Then she stroked his head tenderly.

Suddenly, he was ravenous. He tried to eat slowly but couldn't. When Padma Aunty put a third slice of cake on his plate, he didn't protest and gobbled that up too.

When he came home in December after taking the final ISC exams, Mallika told him her father had started visiting her at home. Yes, she said, her migraines were better. 'It's all because of the Phuknewalla,' she claimed. Then she told him that she was going to some crazy witch doctor called the Phuknewalla, who was supposedly *blowing away* her migraines! It boggled his mind. He couldn't *believe* that Mallika's mothers were OK with it. 'He *does* take away my migraines, I *promise* you, Randhir,' she said earnestly. It was the most illogical, uneducated, ignorant thing he'd ever heard Mallika utter.

But he was only sixteen-and-a-half then. He shrugged it off.

Five years later, when he was going around with Charu, Mallika turned into that gullible, illogical person with *him*. Worse, she turned into someone who had no sense of who *he* was.

Then, a day before Mahima got married, Mallika's naivety led to something much worse. This time, she reached into his deepest self, uprooted his mute heart, and crushed it beneath her feet. That it was Mallika of all people who did it demolished him. After that, nothing in his life was ever the same again.

Mallika: The icing and the cake

1974-1975

I overheard them when I was seventeen. Arnav and Vineet were hanging out as usual on Randhir's terrace, which was right next to my upstairs bedroom window, smoking pot and talking. I was lying in bed and thoroughly enjoying the conversation that was floating down into my room. Arnav was laughing about how he went to Chandni Chowk and got himself a tiger tattoo on his arm and his father hit the roof. Then Vineet began trashing Indian cars – the staid Ambassador, the oomph-less Fiat, and the unprepossessing Standard Herald – and began fantasizing about foreign cars.

I went back to my book.

Ten minutes later, my ears pricked up. Vineet was laughing. 'I tell you – every DU girl is madly in love with Randhir!'

'Yeah, but for Randhir it's only Mallika,' Arnav said.

My heart began to beat very fast. Was this true? Let it be true!

'Hmm,' Vineet said. 'Yeah, I guess. Wonder though, what Randhir sees in Mallika.'

What!

Vineet said, 'I mean she's nice but…'

Arnav said, 'Yeah, nice but… sort of boring, no?'

I shot up in my bed.

Vineet laughed.

Rigid with humiliation, I waited for more.

Arnav and Vineet began talking about Freddie Mercury.

Well, of course. What else was there to say about boring? Nothing. That was *it*. 'He's so bloody *boring*, man,' the boys would say about someone, and that was *it*. Boring was conclusive. Even more conclusive than, 'He's so fucked up, man.' At least fucked up had presence. It had a substantial past, a thrilling future. It had a range of hows and whys. But *boring*? Who cared about the hows and whys of boring? Boring was the adjective without a story.

I wept. It was the bitter truth. I *was* boring. And there was nothing I could do about it. I wanted to kill them for the casual way they'd dismissed me. I wanted to knock them off the roof for being tall and attractive and at ease in their skins. I hated myself for having been so beguiled by their laughter, their vitality, their stupid jokes. For the fantasy that I'd been nursing about beautiful Arnav drawing me out and talking to me.

How could I help being tongue-tied? What to do when I didn't know what to say in social situations? What to say when parties overwhelmed me? To top it all, I was also hopeless at 'getting it.' Once, at Randhir's party, a friend of his had laughingly said to me, 'I've never come across a chatterbox like you,' and shocked, I had replied, 'Really?' and he laughed even more. While it wasn't incumbent upon me to crack jokes, it would have helped if I understood them, because boys spent hours telling the most spectacularly inane jokes the way my friends and I spent hours talking about our emotions. Why then did I go for parties? Well, I didn't really, but once in a while Randhir persuaded me to go for his. Then I would find myself standing mutely, dreaming of sparkling conversation tripping off my tongue like water from a gargoyle. But how much could you fantasize about your witticisms when – even in your own fantasies – you had none?

Clearly, boys thought I was nothing because I said nothing. I wasn't vibrant, vivacious, or radiant, like other Delhi girls. I wasn't animated and confident like Mahima. I wasn't gutsy and articulate like Prabha. I wasn't warm, comforting, and always at ease, like Gauri. I did boring things like reading, going for walks, listening to North Indian classical music on the radio, and gazing out of my balcony. Arnav and Vineet were only saying what every boy thought about me.

I mostly wore sarees because anything else was unaffordable, given how fashions changed in Delhi. That was boring. Lack of money was incomprehensible to those who had it, and incomprehensible was boring. I tutored children every evening so that I could earn money to help Ma pay off the loan she had taken against our house to build my upstairs bedroom. That was boring. I loved the children I tutored, especially Jalpari, the daughter of a scooterwalla who was sharp, cheeky, and full of spunk. No boy was interested in knowing how excited I was at how quickly Jalpari was learning English; they'd find that boring. I studied hard. That was boring. My grandmother, who had great ambitions for me, said I should sit for the IAS exams. I agreed. But what I dreamt of was getting a scholarship to go to America to do my PhD in English. Every year, a handful of students from DU and IIT went off to America on full scholarships, or 'assistantships' as they called them there. I fantasized about this the way you fantasize about winning the lottery. Because, even if I got a full assistantship, we didn't have the money for the plane ticket. People who had money for plane tickets would find that boring.

The only boy who didn't think I was boring was Randhir. Sometimes I secretly fantasized that I was the girl for him. But in truth, I knew very well that I was no Cathy to his Heathcliff.

The boys' lives couldn't have been more different from mine. They went on mad rides on their motorcycles all over Delhi, attended music festivals, acted and debated in college, and went for treks. Arnav was a fantastic actor; I'd seen him on stage a couple of times. He was very well known in Delhi theatre groups. Before that fateful night, listening to Randhir, Arnav, and Vineet talking on the terrace had been far more interesting than listening to Radio Ceylon, the BBC, the Voice of America, or In the Groove. Listening to the boys talking partook of a foreign flavour. It was a different texture, another rhythm, almost an alien landscape. For me, anyway. They were droll; they cracked the most abysmal jokes, laughing so uproariously at their own wit that I couldn't help laughing too. Sometimes I'd hear them making plans to go off on some trek or the other, and then, one day, off they'd go. There were no rules they had to obey, no safety concerns, nothing. They were gloriously free. When the three boys were together, Randhir was no longer my contemplative, sensitive, philosophical Randhir. He became like the others – loud and raucous, cracking endless jokes. Together they were an entity, good-looking, and radiating energy and vitality. Anything but boring.

The story of my mother and Karan and how he came back to us wasn't boring either. Tell me one silent story that is. But no doubt I carried its weight. And of course, weight – even if invisible – was boring. Especially to boys.

The next day, Sunday, my childhood friends, Prabha, Gauri, and Mahima had lunch at home with me. Afterwards, we went upstairs to my room, and my friends asked me for their weekly entertainment – imitations of the boys. This was my forte. I could imitate every conversation that I heard on the terrace. I could mimic how the boys talked and laughed, the rhythm of their voices, and the way they lounged around in Randhir's house. Now, with a sting in my tail, I imitated Arnav talking about his tiger tattoo, and Vineet talking about the Ambassador, the Fiat, and the Standard Herald.

After their laughter subsided, Prabha said, 'Mallika, *please* come with us to TT.'

'Fine.'

They looked astounded. They hadn't expected such a painless capitulation. I wasn't prone to doing things behind Ma's back.

TT stood for Tasty Snacks, a dhaba just outside our colony gates that our mothers had expressly forbidden us to enter. It was painted across the board on top of the dhaba in bright red: *Testy Snakes*. Every time we passed Testy Snakes on the way to the bus stop, we were bathed in the smell of hot frying samosas, pakodas, and kachouris, and it drove us mad with desire. There was no question of stepping inside because it was frequented by all the roadside Romeos and lafangas of Delhi. Every time we passed the dhaba, they looked at us the way we looked at the testy snakes. They muttered obscenities, and one or two would grab their crotches, look at us, and groan. So, there were the lafangas lusting after us, and there we were lusting after the samosas. And that, we had thought, was that.

But now we were seventeen and in our first year of college, and Mahima was eighteen and in her second, and Prabha had decided that *wasn't* that.

'OK,' Prabha said. 'We'll go at three. They'll be sleeping then.' *They* meaning our mothers.

'It'll be safer if we ask the boys to come with us – you think they'll come?' Gauri asked.

I snorted. 'As if!'

The boys would readily have walked us back home if it was late, or picked us up if we were stuck somewhere, or kept us company if we wanted to go for dosas at night. But coming with us to a roadside dhaba called Testy Snakes? As if! Not that they didn't frequent dhabas. Of course they did. They frequented the IIT dhabas, Delhi University dhabas, the Jawaharlal Nehru University dhabas, and the Tib dabs – the Tibetan dhabas. But they wouldn't be caught dead at a roadside dhaba called Testy Snakes, which was frequented by the lower rung of Delhi's population. I might have *looked* like a snob, but the three boys *were* the snobs.

Three p.m. was a safe time. Our mothers would be resting. The dhaba wouldn't be crowded. We would sit in the corner inside the dhaba where no one we knew could see us. Because if it got back to our mothers that we were eating at Testy Snakes, they'd, of course, kill us. We should all take umbrellas, Prabha said. We agreed. Umbrellas always stood us in good stead when dealing with lecherous men.

An hour later, as we walked to Testy Snakes, umbrellas in hand, I saw Gauri stealing a glance at me. She knew I wasn't myself.

But I couldn't tell Gauri what Arnav and Vineet had been saying. Gauri had had a soft corner for Vineet ever since we were in the tenth class in our convent school. I had watched Vineet and Gauri's friendship, full of hope that it would become something more. But instead of falling in love with Gauri, Vineet, after joining St Stephen's for Economics, had gone and fallen in love with a girl from Indraprastha College – Jaspreet – and then proceeded to develop amnesia about his friendship with Gauri. This was when a heartbroken Gauri told me what I had already known: that she loved Vineet. 'Don't tell the other two,' Gauri had said, and I nodded. Prabha and Mahima would have tried to talk her out of loving Vineet. But, as Gauri and I knew, how could you talk someone out of love?

If I told Gauri what I'd overheard, it would be another stab in her heart to know that Vineet, whom she still loved, had been talking like that about me. And maybe I shouldn't have cared about that given that Vineet had dispensed with their friendship, but I did. Every time I saw Vineet, I wanted to yell, 'What kind of friendship is it, that it's so dispensable?'

But I also couldn't speak of what the boys had said because it was too humiliating to utter. And humiliation was a different cup of tea from other emotions. Humiliation burnt a hole in your face; humiliation stole your words; humiliation demolished your very self. Humiliation was akin to shame. Shame was what Ma had experienced when Karan abandoned her and she found herself pregnant. I, Mallika, the bastard, was the living embodiment of shame. But Ma and Shantamama's tapestry of lies had spared me from its grasp; it was easier to bury shame than to feel it.

'Mallika, what's the matter?' Prabha asked.

'Uffho, I'm fine.'

'You're a bit *testy* today.'

We shrieked with laughter. Suddenly, I began to feel more cheerful.

Testy Snakes was less crowded, as Prabha had predicted. The owner, Harinder-ji, was overcome at the sight of our breasts. He wouldn't take his eyes away, even though Prabha and Mahima were in their loosest kurtas, and Gauri and I were in long-sleeved blouses with our saree pallas draped over our shoulders.

Prabha spoke first. 'Bhaiyya, two plate samosa, two plate dahivada and two plate kachouri.'

'Accha ji,' Harinder-ji said to Prabha's breasts.

'And four chais,' Gauri said.

'Bilkul, madam,' Harinder-ji sighed to Gauri's breasts.

We made our way to the only small table at the corner, with two small rickety wooden benches on either side.

'Bloody lech,' Gauri muttered.

The food and tea came in five minutes. Every mouthful was heaven. It was spicy and hot. Our eyes watered, and our noses ran. Only Gauri had a handkerchief, so we all used it for our eyes and wiped our noses on our sleeves and saree pallas. We licked our fingers clean.

'Look,' Gauri said.

We looked. Several men were lounging around at the entrance, throwing us hungry looks.

'Harinder-ji,' Mahima called out peremptorily.

Harinder-ji wiped his hands on the stained towel and came to us. 'Hanji,' he said to Mahima's breasts.

'Tell those men to move from over there.'

Harinder-ji made a half-hearted shooing gesture at the men. The men grinned and stayed put.

'I have an older brother, and he has friends. They will destroy your shop if any of those men come close to us,' Mahima said. Mahima was addicted to Hindi films, and of course, this was the kind of thing the Hero did for the Heroine. Since there was no Hero in her life, or for that matter, any of our lives, her brother and his friends had to do.

Harinder-ji looked affronted. 'Ji, what are you saying, they are just *seeing*.'

Mahima got up. 'I will tell my brother and his friends. Then *they* will also just see.'

Harinder-ji looked aghast. 'Sunno ji, you are giving me threats?'

'Aaj tho' *kya* barish baj rahi hai,' sang one of the men lounging at the dhaba entrance.

Oh? So we were like the long-awaited rain? Bloody idiot.

We held on to our umbrellas and made our way past the men at the door.

One of them reached out for Mahima.

I hit him so hard with my umbrella that he screamed.

We ran.

'There's no traffic, cross, cross,' shrieked Gauri.

We streaked across the road, Gauri and I hitching our sarees high above our ankles.

As we reached the other side, three motorcycles roared out of our colony. Randhir, Arnav, and Vineet, with three girls clinging to them. Hero and Friends waved at us.

'Randhir,' Mahima shouted at her brother. 'Randhir!'

Hero and Friends didn't hear. They turned and sped down the road.

We sprinted inside the colony gates.

'*Idiots*,' Mahima said furiously.

Prabha, who always held the scales of justice high, said, 'Why are you blaming *them*?'

Mahima seethed, 'We were *running*. They should have *realized*.'

Gauri said, simply, 'But boys never do.'

The boys called us the 'quadruplets.' It was the first word I noted down in my little red diary which was full of quotable quotes, *Reader's Digest* style.

The second quote was the one about Mahima, uttered rapturously by one of our neighbours: 'Mahima, oh, she is *so* fear-and-lovely!' As my Shantamama said, 'The gall of these North Indians – criticizing *our* accents when *they* pronounce "fair" as "fear!"'

Fair-and-lovely Mahima absolutely was, with her milk-and-white flawless Punjabi complexion and those hints of pink on her cheekbones. Shantamama had told me more than once, 'Darling, try not to stand next to her, you look extremely sallow.' Mahima was delicate and fine-boned and looked like a fairy. She was intelligent and accomplished in the kitchen. She was doing her BA Honours in Economics from Miranda House but had no intention of studying further – all she wanted were marriage and children. Though she loved Hindi films and knew the dialogues between the Hero and Heroine by heart, it didn't translate into her wanting her own romance. She said, 'Books and films are one thing, but real life is another.' She had complete faith in her parents' choice of a husband for her. Her trousseau was almost ready by the time she was seventeen, from gold payals and bichiyas to dinner and tea sets to exquisite underclothes from Marks & Spencer which had been bought on her parents' one trip to London. Before her bridal undies were packed and put away for her marriage, Mahima had showed them to us and we had touched, sighed, and marvelled. You couldn't get such bras in India, in so many different colours, with such exquisite lace, so soft and silky – even Peter Pan didn't come close, and as for Cross Your Heart, it was always white, always cotton, always boring, notwithstanding that ingratiating little flower between the cups.

Then there was Prabha, who had always wanted to become a doctor and was now doing her pre-med in Delhi. After her pre-med, she wanted to go to the Armed Forces Medical College in Poona and become an army doctor.

'Any woman who wants to live her beliefs is doomed.' This was my Shantamama's gloomy prophecy for Prabha, which I duly noted in my red diary.

Prabha was fair-but-not-lovely. How could fair be lovely when you had such strong opinions and challenged everyone's point of view? The minute Prabha opened her mouth, this fair-and-unlovely girl gave speeches about justice and injustice, truth and untruth, right and wrong. That too, about the lives of women. Who was interested in that? If you wanted to talk about justice and injustice, truth and untruth, right and wrong, then talk about politics, talk about the Emergency, not about women, for heaven's sake!

This was how it went with Prabha.

Prabha: 'But why should I have an arranged marriage? And when I get married, why can't the wedding expenses be split, fifty-fifty?'

Her mother, Anu Aunty: 'So foolishly you talk, Prabha! Even in the West, the girl's side pays.'

Prabha: 'Mumma, why do you keep saying I'm going to be lonely if I don't get married? Mumma, you're married, but you're lonely. Remember, you told me that once?'

Her mother: 'The problem with you is that everything that is inside you, it comes out.'

Madhu Aunty: 'I don't know why that Prabha wants to be a doctor. A lawyer only she should be. Everyone she will argue to death and win every case.'

Prabha: 'Daddy says we should live our beliefs, but Mumma, you and Daddy aren't letting me live mine.'

Madhu Aunty: 'Some things we are all questioning, but this girl, she is questioning every single thing. Listening to her itself gives me a fever.'

Prabha: 'Am I supposed to subordinate my feelings for a role I don't believe in?'

Madhu Aunty: 'Arre, of course!'

Ma: 'But she is right, everything Prabha is saying is true!'

Shantamama: 'But, Padma, of what *use* is the truth!'

Ma: 'But look how she protects her friends – she is their backbone!'

Shantamama: 'Let me tell you, for her husband, that same backbone will become a bone of contention.'

Prabha's paternal grandmother, muttering: 'In my time we never answered back our parents, all this is her churail mother's fault for bringing her up without respect for her elders.'

Once, Prabha overheard a boy call her a 'virago.' She walked up to him and said, 'You boys speak your minds all the time, and *that* has no name, but when a girl speaks her mind, she's a virago?' The boy never spoke to Prabha again. She didn't care.

Then there was Gauri.

We thought Gauri, with her lovely eyes, glowing skin, and utter grace, was beautiful. But what use was it what *we* thought?

'You *must* use My Fair Lady cream, *all* problems it solves,' said Gauri's neighbour lovingly.

What was the point of cooking so well, knitting beautiful sweaters and mufflers, creating lovely flower arrangements, embroidering exquisite handkerchiefs and cushion covers, and being a stupendous Odissi dancer? As far as the world was concerned, none of it bore any weight, given her dark, Madrasi complexion – what man would ever marry her?

Gauri had been our biggest source of knowledge about sex from the time she was twelve. Not that she'd ever had it, but with Gauri, things like that were immaterial. She could listen to two different conversations in two different rooms, one with each ear. She also had an eye on each side of her head and two on the back of it. So, while she was talking to us in Mahima's house, she also knew exactly what the boys were saying and doing in Randhir's room. She knew how many Indian soldiers had fought and died in the two World Wars; she knew Arnav was sleeping with Radha from LSR – Lady Shri Ram College – and Vineet was sleeping with Jaspreet, and she suspected Randhir had slept with at least two girls in Miranda House. She knew all about the mysterious orgasm, notwithstanding the complete absence of sex in books and films and TV. She was in the hostel at JNU, learning Spanish at the School of Languages, and whenever she could, she came over to spend the weekends with the rest of us. Her parents, who had once lived in our neighbourhood, had moved to another colony a few years ago.

And then, there was me.

'*Such* a nice girl! *So adjustable*!' Noted in my red diary, with 'adjustable' underlined.

I was doing my BA Honours in English from LSR. I was not fair-and-lovely, the pinnacle of compliments, but being 'adjustable' was a close second. I was like the ponytailed, blonde, blue-eyed plastic doll that every child had possessed in the sixties – a doll so adjustable that you could pull out its hands, its legs, and its head, and put them all back again, or not, as the fancy took you. In fact, the holes in the torso of this wonderful doll were all the same size, so you could put the arms into the leg holes and the legs into the arm holes! What more could you want in a girl than that? *Such* a nice girl, this Mallika! So quiet, doesn't express her opinions, probably has none – oh, *perfect* wife material!

Randhir was, of course, fair-and-lovely. Not that such a thing mattered if you were a boy. If you were a boy, fair was merely the icing on the cake. Being a boy *was* the cake. But if you were a girl, fair was the cake, and the rest of you, the icing.

Long before that tumultuous day when I blew my nose through all his pristine handkerchiefs, a secret part of me was drawn to Randhir because he was the only boy I knew of who loved books more than cricket. He wouldn't lend his books to anyone. Every time I passed his room when he was home from boarding school, I would see his three bursting bookshelves, a sight that made me sick with desire, for books were always in short supply. Buying books at the rate you read them was unaffordable; libraries were few, and you could only borrow two books at a time. So, on weekends, you did the rounds of the neighbours, borrowing books from various aunties and friends. Each book a person owned was borrowed and read by at least ten or twenty other people. That was how it went.

But not Randhir's books. Before going to boarding school at the end of the summer and winter holidays, Randhir would empty out his bookshelves and lock his books in four large black trunks to prevent anyone from coming to his room and borrowing them. 'He is like that only,' Madhu Aunty sighed to Ma.

From time to time, when Randhir was out, I would gaze at his books from his door through Mahima's binoculars.

'You're mad,' Mahima said.

'Why?' I demanded. 'Don't *you* look at jewellery in a shop window?'

Then came the day when I rushed into Madhu Aunty's house, sobbing. Randhir had said, 'If it's a boy, just tell me. I'll break his neck.'

Then and there, he walked into my heart.

While my whole miserable story came out, he smoked and plied me with one beautiful white handkerchief after another, many glasses of water, and several calming pills; he got me to blow my streaming nose without embarrassment, and, best of all, gave me his absolute attention.

Randhir was a serious-looking teenager. Sometimes almost sullen. But he seemed to find some of the things I said funny. When he laughed, he looked so incredibly handsome that it was almost too much for me.

What I told him about my mother and father was just the bare bones, but those bones were heavy enough. In his infinite wisdom, he understood the nature of my guilt regarding my father. Then, like a magician, he took everything that was unformed and turned it all into words, words so true that they shone. Later, I wrote in my red diary: *You can't force love, Mallika. You can force yourself to do things, but you can't force yourself to feel things.*

A few months after we became friends, Randhir finally said, 'You can borrow my books if you want, but *only* two at a time.'

'Four, *please*.'

'OK, fine, four.'

From then onwards, Randhir kept a protective eye on me. We spoke endlessly to one another about our most precious and most impossible fantasy: going abroad to study. Randhir had a stack of brochures from various universities in America, given to him by friends whose brothers had gone off to study there, and nothing gave us more pleasure than sitting together and leafing through the pages, gazing at the photographs of those impossibly beautiful universities. These brochures appealed to me even more than the occasional Hollywood films we saw, or reading *Time*, *Newsweek*, *Life*, or *Reader's Digest*. It was impossible for Randhir to study abroad because he had to join the family business after college, and it was impossible for me because, even if I got a scholarship, we could never afford the plane fare. So, Randhir and I gazed and sighed and exclaimed over the very same photographs in the very same brochures, month after month, year after year. Randhir kept them hidden in his cupboard in case Madhu Aunty's friends 'borrowed' them, since borrowing often meant never returning.

It was Randhir who told me the story from Plato's *Symposium*, from the speech of Aristophanes. In that story, he said that the sexes were three in number: a man, a woman, and a man-woman, each with four arms, four legs, two faces, and two... Well, two everything.

'Meaning?' I asked, puzzled.

He said, 'Imagine two men joined together, two women joined together, and one man and one woman joined together. That's what constituted the three sexes. And they were so powerful that, to diminish their power, Zeus cut them in half. After that, each half was always seeking the other half so that they could unite and be whole again. So, this could be a man seeking a man, a woman seeking a woman, or a woman and a man seeking one another. *This* is love, Mallika – the desire and pursuit of the whole.'

'Oh,' I breathed.

When I told my three friends this story, Prabha and Gauri were rapt. But Mahima said, 'Two *men* seeking each other? Two *women* seeking each other? Come on!'

'Randhir isn't like other boys,' Prabha sighed. 'He talks differently.'

It was true. Randhir understood the exalted nature of love. He wasn't like other boys.

And then Charu dropped into Randhir's lap like an overripe plum, and I discovered that he was.

Charu didn't love books. Charu didn't love art. Charu's conversation was... Well, she didn't have any. *This* was his other half?

This was not even his other quarter; this was not even a quarter of his other quarter.

So much for the thrilling speech of Aristophanes.

Worse, Randhir became like Vineet. He developed amnesia where I was concerned. He stopped dropping in at my house. As for going together for our regular jaunts to Chachaji's second-hand bookshop at Shankar Market or to the British Council Library – all that came to a grinding halt.

'No personality that Charu has!' Gauri said scornfully. 'I don't know what he sees in her!'

'She's very pretty,' I said wistfully.

'Huh! You're *much* better looking. *And* you have substance. Unlike *her.*' Gauri sneered as she said this. Her sneer, rare though it was, was unrivalled. Prabha's fiery views and Mahima's sharp tongue paled next to Gauri's sneer.

I was broken-hearted. Now Randhir would never marry me. I had always known the chances were close to zero, but they weren't completely zero. After all, he talked to me more than to any other girl. We went to libraries and second-hand bookshops together. We understood each other. How could I not cling to the faint hope that, as I grew up, I would also grow beautiful, sparkle with wit, and turn mysterious? That one day, Randhir, struck by my beauty, dazzled by my wit, and intrigued by my mystery, would fall desperately in love with me?

Fat chance now.

Every time I saw Randhir and Charu together, I felt there was a dagger in my heart – a cliché that felt truer than Randhir's high-flown rhetoric about soulmates. Either Charu was in his house, or they went out together on his bike, or they were returning home from college on his bike. I saw how Charu's arms went tightly around him every time she sat behind him on his bike. But it was in Randhir's eyes that I saw everything. He looked at Charu in a way he had never, ever looked at me.

Charu, who was also doing her BA Honours in English, was in my class at college. She told me she didn't like reading! 'What does Randhir say to that?' I asked, and Charu rolled her eyes and said: 'For heaven's sake, we don't talk about *books*!'

Randhir took Charu for the National School of Drama plays, the classical music concerts – for all the things *I* loved but for which he'd never taken me. Charu told me she suffered through them. She *suffered* through them! And Randhir didn't even know? This ignorance was love?

Madhu Aunty was full of praise for Charu. Randhir was going to ask her to marry him, so much he loved her, but of course, he would have to get a job first. Such a soft-hearted, honest girl; no pretences, no guile, so unlike these Delhi girls, already she was like a daughter in the house.

He was going to marry her. The whole neighbourhood knew it.

I hid my broken heart and tried to act normal. But one day when I was in his room, going through his bookshelf, Charu and he were sprawled on his divan, talking. He took her hand and pretended to read her palm the way these boys sometimes did at parties – any pretext to hold a girl's hand. I saw how Charu's slim, lovely fingers rested on his palm. He said she was ruled by the sun and mercury, and they burst out laughing. I randomly grabbed two books from his bookshelf, said bye, walked out of the door, and almost ran into Arnav. We both stepped back.

'Sorry,' I muttered.

'Sorry,' he said, and I rushed out.

I was going down the steps when behind me I heard Arnav say, 'Mallika?'

Oh, god, no. I swallowed my tears and turned.

'Are you going to the market?'

I shook my head – then I thought, why not, and I nodded. And then I thought, Mallika, you stupid fool, because his reply was: 'I'm going there too, got to pick up some fags. Mind if I join you?'

'OK,' I said.

Of course, I minded. For more than a year, the *nice-but-boring* had been stuck like a thorn inside me. I minded his careless 'Hi,' his sleepy smile, and his gorgeous eyes. I minded that my heart would beat like a hammer every time I saw him. I minded because right now I wanted to go running home and burst into tears and not have to school my expression. I minded because I wanted to hate him for calling me boring, but it was myself I hated for being that.

I minded because I didn't have a word to say to him. I minded because he was happily humming 'Ruby Tuesday'.

'Feel like a Softy?' he said as we reached the market.

'No, thank you.' Did he think we were best friends, walking to the market to eat Softy ice creams together?

In the market, I made an excuse to go to Bittu's Books and said there was no need to wait for me. He went off to the paanwalla to get his cigarettes.

When I came out of the library, he was right there, lighting his cigarette. So, we walked back together in the most horrendous silence. At least, it was horrendous for me, because he was happily humming 'Heart of Gold'.

Charu told me she'd slept with Randhir. 'Don't tell anyone. Promise?'

I was burning, raging, bleeding.

Yet, I couldn't help asking. 'What was it like?'

Sex was the Big Mystery. The kind of books that detailed sex were not the kind of books you could buy or borrow. Since Mills & Boons couldn't talk about The Act, The Kiss was all. The Kiss went on for pages. Of course, there was no kissing in Hindi films, and all Hollywood films were censored. The minute The Kiss ended and the clothes began coming off – cut, cut, cut – we'd hear the crackling, see those familiar scratchy lines across the screen, and that was how every love scene ended, before it even began.

'It's wonderful,' Charu sighed. 'He's so passionate, so tender.'

After that, I pretended that none of this was happening.

I was living my pretence with reasonable aplomb when – a couple of months later – it happened.

We were in the middle of class, when Charu stumbled out of the room, holding her stomach. Excusing myself, I ran after her.

'I'm cramping,' she moaned. 'I'm having a miscarriage.'

'*What!*'

'I'm pregnant with Randhir's baby,' she moaned. 'Help me, Mallika, take me to a doctor.'

I left her leaning against the wall and ran outside the college gates to get a scooter, bundled her in, and took her to the gynaecologist, who had her clinic in the colony opposite our college.

In the reception, I waited for an hour, my thoughts in utter turmoil.

Then the gynaecologist came out and beckoned that I should come into the room. There, she sat next to Charu and said gently, 'That wasn't a miscarriage, Charu, that was a period.'

Charu shook her head. 'It was a miscarriage.'

'No, Charu, you were not pregnant. It was a period.'

'I was pregnant. It was a miscarriage.'

This went on for some time, the doctor saying one thing, Charu the opposite.

After some time, the doctor took me aside and said that not only was Charu not pregnant, but she was also still a virgin. However, she truly seemed to believe that she was pregnant and had had a miscarriage. The girl had gone mental. She needed treatment from a good psychiatrist.

We took the bus home, and Charu cried throughout. 'I *was* pregnant, Mallika,' she whispered when we got off at our colony. 'I've lost Randhir's baby. Please help me.'

'Did you tell Randhir?'

She didn't answer. She kept crying and asking me to help her.

I was frightened. It was beyond my scope. Promise or no promise, I had to tell Randhir.

That evening I went next door and knocked on Randhir's door. He turned from his desk.

'Randhir, I want to talk to you.'

He got up, smiling at me with such affection that I was awash with guilt.

We left home and began walking towards the park.

After five minutes, he said, 'Spill it out, Mallika.'

I didn't look at him. 'It's about Charu.'

Silence.

I blurted it out. 'She said she slept with you and got pregnant and had a miscarriage.'

'*What!*' He stopped in his tracks.

He walked to the parapet at the side of the road. I followed him. We sat.

'Go on,' he said quietly.

I told him everything.

'Bloody hell.'

I didn't have the courage to look at his face.

'You *believed* her?'

'Randhir, you're going to *marry* her!'

He looked at me incredulously.

Oh, god. I should have known. Madhu Aunty had made it up.

'I never slept with her,' he said through gritted teeth.

But how on earth was I to have known that?

'Randhir, she needs help. Something is wrong.'

'Yes, something *is* wrong. She's cracked. She's nuts. She's out of her mind.'

'Don't talk like that about her, Randhir,' I said, appalled.

'She's the one who made up that shit, and you're judging *me*?' He got up. 'We're going home now. You tell Mummy everything. Then *she* can talk to Charu's mother.'

I nodded.

We went to his house where Madhu Aunty, Anu Aunty, Ma, and Shantamama were sitting at the dining table, drinking tea and chatting. I told them everything that I'd told Randhir. They listened, shocked.

Finally, Madhu Aunty burst out, 'I *always* I knew it. That Charu, she hides her cunning behind a sweet face.'

'After singing her praises, now you're saying you *always* knew she was cunning!' Randhir exclaimed.

'Beta, how to tell you something I knew *only* in my heart?'

'Mummy, please answer my question. Why did you keep praising her?'

Ma and Anu Aunty were looking fixedly at the dining table. Shantamama was looking at Madhu Aunty.

Madhu Aunty's eyes filled with tears. 'You do not understand a mother's heart. I was praising her because I thought it would make *you* happy. Your happiness, it is everything to me.'

Before Randhir humiliated Madhu Aunty even more, I said, 'Aunty, what to do now?'

Madhu Aunty got up and said, 'Now I will go and discuss with Charu's parents.'

Ma got up. 'Don't go alone, Madhu. I'll come with you.'

Shantamama, who had been relishing the drama, said, 'I'll also come.'

After they left, Anu Aunty gently said, 'Randhir, Beta, sit.'

Randhir sat opposite her. His face was sullen with anger.

'Beta, all my life I have known you. Now I am telling you like I tell my own children: do not be careless with your words. Words break hearts, Beta. It is worse than breaking things. Your mother has a very good heart.'

Looking like he would burst, Randhir nodded.

That should have been the end of that. But it wasn't. Because the Charu story, which now had a life of its own, had decided to quietly follow me. A few months later, I finally heard its footsteps and tried to flee. But it was too late; it caught me and consumed me.

Arnav: Running

1975

He loved to run. He was in boarding school when he discovered its joys. The trees flashing by him as he ran, the smell of winter in his nose, the feel of the sun like happiness flowing through his body, and the call of the eccentric koyal in the banyan tree, which had established the unique reputation of singing even when it didn't rain. When he heard the koyal, he would stop and whistle the same tune – that long, seductive two syllable note, the high one followed by the low. There would be a short, almost startled silence, and soon enough, the koyal would respond joyfully. Then he would whistle that note again, and the koyal would sing back, and he'd continue his run around school.

The running time was supposed to be punishment time. He was banned from taking part in sports for the entire term after they discovered him with the packet of cigarettes. They hadn't realized the single fag in it was full of dope, or he'd have been expelled. So, the principal gave him two sets of Sanskrit conjugations to learn by heart during sports period every single day. He had to go to the principal's office and recite the conjugations every evening. It was the emperor of punishments – he loved sports with a passion and hated Sanskrit with equal passion. But his frustration didn't last long. What the principal didn't know was that he was a pro at learning by heart. He could mug up anything. If he didn't do well in Sanskrit, it was because he couldn't be bothered. It took him precisely fifteen minutes to mug up the Sanskrit conjugations. Then, while the other boys were on the sports fields, he was out of the study hall and running.

He'd told Mallika about this at Randhir's party. That, and a lot more. He hadn't planned on telling her, or, for that matter, even talking to her. Not after that excruciating attempt some months ago, when he had entered Randhir's room just as Mallika was leaving it with an armful of books and her face scrunched up. Behind her, Randhir and Charu were sprawled on the divan, laughing, as Randhir ostensibly read her palm. By then, Mallika was gone.

What the fuck did Randhir think he was doing? How could he do this to Mallika?

He was so upset with Randhir that he found himself following Mallika and saying her name. Big mistake. She wasn't in tears. She was her usual icy self. Not that he'd have known what to say if she'd been in tears, but he certainly didn't know what to say to the Ice Queen. He asked if he could join her; she said 'OK.' He'd never heard a more ungracious 'OK' in his life. As they walked to the market, the temperature kept dropping. His attempt to (literally) break the ice with a suggestion to have ice cream was met with a no-thank-you that would have put the coldest winter to shame. Then she went off to the lending library, and he nursed himself back to warmth with a kulhar of tea. He'd barely defrosted when she came out of Bittu's Books, and he found himself walking back with her in the most godawful silence.

Impossible to converse with someone so prim and proper. Always saree-clad and serious, she looked as though she belonged to another generation. Like the way their mothers belonged to a realm where their youth was distant enough to have been unlived. As if they had been wives and mothers since birth. That was the kind of always-ness about Mallika. What did Randhir see in her? Of course, what she saw in Randhir wasn't anything to wonder about. Every girl in DU was mad about Randhir, and not just for his looks. 'He's so sensitive,' one of Randhir's classmates had once said soulfully. Arnav and Vineet had found it hilarious; they'd never stopped pulling Randhir's leg about it.

Now, Arnav was at Randhir's party, smoking on the terrace, thinking about the break-up with Radha. About how refreshingly different Radha had been from other girls. About how she had no inhibitions, no care about who thought what, walking into his hostel every weekend without qualms, breezing in and out of his room, saying hi to the other guys without embarrassment. They went for wild motorcycle rides and danced all night at The Cellar; she broke all the rules at her hostel in LSR to spend the night with him. At two a.m., he'd say, 'Let's go watch the planes landing at Palam,' and they'd do that. There was nothing Radha said no to. It was exhilarating till the day it ended, but he hadn't seen that coming.

Feeling more relaxed after the smoke, Arnav came down from the terrace and joined Randhir and his friends, who were having an impassioned discussion about the Emergency which Indira Gandhi had declared the previous month after the Allahabad High Court had found her guilty of election malpractice. In the background, 'Angie' was playing loudly.

Suddenly Randhir nudged him and said in a low voice, 'Hey, listen, man, just go keep Mallika company, I'll come in a few minutes.'

With the utmost reluctance, Arnav turned and looked. Mallika was sitting all alone in a chair in the corner, looking so lost that he found himself making his way to her.

She looked at him so frigidly that it was a wonder he didn't turn into a block of ice. He groaned inwardly. He'd imagined that lost look. He couldn't even make an excuse and leave; he had only just walked over to her. Now he was stuck with her in Antarctica.

'Enjoying yourself?' he asked. Clearly, she wasn't, but a guy had to start somewhere.

The Ice Maiden melted.

'Of course,' said the human girl beneath. 'Can't you see I'm the life and soul of the party?'

Words deserted him.

'You've done your duty. You can go back to Randhir now.'

Laughter was welling up inside him.

'You can tell Randhir you tried your best, but I wasn't amenable.'

She sounded like a schoolmarm reprimanding him. Words like 'amenable.' Talking about 'doing his duty.' He could imagine her wagging her finger as he stood, head bowed down, like a chastened schoolboy.

He burst out laughing.

She went off, her starched saree palla flying past his face as she went.

Randhir, who was supposed to come and relieve him of Mallika-duty, was still talking animatedly at the other end of the room. Not that there was Mallika-duty anymore. He'd screwed up.

Later, after helping himself to dinner, he went looking for Mallika and found her sitting in the back veranda, eating alone. He joined her and said, 'I didn't mean to be rude.'

She shook her head. Then she nodded. Then there was a long silence.

What did she and Randhir talk about?

She plucked Randhir out of his head. 'What was Randhir like in boarding school?' she asked.

'A bloody saint,' he laughed.

Her face lit up.

Then, as he told her his school stories, she did the inconceivable. She began to laugh.

By this time he wasn't making pc; he was telling Mallika about how he began running in boarding school at the age of fifteen and his love affair with that eccentric koyal. He told her about the trouble he and Vineet kept getting into, and the more she laughed, the more stories emerged. He even found himself telling her the thing he'd never told Randhir: that basically he was saving Randhir's ass the day he was almost suspended for that cigarette. He was looking for Randhir's Maths textbook, having lost his own. And there it was, under the lid of Randhir's desk, a cigarette packet with a single dope-filled fag. He was examining it in astonishment when the hostel warden grabbed his collar from behind him, and he was hauled to the headmaster's office.

There was nothing to it, he told Mallika, whose eyes – surprisingly large – were shining at what she clearly believed was his noble deed. The thing was, Randhir had a damn good chance of becoming Head Boy, but a smug, oily jackass named Jaitley was in the running with him. What he, Arnav, knew very well was that someone had hidden the dope in Randhir's desk. In those days, Randhir didn't smoke anything in school – not cigarettes, not dope, nothing. When the hostel warden had materialized like a ghost behind Arnav, what was he supposed to say? 'This isn't mine, someone put it in Randhir's desk?' And if he told Randhir, then Randhir, the saint, would march off to the principal's office and tell him, 'It wasn't Arnav's, Arnav found it in *my* desk.' And then that prick Jaitley, who sucked up to all the teachers, would have become Head Boy. Of course, he didn't say 'prick' to Mallika – just 'that jackass Jaitley.'

'But if Randhir wasn't in the running for Head Boy, you'd still have let them assume it was you, no?' Mallika asked.

'Hey, no need to tell Randhir any of this,' he said, alarmed.

'No, of course not.'

She asked him what music he liked, and he began telling her. He told her how his sister Niharika in New York got him the records and tapes he asked for, and how Randhir and Vineet taped all his music. And then – he must have been mad – he said, 'Yeah, she gets me all my music, but I tell you, I'd give up every record and tape she's given me just to go back to the past and undo that marriage of hers.' Mallika looked at him with concern. He said, 'I don't trust her husband.'

He'd never talked about Niharika with anyone but Randhir. But Mallika's eyes were pulling out everything.

He began talking about his beloved Mishti. How he'd had her since he was twelve, when she was just two months old, a beautiful black puppy. It was just before he went off to boarding school. Mishti was a mongrel of varied parentage – terrier, dachshund, apso, and a few other indeterminate breeds thrown in – he told Mallika; and she had a personality. His mother always took Mishti for her five p.m. walk, but if his mother was even ten minutes late, Mishti went for a walk on her own, carrying her leash in her mouth along exactly the same path that his mother took her. She would take an entire round of the colony, stopping for no one, approaching no one, and completely ignoring the other dogs she encountered. 'Mishti's going for her walk!' children would shout, and Mishti would go past them with her head in the air. Then she'd finally come back home and put the leash at his mother's feet in silent reproach.

No telling Mallika that having a puppy calmed that feeling in his chest. He hadn't known he had that feeling until he got the puppy. No telling Mallika that, after he got Mishti, that feeling diminished. They were inseparable. Mishti knew what lay in his heart even when he didn't. He kept Mishti away from his father, who didn't like dogs, which wasn't that difficult on weekdays because his father was in the office. In any case, Mishti was adroit at avoiding his father. When he went to boarding school a year later, she continued sleeping in his room, his mother wrote. As soon as his father left for work, Mishti would emerge and had the run of the house. Coming home for the summer and winter holidays from boarding school, and now from IIT, meant coming home to Mishti.

He spent the entire time at the party in the back veranda talking to Mallika. It was only later, after Randhir, Vineet, and Mahima joined them, that he realized he hadn't let her say a word about herself.

He wondered what Mallika thought of Randhir's writing. He hadn't asked her; he'd been too busy blabbering about himself that evening. And somehow, he couldn't ask Randhir what Mallika thought of his writing. It seemed as personal as saying, 'I thought Mallika was the one for you,' which he'd already made the mistake of saying after the Charu episode. He would never forget the expression on Randhir's face, as though he, Arnav, had crossed a line.

'Yeah,' Randhir had muttered.

'Then why were you with Charu?' he'd persisted, and Randhir snapped, 'Well, I'm not with her now!' Randhir then shook his Parker pen and started writing. Arnav knew not to ask a question like that again.

Randhir only wrote his stories with a Parker pen. His writing was passionate and compelling, with an unsettling core of darkness. He didn't want anyone else knowing he wrote. Sitting under the banyan tree in school, Arnav would hide Randhir's stories and poems in a geometry textbook, which was the largest textbook they had, and read avidly.

Once he asked Randhir why he'd made one of his favourite characters behave so nastily. Randhir thought, and then said, 'I didn't *make* her do it. Man, *I* was shocked when it happened.'

It was unbelievable. Randhir didn't have the answers, even though he was the one who had created that world?

'I didn't know he'd do that,' Randhir would say, or 'She thinks she'll be happy, but I don't think she will.'

'You're talking as though you're writing about real people!'

'They *are* real.'

'What d'you mean?' Arnav was stumped.

'I mean... they already exist. I just have to find them.'

It had boggled his mind. It had been the most thrilling thing he'd ever heard.

He knew Randhir wasn't frauding, the way he did with girls he wanted to impress. Randhir would never say this to any girl he was trying to impress – even though it would have impressed them hugely – because none of them knew he wrote.

Arnav knew Randhir would have told Mallika: Mallika was the only girl Randhir didn't try to impress. With her, he was himself.

Not long after the party where Arnav had talked his head off to Mallika, he came home one weekend to find no Mishti rushing out of the house to greet him.

'Where's Mishti?'

Ma laughed, 'I came home late. She must have gone for her walk.'

But an hour later, Mishti still hadn't come home.

'Ma,' he said, looking at his watch. 'Mishti should have been back home by now.'

'She should,' his mother agreed worriedly.

Their cook came out of the kitchen as he was going out. 'Have you seen Mishti?' he asked. The cook avoided his eyes. She shook her head.

Then she looked up and said, 'Bhaiyya, I cannot keep quiet anymore. Mishti ran away because Sahib kicked her.'

He stared at her.

'Bhaiyya, Sahib kicked her again and again. And she was howling and howling and running around the house, and your father was running after her, kicking her and kicking her. Bechara Mishti ran out of the house. She was running with three legs. Her fourth leg was not working. This time it was too much, Bhaiyya.'

'*This* time?' Arnav whispered.

The cook was silent.

It was winter and dark now by six. He picked up the torch from the mantelpiece and went out. As he walked, he flashed the torch into every corner, whistling, calling out Mishti's name, but there was no excited barking, no ecstatic whirl of black flinging herself on him.

A teenage boy running back home stopped and said, 'Arnav, you're looking for Mishti? I saw her running out of the gate more than an hour ago.'

'Thanks,' he gasped. He could hear his mother panting behind him. He began walking swiftly towards the colony gate. His heart was beating very fast.

'I'll look this side. You look on the other side of the road,' his mother panted behind him.

He waited for a break in the traffic and then sprinted across to the other side. There was a lot of traffic on the road and a row of houses alongside which he was now walking, whistling, calling. Suddenly, someone was calling his own name. He looked up. It was his mother, on the other side of the road, and she had Mishti in her arms. His heart leapt.

The traffic wasn't giving way, every second dragged. He ran across the road, dodged a car that blared its horn, a cyclist who cursed him, and almost tripped and fell on the other side. He righted himself and ran towards his mother. She was holding Mishti exactly as he did every night: Mishti's head cradled in her neck, his mother's hand behind her head. Laughing, overcome, he flung out his arms.

Tears were pouring down his mother's face. Mishti was still.

He touched Mishti. She didn't move. He walked around so he could see her face. Her eyes were closed. He put his hand on her head. She was cold. He came around to where his mother stood sobbing.

He reached out and took Mishti from her arms. Mishti's head lolled. Her side was broken and bleeding. There was blood all over his mother's saree. He cradled Mishti's head in his neck and held her head in the palm of his hand the way his mother had.

He carried her back home. Ma was saying something. He wrapped Mishti up in his towel and carried her to her favourite tree in their back garden where she had loved to sit, watching life go by. He picked up the shovel lying on the ground and began digging. He kept digging and digging. He could hear Ma weeping. Then he carefully laid Mishti there and covered her up.

Finally, he flung the shovel aside and looked at his weeping mother.

'He's done it before?' he asked her.

'Because I wasn't *there*, Arnav, because I wasn't *there*. I'm so –'

'*Don't*, Ma. Don't say you're sorry. Don't ever say sorry again.'

She was wringing the handkerchief with her hands.

'Where is he?'

'He's praying. Don't disturb him now.'

She was still protecting him.

He went inside the house. His father prayed every morning and evening.

He knocked on the puja room door, then opened it. His father was sitting cross-legged on the mat, in front of the table with all the gods, his hands folded in prayer. He opened his eyes.

'You killed Mishti.'

'I did not kick that stupid dog.'

He stared at his father, and everything came together, his entire life.

'Your prayers are shit.'

His father got up and struck at him. He grabbed his father's hand.

By now he was taller and stronger than his father. He flung his father's hand away and went back to his mother, who was still sitting outside.

'Has he ever hit you?'

'Why should he, when his words do the same thing?'

He looked at her, uncomprehending.

She was the one who laughed every time his father said anything, or made that amused, dismissive gesture with her hand that meant 'oh, come on!' He had always thought it didn't bother her.

'Sometimes to live, one buries the truth,' she said.

He looked at her, his world crumbling around him.

Was the truth ever buried? The truth was in every cell of your being. You couldn't turn away from it because that would mean turning away from yourself, and how was that to be done? The truth, like everything else that was part of you, was too close to see. When the elephant in the room lived with you from the time you were born, it was no longer an elephant; it was just part of your life, as much part of you as love.

Randhir's words, not his. He didn't have the words. Years later, this was what Randhir took out of Arnav's life and out of his heart and put into his own story about a seventeen-year-old boy.

In his story, Randhir wrote the conversation that Arnav did not have with his mother. In Randhir's story the mother told the boy:

Strengthen your heart and face the truth.

What has it changed for you, Ma? The boy said. *You'll always be with him.*

Yes, I am with him, in the way that you see, the mother replied. *But in every other way, I am not with him at all.*

As the boy was grappling with this, the mother said, *If you do not face the truth now, even if you go to the other end of the world, he will always be with you.*

Years later, he, Arnav, read the story and understood.

But now, in this moment, he said, 'I'm going to Randhir's house.'

The house was in darkness, but the light was on in Randhir's room. He knocked on Randhir's bedroom window. Randhir came to the window, then gestured to him to come to the side door. Arnav entered, rushed to the bathroom, and wept and vomited till he felt his stomach was tearing apart.

Once, at sixteen, his father had asked him to get him samosas from the market. 'Take the car if you want,' he'd said magnanimously. Thrilled to be driving, Arnav called Randhir, who was at home with him, and they went off to get the samosas. But when he came back, his father's mood had changed; he was in a temper about something.

'Who gave you permission to take my car?' his father had shouted at him. 'It... You said I could.' Arnav was disoriented. He always felt disoriented when these things happened, and they happened a lot.

'Don't talk nonsense, you're sixteen, and you think I'll give you permission to drive my car?' his father said furiously.

All Arnav's joy went running out of him. He put the keys back in his parents' room and went back to his, where Randhir was looking through his records. Randhir looked up at him and said, 'He did tell you to take his car.' It was on the tip of his own tongue to say, 'Are you calling my father a liar?' He stopped himself.

The night that Mishti died, as Randhir sat at his desk writing, and Arnav lay on the divan, trying to sleep, the floodgates of memory opened. His father saying to his mother, 'Why do you keep saying you want a job, who will ever give you a job? You're not even capable of getting a job as a servant.' His father saying to him, 'You stupid fool, you'll make nothing of yourself in life.' Telling Niharika, 'Arnav is my son, he is the most precious thing in my life, you will always come second.' Niharika never holding it against her father, never. His mother always later saying, 'Sorry, Arnab, so sorry,' as though the fault was hers. From the time they were children, Ma saying to Niharika and him, 'Don't get angry with your father, he's very sorry about what he said.'

Ma saying their father was sorry was the other lie; his father was never sorry, because he lived as though none of it happened. So much so that, when things were calm at home, all of them lived as though none of it happened. His father's behaviour was as much part of their lives as the love that he gave them, the praise that he showered on them for their achievements, the extravagant gifts that he would bestow on them whenever he fancied. His father gave him his motorcycle when he got a high first with seven points in the ISC exams. His father gave Niharika a pair of ruby earrings when she topped her MBA class in Ahmedabad. He gave his wife not one, but three Kanjeevaram sarees when he went down South. His father boasted to everyone about his son's acting. But, once, his father said to him that only sissies acted. After that, he never invited his father to any of his performances.

He didn't know which father he lived with. Was it the one who sang his praises, showered him with gifts, and gave sensible advice? Or was it the other one, the one whose every word, almost every other day, was a shard or a lie?

Until finally, this, his father's biggest lie – 'I didn't kick that dog' – stared at him in the face, and Arnav could no longer hide from the truth.

What happened when you faced the truth? What happened was that the world, your world, came crashing down. Then there was no refuge. That's what Ma had done to him. All her life, she had tried to protect him and Niharika from their father's temper, from their father's words. She was their shield, even when it was cruelty directed at her, a cruelty so casual that it was a part of their lives. But their shield had also protected them from the truth. He didn't have the words to tell her, 'It was you who taught me to shrug, Ma – I learnt from you.' He didn't have the words for any of it.

But Randhir did. These were the very words that Randhir used in his story. And in it, though it would have been easier if the boy's love for his father had died, it just would not.

Arnav threw himself into work and extracurricular activities. He auditioned for a comedy written by an upcoming young playwright in Delhi and got the main part. He worked late into the night. He didn't go home at all on the weekends. Ma came to IIT to see him, and neither of them spoke of what had happened. The months flew by. The play he acted in was a huge success. He began volunteering for a charitable trust called the Indian Conservation Fund, helping raise local awareness about wildlife and environmental preservation. He did very well in his exams. By the time the term was over, he was ready to wind down from all that frenetic activity. Whenever he felt that hard knot inside him, he'd ride his bike to India Gate, park it on the side, and run from there to Rashtrapati Bhavan and back. Or all around Lodhi Gardens. Or from IIT to the JNU new campus.

His Mishti was there, in his heart, but she was also absent, because he didn't go to that place. That place where he could still hold her, her cold nose nuzzling his neck. That place where he could feel her, cold and limp in his arms. He didn't let himself. The only thing he couldn't bury was the sight that he had never seen – his father kicking Mishti again and again, and Mishti – unprotected and abandoned by the one whom she loved the most – running, running, running towards her death.

Finally, he had faced the truth. But facing one truth meant burying another. You faced how it was, but you buried how it felt.

Mallika: Small talk, big talk

1975

My three friends reacted strongly to the Charu story.
'Why did that Charu confide in *you*?'
'Suppose her parents start blaming you?'
'Why *you* – why didn't she tell Randhir?'
'She's not normal.'
'Don't have anything to do with her from now on.'

Ma was no less unequivocal. 'She's *not* your close friend – you owe her nothing. Distance yourself from her. She's ill. It's her parents' responsibility, not yours.'

Shantamama said, 'Why do people always confide their rubbish in you? It's bad for your health – don't listen.'

'Pagli,' said Madhu Aunty. 'Total lunatic.'

Charu never came back to college. After a few months, we heard that she'd gotten married to a very handsome IAS officer and was pregnant. The boy's parents had asked for a very big dowry, but that is what you had to do to get a good boy.

'See, all These Things, they become normal after marriage,' Anu Aunty said.

'Those Victorian women were like that Charu,' said Shantamama. She lowered her voice, 'Too much repression – resulting in hysteria. No outlet, no physical exercise, nothing. That's why exercise is so essential, darling – vigorous exercise – it gets rid of Those Feelings.'

'Arre,' said Madhu Aunty. 'Sometimes even with marriage, These Things do not go away. One girl I knew – such a sweet thing – she was hearing voices and seeing things and all. Totally mental. So, her parents got her married. But even after that, voices and all continued. She ended up in Ranchi Asylum. Electric shocks and all they had to give her – that also did not help. Bas, she has been shut up there for ten years, so sad.'

The Charu story wouldn't leave me. Why had she gone mental? After being so besotted with her, how could Randhir have just dropped her?

How was I supposed to know he hadn't slept with Charu? From what various girls had told me, guys never thought of contraception, and most girls had no access to it. Unmarried girls didn't go to gynaecologists. I knew of girls in my college who had had abortions. It was the most common unspoken story, and, as far as the world was concerned, unspoken meant non-existent.

The Charu story also haunted me because of Randhir. Although Randhir hadn't taken out his anger on me, I had felt his deeper emotions churning below the surface. I felt that a lot. With Randhir it was as though a storm was permanently locked inside him, and the calm on the surface was the story that he had to live. It was rather like the truth about my mother and father, which Ma and I would always have to hide from the rest of the world. After all, what is the deepest truth but a handcuffed, manacled, gagged storm?

I didn't know the truth about my mother and father till I was thirteen.

Until then, my favourite fantasy was that my dead father was alive and would come back to me. I would go to bed every night full of anticipation at the prospect of living this other life with a beloved, adoring father. I would get up every morning imagining that, every time the doorbell rang, it was my father coming back to me.

When I was thirteen, my fantasy came true. My father came back, because he was alive and because he'd found out that he had a child.

It was beyond my friends' wildest fantasies, the story of my father literally rising from the dead to return to his old love and unknown daughter. High passion and heaving bosoms finally leapt out from the realm of books and films into real life! Fate had bestowed upon my friends a real-life romance story, and it was unfolding right next door! My friends buried themselves in the revised narrative: Hero and Heroine had fallen madly in love and were separated by circumstances beyond their control, Heroine had had an illegitimate child – their beloved Mallika – then Hero and Heroine had pined for one another for all those long years, and now Hero had finally come back to Heroine, full of remorse and desperate to see his child.

My three friends had waited with bated breaths for Hero and Heroine to marry.

'Padma Aunty will forgive your father, and everything will end happily,' Mahima said.

'Their love for each other will emerge out of the ashes like the phoenix from the flames,' Prabha declared.

'He has never loved another,' Gauri sighed. 'And now he also has you!'

Of course, it wasn't anything like that. Karan and Ma barely spoke. When Karan visited me at home, Ma and he were always tense, and I was so anxious for them to relax that my anxiety would keep escalating. I didn't know how to talk to Karan. I didn't know what to ask him about his life. How did his mother and sister justify what they had done? Did he still talk to them? All that was unsaid lay between us like a steel curtain.

We began spending two weekends every month with his younger sister, Sita, the one who had never been part of the nasty story, who was more than happy to have me in her home. I took a bus to Central Secretariat, where Karan picked me up and drove me to her home. This way, our neighbours didn't see me being picked up regularly by a strange man. Karan and I went for walks and to bookshops. After dinner, we sat with Sita Bua and her husband. I talked a little, but mostly listened. Afterwards, I could never remember the conversations.

Later, at night, Karan would come to my room and say goodnight, switch off the light, and then sit by my side, looking out of the window. As I was falling asleep, I would feel his hand gently stroking my head. It was something I had fantasized about my entire childhood – my father sitting by me and stroking my hair. But the reality now was that I felt his pain so acutely that my sleep would vanish. I would lie still, pretending to be asleep, all the while, thinking, *go away, go away*, and hating myself for thinking it. Eventually, he would go, and I would be wide awake. Hours later, I would fall into an exhausted sleep. Once, I watched him through half-open eyes as he got up to leave the room. For a moment, he leaned against the wall, and then he hit his head hard against it. I closed my eyes and when I opened them again, he was gone.

I didn't tell Randhir that Karan's pain was the albatross that always hung around my neck. That, as the months passed, I began to feel sick to the pit of my stomach every time my weekend with Karan came closer. Every day, I castigated myself for that sick feeling. I continued spending two weekends a month with him, wanting to love him, wanting to fulfil his need to know his daughter, wanting to mitigate his constant pain, a pain that I felt so greatly that it exhausted me more and more. More and more, I dreaded the nights when he sat quietly next to me, staring out of the window. I dreaded the touch of his hand on my forehead, I dreaded the way his unspoken anguish poured into my body. I began getting a migraine a few days before the weekend with him. By the time I reached Sita Bua's home, the migraine would become unbearable. I didn't tell Ma about the migraines. One day it became so severe that I vomited all day in Sita Bua's house and then found myself crying, asking to go back to Ma. Karan drove me home immediately, and as he sat in the sitting room, Ma massaged my head with Amrutanjan in my bedroom. After Ma went out, I lay in bed, my head bursting and my stomach clenching, waiting for them to start fighting about me.

They didn't. I heard them talking in low tones. Then, after some time, I heard Randhir's voice. Something inside me began to calm down, and it was to the sound of his voice that I finally fell asleep.

The next day Karan came home in the evening. Ma joined us, and he told me, very gently, that there was no need for me to spend the weekends with him.

I nodded, looking down to hide the flood of relief and misery.

Sometimes when a fantasy comes true, its soul can be untrue.

The migraines wouldn't go away. Dr Wadhwa said that I was carrying too much tension. Was I unhappy at school? Was someone in school troubling me? He had heard that I stood first or second in school every term, yes? Was I tense about doing well? I shook my head to all his questions.

By this time Ajji and Shantamama had also come home. So now there was the anxiety of three people in the air. I began shutting myself in my bathroom after school. There I read, studied, and did my homework. Sometimes, after my homework, I spread the towel on the bathroom floor and slept. Ma, Shantamama, and Ajji begged and cajoled. I listened to them, because I didn't know how not to, but after that I'd go back to the bathroom.

In the meantime, Ayah-ji was simmering. Finally, she took matters into her own hands and got the Phuknewalla home.

The Phuknewalla was a man in his forties with tattoos all over his face and an upright, serene bearing. While Ma, Shantamama, and Ajji watched nervously, and Ayah-ji stood like a fierce sentinel next to me, I sat on the sofa in the sitting room. The Phuknewalla stood before me and asked me where the pain was. All around my head and neck, and worst on the left side of my head, I told him. He moved his hand around my head and neck as though he were gathering something, hovered it at the left part of my forehead, and pulled. I felt something rising out of my head, and it moved as though there was a rope attached to it. Then, with his fist still clenched, he opened the front door, stood outside in the veranda, opened his fist, and blew into it, as though he were blowing away dust.

'Tell me,' he said.

'It's going,' I whispered.

Ma was looking at me in disbelief. Ayah-ji was looking like the cat that had licked the cream.

'Drink water and rest,' the Phuknewalla said. Then to Ma: 'I will help her. It will take time. But her mind, it is too heavy. You are her mother. Teach her how to keep her mind peaceful.'

'What can *she* teach Baby about that,' Ayah-ji muttered.

It was after this that Ma took a huge loan against the house and sold the only jewellery she had – her mangalsutra and gold bangles. Then, with Madhu Aunty's advice and help, Ma hired a contractor to build me an upstairs room and bathroom. It was in this room, without the weight of everyone's worry, and with the silence and solitude that I so cherished, that I began to recover.

The building of my upstairs bedroom was going on when Karan began visiting me at home.

But who *was* he to Padma, this tall and handsome man? The neighbours asked.

He was a family friend who wanted to marry Padma, Madhu Aunty assured everyone. His mother was dead against his marriage because Padma was a widow – that too, a Madrasi one, that too, with an unmarried daughter, such a responsibility. That was the situation. But see how he always sat with Mallika and her friends in the veranda, *never* alone with Padma. See how, when he was inside the house, in the sitting room, the doors were always wide open. See how Padma's own mother and sister accepted him. And see how he *never, ever* visited Padma at night. 'See with your own eyes!'

The neighbours saw with their own eyes.

Thus, Madhu Aunty conveyed to all that everything was above board and there was no hera pheri going on. Shantamama said that no PhD could teach you this skill.

Unfortunately, Madhu Aunty's story didn't convince everyone.

I wasn't quite fifteen at the time. That morning, I was at the market next to the knife sharpener. As he sharpened our meat knife, he talked to me about his son, who was doing very well in his government school. I was immersed in his story when a voice floated towards me.

'Padma must be *so* frustrated. Good thing she has found a man, otherwise it will be one of our husbands.' Laughter.

Slowly, I turned. It was Mrs Mittal, one of our neighbours, talking to another woman as they bought fruits from the phalwalla. The knife sharpener gave me the knife. I put it into my cloth bag and went to the fruit cart to buy bananas.

'Mallika, sunno, when is your mother getting married?' Mrs Mittal and her friend were smiling, their eyes shining with malice. The other two women next to them looked uneasy. Ma had been tutoring their children for two years, and they had great regard for her.

'We are all *waiting* for your mother's marriage invitation,' Mrs Mittal continued.

'My mother is already married,' I said.

'I didn't know!' Mrs Mittal exclaimed.

'Why should *you* know? You're not my mother's friend.'

I had the satisfaction of seeing the smile wiped off Mrs Mittal's face.

She gave me a look, paid for half a dozen bananas, and went into a nearby shop.

Her scooter was parked at the other end of the market, under a tree. I saw it two minutes later as I was walking home. I looked around. There was no one about. I crouched down, thrust the knife into one tyre, pulled it out, thrust it into the other, and pulled it out. I did it twice more on each tyre. Then I dropped the knife back into my cloth bag and ran home.

Panting, I entered the house and gave Ayah-ji the sharpened knife. Ma was out with Madhu Aunty. I told Ayah-ji I was going to Gauri's house, rushed to Ma's room, took three rupees from the purse in her cupboard, grabbed my mirrorwork bag from my room, and ran to the bus stop.

The flats in the government colony I went to were neat, clean, and beautifully painted. The downstairs flats had green flower-filled lawns and trimmed hedges. It was not like my colony, with its higgledy-piggledy houses, big and small.

I rang the bell.

Karan opened the door. He was looking preoccupied. 'Mallika!' His expression changed instantly to one of concern. Putting his arm around me, he dropped a rare kiss on my head. 'Are you alright?'

I nodded.

'Your mother?'

I nodded, sat on the side of the sofa, and said, without any preliminaries, 'I was in the market and heard this woman, Mrs Mittal… gossiping about Ma. About Ma finally having found a man. And then she asked me when Ma was getting married. I said, she's already married. Meaning you.'

He didn't look shocked.

'By tomorrow, half the colony will get to know. What'll Ma do?'

He was looking thoughtful.

'Ma's gone out. So, I came here.'

'I'm glad you came. And there's nothing to do. Now the story will be that we're married.'

'But you're not living together,' I said, beginning to panic.

A voice emerged from inside one of the rooms. 'Beta, kaun aya hain?'

He got up. 'I'll be back.'

It had sounded like an old woman. An old woman with a strong voice.

I could hear the murmur of conversation.

He came back in a couple of minutes and sat opposite me again. 'I'll come home this evening. Your mother and I will work it out.'

'Who is that in the other room?' I asked.

There was a brief silence.

Then he said, 'My mother.'

'Why is she with you?'

I felt his withdrawal.

'She's my mother, Mallika.'

'Why isn't she with your sisters?'

He said quietly, 'Because... I'm her son.'

'After what she did to you and to Ma, you let her stay with you?'

'Do you want me to abandon my mother?'

'Well, you abandoned *mine*.'

He looked as though I had hit him.

I could hear myself breathing hard, like I had been running a marathon.

'Why haven't you ever admitted that your mother and sisters betrayed you? Why haven't you ever acknowledged that your mother called my pregnant mother a *randi*? How could you forgive them?'

I couldn't breathe. My chest hurt. I got up and ran to the door, down the stairs, and to the bus stop. I got into the bus that had just stopped there, even though I didn't know where it was going. When it stopped, I got off and waited for the bus that would take me to Central Secretariat.

When I finally reached home, both Karan and Ma were there. He must have driven straight to our house after I ran out. As they talked inside, I sat in the veranda with the *Illustrated Weekly of India* on my lap, watching two policemen arriving at Mrs Mittal's house and examining her scooter as she talked to them, gesticulating furiously. A rush of terror went through me.

Ma and Karan joined me outside. They said they would keep to my story. They would tell the world that they were married but could not live together for some time. They told me to stop worrying. By now, in addition to my terror of being arrested for puncturing the scooter, I felt a deep shame for having shouted at Karan. But the apology in my throat wouldn't come out.

As soon as Karan left, Ma rushed to Madhu Aunty's house.

The next morning, Madhu Aunty went to the market and caught up with various neighbours as she bought fruits and vegetables. Then she dropped in at a couple of houses for chai and gossip. The questions flew towards her like missiles.

'When did Padma get married?'

'Why so secretly-secretly?'

'Why she is not living with him?'

Madhu Aunty then told them the final, inspiring story.

As they all knew, this family friend wanted nothing more than to marry Padma. Padma was so moved by his devotion that recently they had had a registered marriage; only Mallika, Anu, and Madhu herself had attended it. The problem, Madhu Aunty sighed, was that Karan-ji's mother was living with him. He was a good man, a good son, and his mother was, of course, his responsibility. How could he and Padma live together when his own mother would not accept the woman he loved? So, they had decided that, as long as his mother was alive, Padma and he would not live together.

The neighbourhood was ablaze. Mrs Rao had had a secret wedding!

Karan was welcomed with open arms into the neighbourhood. It was what Padma deserved. Such a pity they couldn't live together, but as a neighbour said, his mother would not live forever.

The longer that witch lives, the better for us, Shantamama wrote in her letter from Bangalore.

Now Karan could visit us regularly without gossip. My friends joined us on the veranda every time he came home. Their affection and spontaneity banished his reserve. I had never seen him laughing the way he did with them. I no longer had to rack my brains about how to fill the silences. There were none. I had never been able to speak to him about myself, but my friends did. They said I never understood jokes, I never spoke to boys, I was the teacher's favourite in school because I was so quiet and well-behaved. They were hell-bent on impressing Karan. Prabha wanted to know if he too thought Indira Gandhi had been a terrific Prime Minister during the 1971 war with Pakistan, and how dare the Americans send their stupid Seventh Fleet to the Indian Ocean, and why did the Americans always support Pakistan? And did he too believe it was Nehru's fault that India lost the war with China? Wasn't the moon landing fantastic? Did he believe there was life on other planets? Did he like to eat chaat? Mahima told him about the latest films she and her mother had seen, and why Rajesh Khanna was her favourite actor. Did he think Lal Bahadur Shastri had been murdered in Tashkent after the 1965 Indo-Pak war? How dare the foreign press call him 'little sparrow' when he was India's Prime Minister? Gauri wanted to know if he believed Hindi was India's mother tongue, and how could it be when India had so many languages? Look at all the anti-Hindi riots in the South; Hindi should not be forced on the South, didn't he think?

'Have you seen Mallika's moon album?' Prabha asked him, and he said no. Prabha rushed into my room and came out with my moon album – news items about the Apollo 11 landing on the moon and the front-page news about Neil Armstrong, Edwin Aldrin, and Michael Collins coming to Bombay.

'I didn't know you were interested in this,' Karan said to me, amazed.

My grandmother, Ajji, accepted the sham marriage. Though she had never forgiven Karan for abandoning her pregnant daughter, she had always hidden this effectively under her calm demeanour. Being a practical woman, and one who loved me dearly, she understood my need to know the man who had fathered me. Also, the sham marriage benefited all of us.

But Shantamama's husband, my Naraina Uncle, was upset. When Shantamama told him about Ma's sham marriage and that Karan was now visiting us regularly, he said that he would no longer come to Delhi to see us. His anger against the man who had abandoned my pregnant mother was unbreachable. When we got Shantamama's letter telling us this, Ma was distraught. Naraina Uncle had opened his home and heart to her when she had become pregnant and was disowned by her father; he was a beloved brother-in-law, almost like a father to her. Ma wrote an anguished letter to him. Naraina Uncle replied saying he would always be there for us. However, he would not be a participant in this new web of lies, all of which had their source in the man who had abandoned Ma.

Ma was beside herself with grief.

Then something unexpected happened, thanks to Shantamama, something that made Ma feel somewhat better.

For some time, Shantamama had been trying to persuade me to write to their brother, my Madhav Uncle. 'After all,' said Shantamama. 'You're an only child, and he's your only uncle. You don't have to be estranged just because he and your mother are estranged. He'll be happy to hear from you, I promise. My darling, it is very important to have a man in your life – a brother, a husband, a son. It is true, your father is here, but that is as you know… complicated. Madhav is our flesh and blood. He will protect you. If Naraina dies early, then who will cremate me or Padma but our brother Madhav? If he's alive, of course, and naturally he will be, what with that hardy constitution he has thanks to Amma, who used to feed him all those expensive almonds she hid from Padma and me and fill his plate with all the bits of kidney and liver that Padma and I never got.'

I exclaimed, 'Shantamama! You're thinking about *cremation*? *Now*?'

'Why not? You think we will live forever?'

I asked Ma if she minded if I wrote to my uncle. Ma didn't even hesitate. 'He and I were so close, Mallika. Just because we don't talk, doesn't mean he doesn't want to know you. Write.'

I did, and in ten days, I received Madhav Uncle's reply. It was a loving letter, saying how happy he was to hear from me, hoping Ma was well, and telling me all about his three daughters, whom he hoped I would one day meet – after all, they were my first cousins, almost sisters to me.

I was giddy with joy. I wrote back to him the very same day. Our correspondence began.

Then, in a couple of months, out of the blue, he wrote to Ma. Ma joyfully showed me the letter. It was cordial and affectionate, with no mention of the past. Ma, who had loved Madhav deeply as a young girl, immediately replied.

The only thing was that Madhav Uncle talked constantly about his God. 'The way he goes on and on,' I said to Ma, and she laughed. 'Indulge him.'

It made me so happy to see Ma laughing after the grief that had consumed her about Naraina Uncle.

And so, the years passed. Whenever Karan visited us, the veranda – in full view of the curious neighbours – was alive with the conversation and laughter of my three friends and Karan, with me happily listening. When Shantamama and Ajji came to Delhi, they also joined us. We looked normal and happy, just like all the other normal and happy families around us.

That, in a nutshell, was my story. If anyone were to find out, it would be Big Talk. When Big Talk *was* my life, it left no room for Small Talk.

A couple of months after the Charu episode, Randhir decided to throw a party. He urged me to come, so I said 'OK.' That's what guilt did: it made you do things you hated, to make up for things that weren't your fault. I would go for Randhir's party to make up for Charu, though I still didn't know why it was my fault. If Charu hadn't confided in me, she'd still have thought she was pregnant, wouldn't she?

My three friends, who had been stretched beyond endurance by my ways, spent an excruciating hour training me for the party.

'We're going to teach you how to talk to boys,' Mahima declared.

First of all, I had to look more friendly around boys. 'Try to smile more often,' Prabha said. When boys cracked jokes, I *had* to pretend to understand, Mahima said. I was never, ever to ask them the meaning of the punchlines, Gauri said. I was forbidden from looking blankly at them when the joke ended. 'Just laugh,' Mahima ordered, 'and afterwards, we'll explain.' It was no use talking to boys about personal stuff, they advised me. For boys, serious things had to be political, not personal, so you couldn't talk about being worried about your exams and things like that, because boys didn't know what to say about any kind of worry. I could talk about the Emergency or the Apartheid or the wars with China and Pakistan or Project Tiger – after all, that was one good thing Mrs Gandhi had done. And if they were JNU boys, then I could talk about Marx, Lenin, and Trotsky. 'I don't know anything about Marx or Lenin or Trotsky,' I said. My friends said I was being silly. That was not how one *started* a conversation; one began with small talk.

'But how do you *start* small talk?' I asked them.

They looked at me in despair.

And now, here I was at Randhir's party, sitting all alone with the Doors blaring for company. Mahima had shooed me out of the kitchen. Gauri hadn't come because she had her dance class. Prabha was not allowed to come for the party as punishment for telling her grandmother not to be mean to her mother. Randhir and Arnav were talking and laughing with a group of their friends.

Then Randhir glanced at me where I sat and said something to Arnav.

Arnav glanced at me. Then he began making his way towards me.

As Madhu Aunty said: Arnav, he will do *anything* for Randhir. Tonight, I was the Anything.

Here he was, saying hi. He sat on the moorha next to me, his long legs stretched out. I was several inches above him on my straight-back chair.

'Enjoying yourself?' Arnav said, smiling politely. Then he lit his cigarette without bothering to wait for my reply.

Something in me snapped.

Later, I didn't remember what I'd said. All I remembered was Arnav's laughter, and that familiar feeling of humiliation. I walked blindly towards the door.

Once there, Vineet cornered me and said sadly that Jaspreet couldn't come for the party because her parents were very strict. 'You know, Mallika, when parents are so strict, love becomes complicated. I mean, love should be simple. Acceptance makes it simple. No?'

'Yes,' I said, grateful that *someone* was talking to me on his own accord.

Behind us, a lot of Big Talk was happening.

'Now that she's declared an Emergency, she's using the Maintenance of Internal Security Act to put anyone who disagrees with her in jail. She's arresting thousands of people, and all her political opponents, without warrants – no lawyer to defend them, no trial, no nothing,' Randhir was saying. 'No one cares; where's the outrage?'

'But –' said one of his friends.

'Where's the outrage about our newspapers being censored? When she uses the newspapers and that bloody Doordarshan for personal propaganda?'

'Listen, man, don't talk about these things. I mean, you can be arrested.'

'Don't be ridiculous, I'm talking at home. Look at her posters plastered all over the place, having to listen to that "India is Indira and Indira is India" bullshit –'

'– and the thing is, Mallika,' Vineet went on, 'I'm not very good with words. But all those things described in literature and all – now that I love Jaspreet – I *feel* all those things. When I was doing my BA, I took English as a subsidiary, but they didn't teach us anything useful. We had to read that book by that Brontë woman – *Silas Marner* – godawful book –'

'George Eliot,' I corrected him.

'Yeah? I guess. Actually, I never read the book. Borrowed the comic, you know, *Classics Illustrated*. Read it the day before the exam and passed. Just goes to show!'

A couple of Randhir's friends joined us. I excused myself.

Five minutes later, as I was sitting on the steps in the back veranda, eating Madhu Aunty's food and listening to Eric Clapton, Arnav came towards me with his plate piled with biryani.

He sat next to me. 'I didn't mean to be rude.'

What to say? He *had* been rude.

He began quietly eating with me.

Suddenly my food tasted like nothing. I had no conversation.

After a short while, I said tentatively, 'What was Randhir like in boarding school?'

'A saint!' He laughed and began to talk about their school days.

It was as though he had cast a spell around me. The taste came back to the food I was eating. I felt laughter running through my body all the way to my fingertips and toes. By the end of the evening, and for the years that followed, I was done for.

Arnav: Partners in crime

1975

He came out of Randhir's back door and was walking down the veranda steps to where his bike was parked when Mallika emerged from her back veranda. She ran towards him. Breathlessly but peremptorily, she said, 'Arnav, please give me a lift.'

'Yeah, sure,' he replied, a little stunned. He started the bike and had barely got onto it when he felt her sitting behind him.

'Where to?'

A slight pause, then she said, 'I'll get off at IIT.'

She must have thought he was going back to IIT. But he was going to see his mother. He didn't say so. He'd drop her there.

She held onto him tighter than any girl who'd ever sat on his bike. He was so disoriented that he almost ran into the bus in front of him.

She was still holding onto him tightly when he stopped at the red light near India Gate.

'Are you going onwards from IIT?' he asked.

Another pause.

'To... JNU... To see Gauri.'

'Gauri isn't at JNU – Randhir's taken them all shopping,' he said.

Mahima had got engaged recently. Randhir, with a stiff upper lip, had taken the girls shopping just half an hour ago. How come she wasn't with them? For that matter, how come she didn't know?

The lights turned green.

'Not to worry, I'll take you back home,' he said, turning.

She said, 'Can we stop and sit here for a while?'

Stop and sit at the India Gate lawns? What on earth for?

He stopped. As they got off, he saw that she was frozen to the bone. Her nose was bright red. She was hugging herself. Her eyes were watering and a streak of kajal was running down her cheek. She just had on a sweater and shawl. He was overcome with remorse. No wonder she had wanted to stop. She was freezing to death.

'Mallika, you're freezing.' He took off his jacket and gave it to her. He was wearing a thick sweater under it.

She took it without protesting and put it on.

'Now *you're* cold.' She gave him her red bandhini shawl.

Smiling, he took it and wrapped it around himself. They sat on the lawn.

Of course, she didn't talk.

She hadn't talked that day at the party either when he'd told her his stories. He hadn't realized it at the time because she was laughing so much.

Now, she was looking down at her lap, lost in thought.

'You didn't know Mahima and the others were going shopping?' he asked, lighting a cigarette.

She looked up at him, her eyes wide.

'I mean, the four of you do everything together,' he added.

Her eyes became wider.

Had he said something wrong?

After a whole minute, she said, 'No; sometimes we don't do things together.'

He was just making pc, and here she was responding as though the weight of the world sat on a correct answer! She really was an odd one.

She opened her cloth bag, took a small sleeping puppy out of it, and gave it to him.

Bemused, he took it from her.

It was a little black Mishti. He almost doubled up with the pain.

He gave the puppy back to Mallika. Her hands were ice cold.

'Mallika, what on earth are you doing with a puppy?'

'I found her on the road outside the colony. She was... lost.'

She was looking at him as though – oh, god, no. No.

'Mallika, I can't keep her.'

Her face fell.

The puppy was a female. Black, like Mishti. He tried not to watch how Mallika was cradling the puppy against her neck – the way he had cradled Mishti when she was a puppy. When she was no longer a puppy. When he was home, that was their goodnight ritual: he, sitting on the floor with Mishti in his arms; her face buried in his neck, giving an occasional whimper of love.

'Why can't *you* keep her?' he asked.

'My Ayah-ji was bitten once and had to have fourteen injections in her stomach. She hates dogs. Every time I said I wanted one as a child, she'd threaten to leave.'

The puppy was suckling her chin. 'Poor thing, she's hungry,' Mallika sighed.

He said softly, 'Let's take her home. My mother will find a home for her.'

Mallika literally sagged with relief.

'But why were you taking the puppy to Gauri?' he asked, puzzled.

She thought about this. 'My mother had gone out and I couldn't find Prabha, Mahima, or Randhir,' she said.

'But they'd have come back.' Nothing she was saying was making sense. 'And besides, Gauri's in the hostel, she can't keep a puppy.'

Mallika said, 'But Gauri always knows what to do.'

He blinked.

'Chalo then,' he said. He didn't get it.

They got up, she put the puppy carefully in her bag, and they walked to his bike.

It just came out of him. 'Did I talk too much that day at Randhir's party?'

'No.'

'Yeah, I'd smoked too much at that party.'

Then he realized how it sounded: as if being stoned was the only reason he'd talked to her.

'That's why you talked to me?' To his relief, she sounded amused.

'Of course not.'

Mallika laughed. 'You're quite a storyteller!'

'Me? Oh, no, that's Randhir.'

'Of course not! Not Randhir.'

Not Randhir? What was she saying!

'How can you say that? You know he's been writing stories all his life! I mean, you know how obsessively he does it.'

They were standing next to his bike. He waited for her answer.

She looked away from him and didn't say a word.

After a few seconds, he started the bike, wondering. Did she not like Randhir's writing? How could that be?

By the time they reached home, he – sans jacket – was frozen to death.

Ma greeted Mallika and the puppy with delight. When he asked her if she could find a home for it, Ma answered immediately: 'The Luthras want a puppy for their daughter – they're a very good family. I'll phone them.' She kissed the puppy several times and smiled delightedly at Mallika.

Ma was on the phone, talking and laughing for a few minutes. Then she put down the phone, beaming. 'I'll take her there after lunch. They're so excited. They're all dog lovers, Mallika.'

He watched Mallika smiling at his mother with relief.

'Now you have lunch with us, Mallika,' Ma said.

'But –'

'Come on, Mallika,' Arnav interrupted. 'Just phone Madhu Aunty and ask her to tell your mother you're having lunch here. I'll drop you back after that.'

Mallika hesitated. Then she said, 'OK. Thank you.'

While Mallika was phoning Madhu Aunty from his house, he put on another jacket, took an old towel from the cupboard and a basket he found in the kitchen, and installed the sleeping puppy in his room. He had tried so hard not to touch this little Mishti. But now, alone with her, his resolution disintegrated. He held her, stroked her, and kissed her. Little Mishti blissfully licked his face, his neck, and his hands. This kind of love was pain. He didn't want it.

After Mishti's death, he had spent very few weekends at home. He missed Ma, but it couldn't be helped. The smell of agarbatti wafting out of his father's puja room revolted him. Before, it hadn't cost him anything to be part of the pujas for festivals like Diwali and Janmashtami. He had always seen them as family rituals more so than prayers. But after his praying father sent Mishti to her death, Arnav could no longer be part of it. He refused to join his parents for their pujas during Diwali or Janmashtami. 'I've given up on the boy,' he heard his father complain to his mother. 'Maybe a good wife will sudharo him one day.'

Fat chance.

He fed the puppy milk, took her outside to pee, and finally put her back on the old towel and joined Ma and Mallika for lunch.

Ma had taken a shine to Mallika. During lunch, she chattered away, asking Mallika about her mothers and her stepfather and her college and her saree – oh, it was her grandmother's saree, such a beautiful Kanjeevaram, you didn't get Kanjeevarams like this in Delhi, not even in the emporiums. Ma was beaming ominously at Mallika.

An hour later, driving back to Mallika's home, he took the detour to India Gate again. This spot – where large lawns sprawled on either side of Rajpath with their stunning trees, where at one end lay Rashtrapati Bhavan and, at the other, India Gate – was one of his favourite spots in Delhi. He, Randhir, and Vineet often drove there after midnight and raced each other on their motorcycles down Rajpath, which was empty at that time of the night. Sometimes, even at that late hour, there would be a solitary ice creamwalla with his cart of multicoloured ice creams, and they'd descend upon him, raging with hunger.

As he and Mallika drove past India Gate, Arnav felt the urge to ask her if she felt like some ice cream. He didn't want ice cream, he wanted… He had no idea what he wanted.

He turned, 'Ice cream?' Mallika said, 'Oh, yes!'

Ten minutes later, they were sitting on the India Gate lawns, eating ice cream.

'Please don't tell anyone about the puppy, not even Randhir,' she said.

This was getting odder and odder. 'Why?' he asked.

'Just don't.'

'OK,' he said, both amused and curious. She went back to eating her ice cream.

The Ice Maiden returned when she caught him looking at her. 'What?'

'I've never seen anyone eating ice cream with such relish.'

She laughed, and the Ice Maiden dissolved like mist under the sun.

Before her laughter disappeared, he plunged into a story about the time Vineet had dared him to enter the famously prison-like LSR hostel.

They'd both smoked a lot that day. All he remembered now was emerging from a delicious sleep to find himself in a room full of hysterically laughing girls. He hadn't had the foggiest idea where he was. He swung himself off the bed and almost tripped over the burkha that he was wearing. As he looked at himself in horror, the girls became even more hysterical. 'Arnav, you're too funny,' one of the girls shrieked – he recognized her as a girl called Radha, whom he'd met at the IIT festival. 'Where am I?' he asked. The girls, in a frenzy of laughter, informed him that he was in the LSR hostel. 'But… How?' The girls became more hysterical. They told him that no one had any idea how he'd got inside. A group of girls had come back to the room and found a burkha-clad man asleep on the bed. Fortunately, two of them recognized him from the IIT festival. He was then stuck in the hostel overnight as the guard had locked the main door. The girls smuggled him food from the dining hall, kept him company, and stayed awake all night, laughing and talking.

The next morning, he still couldn't leave as the hostel superintendent was sitting in her office next to the main door, and the girls said that, burkha notwithstanding, she'd notice he was a guy. He had to wait till the afternoon. The superintendent went out, and the girls rushed him downstairs and out of the hostel door.

But it wasn't over. The guard saw him striding down the hostel path towards the gate and accosted him.

'Who did you come to meet?' the guard asked him.

'Sita,' he said in a high falsetto.

'And who do you think you are? Ram? Haraam zaada.' The guard ripped the veil off his face.

There was only one thing to be done. Arnav lifted his burkha and sprinted towards the hostel gate. He was a runner; the pursuing guard didn't stand a chance. He whizzed through the gate, where fate favoured him in the form of another IIT guy who was sitting on his motorcycle, waiting for his girlfriend. 'Khanna, man, get me out of here,' he exclaimed, and leapt astride the bike, burkha and all. Khanna rose to the occasion, started the bike and they were off.

Mallika laughed so much during this retelling that tears were running down her cheeks and she almost dropped her ice cream.

Arnav knew then that ice cream wasn't what he had wanted; he had wanted her laughter.

Of course, he hadn't told Mallika that Radha was the one who had entertained him all night in the LSR hostel and smuggled food from the dining hall for him, nor that she had landed up at IIT the next day. He found Radha next to him as he was half-dozing between classes on the lawn in the winter sunshine. Within a week, she was in his bed. And now, a year later, out of it.

When they arrived Madhu Aunty, Anu Aunty, and Padma Aunty were sitting in the veranda of Madhu Aunty's house, looking grim.

They walked to the veranda and said their namastes.

'Mallika, that Mrs Mittal came home to pick a fight with me,' Mallika's mother said.

Mallika looked pale. 'Why, Ma?'

'Because she's gone mad. She said you stole her puppy.'

Arnav looked at Mallika incredulously, then schooled his expression.

'Some insect she has in her brain about Mallika,' Anu Aunty said.

'Bekaar woman,' Madhu Aunty said. 'Saying she will call police. I said, "Call, call."'

He saw that Mallika had become even paler.

'Arre, Mallika, do not look worried,' Anu Aunty said. 'She cannot do anything.'

'Look,' exclaimed Madhu Aunty, pointing.

A policeman was striding towards them, baton in hand, as though on a mission to destroy evil. A heavy woman was panting and groaning like a goods train behind him, and a plump twelve-year-old boy was beside her, pointing to Mallika and wailing, 'Bloody thief, she's a bloody thief!'

Mallika was looking sick.

Arnav and Mallika sat on the two remaining veranda chairs next to each other.

'She thinks she will win.' Madhu Aunty was now in full throttle. 'She will never win against me, never.'

Arnav had seen the policeman before. He was from the local police station. These days he was often seen making the rounds of the colony. He'd threatened to arrest a fourteen-year-old boy whom he'd seen tearing off the 'India is Indira, Indira is India' poster from one of the shops in the market. The Emergency suited his temperament: he spent a lot of time scaring the shit out of whomever he could.

The trio arrived at the veranda.

'*She*,' Mrs Mittal declared, pointing to Mallika. 'She is the one who stole my puppy. *Just now* you arrest her.'

Shit, he thought, Mallika *had* done it.

But the policeman wasn't looking at Mallika. He was gazing at her mother as though he'd seen a vision of the Goddess Durga herself. He flung his baton into the flowerpots and threw himself at Mallika's mother's feet.

'Sampat Bhaiyya, no need, no need, please get up, get up now,' Mallika's mother protested.

Sampat Bhaiyya refused to get up. He was murmuring things at her feet like a mantra.

When he eventually rose, he explained, 'Both my sons have got into best English medium school.' He then did a namaste with his head bowed down, as though he were in a temple and she were the deity.

'Very good, excellent,' Mallika's mother said. 'Give them our blessings.'

'*You* both give them, Madam. They will come with sweets, and *you* both give them blessings.'

Mrs Mittal pointed to Mallika and shrieked, '*She* is the thief who stole our puppy!'

The policeman glanced at Mallika and did a double take.

Then he threw himself at Mallika's feet.

'No, no, no.' Mallika leapt out of her chair. 'Please get up, please get up.'

'Only because of your mother and you my children have had success,' he said.

He got up, smiling beatifically.

'Very good news, I am very happy.' Mallika's face was red.

Finally, the policeman turned to Mrs Mittal. 'Hanji?' he said disinterestedly.

'What *hanji*?' Mrs Mittal shrieked. 'She's the one – three times I am telling you.'

'Madam, ten times if you tell me, then also I will never believe. Hundred times if you tell me, then also I will never believe. Because such a thing cannot be.'

The boy, Chotu, began to wail.

'Keep quiet,' Madhu Aunty shouted, and Chotu's cry cut off midway.

By now several neighbours had gathered to watch the drama being enacted on the veranda. The policeman was playing centre stage. He turned to face his audience and gestured to Mallika's mother, 'She is Bari Saraswati.' Then he gestured towards Mallika. 'She is Choti Saraswati. Because of their tutoring, my sons have got admission into best English medium school. They have put their life into my children. Such pure hearts they have. Everyone knows.'

Then he turned to the fuming Mrs Mittal. 'And you, Madam, you are talking of Choti Saraswathi *stealing* your puppy? Madam, leave it, all this. If you want, you can go to police station to register complaint. Certainly go. Go, most welcome. But I know truth from falsity. That much even I know.' He turned to Mallika's mother. 'Namaste, Madam.' He turned to Mallika. 'Namaste, Madam. My children, they will see you next time with sweets.' He turned to the audience of neighbours and did another namaste.

Then he picked up his baton from the flowerpots and, without a glance at Mrs Mittal, made a superb exit.

That should have been the end of the open-air drama, but it was only Act I.

'She's a bloody thief, she stole my puppy!' Chotu shouted, rushing towards Mallika.

Arnav leapt up, took Chotu by the collar, and dumped him on the veranda steps. 'Don't *move*.'

'Don't you dare touch my son,' Mrs Mittal screamed.

'Keep your mouth shut,' Madhu Aunty screamed back.

Mrs Mittal shrieked at Mallika, 'We saw you, don't deny, we saw you!'

By now even more neighbours had gathered to watch and listen.

'Mrs Mittal, don't talk such nonsense,' Mallika's mother said calmly.

Mallika spoke. 'You saw me walking across the street. That is all. But *I* saw how Chotu kept kicking the puppy. *I* heard the puppy howling in pain. You didn't even stop your son.'

There were sounds of outrage from the audience.

Ah, Arnav thought, as things began falling into place.

'Liar,' Mrs Mittal shouted. 'Like mother, like daughter.'

There was an electric silence.

'And what is that supposed to mean?' Madhu Aunty said dangerously, rising from her chair.

'No values, that Mallika has, bilkul besharam,' said Mrs Mittal.

They were talking in rapid-gunfire Punjabi.

Madhu Aunty said, 'Besharam? There is no one more besharam than you. The whole world knows what a good, honest girl Mallika is. And you are talking of her *stealing*! Kamaal hain! As for Mallika's mother, *she* earns her own living, *her* money is clean. Not like your father's tainted income tax money. Everyone knows your brainless son got into that school only because your father gave the school so much of his dirty money. Go tell the police. I also have plenty to tell the police about your corrupt income tax father.'

'My puppy!' yelled Chotu. 'She stole my puppy.'

'You were kicking the puppy,' Arnav said to Chotu, wagging his finger. 'I've reported you to the SPCA.'

'Yes, SPCE,' Madhu Aunty said with relish. 'Special Police.'

'Special police for *dogs*?' Mrs Mittal said, trying to muster up scorn.

Someone in the audience laughed.

'Special Police for Cruelty to Animals during the Emergency,' he improvised. 'SPCAE.'

Several people in the audience clapped.

'*Anything* they can arrest you for during Emergency,' Madhu Aunty said.

'Battameez.' Mrs Mittal went to the steps, pulled up her son, and stormed off.

Madhu Aunty brushed her hands together as though to say 'I'm done with you both.'

The audience burst into applause.

Arnav was enjoying himself hugely. This was better than any play in which he'd acted.

Madhu Aunty addressed the audience. 'You believe it? That our Mallika stole their puppy?'

'Impossible!'

'How can *Mallika* do such a thing!'

'Too many lies she tells, that Mrs Mittal.'

Uttering their support for Mallika, the audience slowly began to leave.

No doubt they could all see Mallika's innocence writ across her, Arnav thought. There she sat, quiet, in her mustard and red silk saree, her hair in a long plait, a big bindi on her forehead, and large bruised eyes. Even that bygone film star, Meena Kumari, the Queen of Tragedies, had never looked so sinned against.

'Bechari, just look at her! As though she is capable of such a thing!' one of the neighbours said, echoing his thoughts.

'Chalo,' said Madhu Aunty triumphantly. 'Let us have chai.'

He said his namastes, told Madhu Aunty no tea this time, he had to go home.

'Thank you,' Mallika whispered as soon as the aunties went in.

They went down the veranda steps together and stopped at his bike. She looked at him uncertainly.

'Mallika,' he said, his hand on his heart. 'I swear I'll be your partner in crime anytime, anywhere.'

She laughed, then looked away.

He saw it then.

'Bye,' she said, giving him the jacket that she'd worn.

'Bye.'

It was so clear now. How had he not seen it before? Mallika was shy.

Mallika: A red shroud

1975–1976

After Randhir's party, I went back to my uneventful life of studying, spending time with my friends, and tutoring. For the last two years, I had been tutoring a slum girl, Jalpari, daughter of Gopal, our colony scooterwalla. She was twelve now, sharp as a knife, cheeky, and full of backchat. When she was ten years old, she had come home, asking me to tutor her in English. She would work in an office when she grew up, she had said, with an irrepressible smile, and how to do that without knowing English? Then she had produced five rupees from her frock and asked if it was enough.

'No need,' I had said, 'I'll tutor you.'

'My father said I have to give you money,' Jalpari said firmly.

I hesitated before replying. 'Alright, you give me one rupee every month, and when you get an office job, then you can give me the rest.'

Jalpari's eyes lit up, and she nodded.

She was very quick to learn, full of questions, and hard-working. She told me that her mother didn't want her to learn English; her mother wanted her to sweep and swab at people's houses after school hours and earn money for them. But her father, Gopal, had overridden her mother. I had been tutoring Jalpari for two years. She sat at the dining table with the other children I tutored. But just recently, the mother of a new tuition boy, Himanshu, had asked me, 'Isn't this girl a Harijan?' I looked at her, disconcerted. I'd never encountered such a question before. Another mother who had come to pick up her son said reassuringly, 'This is the daughter of our scooterwalla, Gopal.'

'This slum girl shouldn't sit with our children,' the first mother said, and left.

'I'm not going to make her sit separately,' I said to Ma and Shantamama later, when we were alone.

Ma nodded, looking troubled.

'Just know that you're going to lose this student,' Shantamama said. 'And maybe others.'

'I've never lost a student these two years that Jalpari's been here,' I said. My mothers looked at each other and said nothing.

A few days later, Himanshu came with half a month's fees in an envelope and said, 'Mallika Miss, my mother says I can't come because this slum girl also sits here, and you give her water from the same glasses we drink from.'

I nodded. 'Tell your mother I don't want this,' I said, not taking the envelope.

The next day I went to the market and bought two beautiful oval-shaped steel glasses, and had them engraved. 'For Jalpari to drink water from,' I told my mothers, showing them both glasses.

'But why *two* glasses?' Ma asked.

'One for her, one for me. I've had our names engraved on them, see? Now Jalpari will see that I'm drinking from the same kind of glass as her. And the other children and their mothers will see that Jalpari isn't drinking from their glasses.'

After that, I made Jalpari sit at the head of the table so that none of the other children's mothers could complain about them having to sit next to her. Jalpari was thrilled with her new steel glass, the only one that looked like mine.

I lost another student, but immediately got two more. Shantamama, who was always worried about our precarious finances, was very relieved. Before she went back to Bangalore, she said, 'You're very oblivious, Mallika. Don't you know that your two students, Rajni and Mohit, never drink water in our house because Ayah-ji is a Muslim?' She saw my shock and nodded. 'Yes. Exactly. Your mother tries to protect you from these things. I don't see why. You should know these things happen.'

But there was no time to brood about this incident or ask my friends what they thought because two days later, Mahima got engaged. Shekhar, Mahima's fiancé, was out of a Mills & Boon romance – tall and handsome with a deep voice and a gorgeous whiff of foreign aftershave. Gauri and I fell head over heels in love with Mahima's fairy tale story. How could we not? Mahima, who had always had everything, now had the *ultimate* everything.

The only fly in the ointment was Shekhar's sister, Renu.

'That Renu, total battameez she is,' Madhu Aunty said disapprovingly.

We were thrilled with Renu's battameezi. We had never seen anything like it. Renu's saree blouses and kameezes were cut so low that when she bent down, we could see her nipples (she applied rouge on them, she told us once). She would go into a tizzy at the sight of Arnav and Vineet. 'That too, she's a married woman,' Mahima hissed to us. Once, she arrived at Mahima's house in a red shirt with a neck so precariously low that Madhu

Aunty tossed her a chunni, saying peremptorily 'Wear this, there are boys in this house.'

Of course, Renu knew there were boys in the house. That was the point.

We had never seen anything like it. It demanded a regular viewing.

Whenever we saw Renu's car parked outside Madhu Aunty's house, the three of us would drop in and plonk ourselves in the sitting room. There, we would eat the offerings laid out for Renu – badaam, cashews, and kaju ki barfis, all the things our mothers could never afford – and watch her flirting and giggling with the boys. Sometimes she'd follow Vineet and Arnav to Randhir's room and drape herself on Randhir's bed with her saree palla falling off her shoulders; we could see her from the sitting room. Then Madhu Aunty would say frantically, 'Come and have tea, Renu,' and Renu would come outside, pick up her cup and saucer, and go back to Randhir's room. 'Bilkul besharam,' Madhu Aunty would say. After Renu's first few visits, whenever she arrived, Madhu Aunty ordered the boys out of Randhir's room, and they'd troop out and escape on their bikes. Once, as they left, Renu followed them, perched herself on the back of Vineet's motorcycle, put her arms tightly around him, and went off with them. It was a sight to behold: Vineet's gritted teeth, and Renu's joy.

When the boys weren't around, Renu took to dropping in at my house. She regularly told me all about her husband's passionate lovemaking. I gave my friends a blow-by-blow account of all Renu's stories. 'Have you heard of the bud of pleasure?' Renu asked me. 'No,' I said, and she told me how women had orgasms. I promptly told my friends. Our sex education grew in leaps and bounds.

Of course, I knew Renu lied. But so what? There was nothing malicious about her lies. As soon as she uttered them, they became her reality. Asking if the things she said were true or not was like asking if a book were true or not. What mattered was being swept away, and swept away I was. And the more I got to know her, the more I felt that there was another, almost-invisible Renu who was obscured by the all-too-visible one. She read voraciously. She quoted Shakespeare's love sonnets – not to show off, but because she loved them so much. When I told Renu about my constant quest for books, she promptly lent me several from her collection. On one occasion, when I had a cold, Renu came home with a huge bowl of soup that she had made for me.

'The strangest of people like you,' Ma said. 'I just don't understand.'

'Why *her*?' Randhir asked, astonished when he found out that Renu was visiting me.

'Why not?' I responded. Randhir gave a snort of laughter and went off, leaving me smarting and ashamed for not having defended Renu.

By this time it was no longer entertaining to watch Renu in Mahima's living room, making such a fool of herself over the boys. I saw how they rolled their eyes, exchanged glances, laughed. I stopped going next door to watch the Renu drama. But if I happened to be there, I couldn't avoid it.

One day, when the boys were laughing at an oblivious Renu, Arnav caught me looking at them, and his laughter faded. Ten minutes later, as I was leaving from the back door of Madhu Aunty's house, he entered the kitchen with his empty tea mug and said, 'Mallika, how come that look was for us and not for her?'

It was the first time he had spoken to me in many weeks, after that party. Now, as he asked me this question, my tongue was tied in its usual knots. At last I said, 'You and Vineet were laughing at Renu.'

'And you girls don't?'

Not any longer. Well, *I* didn't.

'Eating badaams and kajus like there's no tomorrow and watching her shenanigans as though you're watching *Chitrahaar!*' he said teasingly.

Shame filled me.

'We don't... I don't laugh at her now,' I muttered. 'Got to go. Bye.' I rushed back home.

He hadn't even bothered to talk to me after that party, and when he did it was about *this*?

Had I really been that deluded at the party? He'd seemed so relaxed and happy talking to me. In fact, he'd shown no inclination to leave my side. More than an hour later, Mahima, Randhir, and Vineet had joined us at the back veranda. The boys began cracking jokes. Keeping my friends' lectures in mind, I'd laughed – even at the ones I didn't understand. The next day, Mahima had said, 'At least now they don't think you're a snob.' I had replied indignantly that Arnav wouldn't have talked to me if he thought I was a snob. Mahima snorted that Arnav was doped out, that was why he was talking to me.

That had hit me hard. 'Well, better to be a snob than boring,' I had said, trying to shrug it off.

My three friends stared at me.

'Who said you were boring?'

'Randhir would *never* say such a thing about her.'

'It was either Arnav or Vineet.'

'Probably both.'

They got it out of me, the conversation that Arnav and Vineet had been having on the terrace a year and a half ago.

They were furious. They raved and ranted about the stupidity of boys. It was very comforting. Then Gauri had said, 'Mallika, *I'll* tell you why you're not boring.' I had looked at Gauri, full of hope. 'You're not boring because you find everyone interesting,' Gauri said triumphantly. She saw our blank faces and exclaimed, 'Oho! Can't you see – boring people aren't interested in others. They're only interested in themselves.'

How reassured I was to hear that!

But I knew Gauri was wrong. As I walked to the market to borrow books from the lending library a few weeks later, I was trying to digest the fact that something that had meant so much to me had meant nothing to Arnav. Mahima was right. He'd only talked to me because he'd been smoking pot. After the party, he'd got involved in a play produced by the Delhi Theatre Group, in which he – as usual – had the leading role. Randhir had taken me for it. In it, Arnav had transformed into a high-strung, neurotic, obsessive middle-aged government employee, in love with an oblivious colleague. He was so funny in his role that Randhir and I, along with the rest of the audience, were laughing almost non-stop. Why would someone so talented, popular, and vibrant be the least interested in talking to me?

I was jerked out of my reverie by the sound of a puppy howling in pain. I looked up to see Chotu, Mrs Mittal's son, in his veranda, kicking his puppy, while his mother – the unforgotten and unforgiven woman whose scooter tyres I had slashed four years prior – also sat at the veranda, filing her nails.

'Chotu, don't do that,' I shouted.

Mother and son looked at me. 'It is *his* puppy,' Mrs Mittal said, and went back to filing her nails. She had disliked me ever since that long-ago day when I had been rude to her. Chotu gave the puppy another kick, and it howled and howled. I walked on to the sound of the howling puppy, feeling I'd burst. A few minutes later, a scooter whizzed past me. Mother and son were on the scooter, probably on their way to the market.

I immediately turned and walked back. Then, hitching up my saree, I ran.

The poor three-month-old puppy was tied to a chair in the veranda, looking miserable. I went to it, knelt, and tried to take the chain off its collar. It cringed in anticipation of my hitting it. I stroked it, and it whined and licked my hand. 'Don't cry, my baby,' I whispered. I looked over my shoulder. No one. But the chain wasn't coming off the collar. And I was so frightened at what I was doing that my hands were shaking. Finally, I unbuckled the collar, left it and the chain lying on the veranda, picked up the little puppy, and put it in my cloth bag.

What to do? Where to go? Ayah-ji wouldn't let me bring it into the house; she hated dogs. I emerged from their veranda to cross the street that ran between our houses when I saw mother and son returning on the scooter. Looking straight ahead, I crossed the street and walked towards my house. I went inside, walked through the sitting and dining rooms, and stepped out of the back door. Arnav came out of Madhu Aunty's back door at the same moment, waved, and went towards his bike. He was putting on his helmet when I reached him and asked him for a lift; he said 'sure,' as though this was the kind of thing we did often together. As usual, he drove like a maniac, almost hit a bus, apologized profusely, and continued driving like a maniac, while I hung on, side-saddle in my saree, desperately holding him with one hand and keeping my cloth bag firmly on my lap with the other.

Thank goodness he didn't find it strange when I asked him to stop at India Gate. What else to do? How could I go back home with the stolen puppy? So there we sat on the lawns: I, overcome by his kindness in giving me his jacket in this freezing cold, enveloped in his smell; he, looking like a beautiful gypsy with my shawl around him, totally at ease and thankfully oblivious. What to do with the puppy? What to tell him? The truth would implicate him in my crime. Yes, I'd committed a crime.

'You didn't know Mahima and the others were going shopping?' Arnav asked, lighting a cigarette.

He was making pc, of course.

Still. I had to answer. Meaning I had to lie.

This was the problem with lies. You could never stop with one. Which was fine if you were Madhu Aunty and Mahima. Lies tripped off their tongues with ease. Not a vestige of guilt did they struggle with. Which wasn't to say I didn't lie. Of course, I did. The very story of my life was a lie. It was a lie that Ma, Shantamama, and I had lived and maintained with such fidelity that it had become the truth along with all the other subsequent lies about my father. Ours was the Big Lie. Big Lies had a place in life because without them there *was* no place in life. Small lies had a place in life too, but Ma and I had little talent for those, much to Shantamama's exasperation.

So Arnav's innocuous question, followed by another innocuous question – didn't the four of us do everything together? – paralyzed me. In other words, he was asking how come I hadn't gone with them.

What to say? Even pc requires an answer, no?

I hadn't gone with them because I was drowning in an ocean of longing. Not going was the only way to keep myself afloat. It was too much – Mahima's beautiful trousseau, all those gorgeous foreign underclothes, perfumes, lipsticks, sarees, jewellery, gold payals, and... everything. Not because I wanted a beautiful trousseau, or a big wedding, or gold payals, far from it. But because, once in a while, I longed for beautiful new things too, and they were always, always, always beyond my reach. There were times when my squashed longings became unsquashed and shot up, shrieking: 'look at me, here I am!' This was one such occasion. So I told my friends I didn't feel like going shopping with them.

'So damn obstinate,' Prabha had said. Mahima and Gauri had concurred.

'Why do you have to do everything that *you* feel like doing?' Mahima had said. 'Sometimes it's good to do things you don't feel like doing if it makes other people happy.'

I do that a lot, I wanted to shriek.

This was the long and truthful answer to Arnav's short and idle questions.

I said that we didn't always do things together, which he seemed to find amusing. His laughter made it easy to take the puppy out of the bag and give it to him.

His amusement disappeared completely. He held the puppy to his cheek for a few seconds and then, to my surprise, gave it back to me.

Thankfully he believed me when I said I'd found it on the road. But I shouldn't have asked him if he could keep it. His mood changed. He refused so abruptly that I felt a little sick in my stomach. That familiar feeling of rejection and humiliation returned. And worry.

Then, out of the blue, he said his mother would find it a home. The relief, oh, the relief!

He was making pc again as we walked back to the bike. I wish he hadn't bothered. Because, unwittingly and carelessly, he crushed me. He confirmed what Mahima had suspected – that he'd talked too much to me at Randhir's party because he'd smoked too much that night. I felt it like a punch in the stomach. Here was the proof, finally. I managed to give Arnav a light and amused response. It took a lot out of me.

But when he told me that Randhir had been writing obsessively all his life, I couldn't even nod, so sharp was my anguish. How to pretend that it didn't matter that Randhir had never told me?

To my great relief, Arnav's mother immediately found the puppy a home, but after that I didn't have the energy to tell her that I didn't want to have lunch with them. I phoned Madhu Aunty and asked her to please tell Ma.

'But why you are in *Arnav's* house?' she asked sharply.

She knew very well that Arnav and I were not friends.

'I asked him for a lift, Aunty, to go to JNU to see Gauri.'

'Arre! But you know Gauri she has gone shopping with the other two.'

'Yes, Aunty, I forgot, and when we were halfway there Arnav told me, and… he had to give something to his mother, so we came here, and then his mother said we must have lunch.'

'But why you asked *Arnav* for lift?'

'Aunty, I… I thought he was going to IIT. And you know JNU is right next door to IIT. I'll come home after lunch, Aunty. Please tell Ma.'

I said bye before she could ask me more questions.

His mother was hospitable, warm, and talked a lot. It took a huge effort to respond to her, but I did, even though all I could think about was the fact that Arnav had only chatted with me at the party because he was stoned, and the fact that Randhir had hidden his writing from me ever since I'd known him. As I chatted with Arnav's mother, I was thinking, everyone has secrets. And of course, Randhir has the right to his. But why was his *writing* a secret? That too, from *me*? All the while I was smiling and nodding at what Arnav's mother was saying, I was thinking, stupid me, imagining all these years that Randhir and I were kindred spirits! First, Charu had proved me wrong. Now, Arnav had proved me wrong again.

Then out popped another thought. How would I brazen it out if Mrs Mittal came home and accused me of stealing the puppy?

By the time Arnav drove me back home, yet another worry was jostling with the rest. Now Arnav was complicit in my crime; if I was discovered, he would get into trouble too.

'Ice cream?' Arnav said as we passed India Gate.

It was as though the gates of heaven had briefly opened to give me some respite from my non-stop thoughts.

So we sat at the India Gate lawns and ate ice cream, and my cassata was like a shot in the arm.

Afloat on my ice cream sea of joy, my thoughts retreated. I asked Arnav not to tell anyone, including Randhir, about the puppy. He nodded indifferently. Boys were wonderful about these things. They just weren't interested. If I'd told any girl such a thing, she'd never have let it go.

I finished the ice cream, and when I looked up, Arnav was looking at me, his eyes smiling, and my cheeks began to burn. He laughed and said he'd never seen anyone eating ice cream with such relish. Then he told me another one of his stories – or rather, he acted it out – about the time he entered the famously very strict LSR hostel. What do you expect? I fell headlong into this story too.

I was still afloat on this story as we drove back home. It was likely that he would forget this time with me too, because storytelling was what he did with everyone, not just me. He was a natural. He could never know that, each time, he stole a bit of my heart.

When we arrived, Madhu Aunty, Ma, and Anu Aunty were sitting in the veranda of Madhu Aunty's house. And down the street to my right were my Consequences, rolling inexorably towards us like tanks at the Republic Day parade, with a policeman leading the march, swinging his baton, and Mrs Mittal and her son following behind him. My thoughts, which had subsided so beautifully after the ice cream, flew into my head like a swarm of locusts.

The drama that followed was witnessed by half the colony, and people talked about it for months. That it ended well was, of course, thanks to Sampat Bhaiyya. The constable had been determined his sons get admitted into a top English medium school and had come to Ma and me a year ago to ask if we would tutor them. Ma and I had decided to subsidize his fees, but when we told Madhu Aunty this, she said, 'Why you should subsidize? Arre, Padma, under the table he is earning ten times as much as you!' Later, Sampat Bhaiyya had confirmed this in as many words.

Over breakfast, as I was thinking dreamily about Arnav's laughter-filled eyes when he'd said he'd be my partner in crime any time, I saw Ma staring at me.

'You *did* steal the puppy,' she whispered.

The toast became sawdust in my mouth.

'Tell me the *entire* truth, from beginning to end,' she commanded.

And so I did.

'Deva,' Ma moaned after I told her what I'd done. 'Finish that toast. Don't waste food. Why didn't you tell me the truth earlier?'

'I didn't want to implicate you, Ma.'

'*Implicate*? I'm your *mother*. What rubbish are you talking?'

Ma took a sip of her coffee and then gasped. '*You* were the one who slashed Mrs Mittal's scooter tyres four-and-a-half years ago!'

I choked over my coffee.

'What kind of a mother am I? I don't even know my own child!' She buried her face in her hands. '*What* would you have done if Arnav hadn't been there? Or if we hadn't known Sampat Bhaiyya?'

There was no answer to that.

'*Never* again, do you hear me? And finish the toast. Don't waste food.'

The next time Arnav came home, Randhir and my friends ordered him to tell them the story. He did. He surpassed himself as Tragedy Queen Mallika; enraged Madhu Aunty; hysterical Mrs Mittal; bawling Chotu; and the abject, ecstatic policeman throwing himself at the feet of Ma and me. He even took on the role of the audience. It was a stellar performance, and everyone howled with laughter.

Later, in the privacy of my room, I performed my version of the entire story for my three friends. They were hysterical with laughter at my imitation of Arnav.

Afterwards it was the happiest time I could remember.

Then Shantamama's letter came, telling us that she had a tumour in her uterus and had to have a hysterectomy. She'd said the doctor believed it was most likely benign, but could Ma come? The date for the operation was fixed for the week after Mahima's wedding.

'Don't worry, a hysterectomy is not a dangerous operation,' Ma assured me. I knew that this was true – at least five women we knew in our colony had had one and recovered – but I began to worry.

Mahima's sangeet was held two days before the wedding. It was an ebullient affair, and the house was full of laughter. Mahima looked lovely in her pink ghaghra, and all the women danced, Renu being the most enthusiastic. Prabha and Gauri and I helped with the serving of the food and drinks. Then I went and sat on the veranda for a breather. Renu joined me a minute later and sighed, 'I wish you were marrying my brother; then I would have you as my sister.'

I smiled at her. She always said things like this to me.

But after a couple of seconds, she seemed to change her mind. 'No, I'm glad you're not. You deserve to be happy.'

'What d'you mean, Renu?'

She leaned towards me. 'Do you like my perfume? My husband goes mad when I put it on!'

'It's very nice. But, Renu, why did you say you're glad I'm not marrying your brother because I deserve to be happy?'

Renu laughed. It was her familiar, loud, slightly coarse laughter. 'Mahima shouldn't get married to my brother.'

My heart plunged. 'Why?'

'Don't know why I'm telling you. I think it's that whiskey I had before I came.'

I could hear the sounds of singing drifting happily out of the living room. 'Renu –'

'My husband, he says, "I like a modern wife," so I drink with him when we go for parties and all. But I just don't like drinking. He drinks a lot, and then he beats me. A real thrashing he gave me today. See?'

Even in the darkness, I could see the marks on Renu's upper arm as she pulled up her kurta sleeve. I gasped.

'He cries afterwards, he says he can't live without me. Every time, he begs forgiveness; he literally touches my feet. Can you imagine, a husband touching his wife's feet? That much love he feels for me. My brother, he is not capable of that kind of love.'

That kind of love?

'The only reason my husband beats me is because he is possessive about me – he doesn't want me to talk to anyone, smile at anyone. That much he loves me.'

'Renu, what were you saying about your brother?'

'I was saying that he isn't capable of such love. My brother, he is a pervert, Mallika.'

Laughter spilled out from inside the house, and someone began playing the tabla.

'A – what?'

'A pervert. About sex. He is abnormal about sex. He is sick.'

I looked at her without comprehension.

My friends and I had never discussed perversion. None of the women who poured out their stories to me had spoken of it. My books had nothing to say about it.

'Everyone in my family knows, and they all pretend they don't know,' Renu added.

'What's a pervert?' I asked.

She laughed. 'A pervert is a pervert, what else!'

'Renu, Mahima's like my sister.'

'I know, I know. I'm so sick of life, Mallika, I'm so sick of life.'

'Renu, *tell* me.'

Renu burst into tears. 'Mallika, don't stop being my friend.'

'Renu, if you can't tell me, then tell Madhu Aunty.'

She wiped her tears with the palm of her hand. 'Are you mad?'

'The marriage has to be *stopped*.'

'It can't be stopped.'

'It can. It *can*.'

'What are you going to do? Tell people "Renu said her brother is a pervert?" When the wedding is in two days? What do you think people will say? They'll say, "Oh, Renu, she's a big, fat liar, how can you believe her?" You think I don't know what they say about me? You believed what I said? Huh? How can you believe me? Huh? Even I can't believe me!'

'I *do* believe you, Renu!'

'Then you shouldn't believe me. It's stupid of you to believe me.'

'It has to be *stopped*.'

'What do you mean, "it has to be stopped, it has to be stopped." Don't go on like a broken record. It can't be stopped, and don't bring me into it, OK? I'll deny it if you do.'

Renu flounced inside, leaving me in the veranda.

'Mallika, Beta,' called Madhu Aunty. 'Come, we need help with serving the sweet dish.'

I went to the kitchen. Prabha and Gauri were alone, filling bowls with khir.

'Prabha, Gauri,' I said breathlessly. 'Renu said Shekhar's a pervert.'

They looked at me, astounded.

'Mallika,' said Prabha. 'How can you believe Renu's rubbish?'

'Mallika, she'll say *anything* for attention,' said Gauri. '*Don't* believe her.'

'Mallika,' Prabha continued. 'Please don't let Renu's lies become another Charu story.'

They were right.

But what *was* a sexual pervert? I wondered this that night as I tossed and turned in bed. I knew the adjective, perverse, but the noun, *pervert*? Once, Gauri had informed us that there were men who burnt their wives with cigarettes. 'Why?' I had asked, and Gauri said, 'They like to do such things.' Was that what Renu had meant? Or did she mean Shekhar would be a wife beater? But how would she know either of these things?

And that was the other thing I didn't understand, the thing that was submerged beneath my worry for Mahima. Renu's husband beat her. And she said it was proof of his love that he begged for forgiveness every time after he did it. She thought this was *love*?

The next morning, I awoke with the certainty that Renu had taken back her words about Shekhar not because they were untrue, but because she had regretted saying them.

I had to tell Randhir. With one day left before the wedding, only he could prevail upon his parents to stop it.

I went next door several times, but Randhir was nowhere around.

In the evening, he dropped in at my house, looking exhausted, and said, 'Feel like going for ice cream at India Gate?'

And so we did. It was a beautiful winter evening, and I could tell he was so happy to be with me.

Then I told him.

And he exploded.

There was no Randhir; there was only his anger. So great was his rage that it was like a red shroud around me. I was suffocating in it. In my whole life, I had never encountered such fury. Ma, Shantamama, my grandmother, and my Ayah-ji nagged and scolded. My three friends and I got irritated with one another and frequently argued. There was nothing frightening about any of this. And Karan had never raised his voice at me. His anger was only for my mother; a frigid, tightly controlled anger. But Randhir's anger choked me. Even as I tried to breathe, I knew that no one had ever looked at me the way Randhir was looking at me: his face twisted, his hands clenched, his body rigid. I could not recall his words any more than you can remember every stone flung at you, but I felt every one of them, physically, on my body. And then he was done. He was no longer twisted and rigid. He was leaning against the jamun tree, looking upwards, as if in prayer, as if I didn't exist.

I stood shivering where I was, with green grass and tall, strong trees all around me, not understanding why, not knowing what I had said wrong, not comprehending his terrible rage.

I still cannot remember his words. But I will never forget that anger and disgust. Yes, disgust. At me. Until that moment, I had not known that it was possible for someone who held your heart, someone whose very heart was in yours, to speak to you like this.

Randhir: Just a normal guy

1975–1976

When he topped the university in his BA Honours second year, Randhir summoned up the courage to tell his parents he wanted to do his Masters, and his father had said, 'That is alright, Beta, do your MA. You are brilliant student.'

He was awash with disbelief and relief.

'I'll work in the factory after that,' he had said, overwhelmed with gratitude that he didn't have to fight this one out.

His father smiled, full of love. 'I know you will, Beta.'

His brother, Akhil, was coming home soon to join their father's business, so it wouldn't all be on him. He would still find time to write. His father would never understand what writing meant to him, but then his father didn't understand what reading meant to him either. Yet he was generous to a fault about spending money on Randhir's books and magazines. Randhir had persuaded his father to subscribe to *Time*, *Life*, *The Illustrated Weekly of India*, and *Imprint*. Randhir was the only member of the family who asked for books and magazines, something his father regarded with fascination. After Randhir read the magazines, they would make their regular rounds – first to Arnav, then to Mallika and her mother, then to Prabha and Gauri. Gauri, the last in line, had strict orders to return them to Randhir as soon as she was done.

Then the bombshell dropped. Akhil, who had been studying in Bombay, got himself a job there and eloped with a Muslim girl, Ameena. He broke the news to his parents in a brief letter, asking them if he could bring his wife home for their blessings.

As Mallika would say, as if!

Hindi films were no exaggeration. The scene at home was exactly like one. His father said Akhil was no longer his son, he could never step into the house, he was lost to them forever. This was accompanied by his mother's histrionics. He and Mahima listened, aghast. Finally, his father said to his weeping mother, 'Remember this – if you go to see them in Bombay behind my back, there is no need for you to return to this house.' He turned to Mahima and Randhir. 'The same goes for you both.'

The next day, he came to Randhir's room and said, 'Beta, in you I have faith. You do not let me down. I hope you will carry on the work that I have put my life into.'

'Yes, Daddy, of course I will,' Randhir replied, and felt the bars of the prison clamp down.

That afternoon, he wrote to Akhil, congratulating him, saying he wanted to meet his wife and that he hoped to do so one day. He told him what had happened at home, making it clear he wasn't of his father's mindset. He posted the letter immediately.

After that, he went to the bathroom cupboard to look at the bottle of pills. He did this periodically. The bottle was still nestled safely behind his Old Spice aftershave.

A boy from a 'first-class' family was coming to see Mahima. Mummy said, 'No need to mention Akhil's marriage to them. We will just say he is working in Bombay.'

'Mummy, how can you hide such a thing?'

'Oho, keep quiet.'

As usual, he had no say.

Mahima met Shekhar a couple of times, liked him, and said yes.

Why Mahima wanted to get married as soon as she finished her BA, he couldn't understand. He'd asked her, and she'd said, in that tart way of hers, 'I want marriage and children. How's an MA going to help with that?'

His parents extolled the virtues of her fiancé, Shekhar – his family and his MBA and his fairness and his good looks and, of course, his wealth. As far as he, Randhir, was concerned, Shekhar was boring as hell, and the sister, Renu, was vulgarity personified.

Every time Arnav or Vineet saw Renu enter the house, they'd dive for cover. She dressed horribly, she called Arnav 'Handsome-One' and Vineet 'Handsome-Two,' cracked the most awful jokes with them, slapped their arms, chucked their chins, and laughed so coarsely that it made him cringe.

The weirdest thing was that Renu had taken to Mallika. She was constantly dropping in at Mallika's place, lending her books and chatting with her. What on earth did they see in each other? What did *Mallika* see in Renu? Sometimes he didn't understand how Mallika's mind worked. Once, Mallika had told him that her Shantamama and grandmother had cursed Karan's mother and sisters and, as a result of that curse, none of Karan's sisters could have children. How could Mallika believe such a thing? But then she also believed that the so-called Phuknewalla actually rid her of migraines. He wanted to say, Mallika, have you ever heard of the placebo effect? But he didn't. If there was one person in the world he didn't ever want to hurt, it was Mallika. He had even kept quiet about that damn Charu affair.

OK, fine, he had liked Charu. But what was wrong with that? She was fun, she was vibrant, she made him laugh. She was the prettiest thing ever. Sure, they spent a lot of time together, but so *what*? Mummy loved his friends coming home and staying on for lunch or dinner. And as long as his bedroom door was open, Mummy was fine with girls hanging out in his room and listening to music. So, fine, he spent more time with Charu than with the others, and OK, they'd kissed and stuff when Mummy was out, but so *what*? It wasn't as though he were sleeping with Charu; most girls drew the line at that anyway. Mummy sang her praises all the time. But as for Mallika – that she had *believed* he'd made Charu pregnant was the limit. She'd thought he was going to *marry* Charu! Didn't she know by now how Mummy fibbed? And then Mallika had the gall to get on her moral high horse, asking him why he was being so harsh about Charu as though this bloody mess was *his* fault! And they'd had to tell Mummy and deal with her dramatics in front of her friends. What a fucking nightmare.

When Mummy had come back home from Charu's house that night, she insisted on giving him a blow-by-blow account of what had happened. Both fascinated and repelled, he had listened.

Mrs Kapoor's reaction to his mother and her friends' recital of the story had been a trill of laughter. She had said, 'Uffho, my Charu, too much Imagination she has, that is the problem!'

They were all so confused by this reaction that they just didn't know what to say, his mother told him.

'Always I tell Charu, "Beta, Imagination is not for real life; it is for books only,"' Mrs Kapoor continued. 'But Charu, she likes to have fun by pretending that her Imagination-Stories are real!'

'Mrs Kapoor,' his mother had said. 'My son, he swore on my name that *nothing* like that happened.'

'I know, I know,' Mrs Kapoor agreed. 'So many times I have told Charu, "Beta, some things girls do not joke about." What is there? I will tell her again. And it is my request… Please do not mention to anyone. People, they are not understanding Imagination except in books and films.'

Padma Aunty said, 'The doctor said Charu needs help from a psychiatrist.'

At which Mrs Kapoor put her hands to her cheeks and exclaimed, 'Arre baba, never – never! If I take her to one of *those*, then who will marry her?'

Which was true, his mother said to Randhir, who would?

Mrs Kapoor then said, 'We will find good boy, we will get her married. Then Imagination and all will settle down. What you will have – tea or coffee or neembupani? Please have, no formality.'

Imagine offering them hospitality after all that! His mother snorted.

He couldn't get over it. How had this gone so wrong? He was just being a normal guy. He was just doing what other guys were doing. And, unlike them, he wasn't shady about it. He hadn't hidden it from his parents; he'd brought Charu home, Mummy had said she loved Charu. And *this* was the result? He could barely hold his despair.

He knew he shouldn't have spoken to Mummy like that in front of everyone. Most of the time he kept his mouth so closely shut that every angry word was swallowed like spit, and every unwanted thought was stamped and crushed into the rot of oblivion. But he hadn't realized how his feelings left its trace on his face till he entered his room and caught his expression in that wretched birthday mirror. For a couple of seconds he almost didn't recognize himself.

He had told Arnav the whole bloody story, and Arnav listened incredulously. He'd never discussed Mallika with Arnav, but this time he couldn't help it. 'Mallika knows me. She should have known better.'

But instead of agreeing with him, Arnav said, 'How?'

'You think I'm going to get a girl pregnant and ditch her?'

'That's not what Mallika said.'

'Well, yeah, but… this thing with Charu, it was… I told you it was *nothing.*'

'Oh, come on. Mallika wasn't the only one. We *all* thought you were besotted with Charu. I never understood. I mean, I always thought Mallika was the one for you.'

He stared at Arnav.

'I mean… isn't she?' Arnav asked.

Randhir muttered something.

'Then why the fuck were you with Charu?' Arnav exclaimed.

He was completely rattled.

The one for him? What did that mean? It meant marriage, that was what it meant.

Oh, god, he never wanted to marry. Not Mallika, not anybody. Did Mallika expect it of him? *Please, please let her not expect it of me.*

During the summer, winter, and Dussera holidays, when Arnav moved back home to his parents from the IIT hostel, he started landing up at Randhir's house late at night.

Randhir would hear the motorcycle in the distance, and then the sound would disappear as Arnav switched off his bike, cruised down the street, and parked next to his house. He'd get up from his desk or emerge from a deep sleep to the sound of Arnav's familiar knocking at his window. Then Arnav would go to the terrace for a smoke and crash on the divan.

Randhir knew that Arnav's father was the source of all this. They had spent plenty of time in each other's homes, and he had observed all the things that Arnav never spoke of. That his father was charming and vicious, loving and ill-tempered, full of understanding and completely empty of it, all in the same day, sometimes in the same hour. It was like walking on quicksand.

Arnav's entire home life was centred around his dog, Mishti, whom he had had since he was twelve. Mishti was his life. Mishti slept on his bed; Mishti and he went for their walks thrice a day whenever he was home for the holidays; he took Mishti to the vet, took care of her when she was sick, bathed her, and checked her body for ticks. He had a sketchbook full of drawings of Mishti. Just once, after Mishti's death, Arnav broke his silence about his father. That night, after Arnav had retched and vomited in Randhir's bathroom, they went up to the terrace together, and Arnav, his eyes bloodshot, told him everything in three sentences: 'My father kicked Mishti, and she ran away from home and got run over. Apparently it's not the first time. So much for all those fucking prayers.'

That was it. Arnav never spoke about Mishti or his father again. If Randhir hadn't known him, he'd never have guessed how broken-hearted he was – he kept himself busy. One time he ran all the way from his house to Randhir's. It took him three hours; he arrived at four a.m. and crashed for the next fourteen hours. Soon after this, Arnav went back to the IIT hostel, to his voluntary work with the Indian Conservation Fund, and to acting. He auditioned and got the main role in a comedy. The play was a huge success. Randhir took Mallika for it, and they were in fits. As the months passed, Arnav calmed down, and as Randhir wrote at his desk, Arnav would sketch on his drawing pad. He had been excellent at drawing, even in school, winning prizes in all the *Shankar's Weekly* drawing competitions every year.

Randhir envied Arnav's ability not to agonize about every damn thing. Arnav just ran and sketched and performed and – lucky guy – even if his thoughts were in hot pursuit, they could never catch up with him. Whereas Randhir's thoughts were always ahead of him, and he was roped to them by the neck as they drove furiously forward, dragging him, arms and legs shackled, behind them.

Mahima's wedding was upon them. He and Arnav were running around doing a hundred things; relatives were crawling out of every which crack. He hadn't a minute to himself. It was driving him nuts.

A day before the wedding, he managed to get away. He went to Mallika's house and asked if she wanted to go to India Gate for an ice cream break. She nodded, looking grave. He knew why: she was worried about her Shantamama's impending operation. Mallika told her mother she was going out with him and hopped onto his motorcycle, saree-clad but wearing a coat.

'I've been wanting to talk to you,' she said as he parked the bike beside the India Gate lawns.

He breathed in the winter air, resting his eyes on the beautiful jamun trees and the endless expanse of green grass. 'Sorry, Mallika, I've just been busy with all the wedding stuff. I tell you – the relatives are driving me *nuts*. They're *everywhere*. They don't bloody stop yakking.'

They began walking down the lawns. At last, he was beginning to feel calm.

'Oh, I forgot!' He stopped. 'Let's go get some ice cream. What'll you have – your favourite cassata?'

'Later, Randhir.' She was looking deadly serious.

He looked at her in surprise.

'What?' He tried to tease her out of her mood. 'Has that Mrs Mittal descended on you with another policeman?' He still hadn't got over the story of Mallika stealing the puppy. That an oblivious Arnav had been her unwitting rescuer took the cake!

'I have to tell you something. Randhir, please believe me.'

She was pale with apprehension.

'Mallika? What's the matter?'

'Shekhar's a pervert. Mahima's marriage must be stopped.'

The blood rushed to his head. 'What the *hell* do you mean, "pervert?"'

They had stopped walking. She was pale. Her throat was moving.

He could feel his entire body trembling.

'A sexual pervert,' she whispered.

He stared at her. She was trembling too.

'What's *wrong* with you? What the bloody hell is *wrong* with you? Do you have no bloody sense in your head?'

She was hunched up, both arms around her body, as though he were hitting her. She tried to speak but no words came out.

'Someone's been talking shit to you, and you've been taken in as usual, haven't you? You listen to every damn Tom, Dick, and Harry and *believe* them. What's *wrong* with you?'

Tears were streaming down her face. 'The wedding has to be cancelled. Tell Madhu Aunty and Uncle that –' She began to sob, unable to speak.

'Yeah, sure. I'll tell them you've been listening to gossip about Shekhar, and therefore we should cancel the wedding. Which is tomorrow. Sure.'

'Listen to me, Randhir. *Please*. You haven't listened to the whole thing. I –'

'Pray, tell me: what is a sexual pervert?'

'I don't know,' she whispered. 'But –'

'That's fantastic. Perfect reason to cancel the wedding.'

'You're not listening to why I'm telling you this, just –'

'I don't want to listen to gossip.'

'It's Mahima's whole life, Randhir, please just –'

'I'm her *brother*. You think I don't care?'

'I know you care, that's why I'm telling you. Randhir, if you come with me, I'll tell Aunty and Uncle. *Listen* to me. I'll tell them –'

'You're not going to tell them *anything*.'

A middle-aged couple had stopped in the middle of their walk to stare at them.

Suddenly, he realized he'd been shouting.

He turned away from her, walked almost blindly towards the nearest jamun tree, and leaned against it. He felt he was going to vomit. He felt the trunk against his back, strong and so comforting that he could have wept. He rested his head against the trunk and looked up at the canopy of leaves, at the glorious branches. The sun was setting, and the birds had set up a virtual chorus. It felt as though the tree was embracing him. He remembered Arnav talking passionately about the Chipko movement in Uttarakhand, where villagers, mostly women, had put their arms around trees and clung to them to prevent them from being logged, and about how this movement had spread to other parts of the country. He felt, in this moment, that he was capable of nothing – not even of saving a tree like those impassioned villagers – for he was the one who needed saving. If he could, he would have hugged this tree and begged it to give him succour. If anything could save him, it was this all-embracing, all-accepting tree; it was all there was for him.

Arnav: Just a kiss

1975–1976

As he drove back home after the veranda-drama featuring Mrs Mittal and her son, it was finally obvious to Arnav that Mallika had acted on her first impulse after seeing that bloody Chotu kicking the puppy. Later, she'd made up that ridiculous story about taking the puppy to Gauri. Why on earth hadn't she simply told him what she'd done instead of giving him all those tortured, long-winded explanations? While he and Madhu Aunty had thrown themselves into their roles with zest on the veranda, Mallika had been trying to hide her fear of the consequences. Just as she tried to hide her shyness. He attempted to push it out of his mind, this strange feeling that all these years he'd wounded her. How could he have? He'd been unfailingly polite to her.

Sure. And in his mind, he'd dismissed her as not worth knowing. He found himself cringing.

He also knew what would happen when he reached home. Ma would ask him about Mallika and ask, why didn't he find someone like her? Meaning instead of someone like Radha, who had been wearing his t-shirt (and nothing else) and eating a guava on his bed in his hostel when Ma had landed up there. He'd been in bed too, sated and sleepy, when he heard the knock on his door. He got out of bed, shirtless, and opened it, and there was Ma, holding a steel utensil and smiling. Then she looked beyond him, and her smile faded.

'Hullo, Aunty,' Radha had said chirpily, her mouth full of the guava.

His mother collected herself and said icily, 'Good afternoon, Radha.'

Ma entered and gave him the biryani that she had cooked without another glance at Radha.

Radha got out of bed and pulled his t-shirt down so that it now reached mid-thigh. She exclaimed, 'Biryani! Oh, it smells so good, Aunty!'

Ma gave her a look and left the room without saying another word. He ran after her.

'Ma, don't rush off like that.'

'And don't say she's just a friend, shameless creature.'

'Ma, don't talk like that about her.'

'You're also shameless.'

'For heaven's sake, Ma, I'm not a kid,' he hissed as they walked down the hostel corridor to her car parked outside.

Just before she drove off, she burst out, 'And she says "hullo, Aunty" in your t-shirt and those bare thighs, "hullo, Aunty" – oh, my, that girl has gall.'

He returned to his room and shut the door. 'Shit.'

Radha laughed. 'No chance of my ever winning her approval.'

'Why should you care about her approval?' He helped himself to a slice of guava.

Her laughter faded. 'You're so bloody oblivious.'

He looked at her, shocked. She'd never spoken to him like this.

'We've been going around for almost a *year*.'

'So?' He was bewildered.

'*So? So?* You've got no brains, or what?' Her voice was getting higher.

What was she talking about?

'Don't you want to *be* with me?'

'I *am* with you.'

'I mean, after you finish IIT?'

He couldn't even think about things one week down the road, and she was asking him about what was *two years* down the road?

'I'm asking about after you get a job,' she said.

Horror began filling him.

'Don't you see a future together for us?'

Shit, shit, shit.

'Don't you want us to get married one day?'

He was aghast.

She burst into tears and scrambled out of bed. 'You're just having fun with me.'

'Aren't you having fun with me too?' he said, trying to lighten the mood.

'That's not what I meant. Don't be *stupid*! You're not serious about me even after a *year*.' Tears were streaming down her eyes. 'Don't you love me?'

Love? It was the last thing on his mind. He *liked* her. He thoroughly enjoyed being with her. He wasn't interested in anyone else. He –

'Well, obviously not,' she said. 'I'm done with you.'

She put on her clothes. Before she left, she asked, 'If you don't love me, even after a year, then why were you with me?'

He had no idea what to say to that. So stunned was he that he didn't even ask her not to leave.

Later, he had told Randhir. 'It just came out of the blue. I'm *twenty-one*. I'm not thinking of marriage!'

'Listen, you idiot, you were with her for a *year*,' Randhir said in exasperation.

'So?'

'If it came out of the blue, it means she's been brooding about it for ages. Didn't you ever notice?'

He shook his head.

'You're so bloody oblivious,' Randhir sighed.

'Look who's talking! What about *you*, ditching Mallika for Charu? That's not oblivion?'

Randhir's face became dark, and Arnav shut up.

He had never told Ma it was over with Radha. But of course, she guessed. You could hear it in the way she began humming Rabindra Sangeet again.

When he reached home, he told his mother not to mention the puppy to Madhu Aunty. 'Mallika stole it from a neighbour who was kicking it and ran with it.'

'Oh, my goodness! Ran to *you*?'

'No,' he said firmly. 'Not to me. She just ran. I happened to be nearby.'

'Oh,' his mother sighed.

He looked at her uneasily.

'Oh, Arnab, you should court her and marry her,' she said, her hands clasped.

Court her? *Court* her! He had to end this right now. But he was laughing so hard that he couldn't speak. 'She's going to marry Randhir,' he said finally and went to his room.

She followed him inside. 'Randhir told you?'

'Well…'

'Mallika told you?'

'Ma! Some things you just *know*!'

Her face lit up. 'Oh, that means you know nothing at all.' She patted his cheek and left his room with a light step.

Mahima's wedding took place at the maidan just a couple of minutes from the house, where a large shamyana had been put up. He, Vineet, and Randhir were busy helping Aunty and Uncle with various last-minute things, and the girls were serving the guests snacks. Randhir was in one of his black moods, so Arnav gave him a wide berth. The girls looked lovely – Prabha laughing, Gauri full of her usual grace and warmth, but Mallika graver than usual. All three graceful, fresh, glowing in their beautiful silk sarees. Mahima looked like a typical bride: too much jewellery, too much make-up, too much everything. Packaged and ready to be presented to another family in all her finery, like his sister Niharika.

They'd had a massive wedding for his sister. No arranged marriage: Niharika had gone and fallen madly in love with her classmate. She'd known him for five years when they did their MBA in Ahmedabad; he was, by all accounts, brilliant. He went on to do his PhD in America, after which they got married. Every time she came home from New York, she declared – more and more loudly – how happy she was. He was sick of hearing it.

Now, at Mahima's wedding, after dinner and before the pheras, he went outside the shamyana to join Randhir for a smoke. Randhir's mood had not lifted. A few minutes later, Mallika came out, looking apprehensive. Randhir saw her and snapped, 'For god's sake, not *now*!' Mallika flinched then went back inside. Arnav looked at Randhir in shock. Randhir, his face dark with anger, ignored his look.

Five minutes later, Mallika came out of the shamyana again and flung a bunch of keys at Randhir. 'If you think I came to *talk* to you, you're mistaken,' she said. 'I came because Madhu Aunty asked me to look for you. She wants two thousand rupees from her Godrej – here are her keys.' She stormed off past them towards her house, the gajra from her bun hanging down her neck.

'What the hell's wrong?' Arnav asked Randhir, flabbergasted.

Randhir picked up the keys from his feet and went towards his home.

Ten minutes later, Randhir was back. 'Listen, Mallika's sitting outside her house; she wouldn't come back with me. I've got to give the money to Mummy. Just walk Mallika back.'

'OK.' So he went to Mallika's house.

She was sitting on her steps in the darkness. Her gajra was still dangling loosely down her neck. He sat next to her.

Before he could speak, she said, 'I can walk back on my own.'

'It's late.' He was trying hard to stop himself from lifting her gajra from her neck and winding it around her bun.

They sat in silence.

After some time, he said, 'Why is Randhir in such a foul mood?'

'He's angry with me.'

'Why?'

'I don't know. Ask him. Maybe he'll tell *you*.'

Tell *him*! About *Mallika*! As though!

The sound of the shehnai drifted down towards them from the shamyana. He looked at his watch. 'Should we go? The pheras will start soon.'

She looked at her own and got up immediately.

'Your gajra – it's falling off.'

She lifted the string of jasmines from her neck, wrapped it around and under her bun, but it fell out again from the side.

'Hold on.' He stood behind her and tucked it under her hair.

'Thank you,' she said, turning. She looked up at him and smiled. He couldn't help it; he touched her cheek with his fingers. She put her hand over his, and her eyes said *yes*. He bent, and, breathing in the smell of jasmines, he kissed her mouth.

Her lips yielded but stayed closed. When he opened them with his own, he heard the sound in her throat, or was it his? How hungry he was for this kiss he only knew as he kissed her. Later, he couldn't remember how long it had lasted. But he remembered how she looked at him after they stopped, those large eyes, glistening with so much emotion that it was as though they were full of tears. He wanted to look away but couldn't, he wanted to run but didn't. He wanted to say, I'm sorry. He wanted to do more than he had already done. He wanted it undone.

He said, softly, 'What *is* it with you and Randhir?'

She blinked as though she were coming into the glare.

His palm was still cupping her cheek. He dropped it. He thought, *I've gone mad*.

Her eyes were full – he saw – with the very same thought.

They turned, almost simultaneously, and walked back to the wedding venue. It was a silent three-minute walk.

She went into shamyana. He stayed outside and lit another cigarette.

For god's sake. It was just a kiss.

Just a kiss? If Randhir knew, he'd wring Arnav's neck. How the hell had it happened?

Mallika: What is forgotten

January 1976

As I open my eyes, I can still feel the impact of Randhir's words on my body. My body is sore. I close my eyes. Brown shoes beating against glass, and I, in utter darkness, suffocating, knowing death awaits me, the worst kind of death. I am screaming, Ma, I am screaming, Shantamama.

I cannot stop screaming.

'Beta, it was bad dream. Just bad dream, Beta, perfectly safe you are.'

Madhu Aunty's arms were around me; my face was buried in her ample bosom.

At last, I let go of Madhu Aunty. I was in Mahima's room, in Mahima's bed. I looked up at Randhir and Arnav, who were standing next to my bed with identical looks of shock.

Madhu Aunty was smelling so strongly and so reassuringly of aloo parathas that my rapid heartbeat began to subside.

Why was I sleeping in a churidar kurta? Where was Mahima?

'Where is Mahima, Aunty?'

Madhu Aunty burst into tears. 'She's gone. My bacchi, my bitiya, she has gone.'

Madhu Aunty was still talking, but for a few seconds I couldn't hear her. All I could hear was that high-pitched sound in my ears, and everything became dark around me. I grabbed Madhu Aunty's hand and said, 'You're lying.'

Madhu Aunty looked at me as though I had gone mad. '*What*!'

Randhir and Arnav were also looking at me as though I'd gone mad.

'Where's Mahima?' I asked again.

Randhir said, 'Gone to Chandigarh, Mallika. Where else?'

'Why has she gone to Chandigarh?' I asked.

They stared at me.

Madhu Aunty said, 'You've forgotten, Beta? That is where her in-laws are, no.'

Mahima had gone to her *in-laws*? When her wedding was just around the corner?

'Why?' I asked.

No one answered. They were looking at me as if something was wrong with *me*.

It was a dream. I closed my eyes. A hospital bed. Doctors asking me questions, me answering them. Madhu Aunty, Randhir, and Arnav in the hospital. In a car with Randhir and Arnav.

When I opened my eyes, I saw that Ayah-ji was lying down on a mattress next to me. She got up and felt my forehead. 'You are alright?'

'I'm fine, Ayah-ji. Why am I here?'

'Because your Ma has gone to your Shantamama for her operation, and you are not well. Go, brush your teeth, wash your face. I will get you tea and nashta.'

Ma had gone to Shantamama? Wasn't she supposed to go after the wedding?

My head was hurting. I looked at my watch. It was noon.

'Ayah-ji, why are you here?'

'To look after you, what else?' Ayah-ji went out of the room.

I went to the bathroom. I was feeling unsteady. My toothbrush and tongue cleaner were in the glass next to the sink.

But there was nothing of Mahima's in the bathroom. No nightie, toothbrush, nothing.

I didn't remember coming here to spend the night.

When I went back to the room, I saw that the framed photos of her parents and brothers and of the four of us as children – Mahima's favourite photos – were all gone.

I was beginning to feel like Alice in Wonderland. I had fallen through a rabbit hole.

I went to Randhir's room. Simon and Garfunkel were on, but for once the music was soft. The curtain was drawn. I knocked on the door and peered in. Only Arnav was there, sitting cross-legged on the divan, smoking and looking through some records. He looked up, his face so soft, so vulnerable, that he seemed almost like someone else.

'Hi,' he said, and I heard the uncertainty in his voice. As though he were not sure how to talk to me. Looking at me as though... as though... I didn't know what.

'Feeling OK?' he said. Very carefully.

I nodded. Then I shook my head.

'Come and sit.'

I entered and sat on Randhir's chair next to his desk.

He got up and drew the curtain to the side. Madhu Aunty's rule when girls were in the room.

'Why has Mahima gone to Chandigarh?' I asked as soon as he sat back on the divan.

Again, he looked at me as though something was wrong with me.

'Arnav,' I begged. 'Please answer my question.'

'Mahima's gone to Chandigarh to her in-laws.'

'That's what Madhu Aunty said. But why?'

As though he were teaching me my ABCs, he said, 'Because she's married.'

'*Married?*'

He stared at me.

'*When?*'

He shook his head like a dog. 'Uh… Three days ago.'

'Where was I when she got married?'

There was another of those peculiar silences. Then he said, 'You were there.'

I shook my head. 'No.'

He looked at me incredulously.

Everything was a dream. I closed my eyes.

After a minute, I opened them. Randhir stood before me, frowning.

Arnav said, 'She doesn't remember Mahima's wedding.'

'Shit. Mallika, do you remember your accident?'

Accident?

The boys saw my expression and exchanged glances. They looked shaken.

'You had an accident,' Randhir said. 'We'll tell you. Go lie down, and we'll come there in a minute.'

It took longer than a minute. Ayah-ji came with breakfast and tea. I felt better after eating. Then, fifteen minutes later, Madhu Aunty came in with the boys, who were carrying a couple of chairs. Madhu Aunty and Randhir told me what had happened, while Arnav sat quietly and listened.

Two days after Mahima's wedding, Ayah-ji came running to Madhu Aunty's house, screaming that I'd fallen down our stairs and hurt my head. Madhu Aunty, Randhir, and Arnav rushed home after her. I was lying at the bottom of the stairs, unconscious. There was a big lump on my head. They took me straight to Safdarjung Hospital.

Later, the doctor had assured them that I would be alright. It was a mild concussion, and I needed to rest, that was all. My vital signs were fine, and though I was disoriented, I was responding normally in every other way. They needed to keep an eye on me and return only if they suspected anything was wrong.

Did I remember any of that?

Not falling down the stairs, I told them. But I remembered the hospital, like a dream.

The next day, the hospital had discharged me. Since Ma had gone for Shantamama's operation, Madhu Aunty and Randhir brought me back to their house.

'Shantamama's operation went off well?' I asked Madhu Aunty, suddenly panic struck.

'It must have. Your Ma has not sent telegram so far; it will come soon.'

'But Ma should have sent the telegram by now.'

'Beta, stop worrying, you know sometimes telegrams come late.'

I knew that. Sometimes they came later than letters.

'What's your last memory?' Randhir asked.

I tried to think.

'Did you take me to India Gate?'

Randhir didn't meet my eyes. His face was flushed. He nodded.

Madhu Aunty, who had been uncharacteristically quiet, said, 'We have to go back to hospital.'

'Aunty, no. Please. Ma can take me when she comes back. I... want to rest.'

'Alright, Beta, alright.'

Randhir took charge now. 'OK, let's see what you remember and what you've forgotten and write it down.' He went out of the room and returned with a writing pad. He asked Ayah-ji to help us, and Arnav to take the notes.

I remembered going to India Gate with Randhir, I said. I didn't utter a word about his uncontrollable, inexplicable rage.

The next day was the wedding. No memory of it. Ayah-ji said that I had spent the morning of the wedding with Prabha and Gauri in Mahima's house. In the afternoon, I had come back home with them. That evening, we had dressed up and gone for the wedding. After the wedding, Ma, Gauri, Prabha, and I had come home, and the three of us had slept upstairs.

No memory of the day after the wedding. Ayah-ji said that Ma left for Shantamama's operation in the morning. Soon after, Prabha and Gauri left. Later in the afternoon, I told Ayah-ji I was going to see Gauri at JNU and would spend the night with her, and I went. But I didn't spend the night with her, I came back home later.

I couldn't remember the following day either, the day I tripped and fell down my stairs.

I did remember the next day, but not very clearly – being in the hospital, being examined by doctors, Madhu Aunty and the boys by my bedside, and driving back home.

So three days of my memory were gone.

'Damn peculiar, never heard of such a thing,' Randhir said.

'Suppose more memory goes?' Madhu Aunty said.

'Mummy, her memory isn't leaking out of a hole in her head!' Randhir exclaimed.

'You know everything? Are you doctor?' Madhu Aunty demanded.

Arnav didn't say anything. He gave me a slight smile, and oddly it was comforting.

They got up to leave. 'Now, rest,' Madhu Aunty commanded.

Don't go, I wanted to say to Arnav. *Please, stay with me.*

Ayah-ji had got me a fresh kaftan, a sweater, a shawl, and undies. I went to the bathroom to have a bath. My entire body felt sore. When I took off my clothes, I saw the bruise on my breast. Had I scratched myself? I touched my neck and felt something. I picked up the stool next to the bucket, took it to the washbasin, and stood on the stool so I could see more of myself in the mirror. Now I saw two distinct marks which had been hidden by my polo necked sweater, one on the left side of my neck and another between the right side of my neck and shoulder. I felt them; there was a slight bump, but neither hurt. Whatever it was, it was healing. It was most likely an allergy. It had happened to Prabha once. She had these welts all over her body and face, and she'd scratched so hard that some of them took days to go. That was what had probably happened to me.

But why was I sore between my legs? It had felt even worse when I peed in the morning. Did I have a boil or something there? Was I getting a urinary infection? Ma got them sometimes; she had described it as a burning sensation. I hoped not. I had better drink lots of water.

After my bath, I asked Madhu Aunty for Burnall.

'Why Burnall?' she asked. When I said I had an allergy on my body, she said, 'I'll give you Savlon – Burnall is for burns.' I told her, 'Ma says Burnall works for everything.' She sighed and gave me Burnall.

Of course, the whole room smelled of it. When the boys came to look in on me, they were dramatic as usual. Randhir sniffed as though he were smelling rotten eggs, and Arnav reeled. I explained about my allergy, and like his mother, Randhir replied, 'Burnall is for burns.'

Tiredly, I said, 'Ma and I use it for everything – it works.'

The boys sat by my bed, and we began playing Scrabble, but neither of them were in a chatty mood. Soon, I began to feel tired, and they told me to go to sleep and left.

I awakened from a dreamless sleep with a sense of terror.

Ayah-ji was asleep on a mattress next to my bed. I could hear Steve

Winwood playing in Randhir's room. I heard a burst of laughter. It was
Vineet. He was with them too.

'Where are you going?' Ayah-ji demanded, opening her eyes as I stumbled
out of bed.

'I'm just coming, Ayah-ji.' I wrapped the shawl around myself and went
to Randhir's room.

They were all there, Randhir, Arnav, Vineet, listening to music, smoking,
talking. They looked up as they saw me at the door.

'Hi, Mallika, feeling better?' Vineet said cheerfully.

'Yes, thank you,' I said, and looked at Randhir.

He got up and came out. 'What's the matter?'

'Randhir, please go to Chandigarh and see if Mahima's OK.'

'I'm going next week. Don't worry. Go rest now.'

There was no anger on his face.

I went back to Mahima's room and got into bed.

Had Renu lied? Please, god, let it be a lie.

When Anu Aunty came to see me later, I told her I was worried about not
having heard from Ma about Shantamama's operation. She told me the same
as Madhu Aunty: stop worrying, the telegram would come.

That evening, Randhir brought Gauri home on his bike, all the way from
JNU. He'd told her everything. I was overjoyed. The boys, Gauri, and I
played a game of Scrabble, and this time the boys cheated like crazy and
made us laugh. After dinner, Gauri changed into her kaftan and got into
bed with me. She told me all about the wedding and how beautiful Mahima
looked in her pink lehenga and kundan set. She described what everyone
was wearing, from their sarees and blouses to every piece of jewellery.
Shekhar's family behaved quite well, and the baraat was just fifteen minutes
late. Shekhar looked so handsome in his sherwani. The ceremony after
dinner was very long, and they all cried when Mahima left with Shekhar
and his family. Madhu Aunty cried so much that Randhir and his father had
to hold her up. Mahima cried a lot too, especially as she hugged her three
friends. She kept saying, 'Write to me, please, write to me.'

'You were looking beautiful,' Gauri said. It was a testament to her love that
she always found me so. 'You were wearing your long gold-plated earrings
with the red stones that look just like real rubies. They looked more real than
the real ones that the others were wearing.' I listened, lulled and comforted.
'Randhir was sullen throughout the wedding. I've never seen him look so
unapproachable. As for Arnav, he couldn't take his eyes off you!' I shook my
head, wishing this were true. 'You never notice these things, Mallika.'

As I was falling asleep, I knew there was something that I had to ask
Gauri. It was nagging me in that insistent way, but I couldn't find it.

Ma came home before her telegram.

Shantamama hadn't had her hysterectomy because the doctors had found she had a heart condition. They said it would be better for her to go to the best cardiologist at the All India Institute of Medical Sciences in Dehli so that he could first clear her for the surgery.

Ma was so worried about my concussion that she wrote to Karan, who was posted to Lucknow.

Karan came to Delhi immediately. We went back to the doctor I had seen at AIIMS, and I went through various tests. Once more, the doctor said that, except for the memory, I was fine. It was unusual, what had happened to me, but not unheard of. Would my memory come back? They couldn't say.

After Karan left, Randhir and Arnav came to see me regularly, Arnav all the way from IIT. They cheered me up with their jokes and laughter. I needed cheering up because I felt anxious and emotional all the time. Especially at night, when I would get up at odd hours with a sense of terror.

The day before he left for Chandigarh, Randhir and I sat on the veranda. Why were you so angry with me? I wanted to ask. But I was apprehensive about even mentioning it.

'I'm sorry for losing my temper with you,' he said, answering my thought.

'Randhir, Renu was the one who told me Shekhar was a pervert,' I said.

He nodded. 'I thought as much.'

'Randhir, I know no one believes Renu. But when she told me, I felt it was the truth. *That's* why I told you.'

'Felt *what* was the truth?'

'Whatever it was that she was talking about. I don't know anything about... these things.'

'How could you believe a liar like her?'

'Because I felt that this time she wasn't lying, Randhir.'

'Cancelling a wedding because you *feel* something is wrong is very different from cancelling it because you *know* something is wrong. That too, the night before the wedding.'

He was right.

'Try not to believe everything people tell you. It's really disturbing how you do that.'

I summoned up my courage. 'Is that why you were so angry with me?'

'I shouldn't have lost my temper. I'm sorry. You did the right thing by telling me.'

But that didn't answer my question.

'I told Mummy and Daddy. They didn't believe it,' he said.

'You *told* them? But...?'

'I told them I'd heard rumours that Shekhar was... not a good man. That maybe we should cancel the wedding.' He shrugged. 'Didn't work.'

I could see that now. Of course, Madhu Aunty and Uncle wouldn't cancel the wedding based on flimsy rumours.

'Well, I'm going to Chandigarh tomorrow. So don't worry.'

Relief rushed through me. 'Randhir, please see if...' I stopped.

'What?'

'If there are any bruises on her body or anything.'

He gave a brief nod. Then, 'Will you try to forget how I talked to you, Mallika?'

I nodded.

'And try to forgive me, OK?' he said in a low tone, looking at the floor.

'Randhir, you haven't told me why you were you so angry with me.'

He got up and said wretchedly. 'I'm sorry. I'm really sorry.' He said bye and left.

But sorry wasn't an answer.

While Randhir was away in Chandigarh, Arnav dropped in twice in the evenings to see me. He chatted about the plays in which he'd acted and his treks with Randhir and Vineet. It was strangely soothing, listening to him. He asked me if I remembered anything at all of those three days, and I said no. To my astonishment, he even gave me his hostel phone number in case I ever needed it.

'Did Randhir ask you to look me up?'

'Of course not,' he said, looking so taken aback that I wanted to bite my tongue.

Randhir came back from Chandigarh and came straight to see me. Mahima was fine, he said. My heart soared. Her in-laws adored her, and Shekhar was extremely courteous and considerate. Mahima was happy. She had no marks anywhere. So *now* would I stop worrying?

I nodded, relieved to the point of tears.

Arnav stopped coming to see me. Randhir told me he was busy acting in a play.

I went back to tutoring. Jalpari had stopped coming, and it worried me. I knew that Jalpari's mother had wanted her to take up sweeping and swabbing, but that Gopal, her father, had encouraged her desire to learn English. I needed to speak to Gopal. I went to the scooter stand a few times, but he was never there. Nor did I see him in the colony.

Ma and I went to the cardiologist at AIIMS with Shantamama's papers to find out if he could clear her for the surgery When we went back the next day, he told us that Shantamama's heart issue was not dangerous and that he'd discussed it with the obstetrician. They had cleared her for the hysterectomy. Ma sent a telegram to Shantamama to come to Delhi at the earliest for her operation.

I couldn't stop thinking about the way Randhir had lost his temper with me. And later, how he'd asked me to try to forget it. How was I supposed to do that? You could try to *remember*, but how did you try to *forget*? I couldn't forget Karan's return into my life, his desire to gain my love. Or Ma's constant grief during my childhood over the lover who had deserted her. Or my own longing for a father. Or my terror when I overheard the two girls calling me a bastard. Or my anger against Mrs Mittal for talking loudly in the market about my sexually frustrated mother. Or the fear I'd always felt about our secret being found out. Wouldn't it be wonderful if such things exited your mind just because you wanted them to? But the truth was that people just stopped talking about it and carried it like a ball of thorns inside them, pretending that it didn't exist, till the pretence became real.

I hadn't wanted Randhir's plea for forgiveness. I had wanted his truth. I had wanted him to tell me *why* he had lost his temper so terribly with me. 'Sorry' didn't mitigate my shock. Randhir had said that I had done the right thing by telling him to stop the wedding. So why, at the time, had he acted as though I had wronged *him*? As though what I had said was his crucifixion?

Besides, what on earth did forgiveness mean?

I knew what lack of forgiveness was. It was what I felt for the three women I had never met – Karan's mother and two sisters, who had separated my pregnant mother from him. It was what I felt for Mrs Mittal for gossiping about Ma. For letting her son kick that helpless puppy.

But forgiveness? Once, when I had asked Ma, she had said, 'When your pain and anger goes, that's forgiveness.' Well, Ma's certainly hadn't gone, so I knew she was still unforgiving of Karan. But though my own shock and pain at Randhir's rage remained, I wasn't unforgiving of him.

As for Karan, I hadn't forgiven him when he came back into our lives six years ago. He had never acknowledged what his mother had done. After discovering her perfidy, how could he have anything to do with her? But despite my anger and pain, I couldn't let him go. And I certainly didn't want him to suffer any more. Thankfully things had eased greatly between us by now, and while I didn't know if I loved him, I did care deeply for him. Maybe that was forgiveness – caring for, or loving, someone who has wronged you?

This was when I realized, with a sense of shock and bewilderment, that I still hadn't forgiven Karan. How was it possible? How could I care for Karan when I hadn't forgiven him?

But I could. I did.

All kinds of feelings and thoughts were jostling inside me. I found myself consumed by a terrible longing for Arnav. I kept thinking about Karan's lonely life and how difficult it had to be for him. I worried about Shantamama's tumour. Ma and I had written to Naraina Uncle, begging him to stay with us during the operation time. I began agonizing about what would happen if he refused. Where would they stay? Who would look after Shantamama? She had to recuperate in our house. Round and round my head they went, my thoughts, round and round.

Neither could I stop worrying about Ayah-ji, whom I had caught crying surreptitiously a couple of times. I kept asking her why, but she said she was fine. I knew it wasn't because she was missing anyone in her village; she was a childless widow and had no love for her relatives, all of whom had abandoned her after her husband died. She had lived with us since we came to Delhi and had a room to herself in the adjoining servant's quarter where she went every night to sleep. She was happy with us, reigned supreme in the kitchen, and had no qualms about speaking her mind. It was only when Shantamama came to Delhi and wanted to cook for me that the kitchen became a warzone. But the warzone was no cause for tears, just fights, which Ayah-ji invariably won. And yes, she had been very upset by my concussion, but I was alright now. Had Ma or I said or done anything to hurt her? I kept trying to figure it out, but couldn't.

Naraina Uncle wrote back a formal but warm letter to Ma, thanking her. Yes, he would stay with us during the time of Shantamama's operation. Oh, the relief, the relief! We would finally be reconciled! We could take care of Shantamama. We would take care of him. He was a good, kind man, and at last he would be back in our lives. Ma and I hugged each other in relief.

One day, as I was coming back from the market, I saw Arnav parking his motorcycle next to Randhir's house. Happiness seized me. He didn't see me, and I went running to him and breathlessly said hi. I was so happy to see him that I could have hugged him. Perhaps he read my face because he looked taken aback, almost apprehensive, as though now I was putting him in the position of having to fend off my hug.

'Hi,' he said, smiling, but his smile was forced. 'Feeling better?'

'Yes,' I replied, my heart sinking. 'And you?' *And you*, oh, god, what a stupid thing to say, what a stupid thing to do, running to him like that!

'Yeah, I'm fine,' was all he said, and then, because I was so mortified and so upset by that forced smile, I began to blabber. I asked him about the wedding, even though Gauri had already told me all the details. But, to my huge relief, he began describing Mahima's wedding – although after some time, I realized that it wasn't her wedding he was describing at all, he was just telling me various wedding stories. But I didn't care because it was wonderful to be laughing with him. Finally, when we stopped laughing, I didn't know what to say. So I blabbered about wanting to remember the wedding because I felt I'd forgotten something important, and I was asking everyone.

He shrugged and shook his head. 'I don't remember anything unusual.'

'OK, then. Bye,' I said, and went back home to spend the rest of the day in the familiar dungeons of self-flagellation.

Little did I know how close to the truth I had come. Because I *had* forgotten something. Something very big.

You see, just because you've forgotten something doesn't mean it's forgotten you.

Mallika: Paagal, lunatic

1976

She had to hide it until it went away.

It was mid-April now. In early January, after Mahima's wedding, she'd had the concussion and lost three days of her memory, and everyone was dragged into it. This time, she'd manage it on her own. No choice – Prabha was in Poona, Mahima in Chandigarh, Gauri far away in the JNU hostel where the phone rarely worked. No one to talk to, to ask, *What's happening?*

Had it been any other time, she'd have told Ma and Shantamama. But now the date for Shantamama's operation had been fixed. The days were consumed going to AIIMS, meeting doctors, having various tests done. The commute to the hospital and back took a lot of time. Ma was still teaching, and Mallika was going to college, but one of them always accompanied Shantamama and Naraina Uncle to the hospital. For the first time, Ma and she were not taking tuitions. They had told their children's parents that they would resume tutoring when the summer holidays began.

Of course, her mothers noticed she wasn't well. Every day, Ma asked her why she was looking so wan and pale. Every day, Shantamama wanted to know why she wasn't eating properly, why she was looking so tired. But they didn't have the time to focus on it, thank god. When she told them that she was tired of them worrying about her, they said, 'Fine, fine.'

It had started like a switch one morning and had not stopped. So far, she had managed to vomit in her upstairs bathroom. She vomited with both her bedroom door and the bathroom door closed so no one heard her. Then she felt nauseous all the time. It was awful, vomiting in the hospital's dirty bathrooms. She carried a large flask of water with lime squeezed into it wherever she went and drank it all day. Fortunately, with all the appointments and tests, they didn't eat all their meals at home together. She would have breakfast early in the morning before anyone else, and what she couldn't finish she would wrap up in newspaper and give to the jamadarni if she saw her on the way to the bus stop. She took lunch with her to college and usually gave that to the beggar outside the college gates. Dinner was the meal she couldn't get out of, so she would force herself to have a little rice, dal, and dahi, just enough not to worry them. Then she would go upstairs and vomit it all out, as quietly as possible.

It wasn't jaundice; her eyes weren't in the least yellow. It was probably some stomach infection, a bad one. It had happened to Mahima once, and poor Mahima was vomiting away for days; Madhu Aunty had been so worried.

She didn't go to Dr Wadhwa, their neighbourhood doctor, because he would certainly tell Ma, and she didn't want that worry on Ma's head.

On top of the nausea, her period was overdue. Her periods were never regular. Sometimes she got them twice a month, sometimes once in three months. They had always been unpredictable. The doctors had said it would normalize once she got married. Ma had taken her twice to a gynaecologist, who both times had examined her and then suggested she go on the pill. But neither she nor Ma felt comfortable with the idea. Gauri had told Mallika that her periods stopped whenever she was worried. Once, Gauri's period had stopped for three months, and the doctor had the cheek to say, 'Has there been any lafda with a boy?'

'Lafda with a boy, what cheek,' Gauri had said to Mallika.

'Well, it happens,' she had said to Gauri. Then Gauri had proceeded to give her a long list of medical reasons that periods stopped, which had nothing to do with pregnancy. A good doctor should know that and not jump to stupid conclusions, Gauri had said.

Mallika had already decided to see the gynaecologist opposite her college in Greater Kailash, the one where she had taken Charu. But she just hadn't found the time. Shantamama needed her. It helped Shantamama so much to have Mallika by her side when they were waiting for the doctor. Shantamama needed a lot of reassurance. For some reason, she seemed to feel that she wouldn't come out of the anaesthesia. 'What rubbish, Shantamama, of course you'll wake up,' she would tell her, and Shantamama's face would brighten up and she'd say, 'When you say it, I believe it, darling.' And though it was a small thing, going to the gynaecologist next to her college, the prospect seemed formidable. No scooter would take her that short distance, but walking would take her half an hour, and that was too much for her in the heat when she was so nauseous.

It was easier in college than at home. It was easier not to pretend, not to school her expression so she appeared calm and happy, not to force herself to eat. At college, she vomited in the toilet, and usually no one saw her even if they heard her. If she was noisy – and sometimes it was impossible to do it quietly – she would wait for ten minutes before she went out so that whoever heard her had gone. It was too much, to deal with concern, to reassure people that nothing was the matter. It was too much.

Then one day, as she came out of her college bathroom, she found herself blacking out. She stumbled to the wall and sank down, put her head between her knees, and stayed like that for ten minutes.

Eventually, she got up. She forced herself to drink a lot of water from her flask. Then she went out of the college gates and hailed a scooter. 'I'll pay you more, just take me,' she told the scooterwalla when he said the distance was too short. And so he took her.

Everything askew. Sixteen weeks, the gynae kept saying, so cold, so disdainful. Not Charu's gynae, another one, at the same clinic. Without even doing a urine test, talking about pregnancy, stupid woman. She was a doctor; wasn't it her job to explain properly? The gynae just asked her when she had her last period, she told the gynae it was towards the end of December, but that her periods were always irregular, this wasn't the only time it hadn't come for months, then the gynae put her hands inside her and came to some bizarre conclusion. Not even gentle hands – it hurt – why can't you relax, the gynae snapped, such a horrible woman. You're not married no, the gynae said, with that look, and she said no, but you haven't done a urine test. I'm a doctor, she said, as though she were God, you're pregnant, or did she say you're not pregnant? *Pagli. Lunatic.* She said, I've never had sex, and that bitch said, you're the Virgin Mary are you? She said, Charu's was a period, not a pregnancy. The gynae said, I don't know any Charu, if you want an abortion, I have a slot tomorrow, already it is late, you're sixteen weeks gone. I can't be pregnant, I've never had sex, she tried to explain. The gynae said, it's a pregnancy, your period will not come, or was she saying it's not a pregnancy, your period will come? She would come back with Gauri, Gauri would ask the gynae all the right questions, and everything would be alright. The doctor was saying, one thousand rupees, do you have it? And obviously, she didn't. Did the horrible doctor think she worked in the Income Tax department, carrying one thousand rupees in her bag? Oh, now she understood. She understood completely, she was awash in relief. This was how some unethical gynaecologists in these private clinics made money, she had read about it in the newspaper. They knew how frightened unmarried girls were, these poor girls thinking they were pregnant when they were not. Then these corrupt gynaes said, you are pregnant, and did a so-called abortion when actually there was no abortion to be done, because there was no baby. This woman was one of those. She could see the corruption in her eyes. Gauri would see it in an instant, Gauri knew truth from lies. She would ask Gauri what to do. Fine, she said to the gynae, what else to say, and the gynae said one p.m. The vomit was rising in her throat, she paid her with almost all the money she had in her handbag. Thank god she had had the foresight to keep money in her bag a week ago. She went to the bathroom, vomited, drank water, and then she sat in the reception and tried to think.

No question of discussing this with Ma and Shantamama, not with the operation around the corner. No strength nor money to go to JNU now to talk to Gauri. She would go first thing in the morning, catch Gauri before classes, leave as soon as Ma, Shantamama, and Uncle went to the hospital. Gauri would sort out all the confusion.

Getting up, going to the bathroom, vomiting again. Drinking water and walking to the bus stop.

The next day, everyone leaving for Shantamama's admission to hospital. Ma and Naraina Uncle would both spend the night there since the operation was the day after that. Kissing Shantamama, telling her she would see her tomorrow. Why are you looking so ill, Shantamama said, have you got fever, Ma said, feeling her forehead, I'm fine, she said. All of them leaving in a taxi. Taking one hundred rupees out of the two hundred in Ma's black trunk. Too ill to travel by bus. Quickly having a bath and wearing her purple batik saree. Taking a scooter all the way to JNU. Reaching there at eight-forty-five.

Gauri's room, locked. Standing there, dazed.

'Are you looking for Gauri?' a girl in the corridor asked.

Nodding.

'She's gone for a dance performance with her dance group to Agra, she'll be back tomorrow.'

Going downstairs. How to come back tomorrow when it was Shantamama's operation? Waiting with the other students for the bus that would take them to the old campus. The bus coming in ten minutes, getting in, and then getting off at the old campus, hailing a scooter. *Pagli. Lunatic.* Sitting in the scooter, feeling faint, giving him directions to go home, closing her eyes, seeing herself rising out of her body, watching her body floating, floating down a river. Floating down a river, her body, thrown in just like that, not even a cremation, she should sink but she's floating. Inside the dead body, life, floating. Her body floating down a river and inside her body life moving, twisting, her body twisting, life a knife twisting, turning. Twisting, turning, the knife, opening her eyes in a scooter in traffic, a knife inside her, someone groaning, the scooterwalla's voice, blood is coming out, blood. Holding onto the bar on the side of the scooter, awful sound. Finally, it has come, her period, finally. *Pagli. Lunatic.* The scooter stopping, the scooterwalla running into a small building, her purple batik saree drenched, holding onto the bar. Pay him, pay him. How long it takes to open her bag, the scooterwalla is back, giving it to him, ten rupees, five rupees, two rupees, one rupee, not sure. Two nurses helping her out. The red knife, twisting, twisting, twisting.

Looming above her, doctors, nurses, masks. Then a clean bed, a clean room. She closes her eyes. When she opens it, there is a new scene, a kind face, gentle eyes. She smiles, oh, the sweetness of her voice, you're alright now, you're alright, come, sit up, good, now drink this soup. She is an angel. Slowly drinking the chicken soup. Have the toast too. She has both. The angel watches her. Don't go, she says to the angel. The angel smiles, where will I go, I'm right here, what's your name? Mallika. Mallika. The angel doctor says, feeling better? Much better, how not to be better with words so soft and eyes so kind. She must tell her before she jumps to the wrong conclusion, she isn't mad like Charu, she isn't a lunatic, she isn't paagal, I didn't have my periods after the end of December, it's happened before, my periods aren't regular, and I was in the scooter this time when my period finally came. The angel listens carefully. Child, it was not a period, it was a pregnancy. *Pagli. Lunatic.* This was what happened when your eyes closed, scenes changed, words got reversed, what she meant was that it was not a pregnancy, it was a period, that's what the gynae told Charu, the gynae told Charu, this is a period, not a pregnancy, that is exactly what she told her, and Charu said, it is a pregnancy, not a period, and then the gynae said again, it is a period, not a pregnancy, and Charu said, it is a pregnancy, not a period. She tells the angel doctor, it was a period and not a pregnancy, she tells her with eyes closed in case the words change. The angel doctor says it is a pregnancy not a period a period not a pregnancy a pregnancy not a period a period not a pregnancy. Mallika, is there anyone who can come and take you home. Randhir. Is *he* the boy? The angel asks. She opens her eyes, and the angel's words kept coming out wrong and then right, Mallika, it was not a pregnancy, it was a period, it was not a miscarriage. That is what happened when you opened and closed your eyes, everything shifted, words came out wrong. She says, I know it wasn't a pregnancy, it was a period. No child, it was not a period, it was a miscarriage, you were pregnant. Poor Charu, how difficult it must have been for her. She spells it out, I've never had sex so I can't be pregnant. The angel's head is tilted slightly to the side, you have never had sex? No, never, how can I lie about something like that to *you*, a doctor, I'm an educated girl, I've never had sex. The angel reaches out and strokes her head, like Ma, like Shantamama. She sighs and closes her eyes, oh, no, no, why did she close her eyes, now when she opens them the landscape will change again, and words will shift like sand dunes in a desert. Does your friend Randhir have a phone? Yes. The phone is next to you, here's my card, phone him and ask him to come here. She opens her eyes and dials Randhir's number and talks to him, then gives the phone to the doctor, and the doctor talks to him. The doctor puts down the phone and says, how long have you known this Randhir? All my life, she says, and closes her eyes. Sleep, I'll wake you up when he comes. Oh, god, she has no money, how much do I have to pay you. The angel says, it is a thousand rupees, but don't worry about it now. She says, I don't have a thousand rupees, and the angel says, one day, when you have it, you can pay me, now close your eyes and breathe deeply. The nausea has gone. She begins to breathe. Now, at last, she knows the reason for the nausea, it was all that old blood accumulated inside her. Now, that blood is out, and the nausea has gone, now breathe in and breathe out, breathe.

Randhir is sitting next to her, rocking a poem in his arms. Her thoughts no longer confused, her words no longer crowding and heaving against each other. Saying, oh, Randhir, at last you wrote a poem for me. Randhir saying, you wrote it for me, I have a gift for you, and giving her a saree and leaving the room with the poem. Looking at the saree, what a beautiful indigo colour. Getting out of bed and wearing the saree, but the saree is drenched in blood. Why has Randhir given her a blood-drenched saree? Shantamama saying reprovingly, you don't look a gift horse in the mouth. She wears the saree. But the blood is now all over her body, she must bathe, but it is an outdoor bathroom, there are no walls in the bathroom, everyone will see her naked, how to have a bath? Why are you so worried, I'm here, says Randhir, so am I, says Prabha, me too, says Mahima, I am also here, says Gauri, all of them holding her tenderly, helping her walk to the wall-less bathroom where there is a big steel bucket of hot water, a bar of green soap, and a yellow mug. Then all four of them turning their backs to her and holding hands, forming a circle around her. Finally, she can take off her blood-soaked saree, blouse, petticoat, and her underclothes and wash the blood off her body. No one can see her naked, she has a wall of friends around her, their backs to her, and her mothers are standing outside the circle, guarding her, it is their Chakravyuha of love, and no one can breach it, absolutely no one, at last she is safe.

Randhir is sitting next to her. Smiling at him with love and relief. Randhir not smiling back. Then the embarrassing thing to say, saying in a low voice, I didn't have my period for four months, and it happened when I was in the scooter. Randhir nodding. Done. Now, no more talking about it. Randhir giving her a large brown paper packet which has *Mriganayani* written on it. Looking at him in surprise and opening the packet. A beautiful indigo saree with a mustard border, brand new, and an old black petticoat. Oh Randhir, she says, I just *dreamt* that you gifted me an indigo saree. He says, the saree and stuff you were wearing... it all had to be thrown, the doctor asked me to get you fresh clothes. It's Mummy's petticoat, he says. He gets up. He is leaving her. Where are you going? Randhir saying, just outside, you change into this, and then I'll take you home. Then Randhir sits down again, what are you scared of? She says, you were leaving me. He takes her hand in both his, the first time he has ever held her hand, he says, I'll never leave you. Relief rushes through her. Randhir, she says, her heart racing, tomorrow is Shantamama's operation. They have to donate blood to the hospital, Naraina Uncle says he's arranged for that from friends, but suppose they don't come? They'll come, he says, stop worrying. She says, the operation is at nine in the morning, I'd have taken a scooter, but... Can you drop me there, Randhir? No, Mallika, he says, you have to rest. I *have* to go, she says, I *have* to go, I'm already feeling better. He shakes his head, no. She should never have told him. She'll take a scooter early in the morning. If he doesn't believe her, he'll stop her from going, he must believe her. I won't go, Randhir, please believe me. He says, I'm going out, you change, and then we'll go home. She says, you believe me, Randhir, you believe me, no? Yes, Mallika, I believe you, now change, he says and goes out of the room. He's lying, he doesn't believe her. She'll have to go to the hospital before he gets up early in the morning, or else he'll stop her. She has to be there to kiss Shantamama before the operation and to tell her, don't worry, you'll wake up from the anaesthesia, and then when Shantamama opens her eyes, she'll kiss her Shantamama again and say, see, you've woken up.

She's still wearing her blouse under the white hospital gown. She wears Madhu Aunty's black petticoat, which is loose and comfortable, and then Randhir's beautiful new saree. It almost matches with her blouse. Then the angel doctor comes and gives her some pills to take at night for the first three nights and asks Randhir to bring her back if there is any problem. After that, Randhir drives her home in Madhu Aunty's car. Charu's was a period, not a pregnancy. As is hers. The difference was that Charu *thought* it was a pregnancy while she *knows* hers is a period. Because she's never had sex. Charu had not had sex either, but thought she was pregnant. That's the main difference between them, Charu was mistaken, and she isn't. Everyone had thought Charu was mad, paagal. That Charu had a weak mind. Well, *she,* Mallika, isn't going to have *anyone* thinking that about her.

'What did the doctor tell you?' she asks Randhir.

He's driving home slowly, in silence. He answers without looking at her. 'She said, some gynae problem.'

She says, 'What else?'

'She said you were… confused.'

'About what?'

'Mallika, you're exhausted, we'll talk later.'

Has the gynae told Randhir what she's confused about? Her blood runs cold. Randhir will think she's turned into another Charu.

'It was a period, nothing else,' she says. It's mortifying talking to him about her period, but better that than Randhir thinking she thought it was a pregnancy. Because then he will think she believes it was *he* who got her pregnant. Just like Charu. And he'll abandon her.

He doesn't answer.

But now she is getting confused again. She *hadn't* thought it was a pregnancy, she *knew* it was a period, she had *told* the gynae this, so why should Randhir think anything? Now she is really confused. Where did the word 'pregnancy' come from? The gynae *couldn't* have said it, because she *wasn't* pregnant. Oh, she knows where it had come from! It had come from *her*! She had been thinking of Charu, and that's when she'd mentioned the word 'pregnant.' And the gynae had thought she was talking about herself. It is all too close to Charu. Randhir shouldn't think she's mad and tell her mothers.

She says, 'Don't tell Ma anything, just tell her I phoned you from college and that you got me home.' He doesn't say anything, which means he'll tell Ma.

He stops at the traffic lights, and she puts her hand over his on the steering wheel. He turns to her, his eyes widening. She lifts his hand from the steering wheel and puts it on her head and says, 'Promise me you won't tell Ma or Shantamama or anyone else, ever.' She is holding his hand on her head so firmly that he can't shake it off. Cars honk behind them.

'Mallika, the light's green,' he says.

'Promise me,' she says. He tries to take his hand away, but she holds it tightly on her head. Several cars are honking loudly behind them.

'I promise,' he says.

'If you tell them,' she says, still not releasing his hand. 'Something really bad is going to happen to me, and then you'll know why it's happened.'

'For heaven's sake, Mallika!' he expostulates.

'*Promise me.*'

'Fine, I promise. But *you* must tell them later.'

'Alright,' she says, but of course it isn't the truth. She lets go of his hand and he shifts gears and begins driving. 'Tell Madhu Aunty I phoned you from college and you picked me up from there.' She closes her eyes. Without opening them, she adds, 'Don't talk to me about this again, ever.'

There is a silence, then Randhir says, 'About what?'

Without opening her eyes, she says, 'About today.' Because then Ma will go to the gynae to find out what had happened to her, and the gynae will tell her, 'your daughter's gone mad.'

'Answer me,' she says.

'I can't promise that.'

'I never asked you about Charu; I've never asked you about your writing. Give *me* that respect. Otherwise, I'll never speak to you for the rest of my life. *I* promise.'

It has taken everything and more to say all this. She has nothing left in her.

They drive back home in complete silence.

She is very weak. He helps her out of the car and takes the house keys from her. They go to the side door, he unlocks and unbolts it, takes her to the downstairs room, and tucks her into bed. Ayah-ji is taking her afternoon nap in her quarter and will be back home in another hour.

It is a blur after that. Ayah-ji comes and fusses over her and gives her tea and biscuits. Madhu Aunty comes. Anu Aunty comes.

She gets up a couple of hours later. Her thighs hurt; her legs are weak. Randhir drops in again and sits with her quietly as she has Ayah-ji's soup. Then he makes sure she has the pill the doctor has given her and leaves. She gets into bed and puts on the alarm for six a.m. She'll leave the house for the hospital by seven, and Randhir won't be any the wiser.

But he was. He had given her the sleeping pill the doctor had prescribed. He had asked Ayah-ji to take the alarm clock away after she slept. So of course she never got up in the morning.

She slept the rest of that dreadful day, and all through the night. When she woke up at ten in the morning, she knew it was too late to kiss Shantamama good luck for the operation. She also knew she couldn't go to the hospital because she felt even weaker; her thighs were hurting and trembling, and she could barely walk to the bathroom.

After ten days of no college, lots of rest, lots of chicken soup, and plenty of sleep, she was better. Then back to college.

Shantamama was in hospital for two weeks, and then she came home to recuperate for a month. A couple of days after she came home, Naraina Uncle went back to Bangalore.

Madhu Aunty had told Ma about Randhir picking her up from college because of her heavy period. Ma took her to the gynaecologist in Connaught Place who had seen her previously about her irregular periods. The gynaecologist said fine, this time she would prescribe the pill to regulate it. Mallika started on the pill, but within three days, she began feeling

nauseous. Terror filled her. Was she becoming mad again? Then she began
to vomit. Ma saw her vomiting and said, 'It's the pill, stop it immediately,'
and she did. The nausea stopped.

But the terror stayed with her like a cactus that kept growing. Its thorns
became her thoughts. Why hadn't Mahima written to her? Could Randhir
have been mistaken about Mahima being happy? She had to save up money
to pay the gynaecologist. How would she do that without Ma knowing?
There were no savings in the bank at all now because the loan had to be
paid every month, and less money was coming in while more was going
out. She wasn't tutoring anymore because she had to study for her own
exams. How would her children do well in their exams without her tutoring
them? How would Jalpari manage without her? Shantamama looked pale,
and her vivacity had faded. Ma looked exhausted, and was continuing her
tuition, plus going to college and looking after Shantamama. She, Mallika,
also looked after Shantamama and helped Ayah-ji in the kitchen, but she
felt her help wasn't enough. Why was Ayah-ji still crying secretly? Had she
or Ma made Ayah-ji unhappy? Had they said anything to hurt her? Had
Shantamama said something sharp to her? Sometimes Ayah-ji forgot to
bolt the side door at night, so Mallika would find herself getting up to
check if it was bolted. Then she'd wake up and check it again in case she'd
only dreamt that she'd bolted it before. She did this every night. Two,
three times a night. After some time, she began checking the front door
too, in case Ma and Ayah-ji had forgotten to bolt it. They also sometimes
forgot to put the vegetables inside the fridge. She would get up in the
middle of the night with the fear that the vegetables would go bad in
the heat. Then she'd check the kitchen and dining table to make sure
there were no vegetables there. And she kept searching for her magenta
silk saree, maroon sweater, and maroon shawl, and she just couldn't find
them.

Then she searched and found the joint account passbook belonging to
her and Ma (which Ma had hidden from her) and saw that there were just
two hundred rupees in their savings account. Of course, they had no fixed
deposits or anything. No gold to sell. It was all her fault. Ma had had the
upstairs room built for her because she had known that it was the only
thing that calmed her down, having her own space. And for that, Ma was
in debt. Why couldn't she be like other girls? Because of her, they were now
without any money. And Ma was making chicken soup every day for her and
Shantamama. She told Ma to make chicken soup for Shantamama but not
for her, and Ma said, 'What rubbish!'

She was finding it difficult to absorb what the lecturers were saying in
class. There was a lot of studying to do for her second-year final exams, and

that was very difficult, even though she was a good student and had come third in the university in her first year. But now nothing was going into her head. She couldn't fail. She *couldn't*. Her head felt funny. Sometimes it felt as though there were two plates that were shifting. Randhir kept checking in on her. She asked Randhir if Mahima was alright, and he said of course she was. She often saw Arnav next door. They were back to waving and saying hi. She longed for him to sit with her, talk to her, just *be* with her. Naraina Uncle came to Delhi again, and Shantamama went back to Bangalore with him.

She'd become like Charu. Ma shouldn't know. That first gynae had planted the seed of terror in her. She had declared Mallika was pregnant with such certainty that Mallika had almost believed it, even though she had never had sex. It was such a terrible shock that she had started mixing up Charu's story with her own. If Gauri had been with her, Gauri would have sorted it out for her. Her mind would have stopped jumping around like a mad woman's. She didn't want Ma and Shantamama thinking she'd gone mental, because it was a temporary thing. No need to worry them unnecessarily. She was fine now.

If Randhir knew she had become like Charu, he would be revolted. Randhir would think she was – as Delhi boys called it – froosth. Sexually frustrated. A hundred times more devastating than being called boring. He would think, with disgust, 'Mallika thinks I made her pregnant.' They could never remain friends after that. She could never look at him in the face. She would die of shame. She would die of shame.

The cactus that had taken root inside her was growing fatter. And taller. She studied for her exams, took them in May, and did terribly. After finishing her very last paper, Ma found her standing at their front door with her hand on the side of her head. She entered the house, saying, 'Ma, I'm feeling funny,' and alarmed, Ma said, 'What do you mean, funny?' and she said, 'My head feels funny,' and Ma said, 'You have a migraine?' and she said 'No,' and Ma said, 'Is it the concussion pain?' and she said, 'I don't know.' Then the rest of her words dropped deep inside her and her thoughts began to descend into that abyss. She wasn't sure how she would climb up to her room, but she held onto the banister, and Ma, who was following her, was saying something, but she couldn't make out what, and she entered her room and took off her sandals and, without washing her feet or her hands, lay down in bed. She closed her eyes, and everything began running out of her mind like water running out of a leaking surahi, and her head became emptier and emptier, and then it became empty.

From then onwards, nothing and no one mattered. She stopped worrying and she stopped thinking and she stopped wanting and she stopped hearing and she stopped doing and she stopped caring and she stopped talking. Like a flower at night, the cactus had closed its thorns and gone to sleep. Finally, blessedly, there were no more thoughts in her head, and no more feelings in her heart. Mental was a benediction like no other.

Shanta: In the hearts of lazy daisies and stem stitches

1976 and earlier

Just before Padma's trunk call came, she was immersed in her fourth rereading of *Pride and Prejudice*. When Naraina and the boys come home in the evening, I'll read out Mr Collins' proposal to Lizzie, she had thought. Laughing, she had looked up from the book and murmured to herself, 'Oh, how happy I am!'

She should not have said it out aloud. Happiness was a treasure to be hidden in the deepest recess of your heart. It was not to be shared with others. It was not to be shared even with yourself.

She was happy because finally Naraina had stayed with Padma and Mallika after so many years, because finally her sister and husband were reconciled. She was happy because the operation had been successful, because she was resting and rereading all her favourite books without guilt about housework, because Naraina and the boys were no longer deaf to her chatter. She had pushed aside that nagging worry about Mallika being so pale and run-down during and after her operation, and that heavy period of hers. Of course, it was because Mallika was worried about her. With what love Padma and Mallika had taken care of her and Naraina. How worn out they were, yet they kept doing and doing.

After resting in Delhi for a month, cossetted by Padma and Mallika, she had come back home to Bangalore. The gynaecologist had said three months rest. Naraina had strongly reiterated it, and so had her sons, Vikram and Varun. So, for the first time in her married life, she was actually resting. Her husband and sons were *talking* to her! They were saying, 'Feeling better, Shanta? How are you, Mummy? I hope you didn't go to the kitchen today, Mummy. I hope you rested, Shanta.' Things like that. And when she told them about the books she was rereading, wonder of wonders, they looked up from whatever they were doing and listened! It was an effort for them, she conceded that, but at least their eyes didn't glaze over every time she talked.

Before her operation, her husband and sons had been deaf to her chattering. She had told Padma it was no wonder more men got deaf in old age than women: they never wanted to hear, so their ears got used to blocking out sound until one day the pretence became real. Padma had laughed and said, 'All pretence becomes real in time; look at mine!' Thank goodness Padma had finally developed a sense of humour about her life.

Well, at least Padma didn't have to contend with grunts. In her own home, not only were her husband and sons selectively deaf, but if they responded, it was not with words, but with grunts: Did you have a good day at work, Vikram? Grunt. How was college, Varun? Grunt. You're looking tired, Naraina, what's the matter? Grunt. The English language didn't hold a candle to the Grunting language, which could express everything and mean anything.

But the discovery of her tumour and, on the heels of that, her heart problem – and then the not-so-easy operation – must have unnerved them. Their selective deafness had abated, and every grunt had been replaced by a word – 'yes,' or 'yeah,' or 'no,' or 'nope' – and even sparse sentences – 'I'm OK,' or 'I'm fine.' After the operation, they saw she was run-down and tired; they had never seen her so. She had always been full of energy and on her feet the entire day, taking care of the house, attending to all their needs and demands, tutoring them when they were in school, mending their clothes, knitting their sweaters and mufflers, and doing the one hundred and one never-ending things that all mothers and wives did. Now, fear for her health had birthed in her husband and sons that wonderful quality, forbearance. Of course, she wasn't foolish enough to think it was a permanent change. So she might as well strike while the iron was hot, because it would begin to cool as she got better, and then deafness, glazed eyes, and grunts would once more reign supreme.

When she returned to Bangalore from Delhi, the iron was hot and steaming; every day when they came home, she would talk to her husband and sons about whichever Jane Austen book she was rereading, and they would listen with heroic patience. They had never read Austen, and never would, but so what? She was living in that nineteenth-century world the way she and Padma had when they were young girls. All the news she had to give Naraina, Vikram, and Varun lay within Austen's pages, so when they came home in the evening and asked her how she was, she told them what she had read.

Oh, what a joy it had been to be reading so sinfully in the mornings! Because it was the doctor who had insisted on her resting, she had got rid of her guilt. That constant, hissing companion had leapt off her shoulder and scuttled to the corner of the kitchen where it now crouched, glowering. She knew it would leap back on to her shoulder the minute she got better, but at least for now it wasn't hissing her inadequacies into her ear. She hadn't read like this since she was a young woman in her parents' home, when she and Padma would lie side by side every night devouring books. She wasn't reading anything new, just her old loves. She had reread all of Austen, saving *Pride and Prejudice*, her favourite, for the last. The others were waiting for her on her bookshelf: Charlotte Brontë, George Eliot, Thomas Hardy, Charles Dickens. And after that, Marie Corelli; maybe hers were not classics like the others, but Shanta had loved her when she was Mallika's age. And of course, Georgette Heyer, whom she could go back to any time. As a young woman, she had read every Austen book at least three times, but rereading them now after all these years was a greater joy. She was going back to a Shanta whom she had forgotten existed. She was transported to her childhood – to her beloved father, whose favourite child she was; to her mother; to the young, passionate Padma who had worshipped her; and their brother, Madhav, who Padma had adored. She was going back to the time before Padma had shattered and broken the family with her pregnancy; the time before Padma alienated Madhav, who had wanted to adopt baby Mallika; the time before their father had disowned Padma. Now, in the quiet of her house, without her husband and two boys, and without guilt, memories of her childhood flooded her, and she found herself afloat in its tenderness.

Naraina and the boys weren't interested in her childhood stories. Once, she had started talking about Appa's dreams for her, and after a few minutes, Naraina had said patiently, 'Alright, Shanta, could you please come to the point?' Point? What point? She was just being nostalgic.

Well, maybe that wasn't all. Maybe she was just trying to say that Appa had had big dreams for her, that he saw her potential, that in her MA finals she had topped the university and been offered a lectureship on a platter. That she hadn't taken it because she got married. Maybe she was trying to say, 'Don't think I have no brains.' But that was not what he wanted to hear. When men said, 'Come to the point,' they meant, OK, hurry up, tell me the problem, and I'll give you the solution. They didn't know that anything wistfully uttered was an invitation for them to understand your heart.

She could hear Padma's voice saying, 'Enough, Shantacca, stop complaining about him. He's an honourable man, what more do you want? Where would I be without him? How often you leave him and the boys and come to Delhi, and he never objects. Why don't you weigh all he's done for me against all your complaints about him?'

She did. In her calmer moments, she did. She knew he was a man of integrity, a man with a strong sense of duty, both in his professional life and in his personal one. Without hesitation, he had opened his home and his heart to Padma when she came to them, unmarried, pregnant, and shattered. Padma had stayed with them, not speaking of the baby, not talking about anything. Shanta had told Naraina she wanted them to adopt the child. He had agreed without a moment's hesitation. Why did she feel she had to ask him? With one more child in their house, they would be even richer, he had said. His words had come straight from his heart, and love for him had flooded her. Padma had stayed with them till Mallika was born. But when that day came, Padma – who had had no love for the baby growing in her womb – could not relinquish Mallika. Then, with the money that Amma had kept aside for Padma's marriage – a marriage that never happened – Naraina had helped Padma buy her little Delhi house and settled her there.

Then, more than twelve-and-a-half years later, Karan had found out he had a child and came back into Padma's life. When Shanta had come back from Delhi after trying to persuade Padma to marry Karan, Naraina had expostulated, 'That he's decided to come back into their lives is bad enough, but now that man wants to *marry* her?'

She was shaken. It was rare for Naraina to show his anger.

'How *dare* he? He leaves her high and dry when she's pregnant with his child, marries another woman, refuses to answer her letters, and then, thirteen years later, he thinks he can whistle and have them back?'

'But Naraina, his mother was the one –'

'If Padma marries him, you will not step into his house.'

'*His* house?' She was confused and frightened.

He let out a sound of exasperation. 'Shanta, have you lost your wits? If they get married, Padma and Mallika will be living with him in *his* house.'

'Oh,' she said at last.

And everything Padma had been saying suddenly began to make sense.

'Padma says she'll never marry him.'

Naraina let out his breath. 'Thank goodness. I don't want to hear that man's name again.'

Amma was staying with Shanta and Naraina those days. Later, Amma had scolded her too. 'Shanta, how could you be so foolish as to think Padma would ever be happy with that man?'

'Amma, Padma will have standing, respect, and security as a married woman.'

'Padma already has standing and respect. She does not need a man for that.'

'And Mallika needs a father.'

'For what does she need a father?'

She looked at her mother wordlessly.

'What can a father give Mallika that you and Padma have not given her?

That Madhu and Anu have not given her? That *I* have not given her? The only financial security that Padma has – her house – is because I gave her the money for it.'

She tried to find a response to this but could not.

'Shanta, he does not even have his own house! His ancestral home will be divided between him and his three sisters. Do you wish him to take possession of Padma's house?'

'Amma, he will not do such a thing!'

'You say this of the man who abandoned my daughter when she was pregnant with his child?'

'But he did not know she was pregnant, Amma.'

Amma ignored this. 'You want Padma to be daughter-in-law to the woman who called her a whore, knowing it was her son who had made Padma pregnant?'

She was silent.

'If Padma marries him, she will have to look after that woman. As his mother grows older and feebler, do you want Padma to bathe this woman who called her a whore, clean the shit of this woman who called her a whore, wash the private parts of this woman who called her a whore?'

'Amma!'

'Why so shocked? This is what a daughter-in-law *does*. This is what marriage *is*.'

As a little girl Mallika would say to her, 'Shantamama, tell me about when you and Ma and Madhav Uncle were small.' By now, Mallika knew all her childhood stories: how Amma had always favoured their brother, Madhav, and how Madhav and Padma had adored one another and spent so much time together when they were students in Delhi. Mallika knew how Shanta had combed and plaited Padma's hair, taught her to wear sarees, advised and counselled her. How Padma had hated housework even as a young girl. How even in those days Shanta had loved to arrange flowers in every room and cook and do embroidery.

She didn't embroider any longer because it was a strain on her eyes. Besides, where did she have that kind of time? But when guests came, she would change the cushion covers and put on the ones that she had embroidered as a young woman – all from designs in those English needlework magazines. Mallika had said to her, 'Shantamama, one day, when you no longer use those cushion covers, will you give them all to me?' She had said, 'For who else, my darling?' As though her sons were interested in keeping her embroidery! When Mallika and Padma had come to see her once in Bangalore, Mallika had asked her to give her the two she loved the most. Back in Delhi, Mallika had gone to

Connaught Place and had the backs of the cushion covers removed and got them framed. All the money Amma had given Mallika for her birthday she spent for the framing! They were so exquisite, Mallika had sighed, they *had* to be displayed – Mallika, who didn't know the difference between a lazy daisy, a satin stitch, or a stem stitch had said they were exquisite!

So now, there they were, in Mallika's upstairs room. One embroidery was of a woman in a bonnet and gown walking in a garden of flowers. The other, larger one was of an English countryside with rolling hills, trees, and flowers, and in the distance, a little village nestled in the hills' folds. 'But darling, no one can see them in your room, why don't you display them in the sitting room?' she had said, and Mallika had responded in surprise, 'But *I* can see them. Every day! And my friends say they've never seen anything so beautiful. It's true, there's nothing as beautiful.' Mallika was rarely extravagant in her praise, and when Shanta heard this, her heart had blossomed like those flowers in her embroidery.

When Mallika had created the sham marriage between her mother and Karan aged fourteen, Naraina stopped visiting Padma. It was at this time that Shanta persuaded Mallika to write to her uncle. Soon after Mallika and Madhav's correspondence began, Madhav, who had not contacted Padma since she was pregnant, wrote to her: a cordial, affectionate letter with no mention of the past. Padma immediately replied.

That long estrangement was over! All because *she,* Shanta had set it in motion!

But a few years later, when Mallika was in college, both Padma and Mallika stopped writing to Madhav and refused to tell her why.

'Promise me you won't mention Mallika's or my name to Madhav. Promise me you won't sing Mallika's praises to him,' Padma had pleaded.

'Uff, Padma, is praising her a crime?'

'Promise me. *Promise me.*'

So, very reluctantly, she had promised.

Madhav must have made one of his nasty comments. You had to overlook these things in life. But Padma could overlook nothing. And Mallika was completely influenced by Padma's views.

After that, she had once made the mistake of complaining to Mallika about Madhav and his wife's nasty remarks and how it hurt her.

Mallika burst out, 'Shantamama, your brother is so mean to you, and his wife is even meaner, but you still write to them, meet them, and give them gifts and all!'

'Mallika, if I want to keep my relationship with my brother, I have to be nice to his wife. You and your mother need his protection.'

'But he isn't protecting you, he's *hurting* you.'

'The way you argue!'

'Shantamama, you keep saying blood is thicker than water. Madhu Aunty and Anu Aunty aren't blood. But they've done *everything* for Ma. What has her brother done? For either of you? *Nothing.* On the contrary he gives you *grief.*'

'*Why* did you and your mother stop writing to your Uncle Madhav?' Shanta asked, for the hundredth time.

Instead of answering, Mallika tossed her head. Like a bull.

Nor would Mallika talk to them about that tall, strapping, handsome boy, Randhir, who spent so much time with her.

'Padma, it isn't good for them to spend so much time together,' she said, for the five hundredth time.

'He's a very good boy, Shantacca. He's devoted to her. And very protective of her.'

'All that is meaningless without commitment.'

'Shantacca, for heaven's sake, they're too young!'

'Shouldn't we talk to Mallika?'

'No. Let it take its natural course.'

She wanted to say, *The way it took its natural course with you?*

Randhir seemed a good boy, but who was to say? Northerners were a different breed. When Padma had first moved into this neighbourhood in the late fifties, there were practically no Southerners here. Everyone in the colony had complimented her and Padma on their looks. 'You look like us only,' one neighbour had said generously. Another had said, 'Say something in your Madrasi language, I want to hear, I want to hear!' As though Madrasi was a language! As though Shanta was a performing monkey!

During the sixties, one of the neighbours had said to her, 'You *must* come for my daughter's wedding.'

Shanta had responded with surprise, 'But you never gave me an invitation.'

'Never mind, you *must* come, you *must* come, *most* welcome.'

Shanta was stumped. When she went back home, she had told Padma about the conversation, and Padma had laughed, 'This is how Northerners talk, Shantacca!'

Anu and Madhu were loyal and true, she would never contest that. But what about that time of her operation when those colleagues of Naraina's from Northern Railways had said, in that typical North Indian way, 'What is there, what is there, *we* are there, *we* will donate blood!' And then neither of them had turned up.

When she had said this, Padma said, 'And *who* donated blood eventually, Shantacca?'

Randhir and that boy Arnav who would look so much handsomer if he shaved regularly.

They had come to the hospital before the operation. Thank God. The hospital wouldn't operate till blood was donated to replenish their supply. So Randhir, Arnav, and Naraina all gave blood, and after that the doctors went ahead with the operation. Padma's blood pressure had shot up; the doctors said she could not be a donor. All this Shanta had found out when she was recuperating in Padma's house later.

'Fine, those boys are Northerners, but they're exceptions,' she said to Padma.

Padma snorted. 'You *never* admit you're wrong, Shantacca.'

Randhir was a good boy. His mother, Madhu, was devoted to Padma and Mallika. It wasn't easy for a boy to take advantage of a girl when their families knew each other so well. Padma was right, Randhir had always been there for Mallika. And though she wasn't entirely happy about the prospect of Mallika marrying a businessman, Randhir was different. He was an intellectual, he read as voraciously as Mallika, he would have his MA; he was Mallika's equal in every respect. Best of all, Mallika would never be short of money. And if Mallika really wanted, she could also work. She could be a lecturer and that would be like pocket money if she married into such a rich family. Or she could be a newsreader on All India Radio; she had a lovely voice, ten times better than that Latika Ratnam's. Mallika would have no lack of sarees and jewellery, though she fervently hoped Madhu wouldn't give Mallika a kundan or a diamond set. These North Indian jewels looked like paste. The single diamond in Amma's nose ring had more shine than an entire North Indian diamond necklace.

But then, how could Randhir have fallen in love with Charu?

After that bizarre meeting with Charu's mother, Shanta had asked Padma, 'How can you be so sure that Randhir loves Mallika?'

'It's over. It was just a fling, just foolishness.' But Padma looked troubled.

'How could Madhu talk about Charu as a future daughter-in-law if she wanted Mallika?'

Padma had said nothing.

'We need to sit Mallika down and ask her if she knows his intentions.'

'Shantacca, let us wait till he finishes his MA and starts working.'

How was it that Padma had not learnt a lesson from her own life and from the Charu affair? It was true that Randhir was deeply protective about Mallika, that he had done a lot for her. But none of that meant anything if he had not uttered the word 'marriage' to Mallika. And Madhu, who had more than enough to say about anything and everything, hadn't uttered a *word* about wanting Mallika as a daughter-in-law.

Once, Padma had told Mallika, 'One should marry a man who knows your heart. A man for whom looks are secondary.'

For whom looks were *secondary*?

'I must say you have a very high opinion of men,' Shanta said. Did Padma think Karan had fallen in love with her all those years ago for her *heart*? Did Padma think Randhir had had his fling with Charu because of *her* heart?

The problem was this: Randhir never looked dazzled or starry-eyed with Mallika.

'You should learn to smile and flirt a little,' she advised Mallika. 'Subtly, of course.'

Mallika laughed, 'Oh, Shantamama!'

Which was exactly what she needed to do with Randhir. Laugh and say, 'Oh, Randhir!' Men didn't want to hear your opinions (as Mallika's friend, Prabha, still hadn't learnt); they wanted you to giggle and make 'oh' and 'ah' noises. They wanted to be dazzled. But when Randhir was talking to Mallika, she would look at him so seriously that, even if he had had the slightest inclination to flirt, it would be thwarted. Mallika was a great thwarter.

Besides her absolute inability to dazzle men, Mallika had no wifely qualities. She was happy to spend hours in her room alone, reading. Very unhealthy. Didn't bode well for marriage. Secondly, she couldn't cook, never noticed if things were messy, wasn't interested in needlework or flower arrangements or housework. Was Randhir aware of that? Because in marriage, men didn't want intellectual companionship, they wanted well-cooked food and a well-kept house, and if you gave them that, then fifty percent of their needs were fulfilled. And if you gave them sex whenever they wanted, then they were ninety percent happy. And if you kept your mouth shut, then they were one hundred percent happy. Knowing your heart had nothing to do with anything.

The phone rang. She stood up and picked it up.

'Trunk call from Delhi for Mrs Shanta,' the operator said in that languid tone, and her knees went weak. She sat down on the chair, holding the phone tightly to her ear. From Delhi. That meant Mallika or Padma. Not dead, Deva, not dead. No coma or anything, Deva, please.

'This is Mrs Shanta,' she gasped, and the operator connected her.

It was Padma. In Kannada, she said, 'Shantacca, don't worry, no one is dead or in hospital or anything.'

She leaned back against the chair in terrible relief. Deva, thank you, thank you.

'Shantacca, I'm phoning from Madhu's house,' Padma continued, still speaking in Kannada. 'This is a three-minute call. Mallika is ill. The doctor says it is a serious illness of the mind. We have to make up a story. Think fast; everyone is asking what is wrong.'

She felt she was going to faint. 'Illness of the *mind*?' she panted, also in Kannada.

'Yes, illness of the mind. She has to see a doctor who treats the mind. Understand?'

'Psychiatrist?' she whispered in English. Thank God no one was at home.

'Yes. I'll write and tell you everything. What to tell people, Shantacca?'

Her mind was paralyzed.

'One minute left,' intoned the operator.

Her brain was paralyzed. Yet she heard the answer clearly, as though someone had whispered it in her ear.

'Tuberculosis,' she said. 'Say Mallika has TB. No one will even come near her.'

'Yes. Yes.'

'Don't even tell your two friends. Never tell them.'

'Never. Never.'

The phone began to purr. The three minutes were over.

After ten minutes, she was still feeling faint, unable to get up from the chair. The house was very quiet. The servant had finished cooking and washing the dishes and gone back to the quarter. She could hear Lata Mangeshkar's high-pitched voice on the radio from her neighbour's house. She heaved herself up, went to the kitchen, and made herself a cup of coffee with three spoons of sugar instead of her usual one-and-a-half. After she drank the coffee with two glucose biscuits, the faintness became better.

Mental. Mallika had become mental. Like Charu. But *how*? *Why*? But 'mental' meaning what? Was she raving? Was she wandering around without a bath and with her hair uncombed, muttering things? The doctor was wrong, he *had* to be wrong.

If Madhu got to know, she'd never let Randhir marry Mallika, even if he wanted to, which he wouldn't. He had already been burnt by that Charu. If Mallika wasn't cured, she would never get married, never have children. After she and Padma were gone, there would be no one to take care of her.

Mallika hadn't been well during the time of her operation. She had been pale and listless and had had no appetite. She had noticed it, and so had Padma, but they hadn't had the time or the energy to focus on it. Besides, she had thought Mallika was worried about the operation. And that heavy period had taken the life out of her.

It was related to the concussion. That was it.

She sat at the dining table, took the writing pad from under the paperweight, and began writing to Padma in Kannada.

Until I come to Delhi, we will write to each other only in Kannada. And even so, I want you to burn all my letters after you read them. I will do the same with yours. Every time you mention the illness, say 'TB.' We will live it and breathe it. Just as we have lived and breathed the other big story in our lives. I prayed to Krishna for you, and I will pray to Krishna for our child, and rest assured, He will help us.

I will come as soon as the doctor permits me to travel. In the meantime, forget your pride and ask Karan for money. There will be a lot of expenses. Make a trunk call to him in Lucknow from the Post Office, since, of course, you can't speak to him about this from Madhu's house. Hug and kiss my child for me. She will be cured. You must have faith. Twenty years ago, did you think you could ever overcome that enormous obstacle in your life? Did it not seem insurmountable? Not only did you overcome it, but you triumphed. Today, you have standing, you have a reputation, you have respect, you have independence, and you have friends who will do anything for you. As a result of which, our child has always been safe, loved, and protected. All those years ago, could we have imagined that such a thing was possible? Keep all that in mind, and know that this too shall pass.

She went down the street and posted her letter.

She was eating lunch when the doorbell rang. It was the postman, late as usual, with a letter from her brother, Madhav. She kept the letter aside to read after lunch.

Madhav had been so solicitous of her when she wrote to him about her operation. He had said she should have the operation in Bombay; he knew the top doctors, she and Naraina should stay with him, she could recuperate in his home, his wife, Ratna, would take care of her. She had been so moved. But of course, it was out of the question. His wife was full of smiles on the outside and full of poison in the inside; imagine being looked after by that witch.

When she was recovering from her operation in Padma's house, she had written to Madhav. Anxious that he and Padma would get reconciled again after their mysterious break in correspondence, she had written to him about how well Padma and Mallika had looked after her, what a loving and caring child Mallika was, and all Mallika had done for her despite her exams looming. And then, in a moment of weakness, she had told him how run-down Mallika had become because she was so worried – the poor child worried too much and it took a toll on her health. And in writing all this, she had unthinkingly broken her promise to Padma.

After lunch, she read Madhav's letter.

She always read her letters twice or thrice. But this letter, she would never read again.

Om,
My dear Shanta,

I am not interested in your endless chatter about your saintly niece Mallika and her so-called achievements, which frankly have no bearing on my life. On my Path towards the Ultimate, which I have walked for several years now (not that you would know anything about it), I am well on the way to living a life of compassionate detachment. I am aware that compassionate detachment is a concept that is foreign to you, but that is not my concern either. I am cleansing myself of all that is poisonous and superfluous, and your letters, so entrenched in the Ego, constantly fling those very things back into my life. To carry poison on the Spiritual Path besmirches the Path itself. I am cleansing myself of all poisons, so that when my day is done, He Who Sees All and Knows All will gaze into my heart and know that the only thing I carry in it is my simple, yet profound love for Him. Kindly refrain from mentioning the names Padma or Mallika to me again. Who is Padma but a stranger, albeit one who is morally bankrupt? Who is Mallika but the illegitimate daughter of this morally bankrupt woman, and, from all your accounts, so highly strung that she could very well end up in a loony bin. Or, who knows, in the same morally reprehensible situation as her mother. Blood will tell.

Let it be known to you that I used the term illegitimate deliberately. That I refrained from using the other, more appropriate word, for fear of offending your overwrought sensibility.

Yours affly,
Madhav
Om.

Half an hour after reading the letter, Shanta was still in the sitting room armchair. She was feeling nauseous, and her head was pounding. She got up slowly, and unsteadily went to the bedroom. There, she thrust the letter under the petticoats in her cupboard. She would burn it later. She got into bed. She had had headaches before, but never one like this – this must be a migraine. This was what Mallika had been dealing with since the age of thirteen. She took a Crocin, rubbed Amrutanjan on her forehead, and covered her eyes with a thin towel.

When Naraina came home in the evening, the migraine was worse. She got out of bed, gave him tea, and sat and asked him about his day.

'Are you feeling unwell, Shanta?' Naraina said as he drank his tea.

'I have a migraine.'

'Are you worrying about Padma and Mallika?'

'I'm not worrying about them. I'll go and lie down now.'

He looked at her in disbelief. 'Yes, of course.'

She got up and went to the bedroom and got into bed again.

It was the first time in her life that she had abandoned him in the middle of his tea. She never got up from their meals until he had finished, even when she was ill. Today, she couldn't do it. She couldn't cry. She couldn't do anything.

Naraina had asked if it was about Padma and Mallika. He never noticed anything about her – he didn't even know the colour of her eyes – but today, he had put his finger on it.

Half an hour later, her older son, Vikram, was back from office and came into her bedroom. 'You're not well, Mummy?' he said.

'No.' She had never said such a thing before. Even when she had that tumour inside her, she had told them she'd be fine, even though she had no confidence that she would.

'What's the matter?' He sat down by her side.

'Headache, Vikram. Go and have your tea.'

'OK. Sleep early. You'll be better by tomorrow.'

He was a bright boy, though lazy, and had done well in school and college without working particularly hard. Good-looking too; some girl or another was always after him. He had lots of friends who came home, loved films, parties, and going to the discotheque. She knew he smoked – she could smell it on him. And he spent money like water: although he earned a good salary and lived at home, he didn't save a paisa.

Ten minutes later, her younger son, Varun, came into the room. 'Ma, you're not well?'

She groaned. The one day she wanted to be left alone, no one would do so. 'Can't talk. Migraine.'

'I'll rub your head.'

He picked up the Amrutanjan from the side table and began rubbing her head with it.

He was good. Very, very good. His fingers were strong and unerringly found the areas of pain. He even went down to the right side of her neck, where the pain was. 'Oh, my darling, you have magic hands,' she sighed after ten minutes, as the stabbing pain began to abate.

'Good.'

'Mallika used to have terrible migraines for so long.'

His fingers paused, then stopped. 'Why is everything always about Mallika?' He got up.

'Thank you, darling,' she whispered as he left.

She shouldn't have said it. He didn't like Mallika. He didn't say it, but she knew it. It was one of her sorrows, that her boys and Mallika weren't close.

Varun was the quiet one, often sulky, the one whom she couldn't always fathom. He had done superbly in school and was now doing equally well in college and planned to sit for the IAS exams after his MA. He was as motivated and hard-working as Mallika.

The boys no longer came with her to Delhi. They would make comments like 'Oh, off to your favourite daughter,' or 'Ditching us again, Mummy?' She had learnt to laugh off their remarks and pretend that she never noticed Naraina's dark face whenever she left.

She castigated and defended herself in equal measure. She was a terrible wife and mother. No, she wasn't – she did everything for them all year round. She was a terrible wife and mother. No, she wasn't – the three of them never spent time with her, she was alone all day, and they only came home in the evenings and, even then, hardly spoke to her. She was a terrible wife and mother. No, she wasn't – they just wanted her around like a faithful dog. She tried to make up for it by cooking everything everyone liked, which drove the servant mad because he didn't like her interfering in the kitchen. Her husband's immense satisfaction at mealtimes placated her guilt. But only temporarily. Guilt had a voracious appetite; it was never appeased, it wouldn't stop hissing in her ear. She invited people for dinner as often as Naraina wanted, she had sex whenever he wanted – which, thank god, wasn't that often these days – she wrote regularly to his parents and sisters and brothers. When his family came to stay, she looked after them lovingly, cooked their favourite meals, and gave them presents she could ill afford. If Vikram said, just as she was going to sleep, that he wanted caramel custard, she made that. If Varun wistfully said that he liked her to sit with him when he was studying, she sat with him at the dining table as he studied late into the night, putting buttons on their shirts, stitching the holes in their socks, darning their pants and sweaters, or knitting them sweaters and mufflers. To be able to guiltlessly do the one thing her husband and sons didn't want her to do, she did everything else that they wanted her to do.

Even so, the guilt never left her.

Nothing to do but pray. She prayed to all of them – Krishna, Ganapati, Anjaneya, Sarasvati, Lakshmi, Durga, Rama, Shiva, Guru Nanak, Jesus, Mary, and St Anthony. She had put St Anthony on her shelf of Gods because he had found several things that she had lost, the latest being her gold chain. 'Please, please, find it, St Anthony,' she had begged, and five minutes later, she found it under the mirrorwork cushion. It was beyond belief; even Krishna wasn't as prompt. In fact, Krishna wasn't prompt at all. He needed a lot of wheedling. Padma's neighbour, Mrs D'Souza, had given her the picture of St Anthony, saying, 'Anything you lose, he will find, just ask him.' It was absolutely true. Before the gold chain, he'd found the cupboard keys she'd misplaced, the back of her gold earring that had rolled behind the table leg, and the chequebook she'd put in the wrong handbag. She loved St Anthony. 'He's not taking your place, don't worry,' she told Krishna. 'But you have no proclivity for finding things.' She prayed to all of them because she'd give them all a chance to help Mallika. Though Krishna had her heart, no question about it, that beautiful, wily man.

She told Naraina and the boys that Mallika had TB. She chatted with them, fed them, mended their clothes, and pretended that everything was normal. But when Naraina and the boys left in the morning, the terror and pain would descend on her like Saturn itself. She had abandoned Lizzie and Mr Collins right in the middle of her third reading of Mr Collins' proposal, and she didn't even care.

She shouldn't have told Madhav that Mallika had become pale, thin, and run-down due to worry. Because of that, Madhav had said Mallika should be in a loony bin. His letter coming on the same day as Padma's phone call was too much of a coincidence. Did it mean his words were prophetic? There were some people who were never cured. They became worse and worse till they had to be locked up in some institution or another. This thought had its tentacles around her so tightly that she could barely breathe.

Amma, she wrote to her mother, *can you come as soon as you can and stay with me?*

Amma came.

The day following her arrival, as soon as Naraina left for the office, Shanta burst into a storm of tears and told her about Mallika.

Amma listened quietly, her face pale.

'Don't mention any of this to Madhav, Amma.'

'Do you think I'm a fool? I never tell them how well Mallika is doing in college, what a good daughter she is. I hope *you* do not.'

Amma saw her face.

'Oho, Shanta,' she said, apprehensively.

She got up and went to her bedroom. She took the letter out from under her petticoats and came back to the sitting room and gave it to her. 'Your precious son's letter.'

She watched her mother's face as she read the letter. It became even paler.

'All his wife's doing,' Amma said unsteadily. Her hands were trembling.

'Amma, don't blame his wife for everything. I have no love for her, but the letter was entirely your precious son's work.'

'His wife has influenced him. She is jealous of Mallika.'

'You always exonerate Madhav, *always*.' Shanta burst into tears again.

'Shanta,' Amma, stroked her hair. 'Mallika will be cured. She will live a normal life.'

'How can you say that, Amma?'

'I know a woman who has healing hands.'

'What?'

'She does not proclaim she is God, or that God speaks to her, or anything. She is not dressed in saffron. She is like us, a middle-class, educated, ordinary woman. A *good* woman.'

'Amma, what is all this nonsense!'

'It is not nonsense. She has a God-given gift of healing.'

'How do you know her?'

'There are many people in my life about whom you and Padma know nothing. Do not interrogate me.'

Shanta bit back her response.

'She does this work on those who are very ill. She never tells them to stop their medicines or anything. It takes time, but those who go to her are helped greatly. I will write to Padma with her address. I am one hundred percent certain that she will make Mallika better.'

One hundred percent certain? This was North Indian rhetoric. Amma never spoke like this.

'By the time you get better, and we go to Delhi, That Man will be gone.'

Poor Karan. He was 'That Man' to both Naraina and Amma. Amma carried her hatred for Karan like an abscess inside her. Although she never showed it, Mallika felt it.

'Problem is this,' Amma continued. 'Mallika, she feels everyone's emotions. That causes her too much distress. It is not a good thing, to be like that, but what can she do? That was how she was born. You see, Shanta, no matter how much love she got after her birth, she was an unwanted child before it. Unwanted by her mother, rejected by her father.'

'Amma, you know very well he did not know Padma was pregnant.'

'No matter that he did not know. Rejection is still rejection. In the womb, the foetus knows everything. In the womb, the foetus feels everything. Mallika, the poor child, absorbed all Padma's emotions when she was in her womb. Padma's emotions were the opposite of love. It is no wonder that the child is the way she is, absorbing the pain around her like a sponge absorbs water. Pain is familiar to Mallika. It is what she has known from conception.'

'But *I* loved her when she was in Padma's womb,' she said, anguished at the thought of Mallika growing in a womb devoid of love. '*I* caressed Padma's stomach, *I* whispered endearments to her – I wanted her to be *mine.*'

'She *is* yours. That is why. In some ways, she is more yours than Padma's,' Amma said. 'That is why *you* give her more joy than Padma. That is why you always will.'

Happiness flooded her. Nothing Amma had said in her entire life had made her happier. She forgot everything else. Oh, such happiness. Ten whole seconds of happiness.

Then the doorbell rang. It was the postman with Padma's second, devastating letter.

Padma: Never say never

1976 and earlier

She was sitting frozen at the dining table after Dr Wadhwa left when her two friends dropped in, full of concern.

'What Dr Wadhwa said about Mallika?' Madhu asked, sitting opposite her.

'Tests results, they have come?' Anu asked, sitting next to her.

'No, the test results haven't come,' she said.

'But what is *wrong* with Mallika?' Madhu asked.

Her mother's instinct must have kicked in. 'She has fever and cough.'

Later, she would know what a prescient lie this was.

'Also a lot of exhaustion and weakness.' Which was true. 'She's sleeping just now.'

This would prevent her friends from going upstairs to check on Mallika.

'Bechari Padma, how tired you are looking,' Anu said. 'Do not worry, Mallika will get better.'

'Yes, Anu. I'll make us some filter coffee.' She got up.

An hour earlier, Dr Wadhwa had dropped in with the test results. He said that everything was 'tip-top.' Then he had given Mallika another check-up, taken her blood pressure, taken her temperature, checked her heart, her ears, her throat, everything. He had tried to get her to talk, but Mallika could barely make a sound or get out of bed.

After she and Dr Wadhwa came downstairs, they sat down. Then he said, very carefully, 'Mrs Rao, I think that this is not in the body. It is in the mind.'

Completely taken aback, she said, 'Dr Wadhwa, Mallika *isn't* pretending.'

He shook his head. 'You do not understand, Mrs Rao. Tell me, is fever a pretence?'

She shook her head, puzzled.

'Is jaundice a pretence?'

She shook her head again.

'Is a broken leg a pretence?'

What strange questions. Once again, she shook her head.

'Exactly. In the same way, a mind can be ill, a mind can be broken. That also is not a pretence.'

She felt weak with shock and terror. Mallika's *mind* was ill? Broken?

'What are you saying, Dr Wadhwa?'

'Mrs Rao, I have known Mallika all her life.'

She looked without comprehension at his kind face.

'I think this is depression.'

'Depression? But… She isn't unhappy, Dr Wadhwa. She's *ill*.'

'Depression is an illness. It is my belief that she has a major depressive disorder.'

She couldn't think.

'Do not feel afraid. Just like there is treatment for illness of the body, there is also treatment for illness of the mind. I will give you the name and phone number of a very good psychiatrist – take Mallika to him. Tonight itself, I will ring him.'

He wrote it down on his pad, tore the page, and gave it to her.

Psychiatrist?

'With the right psychiatric medicines, she will get better. But you must be patient. That is all.'

She couldn't absorb anything. Her hands were cold. 'So she *will* get better?'

'She *will* get better. She *will* finish college. She *will* get married. She *will* have children. She *will* live a normal life, do not worry.'

'But why? Why has this happened to her?'

'That I cannot say. The psychiatrist is the best person for all that.'

Now, he had left, and Madhu and Anu had arrived, full of concern, and Padma told her dearest friends the first lie.

Of course, she knew that if they were told the truth, they wouldn't tell a soul. They would be full of compassion. Yet, without uttering a word, they would relegate Mallika to the place they had relegated Charu. The place where *she* had relegated Charu. The place of no return.

And Randhir's love for Mallika would shrivel up and die.

The next morning, after ten, when she knew Madhu's husband would have gone to the factory, she went to Madhu's house.

'Madhu, could you please book a trunk call to Shantacca? I'll pay you for it. Mallika wants to see her badly.'

More lies. Mallika hadn't even mentioned Shantacca. She hadn't spoken at all.

'Just now, I will book trunk call. But, Padma, I know what is wrong with Mallika. It is anaemia. Such heavy periods she has.'

'Yes, that's possible.' Could this be the story they'd spin?

How would she hide the truth from her two best friends? From Mallika's friends? From the parents of the children they tutored? From the entire neighbourhood?

Madhu booked the trunk call, then made her some chai.

A trunk call was no way to break the terrible news to Shantacca. But the story had to be invented right now.

Miraculously, the trunk call came through in just half an hour.

Silently thanking heavens that Madhu was Punjabi, she spoke to Shantacca in Kannada.

'Tuberculosis,' Shantacca said, her voice throbbing with shock. 'Say Mallika has TB. No one will even come near her.'

When she went home, it hit her.

She couldn't take tuitions if she had been exposed to the so-called TB.

How would she make the monthly loan payments? How could she pay the psychiatrist and afford the medicines?

No choice but to ask Karan, as Shantacca suggested.

She made Mallika sit up in bed, sat by her, and saw to it that a few teaspoons of rice, dal, and dahi went into her. Mallika, her eyes drooping, ate silently and lay down again. She stroked her hair, kissed her cheek, tucked her in under the sheet, and went downstairs.

She ate lunch, told Ayah-ji to eat and, after that, to rest in Mallika's room. She'd be back in the evening, she told Ayah-ji. Ayah-ji was frantic with worry. Padma was exhausted trying to keep her calm. On top of that, Ayah-ji had forgotten to tell her till now, but Jalpari's father, Gopal, had come to the house around the time Mallika had her concussion, and then again when everyone was busy with the operation, asking for her.

'Ayah-ji, I can't talk to him now. If he comes, tell him Baby isn't well and that she can't tutor Jalpari till she gets better.'

The day Mallika had come back from college and collapsed in her room, she couldn't talk, couldn't register what was being said to her, couldn't get out of bed. Terrified, Padma had told Ayah-ji to get Dr Wadhwa. Within half an hour, Dr Wadhwa had arrived on his scooter. Her vital signs were absolutely fine, he had said after examining her. He would send his assistant in the evening to take her blood and urine and send it to the lab.

'But what is wrong?' she had asked.

He had not replied immediately. Eventually he had said, 'Some kind of exhaustion. Just make her eat and drink plenty of water. I will come again tomorrow morning.'

She had slept with Mallika that night. Not that she could sleep. Every five minutes, she would feel Mallika's pulse to make sure she was still alive. Every time she checked, Mallika's eyes were open, looking at nothing. The next morning and every subsequent morning, she and Ayah-ji had to help her get out of bed and take her to the bathroom. Since Mallika couldn't stand, Padma had put a plastic chair next to the sink where Mallika sat and brushed her teeth. It exhausted Mallika, brushing her teeth. When Mallika went to the toilet, Padma would wait outside the door. After that, she filled the bucket with water for Mallika's bath. She helped Mallika take off her clothes and sit on the plastic stool, and would have bathed her too, but Mallika shook her head. She sat outside the bathroom while Mallika had her bath. Bathing, towelling herself dry, and putting on her kaftan must have been like climbing a mountain, because when Padma opened the bathroom door, Mallika would be panting. She would reach out for the bed and collapse on it. Ayah-ji brought her breakfast upstairs, and Padma made Mallika eat a boiled egg, bit by bit. After that, she combed and plaited Mallika's hair. It was the summer holidays, thank goodness, and she was done with teaching.

Ayah-ji was beside herself. Padma kept comforting her, but Ayah-ji wouldn't stop crying and saying it was all her fault, that she hadn't looked after Baby properly and that was why Baby was so ill. She tried to tell Ayah-ji that nothing was her fault, but it was no use.

The test results came, and Dr Wadhwa said what he had probably suspected right in the beginning, the thing that Padma couldn't for the life of her comprehend. It was not Mallika's body that was ill, it was her mind.

It took her two buses and an hour and a half to reach the main Post Office in Janpath. Another forty-five minutes standing in line to book the three-minute trunk call. Then someone behind her said, 'Mrs Rao, what you are doing here?' It was one of her tuition children's mothers. Oh, god, no.

'Namaste, Mrs Kapadia. I have to make a trunk call.'

'I also have to make, chalo, we can talk till then,' Mrs Kapadia said.

Padma nodded, exhaustion filling her at the prospect of talking.

'My brother, he is in hospital,' Mrs Kapadia continued. 'I am making trunk call to my sister-in-law, so worried I am. To whom you are making trunk call?'

'To my husband,' Padma replied.

'Why you are making trunk call to him? Mallika, she is alright, no?'

What time better than now? It would save her telling everyone; Mrs Kapadia would.

'Mallika has TB. That is why I'm phoning him.'

'Hai, hai, poor thing, poor thing! *You* don't have it, no?'

'I will get myself tested. But… You should not be near me, just to be on the safe side.'

'No problem, no problem.' Mrs Kapadia retreated.

Her trunk call came through after half an hour.

It was Karan's direct line in the office. 'Yes?' he said in that deep, clipped voice of his.

'This is Padma.'

'Hullo?'

She shouted, 'This is Padma, can you hear me?'

'It's a bad connection, what's wrong?' She could hear him clearly.

She was phoning to ask him for money. Suddenly she found she couldn't do it.

'Please come to Delhi,' she shouted.

There was a shocked silence.

His voice changed. 'Mallika?'

'Yes.'

'What's wrong?'

How could she shout it out for all to hear – including Mrs Kapadia?

'Padma, what's wrong?'

'Can't say.'

'I can't hear you.'

She shouted, 'I can't say.'

'I'll come tomorrow.'

'Yes, please come. Mallika's at home.' So that he'd know she wasn't in hospital or anything.

The phone began to purr. Her three minutes were up.

'I'll *never* take your money – keep it,' she had said all those years ago when Karan had said he would pay for Mallika's expensive convent school. How upset he had been when she had refused his money for the child that he had presumed was his just because he'd accidentally fathered her.

'Why must you be such a martyr?' Shantacca had said. 'There's no merit in martyrdom.'

She hadn't listened to her friends either when they had said, 'The money is for Mallika, accept it in *her* name, Padma.'

In the years that followed, she hadn't taken even one rupee from him.

During the time Mallika was in school, they had managed because of Amma. Whenever Amma stayed with Shanta – six months of the year – she sent Padma money, all of which went towards Mallika's convent school fees, summer and winter uniforms, and blazer and shoes. When Amma stayed with Madhav, she didn't send money because she didn't want him and his wife to know. After Mallika finished school, things eased, as college was virtually free. Padma had told Amma there was no need to send any more.

As soon as Mallika finished school, she started tutoring children. Shantacca had been anguished. 'How could you have been so foolish as to refuse Karan? See, now the burden is on our child. She's only sixteen, Padma. Every other girl her age is having fun and enjoying herself. But Mallika's become an adult before her time. All because of your false sense of pride.'

She had been distressed too. She had tried to tell Mallika there was no need to do this. But Mallika wouldn't budge. It continued after Mallika joined college. She tutored five evenings a week and deposited the money she earned into their joint account.

After Mallika's concussion, it was Anu who had said gently, 'Padma, Karanji is Mallika's father. You must tell him about her concussion.'

It had not occurred to her to tell Karan. Anu was right. So she had written her very first letter to Karan in nineteen years. It was brief and to the point. It didn't even fill the inland sheet.

As soon as Karan received the letter, he took the train to Delhi. Padma had made an appointment to take Mallika to the hospital in ten days' time, but he knew some big shot and had got her an appointment immediately. Mallika was thoroughly checked, and the doctors assured them that all was well. As for the lost three days of her memory, it was unlikely it would come back.

'Next time, if anything happens to Mallika, please make a two-minute trunk call to me,' he had said, giving her a piece of paper. 'This is my direct line in the office.'

This time, he drove all the way from Lucknow to Delhi and came straight home. It was eleven p.m. when he arrived. 'I've eaten,' he said. 'Tell me what's happened.' He placed his suitcase behind the sofa and sat down. He looked drawn.

She got him a glass of water, which he drank thirstily. Then she sat opposite him and said, 'Mallika has a mental disorder.'

His face had the same expression that hers must have had when Dr Wadhwa had said this. One of absolute incomprehension.

'He said it's probably a major depressive disorder. It's very severe. She can't function. She's completely bedridden.'

And then, as the colour ran from his face, she couldn't say any more.

It had taken everything for her to say 'mental disorder.' Saying it made it real. Even though what she saw was real enough. But it was possible to delude yourself that what you saw was a physical illness. A part of her still hoped that when they went to the psychiatrist, he would say that.

'We have an appointment with the psychiatrist tomorrow,' she said.

'But why has it happened?'

'I don't know. Neither does Dr Wadhwa.'

Finally. Thank god. Finally, she could share this with someone.

'It's my fault,' she burst out. 'I should have seen it coming. I could have prevented it.'

Quietly he said, 'Tell me everything. From the beginning.'

Mallika was good at hiding things. She had hidden her migraines, she had hidden the burden of pain and guilt she was carrying about her father, she had hidden the fact that she had slashed Mrs Mittal's scooter tyres and later stolen her puppy. Padma had guessed about the puppy following Mrs Mittal's accusation after she caught Arnav looking incredulously at Mallika. The next day, it hit her that Arnav was incredulous because he knew the accusation was true. Which meant he'd helped Mallika without knowing what she'd done. On the heels of that, like a photograph in her mind's eye, she saw the scooter with the slashed tyres, and the police looking at it, and Mallika sitting in the veranda, reading a magazine without turning the pages.

All that, she didn't tell Karan. She told him that Mallika was a bit disoriented after the concussion, but she noticed the change in her around the time of Shantacca's hysterectomy. Mallika was eating less and looking pale and tired. But Padma hadn't had the time to focus on her, because they were all so involved with the operation. And she had believed it was because Mallika was worried about the impending operation. Also, Mallika's periods were irregular, and when it would come, it was always so heavy and painful that it would take the life out of her. That was what had happened just before Shantacca's surgery. It must have been really bad, because Mallika actually phoned Randhir from college and asked him if he could come and pick her up and take her back home.

Padma had come back from the hospital, after spending the night with Shantacca in the ICU, to find Mallika extremely weak. After two or three weeks, when Mallika was better and back in college, she took her to a gynaecologist in Connaught Place whom they had been to a couple of times before. This time, the doctor put Mallika on the pill and said that would regulate her periods. But the pill made Mallika nauseous, and then one day she began to vomit. After that bout of vomiting, Mallika was shaking, terrified. That should have told her something was wrong, because what was there to be terrified about? She told Mallika to stop taking the pill, but Mallika remained worried about everything. She was also disoriented, forgetful, had no appetite, and looked exhausted. After her last exam was over, she came back home and collapsed in her room. After that, she hadn't left her bed except to go to the bathroom.

Mallika had stopped talking. She couldn't absorb what was being said to her. She couldn't sleep. She could barely eat. She couldn't *read*. She had asked about Shantacca only once and didn't ask about her friends. She lay on her side and looked at the wall, and if you asked her to turn over, then she lay on the other side and looked out of the balcony.

Dr Wadhwa had done every possible test for Mallika, and everything was normal. Nothing had *happened* to Mallika to cause this. Yes, she had lost three days of her memory after her concussion, but those days had been accounted for.

Karan said, 'I've taken a month's leave. I have the car so we can take Mallika for her appointments.'

Another storm of relief engulfed her. She nodded. 'I've made the bed in the downstairs room, Karan. Stay with us as long as you're here. Also, the story is that Mallika has TB.'

He nodded.

Her blood pressure had shot up during the time of Shantacca's operation. Even after Shantacca left, Padma's blood pressure didn't stabilize sufficiently. Fear of having a stroke and abandoning her child swept over her every day. The only way she could stop thinking those thoughts was by focusing her mind on Randhir. If anything happened to her or Shantacca, he would take care of Mallika.

It didn't matter that Mallika never spoke of her feelings for Randhir. She didn't have to. Theirs was no immature young love. It was a love of the very spirit. Till Randhir came into Mallika's life, Padma hadn't believed such a love was possible between a man and a woman. In her youth, she had believed that she and Karan were soulmates. But her love story with Karan was a run-of-the-mill love story. You believed that heady, desperate feeling was love, but it wasn't. Even if you weren't having sex, it was there, the desire for it, and therefore the desire for him. It consumed you both. All those years ago, she hadn't known the difference between that madness and love.

Shantacca said that Mallika and Randhir were like an old married couple. So? What was wrong with that? What was wrong with *substance*? That trumped the madness of young love any day. They were so close that sometimes Mallika only had to mention his name for the doorbell to ring. And there Randhir would be, smiling, ready to go for a walk with her, or take her to the British Council library.

Initially, it hadn't worried her that Madhu, so voluble about everything and with an opinion on every subject, had never uttered a word about wanting Mallika as a daughter-in-law. After all, Randhir and Mallika were so young, why talk about something so far away?

But then Randhir fell like a ton of bricks for Charu and disappeared from Mallika's life.

And Madhu started talking about Randhir and Charu getting married.

Padma had felt sick with shock. Then came anger.

Anger against those you loved was the hardest anger to bear. She had known this kind of anger only with Karan.

The more she felt Mallika's pain, the more her anger against Madhu and Randhir grew. The greater her anger against them, the more corrosive her guilt. Every time Madhu spoke about Randhir marrying Charu, she measured it against everything that Madhu had done for her and Mallika. Every time she saw Randhir's stupid, dazzled expression when he was with Charu, she measured it against all that Randhir had done for Mallika.

But after the Charu drama, Randhir went back to Mallika. It was Randhir who rushed Mallika to hospital after her concussion, brought her back home and kept an eye on her while she recovered; it was he who picked Mallika up from her college when she was bleeding so heavily, he who had then come to the hospital that same evening to tell Padma not to worry, he who – along with his friend, Arnav – had donated blood to the hospital before Shantacca's operation. Now, he came home every single day to find out how Mallika was feeling.

But even after all this, Madhu didn't mention wanting Mallika as a daughter-in-law.

The next morning, after Mallika had had her bath and dressed, Karan came upstairs, kissed her on her head, and gave her breakfast in bed. She accepted his presence without any reaction. After Padma combed and plaited Mallika's hair, Karan helped her down the stairs. By then, Padma and Ayah-ji had filled two flasks with water and lime juice, chopped an apple, and put some biscuits in a small tiffin carrier. Mallika didn't have the strength to sit up in the back seat of the car, so she lay down all the way to the doctor's office.

The psychiatrist, Dr Roy, was in his late forties, fresh from America. The clinic didn't look Indian. This was what doctors' offices must look like in America: sparkling clean, shining, everything in place, even smelling different. Uncrowded. He had practiced in America for fifteen years, he said. He had an American accent, but thankfully it wasn't a strong one.

He saw how Mallika was and gently asked her to lie down on the sofa opposite him.

Then he said he needed to speak to Mallika alone.

'But we're her parents,' she said.

'Of course. We'll talk after I speak with her.'

She looked at Karan. He was looking taken aback too. Then he turned to her and nodded.

So they exited the room, leaving Mallika lying on the sofa.

They waited outside, each lost in thought.

After half an hour, the doctor came out and called them in. Mallika was still lying on the sofa, her eyes closed.

She couldn't talk much, the doctor said, and he had asked her permission to speak to them, which she had given.

Permission?

She and Karan glanced at each other in astonishment.

The doctor said, 'She is above eighteen.'

'Nineteen is hardly an adult,' Karan said.

'Oh, yes – in India it's twenty-one, isn't it?'

'No, Dr Roy,' she said. 'In India, it isn't anything! Look at her state! Even if she were *thirty*, you could talk to us without her permission!'

Dr Roy smiled faintly.

She told him everything. He took down copious notes. He wanted to know more about Mallika's concussion and lost memory. She went over each day. 'Every moment has been accounted for,' she said. He asked if either of them had ever suffered depression, or if there was depression or any other mental illness in either of their families. She said no. Karan said no.

Yes, it was a major depressive disorder, Dr Roy said at last. Fortunately, she wasn't suicidal or anything.

'But *of course* she's not suicidal,' Padma interrupted, shocked. 'She's got nothing to be suicidal about.'

The doctor paused. Then he said, 'Depression manifests in different ways for different people.'

'But *why* is she depressed?'

He couldn't say why, he said.

He, a psychiatrist, couldn't say why?

Then he spoke about an imbalance in the chemistry of the brain. Something about serotonin. About how it was beyond Mallika's control. People could look after themselves in every way and yet succumb to physical illnesses, and so it was with mental illnesses.

'But how can you compare the two? Mental illness is so rare.'

'It's a lot more common than you think. In India, it's well-hidden because of the social stigma. It's unrecognized, unaccepted, misunderstood. Most people won't go to a psychiatrist or take their children to one. They think the problem will get better on its own. Or they think they can scold their children out of it. Or beat it out of their children. Or you're expected to snap out of it. It's perceived as your fault.' He was watching them carefully as he spoke.

'We'll never do that,' she said.

He nodded, looking relieved.

On the sofa, Mallika wasn't listening. She wasn't even moving.

'What should we do to help her?' Karan asked.

'Don't try to talk her out of it.'

What did he mean, talk her out of it?

'Refrain from telling her she shouldn't lie in bed, or that she should go for a walk or start reading again, things like that.'

'But won't it help her to get fresh air?' Karan asked.

'Yes. Take her outside when she's a little better. Not yet, though.'

Karan nodded.

'Be kind to her,' Dr Roy said.

Once again, she was shocked. How could they be anything else!

'In India, the harshest, unkindest things are done in the name of love. To those who have illnesses of the mind, most of all. And also to those who are deemed ill of mind simply because they are of a different mould.'

Was this what her child would have to go through for the rest of her life? Cruelty and condemnation from those who did not understand and would never understand? She was crying so bitterly by now that her whole body was heaving.

The doctor said, 'This isn't a lifetime sentence.'

'It seems like one,' she wept.

'Certainly not.' He spoke with such assurance that her tears began to abate.

'We've told everyone she has TB.'

To her surprise, he laughed. 'I'm sure that's *very* effective.'

This firmly set the seal on her liking. Maybe he was America-returned, but he did understand how it was in India.

He wrote out two prescriptions – one, he said, for the depression, and the other to help her sleep. He would like to see them back in a week.

Ayah-ji muttered to herself and wept as she worked. After they tucked Mallika into bed, Karan said, 'The doctor says she will become well again, Ayah-ji.'

Ayah-ji burst into tears. 'My Baby's mind was not peaceful, that is why this has happened.'

She looked at Ayah-ji, stunned. Ayah-ji didn't need a psychiatrist to tell her anything.

Karan said, 'Ayah-ji, all of us must have peace in our hearts. That peace must surround Baby. Then she will get better.'

Ayah-ji looked at him as though his words were those of a prophet. Then she wiped her tears and nodded.

Ayah-ji, who regarded most people with suspicion, had grown to regard Karan with grudging respect. For her, his words bore weight. If Karan had said Mallika would be cured, then, as far as Ayah-ji was concerned, Mallika *would* be cured. No one had told Ayah-ji their whole sordid story, and of course she didn't know English, but she knew every single secret in their house.

That night, as Karan slept downstairs in Mallika's old room, Padma lay upstairs in bed with her sleeping child, her arms around her, scenes from the past once again assailing her.

A few months after Karan had re-entered her life, he had said, 'It would be good for Mallika if we got married, Padma. Let's start afresh. Let's give her what she's never had – a proper family life.'

That was when she had felt that high-pitched *kuiii* sound in her ear. 'She *has* a family life,' she had said. 'She has Amma, Shantacca, Madhu, Anu, and her three friends who are like her sisters. I'll *never* take her away from them, *never.*'

'I'm not asking you to take her away from them.'

'How can you ask me to marry you and be part of *your* family and live in *your* house?'

'Mallika and you don't have to have anything to do with them.'

'How? Your mother will come live with you permanently one day.'

His eyes shuttered down.

'Whenever your sisters want to see her, they'll come and stay with you.'

He was silent.

Then he said, 'I'll work that out.'

Bitterly, she said, 'It didn't even occur to you till I mentioned it. You think I'll ever let your mother and sisters come within a mile of my child? I'll never marry you. Never.'

'I see. You'll never marry me, but you'll continue having sex with me?'

She got out of his bed, grabbed her clothes, and went to the bathroom.

It was the first time he had mentioned it. There they were, having desperate sex as though they could make up for all those years, but never speaking of it. She didn't want to think about how, despite her rage, she had still wanted him. He had wanted her no less. She, who had been so circumspect all the years of her so-called widowhood, found herself going to his government flat near Khan Market once or twice a week after college.

She would phone him at work from the college's public phone, and he would come back to his flat for an hour from work. 'I want to talk to you,' she would say, because she couldn't in her own home with Mallika there. He would come back to his flat, and she would join him there, and it would come out of the cauldron, all that she was carrying. He never contradicted her, he never tried to justify what he had done, he never spoke of his family, he just listened. And then, exhausted, she would reach for him, or he for her, and they would end up making love. Or, as he said, having sex. It was always in the afternoons that they met. His servant was in his quarter, most of the men were out at work, and the women were having their afternoon naps; the timing was perfect. Then, still without words, she would get dressed, and he would drive her to the bus stop. 'You can't drop me home,' she had told him right in the beginning. And so it had continued once or twice a week, their desperate, frenetic couplings. As for speaking about it, they never did.

But after he said this, she never went back to his flat.

When she looked back on the old days, she couldn't remember talking with Karan the way Randhir and Mallika talked. With Karan, what she recalled was that hunger – wanting his touch, wanting his mouth all over her body, wanting his limbs around hers, wanting, wanting, wanting. Want or love, she hadn't known the difference.

She knew it now.

She had told her two friends and Shantacca about Karan's proposal and her refusal.

'What is wrong with you, Padma? He will give you security, status, everything,' Madhu said. 'How can you be so selfish, Padma – how can you deny your child her father?' asked Shantacca.

'Padma, it will be so much easier to get Mallika married if she has a father,' Anu Aunty advised. 'Financially also, it will be easier for you.'

'Can't you *see* that Mallika and I will have to live with him and deal with the very mother and sisters who separated us? You're asking Mallika to give up *this* family, which has given her everything, in order to embrace *that* family, which rejected her when she was in my womb?'

Why did no one understand that?

And by then, people were asking her questions about Karan, and the 'family friend' response was no longer holding water.

'You can't come home like this,' she said to Karan. 'My reputation is at stake.'

They were in her sitting room, talking.

'Alright. In that case, Mallika can come to my house on the weekends.'

'I see. So when your neighbours see a young fourteen-year-old girl every weekend in your house, you're going to tell them she's your daughter?'

'Are you asking me to never see her? That's unacceptable.'

'Don't accept it, then. I don't care a damn about *your* acceptance.'

They looked across the room at each other like enemies.

Suddenly, Mallika rushed out of her room. 'What about *me*? What about what *I* want? Am I *nothing*?'

They looked at her, frozen. She had been listening the whole time.

'*I* want to spend time with him,' Mallika said to her.

Then Amma came out of her room. Without even glancing at Karan, she spoke to Padma. 'Mallika has decided. You cannot stop it.'

Padma could hear herself and Karan breathing hard.

'Padma, you are always saying, "I want peace, I want peace." If you truly want peace, then accept what cannot be changed.'

Only then did Amma look at Karan. 'You also,' she said, and went back to her room.

Karan worked it out.

But alas, both she and Karan had been blind to Mallika's intense suffering. Until Randhir, holding Mallika's pain as though it was his, spoke to them. That was when they realized that she was hiding the burden of making both her father and mother happy at any cost.

For the first time since his return into her life, she had felt Karan's heart breaking. For the first time, she glimpsed the agony that he carried and always would. A deep and painful compassion wound its way around her anger.

More than a year later, Mallika had overheard Mrs Mittal gossiping about her mother, and the story that Padma and Karan were married began.

When Karan came home later that evening, he said, 'There's no getting out of it. It's a convenient story. It solves everything. For you, me, and Mallika.'

Madhu established this lie in her inimitable way. And Padma lived it.

It wasn't without its consequences. Her brother-in-law did not return to her house for five years. She felt she had betrayed him, this kind and generous man who had opened his home and heart to her while she was pregnant with Mallika. Finally, at the time of Shantacca's operation, both she and Mallika wrote to him, begging him to stay with them.

Naraina quietly agreed.

After the operation, as Shantacca recuperated in her house, Padma asked Naraina, 'Please, will you come back?' He patted her gently, as he used to do when she was a young girl, and nodded, and she almost wept with relief. Her guilt about Naraina, Vikram, and Varun always dogged her. But once, when she had worriedly said to Shantacca, 'We're taking you away from your children,' Shantacca had burst into tears.

'You mean Mallika isn't my child?'

Padma had comforted her sister and assured her this was not what she meant. She never mentioned it again.

After their convenient 'marriage,' Karan visited Mallika at home regularly. Whenever he did, Mallika's three friends gathered around him like flapping, eager fledglings. She and Karan were polite with each other, but what was there to say? A part of her had barricaded itself against him, and she couldn't get past her own barrier. She certainly couldn't penetrate his. As Amma had said, accept what you cannot change. They both had.

Finally, there was a measure of peace between them.

This time, with Mallika's unaccountable illness, they were both floundering. This time, their lack of words came from the fact that none were necessary. They knew what they had to do. They had to take care of Mallika. Nothing else mattered. Suddenly, it was simple between them. Has Mallika had her medicines? Did she sleep? Should we take her out to the park after a week? What did she eat? You rest, I'll sit with her. A daily malish will do her good. He slept downstairs, she slept upstairs with Mallika. They ate together, mostly in silence, both exhausted. They took turns sitting upstairs with Mallika. He had paid the doctor, and she assumed he would continue to do so. He had said he would deposit a cheque into her account before he left. She hadn't had to ask him for money. He wore his collected demeanour, but she was aware of the deep distress beneath it.

She had asked Mallika only one question. 'Is it alright if Karan keeps you company? You can say no if you don't want him.' When Mallika said yes, she knew it was true because, suddenly, she saw that Mallika no longer had it in her to pretend. Pretence required... strength?

No, not strength; only truth required strength. Pretence required energy. Unending energy. Energy that you eventually ran out of.

As she sat next to Mallika's bed, staring unseeingly at her book, it hit her how much of Mallika's life had gone towards that pretence after Karan's return. The pretence of hiding her true feelings. Padma had, of course, pretended too, but she had only had to pretend he was a family friend, and then that he was her husband. But Mallika had put up a front before her mother *and* father, as well as the neighbours, because she hadn't wanted to hurt either of them.

Hadn't Mallika done this with regards to Madhav too?

One day, in the mood for something light and wholesome, Padma had gone to Mallika's room to browse through her bookshelf. RK Narayan's *Swami and Friends* – just the kind of book she was in the mood to reread – was on the topmost shelf, so she dragged a chair to the bookshelf. When she stepped down, she found there was something in the book.

Two letters. One was her own letter, addressed to Madhav, which she had given Mallika to post some time ago. It was sealed. The other was a letter from Madhav, addressed to Mallika. This had been read. She opened it.

Om
Dear Mallika,

I marvel at how well your mother has trained you. You write to me every month, with every appearance of affection and duty. This has no doubt been prompted by your mother in the hope that I will start doing what she has so cleverly persuaded our own widowed mother to do all these years – send her vast sums of money. It is also possible that you have been writing to me unprompted. After all, the apple does not fall far from the tree. But I am not the simpleton that our mother is. You will get nothing from me. I presume that now, knowing that there will be no monetary benefits to your clever but tedious six-weekly exercise, you will stop writing to me.

If I have written to you all these years, it is because I was deceived. I have been deceived before. Many years ago, your mother betrayed our parents in the most shameless manner. Since then, for years, unbeknownst to me, she has continued sucking the blood of our poor, widowed mother. I have only just discovered her perfidy. I should have known that a leopard does not change its spots.

I asked myself how I could have been so deceived. He who sees all and hears all, the One with a compassionate heart, the One about whom you are distressingly ignorant, gave me the answer, as He so often does these days, for just as I have taken Him into my heart, so has He taken me into His. His answer is this: There is no room for dishonesty when you are on the Path. All is revealed as it is. The Seeker must look at everything unflinchingly. And so I have looked unflinchingly at my foolishness and gullibility. If I have been saved from myself, it is all due to His infinite mercy and compassion.
Affly,
Your uncle, Madhav
Om

She had asked Mallika why she had kept silent.

'I couldn't tell you, Ma – it made me feel ill,' Mallika had answered. 'It still does.'

Padma never wrote to Madhav after that.

She told Dr Roy about this, and about how Mallika kept a lot to herself, at great cost to herself.

'Do you think she was hiding something from you before her breakdown?' the doctor asked.

She shook her head.

'A boyfriend?'

She shook her head again. 'She's secretive, but she isn't deceptive.'

The doctor was making notes.

'She's introverted,' Karan said.

'And shy.'

'She has excellent friends,' Karan said.

'Tell me about her friends.'

She told the doctor about Prabha, Gauri, and Mahima. About Randhir. She didn't speak to him about her dreams of their marriage; she couldn't, not in Karan's presence.

'She said something about two mothers. She said to ask you.'

She and Karan were both silent. In unspoken agreement, they had let the doctor assume the three of them were a family.

Exhaustion hit her. 'You tell him,' she said to Karan.

For a moment, there was no response from him. Then: 'Mallika was raised by Padma and her sister, Shanta. Both women are mothers to her.'

Padma sat back against her chair, feeling the tiredness in every limb.

Karan went on, 'I was married to someone else. I didn't know Padma was expecting my child.'

'Why?' Dr Roy asked.

The crux of it all.

The silence grew.

'I didn't get Padma's letter telling me she was pregnant.'

Even *now*. Even *now*, he was exonerating his bloody mother.

'*Letters*. I wrote him several. His mother read them and hid them,' she said.

Dr Roy looked at Karan with a question in his eyes.

'Why is this relevant?' Karan asked.

'Because your daughter is very ill. All this could well be part of it.'

'*This?*'

'Do you believe such a thing could leave her unaffected?'

'Not at all. But Mallika fell ill two weeks ago. This is an old story.'

'And a relevant one. It must have impacted Mallika deeply.'

'Ask him why he didn't marry me,' she said.

Karan threw her a glance of blazing anger. She stared at him in disbelief. Dr Roy took it all in.

Karan said, through his teeth, 'My marriage happened the day I returned from Delhi at the end of college.'

'You mean… the marriage ceremony?' Dr Roy asked, astounded.

Karan nodded.

'And… You didn't know?'

He gave a brief shake of his head.

He was being given another chance. To finally, in her presence, say the words that she had been waiting for forever: My mother did it.

'How come?' Dr Roy asked.

'None of this is relevant to Mallika's illness.'

Padma said, 'His mother arranged the marriage for the day of his return to Lucknow and lied to him, saying she'd sent him a telegram about it. She said his marriage to… Prema was based on a long-standing understanding with the bride's family. She read the letters I wrote about my pregnancy and hid them. I never heard from him. He never contacted me. My father disowned me, and my sister and her husband took me in. I had the baby and got a job as a lecturer in Delhi. The story was that I was a widow, and that was the story Mallika knew. My sister came to Delhi several times a year to help me bring up Mallika. When she was twelve-and-a-half, Karan found out he had a child and came back into our lives. And all of it *is* relevant to Mallika's health, because she was deeply affected. She used to get terrible migraines when he first he came back. She hid that from us. She never talks about it, even now.'

Dr Roy was looking stunned. 'I see.'

'And now the lie is that we're married.'

That was it, she thought as they drove back home. For today, that was all.

But it wasn't. As she was falling into an exhausted sleep that afternoon, there was a knock on her bedroom door.

It was Karan. The mask he always wore had fallen off, and his entire face was ablaze. He shut the door behind him, pointing silently upstairs. He didn't want Mallika to hear. Standing beside the door, he said in a low voice, 'What was the need to discuss our private affairs with the doctor?'

She sat up in bed, dazed with exhaustion.

'Please refrain from washing our dirty linen in public.'

He turned to go.

'I'll wash every piece of dirty linen with the doctor, including your precious mother's pristine underclothes.'

He turned towards her. For some strange reason, she couldn't see him properly; it was as though she were addressing his moving reflection in water.

'I'm going to tell the doctor every single thing that's affected Mallika. And if you don't want to hear it, then go back to Lucknow. Just make sure to send money into my bank account every month for the doctor, medicines, and transport.'

She lay down again and closed her eyes. When she opened them a few minutes later, thinking, *If only I had slept*, she saw from the tableside clock that an hour and a half had passed.

And she had felt compassion for him! Just because he was suffering for Mallika! Well, she was suffering for Mallika too. That compassion could go into the rubbish bin. She had thought, when he came this time, that there were the beginnings of harmony and peace between them, because they both had Mallika's interests at heart, and nothing mattered more than that. Well, clearly his bloody mother mattered more than that. An insistent voice inside her kept telling her that what had happened to Mallika was an accumulation of painful experiences combined with an inability to speak of them. The doctor needed to know the truth of everything that had affected Mallika. The silence that Karan was demanding of her was a lie. She wouldn't give him that silence. The lies she *had* to live were enough. How could Karan think that the truth about their lives wasn't relevant to Mallika's life? How dare he demand silence to save his bloody mother's face!

She had the words now. She would tell him.

The doorbell rang.

Karan was sitting at the dining table, writing a letter. He didn't look up when she went to open the front door.

It was Gopal, the scooterwalla – Jalpari's father.

'Namaste, Teacher-ji.' Tears were streaming down his cheek.

'Gopal! What has happened? Come inside.'

'Namaste, Sahib,' he said to Karan, entering.

'Namaste.'

'Teacher-ji, Jalpari was playing with her friends in our basti. Two men stopped their car and caught her and took her away. Bas, she's gone. After that, we have not seen her.'

He wiped his face with his sleeve.

'*When?*'

'January.'

'But... it is May now!'

'Teacher-ji, because all three times I came to you, you were not at home.'

He had gone to the police the very day it happened and registered a report. They did nothing. Again and again, he went to them. 'Yes,' they said. 'We are investigating.' All lies. He even gave them money, but he had so little to give.

'I will come with you to the police station,' she said. 'Just wait five minutes.'

He was very grateful, but that would not make any difference. She must not feel bad that he was saying this, but what respect did the police have for a teacher? Now, if she had been a big sahib in the government who knew the police commissioner, or if she had been a powerful MP, or a crony of Sanjay Gandhi, or if she had been a businessman with enough money to bribe them, then they would have looked at the case. She was a good woman, but in this world, what worth did goodness have? Perhaps God knew its worth. But where God lived and where the rest of them lived were two different worlds.

'I will come with you to the police station,' Karan said, getting up.

'That is why I came here, Sahib. You are a big sahib. The police, they will listen to you.'

Karan and Gopal went out together.

Padma's legs were trembling. Slowly, she went upstairs to Mallika's room.

Karan came back from the police station. All he said was, 'It doesn't look good.'

A few days later, she got Amma's letter.

She would come to Delhi with Shanta as soon as Shanta was stronger, Amma wrote. But in the meantime, here was the name and address of Kavya, a woman who worked on those who suffered illnesses of the mind as well as other illnesses. She knew her well and trusted her. Padma should take Mallika to Kavya. Not as a substitute for the doctor, but in addition. God had given Kavya the power to heal the spirit. Illnesses of the mind were ultimately illnesses of the spirit. There was no need to tell Mallika's father; that would cause conflict. Mallika would sense the conflict even if it were unexpressed, and that was bad for her. Therefore they should go to Kavya after Mallika's father left. The child would get better. She was sure of it. She sent her love and blessings.

'I'll *never* pray,' Padma had said more than once to Shantacca.

But that time when Mallika had fallen into a deep sleep after swallowing the Calmpose, she had thought Mallika was dying. She had put her hands on Mallika's body and prayed and prayed.

'I'll *never* believe in those hocus-pocus people who claim to heal you, what utter rubbish!' she had said several times.

She had accepted the Phuknewalla with relief and gratitude.

'I'll *never* take your money, keep your damn money!' she had said to Karan.

And yet here she was.

The moment you uttered the word 'never,' it pretended to do your bidding but quietly hid. Then, with infinite patience, it waited for the time to come when you were desperate. Not merely desperate. It waited for the moment you were so desperate that if someone had said, 'You'll get what you want if you stand on your head,' you'd stand on your head. That was when your 'never' emerged gleefully and stood in plain sight as you did all the things you'd scorned, all the things you'd sworn you wouldn't do.

She would go to this healing woman tomorrow. Find out about her, get a sense of what she was like, see if she seemed trustworthy. And if she appeared genuine, then after Karan left, she would take Mallika to her.

And she would not say 'never' ever again.

Mallika: Deadness, my saviour

1976

As children, Prabha, Gauri, Mahima, and I used to act out 'Mad Mrs Moitra.' Mrs Moitra, one of our neighbours, was mad because she was the only woman we knew who had left her husband. Her husband then took away their son, her parents would have nothing to do with her, and after that, she went crazier. We would see her going to the market, muttering to herself, and she sometimes didn't comb her hair. She lived alone, worked in a bank, didn't care that no one befriended her, and sat in her veranda on weekends painting abstract paintings. Gauri used to say that, late at night, especially when there was a full moon, Mrs Moitra tore her hair and screamed and threw herself on the ground. 'Mad Mrs Moitra' was the crème de la crème of performances, and Gauri and I excelled in this role. We would unplait our hair and pull at it, shrieking, shuddering, and wailing. Prabha and Mahima acted as the affronted neighbours who urged the mad woman towards sanity with sermons, scoldings, and threats. The fact that our mothers had sternly forbidden us to play the game after Madhu Aunty caught us at it one day gave it even more allure.

Someone must have been watching from above and thinking, *You think mental is funny, do you? Alright, my dear, one day I'll give you a slice of that pie, and then you'll know.*

The psychiatrist asked me to lie down on the sofa. I answered his questions, mostly with a 'yes' or a 'no.' Sometimes he wanted more than that. Then, with tremendous effort, I managed a sentence. Between sentences, I closed my eyes and rested, because each one was like running a marathon.

'Take your time,' he said gently. His soft voice, with its American drawl, soothed me.

He asked me what physical activities I could do. I said, 'None.' I couldn't tell him that the exhaustion was so deep that it was in my very bones, in my very marrow. Or that normal, daily activities were impossible. He asked me what feelings I had inside me. I said, 'None.' Despair? Anger? Worry? Fear?

I shook my head in response to each. I neither had the comprehension nor the words to explain that I had felt all of that and more before my collapse, but that when I had descended into my illness, I had swung from feeling too much to the other end of the spectrum, where I didn't feel anything at all. That all emotions had abandoned my heart, all thoughts had fled from my brain, and that my very spirit had dissipated like vapour. He asked me if I liked to read. I said, 'Not now.' He asked me why. I said, 'Can't absorb.' He asked if I had any appetite. I shook my head. He asked how much I slept at night. I said, 'About two hours.' And in the day? 'No,' I said. He asked what I was thinking when I was awake at night. I said, 'Nothing.'

'You're awake every night with no thoughts?' he asked.

I nodded.

He asked if I had ever felt suicidal.

I shook my head.

'Never?' he asked, and I said truthfully, 'Never.'

'Are you close to your parents?'

I nodded.

'Do you have good friends?'

I nodded.

He asked how I did in school and college. I said, 'Well.' But that wasn't true. I had not done well this time. I would fail my second-year exams.

'Can't talk,' I said.

He asked if he had my permission to speak to my parents.

'Yes.'

I felt battered by the effort of answering his questions. I heard his voice, Ma's, Karan's. But I had no idea what they were saying, even though I wasn't asleep. I wasn't awake either. I didn't know what I was.

After that, Karan drove us home. I had a small lunch, took the first dose of my medicine, got into bed, and closed my eyes. Later that night, Ma gave me my sleeping pill and lay in bed with me.

'My love, I've told everyone you have TB, so don't worry, no one will come home or ask questions.'

I nodded, but I wasn't worrying because I had no thoughts.

That night, after the sleeping pill, I slept a little for the first time.

One day ran into another, and every day was the same. I lay in bed, but I didn't sleep. The fan whirred noisily above my head. Randhir sent me his transistor, which Ma plugged into my room. Ma put on In the Groove at eight-thirty in the morning, then Radio Ceylon and All India Radio so I could listen to North Indian classical music. As long as no one asked me questions, their voices were comforting. Ma sleeping with me every night was comforting. Comfort was the only feeling I was aware of. Every other day, before my bath, Ayah-ji gave me a mustard oil malish, her callused fingers hard and loving against my arms, legs, back, and neck. Once a week, Ma massaged my hair with coconut oil before my head bath. Ma got me books in the hope that I would read them. They made me eat small portions every few hours. Food tasted like nothing.

Karan and Ma took me every week to the psychiatrist. I knew that I had a major depressive disorder, though that made no sense, because I wasn't sad. I was... Well, I wasn't anything.

He wanted to know about my concussion. I shook my head. He asked about my three friends and Randhir. I uttered my longest sentence. 'After my mothers, I'm closest to them.'

'Your *mothers*?'

That made me even more tired. 'Ask them.'

Every morning, after my bed tea and biscuits, Karan and Ma began taking me to a park in the colony a mile from ours where no one knew us. Anu Aunty, who was plucking jasmines in her garden, would wave to me, and so would Madhu Aunty and her husband, who would be having tea in their veranda. I would wave back. Karan drove us to the park. Ma said, 'Sit on the grass, it's good for you.' I would sit on the grass, feel the early morning sun on my body, the breeze against my skin, and look at the gulmohar and mango trees. Ma and Karan would walk slowly up and down on the lawn. After an hour, they'd drive me back home.

And so, a month passed. The medicines were working, because now I could get out of bed on my own and didn't need to sit on the stool in the bathroom when I had my bath. I could comb and plait my hair. I could walk down the stairs once a day to eat a meal.

I told Dr Roy that I had been worried about everything before my collapse; every small thing had become big in my mind. That my thoughts wouldn't stop. But I didn't speak about Mahima, or about Randhir losing his temper with me, or about how I'd ended up in the clinic and the craziness of that Charu-like episode.

At home, it was simple to do whatever I was told to do. When Karan said, 'Come, now eat this, Mallika,' I would eat it, though I had no appetite, and when he said, 'Come, let's sit on the balcony,' I would do that. When Ayah-ji said she was going to take out my nazar every morning, I sat back in bed and let her circle my head several times, clutching red chilis, garlic, and rye in her fist, extracting whatever evil had befallen me. Then Ayah-ji would go downstairs and throw it all into the hot tawa and the smell of burning chilis would make the entire household cough.

'How is Shantamama?' I asked Ma.

'*Much* better, almost normal.'

Karan left. He kissed my head and said he would be back soon. And as soon as he left – in fact, the very next day – Ma asked me to get ready, so I did. Then Ayah-ji got us a scooter, and we went to see a lady my mother called Kavya.

That day, I didn't notice how lovely-looking she was, because just like some people made the most of themselves, she made the least of herself. Her smile was warm. She asked me to call her 'Masi.' I went into another room and lay down on the bed. Masi put her hands under my head. I felt heat from her hands fill my head. By the time Masi had her hands on my heart, I was asleep. When I got up, Ma and Masi were sitting next to me, talking in low tones.

During my third session with Masi, she said, 'Beti, something I have to tell you.'

I turned on my side and looked at her.

'This message came for you: don't force yourself to do anything you don't wish to do. Flow like water, or else you will burn like fire.'

I nodded. I had no idea what she meant.

'The other message I got is that the doctor you are going to, he is a good man. He is wise and has a pure heart. Do not stop going to him. Do not stop the medicines.'

This, I understood.

I began sleeping better and the doctor cut down the dosage of the sleeping pill. I spoke a sentence or two more. Food smelled and tasted better.

Prabha came home for the summer holidays, and after that, Mahima came, but Ma said they couldn't see me till I got better.

Once my friends left the colony, Ma and I began going for short walks at six a.m. At first, I couldn't walk for more than five minutes. But every day I walked for a few minutes more, until I was walking for almost fifteen minutes. Not too many people were up and about in the mornings, so I didn't have to engage in conversation. Talking was more tiring than walking.

Anu Aunty and Madhu Aunty were coming home to see Ma regularly, and since I was now sitting in the veranda and no longer contagious with TB, they sat with me and chatted. Ma answered their questions. They didn't ask me much because they saw how weak I was.

I had heard Ma telling Dr Roy how I couldn't go back to college in my state. But taking a year off college was unheard of. No one ever did such a thing; it was like taking a year off from your job – it was inconceivable. You resigned from your job because you had another, better job, not for any other reason. It was the kind of thing people in America and Europe did; you didn't take that kind of time off in India unless you were dead.

Now, with one week left until college reopened, I said, 'Ma, I can go back to college.'

It was the first time I had said I would do anything. Ma said, 'You don't have to, love. I've found out. You can get medical leave.'

'I'm better.'

'You can't read.'

'From today, I'll read one page every day.'

'Alright,' Ma said, reluctantly.

I took out Richmal Crompton's *William* from my bookshelf and slowly began rereading it, sentence by sentence. After one page, my brain couldn't absorb any more, so I put it aside. But the following day, I read one page in the morning, and one in the afternoon. 'Don't tire your brain,' Ma warned me.

I told Dr Roy I wanted to go back to college. 'I read one page the day before. Two pages yesterday.'

He reflected on this.

'My mother teaches English literature. She can help me.'

'Alright. But take it easy.'

I nodded. Everyone took it easy in college. No one studied till the end of the year.

I had lost almost seven kilos. Ma was stuffing me with vitamins, iron, and chicken soup. Anu Aunty gave me a bottle of Drakshasava, which she said was excellent for weakness. Madhu Aunty made me pinne ki laddoo, which was usually given only to pregnant women; it was full of dry fruits and nuts. She said she had made it for Anu Aunty when she was pregnant. I had both every day.

A day before college began, Karan was back home with us. I felt a tug of happiness to see him. He had taken another month's leave so that he could drop me to college and pick me up, so I didn't have to travel by bus. He laughed and said he had a year's leave accumulated. It was nice to see him laughing. I saw Ma looking at him too.

I had thought I would fail my second year exams, but I had passed with the lowest second division, just fifty percent. Back at college, it required enormous effort to focus on the lectures. At home, I would study for half an hour every day after tea, and then my brain switched off. At night, I took my sleeping pill and slept by nine. In college, I had always been quiet, but now I was utterly silent. 'Poor you, you've become so weak and thin after your TB,' one of my classmates said to me. Other than that, they left me alone. Between classes, I sat in the library, sometimes putting my arms on the table, laying my head on them, and closing my eyes. After classes, I would go outside, and Karan would be waiting for me in his car with a flask of cold lime juice.

Karan said that, after he left, I should take a scooter to college every morning. Every morning? I thought, without comprehension. 'I've put money in your mother's account for it.' He also said that, three times a week, Randhir would pick me up after classes. Randhir had insisted.

As soon as Karan left, Ma took me back for the sessions with Masi. I took a scooter to college every morning, and Randhir picked me up thrice a week. We worked out our timetables so I knew approximately when he would come pick me up. I carried a mirrorwork bag in which Ayah-ji packed a lunch of parathas and sabji, biscuits to snack on, a flask of lassi, and another of lime juice. In between and after classes, I forced myself to eat and drink as much as my stomach could hold. Afterwards, I sat in the library. At the appointed time, I went outside, where Randhir would be waiting for me, sitting on his motorcycle, smoking.

'That chap you're going around with, he's *gorgeous*,' one of my classmates sighed.

'I'm not going around with him.'

'Come *on*, Mallika! Who d'you think you're trying to fool?'

Twice a week, I took scooters back home. But many didn't want to go in my direction, and sometimes the wait for a scooter took an hour. Though I always carried an umbrella, I would find myself wilting in the heat, and when I reached home, I would collapse in bed.

Within a week of Karan's departure, Shantamama and Ajji came. They hugged and kissed me, and didn't ask me a single question. Shantamama took Ma's place and slept with me every night.

From time to time, I would hear Ma and Shantamama talking:

'Padma, do you think she is like this because of her concussion?'

'But the psychiatrist said it has nothing to do with the concussion, Shantacca.'

'Suppose the concussion has done something to her head?'

'Shantacca, I beg of you, please stop it.'

'And she's also gone and lost her magenta silk saree, her maroon sweater, *and* her maroon shawl. Left them all in a packet on the bus, Ayah-ji said.'

'Shantacca, don't go on about it. There's enough we have to worry about without that.'

'But her purple batik saree has also disappeared. Could the dhobi have stolen it?'

'Impossible. He's been with us for ten years. It'll turn up, Shantacca.'

'Padma, haven't you heard the saying that a dhobi's wife is the best-dressed woman in the neighbourhood?'

Dr Roy and I were talking somewhat more.

In one of our sessions, he said, 'One of the things that will help you get better is being yourself.'

I looked at him without understanding.

'It's alright to be shy.'

No one had said such a thing to me before. In fact, they had said quite the contrary.

'I was shy at your age. It's quite a disability for a man.'

He, shy? He looked so self-assured, so much at ease in himself!

'You won't feel so out of place if you accept yourself.'

I found myself wrestling with what this meant. I gave up.

'Getting better doesn't mean trying to be like other people. Sometimes it means trying to be like yourself.'

I took out my red diary and pen from my handbag, opened the book to a fresh page, and wrote down what Dr Roy had said. Then I looked up.

He smiled. 'There's no need to put pressure on yourself about anything. Not college, or parental expectations, or the expectations of friends, other family, neighbours. Not even your own expectations of yourself. Do what you *can* do. Not what you feel you *should* do.'

I wrote it down. How was that possible?

'Stop pretending.'

'Pretending?' Exhaustion hit me. 'I *never* pretend.'

He said, 'That's not what I meant. You're tired. We'll talk about it next time.'

When I went home, Ma gave me lunch and I got into bed. I was aware of a truth glimmering at the edges of my being, a truth that was too big for me to embrace. It made me feel my head would burst.

It was quite funny that Dr Roy had asked me, that very first day, if I ever felt suicidal. Feeling suicidal meant having thoughts. It meant having feelings. It meant such utter despair that you jumped from a high building, threw yourself into a river when you couldn't swim, or cut your wrists. It meant having thoughts, the ability to plan it out to the last detail, days and weeks before you did it; it meant knowing how to tie the knot that would snap your neck when you kicked off the chair, knowing what pills to take and how many, and how to buy a whole lot without a prescription and without the chemist getting suspicious. And then, when everything was in place, doing it. I neither had the despair nor the mental capacity to think or plan; I had travelled to a space beyond emotion and thought.

As I slowly emerged from this place, I found myself unable to return to my old self, the self that had felt everything so keenly. Everything was muted. What a relief! It was this relief that I felt more deeply than any other feeling. It was a relief not to care. Not to care whether I talked or not – and when I did speak, not to agonize endlessly about what I had said. It was a relief not to think. Dos and don'ts, shoulds and shouldn'ts, were no longer daily incantations in my mind. There was only one thing I knew I had to do. I had to study.

That meant understanding what I was reading. It was like learning to walk again, one step, two steps, several steps. Slowly and laboriously, I began to read again, and, very slowly, to absorb what I was reading. 'The minute you can't absorb anything, stop,' Ma told me. 'Don't tax your brain.' I only read my textbooks. Ma would sit with me every day before her children came for tutoring and discuss my books with me. Listening to her was better than reading any literary criticism. She did this slowly and patiently every single day.

I stopped castigating myself for things beyond my control, as I had been prone to do. I didn't feel bad about not talking in college. I wasn't thinking obsessively about how much my illness was costing my mother and Karan. I wasn't panicking about how we would manage without the extra income that I earned by tutoring. The Hindi word 'himmat' explained it best: I didn't have the himmat – the strength, the capacity – for such preoccupations. Thinking about these things would have been tantamount to walking with two broken legs.

After I came back from college, I would rest, then study for an hour. On Saturdays, I put in an hour in the morning. No studying on Sundays. Ma would not let me. It still put me ahead of everyone in class because no one studied consistently in college, not even Randhir – it just wasn't done. I was still taking the antidepressants and a lower dose of the sleep medicine. The migraines, which had still come occasionally before my illness, had now disappeared. It was as though the illness had pushed them out of my body along with everything else.

Randhir and I went for a walk one evening, and I asked him, 'What makes you happiest?'

He smiled at me. 'Writing. I write stories. Sometimes poetry.'

That was how easily he finally told me. But I didn't know what to say.

A scooter stopped next to us. It was Jalpari's father's. 'Namaste, didi, kaise ho, tabyat theek hai?' he asked.

I told him I was well. 'How is Jalpari?'

Next to me, I felt Randhir stiffen.

Gopal looked at me, his eyes filling with tears. 'Your mother did not tell you?'

My heart stopped.

'She was playing with her friends in our basti in early January. Two men stopped their car and caught hold of her and took her away. After that, we have not seen her.'

He wiped his face with his sleeve.

January? But this was August.

'Your mother said that she would tell you when you got better.'

Dumbly, I shook my head. I looked at Randhir. He looked as though he'd stopped breathing.

I found the words. 'My father will help. He knows people. I will talk to him.'

'Didi, he helped me. But it was too late, Didi. It was too late.'

I stood mutely next to him at the side of the street.

'Accha, didi, I will go then?' He started the scooter and drove away.

I couldn't move from where I stood. I was having difficulty breathing.

'Come, sit,' Randhir said, shepherding me to the parapet.

I sat.

'Breathe. Slowly. Breathe.'

For five minutes, I breathed in and out.

Then Randhir told me that Ma had meant to tell me in December, after the term was over and when I was better. Karan had gone with Gopal to the police station several times and had later spoken to someone he knew in the Indian Police Service. But it was a dead end.

Randhir walked me home.

I went upstairs. Downstairs, I could hear Randhir talking to my mothers and grandmother. I closed my eyes and didn't open them till my mothers came upstairs with soup. They didn't ask me any questions but sat by my side as I drank it.

I was awake most of the night despite the sleeping pill, despite Shantamama's comforting presence sleeping next to me. My tears were far away. My body felt battered, as though it could feel the pain, but my heart could not. As though it understood that my heart could not withstand the assault of emotions. As though my body, like a mother, had said, 'I will take it, give it to me.' So my heart, my body's child, gave away its pain, and after that, it didn't feel very much at all.

By the time classes got over the next day and I stepped outside the college gates, my head felt funny.

It was Arnav who was there, not Randhir, sitting on his bike and smoking.

He waved, got off, and came towards me. 'I'm taking you home today, Randhir's bike's giving him trouble.'

'Thank you.'

'Thing is, I've forgotten a book in the hostel. Do you mind if we go back to IIT for a couple of minutes, and then we can go straight home?'

'Of course.'

We walked to the bike.

'Hop on, and hold onto me, otherwise you'll fall off in your saree.' He put on his helmet.

I got on, I held on, and he drove to IIT. By the time we reached his hostel, that old exhaustion had me in its grip. I went inside with him, and he asked me to sit in the lobby while he sprinted upstairs to his room. Soon, he came sprinting down.

'Mallika, I can't find the book, I think someone's borrowed it. Can you hang on a few minutes more, I'll – what's the matter?'

'I have to lie down,' I said.

'Shit, I'm sorry – I'll take you home right now,' Arnav said.

'I have to lie down now,' I said.

'Can you walk upstairs?'

I nodded.

'Hold on,' he said, extending his arm.

I held onto his arm, and we went upstairs to his room. There was no space in my head for niceties. I didn't ask his permission; I took off my sandals and lay down on his bed and closed my eyes. A couple of minutes later, he asked me to sit up for a minute, and I managed. He gave me a glass of water. I drank it and lay down again. I felt him cover me. The bed smelt of him.

'Mallika, should I get a doctor?'

'No. Just have to rest.'

I felt his hand on my forehead, and then on my hair. How utterly familiar and beloved it felt.

I fell asleep.

When I opened my eyes, a pretty girl sat next to me. She looked familiar.

'Awake finally?'

I nodded. My head was feeling better. I looked at my watch. I'd slept for *two* hours.

'Here,' she said, giving me a glass of water.

'Thank you.' I drank the entire glass and put it on the desk.

Who was she? Where was Arnav?

I lay down again. If Ma was at home, she'd be worried I wasn't back yet.

'I'm Mohini. I've seen you before somewhere.'

Now I remembered. Mohini was in JNU too; we'd seen each other in Gauri's hostel. 'I'm Gauri's friend. Mallika.'

'Oh, yes, I remember.'

'Where's Arnav?'

'Gone off to minister to your needs,' she said, laughing. 'Are you sleeping with him?'

I was too worn out to be shocked. I shook my head. I heard myself saying, 'And you?'

'Off and on.'

Off and on?

'I already have someone. We're getting married after college.'

I gave this thought, but to no avail.

'It's boring having sex with just one person. You know.'

I didn't know, but now I did.

'Anyway, he knows about him,' she said.

'Who knows about whom?' I asked.

'*Mine* knows about Arnav. We have an open relationship.'

I looked at her enquiringly.

'Meaning we both sleep with other people, but we tell each other.'

'Oh,' I said, trying to wrap my head around this.

'But Arnav doesn't know about *him*. Because if Arnav knew, then he wouldn't sleep with me. He's like that only. You know.'

I didn't, but now I did.

'First, when I saw you here, I thought he was sleeping with you.'

'No, no.'

'That's what he said: "No-no, no way, are you crazy?"'

I felt a slight tingling of indignation. Crazy? Unlikely, yes, but why crazy?

'Not that I minded – I mean, I'm not a hypocrite. I said, "Well, she's in your bed." He said, "It's nothing of the sort; she's not well," and then he told me what happened. Then he said he was going to get some samosas for you, and did I want any, and could I stay with you because he didn't want to leave you alone. He said if you woke up to give you water, and off he went. And here I am!'

'Thanks so much, Mohini.'

'You're welcome. You're Randhir's friend, aren't you?'

I nodded. 'You know Randhir?'

She laughed. 'You can't know one without knowing the other!'

I smiled. That was true.

She said hopefully, 'Not sleeping with Randhir either?'

'He's my friend.'

'So what! He's gorgeous. I'd jump into bed with him if I had a chance.'

'Try it, then.' Mohini was cheering me up.

'I did, yar. I tried to kiss him at the IIT festival, but he wasn't having it!'

'Well, he wouldn't with Arnav's... You know, with Arnav's...'

'Oh, god, I'm not Arnav's anything.'

'He isn't in love with you?'

She laughed as though this was the funniest thing she'd heard.

I sat up in bed and put the pillow behind me, against the wall.

'I had a threesome once,' she said.

'Oh?'

'I did it with two guys.'

'How?'

'What d'you mean, "how?"'

'I mean... Who does what, with whom?'

'You're *so* funny! See, one thing you *have* to know about guys –'

Arnav came into the room with a greasy newspaper tied up with string, a bottle of ketchup, and paper plates.

'You're looking better,' he said.

'I am.' Although I wished he'd come five minutes later.

'We've had a *very* interesting conversation!' Mohini said.

Arnav threw me a quick glance, then handed us our samosas – two each. He poured us a generous dollop of ketchup.

I was hungry. We all were. For a few minutes, we didn't speak.

'Do you have an allergy?' I asked Arnav, noticing a mark on the side of his neck.

'No. Why?'

'That mark on the side of your neck. It looks exactly like an allergy I had after my concussion.'

Arnav touched the side of his neck and froze.

Mohini looked at him and burst into peals of laughter.

Arnav glanced at his watch.

Mohini looked at hers and leapt up. 'Shit. I'm late. Better run. Mallika, see you. Bye, Arnav – watch that allergy of yours!' She was still laughing as she rushed out of the room.

Suddenly, the atmosphere in the room was taut. I swung my legs out of the bed.

'Feeling better?'

I nodded. He threw a book into his backpack. Something was poking me. I took it out from under me. A long silver earring.

'We can take a scooter back home if you prefer,' he said, zipping up his backpack.

'No, we'll go on your bike.' I'd have preferred the scooter, but I didn't have enough money and he'd end up paying for it, and suppose he didn't take the money back later?

He said abruptly, 'What's that on your lap?'

I looked at my lap. It was the earring. 'I think it's Mohini's. I found it in your bed.'

Then I realized what I'd said.

He turned away from me, unzipped his backpack, and said, 'What were you saying about an allergy you had?'

'After my concussion,' I said, getting up.

'What happened?'

'Just these marks, like yours, they went away.'

He zipped up his backpack, then turned and saw my face. 'What's the matter?'

'Tired.' I picked up my bag of books.

Why was he looking so tense?

'I can teach you some yogic breathing. It really helps with tiredness,' he said.

I'd rather he took me in his arms, but if it had to be yogic breathing, so be it.

He opened his cupboard and took out a hand towel. He handed it to me. 'You have kajal all over your face.'

I wiped my face thoroughly, leaving black streaks on his towel. I handed it back. 'Thank you.'

'You've spread it over your face again,' he said, a little roughly.

'That's OK.'

He poured water over the other side of the towel and handed it to me. 'You can't go out of my room with kajal all over your face,' he said.

'Why not?' I took it from him and wiped my face thoroughly.

'Mallika, use your –' He stopped.

'Use my brain? It isn't working.' I gave the towel back to him. 'Do your yogic breathing.'

'What?'

'You're the one who's all tense and hassled, not me.'

He picked up my wooden hairpin from his bed and gave it to me. I gathered my hair, wound it up, and dug the hairpin into my bun

'Why are you so run-down?'

'The TB, the medicines, all that.'

'How d'you manage going to college and back in this state?'

'I take a scooter in the mornings. Randhir picks me up thrice a week.' I sat down on the chair by his desk and closed my eyes, exhausted again.

A minute later, when I opened my eyes, he was sitting on the side of his bed, elbows on thighs, hands clasped, looking at me with an expression that puzzled me. Did he think I was going to cry? I knew men hated to see women cry. Not because it hurt them; that only happened in Mills & Boon romances, in which the Hero took the Heroine into his arms and kissed away her tears – after all, beneath his hard exterior beat a tender heart. But in real life, men were, at their best, embarrassed and helpless in the face of tears, and, at their worst – as Shantamama said – they were irritated or immune. 'Nothing worse than immune,' Shantamama had warned me in dire tones. Perhaps Arnav fell into the first category – the embarrassed. 'Immune,' Shantamama had said, 'comes after marriage.'

Arnav put out his hand.

I looked at it, puzzled, and he said, 'The earring.'

'Oh.' It was in my hand; I'd been fiddling with it.

I dropped it into his palm, and he threw it, with unerring aim, into a bowl on his desk.

'I'm… sorry.' He said it as though he were choking on the words.

'For what?'

He got up from the bed and began putting his books into his backpack. 'At least I could have been a friend,' he muttered.

At *least*?

'But we've never been friends,' I said, puzzled.

He stopped in the middle of zipping up his backpack and looked at me.

'So why should you apologize?' I asked.

'We've *never* been friends?'

But how could he think one conversation at a party (however delightful), the incident with the puppy, and his being in Randhir's house when I had the concussion – while completely ignoring me the rest of the time – was *friendship*?

I didn't want to hurt him.

'Thank you for everything, Arnav.'

'OK, I get it. Chalo, let's go.'

Completely confused, I picked up my bag, and we went out of his room.

Ma would be worried sick.

'I phoned Madhu Aunty. She said she'd tell your mother you were coming home late.'

I gaped at him. Was he reading my mind? 'Thank you.'

When we reached home, my mothers and grandmother were sitting at the dining table, having tea with Randhir. Arnav said his namastes, and we joined them at the table.

'I was getting worried,' Ma said. 'Mallika, go upstairs and rest. Arnav, tea?'

'Thank you, Aunty, I'd love some.'

'I've rested, Ma. I don't need to lie down.'

'Mallika was feeling very unwell, so she slept in my room for a couple of hours,' Arnav said, as though he had to get it off his chest right away.

Ma tried to hide her shock. Shantamama didn't even try. There was a slight ripple in Ajji's calm demeanour. Randhir looked startled.

'He had to pick up a book from his hostel before coming home, but by the time we reached, I wasn't feeling well,' I explained.

I sat back in my chair. Ayah-ji brought tea. Shantamama, in recovering from her shock, recovered her hospitality, and cut a few more slices of cake. The boys were talking to my grandmother and mothers. Their words drifted around me comfortingly.

'So that'll work, no, Mallika?' Randhir said.

I looked at him blankly.

'Darling, you dream too much,' Shantamama said.

Arnav smiled at me.

Randhir repeated himself, 'I'll continue picking you up three afternoons a week, and Arnav will pick you up the other two days.'

I looked at Arnav.

'Yeah, absolutely,' he said.

'So good of you, Arnav,' said Ma.

Arnav looked embarrassed. 'Aunty, it's not a problem.'

'Oh, but you don't have to,' I said, completely taken aback.

'So rude,' Shantamama muttered to me in Kannada. 'No "thank you," even.'

'Thank you so much, Arnav, but there's no need.'

'There *is* a need, that's why he's doing it,' Randhir said.

My mothers smiled at him, full of appreciation for his strong-arm tactics.

'Let me do it, Mallika,' Arnav said, as though I were doing him a favour, not the other way around.

'OK. Thank you.' I was overwhelmed.

'It's too much; why does he have to do this?' I wondered as Randhir and I walked to the market the next evening.

'Because he's a good friend, that's why.'

'Not mine.'

'Yours, mine, it doesn't matter, it's all the same.'

'Such a Punjabi thing to say.'

He looked delighted. 'You already sound like you're getting better.'

So twice a week, Arnav picked me up from college and spent the night at Randhir's. The other three days, Randhir did it. For the entire term. No buses. No bracing myself against probing hands and bodies. No long waits in the afternoon sun for scooters. And no obligatory chit-chatting with Arnav, because I couldn't, and he didn't. Just a 'hi' and a smile from him – the smile that lit up his face, the smile that had once lit up my heart. We barely talked; I was unable to make the effort, and he seemed to take his cue from me.

I hadn't known it was possible for a friendship to grow in mostly silence, but that was what happened. 'The least I could have done was be your friend,' he had said that day in his room, as though he felt it had been incumbent on him to know I was unwell and help me, as though he had let me down, as though he had let himself down. How strange that he would think so, for he had never been my friend. I had always wanted it, but he had never sought it. And as he picked me up from college and dropped me home over the weeks and months, almost wordlessly, a quiet friendship took root. One that I was sure meant a great deal more to me than to him. Rivulets of happiness trickled into me every time I saw him. Occasionally, the rivulets were streaked with pain. It was no doing of his. Yet it was all his. Unbidden, he had stepped right inside my heart, into the very kernel which held my dearest ones. Now, he was lodged there as surely as the others, yet unlike them, for I knew that their hearts – unlike his – also held me in the same way.

I knew this but didn't feel any of it deeply. I wasn't crippled by shyness. Most of the time, there was a dull numbness inside me. It also extended outside me, like an invisible shield. It was nothing like the deadness that I had lived during the worst of my illness, but it was certainly a distant cousin. The deadness of my illness had saved me, because before my collapse, I had felt too much, too sharply. If I had continued feeling like that, I would have gone mad. But instead of going mad, I'd collapsed. Deadness had saved my life, deadness had swaddled me and suckled me and guarded me ferociously. Deadness had been my saviour. Its cousin now kept guard over me. Now, thoughts and feelings no longer coursed like needles through my blood. I was functioning again. And from some distant place, my thoughts and feelings were rationed to me as though I were suffering from malnutrition: in small, manageable portions.

As the term came to an end, I told Ma I was feeling better and that there was no need for her to sleep with me at night. It was eleven months after Mahima's marriage.

I took out my red diary and finally asked Dr Roy what he had meant by saying that I was pretending.

He said that my mothers, my father, and my grandmother had talked to him a great deal. He spoke of the time during which my father had come back into my life. When I spent the weekends with my father, he said, it had been an enormous strain on me. Yet I had pretended that it wasn't, to my cost. That was what he meant by pretence.

'I *wanted* to get to know him.'

'And he wanted to get to know you too.'

I nodded. Exactly.

'Nonetheless. That's one instance when you didn't express your unhappiness to yourself. I've no doubt there are several more in your life.'

I wrote it down.

'What was I to do?'

'I don't know, Mallika. What I do know is that it's a terrible strain to pretend to be happy when you're not. Over a prolonged period, it can become worse than the cause of the unhappiness.'

I wrote that down too.

'Are you so determined to be a good daughter that you've forgotten what *you* want to do?'

I wrote it down.

'Do you speak your mind?'

'No.'

'Why not?'

I had no answer to this.

'Try to do the things that make *you* happy. There's no need to constantly try to make everyone else happy.'

By now, I was feeling exhausted.

He saw it. 'Alright, Mallika. That's all for today.'

'What do you mean, "don't make others happy, make yourself happy?" I've never heard of such a thing!' Shantamama exclaimed as we sat at the dining table, having tea.

'That's what he said, Shantamama.'

'That's because he's America-returned,' Ma said. 'Americans are like that.'

'Darling, don't mistake me, he's a very nice man,' Shantamama said. 'I like him, and I respect him, and I know he's helped you a lot, and ninety percent of the time, he gives very good advice, and I'm *so* grateful to him, but psychiatrist or not, about happiness he doesn't know a *thing.*'

I couldn't see it at the time, but I was no longer pretending. Being so ill meant that there was no room or energy for pretence. After all, it was only when thoughts preoccupied your head and emotions stabbed your heart that you pretended, because you had to hide them. Perhaps that was what I had been doing – unbeknownst to myself – all my life. But now, I had very few thoughts or feelings, so there was nothing to hide. It took energy to smile if I didn't feel like smiling, and to talk when I didn't feel like talking, so I did neither. Even to reassure my mothers that I was getting better was an effort, so I didn't. The question of persuading myself to do something I didn't want to do didn't arise. The deep imperative to not hurt people by saying no, to not be ungracious, to not be rude, to not bring attention to myself by making a fuss, was no longer an imperative. I no longer battled guilt at my inability to talk, at my enormous-yet-futile efforts to converse whenever conversation was expected, or at the inadequacy I experienced every time I stepped beyond my tight circle of loved ones. In fact, I hadn't even realized how constant and insidious that battle had been, nor how it had throttled me as much as my shyness. As for my shyness, this was viewed as a disability by everyone, and as such had I also seen it. But now, I was no longer thinking about it, apologizing to myself and others about it; I was no longer preoccupied by it at all.

My mothers were the ones pretending for me. They were the ones on the battlefield. Their hearts were torn and bleeding. They were fighting, but no one could know. They were fighting, but no one could see. They had to fight with smiles on their faces and easy words on their lips, and they couldn't show that they bled. Their pretence was for my life; their pretence was both a battle and a prayer.

With what abandon and cruelty my friends and I had enacted 'Mad Mrs Moitra' during our childhood! For her visible illness of the mind, she received fear, contempt, and aversion. My illness of the mind was invisible. The Lakshman Rekha of TB that my mothers drew around me proved to be powerful beyond their expectations. The sympathetic refrain in our neighbourhood was 'Mallika has TB, poor thing' rather than 'Mallika has a screw loose in her head, poor thing.' If the outside world had discovered my illness, as it did with Mrs Moitra, they would not have let my lost self return to me. If people had found out, they would have decimated me, even more so than my illness.

Mrs Moitra didn't find her lost self. But I did. It returned over the months like a thin trickle of water from a distant, hidden source. A pristine source. It filled me very, very slowly.

I was blessed. I had not one, but two mothers *and* one grandmother *and* Ayah-ji, for whom I was the world. They averted what would have been a lifetime sentence. What they did was tantamount to lifting a car to save their child who was trapped beneath it.

That my father came back into our lives during this time was the other blessing. As my mothers, grandmother, and Ayah-ji lifted that car, this father whom I had rejected and then kept at a distance – this father who had quietly accepted my rejection and deferred to that distance – bent down, picked me up, and carried me out of danger.

No one asked my father intrusive questions, so he didn't have to lie. But my mothers were asked every conceivable intrusive question, and they lied with such heart and imagination that not only were their interrogators persuaded, but so too were they.

'Has Mallika taken her TB medicines?' Ma would ask, and Shantamama would sigh, 'Yes, Deva, those TB medicines are so strong, but what to do.' Forever, whenever they referred to that time, they said, 'You know, that time when Mallika had TB,' with such ease and conviction that sometimes even I believed I had had TB.

And I had Dr Roy and Masi.

If someone from above, watching our childhood game of 'Mad Mrs Moitra' decided to give me a slice of that pie, all I can say is that I am thankful it was a different slice, for it held love, protection, and help.

The winter holidays began. Prabha and Gauri would come home soon.

I took my red diary out of my handbag and sat on my balcony in the beautiful winter sunshine, rereading some of the things that Dr Roy had said to me. After some time, I idly turned the page to see what I'd written in times past. A single sentence occupied the page before my first Dr Roy quote.

I was talking to you because it's as if you're inside my story, living it with me.

I read it several times. I didn't remember writing it. It was undated.

I turned the page to previous entry. It was a line from Shantamama: 'Stop reading so much, you'll get mental indigestion.' This was dated a few months before Mahima's wedding.

No wonder I didn't remember. I must have written it during one of those three days when I'd lost my memory!

I read it again. The words were very Randhir-ish, but Randhir had been far too angry with me during that time to say anything of the sort. Who could it be?

Well, anyone really. Most likely someone at the wedding with a poetic bent of mind telling me her life story. How strange to have a tangible link to those three days written in my own hand!

Gauri: Knit one, purl one

1976 and earlier

A couple of months after Mallika recovered from her TB, Gauri began knitting a cardigan for her. It was maroon in colour, like the maroon sweater Mallika had left behind in the bus, along with her silk saree and maroon shawl – so unlike Mallika to be *that* careless! She finished knitting the sweater just before the winter holidays began and gave it to Mallika. It fitted her perfectly.

'It's so beautiful!' Mallika kept saying. 'How did you get my measurements right?'

'I don't have to measure, silly. I know without measuring,' she said, which was true. She could just look at someone and figure out what their measurements were, even their measurements for saree blouses. The only person who was better than her was that salesman in the Janpath bra shop. He didn't even look at your chest; he just looked at your face and called out, 'Arre, Chotu, take out Cross Your Heart 32B and Peter Pan 34A.' And when the invisible Chotu threw the two different bra brands from the attic above the shop, lo and behold, Cross Your Heart 32B and Peter Pan 34A were both exactly your size!

Gauri had knitted a sweater for Mahima after her marriage and given it to her when she came to Delhi on her three-day whirlwind trip. This one was not so much to comfort Mahima as to comfort herself, because they'd lost Mahima since she'd got married. After the first few desultory letters, Mahima had stopped writing to them altogether. They missed her terribly. Why didn't she come home for longer periods? They just couldn't understand. The sweater was a light pink, which suited Mahima's fair, almost-translucent complexion. Madhu Aunty said Mahima loved it so much that she wore it more than any of her sweaters, and Mahima had plenty of sweaters and plenty of everything else now that she was married to such a rich businessman. A well-educated businessman too, and there weren't that many of those around. But Mahima wasn't spoilt. She was as generous as her mother, constantly spending her pocket money to buy gifts for the three of them – books, blouse pieces, chocolates, and, when she went to Connaught Place, pastries from Wenger's.

Now, Gauri was knitting a sweater for Prabha, a cream one with cables – a soothing colour to soothe Prabha's constant outrage about everything under the sun. With Prabha, Gauri tended to swing from admiration for her unflinching honesty and courage, to fear for its consequences. But she tried not to express her apprehensions, because that frustrated and irritated Prabha.

Knitting kept her mind from worrying and scurrying. With every knit-one-purl-one that she dropped, her worry dropped too. And so she completed the body of the sweater, finished knitting the arms and stitching it together, bought matching buttons, and sewed them on. Finally, as her friends wore what she had made, she saw with satisfaction how worry – that unnecessary, distressing, unsubstantial but persistent thing – was transformed. It held her friends in a snug embrace; it was no longer worry, it was love.

During the winter holidays, Mallika wore the maroon cardigan and accompanied Gauri for her dance classes at the Bharatiya Kala Kendra. It was lovely to see the happiness on Mallika's face during those times. When Mallika said, 'Gauri, if I could live my life the way you dance, I'd be complete,' she knew that her friend was finally getting better.

When Gauri was seven, her mother had said, 'You have a lot of grace, Gauri, learn dancing.' She was not a pretty child, thin with straggly hair, her features all over the place. Dark too, which was a disqualification for prettiness by all prevailing standards. She was enraptured by the word 'grace.' Perhaps grace was better than beauty?

'No, Mummy,' she said. 'I don't want to learn dancing.'

Mummy was her stepmother. Her birth mother, her Ammu, had died when she was three. Her father had been so bereft after his wife's death that his grief had left no space for her, his three-year-old daughter. He knew she needed looking after, so he was persuaded by his parents to marry again within a year. He had two daughters by his second wife. As children, Prabha, Mallika, and Mahima would ask her a hundred and one questions about her stepmother. Did she beat her? Did she mistreat her? She didn't remember what she had said to them. Her stepmother rarely showed her feelings. She was always fair. It wasn't as if her sisters were petted and coddled more than her. Mummy wasn't the coddling sort. However, Mummy, while treating the three of them with scrupulous fairness in matters of food, new clothes, sweets, and birthday parties, was not fair with her scoldings. She scolded her flesh-and-blood daughters, but never, ever scolded Gauri. Which meant she loved her less, for wasn't it only those whom you loved that you scolded with impunity, in the manner of all mothers everywhere?

'No, Mummy. I don't want to learn dancing,' she had said, and waited for the scolding.

But even then, Mummy didn't scold her.

The next day, Mummy took her to a house in their neighbourhood. Gauri could hear the rhythmic sound of ghunghrus. Her mother deposited her at the Odissi dance class and went home.

She wouldn't dance. She wouldn't.

But her body didn't listen to her. As she stood sullenly in the last row of girls, determined not to follow the teacher's movements, she could feel her body moving, her heart soaring. The dance filled her until she felt she would burst. I'll do it today, and then I'll never come back, she thought. She began to dance.

'Arre,' the dance teacher said at the end of the class. 'You are Saraswati's daughter!'

She told Mummy this as they walked back home after the class, and Mummy smiled.

'Ammu,' she said that night, alone in her room. 'Are you watching me dance?'

Of course, Ammu said, I'm always with you.

She talked to her Ammu a lot. It was comforting to imagine Ammu was talking back to her, even though she knew it wasn't really Ammu, but her own longing heart. That she was loved by Mummy, her father, and her sisters, she had no doubt, but Ammu was the one who loved her the most. And it mattered to have one person in this world who loved you the most. Mallika was the luckiest, because she was loved the most by three people: her two mothers and her father. Mahima was loved the most by her mother. Prabha was loved the most by her father, for, even though her headstrong ways upset him, he admired her grit, integrity, intelligence, and hard work. Randhir was loved the most by his father. Perhaps one day, she would have that. Perhaps one day, she would fall in love with and marry a man for whom she would be the greatest love. It wouldn't happen any time soon, because she couldn't dislodge Vineet from her heart, though god knew she'd tried.

She loved everything about him: his tall, lanky, clean-cut, boyish looks; his thoroughly gentlemanly behaviour with girls; the way he loved to sit and chat with all the mothers and grandmothers. Arnav was excellent at imitating Vineet chatting to the female relatives, opening doors for girls, getting them chairs, and rushing to the kitchen to get them water if they were thirsty. '*Such* a gentleman!' Arnav would sigh in the tone of Vineet's female classmates. When they ate at Madhu Aunty's house, she would listen with delight to the boys' loud, boisterous conversations. They were all performers, they all excelled at imitating one another. But no one was better at acting than Mallika, and even Randhir had no idea!

But no, Ammu had loved Gauri the most. The picture of Ammu that she always had in her mind was from an old photograph of herself at age two, in Ammu's arms. Ammu's hair was in a plait, and there were flowers hanging down it. She and Ammu were looking at each other, laughing. She had looked at the photo every day until she was seven, but after that, it disappeared. She had been distraught. She had searched for it for days, weeks, months, but she never found it.

'Ammu, am I the best dancer?' she would ask Ammu before every class. And Ammu would smile, as though to say, Silly girl! Enclosed in the love of Ammu's smile, she would change into her salwar kameez and put on her ghunghrus, feeling her dance moving towards her like a lover. As her dance teacher chanted the dance beats and the class began dancing, she felt herself flow into something greater than herself, and often Ammu was part of that.

But sometimes, Ammu was absent.

Once, when Ammu's absence was no longer bearable, she had pleaded with Ammu, 'Send me a sign to tell me you're still with me.' This was during the winter holidays, almost a year after Mahima's marriage. That day, an hour later, as she and Mallika sat in the bus that was taking them to her dance class, Mallika took a paperback book out of her bag and gave it to her. It was Enid Blyton's *The Magic Faraway Tree*.

'You'd lent it to me when we were children. See your name. I must have forgotten to return it to you.'

She smiled. The four of them had adored *The Magic Faraway Tree*.

'There's something in it,' Mallika said. 'Open it.'

She opened it to the page Mallika indicated.

The photograph. Ammu and she, looking at each other, laughing, flowers in Ammu's hair.

She looked up at Mallika, the photo clasped to her heart, dazed. Ammu had sent her the sign.

She was three. She remembered crowds of people in her house, but no Ammu. She remembered searching everywhere for her, in the cupboards and under the beds, and how her father wouldn't open the bedroom door. Eventually, she went to the kitchen, where several women were cooking, and she went from woman to woman, looking up at their faces.

'What is it, child, what do you want?' one of the women asked her.

'I want my Ammu.'

There was a silence, and then one of the women put her hand over her mouth and began to laugh, and the others turned away from her and began laughing as though they would never stop. Then the first woman, her back turned to her but still laughing, said, 'Your mother is dead.' She felt someone grab her hand as she turned, but she shook her off, ran, and hid under her bed the entire day. No one came to find her.

That night, Ammu came to her. Ammu held her in her arms in bed. The following night, as she lay in her bed in her room with her Ayah sleeping on the ground next to her, Ammu came again and once more lay down next to her and held her in her arms. Gauri never saw her. She just felt her, felt the warmth and softness of her body and her arms around her. Sometimes she felt Ammu kissing her head. She could always smell her, that familiar night-time smell of glycerine and rose water which Ammu applied on her face at the end of every day.

Then her father's sister came to stay for a month. When her aunt got into bed with her, she had protested. 'No, you can't sleep with me, *Ammu* sleeps with me,' and pushed her aunt out of the bed.

That was that. Her bed was shifted to her father's room, and Ammu never slept with her again.

After the dance class, they went back to Mallika's house, where she spent the night. As they lay in bed, talking, she told Mallika about the sign. 'But... Oh, it's probably just a coincidence.'

'I think your mother did send you a message,' Mallika said.

'You believe in these things?'

'Well... I... don't disbelieve.'

'How come?'

Then Mallika told her about how much Masi had helped her with her weakness after her TB.

'Mallika, my mother's death is like this... wound inside me. Maybe Masi can help with that?'

Mallika nodded. 'I'll take you tomorrow, if you're free.'

'She takes money?'

'She works in an orphanage down the road. A lot of the money she gets goes to that. Give her what you can afford.'

'Does Randhir know about her?'

'No. No one knows.'

She felt her heart thrill. Only she knew! Not even Randhir did!

What do you feel for Randhir, Mallika? The question had been in her heart for years. And because she was so sure she knew the answer, she hadn't asked Mallika; that would have been too cruel. Gauri was sure that, although Randhir loved her, he didn't yet know it. When she had told Prabha this,

Prabha groaned that this wasn't a Mills & Boon romance, for heaven's sake. The problem with Prabha was that she just couldn't see subtleties.

You could talk to Randhir about anything, even your emotions. He listened, with unfeigned interest. You couldn't with other boys. The minute you began talking about your emotions, boys got uncomfortable. They avoided your gaze, they shifted around uneasily, or they changed the subject or made a stupid joke.

And Randhir not only understood Mallika, but also her complicated family circumstances. He was Mallika's protector. They talked endlessly to each other. He accepted who she was unconditionally. What more could you want in a marriage?

And Mallika's love for him was steady, deep, and, of course, unspoken.

She had never understood that stupid Charu business, and how Randhir just forgot Mallika in those days. She had wanted to strangle him. Every time Madhu Aunty praised Charu, she had wanted to say, 'What's so wonderful about her? She has zero personality.' Thank god the affair had been short and come to a precipitous end.

Vineet once told her that at DU Randhir was always surrounded by a bevy of adoring girls. As for Arnav, Vineet said, he was so involved in the theatre and his environmental passions that he didn't have time for anyone. Yet, some girl or the other always pursued him and caught him, and he went along with it without losing his heart.

'Whereas me,' Vineet said. 'I can't *imagine* sleeping with someone I don't love.'

She was a little shocked that he was talking about sex, but also very moved by this confession.

He told her all about Jaspreet. She was his first and last love! His mother and sisters *loved* her! Once he started working, he'd go to her parents and ask them for her hand in marriage.

Its heart and simplicity took her breath away. No boy she knew had this kind of clarity. None of them were looking for the love of their lives.

After that, Vineet had no time for her.

And on top of that, her parents were getting after her to marry. Yes, of course she should finish her degree, but in the meantime, what was wrong in meeting some good boys? There was one in the IAS, and another who was working in America, and both families really wanted her.

'I can't give up my dancing!' she burst out.

'No one's asking you to give up anything, Gauri. We're just asking you to *meet* them.'

'I'll have to give up dancing if I go to America. And if I marry into the IAS, I'll have to follow him wherever he's posted, and then how can I dance?'

Her parents said gravely that, after she finished her degree, the time was right for marriage, and that she should consider it.

In her panic, the words had just slipped out of her, that she couldn't give up dancing. How could she tell her parents the truth – that her heart was with Vineet? That she couldn't sleep with someone she barely knew and didn't love? But when these words came out of her, it was as though her spirit had given another truth that her mind had not formulated – she *couldn't* give up dancing. Till then, it had never consciously occurred to her that marriage might ask this of her.

In the meantime, she fantasized about Mallika and Randhir getting married. She even knew what she would wear for Mallika and Randhir's wedding – her mustard and green Kanjeevaram saree with Ammu's gold and ruby jhumkas.

But on the night of Mahima's wedding, her fantasy came to a halt.

She noticed two things at the wedding. One, that Randhir was in a bad mood. Two, that Arnav was looking at Mallika in a way that she'd never seen him look at her.

After the wedding dinner, and before the wedding pheras began, she had asked Madhu Aunty if she could borrow her house key because she needed to use the loo. Aunty gave her a bunch of keys and showed her which one unlocked the side door.

When she reached Madhu Aunty's house, she saw Mallika and Arnav sitting on the steps of Mallika's house, in front of the veranda. They were talking. It was a little odd to see them together this way. It was more the kind of thing Mallika would do with Randhir; she'd always been shy around Arnav. Why were they here and not at the wedding? They didn't see her.

A few minutes later, when she came out, Mallika was standing with her back to Arnav, and he was winding her gajra around her hair. Taken aback at the intimacy of the scene, she stopped where she was. Mallika turned, then Arnav kissed her. She kissed him back.

That was when Gauri stepped back into the side of the house where they couldn't see her.

A minute later, Arnav and Mallika were walking back to the shamyana.

She waited for a couple of minutes, then headed back, still reeling. When she reached the shamyana, Arnav was smoking outside. Why on earth was he wearing *jeans* for a wedding? No doubt he had on a very smart blazer, but still. They smiled at each other, and she went inside. The pheras had just started, and Mallika was sitting next to Prabha, looking her usual grave self. She joined them and sat on the dari.

'Mallika,' she said, tapping Mallika after five minutes. 'Everything OK?'

Mallika smiled and nodded. Absolutely no indication that anything had happened. Look at the way she was hiding it! She would get it out of her later.

But she didn't get a moment alone with Mallika after that.

A few days later, she heard someone calling her from below her hostel balcony. Going to the balcony, she saw Randhir downstairs. He waved.

'Hi, I'm just coming down,' she said. Something had happened to Mallika; Randhir would never come all the way to JNU to see *her*. She went running downstairs.

Randhir told her about Mallika's concussion and loss of memory.

As she tried to digest this, shocked, Randhir said, 'Will you come home and spend the weekend with Mallika?'

'Of course.'

Arnav was there when they reached Randhir's house, sitting at the dining table, talking to Madhu Aunty. He waved. 'Mallika's waiting for you!'

Was she imagining it, or was that relief on his face?

The boys followed her to Mallika's room, looking as though she were a trophy that they were bestowing upon Mallika. Mallika was overjoyed to see her.

That night, she described the entire wedding to Mallika. When she tried to tell Mallika about the way that Arnav had been looking at her that day, Mallika dismissed it completely.

Throughout the night, Mallika moaned and cried in her sleep. Gauri kept patting and soothing her.

The next morning, Arnav materialized at the door.

'Do you want a lift back to JNU, Gauri?' he asked. 'I'm going back to IIT.'

'No thanks, Arnav. Randhir will drop me back tomorrow.'

'OK, see you both later. Rest and get better, Mallika. Bye.'

He waved and was gone.

And in that instant, she saw the look on Mallika's face, and then that was gone too.

The look that said, don't go.

What was going on?

It was on the tip of her tongue to tell Mallika about the kiss, but Mallika was looking so pale and exhausted that she decided she'd tell her later.

But once again, later didn't come. Gauri went back to JNU. Mallika was consumed with her Shantamama's impending operation. Gauri had her dance performance, which went off very well.

The night she returned from her dance performance, she dreamt about Mallika. Mallika was sitting on her bed looking at her, and tears were running down her face. That was all. However, the next night she had another dream, and in this, Mallika was floating down a river, her hair streaming behind her. She got up with the horrible feeling that Mallika was going to a place very far away and would be lost to them.

She packed an overnight bag, went for her classes, and then, without eating lunch, boarded the bus that would take her to Central Secretariat. From there, she took another bus to Mallika's house.

When she arrived, Ayah-ji said Mallika was not well and not to disturb her. 'For the operation also, she did not go.'

'She didn't go for the *operation*?'

'That only I said. Do not go to her room. She is sleeping.'

She ignored Ayah-ji and went upstairs to Mallika's room.

'No one listens to me,' she heard Ayah-ji saying loudly behind her.

She went inside quietly. Mallika was sleeping. But her face was deathly pale. She examined her for a minute, and then went downstairs and next door to Randhir's house.

Randhir opened the door and stared at her. 'Oh... Come in, come in.'

He went to the kitchen, then came back with a glass of water for her.

She drank thirstily. 'What's happened to Mallika?'

'Oh... very heavy period,' he muttered without meeting her eyes. 'She phoned me from college, and I got her home. But... how did *you* know she wasn't well?'

'I dreamt about her.'

'You came because you *dreamt* about her?'

'Of course. When I came, Ayah-ji told me she wasn't well. Mallika was sleeping, so I came here.'

'Are you hungry?'

'Very. I didn't have lunch.'

Fifteen minutes later, they were both sitting at the dining table, eating Ramu's unbeatable aloo parathas with dahi and achaar and drinking their second mug of tea.

This was the sweetest thing about Randhir. He looked after all of them.

There was a lined page lying next to her. She saw Mallika's name on it and picked it up. The days of Mallika's lost memory were listed, and where she had been on those days. 'Whose handwriting is this?'

'Arnav's.'

She read the note once more. 'It says here that Mallika came to see me at JNU the day after Mahima's wedding.'

'Yeah.'

'Who told you that?'

'Ayah-ji.'

'We never met that day. I wasn't even *at* JNU that day. I mean, it was the day after the wedding, I'd just left her house. Why would we meet again the same day?'

He took the paper from her and read it. 'It says Mallika came back home that night. So when she didn't find you, she must have come back home.'

'But we didn't even make any plans to meet,' she said.

'She wasn't involved with a guy or anything, no?'

She looked at him incredulously.

He began to look uncomfortable.

'Which guy?' she said finally.

'I mean... You know...'

'*You're* the one and only guy she knows,' she said deliberately.

He flushed.

'As though *she's* going to have some hole-and-corner affair!'

'Sorry, I didn't... I mean...'

'And if she *was* with a guy, we'd know.' She got up. 'I'm going to ask Ayah-ji.'

'I'll come with you.'

They went back to Mallika's house.

'Yes,' Ayah-ji confirmed. 'Baby said she was going to see you that day. Yes, yes, the *same* day you left our house. Then Baby came back home because you weren't there.'

'What time did Mallika come back home, Ayah-ji?' Randhir asked.

'What does it matter when she came back?'

She and Randhir glanced at each other. Ayah-ji was being very difficult.

'Ayah-ji,' Randhir said in that beautiful, soft voice that he reserved only for Mallika and Ayah-ji. 'Only you would know when Mallika came back; you take such good care of her.'

'Randhir Baba, I went back to my quarter early, around six in the evening, because Baby had said she wasn't coming home for the night. The next morning at five-thirty, when I came home, Baby was here. Bas? Enough? Satisfied?'

'Bilkul, Ayah-ji, bilkul,' Randhir said soothingly.

After that, they were all buried under exams. As soon as Mallika finished hers, she fell ill with TB. The niggling question of why Mallika had come to see her retreated from Gauri's mind. And she still hadn't told Mallika about the kiss.

The summer holidays began. Prabha was most upset about not being allowed to see Mallika. Mahima came home a day after Prabha left and drove to JNU to see Gauri. She talked about her new friends and acquaintances in Chandigarh, the parties they went to, Shekhar's travels, how his work kept him so busy, and how he showered her with beautiful sarees and jewellery. About her wonderful mother-in-law, who wouldn't let her work in the kitchen, and her wonderful father-in-law, who never interfered in anything.

Then suddenly Mahima burst out that it was so damn unfair that Padma Aunty wouldn't let anyone see Mallika given that Mallika was no longer infectious. 'I mean, I haven't seen Mallika since I got married. As though I'm going to tire her out! Even Mummy thinks it's ridiculous how paranoid Padma Aunty's become about Mallika.'

Mahima had talked non-stop. But for all her talking, Gauri knew that her outburst about Mallika was the only thing that had come from her heart.

The first weekend that she spent with Mallika after her illness was in September.

'Mallika,' she said in the darkness, as they lay in bed after dinner. 'The day after Mahima's wedding, you came to see me at JNU?'

'*That's* what I wanted to ask you about when you came to see me after the concussion!' Mallika exclaimed. 'But I just couldn't remember.'

'Well, I wasn't at JNU that afternoon. I never saw you that day.'

'That's what I concluded, because Ayah-ji said I came back that evening.'

'You never told me you were coming to see me,' Gauri said.

'I suppose I must have taken a chance, but I wonder why I came to see you just a few hours after you'd left my house?'

'That's what I was wondering too,' Gauri said.

Then, suddenly, she knew why Mallika had come to her the day after the wedding. To tell her about the kiss.

'Maybe you wanted to talk to me about something?' she prompted.

Slowly, Mallika said, 'Yes, probably.'

'About Arnav?'

'Arnav?' Mallika sounded startled. 'No, no, about Randhir.'

'Oh,' Gauri said, equally startled. 'What about Randhir?'

Then Mallika told her all about how badly Randhir had lost his temper with her.

'How *could* he?' Gauri was appalled.

'It was the day before the wedding, Gauri. I put him in a terrible predicament.'

'I hope he apologized?'

'He did. But... why did you say you thought I wanted to talk about Arnav?'

'I told you, I caught him looking at you at the wedding.' Well, at least this part was true. 'So, I thought… maybe he… said something… to you.'

Mallika began to laugh. It was the first time Gauri was hearing her friend laugh in months.

'Gauri! You and your imagination!'

Then Mallika told her that Randhir and Arnav were travelling all the way to LSR to pick her up and bring her back home because of how weak she was. For the entire term, imagine, Mallika said. Randhir and she were good friends, whereas Arnav hardly knew her, and wasn't it nice of him to pick her up despite being so busy with his hundred-and-one activities?

Happiness burst inside Gauri. Under the guise of friendship, Arnav was resuming what had begun that night at the wedding!

'What do you and Arnav talk about when he picks you up?' she asked, trying not to show her excitement.

'We can't talk over the noise of the bike. And I'm always so tired.'

Of course. Arnav was keeping quiet about his affection until Mallika got better. When she did, he would confess his feelings for her and resume what had started between them.

After all, if Randhir wasn't going to marry her, then why not Arnav?

Arnav was waiting for Mallika!

She was blissfully afloat on this fantasy when Mallika proceeded to tell her that Arnav had added yet another activity to his hectic schedule, and that her name was Mohini.

Her joy vanished. Grimly, she listened as Mallika gave her a blow-by-blow account of how Arnav had picked her up from college, how she'd been so exhausted that she'd slept in his room, in his bed, and of her meeting with Mohini, Mohini's threesome, and Arnav's oblivion.

'I never thought threesomes and all happened in India,' Mallika said.

'They happen everywhere, Mallika, stop being so naïve,' she said, wanting to hit Arnav.

First, Randhir had rejected Mallika for Charu. And now, Arnav had rejected Mallika for this stupid Mohini. Gauri felt Arnav's rejection of Mallika so acutely that she couldn't tell Mallika about the kiss. The kiss would have meant a lot to Mallika. But obviously it meant nothing to Arnav, who was already onto the next girl. Best for Mallika not to know.

Now, it was the winter holidays, and she and Mallika were going to see Masi.

Masi's house was simple, simpler even than Mallika's. At least Mallika's house – for all its simplicity – had bright mirrorwork cushions and cheerful, inexpensive rugs, colourful tablecloths and bedcovers. Padma Aunty couldn't afford expensive things, but she made up for this with colour, plus the sun streamed brightness into every room of her house, and the framed photographs all over the house – of Mallika, her mothers, her grandparents, and her friends – welcomed everyone who entered. Masi's small house was full of sun too, which was a relief, because otherwise it looked like the home of an ascetic. There was a bench-like sofa, two straight-backed chairs, a small dining table with an off-white tablecloth, and four chairs. Nothing on the walls. No paintings, no photos. Nothing decorative on the mantelpiece. Everything was terribly clean.

Masi, who was probably in her early forties, looked like her house. Clean and unadorned. She wore an off-white cotton saree with a high neck and kolhapuris on her feet. No jewellery, except for pearl studs in her ears; no necklace, not even glass bangles; not a single ring; and no bindi. Was she a widow? Probably. She had skin like milk, glowing and beautiful. She was quite lovely, though you didn't notice it at first because everything about her was so understated.

But warmth radiated from her. She embraced Mallika as though she loved her. Mallika introduced Gauri, and they said their namastes and sat on the hardbacked chairs. And Mallika said, 'Masi, Gauri wants to know if she can have a session with you?'

'Bilkul,' Masi said, smiling at Gauri. 'Come, Beti.'

In the bedroom, a room as stark as the rest of the house and equally clean, she closed her eyes and was asleep in five minutes.

An hour later, Masi touched her gently on her cheek. She sat up in the bed and Masi sat next to her. 'Your mother came.'

She looked at her speechlessly.

'Your mother wants your forgiveness.'

'Why?' she managed to say.

'She feels she abandoned you.'

She was shaken. Yet simultaneously, the sceptic in her thought, maybe Mallika told her my mother died when I was small?

'You were a young child when she went away. After she died, she used to come at nights to comfort you. She said you did not imagine that.'

Stunned, Gauri felt tears gather in her eyes.

'She said she hears you when you talk to her. She says she is always with you, especially when you dance.'

Her tears overflowed.

'Your Ammu was there for the entire time I worked on you.'

She had never told anyone she called her mother 'Ammu,' not even her three friends. Or about Ammu coming to her at night when she was a child.

'You really felt your mother holding you every night?' Mallika whispered that night.

She nodded. 'Later, I kept thinking I must have imagined it.'

Tears began running down Mallika's cheeks.

Gauri opened Mallika's cupboard and took out two handkerchiefs. Mallika's Shantamama had made two handkerchief bags on her Pfaff sewing machine – one plain yellow and the other purple with beautiful leaves embroidered all along its sides. The plain yellow bag had about ten plain, soft handkerchiefs made out of an old cotton saree. 'These are soft on the nose and face, so use them for colds and for crying,' Shanta Aunty had instructed Mallika along with Gauri, who happened to be there that day. The embroidered purple bag held ten exquisitely embroidered handkerchiefs. 'And these,' Shanta Aunty had said, 'are for going out. Weddings, parties, all that. Gauri, see that she doesn't use these for her nose.'

Gauri had laughed and said she would. After that, whenever she came to Mallika's house, she checked the contents of the two bags. Of course, the handkerchiefs were always mixed up.

Now, as Mallika dried her tears, Gauri rearranged the handkerchiefs, putting them into the correct bags.

She told Mallika about her most painful memory: that, as a three-year-old, she had gone looking for her dead Ammu. And how the women in the kitchen had laughed and laughed when she asked them where her Ammu was. 'Mallika, I've never understood it,' she said.

Mallika was looking appalled. Then her expression changed. 'Gauri, they weren't laughing. They were crying.'

Gauri closed her eyes and relived that scene. Yes. They were.

What a mysterious thing memory was. Hers had tricked her, given her so much pain for so long. And Mallika's had gone, three whole days of it. If Mallika's memory came back years and years later – as it always did in books – would Mallika feel tricked too?

For heaven's sake, why was she getting so morbid! She opened her eyes and smiled at Mallika.

A few days later, Gauri and Prabha were sprawled on Prabha's lawn, drinking chai and eating moomphalis. Prabha was talking indignantly about Sanjay Gandhi's slum demolitions and his forcible sterilization policy. But Gauri's mind was on other things. When Prabha paused, she said casually, 'By the way, do you think Arnav likes Mallika?'

'All because he picked her up from college for a few months? Gauri, come *on*!'

'Guys don't go out of their way like that for just any girl.'

'Randhir did it too.'

'That's different. They've always been close.' Gauri paused. 'And I saw Arnav kissing Mallika on the night of Mahima's wedding.'

'*What?*'

She told Prabha everything.

Finally, Prabha burst out, '*One year* it's taken you to tell me!'

'Because I wanted to tell Mallika first.'

'So why didn't you tell her?'

'First, because she was so unwell after the concussion. Then after that, I couldn't meet her, and after the exams, she fell ill for so long. And then when I finally met her, she told me Arnav's sleeping with this girl, Mohini.'

'Then why the hell was he kissing Mallika?'

'I don't think Arnav was sleeping with Mohini in January when he kissed Mallika.'

'That's why you didn't tell her? Because of Mohini?' Prabha asked.

Gauri nodded. 'You know her. She'll really be hurt.'

'That she will. Good you didn't tell her. But Arnav should have.'

Prabha wasn't good at keeping her temper to herself, that was the problem.

They were sitting on Madhu Aunty's lawn, eating moomphalis and oranges in the winter sun. It was a beautiful morning and there were eight of them, some on lawn chairs and others sprawled on the grass – Madhu Aunty, Anu Aunty, Padma Aunty, Shanta Aunty, Mallika, Prabha, Randhir, Arnav, and Gauri herself.

The boys, Prabha, and Gauri were having an impassioned discussion about the Emergency. They were talking about Indira's amendments to the Constitution, putting the Emergency beyond the scrutiny of the courts, then about her doing away with the Allahabad High Court's judgment of her, and about her putting herself above election disputes and giving herself immunity for criminal offences, all under the guise of national security. After that, Prabha began talking about Sanjay using the Emergency to 'beautify' Delhi by demolishing slums with impunity and leaving thousands homeless. 'What about the lack of outrage about the Turkman Gate slum demolitions and shootings?' Gauri asked. Arnav agreed and went on a rant about Sanjay Gandhi's appropriation of power.

Then there was a lull in the conversation. Madhu Aunty looked at Mallika, who had contributed nothing, and said, 'Mallika, Beta, too quiet you have become – you must talk a little more.'

Of course, with Prabha, even an innocuous comment like that was fodder for an argument.

'Why, Aunty?' Prabha asked. 'Why should Mallika talk?'

'Prabha, bas karo,' her mother, Anu Aunty, said.

'Mumma, *please* don't keep telling me to stop! I'm not *arguing*. I'm just having a *discussion*.'

'Fine, fine, discuss, discuss, let her discuss, Anu,' Madhu Aunty said placatingly.

'Aunty, see,' said Prabha earnestly. 'When people talk too much, no one says, "You're talking too much." But when you're quiet, like Mallika, everyone's always saying "You should talk." Why is it OK to have verbal diarrhoea, and why is not OK to be quiet?'

Madhu Aunty gave this consideration. Anu Aunty looked relieved that Madhu Aunty wasn't ruffled. Padma Aunty smiled as she peeled her orange. Shantamama gave Mallika a meaningful look that Mallika didn't see.

'Beta, your arguments, they are too good! Answer itself I cannot find,' Madhu Aunty said, looking struck.

Madhu Aunty was very canny. Since she never had an answer for Prabha's questions, she always took refuge in praising Prabha. If only Anu Aunty could get the hang of that!

'I am making chai – you all also want?' Madhu Aunty said, strategically standing up.

A chorus of yesses.

The rest of the Aunties got up and went to the kitchen with Madhu.

Prabha sighed, 'No one ever answers my questions.' She sounded so forlorn that Gauri felt bad. She said, 'OK, this is what *I* think. When people talk too much, it's still considered normal. But when people are quiet or shy, it's thought of as abnormal. Or misunderstood. People think you're stuck-up, boring – things like that.'

At which point Arnav lazily said, 'Really? I don't think so.'

Prabha said, 'You do. You assume shy people are boring with no brains.'

Mallika froze.

Arnav said, 'Come off it, Prabha, I don't think that.'

Prabha snorted, 'Of course you think that – you called Mallika boring.'

And then there was dead silence.

Randhir looked at Arnav. Arnav stared at Mallika.

Mallika was concentrating on cracking her moomphalis.

'When?' Arnav asked.

His contented, sleepy look was gone. He was asking Mallika.

Mallika looked up briefly and muttered, 'Forget it.'

'Come, Mallika, let's help Madhu Aunty with the tea,' Gauri said, getting up.

'Prabha has no self-control sometimes,' she hissed as they entered the sitting room.

'She said it on my behalf, Gauri.'

Prabha came in. 'God, Mallika, so sorry, I don't know… it just came out.'

'It's OK. Listen, I'm tired. I'm going home to rest.' Mallika waved and went out from the kitchen door.

'You don't always have to prove your point, Prabha,' Gauri said after Mallika left.

'I *said* I'm sorry.'

'Though I don't know how Arnav could forget he'd said it,' she conceded.

'*Exactly*,' said Prabha.

And that should have been the end of it, but of course, with Prabha, it wasn't.

'I'm going to ask Arnav why he kissed Mallika,' Prabha said.

'Are you *mad*?'

'Casually saying Mallika's boring. Casually kissing her. We don't want him to hurt her again in that casual, careless way of his.'

'I should never have told you. I'll never tell you anything again.'

'You talk to him, then. You're more diplomatic than I am,' Prabha said.

'*Me*?'

'Otherwise, I will.'

Gauri took in her breath and let it out in a hiss.

'Gauri, talk to him now.'

Better her than Prabha. Prabha would make his hackles rise. 'Fine,' she said.

'What'll you tell him?' Prabha asked.

'I'll tell him… not to trifle with Mallika.'

'Gauri! He doesn't read Victorian fiction, for heaven's sake!'

Randhir came to the back veranda just then. 'What on earth are you two doing here?'

'Nothing,' Prabha said. 'Where's Arnav?'

'Gone to the market to get fags.' He went back into the house.

'Go.' Prabha said.

Gauri went down the veranda steps. Arnav was strolling to the market ahead of her. She walked reluctantly towards him, thinking how odd it was, this feeling uppermost in her gut that Mallika was in love with Arnav. She didn't understand why she felt this. But sometimes in life, you could feel things without knowing why, without understanding how. Perhaps this was one of those things.

Prabha: Deal with it?

1976 and earlier

They were seventeen at the time. She was doing her pre-med in Delhi, and Mallika was a fresher at LSR. That Sunday, as she and Mallika lounged on her bed rereading two Georgette Heyers, Mumma came in and said that a famous guru was giving a talk in their neighbourhood.

'Guru Maharaj is a very wise and elevated soul,' Mumma had said.

'Oh, Mumma,' she groaned, knowing what was coming.

Mumma said, 'Prabha, education is not only for the mind; it is also for the soul, that is the highest education. Guru Maharaj-ji is talking at seven tonight at Mrs Sahany's house, so we will go. Mallika, you ask your Ma, and you also come, alright?'

'Yes, Aunty.'

'Such a good girl Mallika is, she never argues. Learn from her, Prabha.' Mumma went back into the kitchen.

'Uff, why do you always say yes,' she complained to Mallika after her mother left. She knew that Mallika had no love for these things. She and Padma Aunty never went to temples. They didn't even pray at home. The only time there were any gods in their house was when Shanta Aunty came, because she always carried all the gods in her trunk and established a place for them on the side table in the downstairs bedroom. Then, from time to time, Shanta Aunty would cajole Mallika, 'Come and pray with me, darling,' and Mallika would oblige. She always obliged. Mallika had said yes to Mumma because she couldn't say no.

Mahima and Gauri also joined them for the talk that evening. Mrs Sahany's house was crowded with people, mostly women. Everyone listened raptly to Maharaj-ji. But it was too high-flown for Prabha, all that talk about the mind, the soul, and the infinite. Mumma was very absorbed. Gauri was listening intently; she had always excelled at languages – she used to top the class in Sanskrit, could read and write Kannada, and was now doing Spanish at JNU. Mahima wasn't listening; she had come just for the heck of it. Mallika was dreaming. She saw Mumma glance at Mallika and smile.

Mumma thought Mallika was absorbing everything, but Mumma had no idea that she was in another world altogether.

When the talk ended, everyone was scrambling to be the first to touch Guru Maharaj's feet and receive his blessings. Gauri managed a short conversation with Guru Maharaj. As everyone crowded around them, they discussed how the mind is like a monkey and how meditation was a means to still the mind. The guru was so taken with her that he plucked a copper bracelet out of the air, with her initial, *G*, and bestowed it upon her. There were gasps all around. 'Wear it, it will protect you,' he said, and Gauri promptly did. People were green with envy, especially Mrs Sahany, who had hosted him. She too should have got a bracelet, Mumma said later.

As they walked home, Mumma kept talking about what a great man Maharaj-ji was, so wise, such great truths he uttered. She was talking mostly to Mallika, because that's what all the mothers did. Mumma was talking about how to quieten the mind, and how solitude was necessary to find one's true self, the divine self. And how the world was filled with nonsensical chatter and meaningless activities, and what a waste of time and energy that was. Mallika kept nodding and saying, 'Yes, Aunty,' in her usual way. Mumma then began talking about how important it was to feed one's soul with silence and solitude so that one could hear the wisdom within.

'You believe that, Mumma?' she asked, surprised.

'Bilkul I believe that!'

'But Mallika likes to spend a lot of time by herself. She is quiet. Yet all of you keep telling her *not* to be like that.'

'Everything has to become an argument with you.'

'Mumma, I wasn't arguing, I just wanted to *know*.'

'Even after a peaceful evening like this, you must argue.'

Prabha turned to Mallika. 'Mallika, what was wrong with what I said? You yourself told me that you were tired of people telling you to talk more.'

Mallika didn't say anything.

Then Mumma said, 'Yes, Mallika does not talk much, and she does not like to mix with people. But when you are so young, it is not the time to be like that. When you are young, it is the time to talk, to interact, to meet new people, all that. As you grow older, it is different.'

'But Mumma, Maharaj-ji said it is good to cultivate these virtues from a young age.'

'Alright, alright, you have won your argument. Are you satisfied?' her mother said, sounding tired.

At this point, Gauri deftly changed the subject and began talking to Mumma about the Gita and its place in the Mahabharata, and that started another, calmer discussion.

When they reached home, they had chola bhaturas at Madhu Aunty's house, and then they went to Mahima's room to gossip. Gauri analysed the entire talk and, in the same breath, told them what everyone was wearing, from the size of their bindis to the design of their toe rings. Mallika listened, wide-eyed. Prabha knew all Mallika's expressions. The serene one meant her mind was somewhere else. The blank or icy one meant she was frightened; it was the face she wore at social occasions. The one she had on now meant she was listening, because her eyes were shining. When she said, 'Yes, Aunty, I know, Aunty,' like she had said to Mumma earlier, it meant she was listening out of love for you, not out of interest.

They examined Gauri's copper bracelet carefully. It was very pretty, with a design of flowers around it.

'These gurus and all, they do so much meditation that they have special powers,' Mahima said.

'But why do they use their powers to produce bracelets?' Mallika asked.

'You're too literal, Mallika,' Mahima said. 'You have to see beyond such things.'

'Mallika, why didn't you tell Mumma I was right when we were arguing?' Prabha asked.

'As if I'm going to take your side against Aunty.'

Mahima said, 'Your mother was right, Prabha. This is no age for Mallika to be quiet and all. That's for when you're old, past forty. Mallika doesn't even have any social skills.'

'Of course she does,' Gauri said. 'She's just not talkative.'

Gauri always had the last word.

Gauri had always been convinced that Randhir and Mallika loved each other.

Prabha had told Gauri 'no' hundreds of times. 'Their relationship is completely platonic.'

Gauri said, 'I know nothing's *happened* between them, but they're like… kindred souls.'

'We're also like kindred souls, the four of us,' she reminded Gauri.

'Of course we are, but we're girls, no? If you're like that with a boy, it *can't* be platonic.'

How enraged Gauri was about Randhir's involvement with Charu! Once, she had said to Prabha, 'I know why Randhir's fallen for that stupid Charu.'

'Why?' Prabha sighed.

'He can't see what's in front of his face because he takes that for granted.'

'*That*,' she informed Gauri, 'is straight out of one of your Mills & Boons.'

Then the Charu episode came to an abrupt end, and there was Gauri, crowing with delight.

'Wait and see,' Gauri said. 'Now Randhir will realize how much he loves Mallika.'

Which, of course, still hadn't happened.

It was all very well having these silly fantasies when you were teenagers. But Gauri hadn't outgrown them. When they were young, every story that mattered was a love story. When Mallika's father had come back into her life, the three of them were convinced that the happy ending was inevitable.

But that did not happen. And they didn't understand.

Now, she did. She understood that Padma Aunty couldn't tie herself in marriage to a man who had betrayed her so deeply or become part of a family that had done such harm to her and her unborn child. Years ago, she had heard Shanta Aunty call Padma Aunty a 'women's libber' as though it were a bad word, but what was women's liberation but one's response to injustice?

How lucky Mallika was! Padma Aunty never got after her about marriage, nor was she obsessed about saving up for her marriage and dowry. Instead, Padma Aunty had had a room made for Mallika, a sanctuary, beautifully tucked away at the top of the house with that lovely balcony. She never bothered to domesticate Mallika the way Mumma was always trying to domesticate Prabha. On Saturdays, when all the mothers were in the throes of cooking their family's favourite food, tidying up cupboards and entertaining guests, Padma Aunty and Mallika would take the bus to Chachaji's second-hand bookshop in Shankar Market and then treat themselves to pastries and mutton patties at Wenger's. During the music, dance, and theatre season, they would take the bus all the way to the Mandi House area and attend every event, buying the cheapest six-rupee tickets. They even came home safely at night, because the scooterwalla, Gopal, who parked outside their colony every day brought them home in his scooter. He wanted to do it free of charge since Mallika was tutoring his daughter, Jalpari, for free, but of course Mallika and Padma Aunty wouldn't hear of it. Most of all, she envied the way Mallika and her mothers chattered endlessly with one another.

She just didn't understand why no one liked it when injustice was addressed. Not even those who were subject to it – like Mumma, who bore cruelty from her mother-in-law every day without any support from Daddy. Dadima, her father's mother, had given hell to Mumma all her married life. Mumma had looked after her mother-in-law, catered to all her needs, and been a tender and uncomplaining caregiver every time Dadima had been ill, down to giving her a bedpan and cleaning her up. Yet Dadima continued being nasty to Mumma and called her 'churail' to her face. Every time she heard Dadima calling Mumma a witch, she would fly to Mumma's defence. And Dadima would mutter to Mumma, 'Very nicely you have trained your daughter, very nicely.' Then Mumma would turn to Prabha in exasperation and say, 'Prabha, bas, do not interfere.' In front of Daddy, Dadima was honey sweet to Mumma.

She had asked her mother once, 'Mumma, you say God always answers your prayers, but if He does, then why is Dadima always so nasty to you?'

And Mumma said, 'God answered my prayers long ago, Beti. I never asked Him to change her. I just told Him, let her not change who I am.'

Prabha told this to her friends, and Mallika sighed, 'Oh, how wise she is, Prabha!'

'Wisdom means getting walked over?' she asked.

All she wanted was for her grandmother to treat Mumma with kindness. Why did Mumma get so upset with her, Prabha, for *that*?

And her parents, so narrow-minded about boys. Even the boys *they* knew. Randhir, Arnav, and Vineet were happy to give her a lift on their motorcycles every time they saw her walking to or from the bus stop. But she couldn't accept, because Mumma had forbidden her from taking lifts from boys – even from Randhir, whom she had known all her life.

After getting into every medical college that she had applied to, including the best in Delhi, she had decided to go to the Armed Forces Medical College in Poona. And Mumma and Daddy, instead of being proud of how she had got in everywhere, were upset. Daddy said, 'How could you make such a big decision without consulting us? Do you have so little respect for your parents?' Mummy said, 'This is not independence, this is ziddi.'

It wasn't obstinate; it was the best decision she had ever made. She had always wanted to become an army doctor and live an unfettered life away from her parents. She loved being at AFMC. Yes, the girl's hostel had rules, but they were nothing like the rules her parents had imposed on her. And living in Poona, she realized that Delhi men were a different breed. In Poona, she was never assaulted on the roads or in buses. The scooterwallas took you directly and safely where you had to go, without taking circuitous routes in order to hike up the fare. It was such a liberating feeling to take a scooter at any time of the night by herself, without fear.

It was how she always wanted to live. Without fear.

She had told Karan Uncle this when she was fifteen. He hadn't replied immediately. That's what she liked – that he gave weight to whatever they said. He didn't give the pat, grown-up reply that a girl couldn't do things a boy could because it wasn't safe or seemly.

He eventually said, 'No one can live without fear, Prabha. Whether you're a boy or a girl.'

'But, Uncle,' she said, 'boys can go wherever they wish, whenever they wish. They can go out at night by themselves. They can go trekking and travelling. They can go to Kamani and see a play without thinking if it's safe to come home at midnight. We can never do that.'

'True. *We* take that for granted, don't we?'

That was all he had said. But to get this kind of affirmation from a grown up when you were fifteen was no small thing.

Their mothers would have said, 'Don't think about what you can't do, what is the point?' Or, 'Why do you want to do that? There are plenty of other things to do.' Or they would say, 'Stop arguing, when you get married you can do whatever you want to do.' It was this last refrain – the get-married-and-do-whatever-you-want-to-do refrain – which she found the most puzzling, given that it always came from women who were married and never did what they wanted to do.

She hadn't wanted that to happen to Mahima, to be stuck in a marriage with a stranger before she knew what she wanted in life. All Mahima's opinions and ideas came from her parents. She said yes to the first boy they introduced her to.

'You're so bright and talented, Mahima. You can sit for the IAS, or the Bank exams, or do an MBA. You can have a fantastic career. What's the hurry to get married?' she had asked.

'I don't *want* a career. There's nothing I want more than children. I don't want in-laws and ayahs bringing up my children. With a career, I can't give my children that kind of time or attention.'

'Prabha, it's what Mahima really wants,' Gauri said soothingly.

'I said yes to Shekhar because Mummy's checked his background, his family, everything,' Mahima said. 'And Shekhar's nice to talk to, he's good-looking, he's healthy, he's doing really well in his business, and he comes from an excellent family. What else is there?'

'Compatibility,' she said helplessly.

'Huh! That's such a Western concept! And look where it's got them – divorce after divorce. I *will* be happy. The way *I* want to be happy. Not the way *you* want to be happy.'

And now Mahima was married, and they hardly saw her.

It was bad enough not seeing Mahima, but what *really* upset her was going home to Delhi for the summer holidays and not being allowed to see Mallika. She had tried to explain to Padma Aunty that Mallika was no longer infectious, but her mother was adamant. 'Prabha, I'm so sorry, but she's very weak.'

So every other day during the summer holidays, she and Gauri wrote letters to Mallika about everything that they were doing and reading and all the neighbourhood gossip. They gave their letters to Padma Aunty. Mallika was too weak to write and sent them lots of love, her mother said.

Her mother looked ill. Dark circles around her eyes, sallow skin, pinched lips. Gauri, who noticed everything, said that Padma Aunty suddenly had streaks of grey in her hair. A few times, they saw Mallika and her mother getting into a scooter to go to the doctor. Mallika waved to them as she got into the scooter, but she didn't smile. She looked thin and pale.

A great sadness clutched Prabha's heart.

On top of this, Mahima came to Delhi just one day after Prabha left. She didn't get to see Mahima either. It was *so* upsetting.

Later, she asked Madhu Aunty how Mahima was.

'Perfect! *So* happy she is! Like a princess, her in-laws treat her! Such a good husband, Shekhar is – before even she asks, he gives! *So* lucky my Mahima is!'

'But Aunty, she never comes to Delhi.'

'Beta, because her husband and in-laws love her too much, they cannot live without her.'

What kind of logic was that?

Thank goodness, by the time the winter holidays came, Mallika was much better. It was at this time that Prabha blurted out to Arnav that he'd said Mallika was boring. Then she had managed to push Gauri to confront Arnav about the kiss – high time. Gauri was exasperated with her. Everyone was. That afternoon, wanting to escape from her feeling that no one understood her, she took a bus to the British Council library.

And that was when it happened. The man sitting next to her on the bus squeezed her breast.

Just like that, he did it, gazing straight ahead of him, as though his body didn't know what his hand was doing. She didn't even *think* of the large nappy pin that she always carried in her hand when travelling by DTC buses. Instead of digging that into him, she socked him on the jaw. He was knocked sideways and screamed blue murder. In that instant, as though in slow motion, she saw the men who were laughing, the men whose eyes were avid, and the conductor, who was looking at her as if he'd like to do the same thing himself.

'Batameez,' she shouted, getting up. 'Haraam zaada, kuttha.' The women in the bus were staring at her. 'Get up,' she said to them in Hindi. 'Get up and kick this haraam zaada out of the bus.'

No one got up.

The man she had socked lunged at her.

She ducked, putting her hands over her head.

After a few seconds, she looked up. Two women had caught hold of him, dragged him out of his seat, and were shaking him as though he were a rat. The other women in the bus were moving towards him. One woman with a cloth bag of vegetables took out a big louki and began hitting him with it. Another pulled his hair. The rest had now caught hold of him and were shoving him towards the front of the bus, calling him names she had never heard before. She got up and joined them. The conductor was shouting, and the driver was looking over his shoulder.

'Look where you're going, bhaiyya,' she said. 'Don't look at us.'

By this time, the women had dragged the culprit to the front door, and the bus had stopped. Swearing and cursing, using words she'd never heard, the women threw him out of the bus. Then they went back to their seats, and the bus began to move again.

'Who do you think we are,' the woman with the vegetables said, brandishing her louki at the men in the bus. 'We are not cowards and dirty people like you.' She turned to Prabha, 'Beta, every woman should be like you.' All the women clapped and cheered. 'Beta, what is your name?'

'Prabha,' she said. The woman shouted, 'See, she is the same as her name: she is light. Today, she has shown us her light. Should I tell you why we have seen the light?'

'Tell, tell,' shouted all the women in the bus.

'We have seen the light because today we are one. Never forget this: alone, we are darkness. Together, we are light. Together we are Durga Maata. Together we are Shakti.' More clapping and shrieks of delight.

When she got out at her bus stop five minutes later, all the women waved goodbye to her, and the one with the vegetables waved her louki triumphantly.

Never in her entire life had Prabha felt so vindicated.

It had happened to all of them – her, Mallika, Mahima, Gauri. It had happened to their mothers. It was why their mothers were so particular that they came home before dark, that they didn't travel alone in the evenings, that they dress with decorum. She had tried to explain to Mumma that none of it made a difference. It happened in the day, it happened at night, it happened if you were with a group of girls, it happened no matter what you wore, it happened no matter how you behaved, it happened no matter how old you were, it happened no matter what.

Most of the time, you couldn't defend yourself. The men were too swift. They'd had plenty of practice. They rode past you in two-wheelers and hit your breasts, then drove away laughing loudly. They walked past you, put their fingers between your bums, and were gone in an instant. They walked towards you and felt your crotch as they passed you, then disappeared.

They didn't tell their mothers. Their mothers would have taken it too much to heart. But also, it would have meant more restrictions – 'Don't go here, don't go there, don't wear this, don't wear that, who is that boy you're talking to?' Life would have ground to a halt if they told their mothers every time it happened.

It wasn't as though she could hitch rides, the way Delhi girls did these days. You could see them everywhere in South Delhi, particularly outside the LSR gates, thumbs up, asking for lifts and easily getting them. Mallika told her that there were groups of girls hitching all day outside her college. The bolder ones hitched alone on motorcycles and two-wheelers. She, Mallika, Gauri, and Mahima had done it once, in a nice, roomy Ambassador with a kind old gentleman. They told their mothers about it gleefully, and, of course, foolishly. They'd been forbidden to ever do it again.

She had no intention of telling her parents what had happened in the bus. But she told Gauri and Mallika everything that night.

'You're very brave, Prabha,' said Mallika.

Gauri said, 'Yes, you are. But be careful. Next time, you may not be so lucky.'

She nodded. She knew she'd had a lucky escape. It could easily have gone the other way.

She looked questioningly at Gauri – had she talked to Arnav? Gauri shook her head slightly. Meaning what? That she hadn't? Or that the talk hadn't gone well? She had to find time alone with Gauri. She was dying to know.

The next morning, Gauri and Mallika came running to her house and burst into her room with a copy of the *Indian Express*. On the second page was a news item entitled, 'PRABHA, THE LIGHT IN THE DARKNESS.'

It was *her* story! The woman who had bashed her assailant with the louki had gone straight to the *Indian Express* office and told them the story. The journalist had found out the bus number from her, got hold of the driver and conductor, corroborated the story, and there it was! She, Mallika, and Gauri read it and reread it, full of excitement.

The journalist hadn't described what the man had done to her. The journalist had merely said that the man had 'outraged her modesty.'

'Outraged my *modesty*, my foot!'

'Prabha! He can't say the man squeezed your breasts in the national newspaper,' Gauri said.

Mumma came into her room with a plate of shakkar para and said affectionately, 'So much noise you girls are making!' She put the plate on the bed where they were sitting.

'Look at this, Aunty, *look* at this!' Mallika said proudly, and gave her the newspaper.

Big mistake.

Mumma read the article. Then she looked up, her face grim, 'This is *you*, Prabha?'

She nodded.

Mumma went out of the room with the newspaper. Now she would show it to Daddy.

'Mallika, what's *wrong* with you?' Gauri whispered.

'I thought… she'd be proud,' Mallika stammered.

'It's OK, Mallika,' Prabha said. 'It's OK.'

After Mallika and Gauri left, Mumma asked, 'What did that man do to you?'

She told Mumma.

'Battameez,' Mumma said, under her breath. Then: 'Daddy and I want to talk to you.'

They sat her down and lectured her. Being lucky once did not mean she would be lucky the second time. Never should she retaliate again because the consequences could be very serious. 'If such a thing happens again, just get up and move to another seat. Try not to be so reckless and unthinking,' Mumma said.

If this had been a film, Mumma would have said, 'See how brave she is! There should be more women like her in this world.'

Heroines existed only in films. In real life, the girl who stood up to wrong was reckless, unthinking, and disobedient. Even Daddy, who had always told her to stand up for the right thing, was upset with her.

Daddy had always been her hero. He had unshakeable integrity. He had lost his job once for refusing to do something dishonest that his boss wanted him to do. This, when he had no savings and was supporting a wife, two children, and his mother. Her mother called him 'Harishchandra', and it wasn't a compliment. But Daddy had told Prabha, 'Beti, how you live your life, *that* is your true religion.'

That Mumma hadn't supported her about the bus incident wasn't a surprise. But Daddy? All he had to do was say, 'You are a brave girl, I am proud of what you did, but just be careful.' But he hadn't.

She couldn't bring herself to ask, 'Why doesn't what you said apply to *me*, Daddy?'

After Mummy and Daddy's lecture, she went to Mallika's house and wept in her room. She understood what her parents were saying, she told Mallika. She had just wanted some affirmation from them, that was all.

'I guess I was lucky,' she said, wiping her eyes.

Mallika said passionately, 'You roused all the women in the bus to stand as one. That isn't *luck*. That's *you*.'

Mallika's words almost made up for her parents' reaction.

They stepped out of the house and saw that the three boys were there, between Mallika and Randhir's houses, sitting on their motorcycles and kidding around with each other. The boys waved and said hi, so they stopped to talk. Mallika didn't make an excuse to go off. Now that she and Arnav were friends, she wasn't as shy. Prabha tried to read Arnav's face. If Gauri had talked to him about the kiss, it certainly didn't show. He looked his usual, laughing self, and not a bit self-conscious with Mallika.

'That was gutsy, Prabha,' he said.

'How d'you know?'

'It was in the *Indian Express*!' Randhir said.

'But Randhir, there are hundreds of Prabhas in Delhi!'

'Your mother told mummy.'

Of course, Mumma wouldn't keep it from Madhu Aunty.

'We have to deal with that shit all the time,' she sighed.

How to tell the boys the way men pressed against them in buses? How, as they walked down the street, men in two-wheelers drove past them and grabbed their breasts? How masturbating men in cars stopped and offered them lifts, how men exposed themselves outside their college gates? Girls from South India, Bengal, and Bombay said it never happened there, and it had certainly never happened to her in Poona. In Delhi, she always carried safety pins. Mahima carried an umbrella, Gauri had three sharp wooden juda pins in her hair to dig into any guy in any bus, and Mallika often carried a tiny knife in her saree blouse. It was sheathed in a beautiful carved white case. You just pulled it out, and there it was, with a white hilt, deadly sharp and ready to draw blood. Not that she'd used it; it just made her feel safe, she said. When walking in Connaught Place or anywhere else, Mallika used her elbows. She had jabbed any number of lecherous, groping men in the stomach, and then she'd run. No one could run faster in a saree than Mallika.

How to explain to the boys how pervasive such behaviour was? That it was part of their daily lives?

'They do horrible things to us in buses and on the roads,' she said.

Vineet was disbelieving. 'Come on, Prabha, aren't you exaggerating!'

Mallika spoke. 'Just because it doesn't happen to any of *you*, doesn't mean it doesn't *happen*.'

The boys turned to her, startled.

'If you're one of those rich girls who goes everywhere by car, *then* maybe it doesn't,' Mallika went on. 'But we all go by bus. Or we walk.'

The boys were listening.

'They don't even spare children. My student, Jalpari, was twelve when two men abducted her in a car.'

'How do you know?' Arnav asked abruptly.

Mallika looked stunned at his tone.

Arnav stammered, 'I mean... I meant... What happened?'

By now, Mallika couldn't talk.

Prabha answered for her. 'Jalpari was a girl from the slums who Mallika was tutoring for two years. Her father's a scooterwalla in our colony. He told Mallika a couple of months ago that two men in a car abducted Jalpari right in front of their eyes, in their basti.'

There was another silence.

Arnav said, 'And... then?'

'Jalpari's never come back,' Prabha said. 'Karan Uncle followed up the police report and everything. But what do the police care about a girl from the slums?'

Randhir was looking at Mallika with concern.

Arnav quickly started his bike. 'Got to go, bye.' He put on his helmet, waved, and was off.

Prabha glanced at Mallika and saw her own shock at Arnav's sudden disappearance reflected on her friend's face.

They said bye to Randhir and Vineet and walked to the park.

'The way Arnav just went off,' Prabha said, still shocked. How could he leave as though what happened to Jalpari was nothing? Sometimes, a minute of silence was in itself an acknowledgment.

'I don't understand, Prabha. He's not like that,' Mallika said, sounding distressed.

'Looks like he is,' Prabha said.

Later that day, Mumma gave her two tiffin carriers of gulab jamuns for Padma Aunty and Madhu Aunty. She had just stepped onto Madhu Aunty's veranda when two girls came out of Randhir's house. They were friends of Randhir whom she'd seen on and off. The taller one, Arati said, 'Well, well, we heard all about your bus drama.'

Something in her tone made Prabha uneasy.

'Really, Prabha, you're too much,' laughed the second girl, Deepika.

Arati shook her head. 'What is the *point* of behaving like that, I don't understand.'

Deepika added, 'It happens to everyone.'

Prabha was bereft of words.

'I mean, newspaper coverage and all that, I *tell* you!' exclaimed Arati.

'Why focus on all *that* stuff?' said Deepika. 'There are so many good things happening in our country, we've progressed so much – that's what you need to focus on, not *this* rubbish.'

Prabha spoke at last. 'So… What do you do when it happens?' She was feeling a bit sick.

'We deal with it,' Deepika shrugged.

'I dealt with it,' she said.

'That's not *dealing* with it. That's just calling attention to yourself,' Arati declared.

Deepika shook her head, making a *tch-tch-tch* sound.

'What does dealing with it mean, then?' she asked.

'*Really*, Prabha!' Arati shook her head pityingly.

'Come *on*, Prabha!' Deepika said, as though she should know.

Then, in perfect accord, they turned and walked away.

Slowly, she went inside and gave Madhu Aunty the gulab jamuns. Then she walked to Mallika's house with the second tiffin carrier. She gave Padma Aunty the gulab jamuns, then went upstairs to Mallika's room. Gauri was there too. 'I'm trying to persuade Mallika to come to Randhir's party tonight,' Gauri said.

'I told you, Gauri, I'm *not* going,' Mallika said. Then she looked at Prabha. 'Why are you looking so upset?'

Prabha burst into tears. 'I should never have hit that man in the bus. I should never express what I feel. There's no point.'

Gauri thrust a soft handkerchief into her hands. She cried bitterly into it.

Finally, when she had stopped, Mallika said, 'Prabha, remember as children we had those blank picture books? The picture only became visible when you filled the page with the strokes of a pencil?'

She nodded. She had loved those books.

Lovingly, Mallika said, 'That's *you*. You're that pencil.'

Gauri sighed. 'That's so true.

Her throat was full.

Comforted, she told them about her encounter with Deepika and Arati. Her friends listened, frowning.

'What did they mean when they told me to "deal with it?"' she asked.

Mallika and Gauri looked at each other. It seemed like they had no idea either.

Mallika turned to her. '*Forget* them, Prabha.'

Gauri said, 'They're not worth your thoughts.'

She was feeling vastly soothed and reassured. The miasma of shame that had blanketed her began to lift.

But her question remained unanswered. What had those girls meant when they had told her to 'deal with it?'

Mahima: Of course I'm happy!

1976 and earlier

Home. Finally, she was home. Such happiness was pain. Her heart hurt from it.

The last time – the summer when Mallika had TB – it had only been for three days. As soon as she fell into Mummy's arms, she had felt bereft because she was leaving in two days, and when she left, she and Mummy cried buckets. Even Daddy was tearful. She had slept with them for those three nights, in Mummy's bed, Mummy's body so warm and comforting against her own. From time to time, Daddy, who wasn't usually demonstrative, would stroke her head as though he couldn't believe she were with them again. And Randhir, who never saw Hindi films, had actually offered to take her for one. She had laughed, 'No, silly, not when I'm home for just three days!' She hadn't been able to see Mallika because Padma Aunty was being overprotective as usual, even though Mallika was no longer infectious. Prabha had gone back to Poona. Gauri, she'd managed to see in JNU for a few hours. Gauri had knitted her the most beautiful sweater – she wore it more than any of her other sweaters.

This time, it was late December, almost a year after her marriage. She was home for ten days and was going out with her friends to celebrate. Mummy had said to take her car, so no worrying about recalcitrant scooterwallas, crowded buses, or coming back before it got dark.

First, they went to Chachaji's bookshop in Shankar Market. Prabha and Mallika bought five second-hand books each. But there was a pile of books lying next to them at which they were both gazing hungrily, so she said, 'OK, now don't fuss,' and bought the whole lot for them. She would have bought them more, but she knew they wouldn't let her. Especially since she had already given them expensive foreign gifts – perfumes, lipsticks, and lacy bras (they were all roughly the same bra size). Shekhar kept bestowing gifts on her from his business trips abroad, and every time, she kept some aside for her friends. Of course, she didn't tell Shekhar. She had to take care not to hurt him. He was too sensitive. Not that he ever got angry with her, never. Unlike her; she didn't show it, but sometimes anger exploded inside her for no reason. It was her fault, because she had everything. The only thing she didn't have was acceptance.

Mummy always said that acceptance made life easier. The early years of Mummy's marriage had been so difficult; Daddy wasn't an easy man to live with. Of course, her brothers had no idea. For her brothers, Mummy not talking about her problems meant that she had none. Mummy had told her that once she had accepted that things would not change, everything became easier for her. But clearly, she was a lesser person than Mummy.

As soon as she and her friends sat down for lunch at Triveni, they began asking her questions.

'Are you happy, Mahima?' Gauri asked.

'Of course I'm happy!'

She told them how well Shekhar treated her, how generous he was. How he wanted to be with her all the time, and about the parties and films they went to.

Mallika asked, 'Why haven't you come home for so long, Mahima?'

'What to do? Shekhar really misses me when I'm gone.'

'Why did you only come for three days the first time?' Prabha wondered. 'If you'd come a day earlier, we'd have seen each other.'

'I know, Prabha. I felt so bad. But Shekhar was going away for a business trip and said not to go until he left. He's too attached to me. And this time, I had to pretend that Mummy was ill so that I could come for ten days! I tell you, men and their dependence on their wives!'

When Mummy had phoned her at Chandigarh a few days ago, she had it planned out.

'Beta, how are you?' Mummy said.

She was silent for some time, and then she burst into tears and cried, 'Mummy if you're not well, I'm coming home, I'll come home tomorrow.'

Mummy was silent for just a few seconds. Then: 'Yes, Beta, please come home, I am feeling very ill, high fever I have.' And Mummy put down the phone without talking any more.

Mahima stared at the phone, letting the tears course down her cheeks. Everyone had heard the conversation. Shekhar and her in-laws were in the sitting room. Her mother-in-law said, 'Go to Delhi tomorrow, Beta. I will talk to the driver today. Do not cry, Beta, your Mummy will be alright.'

Shekhar looked upset. Even her quiet father-in-law seemed affected by her tears. She had never known tears could be so powerful. She would use them again. Sparingly. Instinct told her that, if used too often, tears would lose their potency.

'I'll drive you to Delhi tomorrow,' Shekhar said.

'The driver can take me,' she said.

'I'll take you,' he said.

'I'll phone Mummy and tell her.'

'No need. Let's surprise her.'

It was the worst drive of her life.

When they finally parked outside her house, it was noon. Their servant's little daughter was on the veranda and ran inside.

Mahima had to get in the house before Shekhar entered and tell Mummy to hurry and get into bed. But Shekhar said, 'Wait, Mahima! We will go in together, what is the hurry?'

She was done for.

The front door was open as usual, the curtain fluttering in the breeze. They entered. No sign of Mummy anywhere. Ramu greeted them and said, 'Your Mummy is lying down, she is not well.'

They went to mummy's bedroom, and Mummy was lying there, breathing heavily, her face pale, smelling of Vicks, in an old salwar kameez, a towel next to her, her eyes closed.

'Mummy,' she whispered, sitting on the bed and putting her arms around her.

Mummy opened her eyes and whispered, 'How are you, Beta? Shekhar, how are you?'

'Fine, fine. Mahima, I'll be outside.' He went out.

'Mummy, what's happened to you?' she said frantically.

'Nothing,' her mother whispered. 'But Shekhar must think I am ill.'

Mummy had known she would come. Mummy had known Shekhar would come with her. She had kept Ramu's little daughter in the veranda the entire morning. And as soon as the car came, the little girl told Mummy. And Mummy – who had not had a bath, applied lipstick, or combed her hair since she got up – clambered into bed.

'Little bit acting and all is good,' Mummy said after Shekhar had had lunch and left for Chandigarh. 'After all, we have to live our lives, no, Beta?'

Of course, she didn't tell her friends any of this.

And Shekhar was so generous. He had bought a Fiat for her and hired a driver, so when he was at work, she could go wherever she wanted and buy whatever she wished. All the shopkeepers knew Shekhar and his family, and Shekhar paid them later. He never gave her cash.

Unlike her, Mummy had money of her own. From the time she was little, Mummy had been putting aside money in her own bank account: money that her brothers gave her from time to time, money that she saved from what Daddy gave her to run the house, money that Daddy gave her for her birthday and their anniversary. As the money accumulated, Mummy put it into fixed deposits, and the money grew even more. Then, when Mahima was in college, Mummy had opened a tailoring shop in the market. She had named it Dimple Tailors because she'd fallen in love with Dimple Kapadia in her film *Bobby*. She had started with one small space, one tailor, and one Usha sewing machine; now, there were eight tailors, the business was thriving, and she was putting away money from her tailoring business into her own account. She had made Mahima the nominee to the account, not her brothers. Her reason for this: 'They will inherit everything, but what about you?'

When Mahima had first told Mallika that her parents were looking for a boy for her, Mallika had said, 'But don't you want to fall in love?'

'Uffho, Mallika! Why do you think there's no love in arranged marriages?'

Mallika was a romantic. Gauri too. But Mallika was also gullible. Mahima didn't know which was worse, romantic or gullible. Or maybe they were the same thing.

'Falling in love makes you selfish. Look what happened to my brother, Akhil. Fancying himself in love with a Muslim girl and eloping with her, and not even *thinking* of our parents.'

Mummy had actually found out about the affair before Akhil married Ameena. Mummy had gone to Bombay to try and persuade Akhil to break it off. He refused. So when Akhil broke the news about his marriage, Mummy pretended to everyone that it was news to her too.

After that, naturally the responsibility of the factory fell on Randhir.

Mallika hero-worshipped Randhir. She was taken in by all his high-flown talk about Plato and Aristotle, and about love being two halves trying to find one another to become whole. Mallika's eyes had been shining when she told them all that story. And then Randhir got involved with that mad Charu. So much for his exalted talk about two halves making a whole. The truth was more sordid.

When she, Mahima, had got engaged to Shekhar, Mallika and Gauri were so happy. But Prabha had the cheek to say, 'What a waste of your potential.'

She had retorted, 'Prabha, can't you see you're doing the same thing to me that you say your parents do to you? Inflicting your beliefs on me?'

That made Prabha shut up.

It was around the time of her engagement that Mummy had come breathlessly from Randhir's room and burst into tears. 'I was cleaning Randhir's room – so untidy he keeps it – and I found those American university brochures there. He will go, and he will never come back.'

She had comforted her mother, all the while thinking, I have to talk to Shekhar, I can't marry a man who'll take me away from my parents.

A couple of days later, she and Shekhar went to a Chinese restaurant. It was their second meeting. After they ordered, she tried to think of how to say this without giving away her family's secrets.

He was smiling faintly as he said, 'Don't look so worried. Ask me.'

Taken aback by his perceptiveness, she blurted it out. 'I have to be there for my parents. After marriage. Like you're there for your parents, that way.'

'Of course. We all should be there for our parents.'

She sighed with relief.

Shekhar said, 'But your brothers are there for your parents.'

This was the question she had prepared herself for. Because obviously Mummy hadn't told Shekhar and his family that Akhil was lost to them since he'd married a Muslim girl. All she had told them was that Akhil was working in Bombay. And where was the question of telling them Randhir was applying to American universities when Randhir hadn't even told his own family! She could never tell Shekhar the shameful fact that neither of her brothers would be there for her parents.

So she said, 'I also want to be there for Mummy and Daddy. Otherwise I can't marry you.'

She meant it. If it didn't work out with Shekhar, it would work out with someone else.

'Of course, you can be there for your parents! That's not anything to worry about.'

After he dropped her home that day, she had told her parents that she would marry him.

Mallika and Gauri were starry-eyed about Shekhar. And it wasn't as if she were immune to his looks. But more importantly, he was such a gentleman, and he was mature. Courteous to everyone, respectful to her parents. Opening doors for her and always sitting down in a restaurant after she sat, things like that, which so few boys these days did. So unlike Randhir's friends, with their raucous laughter and loud music and sessions of dope up on the terrace. Also, he didn't think that just because they were engaged, he had the right to touch her. She could never understand how people who didn't know each other could start kissing and all straightaway. Besides, *where* did one kiss? The first time Shekhar kissed her was a month after their engagement. It was in the car when he dropped her back home. It was dark, and there was no one outside. He leaned sideways and kissed her cheek, very gently and briefly. It was an alien sensation, the smell and touch of a man. It was nothing like the books made it out to be. If her pulse was racing, it was mostly because she was nervous that someone would see them.

Whenever he came to Delhi from Chandigarh, he would take her for films. He knew she loved films, and although he wasn't particularly fond of them, he was happy to take her. He would hold her hand while they watched, and she loved that. There was a reserve about him that seemed to soften when she talked. She knew he would open up after they got married. After all, Mallika was quiet too, but not with the three of them.

And then they were married, and like in the films, there she was, in the hotel where they were spending their wedding night, in a flower-bedecked bed, she in her wedding finery, and he tall and splendid like the Hero.

But this wasn't a Hindi film.

He smiled at her. But he was looking tired.

'I'm... scared.' She burst into tears.

He put an arm around her and let her cry into his beautiful off-white sherwani. When she finally stopped, he gave her a handkerchief, and she wiped her eyes and nose.

'You're scared of me?'

'Not of you. I can't... I'm not ready to...'

'Alright. How do you manage to look beautiful even when you're crying?'

She felt herself blushing. 'Can we get to know each other first?'

He nodded, looking relieved.

An hour later, as she watched him sleep beside her, his face relaxed and vulnerable, she thought, How lucky I am.

They went to Simla for a short honeymoon. It was like going for a holiday with a friend.

After they returned to Chandigarh, her mother-in-law sat her down and said to her, 'Bas, you are the kind of girl who can sudharo any man.'

She could transform any man? Puzzled, she said, 'But Shekhar does not need to change himself in any way.'

If only she could tell Randhir how kind and sensitive Shekhar was! Because the night before the wedding, Randhir had told their parents her wedding needed to be stopped. He'd heard rumours about Shekhar, that he didn't have a good reputation, that his family wasn't all it was made out to be, all that rubbish. They got into a big fight. It ended with Randhir storming out of the house. She had overheard everything. It had shaken her terribly.

Not long after their arrival home, the doorbell rang.

Randhir stood at the door, grinning. He'd come to Chandigarh to see her!

She couldn't stop hugging him. He smelt of home. Her in-laws and Shekhar welcomed him with open arms. It was so lovely to see her brother's tall, familiar figure at the dining table and in the sitting room, to hear him talking and laughing in her new home. She could see that, below all that talk and laughter, he was quietly assessing everyone. She felt ensconced in that snug, lovely feeling that only your parental family could give you, that feeling of absolute safety. Randhir had done the right thing, coming to see her. It was what every brother should do for a newly married sister, but Randhir was always so preoccupied with himself. Yet now here he was! He could be so charming when he chose. She could see how taken everyone was by his impeccable manners, his intellect, his looks, and the attentive manner in which he listened, as though each person was spouting words of infinite wisdom. In fact, her mother-in-law was talking about the Ikebana style of flower arrangements, her father-in-law about his business, and Shekhar about his admiration for Indira Gandhi and the need for a country like India to have a permanent state of Emergency for it to function. She was apprehensive that Randhir would get into an argument with Shekar about this, but Randhir listened as though he had no opinion about the Emergency at all. That must have taken something. Randhir, Arnav, and Vineet were all fire and fury about the changes to the Constitution, the clamping down on the press, the fact that anyone could be arrested for anything, the demolition of slums and the forced sterilizations. What was the point? What was all their talking worth? At least the JNU students had gone to jail for their views, but these DU and IIT boys just talked and thought they were *so* superior because they were so full of outrage. What was outrage worth if you didn't *do* anything about it?

Shekhar asked about their brother Akhil. Randhir looked surprised and said, 'He's fine.' She gave Randhir a look, and he realized his mistake and said, 'Better.' Because Mumma had told her in-laws that Akhil hadn't come for the wedding because he had broken his leg. Mumma usually hated using illness as an excuse, but what else to say when the bride's brother didn't come for the wedding?

'Come, let me show you the house,' she said to Randhir.

He looked surprised. 'Oh, OK.'

It would make her in-laws and Shekhar happy that she was showing her brother what a large, beautiful house they lived in. This silly brother of hers! He never understood these things! Shekhar accompanied them. Randhir made polite noises, but the only thing he sounded truly enthusiastic about was Shekhar's desk in his study.

'Oh, wow, what a fantastic desk!' he said to Shekhar.

'My grandfather's,' Shekhar said, and Randhir touched it with reverence, the way a woman would touch a pashmina shawl. Raving about a *desk*, of all things!

After everyone went off for their afternoon naps, Randhir asked if she felt like going for a walk, so she grabbed her pashmina shawl, and they stepped out into a beautiful winter day. She was full of love for her brother. She was bursting with questions about Mummy and Daddy and her three friends. Every time she and Shekhar went for a party, she would think of Mallika standing sulkily in a corner, not talking to anyone. Of Gauri, in one of her lovely handloom sarees, charming everyone. Of Prabha, expounding on her views about women and justice. There was no moment when she didn't think of her three friends. But Randhir said rapidly, 'Mahima, if you want to leave Shekhar, then just tell me, and I'll take you home today itself.'

All her joy evaporated. All her excitement, all her anticipation. All her newfound happiness.

'Have you gone *mad*? First, you wanted to stop my marriage, and now, you want me to leave it? After two weeks? Is something wrong with your head, Randhir?'

'I'm just making sure you're alright.'

'Of course, I'm alright. I just don't *understand* you sometimes.'

'Sorry, I put it very badly. I was… I was just worried, Mahima.'

As soon as he said this, her heart began to melt. Those silly rumours were still stuck in his head. He was her brother. It was his right to ask her.

'My in-laws are very good to me. And Shekhar – we're just getting to know each other, but I *like* him. Let me tell you, he's a lot more mature than those friends of *yours*.'

He let out his breath, and his shoulders straightened as though he were finally done with all the problems of the world.

'Good.' He stopped and gave her a quick hug, then let her go.

She found herself swallowing sudden tears. She missed Randhir's hugs. And Mummy's hugs, and the way Daddy put his hand on her cheek or on her head. The way Gauri tucked her into bed on the nights that they spent together, and how in the winters, she and her three friends would snuggle close to one another under the razai on her large bed as they gossiped. Shekhar had taken her words seriously, which was good of him, but it meant that he hardly ever touched her. What she had meant to say on their wedding night was that she didn't want to have sex straightaway; she first wanted to get to know him. And getting to know him meant hugging, it meant affectionate kisses, it meant snuggling in bed, it meant all the ways that you showed one another affection that had nothing to do with sex, but which – she assumed – could ease the path towards it. She had wept in his arms on their wedding night, and he had tended to her tears and spoken of how beautiful she was. But did she have to cry for him to take her in his arms? He hadn't done it since. Not even on their honeymoon. Words uttered by one of her married college mates kept coming back to her. She had said, 'The problem with guys is that whenever you want affection, they think you want sex.' She didn't know how to say to Shekhar, 'Hold me,' without sounding as if she wanted something more.

Randhir told her about Mallika's concussion and her lost memory.

'Mallika doesn't remember my *wedding*?'

'Nothing at all.'

She was stunned. 'So she's OK now?'

'Yeah. A bit... disoriented from time to time, but OK on the whole.'

He was looking so mellow that it just came out of her. 'Randhir, do you want to marry Mallika?'

His head whipped around. His smile was gone. 'Mallika said something to you?'

'Of *course* not!'

She heard him let out his breath. 'Mallika's my *friend*. And anyway, I don't believe in marriage.'

He didn't *believe* in it! Oh, *really*! Randhir was full of theories. Theories about soulmates, theories about following one's dreams, theories about how to raise your children (oh, yes, even that! He had told Mummy children needed the freedom to grow into their true selves). He had theories about Indira Gandhi destroying the nation, theories about the servile Indian mentality, theories about everything under the sun. And now this!

'Then you better tell Mallika before you ditch her and go off to America.'

He stopped in his tracks. 'Go off to America?' he said, very quietly.

'Mummy found those brochures from American universities in your room.'

'I see. Snooping around in my room, as usual.'

'She was *cleaning* your room.'

'Oh, sure.'

Their moment of harmony and affection was shattered.

How *dare* he talk about their own mother in that tone. How could Mallika not see through him?

Mallika had never spoken about marrying Randhir. And it hadn't even entered Mummy's mind. Mummy always said they were like brother and sister. And since she herself wasn't sure anything would come of it, why tell Mummy? Because although Mallika was a very good daughter and friend, she wouldn't make a very good wife or daughter-in-law because she wasn't interested in housework or cooking; all she wanted to do was read and look after her mothers, which was useless when you got married. As for her reluctance to go to parties and meet people – no man would put up with it.

If Mallika had given her heart to Randhir, she wouldn't give it to anyone else. And Randhir would break it. Not deliberately, but because he would go his way, regardless of her. Even if he loved her, it would not be the way that she loved him. Randhir's love was always the lesser. But being Randhir, he was surrounded by an abundance of love.

And now, after her concussion, Randhir had gone and done his knight-in-shining-armour act, taking her to the hospital, getting her back home, like a Mills & Boon Hero. But a Mills & Boon Hero, however selfish and arrogant, changed by the end of the book. His love for the Heroine changed him. That would not happen to Randhir.

'I'm not going to America,' Randhir said. 'Some friends gave me those brochures.'

And he'd hidden them from everyone? Just so he could look at them? What rubbish!

By the next morning, both of them had calmed down. Neither brought up the previous day's conversation.

Now, as they ate lunch at Triveni, Gauri, Prabha, and Mallika gave Mahima the gossip. She got to know about Prabha socking that man on the bus, how Mallika's TB and medicines had taken the life out of her, how Mallika's father had stayed in Delhi for a month, and after that, how Randhir and Arnav had picked Mallika up daily from college. And how Prabha had told Arnav he'd called Mallika boring, and that he didn't even remember, the idiot.

Then, just for laughs, they went to the astrologer in Bengali Market. Prabha, Gauri, and Mallika asked when they'd get married and if they'd ever travel abroad. The astrologer assured them that they'd get married in the next two-to-five years, and predicted handsome husbands and three-to-five trips abroad for each of them. When astrologers said 'abroad,' they didn't mean Ceylon or Nepal, or communist countries like Russia and China, they meant England and the rest of Europe and America. Mahima asked how many children she would have; he said two – first a boy, and then a girl.

They emerged from the session thrilled. She was delighted at the prospect of a boy and a girl; meanwhile Prabha, Gauri, and Mallika were excited because they would go abroad. No one went abroad unless they were millionaires or air hostesses. As for becoming an air hostess – as their mothers would say – why do educated girls want to do ayah-duty in the air and deal with drunk Indian men? Because Indian men always got drunk in planes with all that free alcohol.

Shekhar drank and smoked moderately and never got drunk. He didn't have eyes for any woman but her. He said she was graceful as a swan. He said the kind of things that would have dazzled Mallika and Gauri. But they now made her squirm. Her mother-in-law said that she was the centre of Shekhar's universe. Unfortunately, she was.

Later, after a spectacular Kuchipudi dance performance by Raja and Radha Reddy at Kamani, they spent the night at Mallika's. Oh, what joy to be with her friends again!

During the first few months of their marriage, Shekhar would say, 'What news from your friends?' That always made her happy. She wanted him to like her friends, to realize how important they were in her life. Every time he asked, she would perk up and give him her friends' news. After some time, he'd laugh and say, 'Is that *all* they write in their letters?' as though there was some great secret that she was hiding from him. So she'd show him their letters, so he could see how innocuous they were. Also, she wanted him to see how much they loved her. After all, he was always telling her she was the most precious person in his life. So, by extension, wouldn't her loved ones matter to him too? He'd skim through their letters and give them back to her without comment. And now, after a year of marriage, he would pick them up from her bedside table and read them without asking her, and she felt bad to say, 'Don't.'

The same thing had happened with Mummy's letters.

'Why is she asking if you're happy? Why shouldn't you be happy?' he asked after reading one once.

'It's just a way of talking, Shekhar,' she said. 'It doesn't mean anything.'

After that, she wrote to Mummy, *Don't ask if I'm happy, because Shekhar thinks I've been complaining about him.* And so Mummy never asked her.

But these were small things. She didn't have to put up with a husband who lost his temper with her or – god forbid – beat her. Or one who drank a lot and womanized, like her sister-in-law Renu's husband. Or one who allowed his parents to treat his wife like shit, the commonest story of all.

The only thing was, she didn't like Shekhar's friends. They kept coming home and staying for dinner, and then staying on for a couple of days. After dinner, Shekhar and whichever friend was visiting would retreat to his study to talk over drinks. 'You go to sleep,' he'd say to her. 'I'm shutting the door, so we won't disturb you.' The study was at the other end of the upstairs floor, the same floor as their bedroom. Why didn't Shekhar ever spend time chatting with her the way he did with his friends? Why weren't his friends ever interested in talking to her? When she was with Randhir, Arnav, and Vineet, she always felt included in their conversations; they treated her with affection and respect. But Shekhar's friends – after the initial greeting – didn't bother conversing with her, or even meeting her eyes. She couldn't stand them.

When Renu had come home to see her and Shekhar's parents for a week, she'd asked Mahima, 'So, are you jealous of your dear husband's *friends*?'

Mahima had said sharply, 'Why on earth should I be jealous?'

Renu had laughed that loud, coarse laugh of hers. 'Bilkul budhu you are!'
How *dare* that vulgar Renu call her a fool?

Still, she said nothing to Shekhar. How could she? After all, she wouldn't
like it if he complained to her about her friends.

After they came home from the dance performance, Prabha and Gauri fell
asleep on the divan on the floor. Mahima was sharing Mallika's bed and was
wide awake.

'Mahima,' Mallika whispered.

'Hmm?'

'Shekhar's good to you, no?'

'Yes.'

Mallika sighed with relief.

'But you know, all this sex and all, it's so overrated,' she said. 'Anyway. I
guess I'm used to it now.'

Mallika was very quiet for some time. Then, 'Do you love Shekhar?'

'Uff, Mallika! You and your love-shuv! Everything isn't about love!'

'Not even sex?'

'*Sex* least of all! Don't be so silly!'

'Isn't sex meaningful when there's love?' Mallika asked.

'Huh!' she said scornfully.

She didn't know how people could *enjoy* it. When it had finally happened,
he hadn't even hugged her or kissed her, he'd just rolled over to her side
one night and lifted her nightie and pulled down her panties and lowered
his pyjamas. It hurt like crazy. What *love* was there in this? She had bitten
her lips till they bled and held on to the bedsheet with both hands; he had
been so patient for so long, what was she supposed to say now, after all these
months? That she was still not ready? It was over quickly, and he turned his
back to her and went off to sleep.

That was how it was every time. Brief, painful, devoid of affection or
tenderness. Every time meaning once or twice a month. Once she said to
him, 'Not this time,' and he said, 'Don't you want children?' She said, 'I do.
But it hurts.' He said, 'We can stop after we have a son.' She said, 'We might
have a daughter.' He said, 'We have to have a son.'

'Sex hurts,' she said to Mallika.

Mallika looked at her without comprehension.

Then Mallika said, 'Always?'

'Always.'

After a few seconds, Mallika said, 'Maybe... you should talk to a gynae?'

'I did. I told the gynae it was really painful, and she said I should use
Vaseline. But the thing is – how am I supposed to be prepared with Vaseline

when I don't know when Shekhar wants to do it?' She knew Mallika had no idea about these things, but her anger with the gynae hadn't gone. 'The gynae told me, "You sound as though you don't want to have sex." I said, "I don't." And she shrugged and said, "Well, you're a married woman now."'

For the next five minutes, they were both silent.

'Talk to Shekhar,' Mallika said. 'Tell him it hurts.'

'Of course, I've told him. He's the one who said to go talk to a gynae.'

'Oh.'

Mahima changed the subject. 'Do you know Randhir's going off to America?'

'*What?*'

So. He hadn't told Mallika.

'Mummy found these American college brochures in his room.'

'Oh, *those*. Some friends of his gave them to him. We've been looking at them for years. It's just a fantasy, Mahima, neither of us is applying.'

'Maybe for you it's just a fantasy, but not for Randhir. He'll ditch Daddy and the factory and go off.'

'No, Mahima, he isn't even *thinking* of applying.'

'You think he tells you everything?'

'About this, he'd tell me.'

'Mallika, forget my brother. He's selfish to the core.'

Silence.

'He'll go off to America without even thinking of you. I don't want you to get hurt.'

She regretted it as soon as she said it. It was as though she'd crossed a line.

For some time, Mallika said nothing. Then she kissed Mahima's cheek and said goodnight.

Mallika was the one who kissed and hugged them. She hugged and kissed her mothers every day. Like a child. In every other way, she was anything but a child, but when she expressed her love, the child in her came out. This kind of affection was all she had wanted from Shekhar. Every time they had sat together, holding hands, watching a film, she had longed for that warm, comfortable feeling to be transferred to their bedroom. But after they started having sex, she no longer wanted to hold his hand.

She wasn't one for praying. Nor had she ever been one who, like so many women, had always wanted a son. But after he said they could stop doing it once they did, she had begun praying that she'd get pregnant quickly and have a boy. If she had a daughter, then she'd have to keep doing it. It had become clear by now that he didn't like doing it either, and that he did things to himself before he could do it to her, and that was why he was in such a hurry, and this was the reason it hurt her so much. It was as though he felt that having sex was like taking a bitter medicine. As though he had no choice but to swallow it, to get it over with quickly, and then he was done. Until the next time.

PART II

Arnav: Will you come back to me?

1976

The hijras had arrived the morning after Mahima's wedding, singing, clapping, demanding money. He was asleep with the rest of Randhir's male relatives on one of the mattresses set in rows in the sitting room and awakened to their loud sounds outside the house. Bleary-eyed, he saw Madhu Aunty coming out of her bedroom, muttering to herself, clutching some money in her hand. She went out and was back five minutes later, saying loudly, 'They're asking for more, and saying such dirty things.' By this time, several of their relatives were up and laughing at Madhu Aunty's predicament. Randhir, at the other end of the room, got up and said, 'Just *give* them more, Mummy.' Madhu Aunty, looking highly irritated, went back to her room and came out with more money. 'Here, *you* go and give them' she said to Randhir. Randhir counted the money, looked exasperated, then followed his mother back into her bedroom. He heard Randhir and Madhu Aunty arguing. Five minutes later, Randhir came out of his parents' bedroom and went outside. There was a lot of shouting, laughter, and clapping, and after a few minutes the sounds faded.

An hour later, as Ramu and Madhu Aunty made breakfast, he and Randhir helped with the serving. Randhir had said he'd rather serve food than sit and talk to the relatives. As for the relatives, they were most impressed that a boy was helping his mother in the kitchen.

As Madhu Aunty put the puris in the thali, she shuddered. 'Uff, those hijras.'

'Mummy,' Randhir said. 'Have you ever thought of how they can earn money?'

Madhu Aunty didn't reply.

'Who gives hijras jobs?'

Madhu Aunty, piling puris into two big thalis, still did not reply.

'Tell me, Mummy, *who* lets them live a normal life?'

'Accha, bas, enough of your lectures.'

'Just think about what all they have to do just to survive,' Randhir said.

'*You* think about it. A lot of time and energy you have to think about these things; I have to feed all the people in this house.' She left the kitchen with two plates of puris. 'Arnav, get the aloo sabji and achaar.'

He picked up the donga of sabji and achaar and took it to the dining room.

When they came back to the kitchen, Randhir, who was looking broodingly out of the window, turned to his mother. 'The amount of money you've spent on the wedding! And you couldn't have given them fifty rupees more?'

'Bas, karo, Randhir. If you want to give lectures, give to your father. He only said, "Do not give them more than fifty," and even then, I gave hundred. Why always you are telling *me*? Your father, he is sitting and eating happily. Go give *him* lecture.'

'They're people too,' Randhir muttered. Madhu Aunty made a sound of exasperation and left the kitchen with another thali of puris.

They were people too. Yes, people whom you didn't think about until they were in your face. If you saw them on the roads, you avoided looking at them. If Arnav hadn't thought about them harshly, it was because, for the most part, he hadn't thought about them at all. Not until Randhir spoke. Not until the rest of the day unfolded. As far as the world was concerned, they were freaks, anomalies, objects of derision – men dressed as women, in sarees, with long hair, bright lipstick, and kajal, fully bedecked with jewellery, bangles, earrings, necklaces, their faces closely shaven. Most of the time, they were invisible, until they suddenly weren't, striding along the road, going to shopkeepers as soon as their shops opened in the mornings, asking for money. Sometimes, you saw them in groups, making their way towards a house where they knew a child had been born, or a son or daughter married, and outside the house, they would begin their singing and clapping. No one could refuse them because it was bad luck: the hijras would curse the new-born, or the bride or the groom.

Later that day, just before he left to go back to IIT, Randhir was still brooding. 'How can they help who they are?' he said to Arnav. It wasn't the moment to ask Randhir what he meant. The guy had been in a shitty mood since before the wedding. The story was that they were born like that, of indeterminate sex. These babies, everyone said, were taken away from hospitals by the hijras. The parents were only too willing to relinquish such babies. So the hijras – who always got to know – came to the hospital and took the babies away, and the parents told everyone their children had died at birth. Someone had also once told Arnav that hijras were castrated males. Such were the stories about hijras.

It was as though he were meant to carry this with him into the rest of the day. As though the story that was waiting to happen had already begun.

He left Randhir's house in the late afternoon. Driving out of the colony, he saw Mallika at the bus stop, in a magenta saree and shawl, a handbag over her shoulder, running to catch a bus. In the manner of DTC buses, it had slowed down without quite stopping, several feet ahead of the bus stop, and several people were running, pushing, and shoving each other to get into it. Inside the bus there was barely any room to stand. Outside the bus, Mallika was swallowed by the crowd of people shoving each other to get in. He braked to a halt, got off his motorcycle, and ran towards her. 'Mallika,' he shouted, but by then she was standing precariously at the foot of the moving bus. 'I'll give you a lift, get off at the next stop,' he yelled, intending to follow the bus and pick her up, but she didn't hear the last bit. To his horror, she hitched up her saree and leapt out of the moving bus, landing on her feet like a cat, by which time he had his arms around her in anticipation of her falling. The men in the bus laughed loudly, some whistled, and one of them shouted something so obscene that he felt it jar his body like an electric shock. He steadied her, she looked at him, and he saw their kiss in her eyes. He let her go immediately, and in a few moments they were at his bike.

'Where are you going,' he said, starting his bike.

'JNU.' She sat behind him.

'Hold on,' he said as usual, and after a few seconds, he felt her arm go reluctantly around his waist, holding him lightly. For god's sake, it was only a kiss, he told her silently.

He'd drop her at JNU, and then he'd go home.

Fifteen minutes into their journey, he happened to glance at the taxi next to them. His sister's husband, Abhay, was inside, looking out of the other window.

His sister Niharika was currently visiting from America. After the obligatory week with her in-laws, she was finally at home. But Abhay was supposed to have left for Bombay the previous day to meet an old friend.

Arnav slowed down until the taxi passed and found himself following it.

'Mallika,' he shouted over his shoulder. 'Just taking a detour.'

'OK.'

He followed the taxi all the way to Ashoka Hotel.

'Why are we *here*?' Mallika asked as he parked.

'I'll tell you in a minute.'

They walked into the hotel lobby, and there was Abhay, his back to them, hugging a woman. She was wearing the Air India saree. Arnav stopped in his tracks.

Mallika looked at him, puzzled.

'That's Niharika's husband. With that air hostess.'

She looked at them. They were walking towards the lift now.

'Bloody hell,' he muttered through his teeth.

There was a brief silence.

'Should I... see where they're going?' Mallika asked tentatively.

He looked at her.

'I mean... you have to be sure, no?'

He nodded.

He watched her as she walked towards the couple. The lift opened and all three went in. As they turned, he turned his back to them.

Ten minutes later, Mallika came to him.

'They went into a room together.'

He didn't reply. He couldn't.

She swallowed, 'They were... kissing outside the door.'

There was a burning in his chest.

They walked out of the hotel in silence.

'Going to see Gauri?' he asked, starting his bike.

She nodded.

He dropped her outside Godavari hostel in JNU and then went to the dhaba for chai. He had to think before he went home and told Niharika. He had to calm himself. But he couldn't think. And he didn't feel calm.

He was halfway through his tea when he heard Mallika say, 'Arnav?'

She was standing next to him. 'Gauri isn't there.' She said it comfortingly, as though she weren't talking about Gauri, but about what he'd seen at the hotel.

He found his body beginning to relax. 'Chai?' She nodded. He ordered another. 'Feel like samosas?' She nodded again. 'Are you going to wait for Gauri?'

She shook her head. 'She's gone out. I don't know when she'll return.'

Seeing his surprise, she explained, 'She didn't know I was coming. I just took a chance.'

'I'll drop you home.'

'No, no, not again. I'll take a bus.'

'Oho, stop fussing.'

He hadn't travelled by bus ever since he got his bike when he was a fresher at IIT. He couldn't get over the sight of Mallika caught in that swirling crowd. And those men looking at her as though they were ready to tear off her saree.

'How do you do it, day in and day out? Travel in those buses?' he asked.

'What else to do?'

He felt himself flushing. Why was he such an idiot?

Her chai came, along with two samosas. He'd lost his appetite. 'D'you want mine? I'm not hungry.' She nodded and polished them off. If he hadn't been feeling so sick at the prospect of telling Niharika what he'd seen, he'd have been amused.

He muttered, 'How do I tell my sister?'

There was a silence.

Then she said, 'You're going to tell her?'

He looked at her in disbelief.

'Come on, Mallika. If you were in her place, wouldn't *you* want to know?'

There was another silence.

Then she said hesitantly, 'Sometimes, women don't want to know.'

Again, he looked at her in disbelief.

'If she tells him and he still doesn't stop his affair, then?'

'Mallika, if I hide something like this from her, I'll be complicit in it.'

'I'm not at all saying, "Don't tell her." All I'm saying is, it isn't so simple.'

'I have to tell her.'

She nodded.

'He treats Niharika like shit. My father treats my mother like shit.' A part of him was listening to himself in horror, saying, *Shut up, just shut up*, but he couldn't. 'Niharika's husband talks to her like my father talks to my mother. Putting her down. Dismissing her opinion about everything. Taking her for bloody granted. I don't understand. Niharika spent all her unmarried life with our father, appeasing him. Now, she's doing the same thing with her husband. I just don't get it.'

Then he found himself telling her a shitload of stuff. Randhir knew it all. He'd seen it all. Mallika had no context. Yet he didn't have to explain. Not that he could have even had he wanted to, because he didn't have answers to any of the whys in his life. Why his father behaved the way he did. Why his mother protected his father. Why Niharika's adoration of her father was so much greater than her love for her mother. Why she had fallen so crazily in love with a man who treated her like dirt, and why she continued loving him.

And then the story of Mishti came out. Knowing the situation at home, and being in the hostel, he should never have got a dog, he told Mallika. This was what was still killing him, that it was his fault for getting a dog when he didn't live at home. Mishti's death was entirely his fault.

He kept talking. He found himself telling her he wasn't sure he wanted to be an engineer. What, she exclaimed, then why was he at IIT? Because he was good at it, and it was a great profession, he said. What did he want to be? He didn't know, he said. How long had he known he wasn't sure about wanting to be an engineer? Just now as he was talking to her! He laughed. It was true: only as he talked to her had he realized that being good at something didn't mean you loved it. He wanted to love what he did, the way Randhir loved writing. He didn't know how to explain how restless he felt a lot of the time.

They walked around the hostel campus. Then they sat, had more tea, got up, and walked some more. At some point, he looked at his watch and saw it was past ten.

'Oh, shit, your mother'll be worried! We'd better go home,' he said.

'Ma's gone to Bangalore because my Shantamama's having an operation. Ayah-ji isn't expecting me back, I told her I'd be spending the night with Gauri.'

'Oh. I hope your aunt's operation goes off well.'

'She isn't my aunt. She's my mother too.'

'Sure,' he hastened to say. 'I just meant she's your aunt, by blood.'

'Maybe she's my aunt by blood, but she's my mother in every other way.'

He wondered how her father had died. Or why she and her mother didn't live with her stepfather.

'My father's family is also blood. But they have nothing to do with us. Madhu Aunty and Anu Aunty aren't blood. But they've done *everything* for us,' she said passionately.

He listened, fascinated. It was as if several other girls were hiding behind the one who had looked so frostily at him at the party, one of whom had kissed him back as hungrily as he'd kissed her. Now, they were both behaving as though it had never happened. He pushed away the memory. It was over. It was done.

'Have you ever felt like getting in touch with your father's family?'

'As if!'

'But you're close to your stepfather, right?' He'd often seen the quadruplets sitting in the veranda with him, laughing and talking.

For a couple of seconds, she didn't answer. Then she nodded.

Hmm. Something there too?

'I'm really hungry,' she said. 'Do you feel like aloo parathas?'

Suddenly, he did.

They walked back to the dhaba and ordered aloo parathas.

She enquired tentatively, 'Did you ask Randhir why he was so angry with me?'

For a few seconds, he didn't know what she was talking about. Then he realized she was referring to their conversation on her veranda, the night of Mahima's wedding. Just before he'd kissed her.

'He doesn't discuss you.'

'Oh.'

'What happened with him?'

She didn't even hesitate. 'Renu told me that Shekhar shouldn't be marrying Mahima because he's a pervert. So the day before the wedding, I told Randhir it should be stopped. He lost his temper. Very badly.'

'What did she mean – "pervert?"'

'That's the thing. I don't know. She refused to say. But whatever it was, I *had* to tell Randhir.'

An incident came to his mind, a memory of the time he'd heard another hosteller sniggering about two gay guys in the hostel, calling them 'bloody perverts.'

'Oh, shut up, man, what's your problem?' Arnav had said and walked away, taken aback by his sudden surge of anger. This was how everyone thought, but he had realized in that moment that he didn't.

No doubt Renu would think it was a perversion. But Renu was also a liar. This *had* to be one of her lies.

'Why do you think Randhir was so angry with me?' she asked.

'It was a day before the wedding, Mallika. What could Randhir do?'

She nodded.

'Everyone knows Renu's a compulsive liar. So, stop worrying. I'm sure Mahima's fine.' He was sure of it.

He saw the relief on her face.

'Now, tell me the whole story of how you stole the puppy,' he said, smiling.

She told him. He liked the sound of her voice. Her impulsiveness. That outrage. Her lack of regret.

Their aloo parathas arrived, and they ate hungrily.

'Arnav, you haven't smoked pot today, no?'

He blinked. 'Huh? Uh... No. Why?'

'Oh... Just wondering.'

They continued eating. He began to laugh so hard that he almost choked over his food. 'You think I've been talking to you because I'm stoned?'

'Yes.'

'Mallika, I'm not a bloody dopehead! I just have it occasionally!'

She examined his face gravely.

'I was talking to you because...' he stopped.

She kept looking at him.

'Because... it's as if... you're inside my story, living it with me.'

He saw the astonishment on her face. He was pretty astonished himself.

'I'm just going to get some fags, be back in a minute,' he said, putting aside his plate.

When he came back with the packet of cigarettes, she was writing something in a red diary. She saw him and put it away in her bag. A handkerchief was lying on the ground. He'd been standing on it before. He bent down and picked it up.

'Oh, that's mine,' she said, reaching out.

'Sorry, I stepped on it, it's dirty. Don't put it in your bag – I'll give it to you at home.' He thrust it into his pocket.

They walked towards his bike. It was almost eleven p.m. He said, 'How come you don't like Randhir's writing?'

She looked up at him, astounded. 'Why d'you think that?'

'You said he wasn't a storyteller. That time when we were at India Gate.'

There was a brief silence.

Then she said, 'I didn't know he wrote.'

He looked at her in disbelief.

She forced herself to smile, and then shrugged.

He didn't know what to say. He felt helpless.

'You don't have anything warm on.' He began to unzip his jacket.

'No, no, I'm wearing two sweaters, *and* I have this shawl. I don't need your jacket.' She wrapped the shawl around her head and neck. She saw him hesitate, and said, 'I'm not taking your jacket.'

He started the bike, and she sat behind him. 'Mallika, please hold on,' he urged. He felt her arm go around his waist.

There wasn't much traffic. Delhi roads were almost empty at this time of the night. They stopped at some traffic lights.

That was when they heard the screams.

At a bus stop on the other side of the road, a man was dragging a young girl towards a car. The girl was struggling and screaming.

'It's Jalpari, Jalpari,' Mallika shouted. The next second, she was off his bike, thrusting her bag into his arms, then running across the road. He got off the bike – no time to park it – it fell sideways on the sidewalk, he tried to cross the road but there was a truck coming towards him, then two cars. It took him a minute, maybe two, to sprint across the road, dodging another car and scooter.

Later, this was what he would remember: The sight of Mallika pulling the girl out of the man's grasp, and the girl running, running, running into the darkness. Mallika screaming and struggling as the man grabbed her, hit her several times across her face, and dragged her into the waiting car. Flinging himself on to the car. His body slipping and sliding on the car as he held onto the luggage rack above it. Kicking at the windscreen as the car picked up speed. The car going faster and faster as he kicked at the windscreen harder and harder, guttural sounds coming out of him. Falling. Hitting the road. He was still wearing his helmet. Then a shuddering, groaning, splintering sound, a sound he would never forget for the rest of his life. Screams from inside the car. High-pitched, unrelenting.

Just ahead of him, the car had hit a truck carrying long, sharp, vicious-looking poles. Or rather, the car had crashed against the poles, which in turn had pierced the car, all the way in.

Hands helped him up from the road. He ran to the car. There was someone running with him. He pulled open the back door.

The poles had gone through the car. Through the body of the driver. Some of the poles had gone all the way to the back, over the body of the man who was lying screaming, on top of her.

She was trying to get him off her.

'Do not move,' the man standing next to Arnav said. Mallika stopped moving. Arnav and this man crouched down and slid their hands under her and very slowly, very carefully pulled her out.

The man who had been lying on top of her tried to get up but couldn't. He was bleeding.

They stumbled as Mallika fell onto the road. She was clutching a small, bloodstained knife.

That was when he noticed that the man helping him lift Mallika was wearing a saree, bindi, lipstick, and long earrings.

Mallika stood, swaying against Arnav, still clutching the knife, her saree in disarray, her shawl dragging on the ground. He lifted the shawl and wrapped it around her. He took the knife from her and slipped it into his jacket pocket. He wrapped his arms tightly around her. She leaned against him, unmoving. Her saree was falling off. He grabbed whatever was trailing and clumsily tucked it into her waist.

Hospital. He looked. AIIMS was at the other end of the road.

'Mallika, come, AIIMS is right there.'

'No, no,' Mallika panted. 'Want to go home.'

The man in the saree said, 'This is going to become a police case. Look.'

The driver of the truck and another man were getting rid of the poles from their truck.

'Bas, now they will drive away,' the man in the saree said. 'Run before the police come.'

Police? He found himself unable to think.

The hijra laughed loudly. 'Forgotten it is the Emergency?'

Mallika was moaning. He tightened his arm around her.

'What is your name?' he whispered.

The hijra laughed again. 'So today you know that someone like me has a name! Durga.'

'Bahut shukriya, Durga.'

'Look,' Durga said, pointing.

The man in the back of the car had opened the door and was stumbling out. He leaned against the vehicle, swaying.

'Run,' Durga said. 'Run, before the police come.'

Mallika was frozen, staring at the man who was sliding down from the car onto the road.

'Hurry,' Arnav said, turning her around. He held her hand and ran with her towards his bike, only letting go to lift it up from the ground. Her bag was still there, under it. He picked it up and slung it over her shoulder.

He started the bike, and it roared into life. She got on behind him and put her arm around his waist, resting her face against his back. He could feel her shuddering. He took a detour, found a rubbish dump, and stopped.

'Mallika,' he said. 'We need to get off for a minute.'

They got off. As she stood, leaning against the bike, he wiped the knife carefully with his handkerchief and threw both into the rubbish dump. Then he drove her home.

At her house, he took her bag, opened it, took out the key, and unlocked and unbolted the side door. She held onto him as though she'd never let him go. He was frozen to the bone when they entered, yet he couldn't feel the cold. He felt he was floating, yet his legs seemed weighed down like lead. It was the strangest sensation, to hear the silence around him and the scream inside his ears. To feel as though he had to run away from the sight of her, as though he could never leave her.

She was still holding onto him. With her other hand, she fumbled for the corridor light and switched it on. 'Don't go,' she said. Her hands were bloody. There were bloodstains on her saree. Her face was swollen and red where the man had hit her. She was shaking.

He touched her face. 'I'll get Randhir.'

'Don't get him. Don't get anyone.'

Her voice was rising.

'OK,' he said. 'OK.'

'I have to bathe.'

'Wash your hands first.'

She went into the kitchen, and he heard the tap running.

When she came out to the dining room, he said, 'Sit.'

She sat at the table.

He went to the fridge and took out an ice tray. Then he went to the kitchen and opened the tap and took out the ice into a stainless-steel utensil.

'Do you have a thin cloth?' he asked her. He could barely look at her. At all that blood.

She got up slowly and went into one of the rooms and came out with a thin white towel. Then she sat again. He made an ice pack then sat opposite her and put it on her swollen face. She closed her eyes. He did it for a long time, over her cheeks, nose, forehead, chin, and her right ear.

When he finally stopped, she said, 'Don't go.'

'I'm not going.'

She got up slowly and went upstairs for her bath.

He just kept sitting. The left side of his body, his torso, his arm, and his leg were in pain, yet that pain was a huge distance away.

After an hour, he went upstairs. Her door was open, but the curtain was drawn. He knocked at her door, but there was no response. He drew the curtain to the side and entered. She wasn't in the room. The bathroom door was shut. He hesitated, then went inside and knocked on the bathroom door. 'Mallika?'

He heard her say something. Then the door opened, and she came out in an indigo kaftan, her hair damp and streaming down her back. She put her arms around his waist and closed her eyes. He held her. She was ice cold. He could see there was no geyser in the bathroom, or any heating rod. She'd bathed with cold water in this freezing cold. For almost an hour.

When he let her go, she remained standing outside the bathroom, shivering, her teeth chattering. 'Do you have a dry towel?' he asked. 'And a sweater? And socks?'

She opened her cupboard and took out all three.

He helped her wear the sweater and buttoned it up all the way to her neck. 'Sit.'

She sat on the chair next to her desk. He put on the socks for her and then did the best job he could of drying her hair. He'd never dried a girl's hair before. She had thick, very long hair going down to her hips. After that, he picked up the comb from the side table and combed it as best as he could.

Then he found he couldn't do any more. He hadn't felt so battered in his life. He sat on her bed, and she kept sitting on her chair. She was still shivering, her teeth still chattering. He should make some tea for her. He should get her a hot water bottle. 'Do you have a hot water bottle?' Even to speak was an effort.

'In the kitchen,' she said. 'On the wall.'

He got up, once again with tremendous effort. 'OK, get into bed.'

He lifted the razai without taking off the bedcover, and she got under it. There was a Rajasthani razai on the divan next to the bed, and he picked it up and put it over her too.

'Don't go.'

'I won't go. I'm getting the hot water bottle.' He went downstairs.

The hot water bottle was hanging on a nail on the wall. The tea utensil was right next to the gas and so were the matches, so he filled it up, heated the water, and poured it into the hot water bottle. Then he picked up a cup without a handle lying on the side, went to where he'd left his jacket, took out his cigarettes from the outside pocket and the small packet of dope from the inside pocket, and climbed upstairs.

She was lying on her side under the razai and blankets, still visibly freezing. He tucked the hot water bottle next to her under the razai, then sat on the bed, took out the dope and cigarettes, emptied part of the tobacco from the cigarette into the handle-less cup, and rolled a joint. He lit it and took a deep drag.

'Here,' he said and gave it to her. 'It'll help you. Inhale it.'

She took it from him and inhaled, as though she'd been doing this all her life.

He switched off the light and drew the curtain at the balcony slightly to the other side, so that the smoke would go out. The light from the streetlamps below filtered in through the curtain and kept the room from being completely dark. They shared the joint in silence. After they finished, she lifted the razai, and he took off his shoes, socks, and jacket, and with huge relief, lay down next to her. She moved so that he could tuck his arm under her head, and they put their arms around each other. The bed was warm, and her shivering was beginning to subside.

He was almost asleep when he felt his body jerk, his arms tightening around her.

Suddenly, he was wide awake. Her eyes were open too, resting on his face. She needed to see a doctor. What had he been thinking? He had to get her to a doctor.

She said, 'They were going to take turns with me, in the car,' she said.

He held her tightly.

'The knife was in my blouse. He tore my blouse, and it fell next to me. I used it. I just... kept... slashing... at him.'

The silence screamed.

'Did he...?'

'He didn't rape me.'

Thank you, he repeated in his mind, thank you. He didn't know who he was thanking. He touched her swollen face. He ran his fingers over her cheeks, her nose, her forehead. He stroked her hair, her back.

'I kept slashing at him with the knife.'

'Don't think about it.' He kept stroking her. Her feet were like ice even through the socks, and he rubbed them with his feet.

'Oh, god; oh, god,' she muttered.

He stroked her hair, her cheek. 'He's alive. You saw him stumbling out of the car.'

'But he collapsed after that.'

'He was moving.' He wasn't sure of that at all.

'He was alive?'

He heard the relief in her voice.

'Yes.'

'What should I do?'

'Nothing.'

'The knife?'

'Remember, I threw it. Far away from... there.'

'The knife's sheath. It's in the car.'

'No one can identify it.'

She shot up in bed. '*Jalpari.*'

'She escaped, Mallika. She escaped. I saw her running away.'

She lay back in bed, gasping with relief.

'Close your eyes,' he murmured, stroking her.

She closed her eyes.

Every few minutes, she shuddered.

He held her very tightly.

She didn't stop shuddering.

He kissed her cheek, her ear.

He kissed her mouth.

He stopped.

'Don't stop,' she sighed, and he kissed her fiercely. She made the same sound that she'd made the night of the wedding, but it was deeper, and she melted into him.

He couldn't separate himself from her. His very limbs dissolved into hers. Even with their layers of clothes. He rolled her over and kissed that beautiful neck. Tasting her skin. With his tongue. With his teeth. Her mouth again. What was he doing? God, what was he doing? He tore himself away from her. Her eyes opened.

'No,' he said.

'Why?'

'Mallika, we shouldn't.'

'Why not?' she sobbed. '*Why* not?'

'Please,' he said.

She sat up, unbuttoned her sweater, and removed it, then crossed her arms and took off her kaftan. 'Take it away,' she said fiercely. It was only her silhouette he could see in the darkness.

'Mallika,' he breathed.

'Only you,' she said. 'Take it *away*.' Her eyes were shining with tears.

He saw the huge bruise on her breast. 'What's that,' he whispered, sitting up too.

'He did it, take it away.'

He put his mouth to it, his tongue. His heart. Oh, his very heart. The tears were streaming down her face. He stopped and looked at her.

'Don't stop,' she said.

After some time, he whispered, 'It's cold, get under the razai.' His hands were clumsy as he got rid of his clothes and dropped them on the floor. He slid under the razai. It should stop. He should stop. Because even as she rubbed herself against him like a cat, even as she wound herself around him as though she knew what she wanted, she also didn't know.

He should have stopped because, of course, it was there, his betrayal of Randhir, sepia-coloured against the darkness of the night. He wouldn't look at it. He could hear Randhir saying, 'You're so fucking oblivious, man.' Words from Randhir's recent story whispered in his ear: *What was oblivion but not looking? Not because you couldn't, but because you wouldn't. When you did it long enough, wouldn't became couldn't.* In the morning, it would stare at him in the face.

But it wasn't time to wake up. That was later. There was only now. Now was the tide engulfing them both. This wasn't Mallika. Not this naked girl, asking for more. It was another girl. Another time. Another space. She uttered his name as though he were torturing her. Perhaps he was, because he knew he had to stop, he was trying to stop. She wouldn't let him stop. She wouldn't stop. 'No,' she said, and he stopped again. Her teeth at his neck, she said fiercely, 'Don't *stop*.'

'You said no,' he said.

'Not to *you*,' she said, tears streaming down her face. 'Don't stop.'

His words came from a place deep and unknown. 'Do what you want, do whatever you want,' and she gasped, 'I don't know.' But she did. Even as she clung and shuddered against him, it wasn't enough, for either of them, and in the end, they took each other almost savagely. A soft and constant tinkle accompanied their sounds.

Later, he must have fallen into a deep sleep. It couldn't have been for long, because when he awoke, it was still dark, and someone was soothingly stroking his legs and arms. Light from the half-closed bathroom door fell on the bed. A strong medicinal smell pervaded the room. She was applying ointment to his bruises.

'It's Burnall,' she said. 'Stay still.'

'That's for burns,' he murmured.

'It works for everything,' she said, continuing her ministrations through silent tears.

'Don't cry, Mallika.'

'Now, turn.'

He turned over and felt her apply the Burnall along his back.

'I saw you fall from the car,' she said. She put the tube on the side table and lay down next to him again.

Something was poking his foot. He slid down under the razai and felt around for it. Surfacing, he peered at it. It was her silver payal. It must have been her payals that were tinkling throughout. She sat up, and he wound it around her right ankle, trying to fix whatever it was of one end into whatever it was of the other.

'I'll do it,' she said.

'No.' He felt compelled to figure it out, and he did. So, this was how it was done. Her small gold balis and her silver payals were all she was wearing. Her hair was streaming down her back. He rolled to his side and kissed the inside of her thigh.

This time she didn't say 'don't stop,' because this time he didn't even try to. The words she couldn't utter streamed out of her eyes. He tended to her tears in the only way he knew, in the only way she seemed to want, but if it was tenderness that she had desired when he first got into her bed, it was no longer that she wanted, it was the opposite, it was obliteration, and perhaps it was what he wanted too, because he gave it to her, and she gave it to him.

Later, as she slept, he examined her body to see if she was hurt anywhere else. She whimpered, curling into a ball; he turned her over and felt every part of her back and hands and legs... No, she wasn't hurt anywhere else, it was only her face, thank god. He lay down and covered them both, holding her as she slept, kissing her swollen face till he fell asleep too.

The pre-dawn light entered the room. She was draped around him, her nose in his neck. 'Mallika,' he murmured. She said something indistinctly into his skin. He kissed her all over her face, he kissed her mouth, her breasts, he had to go before it got too late. He got out of bed and picked up her kaftan and sweater from the floor. She sat up in bed, and he helped her put them on. As he buttoned up her sweater, he saw the bloodstains on the sheet.

'You're bleeding?' he said, sickened that he hadn't noticed.

'I'm OK,' she said, covering the stains with the razai.

'Where are you hurt?' he said. 'Show me.'

'Oh, Arnav,' she said. 'I haven't done this before.'

'Done what?' he asked, bewildered.

She muttered, 'I haven't slept with anyone before.'

There was a brief silence.

'Oh,' he said, mortified at his stupidity. 'I'm sorry, did I hurt you.'

'No, never.'

He tucked the razai around her, kissed her cheek, her mouth. Again. And again. 'Arnav,' she whispered, clinging to him.

'Oh, Mallika, you know I have to go,' he said.

'Yes.' She let him go.

She watched him as he dressed. His jacket had bloodstains. He turned it inside out and put it on. She was sitting up. He sat next to her and covered her again with the razai.

'What have you done with your clothes?' he asked. The bloodstains would never go from her magenta saree and shawl.

'I've put them in a polythene bag. I'll have to throw them.'

'Give me the bag. I'll throw it. Far away from here.'

'Arnav, do you think he's still alive?'

'Of course. That knife... was tiny.'

'He'll tell the police?'

'Not after what he tried to do to you.'

If these were lies, then they were the only ones he uttered that night.

She said, 'No one can know. *No* one.'

He nodded.

'Arnav. Even *you* don't know, OK?'

He looked at her, uncomprehending.

'You can't be implicated in this. Just remember, I came back last night from JNU by bus, alone.'

He didn't answer.

'*You were not with me. You don't know. Anything.*'

It was easier not to argue.

He cupped her face in his hands and kissed her mouth.

She whispered, 'Arnav, will you come back to me?'

It had been a spell. He could hear it splintering.

'Arnav?'

He put his arms around her, holding the razai in place.

'Arnav,' she said again, his name a breath in his ear.

The words he didn't have crowded his chest. He couldn't breathe properly. His chest hurt.

'Bye,' he said, the word a mere whisper, his arms tightening around her.

'You mean *goodbye*?' He heard the catch in her voice, the fear.

Over her shoulder, he closed his eyes.

After some time, she unclasped her hands from around him, and as he let her go, she held his face between her hands. He could not open his eyes.

'Arnav, look at me.'

He opened his eyes and looked at her.

'Just the truth,' she said.

'Randhir,' he said.

She flinched, so hard that he felt it in the hands that held his face. Her hands dropped.

From below her balcony came the sounds of someone shuffling and muttering. Their bodies jerked, and then she stumbled out of bed. 'Oh, god, Ayah-ji's unlocking the back door. Go out from the side door. Hurry.'

She ran down the stairs, and he followed her. He turned to the right, she to the left. She grabbed his helmet from the dining table, ran back to him, and, as he unbolted and opened the side door, thrust it into his hands before rushing away. He heard Ayah-ji – 'Baby, why is your face swollen?' – and he softly closed the door and walked to his motorcycle. He started his bike and sat on it, his mind racing. He hadn't asked her who Jalpari was. And... Oh, shit. He'd forgotten. He'd forgotten to take the bag with her bloodstained clothes.

The darkness was dissipating.

Randhir was looking at him from his bedroom window.

He froze.

'Been wandering around all night again?' Randhir said with resignation.

No words came to him.

'You're waking up the whole neighbourhood – switch off that bloody bike and come in, yar, why the hell are you freezing your ass off?'

He'd forgotten his motorcycle was running. His thoughts had drowned out the sound. He turned off the ignition. Randhir opened the side door of his house, the door that faced Mallika's side door, and Arnav went inside.

'What's happened to you?' Randhir was looking at his ruined jeans. 'And why are you wearing your jacket the wrong way?'

'Had a bit of an accident, it's OK, I'm fine,' he said, heading through the house to Randhir's room.

'Fell off the bike?' Randhir said sharply. 'Or did you get hit?'

He didn't reply.

He took off his shoes, lay down on Randhir's divan, and closed his eyes. Suddenly, his limbs were like water.

Randhir threw him a razai. He covered himself, eyes still closed.

How could she be found out? No way the bastard would report it. Delhi was a city without witnesses. During the Emergency, especially. The roads had been virtually empty, as they always were in Delhi at night, and the few who may have seen her dragged into the car couldn't have seen her properly in the darkness. The hijra who had helped them, the only witness... No, the hijra wouldn't. So much didn't make it into the newspapers. Randhir and he would scan the newspapers carefully for the next few days.

What was he thinking? That, after telling Randhir about the accident, he'd tell him he'd slept with Mallika? And after *that*, that they'd be sitting in perfect harmony, figuring out what to do if the police came knocking at Mallika's door?

He couldn't think.

A reprieve. That was all he wanted. A brief reprieve. In this home, which had been his home for years. With this friend, this brother. Who, in this moment, was still his friend and brother.

The shock began to consume him. It came in waves and swallowed him, his body, his head, his heart. All of him. Even in his sleep, he was inside it. He had disappeared into it, his ribs were in pain, every bit of him was in pain.

Someone was shaking him. For a moment, as he opened his eyes, he didn't know where he was, which room, which house, he didn't know what time of his life it was, and then the waters parted, and he rose out of that terrible sleep, and it was Randhir's frantic face before him.

'Get up, man. We have to take Mallika to the hospital.' He rushed out.

Arnav stumbled out of the divan and ran to Mallika's house.

When they got her back from the hospital, they discovered that she'd forgotten the wedding. She'd forgotten the horror. She'd forgotten the night she'd spent with him. Three days were erased from her memory.

And she was looking at Randhir with her heart in her eyes, the very heart that he had seen in her eyes for him that pre-dawn morning as she had asked, 'Will you come back to me?'

Randhir: An indigo and mustard saree

1976

Later, he would remember that when the phone rang, it was towards the end of April, more than three-and-a-half months after Mahima's wedding, and exams were around the corner. He and Arnav were taking a short break from studying. He was telling Arnav that he'd been wanting to go to Bombay to see Akhil and his wife but couldn't do it because, if his father found out, he was screwed. As it was, his father had no idea he and his mother were writing to Akhil. 'Do you miss Akhil?' Arnav had asked curiously, and Randhir shrugged. He felt bad about what had happened, but he and the quiet, uncommunicative Akhil had never been close; they had nothing in common except their mutual love for cricket. 'He *is* my brother,' he had said to Arnav heavily.

The phone rang.

He went to the sitting room and picked it up. It was Mallika. She was raving about Charu, about pregnancy, about nothing being wrong with her. He was grappling with this when she gave him the address of a clinic. He grabbed the pad next to the phone and wrote it down. She said, 'Please don't think I'm like Charu. I *promise* I'm not like her, please don't stop talking to me.' His heart hammering, he said, 'Of course I won't.' Then the doctor spoke to him.

'Randhir, this is Dr Raghunath – can you get a saree and petticoat for Mallika?'

He said stupidly, 'A saree and petticoat?'

'Hers are completely bloodstained.'

For a few seconds, he felt faint.

Then the doctor said, 'She's alright now, you can come and take her home.'

'What's happened to her?' he asked.

'I'll tell you when you come. Can you take her home in a taxi?'

'I'll come by car,' he said.

He ended the call and went to his mother's room. She was fast asleep. Quietly, he took the car keys from where they were hanging behind the door. Saree, the doctor had said, get a saree. Ma's Godrej was locked. No chance of flicking one from there. Not a chance of getting one from Mallika's house either. He went to the back veranda, where the clothes were drying on the clothesline, and grabbed his mother's black petticoat. Then back to his room, where Arnav was studying on the divan. He opened his cupboard and took out a polythene bag into which he swiftly thrust the petticoat. He had no idea how much a saree would cost. He turned to Arnav.

'Do you have any money? I'll return it to you later.'

Arnav took out his wallet from his jeans and gave him a hundred rupee note. 'No change.'

'You're flush, I must say,' Randhir said.

'Yeah, my grandmother's bounty. I heard you talking to Mallika – is she OK?'

Randhir said she was unwell, brushed aside Arnav's offer to pick her up, and rushed off.

He got into his mother's car and drove towards the clinic. Saree. Where did Mallika and Gauri buy their sarees from? A faint memory came to him of Gauri saying she'd bought two sarees at the annual sale at the Maharashtra Emporium. He turned towards Connaught Place.

After buying the saree, it took him forty-five minutes to reach the clinic. His shirt was soaked with sweat. The nurse showed him into the doctor's office.

He sat opposite her. She looked stern and forbidding.

'Did you make Mallika pregnant?'

He thought he'd heard wrong.

'She was pregnant and bleeding heavily when she came to this clinic.'

He looked at her blankly.

'She had a miscarriage. She's lost a lot of blood.'

He shook his head. He kept shaking his head.

'Are you responsible? Have you had sexual relations with Mallika?'

'No. No.'

She examined his face.

'Never.'

'How long have you known her?'

'My whole life. We live next to each other.'

She was still examining his face.

'If there was a boy, we'd know. She wouldn't hide it from us.'

'Well, clearly there are things you don't know.'

He looked at her, dazed.

'Who lives in her house?'

'Just her mother. Her father's posted to Lucknow. And her mother's sister comes a couple of times a year.'

'No boys? No men? Uncles, cousins, father's friends?'

'No. It's just her and her mother.'

'Male servants?'

'No. She has an ayah who's been taking care of her since she was a baby.'

'Is her father a good man?'

He looked at her, appalled.

'My dear boy, don't look so shocked. In my experience, most of these things happen inside the house.'

He could feel the bile in his mouth. 'Her father's a very good man.'

She poured out some water into a glass from a flask and gave it to him. He drank it up.

'She is very weak. But with rest, she will recover.'

He nodded. He couldn't think.

'But mentally, she is not alright. She keeps saying it's a period and not a pregnancy, that she's never had sex. She keeps talking about someone called Charu. She is very confused. For now, don't ask her any questions. Take her home and let her rest. Is her mother at home?'

'Her mother's sister is having an operation tomorrow. Mallika's supposed to go there.'

'Out of the question. She needs to rest.'

He nodded.

'Will you tell her mother?'

He nodded again.

'Is her mother someone who will support her?'

'Yes.'

'She is lucky, then. Most girls have no one to tell.'

He burst out, 'But she *didn't* tell her mother. She *didn't* tell me.'

'She was four months pregnant. She must have got pregnant sometime in early January.'

Early January?

'Come. I'll take you to her. You have the saree and petticoat?'

'Yes.'

Early January. Mahima's wedding. Mallika's concussion. Her loss of memory. Three days lost. Had it happened during that time? But weren't those days accounted for?

Mallika kept talking disjointedly. About Charu, her Shantamama's operation, some dream about him. He wanted to put his arms around her and soothe her. Instead, he gave her the saree and left the room. The doctor gave him medicines for her, including something to help her relax and sleep. She told him she'd thrown away Mallika's saree and petticoat – they were completely soaked with blood. He nodded, fighting a wave of nausea.

Then he took Mallika home. As he was driving, she made him promise not to tell her mothers. He knew he would never be able to break this promise, even though it was made under duress. She said he was never to ask her again about this day. Just like she'd never asked him about his writing or Charu.

How did she know about his writing? Arnav must have mentioned it to her, thinking she knew. The thought came and went.

The next morning, after checking in on Mallika, he went back home to Mahima's room and began to search for the piece of paper on which he and Arnav had logged down the three days that Mallika had forgotten. After an hour of searching, he found the piece of paper inside the book on the bedside table, and he went over Mallika's three lost days again.

The day of the wedding, she was between his home and her own with her friends all day. When the wedding ended, she went back home with Prabha and Gauri, and they spent the night together.

The day after the wedding, she was at home in the morning. After Gauri and Prabha left, and her mother left for Bangalore, Mallika went to JNU to see Gauri. She came home in the evening.

The next day, in the morning, she'd fallen down the stairs. He and Arnav had taken her to the hospital.

He made himself some tea, sat at the dining table, and read the notes again.

But why had Mallika gone to see Gauri the day after the wedding when Gauri had been at home with her that very morning?

The doorbell rang.

It was Gauri. Standing there as though his thoughts had conjured her up. He stared at her.

She said she'd come because she was dreaming about Mallika. Of all things!

He told Gauri a modified version of what had happened to Mallika. He stumbled over it; he'd never talked to a girl about stuff like periods. Then, as they had lunch, she picked up the note paper from the table, read it, and told him that she hadn't met Mallika the day after the wedding.

He asked Gauri if it could be a guy. Gauri was so affronted that he shut up.

Then they asked Ayah-ji, who said that when she had come home early the next morning, Mallika was at home.

No. It wasn't an assault. It wasn't. It wasn't. It was an affair. Mallika had been taken in by some guy. Anyone could fool her – Charu, Renu, anyone. The guy must have asked her not to tell anyone about their affair. Just like Charu had asked her. Just like everyone asked her. Or maybe she was being protective of the guy the way she had been protective of her father, at the cost of her own health and wellbeing. He'd find out. He'd find out, he'd find the guy, and he'd deal with the bastard if it was the last thing that he ever did.

But why had she told the doctor she wasn't pregnant?

Because it was a shock. Obviously.

Still. He had to be absolutely sure.

It was impossible to get Ayah-ji alone. Finally, a few days after Shanta Aunty left for Bangalore, he dropped in at Mallika's house. There was no one at home. Before Ayah-ji could shut the door in his face, he wiggled past her into the house and said, 'Ayah-ji, I want to ask you something.'

She glared at him.

No, Ayah-ji was *not* in a good mood these days.

'Why are you angry with me, hmm?' he said.

Ayah-ji sat down on the floor. He sat on the moorha next to her.

'All alone I am, everyone asks me questions, no one listens to me. Baby isn't well, she isn't eating, she will not listen to me. Her mother, she doesn't listen to me. Everyone is asking me why. How do I know why? I am all alone, and who is listening to me? Everything goes wrong in my life.' Her voice was trembling.

This was, as Mallika laughingly said, Ayah-ji being Mrs Gummidge.

'Ayah-ji, just like you are worried about Mallika Baby, I also am.'

She burst into tears.

'Ayah-ji, why are you crying?'

'Baby made me promise not to tell, do not ask me anything,' she wailed. His heart plummeted.

'She put my hand on her head and made me promise not to tell.' She was weeping bitterly.

'When did she do this, Ayah-ji, when did she make you promise not to tell?'

'Early in the morning. Mallika Baby told me Gauri Baby wasn't there and that she had come back home the previous night. She put my hand on her head and made me promise not to tell.'

'Tell *what*, Ayah-ji?'

'I *said* I cannot tell you. God only knows what will happen to her if I break my promise.'

'But Ayah-ji, Mallika has forgotten everything about that day.'

'Yes, *she* has forgotten, but *I* have not forgotten giving her my promise. She will be cursed if I break it.'

His heart was pounding with fear. It was also hurting him to see her weep so bitterly.

'Here, Ayah-ji,' he said gently, giving her his handkerchief.

She took it and then looked at it. 'As though,' she said, giving it back to him. She wiped her eyes with her saree palla.

'Chalo,' he said. 'Make some sweet-sweet chai for both of us.'

She got up. Soon, he heard the sounds of tea being made in the kitchen.

Ayah-ji was jealous of everyone who loved Mallika, but for him she had a soft corner. This was because before Padma Aunty had come to Delhi, almost nineteen years ago, Ayah-ji had been working for his mother, taking care of the children, and Randhir had been her favourite child. But when his grandmother came to stay with them, Ayah-ji took umbrage at the things she said and gave a very rude retort. Randhir's father told his mother that Ayah-ji had to go. Providentially, Padma Aunty and baby Mallika had just arrived next door and were looking for an ayah, so it worked out perfectly.

Ayah-ji came with the tea, his in a cup and saucer, hers in a steel glass, and they sat drinking it together.

'Very good tea, Ayah-ji.'

She grunted.

'Randhir Baba.'

'Yes, Ayah-ji?'

'The promise I made to Baby... I am thinking.'

He nodded, trying to look indifferent.

'I promised Baby I would not tell her mother. That is what I promised her.'

His heart leapt, but he didn't say a word.

'That means, if I tell you, I will not be breaking my promise. Hai na?'

He nodded again. If he said urgently, 'Yes, yes,' he would lose her.

She started crying again.

'That morning when I came home, Baby was downstairs. Her face was a little swollen. I said, "What has happened to your face!" She said that when she was coming back home the previous night, she fell from the bus. It was very crowded, she said.'

He could hear himself breathing unevenly.

Ayah-ji said, 'At that time, I believed her.'

He began to feel nauseous.

'Then and there, Baby grabbed my hand and put it on her head and said, "Now, promise me not to tell Ma, I do not want Ma to worry, promise me." It was as if I had no choice. I promised.'

He nodded.

'Then I saw the empty ice tray and pathla towel on the dining table. She had come home and put ice on her face. When she came home at night, the swelling must have been even worse. I said, "Sit down just now." I took out ice and wrapped it in a napkin and put it on her face. For one hour I did that, and by the end, her face looked normal. Then I found Memsahib's pain medicine, so that also I put all over her face. Then Baby went upstairs. She came down, holding a big plastic bag, and said she was going for a walk. She went before I could stop her. She came back in half an hour without the bag and went upstairs and slipped and fell. The rest you know.'

'Ayah-ji, why did you say that she was lying to you about falling from the bus?'

'Randhir, Baba, when you fall down on the road and hurt your face, the bruises on your face are different. There was no blood on her face. I have seen so many faces like hers in the servant quarters. Women who have been hit by their husbands. Their faces do not bleed. Their faces are swollen.'

'Did you tell her you knew she was lying?'

'No, Randhir Baba,' Ayah-ji wept. 'Because I realized it only a few days later. That she had not fallen from a bus. That someone had hit her on her face.'

He had done more than hit her on her face.

'Now, I realize that the clothes Mallika Baby was wearing when she went to see Gauri Baby were the same clothes that she was carrying in the plastic bag the next morning when she told me she was going for a walk. Now, I am sure that she threw away her saree, shawl, and sweater. Because they must have been torn, and she did not want her mother to know.'

He wanted to retch.

It had happened to Mallika on her way back from JNU. She had got rid of the evidence. And then fallen down the stairs and forgotten it.

They were all busy with exams. After her exams, Mallika disappeared. Her mother said she was very ill with TB. That was a good one! Of course, he knew it wasn't TB. She'd had a nervous breakdown or something. Maybe she'd told her mothers what had happened at the clinic, maybe not. But there was no way it was TB.

Very, very slowly, Mallika got better. She went back to college, they started going for walks, he picked her up from LSR, but she barely spoke.

Then, as luck would have it, he couldn't pick up Mallika the day after she got to know about Jalpari's disappearance because he had to meet his lecturer. So he asked Arnav, who had been having dinner with Randhir's family the previous evening, if he could.

'Sure.' Arnav helped himself to some dahi. 'How come you were going to pick her up all the way from there?'

'She's very run-down after that TB.'

'Oh.'

'Bechari, no strength she has,' his mother said, putting another roti on Arnav's plate.

'And don't make pc with her, she's too tired for all that,' he told Arnav.

'Such a good boy, my Randhir is,' his mother said. 'Three times every week he is going to LSR to pick up Mallika. In the morning, he goes to university. He finishes classes, then all the way to LSR he goes to pick her up, and then all the way home he comes.'

He groaned to himself. He should never have asked Arnav in Mummy's presence.

'You pick her up *three* times a week?' Arnav asked.

He shrugged.

'Too much weakness poor Mallika is having,' his mother said. 'And too much goodness my Randhir is having.'

'Mummy, please.'

'Too much,' his mother sighed, and thankfully subsided.

Of course, it had to happen the day Arnav picked her up. Mallika was probably still reeling from Jalpari's disappearance. He was having tea with her mothers and grandmother when Arnav finally brought her home. Arnav got it off his chest straightaway, that she'd been feeling very unwell and rested in his room for a couple of hours. She was pale and had that disoriented look about her. Her mothers had their usual worried expressions, which they still hadn't learnt to mask, even though it put so much pressure on Mallika. That's when Arnav said he could pick up Mallika twice a week.

That night as they smoked on the terrace, Arnav said, 'I'd have pitched in if you'd told me earlier. I had no idea.'

'But why should you?' he asked, surprised. 'I mean, you're not exactly bosom buddies.'

'So she said,' Arnav muttered.

'When you pick her up, don't make pc, OK? She's too tired to respond.'

'You've already told me that.'

'And *don't* speed.'

Arnav grunted.

It was on the tip of his tongue to ask Arnav, How come you told Mallika I write? He stopped himself. He didn't want Arnav to know he'd never told her. Besides, he had now, on one of their walks.

He had wanted to tell Mallika he wrote when, at the age of fifteen, she had declared that his father's expectation of him was 'everything.' Why hadn't he? Mallika would have valued his writing as deeply as Arnav. All he had known was that he was protecting his writing the way a mother protected a premature baby – no one could come close to it, see it, touch it. Not even Mallika. He had shared it with Arnav long before he had even known what it was that he was birthing. It was a part of him that had grown and thrived in utter secrecy, while the other part of him, the other secret which even Arnav couldn't know, the one denied its way, continued its wretched, stunted clamour for release.

It was the day of Prabha's outburst – she'd accused Arnav of calling Mallika boring, after which the girls disappeared, and Randhir gave Arnav a piece of his mind. Later that day, as he was watering the lawn with the hose, he saw Arnav and Gauri walking back from the market together. Arnav had a hunted look about him, and Gauri was looking pissed. Randhir hid his amusement. It looked like Gauri had given Arnav a piece of her mind too. Served him right. Arnav hopped onto his bike and went off somewhere, and Gauri came to Randhir and said without any preliminaries, 'Remember we were wondering why Mallika came to see me at JNU just after Mahima's wedding?'

He nodded. Not that it mattered now. The worst had already happened to Mallika.

'Mallika told me she thinks she came to see me because you lost your temper with her. She thinks it was because she wanted to talk to me about it.'

Looked like Gauri was pissed off with him too.

'How could you have thought Mallika was having a sordid little affair on the sly?'

There was nothing to say. He bent and put the hose on the flowerbed.

'And if she *was* having an affair, what is it to *you*?'

'What is it to *me*? To *me*?' he burst out.

'If Charu was none of Mallika's business, then why is Mallika's affair – *if* she was having one, which I *know* she wasn't – any of yours?'

'OK, bye, got to go.' He went into his house.

What was it to *him*! Why did no one bloody understand that there were all kinds of love? That there were many ways of loving? Did it mean he loved her less because he wouldn't marry her? Did it mean she was less important because he wouldn't sleep with her?

This was when it started, that pounding within him. The pounding that went, *all my fault, all my fault, all my fault*. If he hadn't lost his temper with Mallika, she wouldn't have gone to see Gauri that day, and if she hadn't gone to see Gauri, then nothing would have happened to her. But she did go to see Gauri, and the worst had happened to her.

When she had landed up bleeding at the clinic a few months later, and the doctor told her she'd had a miscarriage, what was she supposed to think? Of course, she was convinced the doctor was mistaken because she had no memory of what had happened. Obviously, she didn't want to talk about something so shameful. Nothing more unspeakable than shame. *He* knew that. Mallika was the one who had shown him that shame and he were best friends.

That evening before Mahima's wedding, after Mallika had flung the word 'pervert' at him, they had come back home from India Gate in complete silence. They hadn't even said goodnight. His house was full of relatives who were staying with them for the wedding. At midnight, finally, he went to his parents' room, where they had just got into bed, and he sat on the bed and said, 'I don't think this wedding should take place. I've heard Shekhar's not a good man.'

It had been of no use. No use at all. Which he'd known from the very start.

He'd accused them of not caring for their daughter, for caring more about what people said. Then he'd stormed out of the house.

When he went to Chandigarh to see his sister a few weeks after the wedding, Mahima seemed happy and fond of her husband and in-laws, who were indulgent and loving with her. He was sure her shock and fury at his tentative suggestion that he could take her back to Delhi if she was unhappy was real. So there should have been some measure of relief after he returned from Mahima's house. But, by the time he came back home, he was in the grip of a black despair. That night, he had opened the bathroom cabinet for the bottle of pills.

But the bottle was gone.

Who else but Mummy? Easier for her to get rid of it than ask him about it. Easier for her not to know what or why. Easier for everyone not to know the truth about the ones they claimed to love. Those who claimed to love you were the most fervent keepers of your lie. For if they knew your truth, they would know shame too – the shame of having a son, a brother, a friend like you.

Easier for the shame to be yours alone. Easier to live as though the most relevant thing in your life had no existence. Yes, easier to live that way.

Except when it was not easier to live that way. Because living as though something didn't exist didn't mean it didn't. Living as though he were like Arnav and Vineet and other guys, didn't mean he was.

Arnav: After

1976

Once, Randhir had told him that some things were meant to be, that they were part of a larger picture which one couldn't see at the time. He didn't buy into that shit. Because some things made absolutely no sense, and they never would. They didn't fit into a larger picture, because there was no larger picture. They happened because they happened.

But if he did believe in fate, Arnav would have said that he was fated to have Mallika in his life. Every time she fell into it, she took parts of him with her, parts that he had guarded so instinctively that he almost didn't know they were there.

First, she'd drawn out his stories. But she didn't stop there. He let her take more.

Or perhaps he gave her more. Perhaps there was no difference.

Then, of course, like the kiss that had begun everything, he could never take it back.

At least, that's what he had thought. That he could never take it back.

But then, of course, he had.

Randhir had taken charge at the hospital. He talked to the doctors, found out everything there was to find out about the concussion, acted as though he were already her husband. After they brought Mallika back from the hospital, he had changed into Randhir's jeans, shirt, and jacket, and thrown his torn and stained clothes into a polythene bag. He hadn't thought the waves of shock he'd experienced earlier could continue with such intensity, but seeing her unconscious at the bottom of the stairs, watching her in her hospital bed, and after that, feeling her look at him without recognition and talk to him as though nothing had happened, was the most disorienting experience of his life.

Then they had got to know about her lost memory.

As they played Scrabble, talked, and joked with Mallika, his mind was in that other place, that other time. There were moments when he felt he couldn't breathe. That evening, he went to the terrace and smoked, and soon Randhir joined him.

'So, what happened to you?'

'Fell off the bike,' he said.

'*Again*?' Randhir said. A year ago, Arnav had been speeding late at night, braked to avoid a cyclist who came out of nowhere, lost control of the bike, and had ended up sprawled on the road. Miraculously there were no broken bones, sprains, nothing. 'What happened?' Randhir repeated.

'Forget it, I'm fine now,' Arnav said, and Randhir didn't pursue the subject. He wasn't fine by any means. Far from it. But his head was clearer about one thing. He wouldn't tell Randhir. Not yet. For the next few days, he'd scour the newspapers. He already had been. So far, nothing. He'd wait and see.

A part of him – the irrational part that he didn't trust – was certain the hijra who had seen it all wouldn't utter a word. The other part of him – the trusted, rational part of him – said, but what if the hijra bears witness for money? And yet another part of him – the part he disliked the most, because it was akin to the rest of the world – thought, even if the hijra speaks, who'll believe a hijra?

It was how he was always pulled: not two ways, but three. The rational part of him decided he'd be an engineer. It led him to IIT; it gave counsel to Randhir, who was always torn about everything; and it tempered his own constant restlessness. The irrational part of him had taken over with Mallika. Kissing her on the night of Mahima's wedding was stupid enough, but *sleeping* with her when she belonged to his best friend? As for the part of him that was akin to the rest of the world, it was easier to believe it didn't exist because he didn't want to be like the rest of the world. But after the accident, he knew he was, because all he could think, in desperation and with shame, was that a hijra wouldn't have the guts to go to the police station.

He took himself to the hospital. He'd cracked two ribs. Nothing to be done, they would heal by themselves, the doctor said. He didn't tell anyone.

Best for Mallika not to know the horror of what had happened, and what it had taken for her to defend herself. Remind her of that nightmare, for what? It was best forgotten. As for their night together, it was the worst mistake of his life. It would never happen again.

He had to stop thinking about it. After Mishti, he'd learnt not to think about stuff that should never have happened, things that you could never change.

But what if her memory returned? Then what? Were he and Mallika supposed to collude and decide not to tell Randhir?

If he told Randhir, it would be the death of their long brotherhood.
If he didn't... then what? Drive off into the sunset with Mallika?
Only you, she had said.
Will you come back to me? she had said.
What was she asking him? *What* did she want? *Who* was she?
What had he done. What had he done.

He emptied the pockets of his torn jeans and bloody jacket, which he'd
hidden at the back of his cupboard. Her hanky, which he'd picked up at the
dhaba, came out. He thrust it back into the cupboard and threw the jeans
and jacket into a rubbish dump far from home. He was consumed by a need
to paint the hanky with its embroidered basket of flowers. Usually he didn't
paint, he sketched. But now the urge to see if he could paint it so that it
looked like the flowers were embroidered just wouldn't go away. So he did. It
took him hours. It was one of his few paintings, and certainly his best. The
basket and flowers did look like embroidery.

For the next few weeks, he dropped by to see Mallika. He gave her his
hostel phone number. 'I know you have Randhir's, but you know, best to
have two,' he said. She looked astonished but thanked him. If her memory
came back, she had to know how to contact him. All the while that he
visited her and talked to her, he was ruthlessly sawing the naked, weeping
Mallika out of his body and out of his mind.

Then the winter term was in full swing. He got down to work. He
auditioned and got the main role in a light-hearted comedy about the father
of a bride. He threw himself into his role.

After the play's run ended, he finally dropped in at Randhir's place. As he
was parking his bike, Mallika came running towards him, her eyes alight. In
that split second, he almost moved towards her in the same spirit.

Almost. Because a second later, it hit him. *Her memory's come back, that's
why she's running towards me.* His own memories drenched him, and he found
his body clenching in anticipation of what he had to tell her: *No. We can't.*

All she said was 'Hi.'

Had he imagined her joy? Because now she was looking all matter-of-
fact and asking him if he could describe Mahima's wedding, because, as she
reminded him, she had forgotten.

That was all.

The relief was like a sledgehammer. In high spirits, he found himself
describing the most entertaining parts of every wedding he'd been to,
slipping into the performative zone he always entered on stage, and she
laughed so much that she had to hold onto her sides.

'All that didn't happen at Mahima's wedding,' she gasped. 'You're making it up!'

And he said, 'I swear that happened,' and by then they were both laughing.

After that, there was an awkward kind of silence between them, and then she said, 'Did you notice anything... about me on the wedding day, anything... different?'

'About *you*?'

'I think I've forgotten something important, and maybe... you noticed something?'

He shrugged, shook his head.

She nodded, said bye, and went home.

The police didn't come knocking. There was nothing in the newspapers. Her memory didn't return.

He let the relief wash over him. He buried that horror, that terror. He dismissed that peculiar feeling of loss. He clamped down on that deep sense of having betrayed both Randhir and Mallika. He banked that slow burn of anger. He was fine.

He was *fine*. He was working hard. His voluntary work at the Conservation Fund filled most of his time and tempered his restlessness. He and another volunteer were involved in opening nature clubs at schools in Delhi. You had to catch them young, inculcate a love of nature in these kids. Once you did that, the rest happened. They would experience that love in larger and larger ways for the rest of their lives. No one would have to persuade them about the ills of deforestation, or the damage being done to the environment; no one would have to persuade them to fight for the protection of endangered species. His mother had instilled in him a deep love of nature from the time he was a little boy. That was all it had taken.

He and a group of other volunteers met with the principals of five schools and started nature clubs, headed by one of the senior boys or girls. They took groups of kids, aged twelve to seventeen, birdwatching to the Ridge Road in large groups on weekends and showed films like *Serengeti Shall Not Die* and *Butterflies Beyond Beauty* at the IIC. The children and their parents came in droves. They organized talks by conservationists and nature enthusiasts. Arnav talked to the kids about the Chipko movement. The CF organized buses to take them to bird sanctuaries and wildlife sanctuaries, often for two- or three-day trips. Several teenagers became voluntary wardens at the Delhi Zoo, to the relief of the Director, who had been complaining for a long time about vandals who threw stones at animals, tried to feed them, or thrust their hands into the cages to provoke them. Arnav and an eleventh-class schoolboy once stopped two men who were throwing stones at the flamingos to see which of them could first break a leg. The men stopped, surprised, as though they didn't understand why these peculiar people were interfering with their fun. Such mindless cruelty was mind-boggling to him. But it was everywhere. To see the enthusiasm of the children in the nature clubs was like a tonic to him.

He occasionally saw Mallika, who seemed to have recovered from the concussion, but was paler and thinner. Studying hard for exams, no doubt. But he also saw a sadness in her eyes, and then he felt everything was his fault, as though he had abandoned her, even though he knew her eyes had always held sadness. As though it was Mallika he had betrayed, when in fact it was his oldest, best friend.

Towards the end of April, when he was studying at Randhir's house, Mallika phoned. She wasn't well, Randhir said, he was picking her up from college.

'I can do that,' Arnav said. He didn't even realize he'd said it till he did.

'*You?* Why on earth should *you*!' Randhir looked astonished and rushed off. As though Mallika were already Randhir's wife. Randhir's tone just wouldn't leave him.

But of course, if the husband couldn't pick up the wife, he'd ask the friend to do it, wouldn't he. And a few months later, Randhir did. That was the day Mallika collapsed in Arnav's room. With her, so did Arnav's equilibrium.

She was pale and unmoving. The way she had been in the hospital. There, Randhir was the one who had been doing what Arnav now had to: touching her forehead, stroking her hair, covering her with the sheet. To lie down beside her, take her in his arms, and breathe some life into her seemed so natural that he almost did it. He was rescued from that insanity by a knock on his door. It was Mohini.

When he returned with the samosas, Mallika had asked him right in front of Mohini about the allergy on his neck. Said she'd had an allergy too, just like that, after her concussion. The memory surfaced of Mallika in Madhu Aunty's house after her concussion, telling them about putting on Burnall for her allergy. At the time, he'd had no idea what allergy Mallika was talking about, but the achingly familiar smell of Burnall had felt like a punch in his stomach.

He now realized what the 'allergy' was.

With Mallika in his bed, and Mohini chortling, those memories hit him hard. He'd wanted them both out. Out of his room, out of his life. Yet later that same day, he found himself saying sorry to Mallika. Before he even knew he was thinking it. Sorry for what? For being with Mohini? For god's sake, why should he be sorry for that! No, it was for being so bloody oblivious, for not knowing how unwell Mallika had been. For not being a good friend. He told her so, and she'd looked surprised and said simply, 'But we're not friends.'

Another hard hit.

He'd decided there and then. On the days Randhir couldn't pick her up from college, he would. And he did.

He'd sawed one Mallika off, and she'd disappeared into the ether. But there was a peculiar kind of comfort in the budding friendship with this other one. By the time the winter holidays began, she seemed to have recovered from the weakness of the TB. The last thing in the world he was expecting – as they hung out on Randhir's lawn that beautiful winter day – was an indignant Prabha accusing him of calling Mallika boring.

Mallika, instead of denying it, avoided his eyes and kept eating her moomphalis.

'What the hell?' Randhir said after the girls went into the house.

'I swear, I don't remember saying it.'

'Well, *obviously* you did.'

'Relax. I'll apologize. I'll grovel. Whatever it takes.'

After Randhir ran out of steam, Arnav got up and went inside the house, to look for Mallika. He saw the other two in the kitchen, talking, but Mallika wasn't around.

He must have said it before he got to know her, he thought. He was feeling shitty. He went to the market to get cigarettes.

Which was when Gauri joined him, sounding a little breathless, saying she was going to the market too.

Remorsefully, he said, 'Gauri, I *really* don't remember.'

'You called Mallika boring, and you don't remember?'

He shook his head.

'Calling Mallika boring is like one of us saying you, Randhir, and Vineet have no brains.'

'Huh?'

'But *we* don't judge by appearances.'

'Got it,' he said, unable to hide his amusement.

She saw it. That's when she said, 'I know about you and Mallika.'

He felt his head jerk towards her, as though a puppeteer was wielding it.

'What?'

'I saw you.'

'*What!*'

'I saw you kissing Mallika on the night of Mahima's wedding.'

He tried to recover from the shock. He felt her looking at him, waiting for a response.

'Sometimes… these things… happen.'

'What d'you mean, "these things?"'

'Gauri, it's not a big deal.'

He shouldn't have said that. Big mistake.

'It *is*. For Mallika, it *is* a very big deal.'

'You *told* her?'

'No.'

He felt dizzy with relief. 'Please don't. It's not going to happen again.'

'Why?'

Why? What the hell?

'*What's* wrong with Mallika?'

'Nothing.' He wanted to run.

'Mallika's better than all the Charus and Radhas and Mohinis of the world; what's *wrong* with you and Randhir?'

There was nothing to say.

They walked in silence to the market. There, she went to the general store. He went to the paanwalla and bought cigarettes. She rejoined him, and they began walking back.

He said, 'She's just a friend.'

She was looking straight ahead of her.

'It was a stupid mistake,' he said, under his breath.

She said nothing.

'If you tell her, that's the end of our friendship.'

Gauri refused to speak.

Let her not tell Mallika. Please, let her not tell Mallika.

'Bye,' he said when they reached home.

She didn't even bother to say it back. She went to Randhir, who was watering the lawn.

Arnav got onto his bike and drove off.

What was he supposed to have said? That Mallika's friendship mattered more than the other stuff? That he'd choose Mallika's friendship over every girl he'd gone out with? Try and explain what that meant when he had no idea?

It had become messy with Mohini. She had said, 'I think Mallika guessed I was in love with you,' and he'd said, 'You *discussed* me with Mallika?' She'd said, 'What do you *think*!' and he'd cringed. She'd said, 'I know you don't love me; I don't expect it, silly!' But this talk about love had rattled him. This time, it was he who ended it.

Obviously he wanted to apologize to Mallika, but it had to be done when she was alone. The morning after Prabha's outburst, Madhu Aunty showed him and Randhir the write-up in the *Indian Express* about Prabha bashing up the guy who'd misbehaved with her. As Randhir said, admiringly, 'Man, only Prabha could do this.' When he finally saw Mallika that evening, she was with Prabha, and they talked about the awful stuff girls had to go through on DTC buses and Delhi roads.

But that wasn't all. The girls talked about Mallika's student, Jalpari, and her abduction.

Finally, he knew who Jalpari was. She had escaped from those two men. But he now knew she had never come home.

The horror of that night enveloped him. He felt he was choking.

He couldn't stay. He left, drove to Lodhi Gardens, and went for a long run.

Randhir was having a party that night, but Mallika was absent, so he couldn't apologize. He saw Prabha and Gauri having an intense conversation in the corner of the room; Prabha looked up and gave him a fierce look. *Shit,* he thought, *Gauri's told Prabha about our conversation.* And when he casually asked Gauri why Mallika hadn't come, she said coldly, 'Because she dislikes parties, obviously.' Gauri was clearly still pissed off with him; why did girls put so much weight into small things? Later, he went up to the terrace to smoke and saw Randhir escorting Gauri and Prabha back to Prabha's house. He came down from the terrace around two a.m., feeling extremely relaxed. Glancing at Mallika's side door, he saw that it was slightly ajar. He put out his hand to shut it. Instead, he found himself opening it further. The light was on in her room. Gauri and Prabha were sleeping at Prabha's house. This was the best time to apologize to Mallika. He'd never get her alone otherwise. He climbed upstairs. Her door was open, her curtain drawn. He knocked on the door.

A hand parted the curtain. She poked her head out and looked at him incredulously. In the other hand, she was holding a nasty-looking stick.

'Hi,' he said softly.

She examined him from head to foot, still holding the stick.

'Why on earth are you brandishing that stick?'

'To hit you with.'

'Why!'

'Because it's two a.m.!'

'May I come in?'

She put the stick down and dug her finger hard into his stomach.

'Ow,' he protested. 'I'm real.'

'Mallika?' It was her mother calling out from her room below.

'Yes, Ma?'

'What was that noise?'

'Randhir's party, Ma. Go to sleep.'

He waited patiently.

'What are you doing inside my house at this time?' she whispered.

'I –'

'Softly,' she hissed.

'I wanted to talk to you. May I come in?'

'No. You're high. Go back to Randhir's house.'

'No.' He'd never get time alone with her.

'How did you get in?'

He heard footsteps coming out of one of the downstairs rooms.

She grabbed his arm and pulled him inside. He stumbled and fell with a big thump. 'Oh, shit.'

She bent and clapped her hand over his mouth. 'Shut up,' she whispered.

The feel of her palm on his mouth was like a balm. He'd never kissed a girl's palm. He almost kissed hers, but she was glaring at him, so it was his laugh that met her hand instead.

She went back to the door. Someone was climbing up. She climbed down.

'What's the matter?' It was her mother's voice. 'What's all that thumping?'

'I fell, Ma. I'm OK, don't worry. Just want to drink some water.'

'Didn't you take a glass of water up with you?'

'Finished it.'

'Where's the glass?'

'Oh, Ma, I'll just take another one.'

'So many glasses to wash, why can't you use one glass the whole day?'

Their voices faded. He could hear them murmuring in the kitchen below.

After five minutes, she was back in the room. If her kaftan was white, she'd have looked like a nun. It covered her from head to foot. But the kaftan was red. He could see her payals at her ankles. They'd been softly tinkling throughout. Very distracting.

'Nice,' he whispered, nodding at the embroidery on the wall. He had no idea if it was. Her toe rings were distracting too.

'Thank you, I'm so glad you like it,' she said. 'Please sit. Would you like some tea or coffee? Or nimbu pani? No formality. After all, it's only two-thirty a.m.'

'Oh, Mallika,' he whispered, laughing silently. 'I do love you.'

'Of *course*.'

'I mean, obviously not as in "I *love* you," but as in… as in…' He gave up. 'As in… Well, you know.'

'Yes, I know,' she said through her teeth.

'Like a friend.'

'You think I'm an idiot or what?'

'*Absolutely* not.'

'Now, say what you have to say and go, before my mothers and grandmother find out you're here and kill you.'

'Oh. Yeah.'

'Or before I strangle you.'

'You're talking a lot,' he said with pleasure.

'At night, I take pills that make me talk.'

He collapsed with laughter on the divan. He managed to do it more or less silently.

'I came to say I'm sorry.'

'OK, you've said it. Now, go.'

'About calling you boring.'

'I *know*. Now, please go.'

'I don't even remember saying it.'

'I'm sure you remember *thinking* it.'

He looked at her, stricken.

She looked back at him as though to say, *Well?*

He'd thought she'd brush it away, make it easy for him.

He couldn't even deny it. Of course, he had thought it. Like an asshole, he must have said it to Vineet. He couldn't have said it to Randhir, obviously, and he wouldn't have to anyone else.

She went to her desk and swallowed two pills, then sat on her bed, leaning against the pillow.

'What's that?' he said.

'Sleeping pills,' she said.

'Why can't you sleep?' He'd never heard of anyone their age taking sleeping pills.

She shrugged.

'I'll teach you yogic breathing, then you won't have to take any pills.'

'It helps you?'

'Sure does.'

'Then why do you smoke dope and grass and all those things?'

'I'm not *dependent* on that stuff!'

'If you smoke those things regularly, which you do, then you are.'

'Such a schoolmarm you are!' He found himself saying this with great affection. 'Anyway. Let me show you some breathing exercises. It's great for people who're stressed out,' he said.

'Why d'you think I'm stressed out?'

'You were, that time in my hostel room.'

'I wasn't stressed out. I wasn't well. *You* were stressed out.'

'*Me*? I'm never stressed out.'

'Don't lie. You were rattled because I found your Mohini's earring in your bed.'

He looked at her, stricken again.

'Sorry, Mallika,' he said under his breath.

'What for?'

She was right. What for?

'She isn't my Mohini,' he said.

'How come?'

'Well… you know how these things are.'

'No, I don't. Tell me.'

He said, 'Fizzled out. Chalo. Let me teach you yogic breathing.'

There was something shining on the floor. Her payal. He picked it up, got up and sat on her bed at her feet, and began putting it around her ankle.

'No, no, I'll do it,' she said, trying to move her foot.

He opened the clasp one end of the payal and fixed it onto the other, closing the loop firmly, then looked up and smiled at her. She didn't smile back.

'I know how to do it,' he said, getting up and going back to sit on the divan.

'Practice with Mohini and Radha?'

'No. Someone else.'

'Let me guess. Her name was Keshavi?'

'Never heard that name in my life.'

'Manmayi? '

He looked at her, puzzled.

'Kanvi? Vinodini? Gaurangi? Kanupriya?'

What weird names she was rattling off! They sounded as though they were out of some Sanskrit text!

'Hmm,' he said. 'Obviously there's something I'm not getting.'

'Now, please go. We can talk in the morning.'

'We can't. You're never alone.'

'What?'

'Never.' He counted on his fingers. 'Gauri. Prabha. Randhir. Your mothers and grandmother. Madhu Aunty. Anu Aunty. Your tuition children and their mothers. How am I supposed to talk to you?'

'Oh,' she said, as though such a thing had never occurred to her. 'Please go,' she said again.

She didn't at all sound as though she wanted him to go. Then why did she keep saying it?

He took off his shoes, sat cross-legged, and said, 'I'll show you the breathing exercises, and then I'll go.'

Pranayama had helped him since the night of the accident. That night had created havoc with his sleep, his state of mind, everything. It had replayed in his head constantly. His father's colleague next door was into yoga. He went over and said he wanted to learn something to help him relax during exams, and this colleague taught him pranayama. That helped. So did going for a run in the early mornings. He would drive to India Gate at six a.m., park his bike, and run and run.

He closed his eyes, and began breathing deeply from one nostril, and exhaling through the other, then doing the reverse.

'This is called anulom vilom,' he said, opening his eyes after two minutes. 'It's good for exhaustion. Gives you vitality.'

Her eyes were filled with laughter.

Well, at least one thing was clear. Gauri hadn't told her about the kiss.

'And the next one is bhramari. This one will help you sleep.'

He closed his eyes with four fingers, plugged his ears with each thumb, took in a deep breath, and began to hum as he exhaled. She must have leapt out of bed because the next instant her hand was clapped over his mouth again. He opened his eyes, and she was glaring at him again. 'You ass,' she hissed.

Footsteps running to her room.

She shot out of the door. It was her other mother. 'Darling, what's that horrible sound?'

'Nothing, Shantamama. I had a nightmare, so I was doing some deep breathing.'

'*Deep breathing*? It sounded like a hive of bees!'

'Sorry, Shantamama, I didn't mean to wake you up.'

'What nightmare, darling?'

'That… someone was in my room, and I wanted to strangle him.'

He tried, but he couldn't hold back a snort of laughter. Mallika coughed a few times.

'Do you have a cough, darling?'

'No, no, Shantamama, it's just… It's nothing.'

'Did you do it, then?'

'Do what, Shantamama?'

'In your nightmare. Did you strangle him?'

'No, I was contemplating it when I woke up.'

'Such violent thoughts, darling! You mustn't feel so intensely about things.

No wonder you can't sleep. Now, forget all that horrible, noisy breathing and just think of calm, good things. Goodnight, love.'

'Goodnight, Shantamama.'

He lay back on the divan, putting the mirrorwork cushion under his head. He was feeling happy and sleepy.

Mallika came back into the room and shut the door.

'Darling, why are you shutting your door? Privacy is all very well, but ventilation is more important.'

Mallika opened the door. Her mother's footsteps faded. She shut the door again.

'Ready to strangle me now?' He heard his words slurring slightly.

She sat on her bed and said, with immense sadness, 'Why did you just go off like that when Prabha told you about Jalpari's disappearance?'

His smile faded. The sight that he'd pushed back inside him, of Jalpari running away into the night, came back full force.

'As though it didn't matter,' she said.

The look of betrayal on her face didn't help. 'It *did* matter.'

'Then *why*?'

'Didn't want to hear it.'

'Why?'

'Because it was… *awful.*'

How could he tell her about Jalpari? What would it change? Nothing. Mallika's father had followed it up, to no avail. Couldn't tell her about Jalpari without telling her everything.

She lay down. Her eyes were heavy with sleep. 'When something is awful – you run off?'

He was feeling wretched. He'd also smoked too much. Sleep was hitting hard.

'I hurt you?' he asked.

'Yes.'

'Never meant to,' he whispered.

With difficulty, he got up and walked to the side of the bed where she lay and sat next to her.

'Mallika.'

She opened her eyes.

'I never meant to hurt you,' he said.

Then, before he did something stupid, he got up. He'd better leave.

He stumbled and fell.

Two seconds later, her grandmother's voice rose from the bottom of the stairs.

'Mallika, child?'

He went back to the divan. It was very cold. He covered himself with the Rajasthani razai lying at the end of the divan.

Mallika got out of bed and opened her door. Someone standing at the foot of the stairs was flashing a torch upstairs.

'Yes, Ajji?'

She had two mothers and a grandmother in the house, but it was as if they were three multiplied by three. They were everywhere.

'Child, I've never heard you walking about so much in your room. What are you so worried about?'

'Couldn't sleep, Ajji.'

'My poor child. Learn to lighten your heart. Try and think of happy things.'

Mallika was saying something. Her grandmother answered. He fell asleep.

He woke up in a state of terror. He was in her room, they were on the divan, their arms around each other, her leg flung over his. She was thrashing and weeping. She said, 'Kiss me,' and he rolled over and kissed her. She stopped thrashing, and her body melted into his, her teeth biting his lower lip as though she could hold him to her with this grip. Time stopped. He was in that other time. He kept kissing her – her mouth, her cheeks, her forehead, her ear. Then she went limp, sighed, and lay still. He stroked her hair back from her face. He touched it. It wasn't swollen. Her skin was smooth, unblemished. She was wearing a red kaftan. He was in his jeans and winter jacket, his shoes next to the divan. She sighed again and curled into him.

Thank god. Nothing had happened. Thank god. She'd been asleep when she asked him to kiss her, and then she'd slept through his kisses, even though she'd responded to them. That sleeping pill had knocked her out. Why was she taking sleeping pills anyway? For a minute, he held her close. The alarm clock next to the bed showed it was close to five a.m. He had to go before everyone woke up. He tried to get up, and she made a sound of protest. Her hair, just above where her plait began, was wound around the button of his jacket, and he had pulled at it. Slowly, very carefully, he tried to twist his button out of her hair. It wouldn't happen.

'Mallika,' he whispered, but she was sleeping like the dead. He tried again. 'Mallika, get up.' By now he'd broken into a cold sweat. He lifted her plait, pulled off the rubber band from the bottom, and hastily undid her hair. At last. He was free of her. He didn't feel free of her. He got up, bent down, and picked her up. He put her back on her bed and covered her with the razai. He picked up her limp hand and kissed her palm. Shoes in hand, he quietly went down the stairs. For a few seconds, he stood on the last stair, still hidden from anyone who might be in the corridor. No sounds. Swiftly, he stepped down, took a right, opened the side door, shut it softly, and went up to Randhir's terrace. There, he put on his shoes, and then, his arms on the parapet, he gazed out into the slowly awakening neighbourhood. His heart was beating so hard that he felt it would leap out of his chest.

When he knocked on Randhir's window after coming down from the terrace, he wanted to tell him he'd landed up in Mallika's room in the middle of the night. Like those Catholic boys in the fifth class in their convent school in Delhi who went for Confession – a ritual that had utterly mystified him and Randhir – he wanted to admit everything to Randhir.

Everything meaning *everything*.

Sanity prevailed. He kept his mouth shut.

Another apology to Mallika was due. But Mahima arrived for a ten-day visit, and the quadruplets were stuck together like glue in a flurry of giggles and gossip.

'Ma, have you ever heard of the name, Kanupriya?' he asked in the days after his late-night trip to Mallika's room.

'Of course,' she said.

'What about Keshavi, Manmayi, Gaurangi?'

His mother looked at him wonderingly. 'Where did *you* find these names?'

'I didn't. Mallika rattled them off to me the other day.'

'They're all names for Radha. You know, Krishna's Radha.'

'Oh.'

His mother served him some mutton. 'So learned Mallika is!' she sighed.

He couldn't hold back his laughter. He had to tell Randhir this!

His laughter faded. But of course. He couldn't.

The night of Mallika's abduction would forever be seared in his mind. But that tsunami of emotions – for which he'd never have a name – was buried. He didn't let himself go there. But after he got to know about Jalpari, and after he made that stupid mistake of going to Mallika's room to apologize, and after he found her wrapped around him on the divan, every emotion that he had squashed so ruthlessly jumped out at him, shrieking, 'I'm alive, I'm alive!' *You're fucking dead*, he snapped, and squashed them again.

At the age of five, he had asked his mother what she wanted most in the world, and she had said, 'A world where Mummy can sing.' It hadn't made sense to him – she did sing, she sang to him, she hummed and sang as she went about her work. Now, he understood what his mother had meant, but would he have told her that? It would have been like telling Randhir, 'Hey, that time I almost got expelled from school was because I was saving your ass.' Fine, neither of these were big matters in the scheme of things, but wasn't it even truer when it came to the bigger truths? Big truths, if uttered, could shatter everything. He'd made that mistake a few days after the accident. He'd told his sister Niharika about her cheating husband. She'd just about killed him. How *dare* he talk to her like that about her husband? What did he think – that she was going to leave him? This wasn't America, where you left your husband at the drop of a hat. But this wasn't the drop of a hat, he was having an affair, he said to Niharika, and she said Abhay would get over it. And did Arnav know how difficult it was to get a divorce in India, and what a divorced woman's life was like, and the shame of it? *She* was the one Abhay was married to, he couldn't do without her, she loved him, and she'd never let another woman take him away from her. Let him fuck whoever he wanted to, but *she* was the one he'd always come back to, so Arnav had better shut up and mind his own bloody business, and he dare not mention it to anyone, did he hear her? He heard her. She was screaming. Her face was red and blotched, tears were running down her cheeks, and her nose was streaming. Their parents had gone out; he'd chosen that time to tell her.

After that, she stopped talking to him. When she went back to America, she didn't even say goodbye to him.

He told Randhir the story of Niharika's husband's infidelity, omitting Mallika's presence. He'd lost his sister, he said.

'Listen,' Randhir said, 'I've been writing to Akhil since the day my father disowned him. Not often, every other month or so. Once in a while, he replies. So just write to Niharika. Even if she doesn't reply. At some point, she'll come around.'

Arnav wrote to Niharika every two or three months. She never replied. In her letters to Ma, she always sent him her love. He wasn't deceived by that. He knew Niharika was protecting his mother from the knowledge that she wasn't on speaking terms with her brother.

He had lost his sister. For what? For the truth. A truth that had shattered her and changed absolutely nothing. That was what Mallika had been trying to tell him that night at JNU, just before they were plunged into that nightmare: that some truths were best not told.

But Mallika will want to know the truth, an inner voice whispered.

The truth? That she was abducted and almost raped? That she defended herself by stabbing that man with a knife?

It's the truth.

Tell her we saw Jalpari? When she already knows Jalpari hasn't come back?

Yes. Everything.

Tell her that, after that horror, we had sex?
Everything.
Explain that to Randhir?
Tell her the bloody truth.
For what? For *what?*

Mallika: Coming back to my heart

1976–1977

By the time the winter holidays began, I was back to reading in bed at night. I read slowly. I read books that made me happy. Ma borrowed books from everyone she knew. She got me Jane Austen, Georgette Heyer, Gerald Durrell, PG Wodehouse, and Stephen Leacock, and a book I had never heard of called *I Capture the Castle* by Dodie Smith. Through these books, laughter returned to my heart. Then one of our neighbours lent Ma Charlotte Brontë's *Villette*. When I reached the part where Lucy Snowe buries all the precious letters written to her by Dr John, whom she loves, I abandoned the book. It felt as though I were abandoning a dear friend whose burden was beyond my capacity to bear. I patted the novel and apologized, 'I'll come back to you when I'm better, I promise.'

I began accompanying Gauri for her dance classes. As I watched her and the other girls dance, something inside me that was dark and knotted began to unravel. *I feel pain when I see them dance*, I wrote in my diary. A few days later, I realized: *It's joy, that pain. It's joy.*

And so it was. It was like a burst of colour streaking a dull and muted landscape.

Finally, I read the letters Prabha and Gauri had written to me so faithfully the summer of my illness. *I feel I've lost you*, Prabha had written in one of her letters. Of course she had, because I had lost myself. But I hadn't lost my loved ones. I was coming back because I had all of them to come back to. Including, finally, Karan.

How did you get better if there was no one to come back to?

How, without them, could the early morning light have given me happiness? How, without them, could I have found comfort in the sounds of the milkman coming in the morning; the kabadiwalla on his rounds, collecting old bottles and newspapers; the vociferous chirruping and chirping and cooing and chattering and scolding of birds at sunrise; the sounds of Ma and Ayah-ji talking and arguing downstairs; the sabjiwalla and phalwalla calling out their vegetables and fruits mid-morning; children shouting and screaming as they played pithoo in the evenings? If, in those familiar sounds and rhythms, I began finding myself again, it was because coming back to my heart also meant coming back to those who were in my heart.

Including Arnav.

The morning after Arnav's nocturnal visit, my mothers woke me up at ten-thirty. It was a Sunday morning; I was in a heavy, drugged sleep; I could barely move my limbs. 'At last,' said Shantamama. 'We were thinking you'd never get up.'

I looked at the divan. Of course he was gone. No sign he'd been lying there.

'Come, get up and come downstairs for your tea,' Ma said.

'Uff, very strong scent you're wearing,' Shantamama said. 'Doesn't suit you – too masculine.'

'I agree,' said Ma. 'Who gave you that scent?'

'How come your hair isn't plaited? I hope you didn't wash your hair at night?' Shantamama said.

Suddenly, I was awake.

Ma bent down and smelt my hair. 'Even your hair is smelling of this masculine scent, chee, not at all suitable for a girl.'

Shantamama bent down and smelt my hair. 'Ufff! Too manly!'

Ma smelt my pillow. 'Even your pillow is smelling of it!'

'Oh. Gauri sprayed it on me when she and Prabha came here yesterday.'

'But last night you weren't smelling of it,' Ma said, puzzled.

'I'll come downstairs in two minutes.' I got out of bed and went to the bathroom before more questions came my way.

As soon as I shut the door, I smelt my hair. It was reeking of his foreign cologne.

But he'd fallen asleep on the divan, and I on my bed.

Why was my hair unplaited?

When I came out of the bathroom, I smelt my pillow. It was his smell.

It made no sense that he'd got into bed with me when I was asleep. That was a creepy thing to do, and Arnav wasn't a creepy guy. None of them were. When inebriated or stoned, Randhir talked a lot, Vineet laughed a lot, and Arnav did idiotic things. Idiotic things, but never creepy things.

As I ate breakfast, my mothers complained about how forgetful Ayah-ji was getting. She had again forgotten to bolt the side door last night. Ah. So that was how he'd come in.

I had gone mad. Why else had I found the sight of him standing at my bedroom door at two a.m., insouciantly rocking on his heels, so hard to resist? Why else had I melted so rapidly when he gave me that smile? Why else had I conversed with him at such length at that ungodly hour with my mothers and grandmother springing up like mushrooms every few minutes?

Once, I'd have felt remorseful for not accepting his apology graciously. And vindicated that he'd finally apologized and presumably changed his mind about my being boring. And horrified that he was in my bedroom. And embarrassed at him seeing me in my kaftan (even though it showed no skin). And terror that he'd be discovered in my room, because my mothers would kill him and go to his house and inform his mother about what he'd done, and that would be the end of our friendship. And guilty for harbouring a boy in my room, even though he had come uninvited – but in my mind, it would have been my fault. Once, all of this would have been unexpressed and churning in my bosom.

But all I had felt was a strange delight.

Except when he'd said – in that careless, charming way of his – that he loved me, and then tried to explain what he meant. *Obviously* I knew what it meant. It meant nothing, and I wanted to punch him for it.

I had even let him wind my payal back onto my ankle. Oh, that warm touch of his fingers on my skin! How familiar it seemed. Had he chosen to let his fingers explore more, I'd have let him. Yes, I'd gone mad. And, oh, he had looked so beautiful doing his yogic breathing!

'What's so amusing, love?' Ma asked.

'Nothing, Ma.'

It was such a relief to know he'd gone off when he heard Jalpari's story not because he was callous, but because he was deeply affected by it.

'Why are you now looking sad, child?' Ajji asked.

'Nothing, Ajji.'

And then he'd fallen asleep on my divan. I'd knelt by his side and shaken him. He hadn't responded. I kept shaking him. He continued sleeping. I had pulled his legs, then his arms. He had shrugged me off and continued sleeping. By then, I was staggering with sleep. I lay down on my bed and was out like a light. I dreamt of him. In the dream, I was sinking in a quicksand of terror, and Arnav rescued me from that terror by kissing me. By doing more than kissing me. Even now, I could feel our limbs entwined, his teeth on my neck, the touch of his tongue on every part of my body. Even now, I could feel the desperation with which we made love. Even now, it made my body burn. I couldn't stop thinking about it. I felt that if he so much as touched me, I'd burst into flames, like that girl in the dream.

I told Gauri about Arnav's nocturnal visit to apologize, and the smell of his cologne in my hair. It made no sense because he wasn't the kind of guy who would do something to you while you slept, I told her.

'He didn't *do* anything, silly! He was just overcome by his feelings for you! He got up from the divan and unplaited your hair and buried his face in it! And then he went back to the divan!' Gauri sighed.

'Gauri,' I said severely. 'This isn't *Two Hearts are One*.'

'You don't know anything,' Gauri said, as though she knew everything.

Ever since Gauri had read her first Mills & Boon – *Two Hearts are One* – at the age of twelve, she had been hooked. In the book, Hero and Heroine are forced to spend the night together because their car breaks down, and there's only one room available, with a double bed, which they're of course compelled to share. In bed, they finally kiss. The passionate kiss goes on for two pages, after which he buries his face in her golden hair and groans that he isn't a monk, and they must stop. This was Gauri's favourite part, the Hero burying his face in the Heroine's hair and putting the brakes on deflowering her.

Gauri let out her breath. 'Tell me, what do you feel for Randhir and Arnav?'

I looked at her in shock.

No one had ever asked me such a question. The closest anyone had come to it was Mahima, and she had backed off after a few minutes. Even I hadn't asked myself such a question. What I felt for them was a flowing, endless thing, and putting words to it was like creating a dam to hold it in place. I wanted to feel what I felt without words and explanations. Words and explanations were like chains that imprisoned me. I didn't have freedom in my life, so why couldn't I have it in my heart?

I knew what Gauri was asking me. She was asking me which one I loved. She was asking me to choose. That's what you were supposed to do with love.

'Neither of them is interested in me that way, Gauri.'

'I'm asking about you; whom are *you* interested in?'

'I care for them both.'

'Mallika! Which one would you like to marry?'

Marry? How could I think of marrying either of them, when neither of them wanted to marry me?

Someone was bounding up the stairs.

Prabha burst into my room, her face flushed, her eyes shining. 'Mahima's come!'

Gauri and I leapt out of bed, put on our slippers, ran down the stairs and out of the house.

We spent ten blissful days with Mahima. She came laden with perfumes and undies for us, and on top of that, bought us books from Chachaji's second-hand bookshop. We went out for lunch and a beautiful dance performance. In some ways, it felt like old times. And yet it didn't, due to my slow realization that, although Mahima's happiness at being back home was heartfelt, that was the only real happiness within her. The rest was a sham. Our conversation about her sex life was very upsetting.

After Mahima left, I told Gauri and Prabha that Mahima didn't like sex.

'Oh, that's quite common,' Gauri said with the assurance that she always had about things she'd never experienced. 'Everyone knows sex is overrated.'

'It's not *that*. It *hurts* her. *Every* time. She's talked to Shekhar about it, and she's seen a gynae, but it still hurts. She hates doing it. That's not OK, that's *awful*.'

My friends considered this. But we had no idea what to think. There was no one we could ask. There was nothing we could read. We had zero context.

My illness – like the painting of Dorian Gray – remained firmly locked up in that other room. For the world outside my immediate family, it had been non-existent when in full bloom, and non-existent I hoped it would be forever more. Dr Roy had asked me several times about the days that led to the concussion, and then the depression. I told him the same thing each time: I had been run-down and worried and couldn't concentrate on studying. Talking about the rest would have been like waking up that slumbering cactus. It had been in a deep sleep for months now, its thorns folded inside itself like petals. It belonged to a desert landscape in another country; it didn't belong to me.

However, I was talking to him about other things that mattered to me. I told him about Prabha punching the man in the bus. I told him I felt as though she'd done it for all of us for whom assault was a thing to be regularly endured in silence. That Prabha had shattered the euphemism 'eve-teasing,' which made such experiences sound so frivolous and frothy. I told him that, for two years, I had carried a sharp, small knife in my blouse whenever I travelled alone. In the winter holidays, I realized that I'd lost it, and I felt I'd lost a protector, I told Dr Roy, who was listening with great interest.

I told him about my mothers' brother's letter to me. I knew the letter by heart, because I had read it again and again, each time thinking it couldn't be true.

'I never did anything to harm him,' I told Dr Roy. 'Nor did Ma. After I finished school, we never took any money from my grandmother. What did Ma and I do to warrant such viciousness?'

'Does a woman who is beaten by her husband warrant the beating?'

I shook my head. Never.

'But she often thinks she's done something to deserve it. You haven't done anything to deserve a letter like that. This is about him, not you.'

I told him about my fantasy about studying at an American university. He asked me why I wasn't applying.

'Because even if I get an assistantship, I don't have the money for the plane ticket or to buy the foreign exchange.'

'What about your grandmother?'

'I've taken too much from her.'

He reflected on this.

'Your uncle has inherited your grandparents' house, hasn't he?'

I nodded.

'Then don't feel guilty. The house he's inherited must be worth a lot more than what your grandmother spent on your education. I'm sure that if your grandmother has the money, she'd be happy to help you realize your dream.'

How Prabha would love him! He was a man of her heart!

'How about your father?'

'He's already spent thousands on me. *And* he's supporting his ex-wife.'

'Think about why you feel you don't have the right to ask your father, when he would do everything he possibly could to help you realize your dreams.'

'He told you that?'

'He didn't have to.'

I left his office, my mind spinning.

'Mallika!'

It was Arnav in the market, waving from the paanwalla's booth. As usual, he was buying cigarettes. Or maybe it was dope. The paanwalla was well known for selling that too. He came over to me. 'Going to Bittu's Books?'

'No, no, buying amrood.'

We walked to the phalwalla's cart.

'Sorry about barging into your room that night. But… I wasn't thinking.'

'I could see that.'

'Mallika, don't sound so schoolmarmish! You can do better than that!'

That got my goat.

'Why was my pillow smelling of your cologne?'

He gave me a quick glance.

After a few seconds, he said, 'Was it? So… what did you think?'

I felt my face burning. 'Nothing. My mothers kept smelling the pillow and asking questions.' I began picking up the guavas on the phalwalla's cart.

'Here, these are good,' Arnav said, picking up a couple of green guavas.

'Too unripe.'

'I've noticed you South Indians like them ripe. North Indians like these green ones.'

I'd never heard that one before. But it was a relief to be talking about guavas.

I paid the phalwalla, and we began walking home.

He said, 'That night, you were also asleep next to me on the floor, on your pillow. I managed to get you back into your bed before I split.'

I looked at him in horror.

He was biting his lips, trying not to laugh.

'I had two sleeping pills… by mistake.'

'Yeah. I saw.'

So that was the story of the reeking-of-cologne pillow and hair. What I didn't have the guts to do in real life, I'd done in my sleep. I wanted to die of mortification.

After the winter break ended, I was well enough to travel to college and back by bus. I was also going to see Masi on my own, and a wall seemed to have fallen away from her. We'd chat over nimbu pani or tea. She loved to hear about college and my friends.

This time when she worked on me, I fell asleep as usual and found myself in a strange house. It was the middle of the night. Someone was banging hard at the door. I rushed to it, then stopped, terrified of what I would see if I opened it. The banging would not stop. What to do? There was only one thing to be done. That was to go to the back door, step outside, walk around the house, and peep from the corner to see who was banging so hard on the front door. But when I reached the corner of the house, I lost my courage and went back inside. Once more, I stood at the front door, where the banging was getting louder and louder. Suddenly, my mothers appeared next to me. Together, they said, 'Meet it.'

I put my hand out to open the front door.

'You can open your eyes, Beti.'

Masi was sitting next to me. She gave me a glass of water. I drank it thirstily.

'Beti, I saw you in a house and there is someone banging at your door. But you are frightened and do not open it. Then your mothers come to you and say, in English, "Meet it."'

Absolutely stunned, I said, 'I saw the same thing.'

She stared at me. 'So then. It is very important.'

'But… meet what, Masi? My mothers would never say such a thing to me. They would be the ones opening the door, protecting me.'

'Hold it inside your heart. When it is ready, it will show a part of itself to you.'

'Only a *part* of itself?'

'Beti, a message has layers. The layers grow as you grow.'

This was beyond me.

She smiled. 'Bas, now leave it.'

Tentatively, I asked, 'Masi, where do your messages come from?'

'I do not know, Beti.'

I had asked the Phuknewalla a similar question many years ago. I had said, 'How do you do this?' And he had pointed to the heavens and said, 'I do not know, He only knows.'

Ma had never believed in 'these things,' as she and Shantamama called them. Meaning astrologers, soothsayers, hands-on healers, pranic healers, godmen, and the like. Ma didn't even want to read my astrological chart, so Shantamama kept it.

Shantamama, on the other hand, had mixed feelings about 'these things.' She would say to me, 'It's not healthy, stay away from these things.' Meaning 'these things' had a kind of dark legitimacy, and the less you had to do with them, the better. She conceded that the Phuknewalla had helped me, but warned me, 'Don't be tempted towards more of these things, it can become an addiction' – as though it were a drug.

Now, ironically, Ma the sceptic was in the predicament of 'these things' being an integral part of her life because of me. She could clearly see that 'these things' were working for me, but it sat ill with her. Having succumbed, she chose not to talk about it. Sometimes, at home, I'd say teasingly, 'These things are doing their magic on me, Ma!' and she'd give me one of her reluctant smiles.

As for me, it was simple. The Phuknewalla had mitigated the extreme pain and frequency of my migraines. Masi was making me better. I had no idea what any of this was about. But as Shantamama always said, the proof of the pudding was in the eating. I didn't need to know the recipe.

I was now approaching the end of my BA final year. Randhir was finishing his MA at St Stephen's, and Arnav his final year at IIT. I hadn't seen Arnav for months.

Randhir's euphoria about Indira Gandhi losing the elections, the end of the Emergency, and the formation of a new government was now submerged beneath the weight of his own life. He was trying hard to come to terms with working in his father's factory. It would be fine, he told me, after all, he'd had his reprieve, five years of it, it would be fine.

I knew this life would strangle him. But he was determined to talk himself out of his despair.

Then one day, as I came out of my college gates, Arnav was sitting outside on his bike. He waved and swung himself off, walking towards me, his smile lighting up his face.

'Hi,' I said, my heart singing, Mills-&-Boon style. It had been so long!

'Hi. I'm going to Randhir's house, so I thought I'd chance it and pick you up. Randhir said you usually finish in the late afternoons.'

I was trying to contain my happiness, which was bursting out of every pore of my body.

'Before going home, feel like some ice cream at India Gate?'

'Yes,' I said, allowing my happiness to show freely.

'I've never seen anyone looking like that for ice cream,' he said. 'Chalo, hop on. And hold on.'

He couldn't know how blissfully I held onto him.

At India Gate, we sat down with our ice creams, and Arnav came straight to the point. 'I wanted to talk to you about Randhir. He's miserable. He's wasting his life. He's an academic at heart, he's a writer, and he's throwing it all away.'

'I know,' I said, trying not to feel sad that Arnav was only with me because he wanted to talk about Randhir.

'At some point, he's going to come to you saying he's had it. That's when you strike.'

I looked at him enquiringly.

'Tell him to apply to American universities. That's when he'll do it. When he's stretched beyond endurance.'

'How d'you know?'

'Mallika, I've known him since we were six! He has to do what he thinks is the right thing. Even if it kills him.'

'He'll tell *you* before he tells me.'

'I won't be in Delhi.'

'Why?'

'I've accepted a damn good job offer in Bombay. I'll be going there in a couple of months, after I graduate.'

My happiness whooshed out of me.

'Why not a job in Delhi?'

'Need a change, Mallika. Got to get out. Try something new.'

He saw my bewilderment and said, 'I mean, I love Delhi, but… I really want a change.'

'Why?'

He began to laugh. 'Oh, Mallika! I don't know why. I just do.'

Arnav left for Bombay, with a cheery 'Write to me, OK?' A couple of months later, he wrote me a measly postcard with a few lines scrawled on it, the gist of it being: *How are you, I'm fine, what news, not much news at my end.* I looked at the yellow postcard with indignation. Was this his idea of a *letter?* No one wrote *postcards* to friends! Then I turned the card over and saw that, in that tiny space, he'd drawn a picture of a sparrow and written in tiny letters: *The sparrow at my window.* It was so exquisite that, instead of tearing up his stingy postcard, I put it in a large envelope with my other letters. I had no idea he could draw as well as act.

Arnav's departure precipitated an awful loneliness. As the months went by, I felt more and more bereft. I walked a lot, especially early in the mornings, hearing the old neighbourhood singer devotedly bellowing bhajans, completely off-tune and utterly happy. If only I could be like him, off-tune yet happy. It was true that I loved being with my mothers and could chatter with them endlessly. It was also true that I loved quiet time to myself. But I sorely missed having close friends nearby. Mahima had left us long ago, Prabha was at medical college in Poona and came home only for the holidays, and though Gauri was still in Delhi, she was far away at JNU, and while she came to see me every four-to-five weeks, it wasn't like the earlier days, when the four of us used to spend so much time together. Randhir was completely consumed by his work at the factory, so we also had very little time together. And Arnav wanted me to persuade Randhir to apply to American universities? Arnav could bloody well come to Delhi and do the persuading.

The next time Prabha came home, I found myself talking to her and Gauri about my own dream of applying to American universities.

'God, Mallika,' Prabha said. 'We didn't even *know* you'd been dreaming of this.'

'I thought you wanted to sit for the IAS?' Gauri said.

'Only because going to America is impossible. There's no money for the ticket or foreign exchange, and Ma's still paying back my room loan.'

They looked taken aback. I had never spoken to them before about our financial straits. Not that they didn't know – our lifelong friendship and proximity made these things obvious. But still. We had never spoken about what our parents had or did not have.

Prabha said, 'Ask your grandmother for the money.'

Gauri said, 'Your father will also happily give you money.'

They were saying exactly what Dr Roy had.

But I didn't know how to ask.

After lunch, the three of us went to Chachaji's bookshop, armed with twenty rupees each – all the money we had. As they were browsing the shelves, Prabha suddenly burst out, 'Mallika, look!'

A stack of six Graduate Record Examination books lay where she was pointing on the floor.

'Chachaji, how much for them?' Prabha asked.

Chachaji gave this thought.

'Thirty rupees,' he said finally.

We looked at each other in disbelief. Thirty rupees was nothing for six GRE books, even second-hand ones.

Prabha said, 'We were just talking about your applying, and see, now these books have appeared before you.'

'It's a sign,' Gauri said.

'This is our advance birthday present to you,' Prabha said, looking at Gauri.

'Of course,' Gauri said.

They took out their purses and paid fifteen rupees each.

'Now, you start practicing, and then you ask your grandmother and father when they come to Delhi,' Prabha instructed.

I was almost in tears at their generosity. But how to ask Ajji and Karan?

The answer came a couple of weeks later, but not in any way I could have anticipated.

I was at Cottage Industries Emporium on a Saturday morning, looking for handloom blouse materials for Ma and me, when a voice next to me said, 'Mallika?'

I looked.

I felt myself falling into another space. I was afloat in the river of dreams.

'How are you?'

'Fine, thank you.' I clutched the counter. It was the only thing that held me to this world, it was the only thing that would prevent that river from taking me away. 'How are you?' My voice felt as though it was coming from somewhere outside me.

'I'm well, Mallika. You're looking good. I'm so glad.'

She remembered my name? I saw myself floating away.

'Alright, then. Bye, Mallika.'

'Bye.'

She was at the door when I found myself walking to her.

'Doctor…' I couldn't remember her name.

She turned.

'I owe you money. But I don't have it yet,' I said.

She was silent. Then she said, 'Are you working?'

'I'm doing my MA.'

'Will you work after that? Or get married?'

'Work.'

'Alright. You can give it to me then.'

'How much?'

She hesitated.

'I have to,' I said.

She nodded, suddenly grave. 'One thousand.'

'I'll give it to you. I promise.'

She nodded again.

'Doctor, I'm sorry, I've... forgotten your name.'

'Dr Raghunath.'

'Dr Raghunath, thank you for... everything.'

'You're welcome. Bye.'

As I looked out of the bus on my way home, I was attacked by images of that time two years ago. The horrible meeting with the first gynae, who wanted to make money out of me by saying I was pregnant when it was just a heavy period. Bleeding heavily in the scooter after four months of not having my period, and that knife-like pain. The clinic with Dr Raghunath, and my terrible confusion. Losing my mind like Charu. Then, with superhuman effort, grabbing my mind and getting it back again. Managing to hold onto it for a while, even though it was straining and heaving inside me. Then, as soon as I finished my exams, my body relaxing, the binding around my mind loosening, and it finally escaping from me.

I had thought that old story had gone away forever.

And now it had resurfaced and waved at me in the face, as if to say, 'Just came to say hullo! You think it's up to you? No, my dear, it's entirely up to me.'

When I awoke the next morning, it was with the knowledge that when Karan and my grandmother came to Delhi, I would ask them if they could help me with the money for the plane ticket and foreign exchange. If they said yes, I would apply to American universities. I had the GRE books. I would start practicing right away.

It was as though the previous day I had been standing at one place, and this morning had materialized at another, without any travel between the two.

Randhir: Beta, just tell me why?

1977–1979

He had never understood his sister. He had never known what she wanted, what she didn't, what she dreamt of. It didn't seem to him that she dreamt of anything. How could his sister live without dreams? He had always wondered. But after he finished his MA and began working in his father's factory, he didn't dream either. Perhaps it was better to be like his sister and not have dreams, because if you had them and they died, it was worse than never having had them at all.

It was an hour's drive to the factory, and an hour back. He and his father left early in the morning and came home late at night. Work was continuous. The workers were discontented; rumour had it that they were forming a union. When he told his father that it wasn't a bad thing, forming a union – after all, workers had rights too – his father told him not to talk like a fool. When workers came to him complaining and he listened, his father said he was wasting his time, people of that class always complained, there was no need to listen and give them the wrong idea. He discovered in his father the shrewd, ruthless businessman – the man for whom giving large and regular bribes to government officials to get this licence or that permission was routine. Not that his father did it, one of his employees did, but it was simply how things worked. He also discovered his father as the politician, who had spies amongst the blue-collar workers informing him who was complaining, who was talking about starting a union, who were the troublemakers. It was a world utterly foreign to the life that Randhir had lived. He found it repugnant. He knew he had no right to his revulsion, for it was this that had been his bread and butter, this that had given him his education, his books, his everything. This was his inheritance. It was what his father would one day hand over to him. By then, he would have become his father.

Perhaps he could, over time, if he could also be himself. Be his father in the factory, be himself at home. If he could write. If he could write, perhaps he would survive it. But there was no time or energy to write. Weekdays were impossible. Weekends were spent on endless paperwork and phone calls.

It was what his father had done all his life. It was why none of them had
known him: he was so busy working for his family that he was hardly ever
with them. It was why their mother was larger than life, for she occupied
every corner that their father didn't.

No writing, no reading, no time with Mallika, no going for treks with
Arnav and Vineet – the last one had been a glorious one in Himachal after
they graduated. No time for anything but the business. Arnav was now
working in Bombay, and that was another huge vacuum in his life. On the
weekends, he managed time with Mallika, but it was brief and unsatisfactory.

He didn't get a salary. The factory belonged to them both, what need for
a salary? This is what his father had said. Whatever money there was, was
theirs. Whenever he wanted money, all he had to do was ask. He couldn't
bring himself to tell his father he wanted his own bank account, with a
salary going into it every month, commensurate with the work that he was
doing. It sounded crass, asking his father to pay him. It sounded as though
he didn't trust his father. But he hated having to ask him for money. He
never felt he could ask for as much as he would get had it been a salary;
most of the time, it felt like pocket money. He was working like a dog and
still didn't have a bank account of his own. Soon, they'd hound him to get
married. He couldn't even say, 'I want to marry Mallika, she's the one I love.'
Marrying her would be the biggest betrayal of his love for her.

Was this how he would live the rest of his life?

His despair was profound.

He began collecting sleeping pills again. This time, he hid them with his
diaries in the trunk below his bed, which he kept locked.

After almost a year of working in Bombay, Arnav wrote to Randhir that he
was sick of his job. He couldn't stand Bombay. He was applying for jobs in
Delhi.

For the first time in his life, he found himself envying Arnav. He envied
the freedom Arnav had to leave a job he hated and find another in Delhi.
The freedom to go where he wished, when he wished. The intensity of this
envy – or was it jealousy? – shook him.

'Arnav's lucky, he got away from home,' he told Mallika as they went for
one of their all-too-rare walks.

'Is that why he went away – to get away from home?'

'I think so. Mishti's death was too much for him.'

She looked at him, puzzled.

Oh, shit. He'd forgotten Mallika didn't know.

'Don't tell him I told you. Arnav's father kicked Mishti. Arnav wasn't at
home at the time. The poor dog ran away and got run over.'

He saw the shock on Mallika's face.

'Yeah. I don't think he's got over it. Or forgiven his father.'

They walked in silence towards the park.

After a while, Mallika said, 'How does Arnav deal with it?'

'Arnav doesn't deal with anything he doesn't want to deal with.'

'Oh?'

He went back to the original subject. 'But Arnav could get away, Mallika. I never can. Every day, I hate it more, working at the factory. Sometimes I feel I'm going crazy.'

For a minute, she didn't reply.

Then she said, 'Randhir, apply to American universities. You've always dreamt of it.'

He'd put that dream into an iron box, locked it, and buried it. 'No, I can't.'

Another pause.

Then, 'Randhir, remember how, all those years ago, you told me I didn't have to spend those weekends with my father? That I didn't have to do what caused me so much pain? You even said I didn't have to love him. Now, I'm telling you something similar. You don't have to work in the factory. That's your father's life. Live yours. Just... summon up the... courage.'

He didn't answer for some time.

'Is that courage or cowardice? I'd be running away.'

She shook her head. 'No.'

He said, 'My father's getting older. My brother isn't going to help him. It's only me. And I run away from my responsibilities? How is that courage?'

'Randhir, I also felt I was letting my father down when I stopped those weekends with him.'

'Mallika, a family business is very different from spending weekends with one's father. And, unlike your father, mine will never understand or accept. Ever.'

'Randhir, it's not cowardice. Cowardice is what Karan did to Ma. Giving into parental and social pressure.'

'Oh, Mallika. He's more than suffered for it.'

She said sadly, 'All these years, that's what he's been dealing with. His cowardice. That's why he can never talk about it. I just realized it.'

They turned and began walking home.

'Arnav was talking to me,' she said. 'He said you're wasting your life. That you're an academic at heart and have a future as a writer, and you're throwing it all away.'

All very well to say that. But it seemed dishonourable to pursue what he loved after Akhil had become lost to the family. A couple of months ago, Akhil had written to him that he'd converted.

It is up to you to tell Mummy and Daddy, or not. But you must know that no one, not even my wife, asked me to convert. I have made this decision on my own, for our future. A baby is coming. Our child must have a stable family life without being pulled in two directions. This is my family now. This is my last letter to you. There is nothing more to say, you see. There is no need for you to reply.

Very shaken, he had written to Akhil, saying he understood his decision. But he hadn't heard from Akhil after that.

He hadn't told Mummy or Daddy. As it was, Mummy had been crying bitterly about Akhil's silence. If she knew he'd converted, she'd lose all hope. But he was haunted by Akhil's words – *This is my family now.* How could Akhil not feel that, given that his own family had abandoned him?

But Daddy felt that Akhil had abandoned *them.* If he, Randhir, went to study in America, Daddy would feel irrevocably deserted. It was no way to treat a father who had worked like a dog to give them everything that they wanted.

Everything except their freedom. 'His expectation of you is your *whole life*, Randhir,' he could hear fifteen-year-old Mallika saying.

His *whole* life. Mallika's long-ago words began to ring like a death knell. *His whole life.*

'Where am I going to find the time to study for the GREs?' he said faintly.

Mallika stopped in her tracks. 'You'll do it?'

'I'll give it a shot.'

'On the weekends. Tell your father you can't work on the weekends. And come home earlier on the weekdays. That'll give you a few hours every night to study.'

'What should I tell my father?'

'He knows you write?'

'Sort of.'

'Your happiness matters to him, Randhir. Tell him you'll only be happy if you can also write, and that's why you want to get back home a little earlier. I mean, if you don't get into grad school in America, you'll need time to write anyway, so... you might as well establish it now.'

'I can't hide it from them. The applications will come in the post. Ma'll see them.'

'That's OK. She won't tell your father.'

He looked at her, taken aback.

'Randhir, you're so *ignorant.* She doesn't tell him *anything.*'

'Oh.' He was nonplussed. 'But something like this...?'

'Something like this, *especially*! You think she didn't know about Akhil going around with Ameena? She knew for a year!'

'She *knew*?'

'Of course. Remember, she went to Bombay to see Akhil once? The reason she went was to dissuade him from marrying her, but he wasn't dissuaded. So she came back and acted as though she knew nothing. I mean, better for Akhil to drop the bombshell than her.'

'Mallika, what all do you know about my family that you've never told me?'

'Plenty,' she laughed. 'Anyway, she won't tell your father about your applications. If she tells my mother and Anu Aunty, they won't mention it to a soul. So you're safe till June or July of '79. A little more than a year from now. If it doesn't work out, there's nothing to tell. If it does work out, then you deal with it then. Until then, you study.'

Arnav and Mallika were the only two who knew his heart.

Yet they couldn't see all of it.

He wrote to Arnav about his conversation with Mallika, and Arnav promptly wrote back. *Listen, man, you have one life. Don't waste it. Do what makes you happy.*

Do what makes you happy! What an un-Indian philosophy! Indians were pros at doing all the things that made them wretchedly unhappy. Working in jobs they hated and never leaving. Getting married when they didn't want to marry, to people they didn't want to marry. Staying married when they hated every moment of it, all the while declaring that Indians, unlike Westerners, had such happy, stable marriages. Happiness. That Great Pretence. And you inflicted the same misery that you had endured on your children, because that was how it was supposed to be and that was how it had better be.

But how come Mallika supported him so unequivocally when she never did the same for herself? If her mother had the money, would Mallika have applied to grad school in America? No, she wouldn't, because she'd never leave her mothers and go so far away. Mallika knew that he must follow his dreams but had firmly shut the door to hers.

A few months later, in August, the newspapers were ablaze with the news of two teenagers, a sister and brother, who had hitched a lift with two men and ended up murdered. It was likely the girl was raped. By all accounts, the children had fought for their lives before their bodies were dumped in the infamous forested area of the Ridge Road.

It shook him horribly. More so because of what he knew had happened to Mallika. He put down the newspaper and went next door. Padma Aunty and Mallika were poring over the newspaper at the dining table. They looked up. He said to Mallika, 'I hope you're not hitching lifts like all these Delhi girls.' She shook her head. She was pale.

Padma Aunty, whose face was heavy with grief, said, 'Sit, Randhir, I'll make some coffee,' and went to the kitchen.

'Be careful, OK,' he said, and Mallika nodded.

Two years ago, he had thought the worst had happened to Mallika. But now, he realized it wasn't the worst. She too could have been murdered.

Losing her memory was the best thing that had happened to her. If she thought it was a heavy period, then let her. He'd never tell her the truth.

For his writing sample, he sent the American universities' English departments one academic essay and two short stories that he had published in the *Illustrated Weekly of India* and *Imprint*, under the name 'R Nanda.' Only Arnav knew it was Randhir Nanda. Mallika didn't even know he'd been published. The head of the department in Pennsylvania wrote to him, asking him if he would like to apply for the MA/PhD in English with a specialty in Creative Writing; they were very impressed with his work. Dizzy with joy, he had written back that yes, he did.

Of course, as he'd anticipated, his mother got to know about his applications to American universities because she saw the large packets from the US arriving in the post. 'Mummy, stop getting hassled,' he said to her. 'I have to get admission *and* aid *and* the visa. More than half of the people who have aid don't get visas.'

'You will get all,' his mother said in a voice of doom. 'And then your Daddy...' She didn't complete the sentence.

In February of the following year, he got admission at four universities, including the one in Pennsylvania.

By July, he had full aid for Pennsylvania.

No cause for celebration. Plenty of students with full financial aid weren't getting visas.

By then, Arnav had got a job in Delhi and was – at last – back.

Two weeks after getting his financial aid letter, Randhir received the I-20 form and went to get his visa. He didn't take any bank papers with him because he still hadn't told his parents.

The visa officer didn't ask for bank papers. Instead, he said, 'You're a writer!'

A *writer*? Even Randhir had never thought of himself as a writer. Just as someone who wrote.

He got his visa, and with it, a big smile.

It was as though he'd earned this by working at his father's factory. As though every moment he'd hated had been necessary to balance the implacable scale that weighed what he hated against what he loved. He hadn't merely realized his dream to study in America. He had realized his biggest dream, for the degree gave him the right to write.

'You think I am paying for your plane ticket to go to America to do *English* degree?' his father said incredulously.

For a minute, he couldn't take in what his father was saying.

He looked at his mother. She was sitting on the sofa, her hand on her heart.

Tears were streaming down his father's face. His shoulders shook with the effort of trying to stop them.

'First, your older brother deceived me with that Mussalmaan girl,' his father said. 'Now, you have deceived me with your tactics about English degree. Saying, "I will do BA, and then work in the factory." Then saying, "I will do MA, and then work in the factory." Then quietly-quietly applying to American universities for third-rate *English* degree. No intention you had of staying in the factory. All lies. And now, you are asking me to give money for ticket to America and money to buy dollars to take to America?'

Randhir had never seen his father weep. Not even when he had cut Akhil out of his life.

'But, Daddy,' he whispered. 'I'm not asking *you* to pay for anything. I've earned enough in two years working at the factory to pay for the plane ticket *and* for the foreign exchange.'

'Accha? What about the money you kept asking me for every month?'

He was feeling sick. 'But that was hardly anything, Daddy. That wasn't even... a salary!'

His father wiped his face against his kurta sleeve and made a contemptuous sound. '"Hardly anything," he says. Living a life of luxury in *my* house, eating *my* food, spending *my* money, and then he says, "hardly anything!"'

Randhir was dizzy with shock. 'Daddy, I'm only asking for the money that I've earned.'

'I have put my life's blood into the factory. I have denied my children nothing. You have all lived lives of luxury, lives that I could not even imagine when I was a child. I came to Delhi after Partition. With nothing. Nothing. Everything, I built from scratch. So that you, your useless brother, and your sister would not lack for anything. And then you have the himmat to ask me for the money *you* have earned? After treating it like a government job, after leaving the factory every day at four p.m., after refusing to work on weekends? You have earned nothing, except my contempt.'

That was it then.

'If you want to go to America, then go. I am not stopping you. But if you think I will pay for anything, you are mistaken.' His father got up and went to his bedroom.

For once, his mother said nothing. She just continued sitting on the sofa, breathing noisily.

Randhir went to his room, got his wallet and keys, and phoned Arnav, who was living with his parents. Then he went to Mallika's house and asked her if she felt like some chaat at Bengali market.

'Shit,' Arnav said half an hour later, as the three of them sat drinking tea and eating samosas and chaat. 'Oh, shit.'

Mallika said nothing. She had her worried look.

'Listen, man, phone the admissions office at the university,' Arnav said. 'Tell them you'll come next year. Apply for a lecturer's job here. You topped the university twice; you'll get a job handed to you on a platter. I can lend you six, seven thousand by the end of next year. You can save up a couple of thousand if you live at home. That's enough for the ticket.'

He was so moved by Arnav's offer that for a couple of minutes he didn't speak. Then he said, 'I need to buy dollars. Can't go with nothing. Taxi, Greyhound to the university from JFK, deposit for rent, food for the first month before you get your first pay cheque... all that.'

They were silent.

'Stop worrying about money, money doesn't matter,' he'd said to Mallika the very first time they'd talked. And she'd wagged her finger at him and declared, 'Only people with money say money doesn't matter.' How amused he'd been! He had had no idea. Because he had never needed to think about money. Now, he did. Now, his father's ruthlessness, which he had seen in the factory, was directed against him. It had happened to Akhil too, disowned by his own father.

What a fool he'd been not to insist that his father gave him a salary. But no, he too had succumbed to the Indian mentality of not talking directly about money. Feeling ashamed to ask for what was rightfully yours. Because you didn't do that with parents. Or relatives. Or anyone.

No money, no dreams. That was how it had always been for Mallika.

He'd find out about lecturers' positions at DU. And make a trunk call to the head of the English department in Pennsylvania, who had been so impressed with his stories, and ask for his admission to be deferred. If nothing worked out and he continued to be trapped in this life – well, the bottle of pills was almost full.

'Beta, do not worry,' his mother said as they ate dinner that evening. His father was still at the factory. 'Do not be sad, Beta. I will pay for your ticket.'

He looked up from his plate, stunned.

'Also, you have to buy dollars, no?'

'Yes, Mummy,' he stammered.

'That also, I will give. Lighten your heart, Beta. It is your dream. So you go.'

'Mummy, that's a lot of money.'

'So? I have. It is all *my* money from *my* tailor shop. I will break two fixed deposits.'

He looked at her wordlessly.

'Alright, Beta? All your dreams, you fulfil. You go.'

He felt such shame and remorse for the disdain he carried about his mother that no words came out.

'But, Beta, one thing you promise me.'

His heart plunged. She would ask him to come back after his degree and go back to working in the factory. Or she would ask him to get married before he left. Or both.

What his father had said was true. He had deceived them. He had given the impression that he would join the factory after he finished his BA. Then, after his BA, he'd done his MA. Why hadn't he had the guts to tell his father the truth right after he passed out of school? That he wouldn't work in the factory, that it was not the life he wanted. How was he any better than the guys around him who strung along the girls they were going out with and eventually went in for an arranged marriage with the girl their parents chose for them? They didn't have the balls to be honest, neither with the girl they were going out with nor with their parents. How was he better than any of them?

'Mummy, I can't promise you anything.'

'Beta, I beg of you. Just promise you will not marry American girl.'

He almost laughed. That was easy.

'Mummy, I'm never getting married, Indian or American.'

'Beta, what are you saying!'

'I'm never getting married.'

'But *why*? Beta, I beg of you, just tell me *why*?

Just tell me why. Oh, what a joke!

What had he been *thinking*! How could he have been such a fool as to think there was any merit in honesty? Live your life *honestly*! What a joke! You could only live it dishonestly. Or not live it at all.

His betrayal would be a million times worse than his brother Akhil's. Akhil had been honest with their parents. He'd had the guts to marry the woman he loved. For that honesty, his father had disowned him. Five years ago, if Randhir had told his father he didn't want to work in the factory, his life would have been unliveable. That he'd had a wonderful five years doing what he loved was because he'd been dishonest. You were screwed if you told the truth, because they'd never leave you alone; they'd get after you to change your mind every bloody day of your life. And you were screwed if you postponed telling the truth, because then you'd be accused of lies and deception. They'd get you either way.

'It's alright, Mummy. There's no need to pay for my ticket or anything.'

It wasn't the end of the world. He would work on his back-up plan.

'Alright, Beta, alright. I will not ask you to promise anything. You go. I will pay.'

Suddenly, he wanted to weep. 'Daddy will be upset with you.'

'Yes. He will be angry with me. He will not talk to me. It is alright. Anyway, where does he talk to me? He comes home late, he leaves early. Now, what little talking there is between us, that will become zero. What does it matter? I talk to Padma. I talk to Anu. When Mahima comes home, I will talk to her. What is in my heart, I share with them. When have I ever shared my heart with your father?'

She had never spoken to him like this.

'What is in my heart, he does not know. Never he has known. Or *wanted* to know.'

'Mummy –'

'Beta, tomorrow, I will take out money, you go to travel agent and bank. Nice, big party we will have before you go. Go, Beta. Go with my blessings. I have already lost one son. I will not lose you also.'

His heart was pounding. But one day, I will lose you. I've already lost Daddy. And I'll lose Mahima, who will always take your side. You'll never understand that I didn't choose it. One day, you'll find out the truth about me, and you'll think, *My son's one of those. A pervert.* And then you'll all be done with me.

Mallika: You're *very* old-fashioned

1979

And here I was, at my second boisterous party at Randhir's house. His farewell party.

While Dire Straits blared, a DU boy, Rajesh, who was famous for being fluent in six Indian languages, began talking to me in Bengali.

'I'm not Bengali,' I said.

'Of course you are!'

'No, no, I'm from Karnataka.'

'Oh, my god! You're not like a Madrasi at all!'

Meaning I wasn't quite as dark, my hair wasn't curly, I had a Delhi accent, I was wearing a Bengali saree.

'But there's no such thing as "a Madrasi,"' I said. How did someone who knew six Indian languages not know this?

'Of course, I know that, but I meant that you don't look like a Madrasi.'

I was stumped.

'Your eyelashes…!' he sighed.

I had to put an end to it. 'They're false.'

But there were no false eyelashes to be had in India.

'From America,' I added.

He threw back his head and roared with laughter.

'I love your deadpan sense of humour,' he said.

Arnav walked into the room. I waved. He waved back. I waved again, furiously. To my relief, he strolled towards us and said hi.

Since he was standing opposite us, I stepped back slightly and mouthed, 'Stay.'

He raised his eyebrows slightly, then looked at Rajesh. 'Hey, Rajesh, how are you?'

'Great, yar. Mallika and you know each other?'

'Very well,' I said. Then, 'I was waiting for you, Arnav,' in case he went off again.

'Oh?' said Rajesh.

Arnav's eyes were full of laughter. 'Yeah.'

I found myself smiling back.

'Oh,' said Rajesh, his smile fading, as though that clinched it.

No, no, that's not what we meant, I wanted to blurt out.

Arnav read my expression instantly. His shoulders began to shake.

'Mallika!'

It was Vineet. Oh, good. My forces had belatedly rallied. No more rubbish now about eyes and eyelashes; I was well-fortified against flirtation.

'Hi, Vineet,' I said, so happily that Rajesh did a double take.

'You know each other too?' Rajesh asked.

'Very well,' Vineet said, giving me a big grin.

'I see,' said Rajesh, clearly trying to figure out which one of them it was.

Arnav was laughing so hard that he couldn't speak.

'What's so funny, yar?' Rajesh asked Arnav.

'Mallika,' said Vineet. 'Madhu Aunty's calling you. She's in the kitchen.'

'Excuse me,' I said, and made a beeline towards the kitchen.

Madhu Aunty came out of the kitchen. 'Mallika, Beta, come to my bedroom.' I followed her. She shut the bedroom door, sat on her bed, and burst into tears.

'Aunty,' I put my arms around her. 'What's happened?'

Had something happened to Mahima? I tried to quell my terror.

Madhu Aunty finally stopped sobbing. 'Mallika, sometimes I ask myself, was my Randhir exchanged in hospital with another baby? That only can explain this foolishness of going to America to write stories and poems.'

She was mourning Randhir's departure. Thank god. Mahima was fine.

But how did she know about the specialty in creative writing?

Madhu Aunty said, 'Today, Vineet said to me, "Aunty, Randhir's doing degree in America where he is going to be writing stories and poems."'

Vineet wasn't exactly the soul of discretion. Which meant that, by now, the whole colony knew.

'Aunty, it just means he'll do some extra courses in writing. That's all.'

'But everybody, they will ask me. What to tell people, Beta?'

I squeezed her hand. 'That only, Aunty.'

What to tell people? The perennial Indian question. The question that dictated every moment of your life. What to tell people when you were unmarried and had a child? What to tell people when the man responsible for this reappeared in your life and refused to go away? What to tell people when your daughter was afflicted with an illness of the mind?

In the spectrum of disasters, what to tell people when your brilliant, talented, handsome son went all the way to America to do a useless English degree with a useless specialty in creative writing was a lesser evil. But nonetheless, it was a tragedy.

Madhu Aunty wiped her eyes with a beautifully embroidered hanky and gave words to the next inevitable tragedy that befell Indian boys who went to America. 'Suppose he marries a white girl, then?'

I sighed in sympathy.

'Beta, I am telling you, once this America-keerha gets into their brains, it is very difficult to make these boys come back.'

Of course, Randhir would never come back. But did it not occur to him that he was leaving me behind forever?

'Beta, sometimes Randhir says bilkul ajeeb things. He said to me, "I will never marry. I will never marry Indian girl, I will never marry American girl, no one I will marry." He is telling truth, you think, or he is just saying like that only?'

'I don't know, Aunty,' I said truthfully.

'Beta, one son has gone from us forever. My other son, he is going across the oceans, and he will also never come back – what is this tragedy, Beta?'

My sorrow was making a rapid comeback. After having told myself a year ago that I would never advise Randhir to apply to American universities – and thereby risk losing him forever – I had done exactly that. Because I couldn't stand his pain. Now, he was blithely going to America, and *I* was the one in pain. The chances these days of getting aid and a visa were abysmally low; Randhir was one of the lucky ones. And I was the one who had urged him to apply. As Shantamama always said, altruism is overrated.

Madhu Aunty said, 'About Mahima also I am so worried.'

My heart stopped. 'Why, Aunty?'

'Three years, and still no baby, Mallika. Everyone is asking.'

So they were. 'No good news, no good news?' everyone had asked nine months after Mahima's marriage. Now, after three years, the neighbours were even more concerned. One neighbour had told Madhu Aunty she should tell Mahima it was very bad to go on the pill. Another neighbour had whispered to Madhu Aunty that FLs were very bad for your insides because they were made of rubber, and to tell Mahima to tell her husband not to use them.

'Don't worry, Aunty, I'm sure it will happen soon,' I comforted her.

'Beta, so patiently you are listening to your Madhu Aunty. Mahima, she also listens to me just like this. Chalo. You go now. You should be with young people, not listening to your old Aunty. Such a good girl, God bless you, you will make some man very happy.'

I gave her a hug and got up.

'Horrible cigarettes these boys are smoking, uff,' Madhu Aunty said as I left the room.

She thought that the marijuana floating down from the terrace was a particularly nasty brand of cigarettes.

I went to the bathroom in Mahima's room, sat on the pot, and cried for ten minutes. I'd been crying every night in anticipation of Randhir's departure. Then I washed my face and sat back on the pot, waiting for the redness on my nose to subside.

When I came out, Vineet was lurking in the corridor. 'Mallika! I want to talk to you.'

Vineet was leaving for America too. He had an assistantship for a PhD in Marketing. Vineet and I had become friends because he and Jaspreet had broken up a year ago and keeping his heartbreak to himself had proved to be impossibly exacting. He had needed a lot of comforting, and since males were not exactly proficient at comforting other males when it came to matters of the heart, it had fallen upon Gauri and, in Gauri's absence, me to listen to his woes. We had listened for several months – Gauri because her heart was in pain to see him in pain, and I because I could never resist a love story, be it the beginning, the middle, or the end. And also because I was fervently hoping that, finally, Gauri's unrequited love would be requited.

We went to the back veranda and sat on the steps.

He hummed and hawed for some time.

'I just don't know what to do,' he said at last.

'About?'

'I'm… madly in love, Mallika.'

My sorrow sank. A sharp spurt of rage rose in its place. First, Jaspreet. Now, another girl. Gauri would have to deal with this shit again.

'It's over with Jaspreet, and you've already found someone else?'

He stared at me.

'It was over with Jaspreet a year ago,' he said.

'That's not a long time,' I said.

'That's twelve *months*.'

But Gauri hadn't got over Vineet for five *years*.

'If you love someone, twelve months to get over it is nothing,' I said.

There was a brief silence.

'Mallika,' he said earnestly. 'You're *very* old-fashioned.'

Old-fashioned? How had the standards for love made such a precipitous descent?

'Mallika,' he burst out. 'It's Gauri!'

'Gauri?' I gasped.

'It's her I'm in love with!'

Joy flooded me.

'Do I stand a chance with her?' He was looking at me anxiously.

'You expect her to feel the same way?' Bloody gall. After treating her so shabbily. Of course she loved him, but as though I was going to tell him.

He sighed deeply. 'One can always hope, Mallika.'

Let him bloody well earn her. And in the meantime, let him damn well suffer.

'How long have you known?'

'Today. I knew today. I was just overcome with the realization.'

'Oh,' I said, firmly containing my joy. 'How come?'

'I was waiting for her to come to the party. Then Randhir said she had her dance class and wasn't coming. And I felt... shattered. I realized that without her, everything's...'

'Meaningless?'

'Yes, exactly. Completely meaningless. Absolutely empty.'

I sighed. Would anyone ever feel this way about me?

'But how do you know it's love?'

'Because I can't think of anyone but Gauri. She fills me to... the exclusion of everyone and everything.'

'Oh,' I said, hugging my happiness to myself.

'You know how it is,' Vineet sighed.

He was, of course, speaking rhetorically. But I didn't know. Everyone filled me, but so far, nobody to the exclusion of anybody else. Randhir had my heart. That was one. I'd lost my heart to Arnav. That was another. And then, what about the hearts held by my three friends, Anu Aunty, Madhu Aunty, my Ayah-ji, my grandmother? And my mothers, who had the lion's share?

'Don't tell Gauri,' Vineet said.

I nodded. Let her be oblivious. Let him go crazy with his love. After all, Gauri had suffered for years. But –

'But, Vineet, you're going to America in a week.'

'So what? I'll come back next summer if there's the slightest chance. I'll come back every year for her.'

This was love. No one would come back every year for me.

'Don't tell anyone,' Vineet said.

'Don't Randhir and Arnav know?'

'How, Mallika? I mean, even I knew only today.'

I nodded.

'Is there anyone else in her life?' he asked.

'A lot of JNU guys are crazy about her.'

'Oh.'

'It's not just that she's beautiful. They can see she has a heart of gold.'

'That she does.'

'How come you never saw it before?'

'I always saw it. But she was just a friend before.'

Oh, yes. A friend who you ditched as soon as you got a girlfriend.

'So,' he said apprehensively. 'Is she involved with anyone?'

I was now treading on unchartered territory. I wanted him to have hope. After all, only hope would keep him steady on the Gauri path once he went to America. On the other hand, I didn't want him to think she was his for the taking.

'One never knows about these things,' I said.

'How can *you* not know?'

I racked my brains.

'She's very private about love.'

Which, of course, was a blatant lie.

'Oh. Then… what to do, Mallika?'

He sounded desperate. I felt a wave of exhilaration.

'What to do about what?' Arnav said, joining us in the back veranda. He had two glass bowls of rasmalai with him.

'Nothing,' Vineet muttered.

'You're going to eat all these rasmalais?' I asked Arnav as he sat next to me.

'Of course,' he said cheerfully, putting down his bowls.

'Greedy bugger,' Vineet said.

The whiff of Arnav's foreign cologne drifted towards me. The very same smell he'd left in my room that night.

'What sage advice are you giving him?' Arnav asked.

Vineet shook his head slightly.

'None,' I said, getting up. 'I'm going to get some rasmalais. Want some, Vineet?'

'Rajesh's looking everywhere for you,' Arnav said.

'Oh, god,' I muttered, and sat down again.

'After I rescued you, it took you ten seconds to ditch me,' Arnav said reproachfully.

'Was Rajesh piling onto you?' Vineet asked, perking up.

I said nothing.

'Here,' said Arnav, giving me the bowl with three fat rasmalais.

'I'll get my own,' I said half-heartedly.

'I got it for you,' Arnav said.

'Thank you.' I took it from him, moved.

'Mallika, can we talk about more important things than rasmalais?' Vineet said.

'But –'

'That's fine. He might as well know. I was talking about Gauri,' he said to Arnav.

'Yeah, I know.'

'How d'you know?'

'I'm not bloody blind, yar.' Arnav was smiling faintly and rolling his joint.

'What to do, man?'

'Haven't the foggiest.'

'I mean, what would *you* do?'

'No idea.'

No wonder guys didn't confide in each other if this was how it went.

'Vineet,' I said, eating a rasmalai. 'Drop in at her JNU hostel after seven tomorrow; she'll probably be there.'

'Yeah. I guess,' Vineet said, sounding forlorn.

Arnav finished rolling his joint and lit it.

I was now on the horns of a dilemma. Was I ruining Gauri's chances by not telling her? If he truly loved her, he would come back for her. But if his love didn't last in America, then what was the point of telling Gauri? It would only cause her more heartbreak.

'Write to Gauri from America,' I said.

'Oh,' Vineet said. 'Yeah, OK… It's just that I don't know what to say in letters.'

'You'll be in *America,* and you won't know what to *say*?'

Vineet looked a little abashed. 'I'm a guy, Mallika. Guys aren't good at corresponding.'

'If you're in love with Gauri and going to America, then you'd better become good at corresponding.'

I found myself rapidly dislodged from the horns of my dilemma. He didn't know what to say in letters? And he claimed he was in love? I would *not* tell Gauri.

Vineet said defensively, 'I mean, Arnav doesn't write to anyone either, ask him.'

'*Anyone*?' I demanded. 'Gauri isn't *anyone.*'

'Of course I'll write to her, Mallika. I was just saying.'

'I wrote a letter to you from Bombay,' Arnav said to me. 'And you never replied.'

'That wasn't a *letter.* That was a *postcard.*'

'What's wrong with a postcard?'

What kind of brains did boys have?

'I suppose I should have replied. I should have said, "How are you, I'm fine, not much news from my end, hope you're fine."'

Arnav burst out laughing.

My exasperation dissipated. His laughter always did this to me. But I couldn't forget what Randhir had told me about how Mishti died. If Arnav's father was the kind who kicked a helpless animal, it indicated a cruelty that couldn't possibly be limited to the incident with Mishti. Arnav must have suffered for years. He hid it well. Very well. Was that what Randhir had meant when he said Arnav didn't deal with anything he didn't want to deal with? But who in the world didn't hide things? That didn't mean we weren't dealing with those things.

Suddenly, Vineet quivered, his nose twitched, and his body straightened. 'Gauri!' he whispered.

Gauri was framed in the kitchen window in her beautiful green Venkatagiri saree, chatting with Madhu Aunty. She'd finished her dance class and come!

Vineet shot up and made his way to the kitchen.

I got up when Arnav hissed, 'Mallika, give him some time with her.'

I sat down on the steps again. Oh, well. She'd spend the night with me, so we had plenty of time to catch up.

As Leonard Cohen sang 'Suzanne,' we sat in companionable silence, I eating my rasmalais, and Arnav smoking his joint.

Vineet had talked a lot about his sorrow to Gauri and me over the last few months. The gist of it was that Jaspreet was upset that he was applying abroad for a PhD. She'd said she'd never live abroad. Or give up her career – she had just got into the IAS. Jaspreet had even told Vineet that his mother and sisters had no respect for her. Imagine, Vineet had said to me, his parents and sisters had *loved* her.

'So,' said Arnav. 'Does Gauri reciprocate?'

'Don't know.'

'I see,' he said, looking amused.

'What's so amusing?' I asked suspiciously.

'You. Always.'

I didn't respond. Bantering was even more difficult than making pc. Besides, at this moment, I was horribly afflicted with the sheer physicality of his presence. One of the few advantages of the exhaustion after my illness had been not reacting this way to him. But the night that he had spent in my room, and the resulting dream that I had had of us making love, had caused my desire for him to become almost debilitating.

Now that he was no longer at IIT and studying, he spent even more time next door, and therefore a lot more time with me. I was so sizzling with longing for him that at times I almost couldn't bear his presence. Sometimes, in the thrall of those feelings, my tongue would be tied up in its usual knots, but he didn't seem to notice, or if he did, he didn't seem to mind, and usually within minutes, he'd make me laugh. It was a lot easier for me when Randhir was also with us.

'How are your sister and the babies?' I asked. Niharika had had twins the previous year.

'OK.'

It was strange, how he rarely spoke about them.

'I really dislike my job, feel like a bloody cog in a machine,' he said, changing the subject.

He was already chafing? He'd been working in Delhi for just a few months!

'I'm going to apply to American universities too,' he said. 'For a PhD.'

'Why?' I asked, astonished.

He laughed. 'I want to travel all over the world. How else to do it!'

'You're joking!'

'Not entirely. Want a change, Mallika. Want to see the world. How else to do it?'

Was this how he went about his life, making one impulsive decision after another?

On the other hand, why not? If this was what he wanted, why *not*?

'What a *good* idea,' I said warmly.

'I thought you'd say the opposite.'

'Oh? Am I *that* boring?'

'Mallika!'

'You *did* say it.'

'You've forgotten my apology?'

He was looking at me with so much laughter in his eyes that I knew exactly what he was referring to.

Hurriedly, I said, 'Everyone's going away. I won't have any friends left at this rate.'

'I don't understand. Why aren't you applying too?'

I froze. No, I couldn't tell him that I was. Not yet.

'Has Randhir said anything to you?' he asked.

'About?'

A pause.

'Oh, about… coming back?'

'You know he'll never come back!'

He was looking at me curiously. 'He told you that?'

'Arnav, you know he can never live the life he wants to in India.'

In the silence that followed, I could hear Vineet and Gauri talking in the kitchen and Madhu Aunty laughing. And the clatter of dishes that Ramu was washing. And the sound of 'A Horse with No Name' drifting out from the sitting room.

'Shit, you're not staying here because you want to get married, are you?' He said 'married' as though it was a disease.

I found myself racked with laughter, then said, 'To whom?'

'I mean... you could have an arranged marriage.'

I started laughing again. I couldn't conceive of marrying for any reason but love. And where had love got me!

'I was wondering where you'd both disappeared to,' Randhir said, coming out from the kitchen door. He sat next to me, lit a cigarette, and began to talk with ire about the new Janata government. The Emergency was over, Indira was out, Morarji Desai's government had collapsed, and Charan Singh had just become Prime Minister. Randhir was once again simmering about the state of the country.

But I was happy. Here they were now, on either side of me. Like the new government, it wouldn't last long, but in this moment, I was happy.

When Arnav had mentioned applying to universities in America, the moment had been ripe to say, 'I'm applying too.' But I couldn't tell him or Randhir, because I hadn't yet told Ma and Shantamama.

In March, Karan had come home and he asked me what I wanted to do after my MA. I had said I would start my MPhil and also apply to American universities.

After some time, he said, 'I see.' He was trying to hide his shock.

'But there's no money for the plane ticket, or the foreign exchange, so... I wanted to ask Ajji and you if... if you could...' I stopped, appalled at how crass I was sounding.

'Of course, I'll pay for your ticket, Mallika.'

'Thank you,' I mumbled. 'I'm sorry, I know it's difficult for you.'

'Mallika. Please. Don't talk like that.'

We walked in silence for some time.

'I haven't told Ma and Shantamama yet.'

He looked at me, taken aback.

'After I talk to Ajji, I'll tell them.'

'If your grandmother is unable to help, let me know.'

I continued practicing hard for the GREs and doing abysmally in the Maths section.

Three months later, Ajji and Shantamama had come for the summer holidays. One afternoon, after lunch, I lay down with my grandmother, and we chatted about my friends and college. 'Are you going to study for those competitive exams now?' she asked.

'Ajji,' I said, feeling wretched. 'Will you be very sad if I don't sit for the IAS?'

She looked at me without speaking. I saw the deep disappointment in her eyes.

'Ajji, there's something else I've been dreaming of doing for a long time.'

She sighed. 'What is it, my child?'

'I've been wanting to apply to American universities for a PhD. Of course, I can only go if I get a full scholarship.'

Ajji had put her hand to her heart. 'You will go away from us?'

'I'll come back, Ajji.'

'A PhD is many years, and it is a very long distance, child.' She held my hand and began stroking it. 'Why *America* for English? Why not England?'

'Universities in England don't give scholarships, Ajji.'

'Oh. A long time you have dreamt of it?'

'Years and years.'

'Then why you have never told me or your mothers?'

'Because, even with full aid, Ajji, I will need a lot of money for the initial expenses.'

'How much?'

'About fourteen or fifteen thousand rupees, I think. If I get in, Karan will pay ten thousand for the one-way plane ticket.'

'*He* knows?'

Before her, she meant.

'Ajji, he came to Delhi before you, in March. I asked him then.'

The minutes ticked by.

'Ajji, many Indian students in America come home every year. I will too.'

'Is *that* so? I thought you would not return till you finished your PhD.'

'Never! I'd never go if that were the case!'

Her face brightened.

I should have told Karan this. I would write and tell him.

'It is a very big thing, a PhD from America. Very big thing,' Ajji said at last. 'Who gets scholarships to study abroad? Only the best of the best.'

I let out my breath.

'Child, if you promise never to marry a Northerner, then I think you can go to America.'

I blinked. 'What, Ajji?'

'I have put aside some money for your marriage. Happily I will give to you if you get a scholarship. But that means you can never marry a Northerner. Because these Northerners, they take dowry. On top of that, they ask for so-called expensive "gifts," like suits and silk sarees. In our family, we do not do all this. If you marry a Northerner, then we will have no money for all their demands, that is the thing.'

'Ajji, but I'll never marry someone who expects all that.'

'Child, that is what you think when love blinds you. That this will not happen and that will not happen. But everything happens.'

She was talking about Ma, of course.

'So now you apply.'

'Ajji, when I come back to India, it'll be too late to sit for the IAS.'

'Never mind. You see, child, America is a very rich country. I have heard that even mechanics and plumbers and electricians have houses and cars. Children drive cars to school. People eat almonds and pistas and cashew nuts the way we eat peanuts. People throw away new-new lamps, new-new sofas, new-new clothes, new-new vessels, they just throw. Everyone buys houses. Middle-class people have two cars, two TVs, two everything. So you work there for a few years and save lots of money, and then you come home and put your money in a fixed deposit. I know lecturer's salary is not much, but you will also have very good income from your fixed deposit.'

Ajji, who rarely smiled, was so enamoured by my dollar-rich fixed deposit that she was beaming blissfully. 'Apply to America with my blessings.'

I kissed her. 'Don't tell Ma and Shantamama. I'll tell them in a few days.'

I would tell Ma and Shantamama about my plan to apply to American universities after Randhir's departure. I couldn't deal with the grief of his departure as well as my mothers' shock at my decision.

The main obstacle – money – had gone. But suddenly, I felt grief stabbing my gut.

Randhir was absolutely right. Not everything was about money.

Arnav had had enough of living with his parents. Mrs D'Souza had recently ousted an extremely recalcitrant tenant from her barsati, and Arnav wanted to rent it. He had asked me if I could accompany him when he went to talk to Mrs D'Souza, because she liked me and that would aid his cause. So here we were.

Mrs D'Souza plied us with tea, cake, and biscuits. 'My dear boy, the last tenant, he was one of those *terrible* Punjabis who refused to vacate. With so much difficulty I threw him out.'

'But *I'm* not a Punjabi, Aunty,' Arnav said, consuming his cake in two large bites.

'My boy, I will only rent to a South Indian. They are very peace-loving, non-interfering, modest people. Here, have some more.'

Arnav helped himself to another slice of cake. He was so enjoying it that he seemed to have forgotten what we were here for.

'Aunty, Arnav's half Bengali,' I said, pursuing our goal.

'Oh, these Bengalis! Such fighter-cocks they are! I mean, look at their football games!'

'But Arnav's not like that, Aunty.'

Arnav had shaved, his jeans were not faded, and Mrs D'Souza's orange cake had induced in him such a state of bliss that he looked almost saintly.

'He works with children in schools, opening nature clubs,' I said, warming to my theme. 'And he really has a way with birds and animals.'

'That is most commendable. I am also a bird and animal lover. See my Mithu?'

We looked at her parrot, Mithu, who was taking a walk on the mantlepiece.

'Ah, she's a beauty,' Arnav said wistfully. I could see he was itching to hold Mithu. But Mrs D'Souza said, 'No, my boy, don't touch her! She bites, she only loves me.'

'And you know he's been Randhir's best friend from the time they were *six*,' I said.

'Oh, Randhir! That boy is most unlike a Punjabi,' Mrs D'Souza said.

This was a compliment of the highest order from Mrs D'Souza.

'Aunty, Randhir and Madhu Aunty will vouch for Arnav's character.'

'No need, my girl.'

I smiled at her. Arnav smiled at me. She had come around.

But, no: 'I cannot rent my barsati to you, my boy. I beg of you, do not press the issue.'

Arnav was offered and consumed a third slice of cake, then we took leave of her.

'Mallika, do you have a mirror?' Arnav said as we walked back.

'No.' I wasn't carrying a bag. 'Why?'

'I need to look at my halo.'

We started laughing.

In one of the days that followed, Mrs D'Souza came to our home, weeping. 'Padma, oh, Padma! Mithu's flown away. See, come here, look.'

She took us to the back veranda, where we saw Mithu sunning herself on the roof of Mrs D'Souza's neighbour's house. 'It's the roof of the Nymph! And the Nymph has a cat! My Mithu will be lunch for that cat, Padma, what to *do*!'

Ma and I looked at each other in consternation.

'Nymph?' Ma said.

'The Nymphomaniac, Padma,' wept Mrs D'Souza. 'My Mithu is on *her* roof. Every boy in this colony has lost his virginity to the Nymph! How can you not know!'

'Oh,' said Ma, who clearly didn't know.

Gauri had told us all about the Nymph. She was insatiable, Gauri had said in thrilling tones. How did *she* know, we had asked. Because Vineet had told her, Gauri said. The Nymph had asked Vineet to put a lightbulb high up in her bedroom, and as soon as he got off the ladder, she'd flung her arms around him. Vineet had disentangled himself and fled. And why hadn't she told us before, Prabha and I demanded. Because Vineet had told her in confidence, Gauri said. But later, she'd heard Randhir and Arnav yelling with laughter about lightbulbs, so she thought she might as well tell us since it was no big secret.

I heard the sound of a motorcycle.

I ran out, and to my relief, it *was* Arnav. He had parked between Randhir's house and ours and was taking off his helmet. I went to him. 'Arnav, you can climb up roofs, no?'

He looked both puzzled and interested.

'Mrs D'Souza's Mithu is stuck on the roof of the house behind ours. And there's a cat in that house.'

'Show me,' he said immediately.

He followed me home. 'He'll rescue Mithu, Mrs D'Souza,' I said.

Mrs D'Souza clasped her hands as another flood of tears streamed down her face.

We went to our back veranda, and Mrs D'Souza pointed to the roof. 'That one. See?'

Mithu was sunning herself happily on the water tank.

'The roof of the Nymph,' Mrs D'Souza said in trembling tones. 'Have you made her acquaintance?'

'I guess I will now,' Arnav said cheerfully.

Mrs D'Souza said sternly. 'You must rescue Mithu without making her acquaintance.'

'Of course, Mrs D'Souza,' Arnav leapt down the veranda stairs.

In another minute, he was shimmying up the drainpipe of the Nymph's house as though he'd done it every day of his life. In two minutes flat, he was on the roof. I walked to the other end of the house, where the parrot was enjoying the sun, and watched him walk agilely along the sloping rooftop towards the bird.

'My!' marvelled Ma. 'That boy could be an acrobat in a circus.'

Mrs D'Souza murmured, 'Oh, Mithu, stay where you are.'

Mithu had clearly given up her bid for independence. She stayed where she was, watching Arnav with resignation, and then, as he cupped his hands and went towards her while murmuring something, she docilely walked into his hands. He stood on the rooftop, balanced like a dancer on the sloped surface, stroking Mithu and contemplating his next plan of action. Then he lifted his t-shirt and tucked Mithu in, tucked his t-shirt into his jeans, walked back to the drainpipe, and shimmied down like a pro.

Fifteen minutes later, Mithu was in her cage at her home, and we were in the sitting room in mine, having tea and snacks.

'Do you have girlfriends and all that rubbish?' Mrs D'Souza asked Arnav. Arnav looked at her blankly.

No, I mouthed to Arnav.

'No,' Arnav said.

'No girls allowed in the barsati. If even one girl visits you, you're out.'

'You're... renting it to me?'

'I am, my boy, so don't you make me regret it.'

'Yeah, thank you, I won't,' Arnav said, giving her his beautiful smile.

'And don't say "ya," it's very rude,' Mrs D'Souza lectured.

'Yes, of course,' Arnav said, and transferred his beautiful smile to me.

Randhir: Ayah-ji's arrow

1979

The morning of his departure, he threw the bottle of pills in the rubbish dump.

That evening, he told Arnav, 'Listen, keep an eye on Mallika, OK?'

He knew Arnav would, but he needed to hear him say it.

Instead, Arnav said, 'Meaning what?'

'Meaning exactly that,' he said, taken aback.

'I'm not you.'

He couldn't believe it. 'I thought you and Mallika were friends?'

'We are. But not in the keeping-an-eye-on-her sort of way. That's you.'

'What's your problem, yar, you know what I mean?'

'No, I don't.'

'I mean, like, if she's stuck somewhere at night, or something like that.'

'*Obviously.*'

'*That's* what I meant.'

'But how on earth would I know if she's stuck somewhere at night? I don't keep tabs on where she goes.'

What was wrong with the guy?

'Shouldn't *you* be the one keeping an eye on her?' Arnav said.

He stopped his packing. 'How am I supposed to do that when I'm not here?'

'That's what I'm wondering. Are you planning to spend the rest of your life without her?'

He felt Arnav had punched him.

'Because if you are, then you'd better tell her before you leave.'

This wasn't a conversation he could have. 'What's this, man, a bloody interrogation?'

'I don't get it.'

'There's nothing to *get.*'

Arnav looked at him incredulously. 'Is *that* the way the wind's blowing now?'

'That's the way it's always blown.'

'What bullshit,' Arnav said.

Randhir continued packing. He felt he was going to burst.

'Have you told her?' Arnav asked.

'There's nothing to tell.'

'You better tell her.'

'Don't tell me what to do.'

'You're just going off to America for god knows how long without saying *anything* to her?'

He snapped his suitcase shut. 'You have some bloody gall. Did you say anything to Radha? Or Mohini? Or whoever you're with now?'

Arnav's face clouded with a rare anger. 'For god's sake, yar. Stop bloody pretending.'

There was a silence as they stared at one another.

'I thought you loved her,' Arnav said.

He snapped, 'Yeah, I do. It's just not the kind of love *you're* talking about.'

Another silence. Arnav hadn't taken his eyes off him.

Randhir flung his t-shirts into the suitcase and snapped it shut. 'I'm done with this conversation. OK?'

Silence.

'OK.' Arnav shrugged.

He had xeroxed all his essays and personal statements and put them in a packet for Mallika. He didn't have any hope that she would apply, but just in case.

Mahima had gone abroad, so he couldn't say goodbye to her. It was a relief. Seeing her was never easy. The evening of his departure, he went to say goodbye to Anu Aunty and her family, then Padma Aunty and Ayah-ji. Each goodbye was more difficult than he had anticipated. Padma Aunty was tearful; she hugged him without saying a word. Then he went to the kitchen to take leave of Ayah-ji and put some money into her hands.

She said, 'It is far, this Amreeka?'

He said, 'Very far, Ayah-ji, I have to take an aeroplane to go there. It is across the oceans.'

She looked at his face without comprehension. 'When will you come back?'

He said, 'I don't know, Ayah-ji. The aeroplane ticket costs a lot of money.' He took both her hands in his and said, 'Stay well.'

Ayah-ji kept looking at his face. Then she removed her hands from his, folded her arms, and said, 'You are crossing the oceans without marrying Mallika Baby?'

Ayah-ji's arrow pierced his very soul.

He didn't have a single word to give her.

She opened her hand where his money still lay. She took his hand, pressed the money back into it, and closed his fingers over it. As he continued standing where he was, unable to move, she took the plates from the kitchen counter and went out to the dining room where she began laying the table for dinner.

Mallika knocked on his door as he was locking the trunks that held his books. His bookshelves were now empty, the way they used to be when he was in boarding school. Arnav was standing by the window smoking, and turned, smiling, as Mallika entered. Mallika looked at the bookshelves and began laughing.

'You've hidden your books again!' she said.

He tried to smile. 'You know how it is.'

'OK, I've come to say bye,' she said. She was smiling determinedly. Arnav went out of the room.

'Take care of yourself, OK,' he said.

She nodded. 'You too.' She wasn't looking at him.

He picked up the brown paper packet from his bed and gave it to her. 'Open it later. Just in case you need it.'

She took it from him.

'Bye,' he said, putting an arm around her and giving her a brief hug.

She leaned against him. Her voice was muffled. 'Bye. Safe journey.' She stepped out of his hug and left the room rapidly.

A few hours later, he went to the bedroom to say goodbye to his father. Daddy, who was reading the newspaper in the armchair next to the bed, acknowledged his goodbye with a brief nod of his head. That was all. Daddy wasn't talking to him or to Mummy.

Then, five minutes later, as he and Arnav were loading the suitcases into the dicky of the car, his father came out of the house and said, 'I will come to the airport.' An enormous boulder rolled off Randhir. Arnav drove them there.

Inside the airport, Mummy hugged and kissed him, her cheeks wet against his. His father said nothing, but tears were rolling down his cheeks. Randhir couldn't bear it. As his parents stood crying, Arnav walked a few steps ahead with him. He couldn't stop himself from saying it again. 'Take care of Mallika, OK? Bye.'

Arnav looked him straight in the eye and said, 'Randhir, no hard feelings, man, but I don't believe that crap you gave me about Mallika. I can't take care of her. If you want to, then you come back for her. Bye. Safe journey.'

This time, Arnav's words didn't hit as hard. Ayah-ji's words had already done the deed.

It was his first time in a plane. As it took off, his ears began to hurt, and the words he hadn't uttered to Ayah-ji and Arnav began filling his mind. *Even if I come to see Mallika, I can never come back 'to' her.*

He was doing it again. He was abandoning her again.

He had always been the golden boy. At home, at school, at college. The boy who could do no wrong. The shining example. 'Itna sundar ladka!' the various aunties were fond of saying. 'Such a beautiful boy!' He was the Dorian Gray that everyone saw, whose true ugly image was hidden in a secret room deep inside him. No one knew the truth. He himself had not known for a long time, or perhaps he had just not wanted to look at it. Had he not lived an irreproachable life? Not once had he transgressed. Had he not always done the right thing? Had he not always, always, always turned his head away? Yes, he had, until the day Mallika betrayed him. The day before Mahima's wedding, Mallika had plunged her hand inside his deepest self, grabbed that picture, and flung it at his face.

After that, he could no longer turn away.

Seething with betrayal and shock, he had lost his temper with her. So badly that she had gone running to Gauri the day after the wedding to talk about it. Gauri wasn't there, and she had come back home alone at night. And that was the night the horror had happened to her, which she couldn't remember. A few months later, bleeding and traumatized, she had ended up at that clinic.

That night, after he brought her home from the clinic, after he told his mother and Padma Aunty the lie that had to be told about her heavy period, his body could barely hold the long years of guilt, anguish, and anger of which now Mallika was also a part. He hated himself. He almost hated every single person who loved him for what he was not.

Remorse racked him. Remorse for getting involved with Charu to prove to himself that he was like other men; remorse for hurting Mallika during that time; remorse for losing his temper with her; remorse for not being there for her; remorse for his knowledge that he would never marry her; remorse for not having the courage to tell her why. She had said that her father's act of abandoning her mother had been one of cowardice. And now, so was his. She deserved the truth. The whole truth. He had thought he would tell her before he left for America, but he hadn't. He couldn't. When Arnav had asked him about Mallika, the moment had been ripe to tell him. Arnav – like no other – would accept his truth. But even so, he hadn't been able to.

In his silence lay his cowardice.

How long could you live in denial? What was yours was yours even if you
didn't want it. It had affirmed its existence in the shape of every sleeping
pill that he had collected so carefully for so long. In the gaping despair that
had swallowed him when, after returning from seeing his sister, Mahima,
in Chandigarh and assuring himself that she was fine, he had come home,
reached for the bottle of pills in the cabinet behind the bathroom mirror,
and found the bottle gone.

If he hadn't been in such a rage against Mallika the day before his sister's
wedding, she wouldn't have gone to see Gauri. If Mallika hadn't gone to see
Gauri, nothing would have happened to her, and the incantation, *it was my
fault, it was my fault, it was my fault,* would not be pacing in his mind like that
wretched, crazed panther paced its cage at Delhi Zoo. Ever since Gauri had
told him Mallika had been devastated by his loss of temper, he had felt the
contents of the simmering cauldron inside him leaking out and coagulating
over his spine.

He had heard guys using the word 'pervert' often enough. Said with a
snigger. With that familiar look of contempt. When Mallika had told him
that was what Shekhar was, it was as if she weren't talking about Mahima's
future husband, but about him, Randhir. As though Mallika had seen his
secret, a secret hidden even from himself. The secret had merely needed one
word to shoot out of its hidden place and explode in his face. And Mallika
had known that word.

He knew Mallika had no idea what she was saying, no idea what Renu
had meant. Mallika had only repeated what Renu had said because she was
frightened for Mahima. She was desperately trying to save Mahima from
something that had sounded terrible. She had wanted him to stop Mahima's
wedding. That was all.

But that wasn't all for him.

He had no idea what Mallika would have thought, had he told her his
truth. Perhaps such a thing didn't even have an existence in the periphery of
her mind. Like the hijras. At least a hijra asserted her being in the manner of
her dress, her jewellery, and the make-up she painted over her closely shaven
face. But how was he to assert his being?

By not hiding it.

An unspoken, unlived truth bore no existence. Prabha's truth about the
casual, routine assault of women in Delhi had borne no existence for him.
Until she spoke it.

What would Mallika think of him were he to tell her? Would she be
shocked? Revolted? Heartbroken? Would she feel betrayed? Would she
think he was… unclean, dirty? That he had not fought hard enough to be a
better self, to be a decent, 'normal' man? How could Mallika not think this,

when it was what *he* had felt for so long? From time to time, it was what he felt even now. That he had lost his fight to be a better self, though he knew this was untrue.

If he told Mallika, and if she felt all the things that he had felt, he knew what she would do. She would hide it. The way she had hidden her deep reluctance to spend the weekends with her father. She would hide it and – as her love for him, Randhir, shrivelled up and died – she would keep pretending that she still loved him. Because Mallika would *want* to do the right thing by him. She would *want* to accept him. She wouldn't want to cause him even a tiny bit of distress. And so she would keep pretending to love him until it completely eroded her. And him.

PART III

Mallika: Young lady, is this young man the cause of your distress?

1979

'I can't believe this,' Ma said.

'Have you taken leave of your senses?' Shantamama said.

At the dining table, my mothers had stopped cleaning the dhanya and methi leaves and were looking at me incredulously.

I stopped stringing the beans and stared at them in disbelief.

I had just told them that I wanted to apply for a PhD to universities in America. Of course, I could only go if I got full aid, I said, and then there was the matter of the visa – even students with full financial aid often didn't get one. But if I did, I could come home every year, I said, bracing myself against their pain.

As I spoke, my mothers had looked startled. Then astounded. Then they looked at each other.

Oh, the money. Of course.

'Shantamama, Ma, you don't have to worry about money. If I get aid, then Karan will pay for the plane ticket. And Ajji will give me the money to buy dollars.'

They looked outraged.

'*They* know?' Ma said.

'You've been plotting and planning this behind our backs with *them*?' Shantamama said.

'*No, no*. I wasn't going to apply unless I knew I had money for the ticket and dollars, so I asked them, and they said yes.'

'What is *wrong* with them?' Shantamama said to Ma.

'They just want me to realize my dreams,' I burst out.

Silence.

'Meaning *we* don't,' Ma said.

'No, *we* don't,' Shantamama said. '*They* want you to realize your dreams, while all *we're* concerned about is your welfare, which, of course, is of no consequence. Wonderful.'

'And since when has it become your dream – going to study in America?' Ma asked.

'Always, Ma, always.'

'Always? How come you never said so before?'

I bit my tongue.

'It seemed... impossible,' I said at last.

'*I* see,' Ma said. 'But now that Randhir has gone off to America, it seems possible?'

'You'll go chasing him to America now, will you?' Shantamama said.

'Mallika, have you no pride?' Ma asked.

'*You*, of all people?' Shantamama asked.

I was dumbstruck.

'Randhir? It has nothing to do with Randhir,' I gasped at last.

'Deva, Deva,' Shantamama said, turning to Ma. 'Bad enough that it happened to you, Padma, but I thought Mallika had more sense. Love is *really* blind.'

'Mallika,' Ma said. 'Have you no self-respect? Following a man all the way to another country, who doesn't even want to marry you?'

'Hoping that he will change his mind if you follow him to America, is that it?' Shantamama said.

'Ma, Shantamama, there's *nothing* of the sort between us!'

'But you're hoping,' Shantamama said. 'That's what you'll carry with you to America, along with your suitcases. Hope. Useless, useless hope.'

'We also had hope,' Ma said. 'Hope that he would propose to you before he left.'

'There's no *we* about it,' Shantamama interjected. '*You* had hope, Padma. *You*. Because of *you*, I kept my mouth shut.'

'Have you forgotten Randhir told his mother he'd never get married?' Ma said.

'It means he wants to have a good time without any commitments. All fun with no responsibilities,' Shantamama said.

'Forget Randhir,' Ma pleaded. 'I know he's done a lot for you, Mallika, and I'll be eternally grateful to him, but what is the use of all that when he abandons you like this?' She began to cry. 'I never thought such a thing would happen to *my* child.'

'And don't pretend your heart is not broken,' Shantamama said to me. 'Since he left a month ago you have not been yourself.'

'I thought you and Randhir were kindred spirits,' Ma wept. 'He understands you so deeply. He's so concerned for your safety, welfare, everything. But I misjudged it all. After what I went through, I let the same thing happen to my own child.'

'Ma, Randhir never promised me anything. We were *only* friends.'

Ma wiped her cheeks with her palm. Shantamama took her handkerchief out of her blouse and gave it to her sister. 'I don't know why you never have yours.' Then she turned to me. 'Alright then. Randhir promised you nothing. That was because *his* heart was unaffected. But what about *yours*? If you follow your heart all the way to America, it'll be smashed to smithereens.'

'I'm doing it for myself, Shantamama, not for Randhir.'

'And' – Ma wiped her eyes – 'have you forgotten the other thing?'

Shantamama nodded grimly.

I looked at them blankly.

'The TB, obviously,' Shantamama said.

'But I'm alright now!'

'*Where* are you alright!' Ma cried. 'You *still* can't sleep some nights. You're *still* having those medicines. You've *still* not got back to reading the way you used to. You *still* get tired easily. And this when *we* are there to see to your *every* need. Mallika, why are you deluding yourself like this?'

'Who will look after you in America if it happens there?' Shantamama asked. '*Who*?'

'Shantamama, Ma, why should it happen there!'

'Why should it happen there? Well, why did it happen *here*?' Ma began to weep again.

My throat was full. My chest felt it would burst.

'Even the *doctor* doesn't know why it happened,' Ma cried. 'He clearly told me that, yes, these episodes can recur. And if it does recur, then you'll be alone, in a foreign country... How will you *survive*?'

'You won't even be able to go to a doctor there – paying an American doctor is like buying a gold bracelet,' Shantamama said.

'Not a gold bracelet – a *diamond* bracelet,' Ma sobbed.

I burst into tears and ran upstairs to my room. I rushed into the bathroom and bolted the door, put the lid down, sat on the pot, and wept bitterly.

When I came downstairs an hour later, Ma, Shantamama and my grandmother – who had come back from next door – were all sitting at the dining table.

'Come, child, sit.' Ajji patted the dining chair next to her.

I sat down.

My grandmother kissed her fingers and put them on my cheek. 'Child, let us all talk calmly.'

I looked at my mothers, whose eyes and noses were red, and the tears began trickling down my cheeks again.

'You,' said my grandmother, 'will not be like any of us. I will see to it that you are fulfilled in life.'

'As though I'm not fulfilled,' Shantamama said sullenly.

Ajji looked at her. 'And you are talking about *Mallika* being deluded?'

For once, Shantamama had no response.

'This is the time for honesty,' Ajji said. 'Mallika, do you want to marry Randhir?'

'No.'

'Good. And what about the other boy?'

'*Arnav*? Ajji, he's not interested in me that way.'

'And you?'

'He's a friend, Ajji.'

'Alright. Keep this in mind. Do not wait for anyone. Any man who does not want you is not worthy of you. You will pursue your path, not a man. Understand?'

I blew my nose and nodded.

'But the main concern for your mothers is your health. There is truth in what they are saying. But you are leading such a normal life now that one forgets. So. Next week when you go to the doctor, we will go with you and ask him what he thinks. If he says you will be well enough to go next year, then apply. If he says you will not be ready, then you must listen to him. My child, what you went through was terrible. What your mothers suffered, you can never know. If it happens to you across the oceans, you will be alone.'

'Ajji,' I began to cry again. 'How can I live like that for the rest of my life?'

My mothers and Ajji were looking at me, but their faces were blurred.

'It's bad enough being a girl – you can't do this, you can't do that, you can't go here, you can't go there, it's endless. And now, my health. It's like being tied up and left to live in an airless dungeon for the rest of my life.'

Silence.

Ajji sighed. 'Ultimately, it is what is written on your forehead.'

'What, Amma?' Ma said. 'If Mallika doesn't apply, she can't go. It's in *her* hands.'

'But *after* she applies, it is not in her hands. *After* that, it is fate,' Ajji said.

In my room later that day, I reread Randhir's first letter, an aerogramme. There was so much to tell me, Randhir had dashed off. But all of that later. He was writing to say that he'd found out that, as a student with an assistantship it *was* affordable – if you were very careful with money – to go home to India every year. This was because teaching assistants got paid more in the summer. He wanted me to apply. He knew there were two things holding me back: money and the fear that I couldn't see my mothers for years. Well,

I could ask my grandmother and Karan for the money for the plane ticket and dollars, he was sure they'd give it to me. And I could also come home every year. *Don't relinquish your dreams, Mallika. Please apply.*

Dear, dear Randhir. His letter, arriving on the heels of my decision to apply, seemed almost prophetic. I wrote back, telling him I would be submitting applications.

The next day, I went to the United States Educational Fund in India, the USEFI, to get some more information. I was still trying to digest the fact that Ma had been nursing hopes of Randhir and I getting married, and that she and Shantamama had probably been discussing it for years. Never had they betrayed their feelings to me.

What would I do if the doctor echoed my mothers' convictions about my health? How would I go my way?

But perhaps going my way wasn't the outcome. Perhaps it was simply the act of giving my dreams a chance that needed doing.

'Mallika!'

It was Arnav, parking his bike as I stepped outside the USEFI.

We walked towards each other.

'What on earth are you doing *here*?'

'I'm applying.'

'But… at Randhir's party when I asked you…'

'I hadn't told my mothers, Arnav. I couldn't tell you before I told them.'

He looked puzzled. Then he said, 'If you can wait ten minutes, I'll give you a lift, I'm going home too.'

'OK. How come you're not at work?'

'Took a day's casual leave. If you're free, should we go for lunch to Nirula's? The upstairs place?'

I was putting aside money for the doctor. The upstairs Nirula's was expensive.

'And ice cream downstairs after lunch?' he said as he saw me hesitate.

Spend the bloody money.

Half an hour later, we were at Nirula's. It was the first time I was seeing him after Randhir's departure. He hadn't bothered to drop in to see me after Randhir left.

After we ordered, he said, 'Well? How come you're applying?'

'I've never told anyone, but I've always wanted to.'

He looked at me with surprise.

'I didn't tell you at the party because I hadn't mentioned it to my mothers. Now, I've talked to them about it.'

'But just now you said you've always wanted to?'

'Ma's a lecturer, so all these years I thought that even if I got financial aid, we could never afford the plane ticket. And the foreign exchange.'

I could see from his face that such a thing had not occurred to him. It never did to those who had the money.

'So finally, I talked to my grandmother, and she said she'd help out. After that, I told my mothers I was applying. I couldn't tell you before I told them.'

I didn't mention Karan. I couldn't talk about my 'stepfather' paying for my ticket.

He nodded.

Well, at least *he* didn't think I was following Randhir.

'I haven't seen you for ages,' I said, changing the subject.

'Yeah. My sister had come from America with her twins and husband. I shifted back home after Randhir left so I could spend time with them.'

No wonder I hadn't seen him. And there I'd been, nursing all that hurt.

He said, 'I told my sister about her husband. You were absolutely right.'

'About?'

He was drinking water and, to my surprise, stopped mid-gulp, his eyes on my face. Then he swallowed and put his glass down.

'My sister stopped talking to me three years ago,' he said rapidly.

'Three *years* ago!'

'Yeah. Because I told her I'd... I'd found out her husband was having an affair.'

I stared at him, taken aback at him suddenly confiding in me.

'But... why was she angry with *you*?'

'Well, easier to shoot the messenger, isn't it?'

'What did she say when you told her?'

'She lost it. Said how dare I, she loved him, he could do whatever he liked but he'd always come back to her, shit like that. That I didn't know what it was like being a divorced woman in India, and you didn't get divorced at the drop of a hat... all that crap. This time, when she came with the twins, she offered me an olive branch, and I grabbed it.'

What did he mean, "all that crap?" How could he think that about what his sister had said to him?

'Arnav, your sister wasn't talking crap. It *is* difficult for divorced women.'

He looked at me, startled.

'I mean, my mother wasn't divorced, but she was a widow. That too, in the fifties. She was the *only* widow living alone without parents or in-laws in our neighbourhood. *And* she had a baby. *And* she was a working woman. *And* a South Indian, at a time when people in our colony thought

Southerners were a strange species. If it hadn't been for Madhu Aunty and Anu Aunty, she wouldn't have survived.'

He was listening intently.

'They gave my mother a lot of support, of course, but they also gave her... respectability. She had to prove her respectability every day of her life. A married woman doesn't have to do that because marriage makes her respectable.'

His eyes didn't move from my face.

'So Ma had two married women who took her under their wings. Because of them, she didn't have to build that foundation of respectability brick by brick. She just built *on* it.'

He nodded with complete attention.

'Ma says that she didn't even *look* at the men in the neighbourhood, let alone talk to them. Because as a widow living alone, she knew she was regarded as fair game. That's how your sister would be regarded as a divorced woman.'

'Yeah,' he said thoughtfully. 'I can see that. Though actually what I meant was that my sister's *justification* of her husband's affair was rubbish.'

It was a relief to hear that. It was also a revelation to feel the unexpected contours of a story that I thought I knew, to see that the story I had always been embroiled in was no longer about Ma, that it was a larger story, related to the road that so many women could never take.

'So... you don't feel my sister's anger with me was disproportionate?' he asked.

I thought about how, even now, the prospect of our story being found out terrified me.

'Arnav, I think her anger came out of... fear.'

He let out his breath and nodded.

The conversation felt both strange and easy; it was the kind of conversation I usually had with Randhir.

As we waited for the bill, Arnav asked, 'If you get into an American university, what'll you do after your PhD?'

'I'm coming back as soon as I finish.'

'But –' He stopped. 'I mean... wouldn't you like to teach there for a while?'

'My mothers are here, Arnav.'

'Yeah, but... all our parents are here.'

'But Ma's *alone*, she doesn't have anyone else!'

I could have bitten off my tongue.

He was looking startled. 'Your stepfather?'

'Yes... but... he's posted out of Delhi.'

He looked even more taken aback. Because, of course, that wasn't always going to be the case.

I spoke rapidly. 'His mother lives with him. She's always been dead against their marriage. My mother won't live in that situation.'

Now he'd be thinking, *But then why are they married?*

'Being married allows them to be together at least some of the time,' I added, before he could ask.

He nodded.

'You know,' he said, 'your stepfather really looks familiar. I don't know why.'

The waiter came with the bill. I unzipped my handbag and took out my purse.

'Mallika. Please. Put that away,' Arnav said.

'We'll go Dutch,' I said automatically, opening my purse. My hands were trembling slightly.

'Uff, stop making a fuss.' He put a fifty rupee note on the bill.

I put my purse back into my handbag and zipped it up. It didn't make a damn difference telling myself that there was absolutely no way my slip of tongue could have given away the true story. It didn't make a damn difference that I didn't resemble Karan. It didn't make a damn difference telling myself that if Arnav got to know the truth, it wouldn't matter to him. That he was the last person to talk about it. Because having hidden the truth about your life for your entire life meant that any crack was terrifying. Even if it was someone safe like Arnav who saw that crack.

We went downstairs, and he began walking towards his bike.

The ice cream? He'd forgotten.

'Arnav, the *ice cream*,' I said, stopping in my tracks.

He stopped too and began laughing. My spirit began to revive.

'Chalo.' We turned and went back towards the downstairs Nirula's ice cream place, and this time, he let me pay.

The ice cream at India Gate was fine, but this was the first and only ice cream parlour in Delhi, and everyone was crazy about it. I was reviving in leaps and bounds.

By the time we walked out of Nirula's and crossed the road, I was replete and happy. We strolled back towards his bike. He glanced at me. 'There's ice cream on your cheek,' he said, and stopped. I stopped. He wiped it off the side of my cheek with his thumb. Then he wiped it from the side of my mouth. This was the scene in the Hollywood film where the Heroine opens her eyes and the Hero looks at her with *that* look, preliminary to the long-awaited kiss. Not that anyone could kiss in public in Delhi, not that we would kiss anywhere, because when I opened my eyes, all that his held was surprise. '*Now* I know why your stepfather looks familiar. He looks like you.'

It didn't register for a couple of minutes.

We reached his bike, and he put on his helmet.

'No, he doesn't look like me,' I said, finally.

'Not feature-wise. His eyes. They have the same expression as yours.'

'What expression?'

'That... sadness.'

His face changed. 'Mallika? Why are you looking so scared?'

Too late.

He whispered, 'He *is* your father?'

Behind him, at the other corner, I saw Jalpari crossing the road.

'*Jalpari!*'

I ran to the crossing. Traffic was approaching from down the street, but it was far enough. Hitching up my saree, I ran across the road. '*Jalpari!*'

She didn't turn. Panting, I ran behind her, and as she entered the broad swath of corridor, I finally caught up with her. 'Jalpari,' I panted, reaching out and clutching her arm.

She turned.

I dropped her arm. It wasn't Jalpari.

'Sorry.' Then, in Hindi, I added, 'I thought you were Jalpari.'

She looked at me as though I were crazy and walked away swiftly.

I took a few steps to a pillar on the side and leaned against it, heaving with terror.

'Mallika?'

It was Arnav. He was looking at me worriedly.

'I thought it was Jalpari,' I gasped.

I covered my face with my arm.

'Child, what is the matter, are you alright?' An elderly couple were next to me, and the woman was peering into my face. Her husband – a tall, straight-backed man with steel grey hair, a beautiful military bearing, and an army-style crewcut – was looking at me with grave concern.

'I'm alright.' I was trying my best to stop shaking, but I couldn't.

'Mallika, come, I'll take you home,' Arnav said, his voice low.

'Young lady,' said the gentleman, addressing me with a very English accent. 'Is this young man the cause of your distress?'

'No, no.'

'She's had a shock,' Arnav said.

I lifted my saree palla and wiped my face. Sweat was pouring down.

'Please,' said the gentleman, taking out a spotless white handkerchief from his pocket and offering it to me.

'Take it, take it,' his wife encouraged. 'He's very good at calming ladies in distress. Unless, of course, it's his wife.'

'Thank you.' I tried to smile, took his handkerchief, and wiped my face. I looked at Arnav. He was pale, and his eyes were anything but calm. The gentleman was addressing him. 'Young man, did you say you would take her home?'

'Yes, sir. I have a bike.'

'A bicycle!' He sounded shocked.

'A motorcycle, sir.'

'Indeed.' He gave this thought. 'My wife and I could drive her home in our car.'

'Thank you,' I said, terribly moved. 'But he lives next door to me.'

'Very well, young lady. We will accompany you to the motorcycle.'

'Sir, that's very good of you,' Arnav said, 'but there's no need to take all that trouble.'

'We will accompany you,' said the gentleman implacably.

'No point arguing with him,' his wife said to Arnav. 'He's Taurus, he won't budge an inch. On top of that, an army man. *Very* unyielding combination.'

She beamed at me. She was plump and beautiful, with glowing skin, laughing eyes, and a pink-and-white Sanganeri saree that almost made the summer air seem cool.

Introductions were made; they were Colonel and Mrs Thimaya.

My terror was subsiding. Arnav walked ahead with Mrs Thimaya. Colonel Thimaya walked with me, swinging his walking stick, every inch the soldier. His bearing was so beautiful, and there was such dignity and kindness wafting out of him, that I felt I could walk with him forever.

He stopped. 'Young man, a minute, if I may,' he said to Arnav's back.

His wife and Arnav stopped, and Arnav walked back to us. 'Yes, sir?'

'You mentioned that the young lady has had a shock. If that is the case, she needs a cup of hot, sweet coffee.' He turned to me. 'Young lady, would you like that?'

'I'd love coffee,' I said, wanting to hug him. 'Please, keep us company?'

'Most kind of you, thank you,' Colonel Thimaya said. 'Poovie?'

'Where will I say no to coffee at the Coffee House?' Mrs Thimaya said.

'After you,' Colonel Thimaya said, inclining his head and extending his hand.

My heart began to melt. No one had ever been so gentlemanly to me.

Mrs Thimaya and I walked ahead. 'When Thimmu and I were courting, he used to take me to the Coffee House and buy me coffee with milk *and* cream. Those were the days! So handsome he was. You should have seen him! Youth, good looks, that clipped accent, *and* the army uniform. Such a *fatal* combination! No money, of course, but when you're young you think that doesn't matter.'

I began to smile. She was like sunshine.

We reached the coffee house and found a table.

'After you, ladies,' Colonel Thimaya said, inviting us to sit.

They were a gift. As though the heavens themselves were reminding me that there were good things in this world too.

I didn't know if Arnav saw it, but I was aware that Colonel Thimaya was quietly and unobtrusively assessing him and making sure that I was not in any kind of danger from him. I knew because Ma had done exactly the same kind of subtle assessment with Randhir during my teenage years. Later, she had done it with Arnav, insisting on him having tea and snacks when he dropped me home and chatting with him.

'What happened to you, child?' Mrs Thimaya asked.

My throat filled.

Arnav quietly answered for me. 'Her student was… kidnapped a couple of years ago. Mallika thought she saw her this afternoon and ran after her. But it was someone else.'

'Oho,' said Mrs Thimaya, her face falling. 'How terrible.'

The coffee came, with milk, sugar, and cream.

I put two spoons of sugar in my coffee. 'Put one more,' Mrs Thimaya said. 'It is very good for shock.'

I put another half-spoon of sugar in my coffee. *They* were good for shock.

They asked about our families. We told them. Colonel Thimaya talked about the benefits of an early morning walk when the rays of the sun were most beneficial for the body. And a cold bath in summer and winter, regardless of how cold it was.

'Even when he was posted to Kashmir in the winters, he used to bathe with cold water – can you imagine?' Mrs Thimaya shuddered.

'It is an excellent antidote for the prevention of illness,' Colonel Thimaya maintained.

I returned the borrowed handkerchief to Mrs Thimaya. 'It is full of kajal stains,' I said remorsefully.

'Doesn't matter, by tomorrow it will be good as new.' Mrs Thimaya put it into her handbag.

'Everything about the Colonel is so… impeccable,' I whispered to her.

'So everyone says. When he was serving in the army, he was impeccably dressed because his batman saw to it, and after he retired, he is still impeccably dressed because I'm his batman.'

I began to giggle.

She told me that when she was in Presidency College in Madras, she was the tennis champion. 'I even played mixed doubles. It was considered very daring those days, you know.'

Five minutes later the bill came, and Arnav reached for it.

'Young man,' Colonel Thimaya said. 'May I request you to kindly desist.' Arnav desisted.

Five minutes later, as Arnav and the Colonel walked ahead of us, Mrs Thimaya asked, 'Does that boy want to marry you?'

'No,' I said, shaking my head. 'We –'

'Give him an ultimatum, then. Waiting and pining is all very well in books, but it never does anyone any good. Thimmu made me wait. He was being noble, you see. Nobility is his forte. But nobility always comes at someone else's expense. He said he couldn't marry me without first getting his sister married. Now, thirty-plus years later, his sister is *still* not married. I told our daughter, if I had listened to his noble words, you wouldn't have existed.'

I was still laughing as we said our goodbyes. The Colonel and Arnav shook hands.

As they turned to go, Colonel Thimaya slipped. I rushed to him, and Arnav reached out for his arm. The Colonel righted himself and put up his hand firmly to stop us.

'We thought you'd fall,' I said apologetically.

'Young lady,' he said gently. 'I am a paratrooper. I know how to fall.'

When we reached home, Arnav quietly asked if I was OK.

I nodded. But what I wanted to say was, *Don't go. Stay with me. Hold me.*

We said bye.

I had shut the door against Jalpari three years ago, but she had burst through it finally, as though she were saying, *Look at me*. For the first time, I did. Finally, I wept for her. Finally, I told myself she was probably dead. That if she were alive, her life would be worse than death. Every night, after every bout of weeping, I would think of the Thimayas and feel comforted. Such was the magic they had wrought.

But why had I felt such terror in the first place?

I had felt it once before, when I read about the teenage sister and brother who had hitched a lift and been murdered. The sister had been raped. Randhir had come home that day, looking grim, and told me I should never hitch lifts. The terror that had struck me when I read that news took days to subside. And as I ran after the girl at Connaught Place, it had come back tenfold.

As for Delhi girls hitching lifts, that had come to a complete standstill.

'But of course Mallika must apply,' Dr Roy told my mothers and grandmother.

They greeted this statement with absolute silence.

Ma was paying Dr Roy to treat me, but when Shantamama and Ajji came to Delhi, it was a four-for-one deal.

Shantamama burst out, 'She is going because of that boy, Randhir.'

'She's been talking to me about wanting to apply to American universities long before her friend Randhir began applying,' Dr Roy said.

My mothers looked at me in disbelief. I had spoken to him and not to them?

'But... her health? The depression?' Ma said.

'It's been three years. Mallika's come a very long way.'

'But she's still having the medicines,' Ma said.

'It's just a maintenance dose.'

'But it's very far away, America. There's no money to go running to her if it happens again,' Shantamama said. 'How will she manage?'

'One day, none of you will be there for her,' Dr Roy said bluntly. 'How will she manage then?'

I felt breathless with terror. That such a day would come was inconceivable.

Ma put her hand to her heart as though promising herself she would never abandon me by dying early.

'By then, she'll be married with children,' Shantamama said. '*They'll* be there for her.'

Dr Roy said. 'We don't know if Mallika will marry and have children.'

Shantamama looked pale at the inconceivable prospect of my spinsterhood.

'Better for her to learn how to live without you now than later,' Dr Roy concluded.

On the fourth day after meeting the doctor, as I sat at the dining table cleaning rice, my mothers and grandmother alighted around me like birds of paradise. Shantamama had once said, 'Colour gives courage.' And now Ma was in a green-and-yellow Maharashtrian saree, Shantamama was in a purple-and-green Bengali saree, and Ajji was in a maroon Kanjeevaram saree with a thin gold border. As though they were dressed for a killing, no less.

I was in a burnt orange Kota saree with a narrow mustard border. If it were indeed a killing, I happened to be dressed for it too.

Shanta: The eggs in the other basket

1979

Mallika was cleaning rice at the dining table when she, Padma, and Amma joined her. This batch of rice had even more stones than usual, but Ayah-ji didn't even see most of them and refused to go to the eye doctor. So difficult Ayah-ji was. The time of Mallika's concussion, Ayah-ji had known very well that Mallika had forgotten her magenta saree, sweater, and shawl in the bus, but she'd kept mum till Shanta finally got it out of her. Then she had asked Ayah-ji about the other saree, the purple batik one, that Mallika had lost, and Ayah-ji had retorted, 'What do I know, you think I work in a saree shop?' She was the limit. Padma let Ayah-ji get away with everything.

Mallika put the thali of rice to the side and looked at them, her eyes full of apprehension.

Amma began. 'Child, if you get admission and a scholarship, I will give you the money to buy your dollars. That is the first thing I have to say. Now, let your mothers speak.' She sat back in her chair.

That was the first thing? What was the second? What did Amma have up her sleeve?

'Love,' Padma said. 'We don't want to thwart your dreams. But Shantamama and I don't agree with your doctor. Who will be there for you in America if something happens? Certainly not Randhir.'

'Don't persuade yourself that he will propose if you go to America,' Shanta added.

Mallika said, 'Shantamama, even if Randhir were living in Delhi, I'd apply.'

'How long does a PhD take?' Shanta asked.

Mallika swallowed. Then she said, 'About five years.'

Shanta's heart plunged past her toes, into the very floor.

'Shantamama, I told you. I can afford to come home every year.'

Shanta couldn't look at Padma's face. She just couldn't.

Amma broke the silence. 'Child, the second thing is this: do not think you can have the same kind of friendship with Arnav that you had with Randhir.'

Mallika looked shocked.

There they had been, Shanta and Padma, plotting behind Amma's back about bringing up the Arnav issue, and here Amma was, already pre-empting them.

'You have known Randhir all your life,' Amma said. 'His parents live next to us, and both families know each other very well. There is security in that. But Arnav is a young man living by himself. We know nothing about his family. That day you spent the entire day with him. I am not accusing you of any wrongdoing. But that boy will mistake the hand that you are extending in friendship for something else.'

Mallika's mouth was half-open.

'Does Arnav show any signs of wanting to marry you?' Shanta asked.

'No, Shantamama, of course not.'

'Why "of course?" It's *nice* when a man has serious intentions about a woman.'

'You mustn't go out with him again,' Padma said.

'Do not take lifts with him on his motorcycle,' Shanta said. 'That kind of physical proximity is unseemly. People will start talking.'

'Also, child, there is no need to write to Randhir,' Amma said.

Padma said, '*Uproot* Randhir from your life.'

Mallika was looking dazed.

'What kind of family does that boy Arnav come from?' Amma asked, turning to Padma.

'Good family,' Padma said. 'His father is from UP – he's in the civil service – and his mother is Bengali. She was educated at Shantiniketan.'

'Such a good background!' Amma exclaimed. 'Then why does that boy dress so badly? Whenever I see him, his pants are faded.'

'Those pants are called jeans, Amma,' Padma said. 'His sister in America gets them for him. Those faded jeans cost hundreds and hundreds of rupees. It is the fashion in the West.'

'Imagine,' Amma marvelled. 'Here, you have to be poor to wear faded clothes, and there, you have to be rich to wear faded clothes.'

'I'm not going to break off my friendships with Randhir and Arnav,' Mallika said.

They turned to her in disbelief.

'You've forgotten how much Randhir has done for me?' Mallika asked. 'And Arnav donated blood for your operation, Shantamama. And he came all the way to my college to pick me up and drop me home for four months. Are those small things?'

'We are trying to protect you.'

'I know that, Shantamama. But you're all also angry with them. Because neither of them wants to marry me. But that's no reason to be angry. Be angry if they deceive me, if they lie to me, if they take advantage of me. Don't be angry because they haven't fulfilled your dreams for me.'

They looked at Mallika wordlessly.

'They've *never* deceived me,' Mallika said, her face crumpling. '*You've* just deceived yourselves.'

They stared at her, thunderstruck.

Mallika went back to cleaning the rice.

So. Off she would go to a man who wouldn't marry her? Without a thought for the illness that could afflict her? To a country that would never release her?

Oh, no.

She wouldn't let America take Mallika. When America took you, it took you forever. Her prayers were stronger than America's grasping arms. Why should her child go across the oceans to that vast and distant country, where people spoke English with incomprehensible accents, spelt things all wrong, wasted vast quantities of perfectly edible food, threw away beautiful things – furniture, lampshades, shoes, clothes, and handbags – into the rubbish dump, treated children like adults, allowed their children to backchat, and divorced at the drop of a hat?

Mallika had said that even if she went, she would come home every year. Shanta didn't believe it. And she didn't want to think about Mallika not coming home for years and years. But how not to think about it? For that, she would have to become a man. Wasn't that how men survived, by not thinking about the very thing that was staring them in the face? Was *that* what she was supposed to become?

It wasn't as if she weren't grateful for Mallika's recovery. She was more than grateful, and she told the Devas so every single morning when she lit the lamp. She would have prostrated herself before them every day if it hadn't been for her spondylitis.

The Devas had given her the best birthday present: Mallika's recovery. That birthday, a year ago, Mallika had given her a beautiful golden-and-green cotton Orissi saree.

'Happy fiftieth birthday, Shantamama!' Mallika had said.

'Thank you, my darling.' She had hugged Mallika. 'Fiftieth birthday is all very well, but it's never *said*. I'm going to be forty-nine for the next ten years.'

'Alright, Shantamama,' Mallika had said, kissing her.

Her child's eyes – so dull for so long – were full of laughter. She had seen those eyes and known, at last, that Mallika's terrible, unfathomable illness was truly on the wane. What better birthday present than that knowledge? The saree was beautiful, but nowhere near as beautiful as the brightness in Mallika's eyes.

She had worn the saree that very day. There was even a fall stitched on it – Gauri must have done that. Later, though, when she examined the saree, she knew that Gauri couldn't have stitched the fall, because Gauri's needlework was neat, precise, and beautiful. The fall on her birthday saree, though laden with Mallika's love, was a far cry from neat, precise, or beautiful. The stitches showed clearly on the other side of the saree, and the bottom of the fall was stitched with a single thread, even though she and Gauri had told Mallika a hundred times that you needed to use double thread.

She had told herself that if Mallika recovered from that devastating illness and lived a normal life, she would never ask the Devas for anything else. But now, here she was, already asking for Mallika not to go to America. She couldn't put it that way to the Gods, though. She had to choose her words carefully, because the Gods could answer your prayers very literally sometimes. They were either oblivious or cunning, probably both – oblivious like husbands and cunning like mothers-in-law.

If her prayers failed, as prayers sometimes did with these capricious Gods, the blame would also lie with Padma. Padma had put all her eggs in one basket. All her hopes for Mallika in that one boy, Randhir. She hadn't even considered all the other baskets out there for the picking. So many offers there had been from the mothers of their tuition children, all full of praise for Mallika, saying, 'We have a very nice nephew or cousin, or there's this friend's son, so handsome, such a good job, such a wonderful family.' And instead of saying, 'Why don't you bring him home and they can meet,' Padma would say, 'She's still young, she wants to study more.'

Worse, Padma had given such latitude to Mallika with regards to Randhir. What lesson had Padma learnt after Karan got her pregnant and abandoned her? She had lost her faith in men, yet put all her faith in Randhir. Not a word of caution to Mallika; not once did she say, 'Be careful, no need to spend so much time with him.' Not just that, but she didn't let *her*, Shanta, warn Mallika. And then Padma would spout her cynical theories about men and marriage as though Randhir was above it all.

When Padma told her about Randhir going away to America, Padma had cried and cried. Unlike the TB time, when Padma hadn't cried at all. The TB had broken both of them, but neither had cried. Shanta knew now that tears came from the things that didn't break you. When you broke, every tear stayed inside you, each turning to a sharp, jagged stone, and your eyes remained dry while your organs bled.

After their second talk with Mallika, Shanta did something terrible. She would never forgive herself for it. When Mallika had gone to college, and Amma and Padma were taking their naps, she went upstairs to Mallika's room. And there it was: Randhir's letter, lying trustingly on her desk. She would have felt better if Mallika had hidden it. She would have felt better if she had had to search for it.

She opened Randhir's letter and read it.

It wasn't a love letter. No *Beloved Mallika*, no *My darling Mallika*, no *Dearest Mallika*, nothing. Not even *Dear Mallika*. He wrote, *Mallika, a longer letter will follow, I'm dashing this off before I go for class.* It was very reassuring, that first line, and she took in a deep breath of relief.

And then that breath got caught in her chest. The boy was calling Mallika to America. Giving her the solution to the money problem. She could ask her grandmother and her father. The scholarship would be enough for her to come home every year. *More later, Randhir,* he signed off. This boy, for whom Mallika was not a beloved or a dearest or even a dear; this boy, who didn't even end the letter with love; this boy, who had no intention of marrying her; this boy was calling her to America? How *dare* he?

Putting the letter back in the same spot on the desk, she went downstairs. It made her feel sick, what she had done. So much so that she retched into the sink in the other bathroom, but only bile came out, and after that, she cried and cried.

She washed her face, dried it, and then went to Padma's room and told her what she had done.

'Karan's mother read my letters to him,' Padma whispered.

'You're comparing *me* to that witch?'

Padma said nothing.

She told Padma what Randhir had written.

Padma's face was twisted. 'He's good at dispensing advice to her.'

'In short, he's calling her to America because he thinks that'll be good for her, but he doesn't want to marry her?'

Padma nodded. Then she said, 'Shantacca, I'm part of it now. But please. Never read Mallika's letters again.'

'Yes, you *are* part of it now.'

Padma wiped her eyes. 'He knows her so deeply, and still...'

Shanta sighed. What did knowing someone have to do with loving someone? As if men wanted to *know* the women that they had affairs with. Or the women they married. Before marriage, men wanted pretty, intelligent women who made them heady with desire, and after marriage, they wanted those very women to transform into good cooks, superb housewives, and docile daughters-in-law. Not to mention, women who were ever-willing to have sex, whether they desired it or not.

That Mallika, of all people, would stoop so low as to follow a man who didn't want her all the way to America belied belief. For this foolhardiness, Mallika, who was so conscientious about money, was taking inconceivable amounts of money from her grandmother and Karan. Even worse, Mallika didn't seem to realize what she was doing. The girl had become blind! Shanta had always known that this kind of love was blind – she had seen its folly everywhere. But that Mallika should teeter in its grip was beyond comprehension. Equally frightening was Mallika's inability to understand that she couldn't manage the illness if it came upon her in a foreign country. That Dr Roy had said she should apply was a big shock. So what if he had Indian blood? In every other way, he was American.

Mallika went for her usual walk the evening after their talk, and then went off to India Gate with that boy Arnav without so much as asking their permission. When she came back, she was holding a Cadbury in her hand, and her eyes were shining. 'Shantamama, let's eat it before dinner.'

'Oho, if you were going to the market after India Gate, you should have told me. I wanted some black thread.'

'I didn't go to the market, Shantamama. Arnav gave it to me.'

'*I* see. You're already at *that* stage?'

'Shantamama! We're at no stage! He happened to have it with him!'

'*Happened* to have it with him? Men don't buy chocolates for themselves, my dear.'

Mallika gave a long-suffering sigh.

Those shining eyes were not for the chocolate. Those shining eyes were for Arnav.

It was starting all over again. Now, with this boy.

Mallika had given her heart to Randhir, and what was Randhir doing with it, pray? Calling her to America without proposing marriage, that was what he was doing with it. Mallika was missing nothing by not marrying Randhir. If she married him, then when he came back to India, he would spend his life in his father's factory with no time for her. And Madhu would bestow upon Mallika those paste-like North Indian diamonds, that ubiquitous kundan set, and those hideous nylon sarees from London. As though Mallika would touch those nylon sarees with a bargepole! As for the other boy, Arnav, he was seducing Mallika with chocolates. He was getting away cheap; he would give her the chocolates, and she would give him her heart.

Padma was not practical. But she, Shanta, was. She had always had an alternative plan. It was time to set her long-standing idea in motion.

She had her old faithful box camera with her. It was better than any of those new-fangled cameras. She asked Mallika, Padma, and Amma to wear nice sarees and lipstick so that they could take photographs outside on their little lawn as well as inside in the sitting room. She dressed up too. She insisted Mallika wear her long earrings with the red stones; they looked like rubies. Not that you could make that out in a black-and-white photo, but still. And she did something terribly extravagant – she finished the entire reel of twelve. In addition to the group photos, she took three full-length photos of Mallika and two of her profile. Each time, she made Mallika laugh. Padma could never make Mallika laugh. Padma would just say, 'Now, smile.' As though! Unfortunately, Mallika had taken after Padma; for all the humorous books she read, she couldn't joke to save her life.

A week later, and oh, my! What photos! Her old faithful box camera had surpassed itself!

She would place two of Mallika's photos in her sitting room. Not on the mantlepiece, which had so many other family photos. She would put Mallika's photos on top of their television and throw a few parties with people she knew who had eligible sons, and everyone would say, 'Who is this beautiful girl?' And she would say, 'Oh, that's my daughter, Mallika, the one my sister and I raised together.' And they would say, 'Oh, what is she doing?' And she'd say, 'She's completed her MA in English, and she's doing her MPhil, and after that... let us see.' And they'd take a good, long look. Then, in due course, they would speak to her of their son or nephew, and would her niece be interested in meeting him? And she would say, 'I don't see why not.'

It happened exactly as in her fantasy. Two months after she returned to Bangalore, she had *three* offers for Mallika. One, a Delhi boy in America who wanted to come back to India in five or six years; one, a Bombay boy in America who wasn't sure about when or if he'd come back; and lastly, a well-settled Bangalore boy with a marvellous job.

Three offers in two months. She felt drunk with triumph. Now she could thumb her nose at that jobless Randhir and that houseless, carless Arnav.

Yes, it was true that Mallika had forsworn an arranged marriage. But she would see to it that Mallika met these boys accidentally. She would plan it meticulously.

The Delhi boy in America, Bharat, was the best. Though his father was from UP – like that boy Arnav's father – his mother was from Karnataka, so Mallika wouldn't have to contend with a North Indian mother-in-law. He was the best looking of the three, the best age (five years older than Mallika), had the best job and the most money – thirty-five thousand dollars a year, and she felt faint when she translated it into rupees – and a car and a house of his own. Why, even she and Naraina didn't have their own house! In a few years, Bharat wanted to come back to India. They could get married, and Mallika could continue with her PhD under her husband's protective auspices, and when she finished, they would both come back to India. If Mallika didn't go to America, she could meet him when he visited India. He was one of those idealistic men who wanted to return to his country. Mallika liked idealistic men. Which could be a dangerous thing, because idealism without money was fatal to wives. But when idealism was borne aloft on money's radiant arms, oh, how brightly it shone!

Mallika: Self-delusion and chocolate

1979

That evening, after the talk with my mothers and grandmother, I went for a walk.

I understood that they wanted to spare me grief. But what was I supposed to tell them? That yes, while it was true that neither Randhir nor Arnav wanted to marry me, it was also true that I could never ever feel for any man what I felt for them? What was I supposed to do? Tear open my heart and say, 'Begone with you,' and out they'd run, and I'd be done?

I was also trying to come to terms with the fact that Arnav knew about my father. He wasn't a fool – by now, he'd have seen through the story of Ma's 'widowhood' and come to the obvious conclusion.

I was pulled out of my thoughts by a terrible sound. It was something between a baying and a bellowing, coming relentlessly from the house down the road where a young couple and their little son lived. I ran towards the sound, accompanied by another neighbour, Mrs Kapadia, who was also out on her evening walk. From the opposite side, I saw Arnav running. We reached the house together and ran up the veranda steps.

We stared at the veranda floor. It was two-year-old Subramanium making that terrifying sound as he rolled from one end of the veranda to the other. His mother, Yamini, was crouched on the floor next to him. 'He isn't hurt, he's having a tantrum.'

'Hai Ram,' said Mrs Kapadia. 'Yamini, he is sounding like dog who howls when someone has died! Why?'

'I don't know why.' Yamini got up from the floor, while the child continued to roll and bellow, and sat wearily on the veranda chair.

'Little bit strict you have to be with him, Yamini,' Mrs Kapadia said.

'But he does not listen.'

'Talk and all is useless with children. One smack on his bottom, and he will stop.'

'It doesn't work.'

'You Madrasis, you are too mild. Give him a *hard* one.'

As Subramanium rolled bellowing towards me, I went down on my haunches next to Arnav and put out my arms, unable to bear the little one's huge misery.

Subramanium stopped baying and looked at me, tears streaming down his face. Then he got up and crawled into my arms.

'Chalo, here is solution!' Mrs Kapadia said. 'When tantrum happens, you call Mallika.'

Mrs Kapadia waved goodbye and went off on her walk. Yamini looked at me wordlessly, and I saw the desperation in her face. 'Should I take him to the park? Then you can rest.'

'Oh, Mallika! Thank you. My husband is on tour.'

Subramanium's little body was shuddering against mine. But he wasn't bellowing any more.

'You've found your calling, Mallika,' Arnav said as we walked down the road.

Subramanium glared at him.

'Understand what I'm saying, little fellow?' Arnav asked.

Subramanium growled.

'Where have you been all these days?' I hadn't seen him since that day in Connaught Place.

'Oh, acting in a play. I go for practice after work. And all day Saturday. Spend Sunday with my parents.'

It would have been nice if I was also on his list of priorities. A wave of sadness swept over me.

Subramanium kissed me. I stopped. He solemnly patted my cheek. As if to say, *I know.* We looked into each other's eyes, and I saw that he did. I was shaken.

'He's in love with you,' Arnav said.

'No come park,' Subramanium said, looking at Arnav.

Arnav stopped in his tracks.

They took each other's measure.

'Yes, come park,' Arnav said.

Subramanium bellowed.

'Subramanium,' I said, stroking his back. 'Let him come.'

He glared at Arnav.

In the park, we sat on the grass, but Subramanium refused to get off my lap. He lifted my plait and examined it carefully.

'Mallika,' Arnav began. 'That day in CP –'

Subramanium bellowed so loudly that an old man walking in the park stopped in his tracks. Then, seeing that Subramanium wasn't being assaulted, he continued on his way.

'Subramanium,' Arnav said, man to man. 'I want to talk to Mallika.'

'No,' Subramanium said.

Arnav roared with laughter. Subramanium got off my lap. He sat by my feet and began examining the payal on my left foot.

'He's staking his claim,' Arnav said. He lay back on the grass, took a crumpled packet from his jeans and a box of matches from his shirt pocket, and lit a cigarette.

While Arnav smoked, Subramanium pulled out grass and gave it to me. He examined my fingers, one by one. He didn't utter a word except for a small, warning growl when Arnav glanced at us.

Half an hour later, we got up and strolled back. I handed a sleepy Subramanium back to his mother, and Arnav said, 'Feel like ice cream at India Gate?'

I could hear the voices of my mothers and grandmother telling me to have nothing to do with him.

'Yes,' I said.

I rushed back home, told my mothers I was going to India Gate with Arnav, ignored their outraged expressions, and rushed out where he was waiting for me on his motorcycle.

He got us our ice creams, and we strolled down the lawns, chatting of this and that. Then he said, 'You know, I've realized, you're damn impulsive.'

'*Me?*'

'That day in CP – the way you ran across the road! And what about stealing the puppy?'

'And when *you* came into my room in the middle of the night? *That* wasn't impulsive?'

'Why didn't you chuck me out?'

'So that was *my* fault, you coming to my room?' I was incoherent with indignation.

'It was *entirely* my fault. I just don't get why you didn't chuck me out.'

'I suppose you've forgotten that I tried? I kept telling you to go, and you kept refusing. Then you fell asleep. I pulled your arms, your legs, everything. You didn't budge.'

He laughed. 'Did you really? Actually, I'm glad you didn't chuck me out. It was the most entertaining night I've ever spent.'

'Falling asleep in my room was worse than impulsive, it was stupid.'

'If *that* was stupid, then what was falling asleep with your arms around me?'

'*What!*'

'Never mind, at least you're not shy in bed.'

I pushed him hard. He fell into the lake.

With immense satisfaction, I watched him floundering and gasping in the water.

He heaved himself out and stood next to me, completely drenched. Then he fumbled in his pocket, took out an unopened bar of Cadbury, and gave it to me.

'What?' I blinked.

He shook his head, and droplets of water flew into my face. 'I was going to give it to you earlier. But I didn't have the guts to, in front of Subramanium.'

I took it from him without comprehension. 'Arnav! I just pushed you into the lake!'

The next minute, he'd picked me up and swung me towards the lake.

I shrieked.

Three men watching us whistled and hooted.

He put me down gently. 'Did you? Imagine, I never noticed.'

We walked back to the bike – Arnav wringing his t-shirt and wiping his face with his palms, and I dizzy with joy at having been in his arms for five seconds.

He said casually, 'Why were you looking so terrified that day, after you realized it wasn't Jalpari?'

'I don't know.'

We strolled towards his bike.

'I felt I was going to die.'

Only after the words came out of me did I realize that it was so.

We reached his bike. 'You're fine, Mallika. You're absolutely safe,' he said gravely.

There he stood before me, completely drenched, his words so unexpected and so comprehending of that irrational terror that I didn't know what to say. Then he gave me the sweetest smile and asked, 'Aren't you going to eat your chocolate?' Had I been another girl, I'd have hugged him there and then. But alas, I was only me.

The next day, Arnav dropped in, said his namastes to Ajji and my mothers, who were at the dining table shelling the peas, and sat decorously on the sofa.

'Listen, Mallika – Randhir wrote and said you're going to fail in the Maths section of the GRE.'

I nodded. That part was going very, very badly.

'I can help you with that two or three times a week.'

I wanted to leap out of my chair and hug him. 'But what can you teach me in one-and-a-half months? We have to take the GRE in October.'

'I'll give you some tips.'

Suddenly, I felt three pairs of eyes from the dining room boring a hole into my head.

No chance.

'Your idea, it is very good, Arnav. Thank you. On teaching days, dinner you have here only, alright?' Ajji said.

Arnav thanked her, looking delighted. Between us and Madhu Aunty, with whom he ate at least twice a week, his bachelor life would be most flavourful.

My mothers grimly went back to shelling the peas.

My grandmother's ambition for my admission into an American university had overridden her apprehension about my friendship with Arnav. She had deliberately signalled her approval to him in my mothers' presence. Now, my mothers, despite having plenty to say, would have no say.

Arnav began tutoring me. His presence, right next to me thrice a week, made me so heady that I felt I was floating. Ma tried to (literally) put distance between us. She told me that I would sit at the head of the dining table, and he next to me at the other side. So during our sessions, the corner of the table was nicely wedged between us. Arnav was patient and funny. He made up jokes on the spot about my mathematic inabilities, and our laughter dissipated my frustration at being so slow. Ma sat in the sitting room, correcting her student papers or writing letters, and also, of course, listening to us. Sometimes when I went for my early morning walks, Arnav would join me on my last round, sweaty and panting from his run, his face lighting up to see me. That look made me all shivery, and up I went, flying even higher.

The rest of the time, we were busy studying, writing to various universities, and getting our applications and essays ready. He was still working, and I still doing my MPhil and tutoring my students. The loan against the house had *finally* been paid off. I was also putting aside cash every month to pay Dr Raghunath. I hid it in a box under my bed, which also contained my notes from my BA and MA, in a brown paper envelope.

Then October was upon us, and we took the GREs. I had no idea how I'd done.

In December, Mahima came home for a few days. Prabha and Gauri were also home for the holidays, and we were joyous to be together. Mahima had lost weight and started smoking. Almost every night, she came to my room after Ma went to sleep and smoked on my balcony. She said, 'I know I shouldn't, but it keeps me calm.'

'Calm? What d'you mean "calm," what's happening?' I asked, and Mahima looked exasperated.

'Nothing, Mallika. Why d'you always get agitated, I'm perfectly happy.'

As one of our neighbours had said, 'Marriage, it is adjusting-vadjusting only, what else is marriage?' Mahima had adjusted-vadjusted.

After my three friends went back to their lives, Arnav returned to mine and said, 'You forgot me.' He said it in his usual, laughing way, but up I went, up, higher and higher, floating away on the thought that perhaps he *had* missed me.

In April, the letters from America began to come. Arnav got into three universities in America, including Randhir's one in Pennsylvania. I got into just one – also Randhir's university. We couldn't believe it. My mothers and grandmother said they were proud of me and left it at that. As we all knew, admission without aid was of no consequence.

In late June, Arnav flew into Madhu Aunty's kitchen, where Ma and I were sampling her kadhi, and flung his arms around me. 'I've got aid at Randhir's university!' he burst out. 'Oh, Mallika, you better get aid too!'

He let me go, and we all congratulated him.

Ma scolded me soundly when we went home. 'What does he mean by hugging you like that – that too, in front of us!'

He'd hugged me! He'd hugged me! I was flying higher and higher.

Then Randhir wrote and said he was coming back in the summer only because of me.

Higher and higher I flew.

You see, self-delusion is like chocolate; it keeps you going.

Padma: So many hankies

1979 and earlier

She had been so happy. In her entire, life she hadn't known such happiness, not even that eternity ago when she was madly in love with Karan. With Karan, it had been like being drunk. But the happiness that she allowed into her heart after Mallika recovered was like the sound of a singing bowl; it filled the empty space inside her so deeply that it became an exquisite, echoing feeling that radiated out of her.

It had taken two years for her to allow happiness to have its way. Those days when Mallika was so ill, every tiny sign that she could be getting better had created a crack on her parched body through which happiness would squeeze in, a happiness that was intense and untrustworthy. It would squeeze in when Mallika began doing small things like going to the balcony on her own, or speaking one sentence, or eating three mouthfuls instead of two. Happiness would say, See, this is a harbinger of better things to come. But when the better things didn't come immediately – like Mallika comprehending what was being said to her, Mallika talking, walking, reading, smiling, and wanting – yes, Mallika wanting *something*, wanting *anything* – then it would retreat, that traitorous happiness.

Kavya's serenity had anchored her those days.

'How do you know my mother?' she had asked Kavya the very first time they met.

'Many years ago, your mother gave me great help and strength. Since then, we have been writing to each other.'

She had waited for Kavya to say more, but she didn't. She had then asked awkwardly, 'So… what is it that you do?'

Kavya smiled faintly and said, 'I don't know. It does not come from me.'

Considering that this was the most unsatisfactory answer she had ever received, why had she returned with Mallika?

Perhaps because she had felt that Kavya wasn't being deliberately vague. That, on the contrary, she was being utterly truthful. It was a truth Padma didn't understand, but what was new about that? She didn't understand how the Phuknewalla had healed Mallika of eighty percent of her migraines. She didn't understand why Karan had never acknowledged his mother's betrayal. She didn't understand how Mallika, of all people, could have slashed Mrs Mittal's scooter tyres or stolen her puppy. She didn't understand the hard shell of religion which enclosed the poison inside her brother Madhav. She didn't understand why she had kept having sex with Karan in the immediate wake of his return, when all she could feel for him was that terrible anger. She didn't understand why Mallika had a major depressive disorder. And now, well, here was one thing more.

Kavya asked Mallika to call her 'Masi.' After her first treatment, Mallika had slept for ten straight hours. The next morning, she had the best breakfast she had had since her collapse – half a piece of toast and a whole egg. And three hours later, an entire glass of lime juice.

After that, she had taken Mallika to Kavya every single week. There was a box on Kavya's dining table where you could put in whatever money you could afford, and every time Padma put money there, she was thankful for the money that Karan had put into her bank account.

There was an invisible armour around Kavya which preempted intimacy. Padma had no idea if she was a widow, whether she had ever married, or whether she had renounced marriage to live like a hermit. As for Kavya, she showed no interest in Padma's life and no curiosity about the fact that Mallika's father went unmentioned.

As Mallika had slowly come back to herself, thanks to Dr Roy and Kavya, so had her determination. She would go back to college, she said. Her studies were the one thing on her mind, the one thing she clung to.

She, Padma, lived with the constant fear of Mallika relapsing and the anguish about what had happened to Jalpari. She had meant to tell Mallika about Jalpari when she was stronger. But Mallika had found out too soon, and a day or two later, the shock sunk in. When Arnav dropped her home from college that first afternoon, he'd said that she had rested in his hostel room. Padma was so relieved and grateful that she didn't dwell on this shocking fact. Then Arnav overwhelmed them all by saying he'd pick her up twice a week. It would have been hypocritical to protest. Anything that would help Mallika, anything. And Arnav was Randhir's friend, and Randhir would never let any harm come to Mallika. Mallika did not relapse. Padma watched Arnav like a hawk, asked him in for tea when he dropped Mallika home, chatted with him. He told her about his family, his interest in environmental issues, his love for acting. He picked up Mallika and brought her straight home. She was reassured.

She asked Dr Roy if Mallika's depression could come back. He had said, yes, it could, but Mallika was doing very well now and to focus on that. She did. After Mallika completed the first year of her MA, she, Padma, finally allowed herself to feel happiness. Happiness and gratitude. Hereafter, they would always come together. She allowed herself to feel it when Mallika smiled, when her eyes lit up, when she spent time with her friends, when she read a book, when she ate food with enjoyment. Soon, happiness filled Padma's very being. Shantacca felt the same way, but they didn't speak of it. Anything so precious was not to be talked about. That they saw it reflected on each other's faces was enough.

Her newfound happiness camouflaged that old current of disquiet. This surfaced when Karan – during one of his brief trips to Delhi – had asked her about Randhir. He was staying with her, as he had done since the time of Mallika's illness. Mallika had gone to bed. He had turned from the sitting room window where he was smoking – he had started again – and said, 'Is Randhir going to marry Mallika?'

She looked up from the *Illustrated Weekly of India*. 'I know he will.'

He was quiet for a while. Then he said, 'What does his mother say?'

That old, familiar disquiet surfaced.

'We don't talk about it. It's too early.'

'Why is it early? Randhir has started working in his father's factory. Have you thought of asking him?'

'Karan, how insulting that would be. It's so clear how he feels. And Mallika has another year to finish her MA. He'll come to it on his own.'

'And if he doesn't?'

She was finding the conversation extremely difficult. 'How can he not? *You've* seen how much she matters to him.' She put the magazine down, trying to dispel her rising anxiety.

'Has Mallika ever mentioned anything?'

She shook her head. 'You know how she is.'

Karan stubbed out his cigarette and didn't pursue the topic.

It was the first time he had asked her anything personal about Mallika. It was an indication of what a wide chasm they'd both crossed. That they had crossed it at all was entirely his doing, although it had been the last thing on their minds. When he had first come back into their lives, he had wanted Mallika's love. His hunger had crushed Mallika, who wanted to give it but couldn't. But by the time Mallika fell ill, Karan was no longer hungering for her love. He was just giving her his. After their one fight following the first meeting with Dr Roy, neither Padma nor he had had it in them to continue flogging that old, dead, rotting horse. For dead and rotting it was, and dealing with the enormity of what had happened to Mallika meant leaving that old carcass behind. What she had experienced of Karan during Mallika's illness had diluted her long-held, burning desire for that acknowledgement of his mother's perfidy. It was not a decision; it had just happened.

Now, Karan's unlikely gift to her was faith. Faith that the things you thought were irrevocable and irreparable were not. That when it happened, it was in ways you couldn't even imagine.

Yet her happiness was taken away, and not because Mallika's illness returned. Madhu had come home, burst into tears, and told her Randhir was going away to America to study.

As she gave Madhu several hankies to weep into, and as Mallika made coffee for them, Madhu told her about the drama at home. 'I am paying for his plane ticket. To keep this son, I have to let him go to America. I will pray he comes back,' Madhu wept. 'But this is what I have seen, Padma: that when America catches hold of you, you never come back.'

After Madhu left an hour later, fortified with two cups of coffee, several murkus, and three hankies, Padma looked without comprehension at Mallika. Then Mallika told her that she'd known about Randhir's applications for a year.

That night in bed, she went over all the years of Mallika and Randhir's friendship. All these years, she had depended on him for Mallika's safety, protection, and care. She was sure Randhir would never go to America without saying to Mallika, 'I will come back for you, please wait for me.'

But that was what he did.

Soon after, Karan came to Delhi. He always made sure to come when Amma and Shantacca were not with her. She missed the Karan she had leaned on during Mallika's illness, and the unwavering togetherness that had come about during that time. Now, a constraint was back, although it was nothing like before.

'Mallika told me Randhir's gone to America,' Karan said. They were in the sitting room, and Mallika had gone to bed. 'Mallika said she's known about his plans for a year. What did she tell you?'

'Nothing. She won't talk.'

'If he said nothing before leaving, then he isn't going to marry her.'

She stared at him. 'He may come back and ask her and –'

'For god's sake, Padma. Don't fool yourself.'

She felt her hope screeching to a halt.

'Didn't you think so too?' she begged. 'That they... were...'

He said, very quietly. 'Yes.'

'Then why?' she asked, her anguish spilling over.

He made an I-don't-know gesture. Taking a last drag of his cigarette, he stubbed it out and said, 'She mustn't wait for him. Please, make her understand that.'

'When Shantacca comes in two weeks, we'll talk to Mallika together.'

'You're going to wait *that* long?'

'Shantacca's equally her mother, Karan.'

He looked at her as though he were going to say something. Then he nodded and got up. 'Goodnight.'

'Goodnight.'

If Randhir thought he could whistle and Mallika would go running to him with her tail wagging, he was mistaken, she thought. Mallika had her pride.

Then Mallika dropped her bombshell about applying to American universities, and they discovered that she did not.

After this Shantacca did something terrible. She went upstairs to Mallika's room and read Randhir's letter. And she, Padma, did something equally terrible. She listened to the contents of that letter. In one shot, they both betrayed Mallika.

When Shantacca told her of the letter's contents, she wanted to shriek, *Randhir, you want to take my only child away from me to another country for five years, but you don't want to marry her?*

She should have cautioned Mallika from the time she was a teenager. She should have asked Mallika about her feelings. But she had treated their relationship as sacrosanct.

She believed Mallika when she said Randhir had never deceived her. But a boy did not deceive you merely by lying to you. If he gave you the impression, even without words, that you were his soulmate, then left for another country without any commitment, that too was deception. Wordless deceptions were the worst.

What had broken her heart was that Mallika recognized and accepted that neither Randhir nor Arnav wanted to marry her. Didn't the question of why they did not love her not occur to her? Did she think she wasn't worthy of their love? Did she feel she didn't have the right to expect it? Did she think so little of herself?

Randhir continued writing to Mallika, his letters arriving in thick envelopes which, had they been Indian envelopes, would have burst their very seams. Arnav continued tutoring Mallika, laughing with her over her incompetence in Maths, walking with her and spending time with her. Mallika was going the same way with Arnav as she had with Randhir. Or rather, *Arnav* was going the same way with her as Randhir had – attached to her, but with no thought of marrying her.

'Love, be careful with that boy.'

'Ma, I've told you, Arnav's my *friend*.'

It was no use. And now, Amma's fait accompli was ensconced in their dining room thrice a week tutoring Mallika in Maths and happily eating with them.

When she dropped in at Madhu's house for a chat, their servant, Ramu, was on the phone. He said to her, 'Memsahib has gone to her tailor shop. Randhir Bhaiyya is saying he will talk to you.'

She took the phone from him. 'Randhir, is everything alright?'

'Everything's fine, Aunty, I just phoned to say hullo to Mummy, and Ramu said you're here.'

She had loved this boy from the time he was sixteen. She missed him. She wanted to weep.

'So lovely to hear your voice, Randhir. We miss you so much.'

'Yes, Aunty, me too. Mallika's applying, no?'

'Yes. Arnav's tutoring her in Maths.'

Randhir burst out laughing. 'He told me in his letter. He said Mallika's Maths skills would try the patience of a saint!'

She laughed too. 'This is expensive, Randhir, phone after half an hour. Mummy will be back from the market by then.'

'No, no, I want to talk to you, Aunty. How is Mallika?'

'She's fine. Studying hard.'

'I wrote to her that she *must* apply to my university. The English department gives assistantships every year to Indian students from DU.'

'Oh.'

'You won't have to worry about her if she comes here, Aunty. I'll keep an eye on her.'

That loving, familiar tone which ultimately meant nothing.

She took in her breath and said it. 'Randhir, do you want to marry Mallika?'

Dead silence.

'Because if you don't, then you should make that clear to Mallika.'

Still, that dead silence.

'You don't want to get married to her, Randhir, and yet you call her to America?'

'Does Mallika think –' He stopped.

'Mallika never says anything. But I'm her mother. I know her. So please, make it clear to her.'

'That would be very presumptuous of me. We've never talked about marriage. Or anything of the sort.' The warmth had gone from his voice.

'I thought you loved each other.'

'We're friends, Aunty. We've never said or done anything to the contrary.'

No, it wasn't that the warmth had gone from his voice. It was that he was trying very hard to keep his voice from breaking.

'She's applying to American universities because of you, Randhir.'

'No, Aunty. She's wanted to study abroad forever.'

Forever? Mallika had told him, and Dr Roy, but not her?

With difficulty, she found the words. 'She's still very fragile after that TB. There'll be no one for her if her health… isn't good in America.'

Another silence.

'Alright, Randhir. Bye.'

'I'm sorry, Aunty. I'm *so* sorry.' His voice broke.

She put the receiver back and sat down on Madhu's sofa. She could never discuss any of this with Madhu. Taking out Shantacca's hanky from her blouse, she wept into it once more. She had once thought Karan had imposed a sentence of silence on her. She now knew that silence was also a sentence that you imposed on yourself to keep your friendships.

Mallika: Rama, Lakshmana, and Surpanakha

1980

Randhir and Vineet came home for a month in July, and the morning after his arrival, Randhir dropped in and greeted me with a big hug.

'Now *he's* hugging you too? What is all this nonsense?' Ma demanded after he left.

Randhir threw an I'm-back-from-America party.

'Imagine, I already have a Volvo *and* a credit card,' Vineet said. We were on the terrace. Downstairs, 'Stairway to Heaven' was blaring into the night.

'What's a Volvo?' I asked.

There was a stunned silence.

'It's a *car*, Mallika,' Vineet said faintly.

'But… how would I know? I haven't been to America.'

'It's a Swedish car,' Arnav said.

'How are we to know about foreign cars when there are only three cars in India?' Prabha said, taking a drag from Arnav's joint. She was here for a month on holiday from Poona

'I knew what a Volvo was more than a decade before I went to America,' Randhir said.

'How?' I asked.

The boys looked flummoxed. But then, so was I.

Gauri, who had come from JNU to spend the weekend with us, also rose to my defence. 'Yes, how? You don't see foreign cars here, even on TV.'

'You don't have to see things to know about them,' said Arnav.

'Do you know about the Nutan?' Gauri asked.

'She's an old-time actress,' Vineet said.

'I didn't say Nutan, I said *the* Nutan,' Gauri said.

The boys looked at her blankly.

'See,' Gauri said triumphantly. 'The Nutan's right *here*, in India, in *every* house, and you people *still* don't know.'

'It's a stove,' I said. 'When the gas cylinder finishes, that's what our mothers use until the next cylinder arrives.'

'You're comparing an Indian *stove* to a Volvo?' Vineet said.

'You expect us to know about Swedish cars when we've never seen any,' Gauri said. 'But *you* don't know about the Nutan feeding you right here in India.'

'*That's* ignorance,' Prabha agreed.

I wanted to hug my friends.

'*And* it's air conditioned *and* has a music system,' Vineet said blissfully.

'How can you afford to buy cars as a student?' I asked.

'Because it's America,' Vineet said.

'He took a loan,' said Randhir.

I gasped. 'But you're a *student*!'

'In America, they give loans to everyone, even students,' Vineet said breezily.

Gauri, Prabha, and I tried to digest this information.

'It's a *good* thing to take loans in America,' Vineet assured us. 'You build up your credit history.'

We looked at him blankly.

Randhir explained. 'Credit history means your track record of taking and returning loans.'

I looked at Gauri and Prabha, who appeared as astounded as I was feeling.

'If you *don't* take loans, you won't have a good credit history, and then when you get a job, you can't buy a house,' Vineet said.

'None of this makes sense,' Gauri said, shaking her head.

'So... what exactly is a credit card?' I asked.

'Oh, it's like a loan from the bank,' Randhir said.

'Yeah, you buy *everything* with it,' Vineet said.

'You take loans to buy *everything*?' I was stunned.

'Mallika, you really have to get rid of your Indian mentality,' Vineet said.

'You pay back the credit card every month, Mallika,' Randhir said.

'Oh,' I said. 'But still. Don't people end up buying more than what they can afford?'

Randhir laughed. 'Exactly.'

'Then?' I asked.

'Then you pay interest,' Randhir said.

'Do you pay interest on your card?' I asked Vineet.

'Who doesn't?' Vineet shrugged.

'Oh, my god,' Gauri said. 'What a way to live.'

'You're both such dehatis,' Vineet said, looking at her dreamily. She was looking radiant in a rust-coloured saree with an embroidered black border from the Karnataka Emporium. Vineet hadn't been able to take his eyes off her all evening.

Vineet had been writing regularly to Gauri. She seemed unaffected by this. She had been hardening her heart with a vengeance. I, alas, had had no luck in that area. My heart had become soft as putty after all these months in Arnav's company, and Randhir's arrival had precipitated such rapid melting that it was a wonder it could beat at all.

The boys were raucous with joy at being together. Now, Randhir and Arnav had just one thing in mind: that I should get aid at *their* university. 'We'll be crushed if you don't,' Arnav had said, making my heart leap even though he'd said 'we' rather than 'I.' 'But you *will* get aid. I'm sure your letter's got delayed in the post.' Which was possible; this often happened with letters from abroad.

Vineet turned to me. 'Mallika, let's practice for your visa interview.'

'But you know I don't have aid.'

'If you get it, you should be ready with your answers.'

'I know the answers.'

'No-no-no, you're very old-fashioned.'

Prabha took a drag from Randhir's joint, and Gauri looked at her worriedly.

'OK, so I'm the visa guy at the American Embassy,' Vineet said. 'First question: why do you want to do your PhD in America and not in India?'

'Because it's a wonderful opportunity to study in another country and travel and have new experiences and... everything.'

'Completely wrong. Say, "Because I'll have better job opportunities when I return to India." Point being, you're coming back. That's what they want to hear.'

'Hmm.'

'OK, next question. How do we know you'll come back to India?'

'Because I'm an only child, and my mothers are here.'

'Say "mother," not "mothers."'

'Oh, so they're not going to give me a visa if I say "mothers?"'

'Mallika, you're a bookworm, so I'll give you a book analogy. When you read a book, you have the main story, no? You don't want to hear the stories of all the various lafangas in the book, do you?'

'I do.'

'Well, Americans don't. They want the main story. Don't go all Indian on them.'

'Having two mothers *is* one of my main stories.' I was feeling somewhat agitated.

'One *of*?' Vineet asked. 'A main story is a main story. That's *one*. Not one *of*.'

'You're wrong. It's *one of*.' I was feeling more agitated.

'Mallika, you're not just old-fashioned, but you're also damn obstinate.'

'She's absolutely right,' Gauri said. 'Westerners want to fit Indians into *their* categories. Like this Indian girl who was born and bred in America and informed *me* that Brahmins don't eat meat. Why should Mallika subscribe to that kind of thinking?'

'Absolutely. Why should Mallika lie about something so fundamental in her life?' Prabha said.

'Because she isn't Gandhi, and this isn't the freedom movement,' Vineet sighed.

Randhir and Arnav leaned back against the parapet, listening lazily.

'OK,' Vineet continued. 'Next question: do you have property in India?'

'No.'

'Your house, Mallika, your house!'

'It's my mother's house, Vineet.'

'Same thing, Mallika. Say, "My mother has a house." You've already said you're an only child. Obviously it'll be yours one day.'

One day? Now I was supposed to offer that one day to the visa officer like prasad?

'Next question: what's to stop you from marrying an American and becoming an American citizen?'

'I'm not getting married.'

'You're not getting *married*?'

'No.'

'Don't you want *children*?'

'No.'

'But don't you want… *love*?'

'I have it.'

'No, but after your mothers? You'll be all *alone*.'

'No, I won't.'

Vineet tried to grasp this. He couldn't.

Actually, neither could I, but what else to say?

'No way the visa guy will believe someone like you doesn't want to get married.'

'Someone like me?'

'You know, your type.' Vineet made an all-encompassing gesture.

My Type. The saree, the bindi, the long hair. He was probably right. If Indians saw me as a type, which they did, then why wouldn't Americans?

'I'm going downstairs to get some coffee,' Prabha said.

Vineet was thinking deeply. After a minute, his expression changed, as though a lightbulb had gone off in his head. 'I have a fantastic idea, Mallika! Just take Randhir or Arnav with you. Wear a ring and say your fiancé is waiting in the hall. Produce him if they ask. If the visa guy knows you're not going to take one of theirs and become one of them, you'll definitely get the visa!'

Randhir and Arnav were looking extremely amused.

'Not a bad idea,' I said slowly. I looked hopefully at Randhir and Arnav. 'Will you do that for me?'

Their amusement dissipated.

'I mean, how will the visa officer know you're not?' I asked.

'Actually,' said Arnav, 'they have all our information on file.'

'Yeah,' Randhir reiterated. *'Everything.'*

'I can say we got engaged now, in July.'

'If they find out it's a lie, we're fucked,' said Arnav.

It was the first time Arnav was using that word before me, which was an indication of how deep his shock was.

Gauri looked at him disapprovingly. She hated bad language.

'"Fiancé" sounds fishy; they'll say, "How come you're not getting married before you go?" I mean, that's what Indian couples going to grad school do,' Arnav said.

'Yeah,' Randhir said. 'These visa guys always want to see a marriage certificate.'

'Yeah, they know no Indian parent is going to send their daughter off to America with a fiancé – they know in India, marriage is the only way,' Arnav said.

I sighed.

There was a charged silence.

'I mean, I can do it, Mallika,' Randhir said, as though he were being marched off to the gallows. 'It's just that… I might be gone by the time you hear about aid.'

He hoped.

'If you think it'll help, I'll do it,' said Arnav, as though he were also facing the hangman.

'Mallika, I'm hungry, come downstairs with me,' Gauri said, grabbing my arm.

Walking down the stairs, I began to rock with laughter. 'Did you see their faces at the prospect of being my fiancé?'

'Oh, my god! You were *pretending*? Mallika, even *I* believed you!'

We went downstairs to Mahima's room and shut the door, both of us laughing hysterically. Then we saw that Prabha was lying on Mahima's bed, eyes closed. She opened them. 'I'm fine, just sleeping.' She closed them again.

Gauri and I sighed with relief and sat down on the bed.

'Gauri, do you and Prabha know what a Volvo is?'

'I know only because Vineet's been fantasizing about cars with me since I was sixteen.'

'I know because I like cars,' Prabha murmured.

There was a knock on the door.

It was Vineet. 'Hi, what's going on?'

'Nothing,' Gauri said.

Vineet gave me a meaningful look as we came out of the room.

Oh.

'You both catch up, I'll join you later,' I said, going to the sitting room. Excited anticipation filled me. It looked like Vineet was going to bare his heart to Gauri! At last!

'Wish You Were Here' was blaring, and at the other end of the room, I could see Rajesh of the six Indian languages waxing eloquent. I rapidly helped myself to naan, butter chicken, dahivadas, and aloo gobi from the dining table and escaped to the back veranda before Rajesh saw me.

Within five minutes, Rajesh was ensconced cosily next to me on the back veranda steps.

'Great to see you, Mallika. Orissi saree this time, hanh? You're looking damn good.'

'Thank you.' Why didn't Arnav or Randhir ever say I was looking damn good?

He leaned back. 'Is that your real hair or are you wearing a parandi?'

'The entire thing is a parandi.'

He roared with laughter. 'Mallika, your deadpan look is too good!'

Preempting flirtation was a losing battle.

'So you and Arnav both have admission at the same university as Randhir?'

I nodded. 'I haven't got aid, though.'

'You'll get it, you'll get it.' He whispered, 'So which one of them is it?'

'Huh?'

'Which one of them are you going to choose? Randhir or Arnav?'

'Both.'

He roared with laughter. 'Come on, Mallika! You're not the type!'

The Type. Again.

Rajesh got up. 'I'll be back in two minutes, I'll just get some food.'

I went to the kitchen, put my plate in the sink, slipped out of the back door, and went to my own house, where I sat in the back veranda at an angle where Rajesh wouldn't be able to see me. I had to sort out the wheat from the chaff.

OK, so Randhir and Arnav cared for me. They missed me when I wasn't around. They were delighted every time they saw me. They gave me fraternal hugs that made me fly. They protected me. They wanted me safe and happy and well-fed with ice creams. And then, they would leave me and get on with their lives, knowing I'd be there for them whenever they returned, wagging my tail joyfully. But if they were to get engaged to me, then they'd be fucked.

After flying so high, I'd finally crashed.

Maybe it was true, what I had told Vineet – that I wasn't going to get married and didn't want children. If I could never feel for any man what I felt for those two, then how could I get married? How could I live, eat, and sleep with a man I didn't love, or bear his children, or smell his bad breath every morning?

Randhir materialized and planted himself next to me. 'I knew you'd be hiding here,' he said affectionately.

We had spent hours and hours talking about his university, and he'd showed me tons of photos of his friends and the beautiful campus. Now, we sat in silence. He'd better not start ranting about Indira Gandhi having been voted back as Prime Minister and the state of the country, I thought. The state of Mallika was what I was preoccupied with.

He lit a cigarette. 'You didn't mean it, no? That you never want to get married or have children?'

'I meant it.'

'I'm not getting married either.'

'You'll change your mind when you meet the next Charu.'

'Charu didn't mean anything to me.'

'Then why were you with her?'

Imagine. It had taken me four years to ask.

He shrugged.

Why was it that when you asked a male friend a personal question, he gave you a shrug, a one-liner, silence, or a stupid joke, whereas when you asked a female friend, she gave you reams and reams of explanation?

'Why don't you want to get married?' I asked.

He didn't answer immediately. Then he said, 'Because I want to live *my* life.'

In short, a selfish life, Shantamama would say.

But why not? I found myself questioning Shantamama. Better to live a selfish life as an unmarried man than to live the selfish life of a married man.

'Arnav's become a good friend, no?'

I nodded, a little surprised by the sudden change of subject.

'Yeah. He's a little careless and oblivious sometimes, but he'll grow out of that. He's a damn good guy at heart. He'd be a fantastic match for you.'

I couldn't believe it. He wouldn't marry me, so he was passing me onto his best friend?

'In case you change your mind about marriage,' he said apologetically.

'Why don't you suggest it to him? I'm sure he'll be overcome.'

'No need to get hassled, Mallika. I mean, think about it: this way, the three of us will always be together!'

You think I'm looking for a ménage à trois? I wanted to shriek but didn't, because I didn't know how to pronounce it.

Randhir gave me an uneasy look.

Arnav materialized before us.

'Got to help Mummy, see you soon,' Randhir said with relief, and disappeared.

'Madhu Aunty's rasmalais are laid out,' Arnav said. 'Thought I'd call you.'

Ah. I needed a heavy dose of something sweet.

Arnav sat next to me. 'You didn't mean it, did you? About not getting married?'

'I did.' I got up. 'Let's go and have rasmalais.'

'Just *ask* him and get it over with, one way or the other.'

I looked at him, baffled.

'I wish you'd just speak out, Mallika. Is it *that* difficult for you, even after all this time?'

Surely he couldn't be –

'Mallika, *ask* Randhir. Or are you going to just keep waiting for him?'

I felt apoplectic. 'Who do you and Randhir think I am? Surpanakha?'

'Surpa – who?'

'You know what a Volvo is, but you don't know who Surpanakha is?'

Gauri materialized. She was glowing. 'Mallika! I was looking everywhere for you!'

She was bursting with news.

The three of us went back to Madhu Aunty's house and helped ourselves to rasmalais. Then we joined Randhir, Vineet, Prabha, and a group of other friends in the back veranda. Vineet whispered to me, 'Today's the happiest day of my life!'

I wanted to shout out with joy. Finally!

'Mallika,' Arnav said. 'What did you say, who was that person – Surpa-what?'

'Surpanakha.'

A few people in the group began to laugh.

'Why are you talking of Surpanakha, of all people?' Rajesh said.

'Such an *awful* story,' Gauri said.

'Actually, it's quite funny,' Rajesh said.

'Yeah,' said another friend. 'Have any of you watched the Ramleela dance drama at the Feroz Shah Kotla grounds? That scene with Rama, Lakshmana, and Surpanakha is hilarious!'

'What's the story?' Randhir asked.

'Surpanakha is Ravana's sister, who falls in love with Rama,' Gauri said. 'But Rama says he's already married to Sita and can't marry her, and tells Surpanakha she can have his brother. So Surpanakha goes to Lakshmana, who says he can't marry her and sends her back to Rama. The brothers keep sending her from one to the other, having a good laugh at her expense.'

Arnav clearly hadn't got it.

Well, he hadn't heard Randhir's suggestion to me.

'It's damn funny, yar,' Rajesh chortled.

'What's so funny about a woman being humiliated like that?' Prabha asked.

'Come on, Prabha, where's your sense of humour?' Rajesh said good-naturedly.

'And then Lakshmana cuts off Surpanakha's nose with his sword,' another girl said.

'Is that funny too, Rajesh?' Prabha said.

'Indian mythology is full of stuff like that – you can't take everything so seriously,' Rajesh argued.

'Actually, it's Hindu mythology, not Indian mythology,' Gauri said.

'Same thing,' Rajesh said.

There was a silence.

'How is it the same thing?' one of Randhir's friends asked.

There was another, longer silence.

'And why shouldn't we take stories like this seriously, given how Rama's worshipped as the perfect example of righteousness?' Prabha said.

'I'm going to have some rasmalais,' Rajesh said, and escaped.

'Rasmalais, oh, fantastic,' someone else said.

The group broke up, leaving Randhir, Arnav, and me together.

Arnav was looking at me as though I were Brutus. 'Mallika, how on earth do *Randhir* and *I* make you feel like Surpanakha?'

'Mallika said that?' Randhir exclaimed.

'Yeah,' Arnav said. 'I mean, when have we *ever* laughed at you or humiliated you?'

'Yeah,' Randhir agreed, shocked. 'When?'

Speak up, Mallika.

'You' – I nodded in Randhir's direction – 'said Arnav would be a damn good match for me if I changed my mind about marriage. And you' – I nodded in Arnav's direction – 'said I should ask Randhir what he felt and not keep waiting for him just because I can't ask.'

Randhir and Arnav stared at me. Then at each other. Then back at me.

'I'm not planning to marry either of you. So no need to toss me so generously from one to the other.'

I went into the house, carrying their shocked faces with me.

Dr Roy was absolutely right. I needed to speak my mind more often.

Of course, as you know, it wasn't my mind. But at least I'd saved face, hadn't I? And so, I dried my tears in Mahima's bathroom and went out to brave the crowd.

Back in my house for the night, Gauri, Prabha, and I talked and talked.

Vineet had indeed bared his heart to Gauri. He said he had loved her all his life as a friend and had not realized when it had become more than that. Yes, of course he had loved Jaspreet, but that was over. Jaspreet was a young love. What he felt for her, Gauri, was a mature love. He wanted to marry her. He wanted her to meet his family before he went back to America. He said they should get married within a year. He simply didn't know how he would live without her in America, already he couldn't bear it.

Prabha and I listened, stupefied with satisfaction at the happily-ever-after. Prabha, although fond of lecturing us on our romantic notions, did have a few of her own, one of them being that there could only be one true love in your life, a notion that we all shared. Yes, there were two in mine, neither of whom was madly nor even moderately in love with me, but even if that changed, I could only end up with one, no? As even Rajesh of the six languages knew, I was the type.

'Did he kiss you?' Prabha asked.

'Of course. Not too long, though. You know how it is. No place.'

'No place' was the unfortunate story for most Indians in love. And for those who had a place, like Arnav, there was usually a Mrs D'Souza. It was a wonder that unmarried couples managed to have sex at all.

The next morning, my friends and I were finishing a late breakfast with my mothers and grandmother when the postman announced his arrival with a loud knocking at the door.

'From Amreeka,' the postman grinned, handing me a letter.

'Have you got aid? Have you got aid?' Prabha was by my side.

I opened the letter. It was from Randhir's university in Pennsylvania, but it didn't say anything about an assistantship. It was some kind of a signed form.

'What?' said Shantamama, her hand on her heart. 'Quickly, tell us.'

Ma was very pale. Ajji was the only one who looked calm.

'No aid. It's just some form.'

'Randhir'll know,' Gauri said.

Prabha, Gauri, and I rushed next door with the letter.

Randhir and Arnav were at the dining table, bleary-eyed after the party, eating a late breakfast of gobi parathas.

'Randhir, what's this? No, don't touch, your hand's oily.' I held it before him.

He looked at it from top to bottom. Then again, from top to bottom. He looked up at me and gasped, 'You've got aid! This is an I-20. You've got aid!'

Arnav gave a shout of joy. 'I *knew* you would!'

As I held the form for Arnav to read, Randhir explained. You needed the I-20 to apply for a visa. If I had got it, it meant that I had aid. I had written to the university accepting the admission on the condition that I had a complete tuition waiver and a teaching assistantship, hadn't I? Well, it looked like the aid letter had got lost in the post. We had to phone the English department tonight.

We rushed back home and told my mothers and grandmother.

All three were grave and silent.

Ajji said, 'The letter, it will come when the time is correct for it to come.'

She and my mothers then proceeded to go about their day.

That night, Randhir booked a trunk call from his phone, and I spoke to the English department secretary, who said that my aid letter had been sent a month ago. They would send another letter right away.

The next morning, the original aid letter arrived. I looked at the date. It had taken *five weeks* to come to India, instead of the usual one-to-two weeks.

We went rushing to Randhir again. Arnav was there too. They said I should apply for the visa the next day. 'OK, which of you will be my fiancé?' I asked. I was joking – but the boys looked at each other with resignation.

'Heads or tails?' Randhir asked, taking out a ten-paisa coin.

'Tails,' said Arnav, and Randhir tossed the coin. Tails it was.

'Here – wear my ring, it looks real, but it isn't,' Gauri said, taking it off her finger and putting it on my left ring finger. She was biting her lip, trying not to laugh.

I already had all my papers ready, including Ma's house papers, thanks to Arnav, who had advised that I should be prepared with them in case I got aid.

The next morning, Arnav drove me to the American Embassy.

My name was called around one p.m.

The visa officer was young, blue-eyed and blonde. He looked at my papers and said, 'What do you plan to do with your PhD?'

'I'd like to return to India and teach.'

'I see.' He looked at my papers again. There was no expression on his face.

'Are you saying you won't work in America?'

'No. I'm an only child.'

'What do your parents do?'

'My mother teaches English at Delhi University. She's a widow.'

My Shantamama was my mother too. I hadn't mentioned her. This was *awful.*

'So is it just you and your mother?'

'I have two mothers,' I said with great relief. 'She and her sister brought me up.'

There was a twitch of surprise on his face.

'You could marry an American and never return.'

'I don't want to marry.'

Another twitch. 'An Indian woman who doesn't want to marry!'

He was no better than these Indian boys. I was The Type to him too.

'There are many more opportunities for you in America.'

'In India, women become Prime Ministers.'

His brows flew up to his forehead. 'Is that so?'

Two minutes later, I was back in the hall. I waved to Arnav. He got up and came to me. 'He wants to talk to my fiancé,' I said.

'Shit. OK.'

I began to chuckle. 'I was joking, Arnav.'

He gave a shout of laughter. 'You're good at this, you know.'

'Arnav. He didn't give me the visa.'

He stopped laughing. '*What?*'

'So that's that.'

He didn't say a word.

I hopped onto his bike, and we made our way to Nirula's, where we were to meet the others for lunch.

Randhir, Vineet, Prabha, and Gauri were halfway through lunch when we arrived. They looked at me, full of expectation, as we went to their table.

'I didn't get it.'

It wasn't a very animated lunch. Randhir was bitterly disappointed and didn't talk. Nor did Arnav. Vineet was the only one chatting and joking. Gauri and Prabha and I enjoyed his jokes; I certainly needed the laughter. I knew Gauri and Prabha were disappointed for me, but another part of them, I could see, was relieved I wasn't going away. As for me, all I could think of was that this would be my goodbye to Arnav.

'What have they stamped on your passport, Mallika?' Randhir said. 'Show it to me.'

'I don't have it.'

'What d'you mean, you don't have it?'

'He said to collect it after four.'

Arnav put down his fork. 'He said what?'

'To collect it after four.'

The boys stared at me in disbelief.

'That means you've got the bloody visa, Mallika,' Randhir said.

'If they reject it, they stamp that on your passport and give it to you there and then,' Vineet said.

My heart began to thud. 'Are you sure?'

'What did the guy say?'

I told them about the interview. 'And then he said, "You haven't persuaded me." Then he said, "You can collect your passport after four."'

'You've *got* it,' said Arnav.

'Oh, my *god*, you've got it,' said Randhir.

'Of *course* you've got it,' said Vineet.

After lunch, the others headed home, and Arnav and I drove towards the American Embassy to collect my passport. There was a lot of traffic, and a DTC bus was just behind us. Ahead were four cows, draped across the road in the kind of bovine bliss that seems to assail all cows in the middle of traffic. Suddenly, a little boy ran across the road right in front of us. I was holding on to Arnav with one arm and as he braked, I instinctively put my other arm around him. I heard the screaming sound of the bus behind us braking.

The bus hit our motorcycle anyway.

We flew off the bike.

And I mean *flew*. We were flying, Arnav and I, my arms wrapped tightly around him. Everything slowed. Scenes from my life flashed around me. *Ma, Shantamama.*

We descended, landing on the carpet of cows.

The carpet mooed and protested. A couple of cows, still mooing, began to rise from their haunches. We slid off them onto the road, my arms still around Arnav. He was saying something. People were milling around us. Everyone was talking. Everything was silent.

The silence broke.

'Mallika, are you OK?'

A crowd around us, exclaiming, blabbering, shrieking.

Arnav was feeling my head, my shoulders, my arms.

The cows had settled down around us again.

We were surrounded by a huge crowd. A man in a saffron kurta had taken centre stage. 'This is God's mercy,' he was saying in Hindi. 'Look, these cows have saved their lives. This is gau matha's kripa. Dekho' – he pointed to us – 'can this happen in any other country? Never. Such a miracle can only happen in our Hindustan. Tell me why?'

Someone in the crowd shouted, 'Because only in Hindustan is the cow our mother.'

'Shabash!' said the saffron man. 'Only in Hindustan do we revere the cow. Bolo, gau matha ki?'

'Jai!' shouted the crowd.

'Got to get out of here,' Arnav muttered, his arm behind me. 'Come on, Mallika.'

But we couldn't move. The crowd pushed us back towards the cows.

'Gau matha ki?'

'Jai,' roared the crowd.

'Gau matha ki?'

'Jai,' shrieked the crowd.

'Fuck,' said Arnav under his breath.

Twice now.

'We have witnessed a miracle today,' saffron man said. He rushed across the road where a man was sitting with a pile of coconuts and agarbattis.

The crowd made loud sounds of approval and delight. Traffic had come to a complete standstill. Cars, buses, scooters, and trucks honked furiously. No one cared.

Saffron man returned with a coconut and a smoking agarbatti. He thrust the agarbatti into my hand, prostrated himself before the cows, broke the coconut on the road, and poured the coconut water all over the cows, chanting a mantra.

Then he turned to us.

'Saubhagyavati,' he continued in Hindi, his hands folded. 'Show your gratitude to gau matha.'

Clearly saffron man saw me as The Type too. The Sati-Savitri-married Type.

'Bolo, bolo,' he said.

'Thank you,' I murmured to the cows.

'Saubhagyavati,' said saffron man, shocked. 'You are a Hindu naari. This is no way. There is no diya, but you have the agarbatti, do you not?'

What on earth was he talking about?

'Bechari,' saffron man explained to the crowd. He took the smoking agarbatti from me and circled the cows with it three times. 'Like this,' he said to me, giving me the agarbatti.

I fainted against Arnav.

Arnav stumbled but managed not to fall. 'Mallika,' he gasped, his arms tight around me.

'I'm OK,' I murmured into his ear, then half-closed my eyes and lay still.

Like the waters of the sea, the crowd parted.

I was picked up and deposited at the bus stop. Arnav sat next to me. I let my head loll on his shoulder. He put his arm behind me.

After a few minutes of bliss, Arnav murmured, 'All clear.'

I opened my eyes. He was looking at me, his eyes full of laughter. 'Saubhagyavati, chalo, I have to get the bike towed.'

It was too late to collect the visa. Arnav said he'd take me the next morning, but I said no, I'd do it on my own.

I had an early breakfast and took two buses to the American Embassy, where I picked up my passport with the brand-new, shining American student visa.

As Shantamama always said, a miss is as good as a mile, and since we hadn't died, I could now happily relive flying on the motorcycle with my arms around Arnav as though we were one, his arms holding me tight when I fainted, and the feel of his arm around me for five whole minutes at the bus stop. I was sure, though, that his thoughts hadn't kept him awake all night the way mine had.

I was right. Ma and I were drying clothes in our back veranda when I saw a girl shimmying down the drainpipe of Arnav's terrace. Ma was facing me so she didn't see, and I prayed she wouldn't turn. The girl reached the bottom without any mishap, walked towards us leisurely, stopped and said, 'Mallika! Is that you?'

It was Mohini of the I-once-had-a-threesome fame, who was looking extremely pretty and utterly delighted to see me.

Ten minutes later, Mohini was ensconced in our sitting room.

'Phew! I almost got caught by that Mrs D'Souza.'

'Oh.'

'Yeah, I spent the night with him, and she came bounding up the stairs this morning and banged at his door. I grabbed my bag – thank god I was dressed – and split.'

'How did you manage to get into his room?'

'I'd come to spend the night with a friend in the colony and found out he lives here. I went to his barsati around eleven. Mrs D'Souza must have been asleep.'

'You slept with him?'

'What d'you think, Mallika? That we lay chastely side by side all night!'

The balloon I'd been floating in all last night and this morning burst.

'Virtue is damn boring, Mallika.'

True. If only I knew how to go about changing that.

'Try him, he's delicious.'

'Well, since he comes so highly recommended, maybe I should.'

She burst out laughing. 'Oh, there he is.'

Arnav was at the door, looking a little apprehensive.

'Hi,' I said.

He came in. 'I just came to find out if you're OK after yesterday.'

'I'm fine.'

'Mallika said she'll try you since you come so highly recommended,' Mohini chortled.

Arnav froze.

'I didn't… I meant… I didn't mean… I was joking,' I stammered.

Mohini blew me a kiss and got up. 'See you both next time I come.' She gave Arnav a radiant smile and left.

'What was all that about?' Arnav said furiously.

'You, obviously.'

'Obviously?'

'She told me about sleeping with you.'

I meant to say she told me she slept with you. *About* sleeping with you sounded ominous.

Clearly, he thought so too. He was deprived of speech.

He sat down.

'It didn't mean anything,' he said, after thirty seconds of silence.

But it had happened. It had happened on the heels of him being so bitterly disappointed about my not getting the visa, and his joy when he discovered that I had, and his arm around me in the bus stop.

I said, 'How can it not mean anything?'

Helping himself to a murku from the table, he rapidly changed the subject. 'I came to find out how you're feeling – sometimes the pain comes the next day.'

Well, it certainly had.

He finished the murku and helped himself to another. 'It didn't mean anything to her either.'

'How come?'

He got up. 'I'll see you later. Bye.'

He left.

Before I could run upstairs and burst into tears, he was back.

'Because everyone isn't like you,' he said, and left.

I rushed upstairs to my room and buried my burning face in my hands. It would have served me right if he'd said, 'It's none of your business.'

Obviously I knew they'd slept with each other because that was what people did. Obviously love wasn't always a part of this equation, neither for men nor for women. I wasn't such an idiot that I didn't know that. Perhaps what I was asking him was something quite different. Perhaps I was asking him about us. How stupid of me. Because it was true, what Arnav said. Everyone wasn't like me. *My* world wasn't *the* world. In Vineet's words, I was old-fashioned. Meaning stupid. Meaning boring.

Randhir returned to America. Arnav and I went to the travel agent with our bank drafts and booked our tickets. The following day, we purchased our dollars.

My mothers and grandmother had received the news of my visa calmly. Strength seemed to rise in them like sap. They got busy. They bought me small packets of masalas, one bottle of coconut oil, five packets of dal, and Aristocrat and VIP suitcases. Ma – even before I got the visa – had already had three sweaters knitted for me by a lady in the neighbourhood and had had ten handloom skirts made for me by Madhu Aunty's tailor. Bedsheets and towels. A year's supply of the depression medicines and sleeping pills from various chemists. Ayah-ji refused to believe I was going across the oceans and that she wouldn't see me for a year or more.

I said goodbye to Masi. I was overwhelmed and inarticulate. We hugged and hugged. I thanked her for everything and said I would write to her. She asked me if I had any thoughts about the dream that she and I had entered when she had worked on me a few months before, the one with the banging on the door and my mothers commanding me to 'meet it.' I shook my head. It was one of those things – like so many others in my life – that I didn't understand. Yet it lay inside me quietly, as distinct as aquatic life under clear waters, a vision that I looked at from time to time, with wonder more than curiosity.

Saying goodbye to Dr Roy wasn't easy either. He asked me to stay with the small dose of antidepressants that I was taking for at least another couple of years. He gave me the name and phone number of his good friend, another psychiatrist in Philadelphia, and said if I ever needed to, I could phone him without hesitation. He said he had already spoken to him about me. I thanked him, my throat choked up. He shook hands with me, wished me well, and said he was certain I would do very well in life.

It was now time to pay Dr Raghunath. I finally had the thousand rupees in a brown paper envelope in the box under my bed.

I pulled the box out from under the bed, took out the envelope, counted the money, and put it in my handbag, into the large, zipped inner compartment. Then, after ten a.m., when it was likely to be less crowded, I took two buses to the gynae's clinic. Unfortunately, the buses were still crowded that morning, and I had to go standing all the way. From the bus stop, I walked fifteen minutes to the clinic, which was well inside the colony. At the car park, I opened the zip compartment of my handbag, just to double check.

The envelope of money was gone.

No. Impossible.

I checked every inch of my bag.

Then I saw it. A large, beautiful cut on the other side of my bag. Someone in one of the two crowded buses had quietly and efficiently cut through the bag, all the way into the zip compartment. All the money I had collected for so long was well and truly gone.

On my two return buses, I was able to obtain window seats. I spent the entire journey facing the window with my hand shading my eyes, weeping. In the first bus, there was a young man next to me who kept saying, 'Madam, you tell me only, I will help you.' I shook my head and continued crying, while he kept clicking his tongue in sympathy. In the second bus, there was a white-haired woman in her seventies next to me who asked me compassionately if someone had died. I shook my head. She said, 'Beti, think of what you will feel if the person you love most in this world was dead. And then think of the problem you are having now. Is the problem you are having now worse than that?'

This made my tears stop short.

The loss of one thousand rupees was nothing compared to the death of my mothers. Nothing.

'Dekho,' said the old woman, seeing my face and nodding her head in satisfaction.

By the time the bus reached home, my tears had abated.

I walked home from the bus stop, ran upstairs to my room before anyone could exclaim at my red eyes and nose, washed my face, sat on my bed, and thought about what I should do.

When people say you have choices in life, they're thinking of choices in a very different way from the way my mothers, my friends, and I thought of choices. Some choices simply didn't exist. Like, for example, leaving your marriage. That was the world we lived in. But within that world, there was also *our* world. In *our* world, we couldn't conceive of not returning money that we owed. I *had* to return the money. And I had to return it before I left for America.

True, I had not thought of the money till I ran into Dr Raghunathan. This was because that entire experience existed in another reality. Then I met the doctor, and the money I owed her became real.

How did the rest remain unreal?

It didn't. The rest had also become real to me the day I ran into Dr Raghunathan. This was my reality: The first corrupt gynae had lied to me about a pregnancy. I had a very heavy period the next day. The second gynae tended to that heavy period. I became temporarily crazy. Then I recovered.

Randhir had gone back to America. Prabha was still in Delhi, and Gauri was back in JNU, but neither of them had that kind of money. Arnav, however, had been working for two years. Perhaps he did? I would return it to him in America. Returning was the easy part. The difficult part was asking him for such a large amount just two days before our departure without telling him why I needed it. Arnav was packing and winding up to move back home for his last night. The only time I could have alone with him before he shifted back home would be early the next morning.

I had to lie to him. I practiced the lie all night. That I had to return the money to a friend because I'd borrowed and lost her gold chain. If Mrs D'Souza caught me, I'd say I was calling him for a walk.

I got up very early, had a quick bath, and dressed. Using my small hand-held mirror, I dabbed a spot of lipstick on my pale cheeks and spread it with my palm. Then, for good measure, I applied a coating of lipstick. The colour was too dark. I applied Vaseline on my lips to lighten it. The paler I looked, the sooner he'd see how overwrought I was. It was still dark. I quietly went out of the side door, locked it from outside, walked swiftly to Mrs D'Souza's house, and climbed up the stairs to Arnav's barsati.

Randhir: Darpoke?

1980

As his flight to New York took off from Palam airport, he was aware for the first time in his life that the cloud which had always enveloped him was lifting. He could feel it, physically. It felt as though his eyesight had improved overnight and that every colour was brighter, every angle and curve of every object in the plane sharper. It was no longer a blur of people; every person was clearly himself or herself. Even the smell of the plane dinner wafting down from the other end seemed appetizing. His muscles were beginning to relax, as if they were, drop by drop, releasing something long held.

How come he was feeling *now* what he should have felt the previous year? The cloud hadn't lifted when he first left for America. Nor had it lifted when he looked around him in wonder at the beautiful college town where his university sprawled in all its loveliness. Nor when he plunged so completely into his writing life. Nor, for that matter, a few months ago, when he'd fallen desperately in love with Cameron, a student at Columbia, and had embarked on his first, heady relationship. In America, he had all the privacy he wanted, there was no one telling him what to do, no one judging him, no one cared a shit. Yet the cloud, like a haze around him, wouldn't go.

Nor had he felt the cloud lifting during his four weeks at home, even though his parents weren't putting any pressure on him regarding the family business or marriage. On the contrary, he had felt racked with guilt at their silence. He'd been thrilled about Arnav getting his visa and ecstatic when Mallika got hers. But even then, he hadn't had this feeling of... What was it? Freedom? Yes, that's what it felt like, even though he didn't know why. It was as if his body understood what had changed even though his mind did not.

'You're happy in America, no?' Mallika had asked him the night after he came to India, as they and Arnav chatted on the terrace after dinner.

'Oh, *yes*,' he'd answered.

He was happy, despite the haze enveloping it. Happiness for him was the double life: living one in America, living another in India – the life in India no longer unbearable because he knew it wasn't his *whole* life.

He was doing phenomenally well at school, as were the sprinkling of other Indian students across its various departments, all nurtured and encouraged by their professors and given help every step of the way. He'd been reading voraciously about things he'd known only superficially – the civil rights movement, the Vietnam War, the fight to legalize abortion, to name just a few. He had observed with astonishment how religious Americans were, discovered with shock that many kept guns in their homes, and most baffling of all, that most Americans didn't believe the government should 'interfere' by legislating on things like healthcare or maternity leave. A year of living in America, of reading, and of talking to his fellow students wasn't sufficient to answer the question every Indian neighbour asked him: what is America like?

Where to begin except with his university, which he loved? The university wasn't America, but it was certainly *his* America.

'So you like America?' Mallika had asked him.

He began to laugh. 'I don't think I know America yet, Mallika. I just know my university. I love it. And... I think I'm just about starting to discover New York. Though I think of New York as... another country. You know, I can see you at my university.'

'Umm,' Mallika said.

'You're going to be with us, wait and see,' Arnav said.

Mallika smiled at Arnav without answering. She still didn't have news about aid and refused to talk about it. Superstitious as usual, Randhir thought fondly. The extent to which he had missed Mallika and Arnav the year he'd been away had taken him by surprise. He'd felt bereft without them. This summer, he had come to India for them, not for his parents. When he'd booked his plane ticket, he'd had no idea that Arnav had aid, or that Mallika would get it, and that they'd be flying on his heels to College Town.

As they chatted on the terrace, he made Mallika and Arnav laugh by describing his new-age roommate Dave from California and told them how encouraging and kind his professors were, how much he was enjoying his classes, and how teaching was no big deal. Earlier, in his room, he'd shown them photos he'd taken during that stunning golden autumn and that white, white winter. 'You're in those brochures now,' Mallika had said wistfully, and he nodded. 'That's exactly how I felt when I arrived,' he'd said. He didn't tell them that he'd got straight As in all his courses, that his professors were totally taken with his writing, and that his students – if their evaluations were anything to go by – seemed to love his classes. Nor did he tell them that in his second semester, on a trip to New York with friends, he'd met Cameron at a party and ended up spending the night with him. They were both badly, madly smitten, and he'd been twice to New York after that. He knew he was just the latest in Cameron's long list of lovers, but he didn't care.

But over all this lay that cloud; not a black one by any means, more like a mist through which he lived his burgeoning happiness.

'What's the writing like?' Arnav had asked, handing Randhir his joint.

Randhir took a drag. 'I'm doing it all the time. I…' He tried to find the words. 'I feel I'm… going crazy with it, it's like this overflow. I mean… it's almost too much.'

'Fantastic, you *totally* have it now,' Arnav said with satisfaction.

Arnav knew how it was.

Mallika asked Arnav, 'You mean his writing?'

'Yeah.'

She looked at Randhir. 'You didn't have it before?'

It was the very first time she'd asked about his writing.

He shook his head. 'Not in the same way.'

Before he went to America, writing had been his shameful indulgence, his guilty secret. Long before his mother found out he wrote, he'd known how his parents would view his writing: as self-indulgent, as a waste of time, but fine, he could do it as long as it didn't interfere with the things that really mattered – the family business, running the factory, getting married, producing children. What made it shameful, he had realized during his months in America, was not what *they* thought of his writing, but what *he* thought. What made it shameful was that he had felt the same way as his parents, that it *was* self-indulgent and a waste of time. Perhaps that was why he had never shared it with Mallika. Because after telling her he wrote, he would have had to say to her what he'd never had to say to Arnav – don't tell anyone about my writing. The prospect of uttering those words felt like a betrayal of something greater than himself. He'd never had to say it to Arnav, who had been part of it ever since he began writing as a teenager and knew exactly how it was.

'When do you write?' Mallika asked him. And then, before he could answer, 'And where?'

He heard the longing in her voice to enter a world she knew so little about, a longing he'd responded to ever since he'd known her. He said, 'All the time, Mallika. Every day. In my room, in the dining room, in our backyard. In the park. Between classes. When I'm walking. When I'm sitting. That's what writing is, Mallika. That's what no one understands. That it's all the time.'

Mallika's large eyes were listening, consuming every word he was saying, the way she had on the very first day they had discovered each other all those years ago.

He was writing so prolifically that it felt he was running an Olympic race where the racetracks kept changing, trying to catch up with one story running ahead of him, another story sprinting off to the right, a couple of poems skidding furiously forward to the left. Fragments of poems, stories, and ideas littered his notebooks; sometimes when he went through them, he found stuff that he couldn't even remember writing, as though a benign angel had created them for him while he slept. His notebooks were strewn over his desk, his bed, and his bookshelf. He no longer had to hide his writing or lock up his notebooks in his cupboard for fear of his mother snooping; he didn't have to anticipate someone barging into his room without knocking or wince every time he heard his mother indulgently call writing his 'hobby.'

It wasn't his bloody hobby; it was his life. He was living his life. Finally. The feeling was so heady that sometimes he actually felt dizzy with it. Paradoxically, he had never felt so anchored; never had he felt his feet planted so firmly on the ground. No, *in* the ground, as though they were sprouting roots. Even Cameron, that beautiful, flighty, tempestuous man, didn't anchor him like his writing. In fact, Cameron didn't anchor him at all – with Cameron, it was madness, with Cameron, he was Icarus soaring before the fall. If anyone were to ask what Cameron was like, he wouldn't have known how to answer. Cameron was the sun to his Icarus, the end was inevitable.

As the three of them had laughed and chatted on the terrace, he'd observed how close Mallika and Arnav seemed to have become since he'd left for America. It wasn't anything obvious; just the way Mallika's body was so relaxed, and the way they talked as if they'd known each other forever. Had Arnav supplanted him? Had she started talking to Arnav the way she did to him? Did she seek him when she wanted to unburden herself, or when she needed counsel? After Arnav had told him so categorically a year ago that he had no intention of keeping an eye on Mallika, was *this* what had happened?

A couple of days later, he took Mallika out for lunch to a Chinese restaurant. At some point, he casually asked, 'Arnav's a good friend now, isn't he?'

Mallika nodded.

Why was she just nodding? Was she hiding something?

'So... you've told him about your father and... all that?'

'Of course not! I don't confide in him, Randhir!'

'He's totally trustworthy,' he said guiltily.

'I know, but I'm not at home with him the way I am with you.'

Relief swept over him.

'But, Randhir, he knows about Karan. Last year, he guessed.'

'*How?*'

'We were out for lunch and he casually mentioned that I resembled Karan. I just couldn't hide my expression, and he saw it. He said, "He *is* your father."' She let out her breath as though it had just happened.

'And then?'

'And then nothing. I didn't tell him, and he never asked.'

Randhir nodded. Arnav would have put two and two together. He was no fool.

Before Randhir had left for America last year, Arnav had asked him point blank about Mallika; it had been the perfect moment to tell Arnav about himself. It would have cleared up the misunderstanding that had been building up between them about Mallika. If telling the truth was only about trust, he'd have told Arnav right off, that day. But when was telling the truth only about trust? For when your truth crouched in the shadowed muck, the muck that even those closest to your heart likely regarded with disgust, how were you to point to it and say, *Look, that's where I live.*

Even this summer, he couldn't tell them. And it all came to a head at his party. They were on the terrace, listening with huge amusement to Vineet interviewing Mallika in anticipation of her student visa interview. He glanced at Arnav, who was laughing, but with an expression of such tenderness that Randhir reeled. He looked away immediately.

He'd never seen Arnav look this way at any girl. What the hell was going on? *Was* anything going on? Had something happened after he'd left for America? But Mallika wasn't Arnav's type. Arnav had a type that he went for. Or rather, they went for him, and Arnav was only too happy to oblige. His type was a little... wild. The total opposite of Mallika. Surely Mallika wasn't attracted to Arnav – nothing in her demeanour showed it! On the other hand, if Mallika felt anything for Arnav, it wasn't as if it would be written on her face. She hid things well, his Mallika.

His? Yes, *his*.

Mallika had always been his, and Arnav knew it. How could he have explained to Arnav a year ago, the day he'd left for America, that though he could never marry Mallika, he *was* committed to her, totally and irrevocably? He couldn't even explain it to himself.

But Mallika's not yours.

The voice inside him was a like a slap in the face. No, she *wasn't* his.

She could have been. She *would* have been, in every sense of the word, had he pursued it. Yes, pursued *it*, not pursued *her*. It was the idea you pursued, not the person. The idea of being like everyone else, the idea of so-called normalcy. If you weren't like everyone else, you sometimes pursued the idea even more fervently, acting like all the guys around you. Hadn't he done this with Charu, without quite understanding what he was doing? All the while, absorbing Mallika's deep hurt, her sense of betrayal? What a relief it was when Charu went nuts, because he didn't have to continue the bloody façade.

Perhaps he had instinctively known that he could never do to Mallika what he had done to Charu – use Mallika to continue his self-deception. Had he done so, he would have had to carry it to the very end. He'd have had to marry Mallika. Marry her and live his lie forever, or like other men, live his truth covertly. And Mallika would eventually have found out, or he would eventually have told her, and by that time, their love would have died a prolonged, wretched death.

On the terrace at his party, he realized with a sense of impending doom that his relationship with Mallika would dissipate the minute she got married. And she *would* get married. She was traditional, conventional, keen to make her mothers happy, always trying to do the thing her they expected of her. Even if her mothers were saying two diametrically opposed things, Mallika wanted to oblige them by doing both, ending up in one of her tizzies. She was the ultimate marrying-and-having-children kind of girl. Then, after she got married, he'd lose her forever. For which husband would accept their relationship?

As these thoughts rocked his head, he heard Mallika informing Vineet that she wasn't planning on getting married.

Soon after, she disappeared from the party.

After which, he and Arnav screwed up everything.

Randhir found Mallika next door, in her back veranda, sitting on a cane chair and frowning into the night. He sat with her and drew her out of her thoughts. He asked her if she meant it when she said she wasn't going to marry. She said she did. He didn't believe it for an instant, but it was a relief to hear it. It gave him the opening he had been waiting for. He said he wasn't planning to get married either.

There. It was done. Now – if she were waiting for him – she'd stop waiting. And he could stop feeling he was deceiving her.

Mallika didn't look wounded by his declaration.

The relief was enormous; he found himself in a jocular mood, and recalling Arnav's expression on the terrace, he found himself telling Mallika that Arnav would be a fantastic match for her if she changed her mind about marriage.

As soon as it came out, he knew he wasn't joking. If Arnav and Mallika married, he'd never lose Mallika.

To say Mallika was affronted by his suggestion was an understatement.

Within a couple of minutes, Arnav joined them, and Randhir beat a hasty retreat.

But how was he to know the issue was also on Arnav's mind? That he would tell Mallika that, instead of waiting for Randhir, she should ask Randhir what he felt for her?

It wasn't long before Mallika informed them of what they each had said to her. She'd then declared that she had no intention of marrying either of them and stalked off.

He turned to Arnav furiously. 'What the hell, man?'

Arnav gave him a look of disbelief. '*I* should be saying that to *you*.'

This thing had to be put to rest once and for all.

'I told her I'm never getting married,' Randhir said.

'You told her you're never getting married, or that you'll never marry *her*?'

'Same thing.'

'Not the same thing.'

'It's exactly the same thing.'

'Bullshit. So now you're passing her onto me?'

They stared at each other.

He couldn't hold Arnav's look. He left and joined some other friends.

It was the most unpleasant thing Arnav had ever said to him. In fact, it was the *only* nasty thing Arnav had ever said to him since they'd become best friends in 1960, on their first day in Class One, Section B, at the age of five-and-a-half.

Neither of them referred to the incident after that.

His fault. None of it would have happened had he been upfront with Arnav and Mallika. Arnav's anger was justified. Whether Arnav felt anything more for Mallika or not was irrelevant for now. For now, all that mattered was Randhir's truth, which he still couldn't bring himself to tell them.

He didn't know whether this was because of what the truth was, or because of his terrible confusion about Mahima's marriage.

Shekhar had come to New York a few months ago, and at Mahima's behest, Randhir had driven to there to meet him. He spent the weekend with Cameron and took a few hours off to see Shekhar for lunch. Shekhar came laden with homemade sweets and matri for him, talked about the family business, and was full of praise for Mahima. Randhir talked about his university. On the surface, all was amiable and easy. But inside, he felt like crap. It was a constant mantra in his head – *please let what Renu said to Mallika before the wedding be a lie*. It was a wish so intense, a wish that he had visited and revisited so often since he left India that it almost felt like a prayer.

During his summer visit to India, Mahima and Shekhar came home to see him for two whirlwind days. Between the quadruplets and his parents, he had no time alone with Mahima or Shekhar, and he was thankful for it.

'I'm sorry I came for such a short time, don't be hurt,' Mahima whispered to him as they hugged each other goodbye.

He wasn't hurt, he was relieved. It was a relief which came with a hefty dose of self-loathing. If his sister was in an untenable marriage, it was his responsibility to get her out of it, because his parents never would. Yet here he was, relieved that there had been no time or space to ask her about it. What a useless brother he was!

A useless brother to Akhil too. While it was true that Akhil had stopped writing to him, he, Randhir, should have gone to Bombay to see him and his family. But it had felt like too much, doing it behind his father's back, not knowing where to stay in Bombay, not having the money to stay at a hotel, not sure if Akhil would welcome him... Everything seemed too much.

During this visit home, his father had begun talking to him again. He talked as though Randhir had never left India. Not once did his father ask him about his life in America. His mother chattered endlessly as usual, gave him the gossip about the colony, so nice that Arnav was also going to the same university – it would be too much if Mallika too went there, but life was full of coincidences – was he happy now that he was writing stories-shories? This last, loving question made him shudder so intensely that it was a while before he could nod and say, yes. All the things his parents *didn't* say lay heavy on his spine: When will you come back to India? You should start thinking about marriage, next time you come we will show you some very nice girls. If you will not take over the family business, then who will? In short, though his parents were being exactly what he had desperately hoped they would be about his future – silent – their silence brought him no reprieve. He was a worthless son. He didn't have the balls to tell his parents that he had no intention of coming back to India. He was repeating the same pattern he'd sworn to break. He had thought once he left India that he'd fought and won his biggest fight. But no, this could be the fight of a lifetime.

The wall that had risen between him and Padma Aunty hurt like hell. She tried not to show it, but he felt it. She'd loved him like a son, trusted him, had had faith in him. All gone after that agonizing phone call when she'd point blank asked him if he intended to marry Mallika. It hadn't once occurred to him that she thought this way about their relationship; he still hadn't got over the shock.

Nor had he got over the shock of his farewell to Ayah-ji almost a year ago. He envied Arnav's ability to shut out things he didn't want to think about. If only he had some of that ability. When he'd come home this time, Ayah-ji refused to talk to him. He felt like a bloody worm. He was brooding about this as he returned from the market with a bagful of mangoes, when he'd seen Ayah-ji walking ahead of him. He walked swiftly and joined her. 'Namaste, Ayah-ji, how are you?' he asked for the hundredth time. She grunted without looking at him.

Undeterred, he continued chatting with her, asking her about her health (she was alright), her new spectacles (they were alright), how hot the weather was (grunt), until finally he said, 'Do not worry about Mallika, I will look after her in Amreeka.'

This drew an immediate response. 'Now you will marry her?'

He should have been prepared for this.

'Accha,' Ayah-ji said, the intonation clearly meaning, *So you still won't? I see.*

'Ayah-ji,' he said carefully. 'I will never marry. I will marry no one.'

'Why not?' She was finally looking up at him.

'It is not my path. I cannot be a good husband. I cannot be a family man. I do not want children.'

They were approaching the parapet next to his house. 'Sit,' Ayah-ji said.

Obediently he walked to the parapet and sat. She sat next to him.

'Have you told Baby?'

'Yes, Ayah-ji.'

'What did Baby say?'

'Nothing, Ayah-ji. She did not look sad.'

'Baby hides everything. That much also you do not know after all these years?'

He was feeling utterly wretched.

'Tell Baby the truth,' Ayah-ji said.

His head jerked as he looked at her.

'What, Ayah-ji?'

'The people in our hearts' – she hit her heart several times with the palm of her hand – 'they must be told the truth.'

She got up and began walking home.

He got up and joined her. He could barely speak. 'Meaning... what truth, Ayah-ji?'

'How do *I* know what truth. *You* know. That only.'

He swallowed. What could she mean?

'Your whole life, you'll be a darpoke?' Ayah-ji demanded as they reached their homes.

Would he be a coward his whole life?

His *whole* life. Ayah-ji's words, so much like Mallika's, sounded like another death knell.

Ah, the monster that shackled your tongue was fear, always fear. The longer you waited, the bigger that monster grew. How beautifully it fed on your silence.

In boarding school, at the age of sixteen, he had won the President's Gold Medal for his essay, 'Courage.' Without even knowing the source of his words, he had written with passion about the courage to be yourself. Now, nine years later, he still hadn't found it. Ayah-ji had peered into his heart and seen this. He had no idea what else Ayah-ji had seen, but *that* she had.

He would tell Mallika and Arnav. Not here in India. In America, where the air didn't suffocate him. He was leaving in a few days, and they were arriving on his heels; it would have to be in America. It would fall differently, his secret, in America. It would have another resonance. Not only would he have the space to speak of it, but they would have the space to receive it. Arnav would be shocked, but he'd accept it. It would take Mallika longer, her shock would be greater, but she would eventually accept it too. He still didn't know what Ayah-ji had meant, but his apprehension that Mallika would be disgusted at his truth and that her love for him would eventually die had dissolved.

It was dark. The lights had dimmed in the plane and the people around him were asleep. He closed his eyes, and it came to him, the reason this cloud which had always surrounded him was finally dissipating. It was because of the knowledge that, very soon, he would tell them. *They* were his anchors as much as his writing; he hadn't realized to what extent till he left India and found himself with that hole in his heart that was shaped like them. It was *their* acceptance that he needed more than anyone else's. The rest of the world would matter infinitely less once he told them. Once he told them, he would at last be free.

Mallika: That tongueless story

August 1980

Carrying that tongueless story and my lies, I knocked on Arnav's door. As I knocked for the third time, I heard a sound from downstairs. I pulled down the handle and pushed. It wasn't locked. I rushed in and shut the door.

Arnav was asleep. He was naked. I grabbed the door handle again to run out of his room, then saw that the sheet covered him up to the waist. Maybe he wasn't? Indians didn't sleep naked, did they? That was what people did in Hollywood films, even if they were sleeping alone, even if it was snowing outside. My friends and I had discussed it – none of our parents slept naked even when the electricity went off. I sat on the chair next to his desk and gazed at him as I never could when he was awake, at that beautiful brown body, long arms, his unshaven cheek, and those eyelashes closed in blissful sleep. He looked so vulnerable that my fear began to dissipate, and longing filled my heart. The fan was whirring full-speed, but his room, which opened onto the terrace, was hot.

'Arnav,' I whispered.

No response. The fan whirled noisily.

'Arnav, wake up.'

No response.

I got up from his chair, knelt next to his bed, and peered into his face. If I wasn't such a wimp, I would kiss him awake.

He opened his eyes right into mine.

I swayed back.

For a moment, he was still. Then, 'Mallika?' in disbelief.

I attempted to leap up and return to my chair. Instead, I slipped and found myself slithering on the floor like a dying fish. My saree pleats were in the way. Not just my saree pleats, everything was in the way – his bare body, his lovely smell, his expression, my mortification.

He got up and my heart leapt to my throat... But he was wearing shorts. Looking at me as though I'd gone mad, he silently gave me his hand.

I grabbed it, heaved myself up, and sat back on his chair. I was sweating.

'I'm sorry I barged in like this,' I gasped. 'I wanted to talk to you alone.'

His sleep had vanished. He gave me such a searing look that I felt myself beginning to burn. As if he could see right through me, as though he knew exactly what I had been thinking that moment before he opened his eyes. I wanted to tear my eyes away from his but could not.

'Hold on.' He got out of bed and went to the bathroom.

I put my hands to my flushed cheeks and took a deep breath. Calm down, Mallika, calm down.

I closed my eyes and began to breathe deeply.

My heartbeat began to subside.

I smelt Vicco Vajradanti toothpaste.

I opened my eyes. Arnav was sitting on the bed, wearing a t-shirt, and looking at me unsmilingly.

'I needed to talk to you alone, that's why I came up.'

He nodded. His silence was unnerving.

'I'm sorry. I knocked several times. Then I thought I heard Mrs D'Souza, so...'

'That's OK.' He spoke abruptly.

I was losing my nerve again.

He was still looking at me, and there was nothing friendly in his look.

'Do you have a thousand rupees to lend me?' I blurted out.

He frowned as though he couldn't hear me properly. 'What?'

'A thousand rupees. Do you have it? To lend me?'

He was still frowning slightly, almost as though he didn't understand.

After a minute, 'You want to borrow a thousand rupees?'

'Yes. If you don't have it, it's OK. I'll... go.' I got up.

'No, no, sit, don't go.'

I sat.

'I have it.'

I took in another deep breath. 'Could you give it to me by this evening?'

'This... evening?' He shook his head like a dog shaking off water.

I nodded.

'OK.'

That was it? Just OK? No questions? Thank god. Oh, thank god.

'Thank you.' I took in a couple of deep breaths.

'Is *that* all?' he asked, as though a thousand rupees was nothing.

'That's all.'

He nodded.

'Thank you. Can I return it to you in instalments in the next year? Ten dollars a month?'

'Hmm.' He was thinking. Then, 'Yeah.'

'Arnav, when you come home, please… make sure no one sees you giving it to me.'

He came out of whatever he was thinking. 'OK.'

I got up. Thank god. No questions, no explanations, no lies. Thank god.

He said, 'Why so much? What's wrong?'

The lie I had practiced so hard slipped out of my mind like an eel.

The silence stretched.

I stammered, 'I need it for a friend.'

'Are Gauri and Prabha OK? Mahima?'

'They're all fine.'

'Then which friend?'

'A college friend. You don't know her.'

'You're lending *that* kind of money to some vague college friend?'

'She's a *good* friend.'

'You don't have any other good friends.'

I finally remembered what I'd practiced so hard.

'I do. I have a good friend in college. I'd borrowed her gold chain for… a wedding and… I lost it. I have to pay her back.'

He looked at me in wonder. 'God, Mallika. You're such a lousy liar.'

I couldn't pretend any more. All I could do was look at him, unable to hide my despair.

He let out his breath. 'OK, Mallika. Tell me.'

I sat back against his chair, exhausted.

'Mallika,' he said softly. 'Just trust me.'

Of course, I trusted him. But what did trust have to do with it? One word, and this thing would be right next to me, its salivating mouth gaping open like a cavern.

Then why was there a voice inside me clamouring, *Tell him, Mallika, tell him*?

I clasped my hands together in my lap and held myself rigid with the effort to stop my trembling.

He saw it, though. He reached across and took my hands in both his. 'It's OK,' he whispered.

I let my hands fall into his with relief.

We sat like this for a while. I was still trembling.

'Arnav, please don't mention this to Gauri, Prabha, or Mahima.'

Even saying this felt like a betrayal.

'OK.' He was holding my hands very tightly.

'Or Randhir.'

His hands loosened slightly.

'Mallika, look at me.'

I looked up. He was looking flabbergasted. 'You're not going to tell *Randhir*?'

'How can I when he's in America?'

'I mean, you'll tell him when we meet him, obviously.'

What did he mean 'obviously'?

'No,' I said.

'Why not?'

'What for? I need the money *now*; I won't be needing it *then*.'

He looked stunned. 'Don't ask me not to tell Randhir.'

Why was he acting like this?

'If you don't tell him, I will,' he said.

What was *wrong* with him?

'For god's sake, Mallika. Randhir has to know.'

'Why?'

He was looking at me as though... I didn't understand his look.

'I mean, of course I'd have told him if he was here.'

'Here or there, wherever, I don't understand why you're keeping it from him.'

'Because it's none of his business.'

He heard the anger in my voice, and his expression changed, as if he understood. 'It *is* his business, Mallika.'

It finally hit me.

'Because?' I asked.

For a full minute, we looked at each other.

'*Say* it,' I said.

'You're pregnant, and that's why you want the money,' he said under his breath.

'*I'm not.*'

I got up and moved towards the door.

He was up and standing at the door before I could open it.

I stepped back. He stepped forward at the same time and put his arms around me.

'I'm sorry,' he said into my hair, holding me tightly. 'I didn't mean to... I meant to... I'll get you the money this evening.'

I closed my eyes against that old story and leaned against him, still trembling. I didn't want to go anywhere. I wanted to stay here, enclosed within him.

He dropped his arms.

'Go,' he said under his breath as I stood there, unable to move, unable to think.

So much so that I said, 'Where?'

'Home,' he said as though there were nothing stupid about my question at all.

Opening his door a crack, he looked out. 'All clear.' He opened it fully. I went out and stood at his landing. The door shut quietly behind me. I closed my eyes. I was breathing as though I'd been running.

'I must say, you're breathing very heavily, my girl — that too, with eyes closed. What all have you and Arnav been up to?'

It was Mrs D'Souza.

She interrogated me. She expressed her belief in my virtue despite all evidence to the contrary. She told me all about America's influence on her son and about lustful men. Arnav came bouncing out of his room saying I'd come to call him for a walk. I phoned the dentist and the gynaecologist. Madhu Aunty listened to the conversation and interrogated me. I went to the Phuknewalla. Finally, I went back to my room with absolutely no idea what I'd say to my mothers when Mrs D'Souza and Madhu Aunty informed them of my transgressions.

I fell into an exhausted sleep.

When I woke up, my migraine had gone. I went downstairs to find Arnav sitting on the sofa like a fly trapped in a web of colourful spiders. Surrounding him were Ma, in a bright yellow Bengali saree; Shantamama, in a Venkatagiri purple saree; Ajji, in a Kanjeevaram off-white saree with a green border; Madhu Aunty, in a rust-and-green khadi work salwar kameez; and Anu Aunty, in a rose pink Sanganeri-print saree. Mrs D'Souza was wearing a frock with flowers in every colour. Arnav was in his inevitable jeans and t-shirt, but he'd shaved in deference to the household of women, and one long leg was decorously crossed over the other. He saw me and said, 'Hi.'

'Arnav told me *everything* this morning,' Mrs D'Souza said. 'My girl, I must say you are a dark horse!'

I glanced at Arnav. He looked insouciant, but his ears were slightly red.

'And everything Mrs D'Souza told us,' Anu Aunty said, looking at me thoughtfully.

My mothers and grandmother said nothing, but they were scrutinizing my face with peculiar expressions.

What yarn had Arnav spun?

I asked the aunties if they'd have tea or coffee or nimbu pani.

Mrs D'Souza would have coffee. Anu Aunty and Madhu Aunty would have tea. Arnav said either was fine.

In the kitchen, I put the water and milk to boil, took out the Green Label and Red Label, and put the decoction and milk on the gas. What was I supposed to say when they started interrogating me?

Arnav came into the kitchen and gave me an envelope. I took it and thrust it into the waist of my saree, brought my palla around it, and tucked it in.

'What did you tell them?' I whispered.

'I told them I'd help you with the tea.'

'*No, no*, about my coming to your room,' I said. 'Oh, that... Listen, you're not going to like it, I told them –' He stopped as Ma came into the kitchen. 'No need to be in the kitchen, Arnav, I'll help her,' Ma said, taking out the cups and saucers from the shelf.

Arnav went out.

'So you went to his room at five this morning?' Ma asked.

I nodded.

'I can't believe it. I just can't believe it.'

I spooned the tea leaves into the boiling water and milk and said nothing.

'How could you be so foolish?'

I switched off the gas, covered the tea, and said nothing. 'If you wanted to talk to him privately, why couldn't you have just gone for a walk with him?'

'I wanted to,' I said truthfully. 'But people keep coming home to say goodbye.'

'So? Why couldn't it wait? What was the hurry? After all, you're both going to America.'

What on *earth* had Arnav told Mrs D'Souza?

'Ma, don't be upset. You know I'll be staying in the same house as Randhir and Arnav in America till I find a place of my own.'

'That's in America. This is India.'

I poured out the tea, spooned in sugar, stirred the tea and coffee, took out a plate of biscuits and some murkus, and put everything on a tray. As I picked up the tray to take it to the sitting room, Ma said, 'Tell me the truth. Why did you go to his room?'

I put the tray down. 'To talk. About... It was confidential.'

'You tell *him* confidential things?'

I was silent.

'That too, at five a.m.?'

'I told you, Ma. I didn't get any time alone with him.'

'What is so big that you have to hide it from *us*?'

'Ma, the tea's getting cold.'

'Don't think you can keep it from us indefinitely.'

We went to the sitting room. Arnav was chatting with Ajji. I served them tea, coffee, biscuits, and murku and took the tray back to the kitchen to rinse it.

'Mallika, Beta,' said Madhu Aunty from behind me.

I put the tray away and turned to her.

'He is a very good boy, Arnav,' Madhu Aunty said, planting herself squarely in front of me. 'Why no? Why not yes?'

What on earth to say? I said nothing.

'You do not think he is good boy?'

'He is,' I said truthfully.

'Then?'

Silence was my only choice.

'Which friend of yours you are taking to gynaecologist for abortion?'

This complete change of subject disoriented me. What was she talking about?

She looked back at me, her face stern.

Oh. She was talking about my appointment with the gynaecologist.

'I'm not taking anyone for an abortion, Aunty.'

'Mallika, that Charu you took to gynaecologist. Now, someone else you are taking to gynaecologist. Someone who is pregnant?'

'No, Aunty, no.'

'Then why you are going to gynaecologist? You tell me, otherwise just now I am telling your mothers.'

The lie came to me unbidden.

'Boil, Aunty,' I said in a low voice.

'Boil? Where?'

'There, Aunty.'

'*There*? But how?'

'I don't know how, Aunty.'

'Oho. It must be this heat.'

'Must be.'

'I know why. You are wearing those horrible new-type nylon knickers.'

'No, Aunty, I only wear cotton.'

'Theek hai, for next two days, do not wear knickers. Anyway, what is the need for knickers under sarees? *We* all never wear knickers – *we* never get boils and all over there.'

'I have to go to a woman doctor, no, Aunty?'

'Of course, woman doctor only you have to go to, but why you did not tell me?'

I said nothing.

'See, Mallika, shyness and all, it is not good, look where all my mind went. I am your Madhu Aunty, no need for shyness with me. You go tomorrow to gynae, and she'll prescribe ointment or something. Yes, I know, sitting in plane for twenty-four hours with boil *there* – very difficult.'

I nodded.

'But why you did not tell your mothers?'

'They... worry too much. And now that I'm going to America, they'll worry even more.' This was true. 'Please don't tell them.'

'Uffho, Mallika. Too much you are. Alright, I will not tell them.'

I nodded, unable to speak.

'Beta, till you leave, no knickers, alright? That place, it needs ventilation.' She gave me a hug.

She let me go and exclaimed, 'You are crying! Why you are crying?'

'Because I'm going to America.'

'Yes,' she said, her lips trembling. 'I will miss you more than my own son.'

We fell into each other's arms and held on tightly to one another.

This boil story was my first ever lie to Madhu Aunty. And she believed me. Of course I was crying.

When we went out, Arnav had gone, but Mrs D'Souza and Anu Aunty were still there. I excused myself, ran upstairs, took out the brown envelope from my saree, and hid it in my bookshelf.

When I went downstairs ten minutes later, I was greeted rapturously by six children whom I had tutored, and their four mothers. Five hours later, at ten-thirty p.m., the last of the visitors left.

'Shantamama,' I said as we finally sat down to dinner. '*Please* don't ask me anything. I'm very tired.'

'What to ask? The deed is done.'

'No deed was done, Shantamama.'

'You went to his room at dawn, that's deed enough.'

The four of us ate dinner in silence.

'That too, wearing lipstick and rouge and a new blouse,' Ma said ominously.

'For *this* kind of thing, one should always be dressed properly,' Ajji said. 'However, that does not mean what you did was correct, Mallika.'

I took refuge in silence. What on earth had Arnav told Mrs D'Souza?

'But why are you taking sandwiches?' Ma asked as I zipped up my brand-new handbag the next morning, one that Madhu Aunty had gifted me a year ago. 'Surely the dentist won't take so long?'

'Some... work after that.'

'What work?' said Shantamama.

'I... have to get some bras.'

'Child, surely you can buy brassieres in America?' said Ajji.

'Ajji, they're very expensive there, hundreds and hundreds of rupees.'

'Chee, surely that boy Randhir hasn't also been telling you the cost of brassieres in America?'

'No, Ajji, of course not! I'm going now – bye, Ajji, bye, Shantamama, bye, Ma.'

'Darling, why are you using your brand-new handbag? Use it in America, not here.'

'Bye, love, have you put the money for the dentist in your bag's inner zip?'

'Bye, darling, but why is your plait so tight? It makes your face look very thin.'

'God bless you, my child, do not buy nylon brassieres, they are very bad for the skin.'

This time, no buses. I took a scooter all the way to the dentist.

An hour later, I stepped out of the dentist's office with two new fillings and a swollen jaw when a car beeped and stopped next to me. *Bloody Delhi men*, I thought, not looking.

'Mallika.'

It was Arnav in the car, squinting against the sun. 'I'll give you a lift home.'

Oh, no, no.

'Oh… I'm not going home right now, I have some… work.'

'I'll drop you.'

He opened the door to the passenger seat, and I got in. 'How come you're in a car?'

'It's my father's.'

'So… how come you're in the car?'

'So I could start moving my stuff back home.'

'But why are you here, outside my dentist's office?'

'I had some work here and saw you.'

I didn't believe him. He'd followed me.

'You've to turn right here, and then right again over there,' I said.

He parked the car under the shade of a tree, just outside the clinic. I stared at it and saw myself in the scooter, holding onto the side bar as I bled.

I couldn't do it. I couldn't enter this place.

Arnav had got out of the car and was opening my door.

I got out.

We were under the shade of the tree. I looked up at him, the sweat running down my back. I had to tell him to go back.

'Chalo, let's go inside before we burn up.'

I found myself walking inside with him. I didn't look at the building, at the familiar corridor, the reception. I focused on the feel of my handbag on my shoulder and Arnav next to me. He sat at the reception, and I spoke to the receptionist. Yes, Dr Raghunath would see me. I went into her office.

'Thank you, Dr Raghunath.' I gave her the envelope. 'I'm sorry this is so late.'

'Thank you, Mallika. Sit down, please, sit down.'

'I have to leave, doctor, I have some work… But thank you for everything.'

For a few seconds, she said nothing. Then she looked at me and opened her mouth.

I looked at her in terror.

'Good luck to you, my dear.'

'Thank you.'

Outside at the reception, Arnav was flipping through a magazine. A matronly woman in her thirties in a bright red salwar kameez sat next to him.

Arnav looked up at me, startled. 'That was fast.'

I nodded.

'You two are married?' the woman said, assessing me.

Arnav got up. 'Wait here, I'll get the car to the door.'

'No, let's go.'

'You two don't *look* married,' the woman said as we turned to go.

'Unfortunately, *you* do,' Arnav said.

Her eyes widened in shock.

It was the nastiest thing I'd ever heard Arnav say.

We walked in silence to the car and got in. It was radiating heat.

'There's a Chinese restaurant nearby. Feel like lunch there?'

I nodded.

It was air conditioned and cool in the restaurant. Drinking a glass of water helped, and so did the hot and sour soup that followed, even though it was the height of summer. We didn't talk. Halfway through my chicken chow mein, I began to feel better. It was done. I had entered the nightmare briefly, and now, I was out of it.

'Feeling better?'

I looked up from my food and nodded.

He scanned my face.

'Arnav, I'll return the money within a year.'

'I know you will. Stop worrying about it.'

He had given me a huge amount of money. He had lied to Mrs D'Souza to protect me. He had somehow followed me to the doctor's office in his father's car to bring me home safely because he thought I was having an abortion. I owed him the truth. Whatever I knew of it.

Besides, if Arnav told Randhir, Randhir would break the silence I'd asked of him. After today, I never wanted to revisit that time again. Never.

'I had the money, but when I was on my way to the doctor to pay her, I was pickpocketed in the bus.'

'Shit. You should have taken a scooter.'

I nodded. I had done nothing but curse myself for not doing so.

'Why did you owe the doctor so much money, Mallika? What happened?'

'Some gynaecological issues. I didn't tell my mothers. They worry too much.'

'When was this?'

'Last year.'

I wasn't going to tell him it was four years ago. Last year made my narrative simpler.

'Now, no need to tell Randhir,' I said.

He continued eating.

I stopped eating and stared at him.

He looked up and said, very calmly, 'I have to.' Then he went back to eating.

So now he thought Randhir had made me pregnant last year before he left for America.

'Where do you think we had sex?' I asked furiously.

He jerked up from his food and looked at me.

'In his house? In mine? With our families breathing down our necks?'

He put his fork down.

'Or in some seedy hotel?'

He couldn't hide his shock at my words.

'Use your brain, Arnav. Randhir wasn't in the hostel like you were. He didn't live in a barsati by himself. Even were we so inclined, he and I don't have the opportunities *you* do.'

I'd robbed him of words. I was trembling.

'If it wasn't Randhir, then who was it, Mallika?'

I was blind with rage and terror.

'Madhu Aunty also thought I was pregnant. She asked me if it was Randhir or you, because which other boy do I know? Well, since you seem to be so convinced I was pregnant, *you* tell me – was it *you*?'

His face was a blur. I got up and ran out of the restaurant.

It was burning hot. There were no scooters to be seen anywhere.

I walked to his car, which was parked under a tree, feeling my anger whooshing out of me as rapidly as it had come, leaving me with that old exhaustion.

He was sprinting out of the restaurant. He saw me next to the car and came towards me. Silently, he unlocked my door and opened it. Then he went to the other side. We rolled down our windows; it was like a furnace inside.

'I'm sorry,' I said. 'I shouldn't have said that.'

He didn't answer. He was looking straight ahead of him, at the windscreen.

'It was years ago, Arnav; it's all water under the bridge now. I don't want to talk about it.'

He turned. His t-shirt was damp with sweat. 'Years? But you said it was a year ago.'

'Oh, fine, it was four years ago; how does it matter when?' I wiped the sweat from my neck with my saree palla.

'When exactly?' he asked.

I looked at him in surprise. His tone sounded strange.

'A few months after Mahima's wedding. End of April, I think.'

He was utterly silent.

And suddenly I felt something inside my body giving way, and words began trickling out, as though they had been waiting for him to ask.

'I was in a scooter and started bleeding very heavily and landed up at this clinic.' I looked down at my lap, at my limp and rust-coloured cotton saree. It was strange. This was the first time I was talking about it, and I didn't feel that terror threatening to swallow me up.

That was not when it had begun, of course. It had begun with that awful nausea, followed by the encounter with that first, horrible gynae, but that was all too much to tell him.

'And?'

'After the gynae attended to me, I phoned Randhir. He came and took me home.'

'No, I mean... what did the doctor say the problem was?'

I smoothed my saree pleats slowly. 'It's a blur.' I still couldn't look at him. 'I hadn't had my period for a few months. But that had happened before. They're irregular.'

This was the second time I was talking about periods with a man, and it was far more difficult than with Randhir.

'Remember Charu? Randhir told you everything about her, no?'

'Yes.'

'Charu was convinced she was pregnant even though the gynae kept saying it was a period. I must have been in quite a... state, because... I couldn't make out if the gynae was saying it was a pregnancy or a period. It was almost as if... I'd become Charu. I thought I'd gone crazy.'

I looked up at him. He was looking so dazed that I balked. 'You too think I'm like Charu?'

He shook his head.

And suddenly more words began coming out, and they no longer filled me with shame.

'I must have been crazy to think the gynae was saying it was a pregnancy' – I looked down again – 'when I'd never… been with anyone.'

He was utterly silent.

'How could I have been confused about something like that? I thought I was going mad. I was so terrified that I'd become like Charu that… I… I never talked about it to anyone.'

'Randhir?' His voice sounded strange.

'He knew I'd been… bleeding. But he didn't know what was going on in my mind.'

He sounded suffocated. 'Randhir must have talked to the doctor.'

'I suppose so. I don't know.'

What did that have to do with anything? Was he trying to change the subject? Apprehension filled me.

'Are you going to tell Randhir?' I asked, still unable to look at him.

Silence.

Then, 'Tell him what? Randhir… knows.'

'Arnav, I just *told* you. Randhir knows I… landed up in the clinic because I was… bleeding, but I never told him… what was going on inside my head.'

I could hear him breathing unevenly.

'Don't tell Randhir. *Please*. If you tell him, he'll despise me.'

Once again, that awful silence.

Then, '*Despise* you?'

'For losing my mind. For becoming like Charu. For imagining…' I couldn't say it.

I could hear us both breathing.

I let out my breath. 'For imagining the pregnancy. Randhir'll think I imagined it was him. Like Charu.'

I heard him take in a shuddering breath.

He said under his breath, 'You're *not* like Charu. Randhir will never think that. You *didn't* go crazy. I *promise*.'

He believed me. I heard it in his voice. His promise was like a vow.

That was all I needed. Someone trusted, who, knowing what had been going on in my head that day, still believed I hadn't gone crazy.

If Arnav believed it so absolutely, then how could Randhir not?

Randhir needed to know the entire truth. Once he knew, it would never come back to haunt me, and I'd be done with it forever.

I looked up at Arnav, finally. He was looking out of the window. There were beads of perspiration on his face.

'I can't talk about it again, so will you tell Randhir for me?' I asked.

'Yes.'

He was still looking out of his window. His fist was clenched. As though he had gathered that darkness inside me and taken it inside him. As though it was now too much for him the way it had been too much for me.

I was so moved by how hard he was taking it that I couldn't say a word.

Finally, I touched his arm gently. 'It's OK, Arnav. I'm fine now. Let's go home.'

He looked at me. There was no colour in his face.

He looked away immediately and started the engine. Knocked out by the surfeit of emotions contained in the car, I closed my eyes and leaned back against my seat. We drove home in silence.

Gauri: Goodbye

August 1980

Now, Vineet was back in America, and she was on the bus, going to say goodbye to Mallika. Looking out of the window, she thought of how, after confessing his love to her on Randhir's terrace, Vineet had rushed home and told his mother and sisters that he wanted to marry her. You've told them, but you haven't asked me, you idiot, she wanted to say later, but she didn't, because she was so disarmed by his straightforwardness, by his absolute certainty that he wanted to live the rest of his life with her. It felt small-spirited to say, 'Vineet! You should have asked me first!' Mallika's example was always before her – the fact that neither Randhir nor Arnav had shown any desire to marry her, even after all these years. So what if Vineet hadn't asked her? Her answer would have been yes anyway.

Vineet had come home and met her parents too. Now, finally, her parents were no longer unhappy on her account. She had fulfilled their dream for her: a good boy.

They had decided to get married the following year.

She had dreaded telling him, but she had to. She had said, apprehensively, 'I can't live in America, Vineet.'

He had answered without hesitation. 'We'll come back after my PhD.'

She hadn't expected it to be so easy. But here he was, not even questioning her desire to live in India.

She wanted him to understand why.

'Vineet, my dancing is everything to me. I can't give it up after marriage.'

He looked surprised. And a little hurt. 'Am I asking you to do that?'

'No, but...'

'Ours isn't going to be that kind of marriage, Gauri, you should know that.'

She had felt so guilty for bringing it up. She was also overwhelmed that he'd agreed to come back to India without hesitation.

They went to Bharatpur for the weekend. There was nowhere else to be alone. She was back in the hostel, so her parents didn't know. Being together, physically, was new and urgent and all-consuming. But despite that, they didn't have sex. Even with all that pleasure, it was too painful for her. 'It's OK,' Vineet said. 'It doesn't matter.' It was such a relief that it didn't bother him. She had heard from some newly married girls that it could take time – for some, it had taken weeks. It looked like she was one of them.

Vineet, laughing, had told her how he'd confessed his love for her to Mallika. She laughed too, but said nothing. She knew Mallika had been protecting her. Because Mallika wasn't sure Vineet's love would last in America. Not that Gauri could have told Vineet this. Her long love for him was a part of her she somehow couldn't relinquish to him, even though it was about him.

A day before he left, he said, 'Gauri, after I finish my PhD, I really want to work in America for a couple of years... How about if we return to India after two years?'

She hesitated.

Then she thought, If he's willing to return to India for me, then staying a couple more years in America for him is the least I can do. She nodded.

She had bought *Villette* – she and Prabha knew Mallika wanted to read it, so this was their farewell gift for her. When she arrived, it was five in the evening, but Mallika wasn't at home. Mallika's mothers and grandmother were so happy to see her. Padma Aunty made her tea, and Shanta Aunty gave her the chocolate cake that she'd just baked and the most delicious egg-and-cheese toast with dhanya and green chilis. Mallika's grandmother gave her homemade banana chips. They told her Mallika had gone to the dentist because Randhir had made a trunk call from America to say American dentists charged as much for a tooth as the cost of a plane ticket to America, imagine!

So, they chattered away, and then, after a while, a silence fell.

She looked up from her plate to find the three women exchanging glances. Then Padma Aunty said, 'Gauri, is something going on between Mallika and Arnav?'

She almost choked over the chocolate cake. 'Why, Aunty?'

'Because Mallika went to his barsati at five in the morning yesterday. Mrs D'Souza saw her.'

Her jaw dropped open.

They saw her shock. 'See,' said Shanta Aunty. 'Her also, Mallika hasn't told.'

'What did Mallika say?' Gauri asked, unable to believe this.

'She isn't denying it, but she isn't saying why,' Shanta Aunty said in dire tones.

'She just won't answer our questions,' Padma Aunty said.

Going to Arnav's room at five a.m.? For Mallika, that was an act of desperation. But not desperation for sex, definitely not that.

'*One hour*, she was there,' Shanta Aunty said in the same dire tones.

The answer came to her.

'She went to *talk* to him, Aunty.' That was it. There was something urgent Mallika had to talk to Arnav about. And she hadn't had the time nor the privacy to do so anywhere else.

She saw the relief on the faces of Mallika's mothers and grandmother.

'That is what she told us,' Padma Aunty said.

'But talk about what?' Shanta Aunty said.

She had been wondering about that too. 'Something confidential,' she said.

'See,' Mallika's grandmother said. 'Gauri knows our child.'

Then Padma Aunty said, 'Arnav told Mrs D'Souza he'd asked Mallika to marry him, and that she came upstairs to say no to him. Because she wanted to spare his feelings and do it privately.'

She wasn't able to hide her expression.

Shanta Aunty said, 'See, Gauri doesn't believe it. That boy made up the story.'

Gauri said hastily, 'I – no, it *could* be true. I haven't talked to Mallika for ages.'

Not bad, she marvelled. Arnav was trying to protect Mallika. Not bad at all.

But why had Mallika gone to his room in the first place?

At that moment, Mallika came into the house, looking very tired.

And in that instant, Gauri knew why Mallika had gone to Arnav's barsati.

'What did the dentist do?' Padma Aunty asked.

'So late you are, we were getting worried,' Shanta Aunty said.

'Did you get the brassieres?' Ajji asked.

Mallika said, 'I finished all my work.'

'Sit and eat,' Shanta Aunty said.

'I'll make you tea,' Padma Aunty said, getting up.

Ayah-ji, who was clearing the table and understood a few words of English, said, 'Why *you* should make? *I* will make.'

Ayah-ji was becoming more belligerent and possessive by the day.

'Yes, Ayah-ji, you make,' Mallika said.

Ayah-ji gave a snort and carried the tray of cups and saucers out of the sitting room.

Mallika ate hungrily and answered a barrage of questions. Yes, the dentist had filled two small cavities; she hadn't even known they were there. No, she hadn't taken the bus, Arnav had picked her up and dropped her, he'd had work that side too. Yes, he was moving back home today.

Mallika had eaten everything on her plate and was now finishing her tea.

'So he told a lie to cover up why?' Shanta Aunty said.

'What, Shantamama?' Mallika asked, puzzled.

'What need to cover up, unless, of course, the truth is not pretty?' Shanta Aunty pressed.

'Who is covering up what?' Mallika asked.

Oh, god, Mallika, why are you such a tube light? Gauri thought.

'Arnav is covering up why you went to his room, obviously,' said Padma Aunty dryly.

'So Arnav does not want to marry you?' her grandmother asked, frowning.

'*Marry me!*' Mallika looked stunned.

The three women looked at Mallika with varying expressions.

'Why on earth do you think he wants to marry me?' Mallika asked.

'Because he said so, my dear,' said Shanta Aunty, in her driest tone.

Mallika opened her mouth, then closed it.

'He told Mrs D'Souza you went to his room to say no to his proposal of marriage,' her mother said. 'Because it was the only time you could get alone with him and you did not want anyone to know so that his feelings would not be hurt.'

Not bad at all, Gauri continued to marvel.

Mallika was laughing so hard that she almost choked over her cake.

Her mothers and her grandmother were not laughing. They were looking deadly serious.

Mallika managed to say, 'No, no! He doesn't! That was for Mrs D'Souza's benefit!'

Then she dissolved into laughter again.

'She finds it funny. It looks like she is ready to go to America. Where Such Things are of no consequence,' Shanta Aunty said.

'So why did you go to his room?' Padma Aunty asked.

Mallika stopped laughing and wiped her eyes.

The silence stretched on.

'Go, pack now,' her grandmother said. 'Enough of all this.'

Gauri and Mallika got up and went up to her room.

Gauri shut the door, crossed her arms, and said, 'I know why you went to his room.'

Because Mallika's memory had come back, and she remembered the kiss.

'You wanted to confront him, no?' Gauri asked.

Mallika looked at her blankly.

'OK, fine, not *confront*. You wanted to *talk* to him about the kiss.'

'What?'

'I saw you both kissing that night of Mahima's wedding. I was coming out of Madhu Aunty's house.'

Mallika looked shocked. 'You never told me.'

'You were so unwell after the concussion, Mallika. I thought I'd wait for your memory to come back. Then you fell ill with TB. Then Arnav got involved with that stupid Mohini. So I told Prabha. We decided we didn't want you to get hurt.'

'Oh.'

'Then Prabha said she was going to talk to Arnav about the kiss. I told her not to. I mean, she'd really have made his hackles rise. So she said, "Fine, you talk to him." So I did.'

'*You talked to him about it*!'

'Otherwise Prabha would have done it.'

She hadn't told Prabha – and she certainly wasn't going to tell Mallika – that she'd messed it up. Even now, she shuddered when she thought about that conversation. Of how she'd brought up the girls in Arnav and Randhir's life and said how Mallika was superior to them! She'd lost control. And she had thought that *Prabha* would mess it up! By the end of it, she was so frustrated with Arnav, so upset with herself, and so close to tears that she couldn't even speak. That night, when she had told Prabha about her conversation with Arnav, Prabha had been very indignant that he'd brushed aside the kiss as though it was nothing. 'Good thing you talked to Arnav,' Prabha had said. 'At least now he knows he has no business kissing her so casually.'

'What did Arnav say when you talked to him about the kiss?' Mallika asked.

'Something stupid like "these things happen." What did he mean, "these things?" He said it wasn't a big deal. I said it was for you. He looked really apprehensive, as if he thought I'd told you, so I said no, I hadn't. He said, "Don't worry, it's not going to happen again." He said what happened was a mistake; that you were a good friend, and if I told you, it would end your friendship. Bas, that's all.'

Gauri still didn't understand why he had called kissing Mallika 'a mistake.' Why couldn't their friendship have become something more?

Mallika was looking dazed.

'Prabha and I thought it was best not to tell you. I mean, he was going around with Mohini after that. We didn't want you to get hurt. Besides, you'd become friends. Why spoil that?'

Mallika still said nothing.

'So how did it happen, Mallika?'

'I don't know, Gauri. My memory hasn't come back.'

Gauri clapped her hand to her mouth.

'Gauri, do you really think I'm such an ass that I'm going to ask him about a stupid kiss that meant nothing to him and happened *four* years ago!'

They heard footsteps coming up the stairs, and Prabha came in. 'I hope I haven't missed any of the gossip,' she said, smiling.

'No gossip, Prabha, just trying to think what to take to America,' Mallika said quickly.

Meaning Mallika was trying to change the subject because she didn't want to tell them why she went to Arnav's room, Gauri thought. Tonight, she'd tell Prabha. Then wait and see. In the morning, they'd get it out of Mallika.

Mahima: Goodbye

August 1980

She hadn't planned it. She didn't even know she was going to do it. Shekhar and his father were away at work. When her mother-in-law went for her afternoon nap, she went upstairs to her bedroom, thinking, I want to say goodbye to Mallika, and I want to see Mummy and Daddy. Then she found herself picking up her handbag and tossing a pair of gold earrings into it. The rest of her jewellery was in her mother-in-law's Godrej, since her mother-in-law said it was safer there. She never had any cash either and might need the earrings for petrol. Then she took the car keys from the drawer in Shekhar's so-called study – by now, she knew very well what sort of studying he did there – then went downstairs, filled an empty orange squash bottle with water, picked up a packet of biscuits, got into the car, which was parked in the driveway, and drove towards Delhi.

She hadn't been able to say goodbye to Randhir when he left for America – Shekhar had lovingly asked her to accompany him to Singapore, saying how much he missed her when he was away from her, and she'd finally given in. When Randhir came home this time, her mother-in-law lovingly said they were having a big puja, and she was the daughter of the house, and how could they have it without her? So she saw Randhir only for two days, and even then, Shekhar came along with her like her tail. In those two days, she had had no time alone with her brother, her parents, or her three friends. Shekhar was always there. She might as well not have gone. Now, if she told them she wanted to go to Delhi again to say goodbye to Mallika, they'd lovingly stop her again. How could they act so loving after everything that had happened? Hypocrites. She *would* say goodbye to Mallika. She *would* see Mummy and Daddy. No point asking Shekhar or her in-laws anything. Asking was too tiring.

She couldn't tell anyone the truth. And when you couldn't tell the truth, then what was there to say? When you couldn't tell the truth, there was nothing to talk about except the parties you went to, the films you saw, the new jewellery and sarees you bought, what you'd learnt to cook, and what so-and-so's gossip was. Those things, people understood very well. But no one understood the truth. No one wanted to hear it. Even Mummy. Mummy always said, 'You're happy, no, Beta? Of course you're happy, why am I asking.'

In her married home, she had plenty of time, yet there was no space to think. Only love allowed you the sanctuary to think. But when love was a sham and that sham was your life, then even your thoughts were not safe. Living with an awful truth was like living with cancer or any big illness; it became the way it was, nothing more, nothing less. Every truth, however unpalatable, became routine when you lived with it long enough.

During the first year of her marriage, she had believed that a good marriage was just a matter of strategy. Her strategy had worked quite well, at first. Those early days, she hadn't known what Shekhar was up to. Those days, he hadn't been brazen about it. She had practiced the strategy in front of her bedroom mirror. She had watched herself in the mirror as her eyes filled with tears and she whispered, 'Don't leave me and go on tour, Shekhar, I miss you so much.' She practiced crying silently. The mirror told her she looked quite lovely, even with tears brimming in her eyes or trickling down her face. Shekhar always said she was beautiful. He loved buying her new sarees and jewellery, and when he saw them on her, he gazed at her as though she were an exquisite work of art. He was lavish with his compliments. 'You're so beautiful, I love you so much, you light up the house.' Those early days, she had reciprocated generously with her entreaties to him not to leave Chandigarh for his work, and with her wordless tears when he did. She had become really good at it. She was totally accomplished at fussing over him: before he went off for work, adjusting his shirt and telling him to eat a proper breakfast or have another paratha or drink some more lassi, and in the evening, urging him to eat more at dinner and noticing when he was looking tired and massaging his head if he had a headache. He basked in it; his parents watched it with satisfaction. Then, after some months, she would say, 'Please take me to Delhi, Shekhar,' and sometimes, he would.

But as time passed, Shekhar grew immune to her entreaties. He would say, 'Why do you always want to leave me?' Or 'Go later, I'll miss you too much.' Later never came.

He was always so happy when she came back from Delhi. The situation reminded her of the Barbie doll that her mother's brother had got her from America when she was a child. The doll was so beautiful that she and her three friends would play with it every single day, handling it with reverence, gazing raptly at its beautiful, grown-up face; its slim, curved body; and its lovely blue eyes. Each friend was allowed to hold the doll for three minutes, bas. Ultimately, the doll belonged to her, and it was up to her to share or not to share. Now, it was Shekhar who decided to share her or not to share her, and for how long.

Then, some months ago, she had discovered that she was pregnant. Happiness had flooded her. Shekhar and his parents were ecstatic. 'Wait for four months before you tell your parents,' Shekhar's mother said, and though it irked her, she agreed. She prayed it would be a boy. She told Shekhar, 'No need for us to do it now.' He said, 'OK,' and the sex stopped. Thank God.

A few months later, she woke up suddenly at night. She looked at her watch. It was three a.m., and Shekhar was not next to her. Still talking and drinking with that friend of his? She was tired of his friends coming and going. Shekhar talked more to them than he ever did to her. She turned and was going back to sleep when she heard sounds at the other end of the corridor. They were the strangest sounds she had ever heard, a kind of grunting and groaning, as though someone was in pain. Something had happened to Shekhar. She leapt out of bed and ran towards the study, where the sounds were coming from. She didn't even think, she pulled down the handle, and the door opened, and there were two naked men on the bed doing god knows what on top of each other and making those terrible sounds. One of them was Shekhar. She shut the door and ran back to her room in a state of terror. She went into the bathroom and bolted the door. She pulled down the lid and sat on the pot, shaking.

No one had ever spoken of such things to her. She'd never read of such things. Such things were not talked about on Doordarshan, the single government TV channel, and never seen in films. Even she and her friends had never discussed it. On rare occasions, someone in college made a veiled comment like, 'he's one of *those*,' or 'she's like *that*,' meaning that someone liked to do stuff with others of their own sex. What they did, or why, Mahima had no idea.

But now, it was happening in her very household, and it was her husband. He was married to her, but he was doing stuff with other men. That glimpse of him was also shocking because it was the first time that she had seen him naked. He never took off his clothes when he did it to her.

Not long after this, she had a miscarriage.

She was heartbroken and exhausted. She had thought that if this child came, she would have someone to love, someone who was truly hers. If it was a boy, she wouldn't have to have sex ever again. But now her child was just a mass of blood.

They didn't want her to go home. Her mother-in-law said, 'I am like your mother now, *I* will take care of you.' Which she did, with a great deal of love. 'Go home later, when you're stronger,' Shekhar said. He was going off to New York on some work, and when she had asked him if he could meet Randhir, whose university was just a few hours from the city, Shekhar had said that of course he would. Her mother-in-law even packed some homemade laddoos and matri for Randhir which Shekhar took with him to New York.

She was in bed for a month, unable to muster up the energy to get out, to talk, to walk. The doctor had said she was depressed and needed sunlight, walks, and nature – perhaps they should take her to a hill station to recover, what about Nainital or Ooty? But she didn't want to go anywhere except home, and 'home' meant her mother. And if she couldn't go home, then she wanted to be left alone. When Shekhar returned from New York, she told him, 'Don't sleep with me,' and he said, 'I love you,' and started sleeping in his study.

After his I-love-you, Shekhar's affairs, or whatever they were, started again.

She used to overhear her brothers and their friends casually using words like 'fuck;' she hated that kind of language, and they never used it in her presence. But now, in her mind, she used it too. She used it in her mind every time Shekhar said, 'I love you.' What did 'I love you' mean when he said it? It meant 'I will do with you *as* I please.' It meant 'you will do *what* I please.' It meant 'I will fuck *them* when I please, and I will fuck *you* when I please.'

This was how her mind began to talk. It talked non-stop. Even when she wanted it to stop, it wouldn't.

She recalled how, in the first month of her marriage, her mother-in-law had lovingly said, 'You are the kind of girl who can sudharo any man.' You are the kind of girl who can make any man turn over a new leaf.

Now, she understood. Her mother-in-law had meant that if she was a good wife then Shekhar would love her so much that he wouldn't want to be with men. Her mother-in-law knew. But she loved her son obsessively, a hundred times more than her daughter, Renu. As for Shekhar, his mother was the only one he ever listened to. His father no doubt turned a blind eye because he couldn't run the rapidly expanding family business without Shekhar, who was an astute and efficient businessman. Everyone knew, and everyone pretended that it wasn't happening. Even after his marriage. She, Mahima, was the casualty. As Prabha had once said, wives always were.

A month or so after her miscarriage, they were eating breakfast when her mother-in-law said, 'How are you feeling, Beti?'

It just came out of her.

'You let Shekhar do whatever he wants to keep him happy, but no one cares about keeping *me* happy. And I'm supposed to keep *quiet* on top of that?'

Everyone at the table froze. Her mother-in-law's eyes were wide with shock. Shekhar stopped eating and looked at her incredulously. Her father-in-law's eyes became cold as ice.

'*My* happiness is a small thing. All I want is to see Mummy and Daddy two or three times a year, and even asking for *that* is too much for all of you? Even after I've lost my child?' She got up and ran upstairs to her room, weeping.

Her mother-in-law followed her to her room. 'Beti, that was no way to talk,' she remonstrated in her gentle way.

No way to *talk*? What about telling your son that was no way to *act*?

She held back her words. After a few minutes, her mother-in-law left the room.

That night, before they went to bed, Shekhar said, 'That was a very insulting way to talk in front of my parents.'

'I know what you're doing.'

'That means nothing. It's you I love.'

'Then why do you do it?'

'You'll never understand.' Then, to her shock, he began to weep.

She stood where she was, not knowing what to think.

Finally, he looked up at her, his face still wet. 'How could you betray me like this? How could you?'

'*I* betrayed *you*?' she said in disbelief.

'You're my *wife*,' he said, his voice cracking. 'You're my *wife*.'

She turned her back to him and tried to empty her mind.

The next night, at the dining table over dinner, her father-in-law talked casually about his ties with the Congress (I). She had always known about it, but it had been of no consequence to her. All politicians were corrupt, any party in power was corrupt, Indian politicians were the worst. If her father-in-law was hand-in-glove with corrupt politicians, so be it. She wasn't like Randhir and his friends, who went on and on about politics and the ills of the Emergency even now, when it was over. What had her brother and his friends changed with all their talk? What had Prabha changed with her talk? Talk changed nothing.

Now, her father-in-law was talking about someone's body being found on the railway tracks because he had got on the wrong side of a politician. That was too much, even for her. 'How terrible,' she said, shocked. Her father-in-law looked at her, his eyes colder than ice. He said, 'You think it cannot happen to people who have stabbed me or my family in the back?'

No, she thought that night as she tried to read *Eve's Weekly*. *No*. She had been imagining the implication. No, he didn't mean he would do something to Daddy.

Shekhar came to bed as she tried to read. After some time, he said, 'Your family hid many things from us.'

She looked at him.

'Your eldest brother, Akhil, married a Muslim girl before our marriage. Your parents hid this from us when we offered for you. There is a name for this. It is called stabbing us in the back.'

Her magazine slipped out of her hands.

'We have known this for a long time. But I told my parents, "How is it her fault if her parents hid it from us? She is innocent." That is how I protected you all this time.'

Her hands were suddenly cold. She sat up in bed and drank a few sips of water from the glass lying next to her. Her hand was shaking.

'I have protected you; yet you stab me? You stab my mother and my father?'

She thrust her shaking hands under the sheet.

'If your father is safe and sound and carrying on with his business without any problems after he lied to us, it is because of our goodness,' Shekhar said.

She looked at him finally. His eyes were as cold as his father's had been.

'All that can finish in one minute,' Shekhar said.

She put her book on the table and switched off her bedside lamp.

He did not switch off his. 'And your brother, Randhir, what do you think he is?'

She turned to look at him with dread. Now what was he talking about?

He examined her face. 'Oh, I see. You don't know?'

Know what? What had Randhir gone and done now?

'He and I, we are cut from the same cloth.'

At first, she did not understand.

After a minute, it hit her.

'No,' she burst out. 'Randhir's not like that.'

He snorted.

She turned her back to him and closed her eyes. She could hear her heart pounding in her ears.

He said, 'You know I saw him once when I went to New York. But I saw him for a second time, with another man. They were embracing. He didn't see me. That was when I knew.'

She was breathing as though she had been running.

'I wonder what your parents would say to that?' he said thoughtfully.

She panted, 'Randhir's gone out with girls.'

'And I have a wife.' He switched off his bedside lamp.

She would have to bear the shame, just as she bore Shekhar's name. She had to spare her parents from it. Her in-laws and Shekhar would bring shame to her parents by telling everyone that Akhil had been married to a Muslim girl for five years. And if it was true, what Shekhar had said about Randhir, then more shame awaited them. On top of all that, if she left Shekhar, her poor parents, who had done nothing to harm anyone and given all of them so much love, would have nothing but shame from all three of their children.

And her father-in-law would arrange to finish off Daddy and throw his body on the railway tracks.

If only she could tell Prabha, Mallika, and Gauri all this. Not to change anything, no. Just to unburden her heart, that was all. But now, because of Randhir, she couldn't. If she talked to them about Shekhar being a homosexual, and if Randhir was one too, and if her friends found out – oh, the shame of it! On top of all that, her friends would blame Mummy and Daddy for marrying her to Shekhar. And it wasn't Mummy or Daddy's fault. They had chosen Shekhar for her with so much love and care. Of course, Prabha, Mallika, and Gauri wouldn't *say* her parents were at fault, but they would certainly *think* it. She didn't want them thinking anything of the sort.

She reached Delhi without any mishap and finally parked outside her house. As she entered her mother's house, she felt she was dreaming. Mummy came out of the kitchen and gasped. 'Beta?' She threw herself into mummy's arms. They couldn't stop hugging. Daddy was there too, his face wreathed in smiles, and she hugged him.

'How did you come?' Mummy asked.

'I drove, Mummy.'

'Arre! Alone!' Mummy expostulated.

'The driver was on leave, and Shekhar was travelling, and… I was feeling homesick,' she said. 'And I want to say goodbye to Mallika.' She would stay at home for a couple of weeks and then go back. She wanted her mother's love. Her father's love. Her friends' love. For two weeks, that was what she wanted. That was all.

She chatted with Mummy in the kitchen as she made parathas for her. Mummy never let Ramu cook when she came home. In twenty minutes, Mummy made her favourite karelas. Then Mummy and Daddy sat by her and watched her eat, their faces shining with love. Already, she was feeling better, so much better.

The phone rang.

She stiffened.

Mummy went to pick it up.

She could hear the murmur of Mummy's voice, uncharacteristically low.

Then Mummy came to the door and called Daddy. Daddy got up from the dining table and went out.

Suddenly, there was no taste in the food.

Ten minutes later, Mummy and Daddy came back to the dining room, looking shaken.

'Beta,' Mummy said. 'Shekhar just phoned from Chandigarh.'

Mummy sat down opposite her. Daddy sat down next to her.

'Beta, you left your house without telling your husband and in-laws?' Daddy asked.

'They never let me come home, Daddy. I only came for a few days.'

'Beta, how could you do such a thing?' Daddy's voice was full of incomprehension.

She was beginning to feel slightly nauseous.

'Beta, is he beating you?' Mummy asked, her voice trembling.

'No, Mummy.'

It was the biggest mistake of her life that she told them the truth.

'Then, Beta, you have to go back tomorrow. Shekhar said if you go back by tomorrow, they will forgive you. Otherwise, they will never take you back.'

'Then let them not take me back, Mummy.' She began to cry.

Mummy was also crying. 'Beta, you must go back. That is your home now.'

'This is not my home, Mummy?' It was not a question. It was an entreaty.

'Bitiya, you are a married woman now.' Mummy wiped her eyes with her palm.

'Shekhar has… many… affairs.'

Mummy closed her eyes. Daddy made a sound of distress.

Then Mummy looked at her. 'It happens, Beta. Let it be.'

'Mummy,' she sobbed.

'Beta, such a good girl you are, such a good wife. Even your mother-in-law says you are the best Bahu. Wait and see. Your goodness, it will change him. Your goodness, it will sudharo him.'

'Beta,' her father said. 'Your Mummy is saying the right thing.'

'Mummy, Daddy, I'm not happy.'

'That is no reason, my Bitiya,' Mummy said. 'Happiness will come. Chalo. Tomorrow morning, we will take you back to Chandigarh.'

'I have to say goodbye to Mallika.'

'Best if no one knows, Beta,' her father said, his voice heavy with grief.

'I have to say goodbye to Mallika.' By now she was weeping uncontrollably.

'Alright, alright, do not cry, my Bitiya,' Daddy said, his voice choking. 'Tomorrow morning, you go for five minutes and say goodbye to Mallika.'

'Yes, she will not tell anyone,' Mummy said. 'After that, we will drive you back to Chandigarh and come back in taxi. Remember, my Bitiya, acceptance is the biggest thing. Then happiness will come. Acceptance is the only thing, my Bitiya. It is the only thing.'

Prabha: Goodbye

August 1980

All this time in Delhi, she'd been wanting to talk to Mallika and Gauri about Shantanu. But she hadn't known how to bring it up without them having a fit. It wasn't as if she could say right off, 'You know, I'm sleeping with this boy in my class, and I really, really like him, but I don't know if I want to marry him, and I'm not sure if I love him.' She, like Mallika and Gauri, had always equated sex with love, till she met Shantanu and tumbled happily into his bed. She had postponed telling them, and now, there was no time with Mallika leaving for America in two days. She had wanted to talk to them about her confusion. Randhir's story about two halves looking for each other in order to become whole didn't seem to be it. Would Gauri know? After all, Gauri loved Vineet. And Mallika... Well, she still wasn't sure if Mallika's love for Randhir was what Gauri made it out to be, but when Mallika listened to her, it helped Prabha sort out her thoughts.

She was thinking this as she and Gauri sorted out Mallika's things into two piles. 'The pressure cooker, masalas, toiletries, sheets, and towels go into one suitcase, and your clothes into the other,' Gauri said, taking charge. 'You don't want your clothes smelling of haldi and jeera.'

Mallika's mother had swung into action even before Mallika got the visa. Padma Aunty had had pure wool sweaters knitted for Mallika, and had had colourful handloom skirts, new handloom blouses, and petticoats stitched by the tailor. Mallika was taking her old silk sarees too.

'Why on earth are you taking sarees to America? Randhir said you can't wear sarees in the snow,' Prabha said.

'I'll wear them in the summer,' Mallika said in her obstinate way.

'What about razais and all?' Prabha asked, and Mallika said Randhir would lend her one till she bought one there.

'He said that in America I can get furniture for a few dollars at something called "garage sales,"' Mallika said. 'And we can easily get couches, chairs, and so on at the dump. Ma and Shantamama were so shocked!'

That night, as Mallika slept, Gauri told Prabha how she'd finally told Mallika about the kiss.

'What was her reaction?' Prabha asked.

'Shock. Then she said, very scornfully, that she wasn't going to ask him about a four-year-old kiss.'

'She's right. They're good friends now, what's the point of spoiling that?'

'I suppose so.'

For a few moments, neither spoke.

'Gauri, tell me, how do you know you love Vineet?'

'How do I *know*? I just… I *know*!'

'I mean, what *is* love?'

'Must you analyse everything! It just means you want to be with him for the rest of your life.'

Well, she couldn't imagine being with Shantanu for the rest of her life. Even though he was so gentle and thoughtful, and so ready to listen when she talked about the issues that mattered to her. In fact, he was the only boy she knew who listened to her as though he really wanted to understand. She *should* love him. She *should*. *Why* didn't she?

'By the way, Mallika went to Arnav's barsati for an *hour* at five a.m. yesterday,' Gauri said.

Prabha came out of her thoughts. '*What*! Why?'

'She wouldn't tell me.' Then Gauri related what Mallika's mothers had said.

'We'll get it out of her tomorrow,' was Prabha's response.

But at seven a.m., before they could ask Mallika anything, the bedroom door opened, and it was Mahima!

They shouted with joy and hugged her, and she hugged them back fiercely. She said, 'Mallika, I'm here to say goodbye to you, and then I have to go back to Chandigarh.'

They stared at her.

'What d'you mean you have to go – when did you come?' Prabha asked.

'I came last night, but I wanted to spend time with Mummy and Daddy too.'

Mallika said, 'You came to Delhi for *one* night?'

Mahima's eyes were red. 'I got into the car and drove home from Chandigarh yesterday. Didn't tell Shekhar or my in-laws.'

They looked at her in disbelief.

'I was homesick. If Shekhar can do whatever he wants to do, then why can't I do something simple like seeing my parents and saying goodbye to you, Mallika?'

They were wordless with shock.

'The in-laws phoned last night. Mummy managed to placate them. They said they'd accept me back only if I returned today. So Mummy and Daddy are taking me back to Chandigarh. Mallika, have a safe journey and keep writing to me, OK? Don't *ever* stop writing to me.' She hugged Mallika.

'Mahima, what's wrong?' Prabha asked.

'Nothing. I was homesick. I have to go.' She hugged them all. Tears were running down her cheeks as she rushed out of the room.

They looked at each other and ran down after her.

At Mahima's back veranda, Uncle was sitting in the driver's seat of the car Mahima had taken, and Madhu Aunty next to him. Mahima clambered into the back seat, Madhu Aunty gave a forced smile and waved, and the car drove away.

They went back to Mallika's room without talking.

'Oh, god,' Gauri said, sitting down on the bed.

Mallika sat next to her. 'Do you think it's something to do with what Renu said all those years ago? That Shekhar's a pervert?'

'I don't even know what Renu meant when she said that,' Prabha said.

'Maybe it's the painful sex?' Mallika said.

'No one leaves their marriage because of sex,' Gauri said.

'How do we know that?' Mallika asked. 'People never talk about these things.'

'In a marriage, everyone is hiding something or another,' Prabha said. 'I'm going to visit her in Chandigarh, and I'm going to find out.'

'I'll come with you,' Gauri said.

'Winter holidays, Gauri, we'll go for two days.'

There wasn't anything to say after that. They went back to helping Mallika with the packing. Prabha's confusion about Shantanu retreated to the background. Now wasn't the time to talk about it.

Gauri said, 'So. Why did you go to Arnav's room, Mallika?'

Mallika sat down on the bed. 'I'll tell you, but don't mention it to Ma or Shantamama,'

It was strange, Prabha thought, how close she was to her mothers and yet how much she hid from them.

'Remember that time when Shantamama was going to have her operation?' Mallika said. 'And I couldn't go because I had a very heavy period? Well, I was in a scooter...' Here, Mallika paused. 'Because I wasn't feeling well. In the scooter, I started bleeding heavily. You know how my periods are always delayed. The scooterwalla was passing this clinic, and he took me there.'

Here, Mallika paused again.

'Afterwards, the doctor phoned Randhir, and he came and took me home. I'd have told Ma, but Shantamama's operation was the next day, so I asked Randhir not to mention it to them. The doctor had said I could pay her later. After I resumed tutoring, I began putting money aside to pay her. By last month, I had it all. Then, on the way to the doctor's clinic, I was pickpocketed in the bus. I can't go to America without paying the doctor. So I went to Arnav to borrow the money. He gave it to me. I paid her back. That's it.'

'You should have taken a scooter to the doctor's clinic,' Prabha said, shocked.

'I know, I know.'

'How much money?' Gauri asked.

Mallika said, 'I'm not telling you.'

'That means that gynae charged an arm and a leg,' Gauri said.

'You told Arnav why you wanted the money?' Prabha asked.

'I told him I'd lost a gold chain I'd borrowed from a friend and had to pay her before I left.'

'He must have seen right through your lie,' Gauri said.

'He did. But he gave me the money anyway. I mean, lent me the money.'

'Why didn't you tell us all this before?' Prabha asked.

'None of you were there when it happened. And later, there was Shantamama's operation. Then my second-year exams. Then the TB. Then months of weakness… By then, I didn't even want to *think* about it, let alone talk about it. I still haven't told my mothers. It's over now. It's finished.'

And suddenly, out of the blue, a scene replayed in Prabha's mind: the two girls, Deepika and Arati, after they heard of Prabha punching the man in the bus, saying, so contemptuously, 'deal with it.' She had been so shaken, so bewildered. She had never stopped asking herself what those words had meant. It was true that Randhir, Arnav, and Vineet had been blind about what girls had to go through in Delhi, but at least their blindness wasn't feigned. But when the very ones subject to this kind of violence feigned blindness, advocated silence, and condemned those who defended themselves, then what to do?

But now, finally, she understood what those girls had meant. 'Deal with it' meant, keep your mouth shut. It meant, put up with it. It meant, don't make a scene. *That's* what those two girls had meant. *That's* what Mallika had done. *That's* what Mahima was doing. When someone told you to 'deal with it,' what they meant was, hide it. What they meant was, accept it. What they meant was, don't talk about it. What they meant was, pretend it doesn't happen. All of which really meant, *don't* deal with it.

Arnav: Wishing it

August 1980

She was whispering his name, asking him to wake up. He didn't want to. He wanted to stay in bed with her. She was next to him, but he couldn't see her because his eyes wouldn't open. He couldn't put his arms around her because they wouldn't move. He wanted to say her name, but it was stuck in his throat.

She was kneeling by his bed, looking at him. Her eyes were full of sadness. What was she doing outside his bed?

His sleep vanished.

Mallika?

In his room?

In the bathroom, two minutes later, he leaned against the door, trying to breathe. He looked at his watch. It was five-ten a.m.

All the pranayama he'd done since that time hadn't prepared him for this moment. He tried to breathe slowly and deeply. He tried to count every breath. He knew why she was in his room. She was here to tell him her memory had come back. To say, *Why didn't you tell me?*

He couldn't remember why.

Think. *Think.* There's an answer. More than one. *Think.*

He couldn't remember.

He washed his face, brushed his teeth, wore the t-shirt that was hanging on the door.

The thoughts that had come to him four years ago began to resurface.

He hadn't told her about the horror of what had happened to her that night, and what it had taken for her to defend herself, because… what was the point? Why would she even want to know something so gruesome, so terrifying, when her mind had erased it?

He hadn't told her they'd slept together because she had always been Randhir's. As much as Randhir had always been hers.

So?

He'd betrayed his best friend. If Randhir came to know, he'd lose Randhir forever.

You're going to tell her it was because you'd lose Randhir?

His thoughts came to a halt.

Then they began again. They would never have slept with each other if they hadn't lived that horror together. That was all it was – a mistake. He had sworn it would never happen again.

What has that got to do with anything?

His thoughts came to another halt.

Then they began again.

What about Jalpari?

But he hadn't even known who Jalpari was.

You knew later.

But when he had got to know who Jalpari was, he'd also got to know that she had not returned. That Mallika's father had followed it up with the police to no avail.

He came out of the bathroom and found her on the chair opposite his bed, eyes closed, breathing deeply. Already, he was finding her distress hard to take.

He sat on the bed, facing her, bracing himself.

She opened her eyes and began to speak.

She was rambling. About Mrs D'Souza, about money... What was she talking about?

About a thousand rupees?

Did he have it? Could she borrow it?

Her memory hadn't come back.

Relief hit him.

Then – a *thousand* rupees?

That was a *lot* of money. It was two-thirds of his monthly salary as an engineer.

This evening?

He knew why before he even asked her. There were a couple of guys at IIT who'd had to find exactly that much money. You didn't take a pregnant girl to an unsanitary government hospital for an abortion. To have it done at a private clinic cost a thousand rupees.

She was giving him explanations. She'd made up a story. She was a lousy liar. She was flushed, her voice was shaking, he was sure she had no idea she was wringing her hands.

He wanted to kill Randhir.

He also wanted to kick himself. He should have kept his bloody mouth shut. He should have said he'd give her the money and left it at that instead of asking her questions. So what if she denied being pregnant by Randhir? What mattered was that Randhir had left her in this predicament and gone off to America. She was almost reduced to tears by his questions. She was on the point of leaving his room when he pulled her into his arms. He hadn't meant to. She sank into his embrace. As though it was this she had come for. And of all the times for it to happen, his desire for her, which he'd always held on such a tight leash, returned. Here she was, pregnant with Randhir's baby, and all he could think of –

He let her go. She looked at him, her eyes heavy, as though they were in the throes of lovemaking. He turned her around and opened the door, appalled at what they'd almost done at a time like this.

Yes, what *they'd* almost done, not what *he'd* almost done. She loved Randhir, but she wanted him too. She always had, even if she didn't know it. He himself hadn't known it until this moment. Until this moment, he hadn't known that the reason she wanted him was because she couldn't have Randhir. That he should be Randhir's substitute, was, he supposed, inevitable.

He didn't have the thousand rupees. He'd paid for his plane ticket and cleaned out his bank account. His parents had given him money to buy dollars, and Ma had given him some extra that she'd bought from Niharika over the years. There was nothing to do but sell a hundred dollars in black. He took five unfamiliar twenty-dollar notes with him to Mohan Singh Market in CP, and within five minutes, sold them to a plump, overfriendly guy who talked too much and seemed exceedingly comfortable with the nature of the transaction. Afterwards, the guy even had the bloody presumption to say, 'Chalo, should we have chai-samosas?' as though celebrating their black-market transaction. Arnav said he was in a hurry and split.

More fraught with danger than any black-market transaction was the act of giving the money to Mallika in the nest of her mothers, grandmother, and aunties. When he arrived, it was pretty obvious that Mrs D'Souza – who seemed to have swallowed the story he'd spun about Mallika declining his proposal – had told everyone. He could see it on their faces as they conversed with him about everything but that. Somehow, he managed to find Mallika alone in the kitchen and give her the envelope of money. She rapidly slipped it inside her saree, briefly revealing a smooth curve of waist, navel, and hip, a sight that so distracted him that he forgot to tell her about the proposal story he'd made up; then her mother entered, and it was too late.

After an excruciating tea and pc with the hospitable, suspicious aunties, he went back home and packed. Not much to pack. The bed, desk, and chair belonged to Mrs D'Souza. It took an hour to stuff his clothes, sheets, towels, a few kitchen utensils, and his tapes of music into three suitcases. His sketchbooks too, including the one full of drawings of Mishti, which he hadn't looked at for years – he'd take these to America.

He drove home on his bike, and after half an hour of pleading with his father – something he'd sworn he'd never do – returned to his barsati with his father's car.

Arnav's head was bursting. So much for all Randhir's declarations of there being nothing of the sort between him and Mallika.

What had Arnav got himself into?

Why the *hell* had he kissed Mallika the night of Mahima's wedding?

Or had it started with the puppy that she stole?

As for that fateful night, he'd become a pro at not thinking about it. He'd even managed to knock that awful expression of hers out of his head, the one she'd been wearing as she entered Randhir's room after her concussion, talking to Arnav politely, tentatively, as though he were nobody. Totally chilling.

But after that? Afterwards, why hadn't he let things slide back to the way it had been before the kiss, and before the stolen puppy?

He'd tried, and for some time, he'd succeeded. He'd acted in a play, thrown himself into his volunteer work at the Conservation Fund, and went less often to Randhir's house. But when Randhir asked him to pick her up from her college, how could he say no? Then she collapsed in his room, and after that, it had become too damn confusing. He'd felt as though the state she was in was all his fault, even though she told him it was the TB – so bloody weird. Picking her up from her college twice a week had decimated his resolve to avoid her. Because he became fond of her. Nothing wrong with that; he could handle the affection, it was easy.

It was always easy until it wasn't. That became the pattern.

Like an ass, he'd landed up in her all-too-familiar room in the middle of the night, ostensibly to apologize, but really because she had this invisible rope around his neck and was yanking him towards her. And there she was, at that ungodly hour, chattering away with him, telling him to leave without meaning it, beguiling him with every word. Ending up asleep and entwined around him, asking him to kiss her; had he not suddenly realised she was half-asleep, they'd have done more than kiss, even with the threat of those mushrooming mothers.

Going to Bombay had changed nothing. Mallika didn't understand why he was going, and neither did he. He just knew he had to get away. No way was he going because he was running away from her, that was rubbish. It was his restlessness. His restlessness had plagued him ever since he could remember. The only one who'd kept him grounded was Randhir, but soon Randhir was going to disappear into that wretched factory. Bloody awful predicament; he felt Randhir's pain viscerally. So he'd left. But he disliked Bombay, and he hated his job, and he missed Randhir and Mallika like crazy.

When he returned from Bombay, his parents were happy to have him back home with them but bemoaned his lack of steadiness. On and on they went, 'You can't change jobs so often, you need to grow up, settle down.' He and Randhir had often laughed about this business of 'settling down.' Meaning, stay in the same job for the rest of your life even if you hate it, live in the same city because you've always lived in it, live at home with your parents because that was what everyone did, and of course, get married. Settling down sounded like the sounded like the clanging of prison gates prison gates.

And what a pain, staying with his parents after he returned from Bombay – 'Your music's too loud, you never spend any time at home, where are you going at this time of the night?' It never ended. Staying at home and coming back late from work meant no time with Randhir or Mallika except on weekends, and even so, Randhir was busy. As for telling his parents that, within a few months of joining the Delhi job, he was sick of it and had decided to apply for a PhD in Engineering to an American university – that was out of the question. Telling them that he was doing it because it was the best way of travelling the world? What a laugh!

Then his father decided to have a havan at home to give thanks for Arnav's new Delhi job. There had been a time when he'd yawned his way through his father's havans for his mother's sake – because if he didn't do it, his father would take it out on his mother. But after Mishti's death, he was done with his father's prayers. He told his parents no. 'But this havan is for *you*,' his father said. Arnav had made the stupid mistake of saying, 'I'm an atheist.' His father snorted, 'You stupid boy, you have no life experience, you don't even know what that means,' and went on his usual spiel. Said he'd never known anyone so cussed, called him an ingrate, an ignoramus, et cetera, et cetera. Then his mother took him aside and said, so what if he didn't believe in havans, she also didn't believe in them, what did it cost him to make his father happy? 'Ma, I can't,' he said, even though he knew his father would now proceed to take out his anger on her. He was tired of protecting her; he'd lived that lie long enough, he couldn't live it anymore.

Then, thanks to Mallika and the parrot, he'd found refuge in Mrs D'Souza's barsati. After that, Randhir left for America, and he told himself he was getting too damn fond of Mallika. He'd better minimize his time with her, he thought.

Easy to do initially, because his sister, Niharika came from America with her husband and twin babies after three years, and he'd moved back home again for a while. As soon as he hugged his sister, she kissed him and said, 'You're such a sweetheart to keep writing to me, you're the best brother.' It was her olive branch, and he had grabbed it. Though he went to work every day, he had the evenings and weekends with her and the babies. It felt as though they had never been estranged. The only difficulty was being polite to his brother-in-law. But if being a bloody hypocrite was what it took to keep his sister, he'd be a bloody hypocrite.

A couple of days after his sister left, he took an hour off from work to go to the USEFI and saw Mallika coming out of the building in one of her colourful sarees, giving him a smile that immediately and effectively demolished his resolution to keep her at a distance. Suddenly, he felt crazily happy.

Within the hour, his happiness vanished. Who did she think she was kidding, saying she was applying to American universities because she'd always dreamt of studying in America! That it was because of lack of money for the plane ticket that she hadn't applied earlier! Hadn't her grandmother given her the money when she asked? If she had wanted, she could have asked her grandmother earlier. But she hadn't, because she thought Randhir would marry her and take her with him to America. That hadn't happened, so now Mallika was following him, for god's sake.

Shoving aside his frustration, he began talking to Mallika about his brother-in-law's affair, forgetting that the girl who knew about it was not this Mallika, but the Mallika in the ether. Once he realized who he was talking to, his blood ran cold. But to his relief, Mallika didn't notice he was blabbering. Instead, she began talking about her mother's early life as a widow and how tough it was for widowed and divorced women. He was sucked into what she was saying, glimpsing, for the first time, the constrained world in which Mallika had lived. When she said that his sister's reaction had come out of fear, it struck him how true this was, and he wanted to hold her earnest face between his hands and kiss her.

And that wasn't even the half of it. Because after her ice cream, which he enjoyed watching her eat as much as she enjoyed eating it, and after he'd wiped some off her soft, smooth cheek, and after he saw the fear in her eyes as she realized he now knew that her stepfather was her father, she screamed.

'Jalpari!'

And ran after a girl crossing the road.

In that instant, he was transported back to that long-ago night. He was back in that nightmare. Daylight turned to darkness as he ran after her — something terrible was going to happen to her. Then darkness turned to bright afternoon light; the young girl had disappeared, and Mallika, her face ravaged with terror, was leaning against the pillar, panting that she thought the girl was Jalpari.

He would forever be grateful to the Thimayas for rescuing them both from that moment.

That night, he couldn't sleep. Mallika's terror wouldn't leave him. He didn't understand it. Distress he understood, but why *terror*, when her memory of that night had gone?

Had her memory come back?

He shot up in bed, holding his head in his hands.

After she shoved him into the lake, he summoned up the guts to ask her why. She said she had felt she was going to die. But she didn't know why.

Her memory hadn't come back.

But the memory of the terror had. *How?*

That deceptive calmness gathered them into its fold once again. Sometimes, as she went for her walks, he joined her simply because her presence soothed him. By the time he started tutoring Mallika for the Maths section of the GRE, she was entrenched in his life. If he was going to America, he wanted her there too. On the very first day of tutoring, she asked him what an isosceles triangle was. 'But this is *basic*, Mallika,' he said in disbelief, and she said airily, 'I guess I've forgotten my basics – I did Maths in the ninth!' That very night, he wrote to Randhir. *It's all over man, she's going to fail the Maths section of the GREs – her Maths fundas are zero.*

Mallika was totally bindaas about failing in Maths. 'I don't see why my Maths scores should matter to the English department,' she said, a statement that made no sense given that it *would* matter. Sometimes, the things she said defied logic.

'I used to get bad migraines but the Phuknewalla who lives behind us, he's more or less cured them,' she said once.

'The *who*?'

'Phuknewalla. He was born with this gift of taking away headaches – Arnav, he literally takes it out of your head, without even touching you, and then he blows it away, like this.' And she moved her hand in the air, made it into a fist – as though it was holding something – opened her fist, and blew into her palm. Then she looked at him and gave a peal of laughter. 'Randhir doesn't believe it either, but he pretends to.'

Since there was no answer to her flabbergasting belief that someone could blow away migraines, he gave her none. Besides, he was, as always, beguiled by her laughter.

Then dinner. Between his meals with Mallika's family, Madhu Aunty, and those that his mother packed for him, he rarely had to get food from outside. He enjoyed observing Mallika in her home as they ate together. Everything centred around her. Her mothers and grandmother were constantly giving her advice, talking to her, talking about her, urging her to eat more, it never ended. The wonder was that Mallika wasn't suffocated; on the contrary, she seemed totally comfortable with it. Yet, even with the non-stop talking and Ayah-ji's constant grumblings, it was a peaceful house. He wondered about that, given his recent insight into Mallika's life. All he had to do was substitute the words 'unmarried mother' for 'widow' to know that Mallika and Padma Aunty's lives had probably been a lot tougher than Mallika had indicated. What Arnav understood by now was that the man who had made Mallika's mother pregnant had finally done the right thing by her and married her. Still. Why didn't Mallika's mother live with her husband? Mallika had explained that her father's mother, who was living with him, was against the marriage... But no, it didn't gel.

By the time Randhir came home from America, Arnav had got admission and aid at the same university. To his astonishment, his parents were thrilled. His father was full of praise for him, said he'd finally grown up, sighed that he'd miss him, but that he was proud of what he'd accomplished all on his own.

Initially, it was like old times when Randhir came back, the three of them together; it was perfect. Mallika and Randhir were bursting with happiness to be reunited. Mallika even enjoyed Randhir's party, though, of course, she was bullshitting when she told Vineet she didn't want to marry.

But when he and Randhir each gave Mallika advice about the other, the harmony was shattered.

That incident left a nasty taste in his mouth. He should never have accused Randhir of passing Mallika onto him, Arnav. But it had just come out of his mouth. He felt as though he'd tainted his friendship with Mallika by speaking of her like that.

The day of Mallika's visa interview started innocuously enough, with Mallika emerging from the interview saying the visa officer was calling Arnav to ask him about their engagement. As he braced himself to go in and lie through his teeth, Mallika gave one of her peals of laughter and admitted she was teasing, and in the same breath, told him her visa had been rejected.

He was stunned.

Didn't she care? How could she laugh and tease him like that?

Later, at Nirulas with Randhir, Vineet, Gauri, and Prabha, he could barely eat or talk. It was mind-boggling to him that the prospect of being separated from Mallika felt worse than when Randhir had left for America. When Randhir had left, he had been bereft, but he hadn't felt he'd lost him. But he'd lose Mallika for sure. It was goodbye. A final one. Two different paths, two different worlds, oceans between them. This time when he left, she wouldn't say, *Only you*. This time when he left, she wouldn't ask, *Will you come back to me?*

Those baffling words now slipped out of that dream and into his head. She had spoken as if one shared trauma and one night together had bound them forever. What had she *meant*? What had she been about to say just before they heard Ayah-ji downstairs?

He glanced at Mallika. She was eating and chuckling at something Prabha was saying. No doubt she would want ice cream soon after. Not a care that she hadn't got the visa.

Then they discovered she *had* got it.

Randhir was delirious with excitement. He said it was the best bloody thing that had happened in his life.

It was the best bloody thing that had happened in Arnav's life too. He hadn't known till this day that it would have gutted him to be separated from her.

After that, he felt he was flying. And then he *was*. With her. It was crazy how exhilarating it was, soaring off the motorcycle as though they were one, as if he had wings and was taking her for a joyride on his back. He felt her arms tight around his waist, her cheek on his shoulder, the weight of her body behind his. What must have been a few seconds seemed endless; time took on another shape. His thoughts found him. They were lucid, unmistakeable. She was his thoughts. She was all around him, everywhere inside him. It seemed completely natural that, if they were to die, they would die together.

He came down to earth. Literally. His exhilaration turned to terror. It wasn't unlike that old time. Four years ago, he had thought she would be raped and finished off, her body thrown somewhere far away. This time, he thought he'd killed her.

The road below them was moving – it wasn't the road, it was cows. *Cows*. They'd landed on *cows*. His terror turned to full-blown relief. She was alive.

Only with her. First, she stole a puppy, earning his immediate devotion. Then her large, pleading eyes had persuaded him to climb up onto a roof and rescue a parrot. Now, cows. This time, as the crowd of fervent cow worshippers cheered and chanted, and as the saffron-clad man tried to get her to pay homage to the cows, she fainted so convincingly into his arms, that, for a heart-stopping instant, he didn't know she was pretending. Later, sitting on the cement seat at the bus stop, he held her firmly. It felt nice to hold her. Very nice. The people at the bus stop said his wife would be all right soon, she wasn't hurt, he should not be worried; a middle-aged woman ordered the peering crowd to move away, to give her some air. Soon, Mallika opened her eyes; they were shy but also laughing, and he wanted to kiss her. This had been the constant danger after that long-ago night – the forever-on-the-brink kiss, the kiss that lay like a chasm between him and the girl who had given her heart to his oldest and best friend. Not that he, Arnav, could have kissed her even if she was free of Randhir, because every time he wanted to, they were outside. For that matter, every time they were inside, there were mothers, aunties, grandmothers, friends, and tuition children. They *had* been alone that time – more than three years ago – in his IIT hostel room, and she'd been in his bed, but all that had happened was that she had made him feel like a bloody jerk by talking about the 'allergies' on his neck in Mohini's presence. As though he'd betrayed her by being with Mohini, as though he owed her his lifelong fidelity because of that one night.

They'd also been alone the night he went to apologize for calling her boring. That night, in her sleeping-pill-induced sleep, she had asked him to kiss her – nothing chaste about that kiss. Was she dreaming he was Randhir? Later, she didn't remember it. She was good at forgetting. She was bloody good at it.

They were too much, his thoughts. That night, Mohini came up to his barsati. The relief.

By the time Mohini climbed down the terrace drainpipe, and by the time Mrs D'Souza checked every corner of his room, bathroom, and terrace to make sure no girl was hiding there, his relief had dissipated. A sense of dread hovered around him. He didn't want to see Mallika. But suppose she wasn't OK after the accident? The invisible rope she had around his neck twitched, and off he went to her house.

And what a ghastly sight – Mohini talking animatedly to a wide-eyed Mallika, giggling 'Mallika said she'll try you since you come so highly recommended.' She'd been giggling all night; the sound had driven him nuts. It drove him crazier that Mallika had made such a bitchy remark about him to Mohini. And after Mohini breezed off, she had the presumption to say that Mohini had told her *all* about sleeping with him. Why the hell hadn't he left? But no, he'd sat down with Mallika. Why? He didn't owe her any bloody explanations. And Mallika, with that astounded, self-righteous expression, asking him how it couldn't mean anything. Everything wasn't about love for god's sake, what a stupid question, and none of her damn business anyway. He left. Then, like a fool, he returned and told her that everyone wasn't like her; this was true, but why the fuck did he feel he had to say it?

And why had he continued feeling like shit even after that? After Randhir left, Mallika retreated into her shell and barely spoke, not even during the two days that they spent together booking their tickets and buying dollars. Over a late lunch at Triveni, he asked her if anything was the matter. She said, 'Just... you know, leaving India.' He nodded. Of course it was that. Naturally, she'd miss her mothers like crazy. What a relief.

His relief didn't last long. She came up to his room at five a.m. to borrow a thousand rupees.

The morning after he gave her the money, he was in his father's car by eight a.m. He'd parked it across the road from her house, and she didn't even look at it as she walked to the scooter stand, holding her umbrella over her head. She got onto a scooter, and he followed it all the way to a dentist's clinic. *Dentist?* Was he being irrational about why Mallika had wanted a thousand rupees? Sometimes he could be, like the time a few years ago when he'd thrown away the bottle of pills in Randhir's bathroom cabinet. There was no reason to do it, except for one casual conversation during which Randhir had said he understood why that DU guy had taken his own life – because everyone thought the guy was perfect. He'd almost felt Randhir was talking about himself. After that, every time Arnav opened Randhir's bathroom cabinet to use the Old Spice, something inside him would scream, *Get rid of that bottle!* Even though he knew Randhir was hiding nothing, even though he knew Randhir's occasional black moods were of no consequence, even though he was sure that suicide was the last thing on his friend's mind. Finally, before Mahima's wedding, he'd taken the bottle out of the bathroom cabinet and thrown it into the colony rubbish dump. Randhir had never asked him about it; later, Arnav was sure he'd been paranoid. Maybe he was being the same with Mallika?

When Mallika came out of the dentist's office, she walked past the car without seeing him once again. He drove towards her and stopped. She looked at him fiercely. Then, when she saw he wasn't some lecherous stranger, her fierceness turned to apprehension. He didn't listen to her protests, she got into the car, and within a few minutes, they arrived at another clinic. When they got out of the car, she looked up at him. He just couldn't meet her despairing eyes. He hustled her inside.

He *was* right. It was a gynaecologist's clinic.

He wanted to say something to her before she went inside, but he didn't know what, and she went in so quickly. How long would it take? He sat at the reception, feeling queasy.

She was out in less than five minutes. Ready to go home.

What the hell was going on?

At the Chinese restaurant, he was thinking hard, but to no avail.

So he asked her if she'd gone to this doctor just to pay her. She said yes.

That meant she'd had the abortion a few days earlier but hadn't had the money then.

Of course, she hedged when he asked her. 'Some gynaecological issues' didn't cut it for him. He asked her when she'd had those issues.

She said last year.

So not this time. It must have happened before Randhir left for America last year. Randhir couldn't have known when he left that she was pregnant. She couldn't have known either, or else she'd have told Randhir.

He couldn't believe she wasn't going to tell Randhir now. It made no sense. He said he would.

That was when Mallika started losing it. *Really* losing it. Asking him where he thought she and Randhir had had sex, in which house, in which seedy hotel, stuff like that. Saying that she and Randhir didn't have the opportunities for sex that *he* had, and didn't he have any brains, and what was he thinking?

What was he supposed to say? That his mind didn't go there?

She was so emotional that he almost believed her.

But who else could it be? That was the thing. There was no one else.

Which was what he asked her: if not Randhir, then who?

She began to tremble. When she spoke, her voice was shaking so much that her words came out in gasps. 'Since you seem to be so convinced I was pregnant, *you* tell me – was it *you*?'

It was not his friend Mallika, her face contorted, who was uttering these words. It was the girl in that four-year-old dream who was confronting him for making her pregnant and abandoning her.

That girl disappeared.

He sat fixed to his chair.

Slowly, things came back into focus. He was in a restaurant. People were staring at his table. He was alone.

He rushed to the counter, paid the bill, ran outside. No, she hadn't gone off in a scooter, she was there, leaning against the car.

They got into the car. Inside it, he couldn't speak. He couldn't even look at her.

She was apologizing, she didn't want to talk about it, it was water under the bridge, it was four years ago.

He looked at her.

She was looking down at her lap. Sweat was running down her neck, and the back of her sleeveless blouse was damp with it. Her hair was piled high behind her head with two long wooden hairpins holding it in place, their sharp ends jutting out of her bun. Her orange saree was limp, her hands were clasped tightly on her lap. Yes, she said to his question, it was four years ago, a few months after Mahima's wedding, around the end of April.

Then, as he stopped breathing, she told him.

Every word she uttered wrote itself inside him. It was like that. And it was like looking at the writing on the page inside him and not really knowing what it held, even though he knew the language, even though he understood every word. The page held more than her words, more than his questions; it held more than his comprehension that he had made her pregnant and then abandoned her, leaving her to go through it all alone and then be rescued by Randhir, and to believe, all these years, that she had gone crazy and imagined her pregnancy.

Her words held a lot more than that. But the rest of this truth would have to wait for him till he could get back to himself. He felt very far away from himself.

So far away that, this time too, he couldn't tell her the truth. What few words he had, he gave to her: he promised her she was not like Charu and that she had not gone crazy. He spoke these words from his very heart. Not that she would believe him. She would think it was his comfort he was giving her, not his conviction.

But she believed him.

They were looking at each other, and he saw her face transform. He had never seen that kind of relief on anyone's face. She believed him completely.

After he dropped her home, he went to his barsati, loaded the car, got the place cleaned by the woman who did his jhadu-pocha, gave the keys to Mrs D'Souza, and took leave of her. She wished him luck and said many things to which he nodded and smiled without understanding. Then he took leave of Madhu Aunty and Uncle. Aunty wept a lot, said she would miss him like a son, kept hugging him. She gave him several packets of dals and masalas for Randhir – it was very expensive in America, no nearby Indian shops, she kept saying, and he kept nodding. He didn't take leave of Mallika's mothers and grandmother since he knew he'd meet them at the airport. Then he drove home, unloaded the car, repacked two suitcases to take to America, packed his in-flight bag, listened to his parents' advice about how he should maintain his Indian values in America, had dinner with them, and then, turning a deaf ear to their protests about how little time he had left with them, he drove his motorcycle to Rajpath. There, he parked his bike at the India Gate end and began running down Rajpath towards Rashtrapati Bhavan. The jamun trees on either side of those glorious, sweeping grounds felt like a benediction even in the darkness. Rajpath was virtually empty at this time of the night, as empty as the roads had been four years ago when, in another part of Delhi, two men had grabbed Mallika and thrown her into their car.

That night – forgotten by her and unacknowledged by him – had always been there between them. How could he ever have thought he'd quenched it? The horror of what happened to Jalpari, and then to Mallika, and Mallika's bloody defence of herself – it had all happened. They had slept together. That had happened. However hard he had tried to live as though none of it was real, all of it had happened.

It was not just she who had wanted obliteration that night, he had wanted it too. Only one night, but he knew her body, every bit of it. Even though he had barely seen it in the darkness, he knew it better than any other; even though he had known others longer. 'Take it away,' she had said. If her memory ever came back, she'd know how thoroughly he had taken it away. If her memory ever came back, she would know she had done the same for him.

Mallika had asked him if the man had died, and he had said no, and she had believed him. It was possible that he hadn't died. But it was also possible that he had, either that night or later. This had been Arnav's fear, that with a knife so small that it fitted into her blouse, she had saved her own life and inflicted enough damage to have taken her attacker's. For days, he had scoured the newspapers; for weeks, he had waited for Randhir to tell him that the police had arrived at her doorstep. This, his greatest fear, he had managed to forget about until now.

As he ran, a solitary figure in the darkness, he knew that Randhir would know that Mallika had been pregnant. Because there was no way Randhir wouldn't have talked to the doctor. But what sense had Randhir made of Mallika's pregnancy when Mallika had refused to talk to him? What conclusion had Randhir come to?

Then another realization. That he had been with Randhir, studying for exams, the day Mallika phoned from the clinic. Randhir had come back to the room and said he was picking up Mallika since she wasn't well. Arnav had even offered to do it instead. To this day, he could remember Randhir's tone as he said, '*You?* Why should *you!*'

True. Who was he to Mallika at that time? Between her loss of memory and his absolute determination to quench his own, they were nothing to each other. Ever since that night, he had fought it, his feeling that he'd betrayed her. He hadn't even known how much this fight had angered him. Her love for Randhir had let him harden his heart against her. Every time he had wanted her, he had worn his anger like a shield.

But had he told Mallika about that night, she would have contacted him, not Randhir. Had he told her about that night, she'd never have thought that she had gone crazy. Had he told her about that night, she would not have been alone and bleeding in a scooter on some Delhi road. That was the worst of it – that she had been alone because he had abandoned her.

Going to America heralded the end of his closest friendships. Mallika and Randhir would have nothing to do with him after he told them.

But he had a brief reprieve. About twenty-four hours with Mallika on the flight, maybe a little more with the stopover. She'd probably sleep through the flight, but she'd be right next to him. She'd be happy to be with him. She was always happy with him and Randhir and her three friends. Until they reached America, she would still be his friend.

After they landed, after she had a good night's rest, he'd tell her everything.

The only certainty now was that, until the moment when he told her, he would still have her. Have them. He couldn't imagine his life without Mallika and Randhir, but for this brief time, he would have their friendship. He would live this time as though it would never end.

Was it possible that, after he told them, it wouldn't be the end? Could their friendship beget forgiveness? Could such a miracle happen? He couldn't pray, but he could wish it. He did wish it, and he wished it, and he wished it.

Mallika: Goodbye

August 1980

'While you're staying with Randhir and Arnav, wear kaftans to sleep, not those skimpy Janpath nighties,' Ma said the next morning.

'And wear a bra under the kaftan; you may be small, but still,' Shantamama said.

'And do not leave your hair loose at night, make sure it is tied in a plait,' Ajji said.

'And use their bathroom first thing in the morning, before they do,' Shantamama said.

'Don't enter their bedrooms under any circumstances,' Ma said.

'Familiarity breeds contempt,' Shantamama said.

Karan arrived on the heels of their early morning instructions. Urgent work had prevented him from coming earlier, and I could see he was deeply upset that he had so little time with me. 'No, you're not staying with your sister, you're staying here, sleep in my room,' I said. 'I'll sleep with Ma and Shantamama.' He kissed my head and said, 'Alright.' That he was agreeing to stay under the same roof as my grandmother was a testament to how deeply he felt my impending departure. He and Ajji said their cool namastes. He greeted Ma and Shantamama, and then turned towards Prabha and Gauri with scarcely concealed relief and gladness. My friends, more than anyone else, had the ability to make him feel at home.

On Karan's heels came two neighbours, three tuition children, and one grandmother to say goodbye to me – one for the first time, three for the second time, and two for the third time. Ma asked Ayah-ji to make tea. Ayah-ji refused and went upstairs to my room. Shantamama and Ma went to the kitchen to make the tea and snacks, and the visitors settled down to chat with me.

Madhu Aunty and Uncle were back from Chandigarh. 'Too homesick Mahima was, so just for one day, she came, nothing to worry about, she is fine,' she assured us.

Prabha, Gauri, and I were not assured. The conversation Mahima had had with me about sex the first time I met her after her marriage was uppermost in my mind. Was that why she had run away and come home? Did people leave their marriages for *that*?

Prabha and Gauri took leave of Karan, my grandmother, and mothers. The three of us went to the veranda where we hugged each other goodbye.

'How *can* Mahima be fine,' I whispered to them.

Gauri said, 'Mallika, stop worrying, we'll go see her.'

'We will,' Prabha said tearfully. 'And write *long* letters to us.' Prabha was leaving for Poona again soon.

'Get to know other Indian boys in America,' Gauri advised. 'Don't keep waiting for these two.'

I wiped my face with my palm and went inside.

The visitors commiserated at my red eyes and then talked continuously. They left after an hour.

I rushed upstairs to do some more packing and added several undies to my air bag in case the plane got hijacked.

The bell rang. More visitors.

'Mallika, come downstairs,' Shantamama called.

This aggressive onslaught of affection continued till eleven-thirty p.m. Periodically, I hinted that I had so little time with my mothers and would miss them so much. The visitors agreed heartily and stayed on.

Karan had spent the entire time reading at the dining table. Now, he was asleep in my room.

Ma made the two beds. I would be sleeping with them. Shantamama took out something wrapped in an old bedsheet from her trunk and gave it to me. 'For you. Open it,' she said, sitting on the bed and patting the space beside her. I sat down. The bedsheet was smelling of neem leaves. I opened it carefully.

It was Shantamama's exquisite mustard Jamavar shawl. 'You better have it before my sons get married and my daughters-in-law begin eyeing it,' she said. 'It's an heirloom. No one makes shawls like this anymore. You can't buy it for love nor for money. Look at this work. See. It's priceless. Pack it carefully and take it to America.' She wiped away a tear.

Ma sat on my other side, gazing at the Jamavar. 'So beautiful, Shantacca, but you've hardly ever worn it.'

'I know, Padma. I used to keep saying, "For a special occasion, for a special occasion," but that special occasion never seemed to come. That's what happens with these expensive things. Mallika, wear it in America. Don't wear it as a scarf, I beg of you. Wear it with a saree for special occasions.'

I burst into tears.

My mothers put their arms around me. We all wept.

Finally, we got into the two beds, which had been pushed together. I slept between them. Ma kept caressing my back. Shantamama kept stroking my hair. Eventually, I slept.

I opened my eyes to bright sunshine. I was lying alone on Ma's bed. My last day at home. My last day in India. My last day with my mothers.

Mrs D'Souza dropped in to say goodbye as I ate breakfast and sat opposite me at the dining table, talking about her parrot, Mithu. As soon as I finished eating, wondering how to tell her I needed to pack without sounding rude, Karan said, 'Mallika, go finish your packing.' With great relief, I got up and said goodbye to Mrs D'Souza. She kissed me on both cheeks and gave me a keychain with St Anthony on it. 'He's my most beloved saint, my dear. He will find anything you want, take him with you to America.'

Two minutes later, Karan came upstairs and knocked at my door.

'I'll hold them at bay, Mallika, no need to come down.'

'But then they'll come again tonight, just before I leave,' I said despairingly.

He smiled. 'That they will. But for now, finish your packing.' He went downstairs.

The bell rang.

He held them at bay.

Ayah-ji refused to leave my room. She sat on the stool, looking at my suitcases as though they were snakes.

Shantamama came upstairs. 'My darling, now, don't get upset, I'm not forcing you, I'm just *telling* you. There's this wonderful boy, Bharat, in Washington. About five years older than you, good job, so fair and handsome, earning very well, idealistic too. He wants to come back to India. He –'

'Shantamama! No!'

'Darling, am I asking you to marry him? Will anyone ever force you into marriage? All I'm saying is, keep an open mind. If he contacts you, please meet him. For my sake. Please.'

I hated Shantamama to beg. That too, on my last day. 'Alright, Shantamama.'

'Thank you, my darling. He has a house and a car, imagine – so young, and he has all that.'

I nodded.

'So well-settled, unlike Randhir and Arnav. You want to see a photo?'

'No, Shantamama.'

'Alright.' She gave me a Cadbury. 'Put this in your handbag.'

I kissed her and put it in my handbag, tears flooding my throat again.

The bell rang.

Shantamama kissed me again. 'Karan is being very firm with the visitors. To the point of rudeness. What's the use? They'll all be back tonight.' She went downstairs.

Ma came upstairs. 'Here,' she said, giving me several packets. 'These are your TB medicines. A one-year supply. Shantamama and I went to four chemists, including two in Connaught Place, and got them. Your dose may be small these days, but never forget to take them daily. Keep all of them in that bag you're carrying with you. You can't risk your suitcases getting lost.'

I took them from her and put them in my sturdy mirrorwork carry-on bag.

'This – put in your handbag,' Ma gave me an Amul chocolate.

Tears choked me yet again. I put it in my handbag.

She sat down on the bed. 'Why did you go to Arnav's room?'

I sat down on the bed too. We looked at each other tiredly.

'To borrow money. I had saved up a lot in cash. It got stolen on the bus.'

Ma's hand went to her mouth in shock. 'Saved up the money for what?'

I told her the story I had told my friends, about getting my overdue period in the scooter and landing up at the clinic.

After I finished, Ma kept looking at me, her face pale. 'But why didn't you tell me?'

'Because Shantamama's operation was the next day. And then Shantamama was recuperating. And then I was studying for my exams. And after that, I fell ill.'

'You could have told me after *that*.'

'Ma, I couldn't even talk, let alone think.'

'How much money did you lose?'

'Don't ask me, Ma.'

'Ramaa! *That* much!'

'It was a private clinic, Ma.'

She put her arms around me, and I sank into them. 'Even now, your periods are not regular. Suppose you have heavy bleeding in America?' she said into my hair.

'See, Ma, you're already worrying. That's why I didn't tell you.'

We let each other go. 'But why were you in his room for an *hour*?'

'Because he was asking why I needed so much money, and then I had to make up a story about losing someone's gold chain, and he knew I was lying, and... all that.'

'So eventually you told him?'

'No, Ma, how could I? But he gave me the money anyway.'

She got up with a sigh. 'What a good boy Arnav is. *Such* a pity.'

She was at my door when she turned and said, 'I'll return the money to Arnav.'

'Ma, absolutely not. I'm returning it, it'll be easy – five, ten dollars a month.'

After lunch, while Karan kept guard in the sitting room, I lay down between Ma and Shantamama, so exhausted that I fell asleep. I slept for an hour then got up feeling rested but bereft.

After tea, I went to say goodbye to Mahima's father, then Prabha's father. They gave me their blessings. 'Do not worry about your mother, we will look after her,' Mahima's father said. 'There is no need to worry about your mother, we are there,' Prabha's father said. I said goodbye to Prabha's younger brother, Anirudh, who was being tutored at the dining table, and to Anu Aunty's mother-in-law, who shed many tears and said to Anu Aunty, 'Such a nice girl this Mallika is, may she have a long life and success wherever she is. Look at Mallika, so polite and well-mannered she is, so well brought up by her mother. Hai Ram, what to do, there are some mothers who do not know how to bring up their daughters. Accha, get me half a cup of tea, and don't count every grain of sugar that you put into it.'

Shantamama was standing with folded hands before the prayer table, talking in Kannada to the Gods when I returned home.

'Deva, Deva, make Mallika amenable to meeting Bharat, such a good boy he is, make them fall in love with each other and live as happily ever after as is humanly possible in a marriage. And Deva, please let Randhir and Arnav have less influence on her – unless, of course, one of them wants to marry her – who knows why neither does. Deva, may she do well in her studies and not look so unapproachable all the time, otherwise which boy will look at her, let alone marry her? Please don't let her fall in love with a white boy, Deva, she should know that there are no Darcys in real life. May she believe in you, and till she does, Deva, I beg of you, accept my prayers on her behalf.'

Anu Aunty said that, now I was going to America, I must keep an open mind about marriage: maybe I would meet a nice Indian boy there, and if not, my mothers would find a nice boy for me when I came home to India. I must not become like Prabha, who refused to meet any boys. 'And, Beti, put this Hajmola in your handbag, it is very good for gas.'

'Beta,' said Madhu Aunty. 'Keep your Indian values, do not postpone marriage. There, in America, if you find a good Indian boy, you tell us, otherwise we will find for you. Do not become like Prabha. I am telling you, she will end up a spinster. Accha, here, take this deodorant in your handbag, a friend got me from London, imagine, bilkul no sweat or smell for twelve hours!'

Ma slipped Vicks into my handbag. Ajji put toothpicks into it. Ayah-ji put a black stone into it, to ward off bad luck. Ma put two handkerchiefs into it, and a small mirror she had got for me ('Your kajal always runs when you cry, wipe your face properly at the airport'). Madhu Aunty put Pudin Hara into it in case I had stomach problems on the plane. Shantamama said my handbag now looked like a toad.

Karan came upstairs and sat with me. Quietly, he said, 'I've never been able to say the things you wanted me to say, have I?'

'It's alright,' I whispered. It no longer mattered.

'Love may die. But... your fidelity to those you have loved may not. How do you speak of those things? That too, to the two people you've... abandoned?'

I looked at him, stunned.

Then I began to sob.

He put his arms around me.

I had finally received my father's truth.

Finally, alone in the bathroom as I had my bath, my thoughts steadied.

When I came out of the bathroom, Ayah-ji was in my room with my food on a plate so I could eat without being assailed by more visitors. Karan came upstairs a few minutes later. 'If you run out of your medicines, I can arrange for them to be sent to you through someone.' I nodded. I was in such pain by now that I couldn't speak.

Karan carried my suitcases to the car. I went downstairs. Ayah-ji was crying bitterly. We hugged for a long time. I put some money into her hands. She gave me a knotted handkerchief. 'You will need this in Amreeka,' she sobbed. I went to the bathroom in Ma's room to have another cry. I unknotted the handkerchief and found that Ayah-ji had given me forty rupees in five-rupee notes. Oh, my Ayah-ji. My chest hurt.

I switched off the light and opened the bathroom door to see Ma sitting on her bed in the darkness, her hands on her face. Karan entered the room and sat next to her. I drew back.

'Padma,' Karan said.

Ma said, 'Amma and Shantacca are leaving in a couple of days. Will you come and stay with me after that?'

Karan did not answer.

I looked out once more.

They were kissing, their arms tight around each other. This was no tentative kiss.

Stunned, I drew back and quietly shut the door.

Ten minutes later, someone knocked. 'Darling?'

I came out.

'Darling' – Shantamama wiped her eyes – 'promise me one thing. Promise me that you'll start praying – it'll give you strength.'

I nodded.

'Don't nod just to appease me. Just talk to God. Doesn't matter which god, what god – there's only one God. He listens. Say whatever is in your heart to Him. Believe me, He talks back.'

I nodded.

'I've put four agarbatti packets in your air bag. Light them when you pray. Do it for my sake. It isn't as though I'm asking you to get married; I'm just asking you to pray.'

I nodded.

'Even Americans pray. Randhir told your mother they go to church every week. Even *we* don't go to the temple every week. Or every month, even. In fact, hardly ever. So if *they* can do it, why can't you?'

We hugged and kissed.

Ma came in, and Shantamama went out.

'Love,' said Ma, 'Don't worry about us. Alright? We're healthy, we're surrounded by good friends. Fulfil your dreams, love.'

I nodded.

She put her arms around me. 'Keep healthy,' she wept. 'Eat properly. Be safe.'

We went to Ajji and Shantamama's prayer table. Ajji lit the lamp and agarbatti. Rama, Lakshmana, Sita, Hanuman, Saraswathi, Lakshmi, Ganapathy, Shiva, Jesus, Mary, and St Anthony were on one side. Ajji, Ma, Shantamama, Anu Aunty, Madhu Aunty, Ayah-ji, and I were on the other.

'All our blessings are with you,' Ajji said, her voice calm and soothing.

'All our prayers are with you,' said Anu Aunty.

'All our love,' said Madhu Aunty.

Ma and Shantamama didn't say anything.

One by one, they all hugged me, and I felt their tears on my face. I touched Ajji's feet and gave Ayah-ji a final hug.

We emerged from Ajji's room to the sitting room, where two Loving Neighbours were still sitting, teary-eyed.

We walked out of the house that I had lived in all my life and got into Karan's Ambassador. He and Ma sat in the front, and Shantamama, my grandmother, and I at the back – I, sandwiched between them. The two neighbours, determined to be with us till the end, stood waving along with Ayah-ji, Madhu Aunty and her husband, and Anu Aunty and her husband. All the women were weeping.

We drove out of the colony. Blinded by tears, I could barely see it. My grandmother put her arm around me. 'My beloved child. You will always do well in life. Look how you have conquered your illness.'

'Only because of all of you,' I sobbed.

'We could not understand.' Ajji wiped her eyes. 'So bad we feel, even now, that we understood nothing of what our beloved child was going through.'

'You all understood everything.' I put my arms around her.

What I meant, I realize now, was that they accepted everything. I did not have the words to say, 'Your acceptance is what matters.' To say, 'Acceptance is a greater thing than understanding.' Because understanding – however hard you try – may or may not come. My mothers', my grandmother's, and my father's love for me begat acceptance in their hearts. Acceptance of what I could not help, of what I could not change, of what was beyond my control. None of them, who protected me so fiercely, understood what was happening. Just as I did not that day when Randhir lost his temper with me. The jamun tree against which he leaned, in utter despair – the tree that did not understand – was his sole support. My mothers, my grandmother, my father, and my Ayah-ji, all of whom had no comprehension of illnesses of the mind, were like that tree for me: their bodies that solid trunk, their arms that canopy of branches and leaves. Thus accepted, thus cocooned, and thus loved, I survived.

Mallika: Taking it with us

August 1980

We were in the air.

This was my first time in a plane, and Arnav's second. I couldn't figure out the seatbelts, air-conditioning vents, lights, nothing. Arnav figured out everything. It was five a.m., and the plane had taken off half an hour ago. My stomach growled so loudly that Arnav took out a big bar of Toblerone from the seat pocket in front of him and gave it to me. I opened it and broke two pieces, my mouth watering.

'Where did you get it from?' I asked. You couldn't get foreign goods at Indian airports.

'It was lying at home, my sister bought it when she came.'

'I thought you didn't like chocolate,' I said.

'You do.'

'You've got it for *me*?' I asked.

'Who else?'

'Thank you.' I broke myself another two pieces. Chocolate and Arnav were a happy combination.

As soon as I'd seen him at the airport, waiting for me with his parents, I'd felt happiness trickling back into me. He was looking somewhat un-Arnav-like; that sunshine look was strangely shadowed. I hadn't realized he would feel so deeply about leaving his family. My family and his had made their introductions. 'Wipe off your kajal, it's all over,' Shantamama had wept as we said our final goodbyes, but I'd forgotten. Now, my mouth still full of chocolate, I opened my handbag, took out the brand-new hand mirror and handkerchief, and wiped off the kajal, which was indeed all over. Then I wiped chocolate from around my mouth.

'What?' I said to Arnav, who was watching me as though he hadn't seen me for a long time.

'Nothing,' he said. I put another piece into my mouth.

I'd never seen so many white faces. All of them were expressionless. Indian faces were never expressionless; every Indian face showed what it felt. I chewed over this observation along with the chocolate. The other difference was that the whites were talking softly and the Indians loudly. Also, the whites were contemplatively sipping their wine, whereas the Indian men were glugging it down as if there were no tomorrow. And now I came to think of it, there was one more difference – the whites, as they boarded the plane, had been almost languid, whereas the Indians had been in a desperate rush to board, as though the plane would depart before they could get on, like a DTC bus.

I leaned over Arnav and offered the Toblerone to the young man sitting next to us, Harish. He was our age, or thereabouts, and had hailed Arnav with great familiarity as we had stood in line to check in at the airport. 'We are good friends, Arnav and me,' he had said, with a wink at Arnav, and then announced that, since we were all going to the same university, we would all sit together, oh, so wonderful! Arnav had looked strangely unenthusiastic at the prospect. So here we were now, all sitting in a row. Harish's plump countenance was looking somewhat green.

'No thank you, no chocolate, very vomit-y I am feeling,' Harish said miserably.

Poor boy. I opened my bag and took out the Hajmola that Anu Aunty had given me. 'Here, try this.'

He looked as though the heavens had opened. 'Thank you, thank you.' He took the bottle from me, poured out several small golis, and tossed them into his mouth.

A few minutes later, after Harish went to the bathroom, the smell of fart pervaded our area.

I looked at Arnav, shocked. Surely familiarity didn't breed contempt *this* rapidly?

'It's not me, it's that bloody Hajmola you gave Harish,' Arnav said, outraged.

'I never said anything.'

'You looked it.'

How was I to have known that the Hajmola meant for gas also smelt of it?

Harish came back from the bathroom and sat down with a big sigh. 'So sad I was, leaving India. But now, Bhagwan has sent me two friends.'

I smiled at him. I liked the way he spoke from his heart.

Arnav didn't seem to be of the same mind. 'Feeling better?' he asked, without warmth.

Harish shook his head. '*Very* vomit-y.'

'Here –' I leaned over Arnav and gave Harish the bottle of Pudin Hara that Madhu Aunty had given me.

'Thank you, perfect.' He shook a few drops into his glass of water and drank it.

'Head is also aching,' he said hopefully.

Poor boy. 'Here.' I took out the Amrutanjan from my handbag and gave it to him.

'Mallika, bahut thanks, only Amrutanjan helps my headaches.' He took the jar from me and applied Amrutanjan liberally to his forehead and temples.

Our section of the plane was beginning to smell extremely pungent.

'Haahh,' Harish sighed loudly and closed his eyes.

Our food arrived an hour later. We ate hungrily, even Harish. He had slept for an hour and assured us he was much better.

'So what have you got admission for?' I asked Harish.

'For MBA.'

'You have aid for an *MBA*?' Arnav exclaimed.

How come he didn't know when Harish was supposed to be his friend?

'Arre bhai, where you can get aid for MBA!' Harish said.

'You're *paying*!' Arnav and I said simultaneously.

'My father, he is arranging all that.'

'Oh. What does your father do?' Arnav asked.

How come Arnav didn't know?

'My father, he is… I should say… Jack of all trades. With specialty in law and order.'

'He's in the police?' I asked.

'What police are knowing about law and order? But all police, top to bottom, report to him.'

'So… what's his profession?' I asked.

'Have you read book, *Godfather*?' Harish said.

I nodded.

'That only.'

'Pardon?'

'My father, he is that only.'

I looked at Arnav for help.

He was no help. His shoulders were shaking with laughter.

I turned to Harish.

Harish explained, 'For example, unscrupulous tenants, they take advantage of Rent Control Act by never vacating rented house, no? Then owner of house, he comes crying to me. Now, see, I am big believer in non-voilence. But if tenant is not vacating, then how non-voilence will work?'

Voilence! I could hear Shantamama saying, *Such peculiar accents these North Indians have!*

'Nothing serious we do at first – one or two windowpanes are broken, some phone calls are made, like that. And if that does not work, then a little persuasion we do.'

Suddenly, an idea burst inside me like fireworks.

'Are you still...' I tried to find the words. 'Working for your father's... business?'

Harish sighed. 'Yes, indeed. But after MBA, I will leave and start my own business.'

Yes, this was meant to be. I would ask Harish. But how? The conversation was being conducted over Arnav's recumbent body, and he was very much awake.

Harish said, 'The key to my father's success is Philosophy of Truth.'

'Oh?' I said enquiringly.

'When you tell untruth many times, it becomes the truth.'

'Oh.' I found Harish's Orwellian philosophy of life very appealing.

'My father speaks what he thinks. And what he thinks, many people also think, but do not say. So when my father says what he thinks, he is speaking the people's truth. That is why they love him.'

'I see.'

'So, you see, that is my father's success story.'

I nodded then glanced at Arnav, who was yawning.

'Arnav,' I said. 'Would you like my window seat?'

'You want to sit in the middle seat?' he said, surprised.

'Easier talking to Harish if I'm next to him rather than over you when you're sleeping.'

'Oh. OK.'

I told Harish. We all got up, and Arnav sat at the window, and I in the middle.

'How come *you're* so keen to talk to a stranger?' he whispered as soon as we settled down.

'I'm wide awake,' I whispered. 'And he's very interesting to talk to.'

'Don't get taken in. He's a shady guy. And he's bullshitting,' he whispered, closing his eyes.

I turned to Harish, but he was sleeping.

I was tired but my brain was wired. So was my body, with Arnav so close to me. I could smell his cologne, his breath smelt of peppermint, and his arm rested comfortably next to mine. I could barely look at those beautiful brown eyes without wanting to kiss them.

Half an hour later, Harish muttered, 'I cannot sleep.'

'Nor can I,' I said, turning to him.

'Arnav, he is your friend, or...?' Harish enquired delicately.

'Very good friend.'

Arnav was asleep.

'Harish, I was wondering... I need some help.'

'Ask. It will be done.' Harish sat up, looking alert.

'Talk softly,' I whispered.

'Bilkul,' Harish whispered back.

'It's complicated.'

'Complicated is my specialty.'

'Don't tell anyone.' I gestured silently towards the sleeping Arnav.

'Never.'

'Do you take money for your services?'

'Mallika, do not insult me. You are like my sister.'

I was very moved.

His eyes were gleaming with anticipation.

'My best friend, Mahima, she is married in Chandigarh and...' What to say?

'Husband is bad to her? In-laws are bad to her?'

'I'm not sure what the problem is, but there's definitely a problem.'

'In short, you want investigation, not action?'

'Yes.'

He took out a notebook and pen from his shirt pocket. 'Name and address of party?'

I gave him Shekhar's name, took out my address book from my handbag, and gave him the address.

'Rest assured. Investigation shall be done.'

'How?'

'My man will get job in that house. As servant or cook or gardener or chauffeur.'

'And then?'

'Servants can find out everything.'

'My friend's in-laws have contacts with the Congress (I).'

'Every politician, he is in my father's pocket.'

I let out my breath.

'Now the problem, it is not yours,' he said, putting his notebook inside his pocket. 'Go to sleep with light heart, Mallika.'

Which was exactly what I did.

As soon as we disembarked at Amsterdam, Arnav grabbed my mirrorwork bag from me, slung it over his shoulder along with his own, and then the three of us sprinted to change planes. There was just half an hour till the next flight departed. No time to absorb my first time in a foreign airport, although I looked wistfully at all the perfumes and chocolates as we ran on shining floors past squeaky-clean walls and dazzling, glittering shops. Everything around us smelt un-Indian and exotic. Harish panted that his chest was hurting.

This time, Harish had a seat far ahead of us. After Arnav and I found ours and everyone else was seated, I went to check on Harish.

'What's wrong, Harish?' I asked.

'My chest is hurting too badly.'

I took out a strip of Crocin from my handbag and gave him two. 'Have one after you eat, and then after eight hours, have another,' I said. The poor boy was pale with pain.

'Thank you, Mallika, you are a very good person. I hope Arnav is also a good person.'

He saw my shock.

He spoke rapidly. 'Arnav, he was engaged in unlawful activities two days ago. He was selling dollars in black at Mohan Singh Market in Connaught Place.'

'What *rubbish*, Harish!'

'*I* also was engaged in unlawful activities there,' he said reassuringly. 'Arnav, he was selling dollars; me, I was buying dollars. Ninety dollars I bought from him. I gave him one thousand rupees. Very big profit he made out of me; dollar is worth less than eight rupees. That was how we met.'

By now, I was speechless.

'You have very good heart,' Harish said emotionally. 'That is why I am telling you.'

I went back to my seat. Arnav looked at me enquiringly.

I closed my eyes and tried to think.

Arnav said, 'What shady deal were you making with Harish on the last flight?'

'No shady deal.'

'I heard every word.'

'You were *pretending* to sleep?'

'*Trying* to, was more like it.'

I closed my eyes and tried to think again.

'Mallika, you trust that gunda within half an hour of meeting him?'

'He's a gunda?' I opened my eyes.

'He was bullshitting, Mallika!'

'Was he bullshitting when he told me you were selling dollars at Mohan Singh Market?'

His expression was answer enough.

Now, I knew. That when I had asked to borrow money, he didn't have it.

'Arnav, you sold your dollars in black to give me the money?'

'Uff, no big deal, Mallika.'

'Arnav, you could have been arrested, you could –'

'Mallika – Harish is a damn smooth operator. We accomplished the transaction in two minutes flat. Which was a lot quicker than you managed when you stole that puppy!'

'But now you'll run short, and then –'

'Mallika, relax. My mother's been buying dollars from Niharika every time she comes to India. Ma gave me some dollars in addition to what I got from the bank.'

I didn't believe him.

'What's going on with Mahima?'

What to tell Arnav?

The silence grew.

Arnav said, 'Mallika, you can talk to *Harish* about Mahima, but not to *me*?'

'It's not that. It's that Harish can *do* something. You and Randhir can't.'

The plane began to fall. Someone shrieked. I clutched hold of Arnav's arm.

He put his arm around me. No, no, no; what would my mothers do if I died?

I moaned into his underarm.

'What?' he murmured.

The plane kept falling. I could hear a couple more shrieks.

Someone was saying something on the speaker.

'Mallika. It isn't going to crash. It's just bad turbulence.'

He was lying to calm me. What a terrible idea it had been to go to America. For what?

'For nothing. For nothing,' I muttered into his underarm.

'Never mind.' He sounded horribly cheerful. 'Maybe there'll be some Dutch cows below.'

What a pathetic attempt at humour in the face of death.

The plane stopped falling.

My nose was still buried under his arm, which was firmly around me.

I emerged from his underarm, my heart still pounding.

He removed his arm. 'Take a few deep breaths.'

I took a few deep breaths.

'Now, tell me about Mahima.'

'She came to Delhi without telling her husband and in-laws. Her in-laws said they'd take her back if she came back the next day. So Madhu Aunty and Uncle took her back after she said goodbye to me. We saw her for about five minutes.'

He was frowning. 'That's awful. Tell Randhir. He'll do something.'

'He can't do anything. Mahima refuses to talk about it.'

'But what can *Harish* do?'

'He'll... install someone as a servant in Mahima's house, who'll find out what's going on.'

He looked at me in disbelief.

'Arnav, something is very, very wrong. I just *know* it.'

Then, for a long time, Arnav lapsed into thought.

Finally, he said slowly, 'You told me that Shekhar's sister Renu told you that Shekhar was a pervert?'

I nodded.

'Oh, shit,' Arnav said under his breath.

'What?'

He looked at me.

Then he said, 'Nothing.'

I needed to sleep. 'How do you incline this chair?'

He did it for me, and then for himself. We lay back, and I closed my eyes.

After a minute, I opened my eyes and turned to him. His eyes were closed.

'Arnav.'

He opened his eyes and looked at me.

'*I* never told you that Renu said Shekhar was a pervert.'

His eyes were apprehensive.

'Did Randhir tell you?'

His body was tense. He didn't answer.

'Randhir didn't tell you,' I said slowly.

He said nothing.

'Then who told you?' I knew the answer but wanted to hear it from him.

'You.' He closed his eyes against my face.

'Arnav?'

He opened his eyes and looked at me. As though he had to. As though he had no choice now.

My heart was beating very fast. I must have told him on the night of Mahima's wedding. That night when he'd kissed me. The kiss that Gauri had seen. The kiss that he didn't know I knew about.

'What all did I tell you?' I asked.

Another silence.

I heard him letting out his breath.

He said, tonelessly, 'You told me that Renu had said Shekhar was a pervert. So you told Randhir. You wanted to stop the wedding. He lost his temper with you.'

He wasn't looking at me. He was looking straight ahead.

'Why didn't you ever tell me I'd talked to you about it?'

'I didn't think there was any point.'

'Why? Because you kissed me after that? Or was it before that?'

His body jerked.

The lights were off in the plane. Everyone was asleep. We were talking in whispers. I could barely see his face.

'You *remember*?' he said under his breath.

Why? Did he think I was going to hold him to a bloody kiss that meant nothing to him?

Something suddenly clicked.

I bent down, picked up my handbag, and unzipped it. I took out my red diary, flipped the pages till I found it. I read it out to him: *I was talking to you because it's as if you're inside my story, living it with me.*

I looked up at him.

He looked as though he'd stopped breathing.

'You said this to me, no?'

He gave a slight nod.

'What were you talking to me about?'

He didn't answer. But he didn't remove his eyes from my face either.

'Arnav,' I said. 'Just the truth.'

He winced.

Then he said, 'What do you remember.' It wasn't a question. He was stalling for time.

'I don't remember anything. But a couple of days ago, Gauri told me.'

Another silence.

'Told you I kissed you?'

'Obviously, what else!'

Once more, he let out his breath.

'Arnav, tell me *everything* that happened on the night of Mahima's wedding. *Everything.*'

He took in his breath once more and said, 'You had a bunch of keys that Madhu Aunty gave you, and you threw them at Randhir outside the shamyana. Then you stalked off home. Randhir asked me to walk back with you, so I went to your house. You were sitting outside on the veranda steps. I joined you. We talked.'

Everything was dark and quiet. The air hostesses were no longer going up and down the aisles. In the distance, a baby gave a small wail then subsided.

'We got up to go back to the wedding, and I kissed you. That's all that happened on the night of Mahima's wedding.'

So. Several sentences describing what happened before the kiss, and one sentence about the kiss. The kiss was a that's-all.

But what had he been talking to me about that night as we sat on my veranda steps?

'You said it was as if I were inside your story, living it with you. What were you telling me?'

'Everything… that mattered to me.'

Then I saw it on his face. That I had hurt him terribly at that time.

'I'm so sorry, Arnav,' I said, shaken.

Silence.

He said, 'What on earth do *you* have to be sorry about?'

'I forgot everything you told me.'

Another silence.

'How could you help it? Let's sleep now.'

He said this tenderly. That was why I asked.

'Why did you kiss me, Arnav?'

It would have been better if he hadn't answered. But he did.

'I never should have.'

'What d'you mean?' I whispered.

He didn't answer. He wasn't even looking at me.

'Arnav? Tell me what you mean.'

'Forget it, Mallika.'

Forget it? That was what got my goat.

'But I *have* forgotten the kiss, Arnav. And I'd like to have one I can remember.'

I didn't even know what I was going to do until I did it.

I couldn't see his face in the darkness as I lifted up the armrest between us and slid across and over him, wrapping the blanket over us both. I looked around. Everyone was asleep. My mouth landed on his cheek, and I moved it till I found his.

Not in the plane, not in the plane, shrieked Shantamama.

I didn't give him a chance. Or maybe this was the way he liked it, girls always taking the initiative, he not caring one way or the other until it happened, and when it happened, going along with it because it was fun. No, no, it was more than fun – it was fire. No wonder he never said no. Maybe this was the only way. I kissed him as though I'd been doing it all my life. I tasted his tongue. He had his arms around me as I half lay over him, my thigh between his, and we kissed and rocked against each other as though the plane was, indeed, going to crash, and this was our last time. I heard the sound in his throat – no, he didn't stand a chance. Why hadn't I done this before? This was all it took. He kissed my throat with his teeth, he kissed every bit of skin there was to kiss – not that there was much at all, I had a full-sleeved, high-necked sweater on. But he was quite thorough, his hands under my sweater stroking my back. He was making me shiver, or was it something else? I was shivering all over; who would have thought a mere kiss would do this to me? I found his mouth again. It went on and on and on.

Then, even though his hands were still stroking my back, I stopped. I moved back to my seat and lowered the armrest between us.

What was there to say? I thought, as I closed my eyes and lay back, putting the blanket around myself. It was just a kiss. I wouldn't make it bigger than what it was.

But he had sold his dollars in black for me, risking arrest, and that was bigger than what *he* made it out to be. *And* in the car, he had listened to my long-buried story as though nothing in the world was more important than that, and he had been deeply affected by it. It wasn't the whole story, but what need for him or for Randhir or for anyone else to know that, a month later, I'd lost my mind again? That I'd lost it in a very different way, but for a much longer time? No need for them to know. *Arnav* didn't think I was like Charu, and he would talk to Randhir, and Randhir would know that I wasn't like Charu, and then I would finally be rid of the story.

And I would kiss Arnav again in America, before someone else did, and let it go where it pleased and enjoy every moment of it for as long as it lasted, which probably wouldn't be that long given his predilection for running, but at least I'd have it.

'Mallika.'

Now he would tell me one more thing I didn't want to hear. I didn't open my eyes.

I didn't realize I'd raised my hand to stop him until he took it in his and covered it with his other hand.

'I never meant to betray your trust,' he said.

I opened my eyes. What on earth was he talking about?

His brow was furrowed. 'By not telling you… about our… conversation and stuff.'

'Arnav!' I began to laugh. 'You haven't betrayed my trust, for heaven's sake!'

He shook his head.

I was very moved. Not only had he taken my story of that old experience at the clinic hard, but now, he was taking it hard that he hadn't mentioned a four-year-old, forgotten conversation to me? Yes, I was puzzled and upset that he hadn't, but betraying my *trust*? That was a bit much!

Whatever. I was loving the feeling of his hands holding mine.

'Have you forgiven your father?' he asked.

I stared at him.

He looked at me gravely.

Of course, I knew he knew that Karan was my father. He had known for almost a year. I was aware that he must have come to the obvious conclusion about Ma's 'widowhood.' But he had never mentioned it. Now, his question wasn't a mere step towards confirming the answers; it was a massive leap. Oddly, it didn't seem out of place.

Forgiveness. I had agonized about it for months after Randhir asked me to forgive him for his loss of temper. For all that, I had still not understood this business of forgiveness. Now, it came to me with a kind of disbelief: I had forgiven Karan. He had spoken his truth to me today, but unknown to me, I had forgiven him long before that. I no longer held him to account for what all he had allowed his mother to get away with. I still felt the pain, but I didn't hold my pain against him. I didn't hold anything against him.

'Yes, I have,' I said, wonderingly.

He nodded and looked down at our clasped hands.

He looked up again. 'What did it take for you to forgive him?'

This was no casual question. I was sure it had to have something to do with his own life.

Then I knew. Randhir had told me about Mishti. I knew without a doubt. He was wondering if he could ever forgive his father for what he had done to Mishti.

'I didn't try to forgive him. It just... happened,' I said.

He was very quiet after that.

But I couldn't stop thinking about it.

'Arnav?'

He was looking ahead, thinking. He turned to me.

I said, 'He stopped expecting me to... love him back. He just... kept loving me.'

He let out his breath.

'Mallika, when I said I never should have kissed you, I didn't mean it the way it sounded.'

I looked at him questioningly.

'I *will* tell you why. There's a lot... to tell you. But... can we wait... to talk till after we reach America?'

So he hadn't dismissed that long-ago kiss at Mahima's wedding. It sounded like there was a longer story to it. Could that mean that he finally loved me? That he would, in due course and with exquisite detail, describe the long and complex path towards me, his true love? Could it mean that, when we finally had the time and space for ourselves in America – without the blooming of mothers, grandmothers, aunts, and Mrs D'Souzas – he would give this telling the time and weight that it deserved? Interspersed with many kisses? Bliss! Of course, I could wait for it. It was right out of a book. Finally, we were on the same page!

'Yes,' I said, happiness rushing through me.

His hands tightened around mine. He looked at me as though he were committing my happiness to memory.

I fell into a deep sleep.

'Mallika. Mallika.'

I opened my eyes and looked at him sleepily. He needed a shave. His eyes were brimming with excitement. Beneath that excitement lay something else, but I didn't know what it was.

'Look at you. You slept *all* the way.'

'Hmm?' I was still befuddled.

'Look. Look out of the window.'

I leaned across him and looked.

New York, her arms open, rising from the waters to greet us.

Acknowledgements

This book is born of the life my friends infused into me and mine. Over the long years, some of you took care of my parents when I couldn't be with them, some of you took care of my daughter when I couldn't be with her, and all of you took care of me when I couldn't be there for myself. My eternal gratitude to (in the order that I got to know you): Neeta Tolani, Nandini Ramchandran, Sarita Varma, Anjali Mahajan, Kiran Grewal, Nandita Gupta, Judy Nichols, Ruma Mitra, Aru Narla, and my very dear Barb.

And a million thanks to:

Malvika, for her unflagging belief, for reading draft after draft, for her astute and wise feedback, and for her absolute love and support. I couldn't have done this without you.

Padmini Mongia, for decades of loving dedication to my writing and to this novel, and for her unique perspective, her unflinching honesty, and the generosity of her time. No one has contributed more to my writing than you.

Olivia Martin of United Agents, for loving the book enough to want it, for reading it with such care, and for all the work she put into getting it out there. This is your baby too.

Charles Walker of United Agents, for his generous response to an old novel, and his readiness several years later to look at this new one.

Wendy Cope, for her generous help.

Jenna Gordon, editor at VERVE Books, for her tireless work and incredibly insightful feedback. You are that rare editor whose instinct about my writing resonates with my own.

Elsa Mathern and Sarah Stewart-Smith, for all their wonderful ideas and work on the book covers for the two editions.

Ellie Lavender, for all her wonderful work and for being so accommodating about the things that matter to me.

Hollie McDevitt, Sarah Stewart-Smith and Paru Rai, for all their hard work on the campaign.

Jennie Ayres, for her thoughtful and very helpful feedback.

The entire fantastic team at VERVE Books.

Parvathy Appachana, Monisha Mukundan, Sunita Singh Maclaren, Anjana Sharma, Anu Aneja, Elizabeth Cook, Annie Paul as well as (once again) Malvika, Paddy, Ruma, Kiran, Nandita, Judy, and Barb for putting in the time and care to read and comment on a long-ago draft of what I thought would be this book, but which turned out to be another. It is on the shoulders of that book – which I put aside – that this one stands.

Victoria Gould Pryor, my agent for more than two decades, for the enormous love and dedication she put into my writing, for her friendship, and for her support which continues to this day.

Vivek Sinha, Sonali Sinha, Sonya Gill, Raju Agarwal, Namita Mukherjee, Rachna Murvanda, Madhu Murvanda, Jyoti Nair, and Sherrie Summers, for great support during crucial times.

My very dear cousins, Uma Kushalappa and Meenakshi Kushalappa, for huge support throughout.

My parents, Parvathy Appachana and ST Appachana, the best writers of all, whose long, funny, vibrant, irreverent, observant, wise, idealistic, and absolutely delicious letters kept my heart and spirit alive.

In many years of little writing, each artists' residency was an oasis. I would like to express my heartfelt gratitude for the fellowships I received at the following retreats:

Hawthornden Castle, International Retreat for Writers.

The Millay Colony for the Arts. A special thanks to Gail Giles, the Admissions Director, and Ann-Ellen Lesser, Executive Director at the time, for so much kindness and help. When I had to leave within three days of my arrival, Gail said she'd keep a place for me whenever I had the opportunity to return. Thanks to Gail, I had that opportunity six years later, when I returned as a 2001 Norman and Betsy Samet Fellow. My thanks and gratitude to Norman and Betsy Samet for the fellowship which so solidly supported my writing.

The Virginia Center for the Creative Arts.

The Wurlitzer Foundation.

The Oberpfälzer Künstlerhaus artists' colony.

Finally, I am forever grateful to the National Endowment for the Arts for the creative writing fellowship I received in 1995. That fellowship led to a series of unexpected miracles and ended up giving me more than two decades of support. Thank you, thank you, thank you.

Book Club questions for *Fear and Lovely*

1) *Fear and Lovely* is a story filled with secrets and silences. What are some of these, and how do they impact the characters? Is staying silent the same as telling a lie?

2) Which character do you most relate to, and why?

3) What do we gain from Mallika's first-person narrative voice? Do you think she is more driven by her head or her heart?

4) How are family dynamics depicted in the novel?

5) Discuss the characters' varying attitudes towards marriage. Are there any positive models of marriage in the novel?

6) Discuss the depiction of mental health issues and treatment. Do you think the stigma around mental illness in this community worsens its impact on the characters who experience issues?

7) How important is female friendship in the novel? And how does it differ from the way the women and girls relate to male characters?

8) What is the role of spirituality in this story?

9) Forgiveness is a recurring theme, particularly surrounding Karan. How much do you think Karan was to blame for the breakdown of his relationship with Padma?

10) Is Arnav's silence about what happened when Mallika lost her memory understandable? How do you think she will react upon finding out the truth? Do you think she is capable of forgiving him – and do you think she should?

11) What does the US represent to different characters? Do you think Mallika will ultimately return to India?

VERVE BOOKS

Launched in 2018, VERVE Books is an independent publisher of page-turning, diverse and original fiction from new and exciting voices.

Our books are connected by rich, story-driven narratives, vividly atmospheric settings and memorable characters. The list is tightly curated by a small team of passionate booklovers whose hope is that, if you love one VERVE book, you'll love them all!

VERVE Books is a separate entity but run in parallel with Oldcastle Books, whose imprints include the iconic, award-winning crime fiction list No Exit Press.

WANT TO JOIN THE CONVERSATION AND FIND OUT MORE ABOUT WHAT WE DO?

Catch us on social media or sign up to our newsletter for all the latest news from VERVE HQ.

vervebooks.co.uk/signup

📷 f 🐦 ♪ **@VERVE_Books**